W9-CQR-892

FOR TIME AND ALL ETERNITY

For Time and All Eternity

PAUL BAILEY

DOUBLEDAY & COMPANY, INC.

GARDEN CITY, NEW YORK

This is a novel. It is an attempt to portray with truth and fidelity the great Mormon anti-polygamy crusade of the 1880s, but, with the exception of a few actual historical personages, all characters in this book are entirely imaginary and fictitious. In no way are they the portraits of any actual persons, living or dead.

Copyright © 1964 by Paul D. Bailey
All Rights Reserved
Printed in the United States of America

To my grandmothers . . .

who lived their lifetimes

in the "Principle" . . .

PART ONE

The Gentile

EVEN IN MIDMORNING THE EASTERLY STRETCH OF AMMON'S WALL, WHERE it caught the earliest sun, was warm to the flesh, and the top crust of it, where Nancy Corey walked, was dry and powdery to her bare feet. Although the town, with necessity's frantic labor, had been walled less than ten years ago, already the bite of mountain winter, and the soluble erosion of countless spring and summer rains, had chewed into its six-foot adobe breadth until the top walk was as pocked and weathered as the ground, twelve feet below.

In Ammon there was nothing odd about walking the town wall. Even Nancy was old enough to remember that in the beginning—when Brigham the Prophet had ordered the towns of Utah Valley and southward to "fort up" against Walkara and his restive Utes—the men had walked it as a vigilant duty. But the Indian scare to Ammon had come and gone, and in time the town's children had claimed the wall's high and sightly reaches for their own noise and foolery. Their claim on the wall this day had passed, or was yet to come. In this hour most of Ammon's children were out to the fields, or watching stock under the nervous eyes of their fathers. They'd had the wall in the morning. It would be theirs again late afternoon.

The time was Nancy's, and Nancy was fifteen and already a stay-to-home woman—except in her frets against some of the willing attitudes most people expected of her. There was shame, of course, in this sneaking away. But she, and quite often Flora, her half sister, kept morning tryst with the wall. Here they could walk, talk, look and—by lying flat on their bellies—hide again like children, to giggle while their mothers cackled like nervous hens for their return to churn or washtub. Here they could listen to the gabble and shrieks of the married women as they nagged their way through the morning tasks. Here they could talk over their times as children. Here they could darkly whisper the newer fears of the men who were trying to favor them.

Here, too, one could look out across the green squares of the farms—west and south to the lake; north and east to the snowy mountains and Old Timpanogos. Or one could turn back on all this, peer downward over the mud-and-log huts clustered around the big square like wasp nests, and into the pounded earth and puddles of Ammon's public corrals. One looked in that direction only when one had to. There, certainly, at the northeast house line, would be Mother Corey—and there, too, for Flora, would be another Mother Corey. For both Mother Coreys were married to the same man.

Nancy had toed her way up the ladder like an agile cat, but her thoughts this morning were black and hellish. On the wall-top she had expected to wait for Flora, and she had a snootful to tell her. But as Nancy's bare feet plodded the wall toward the southeast corner, she felt the cool updraft of the breeze on her equally bare legs, and she hoisted the shapeless sack of her Mormon skirt to the feel of it. Then she saw Flora, and she knew that somehow Flora had outranged Aunt Millie's venom a little ahead of time. Flora was bellied down on the wall, peering intently over its outer side, unmindful of the fact that her own dress had blown immodestly high and leggy. Nancy took a few more fast strides toward her half sister, stopped, and putting two fingers to mouth blew a shrieking whistle that could have been heard a mile.

At the sound of it, Flora's buttocks went up as though they had been shaved with an arrow. She wriggled back from the wall's edge like a startled trout. Nancy caught the frantic wave of Flora's hand, and knew instantly it was a caution for silence. Hurriedly Nancy strode to the wall's corner, anxious to know now what curiosity could possibly be holding Flora flat on her face. At the east turn, Flora furiously waved her down. Nancy finished the remainder of the distance to the girl's side by belly-crawling like an Indian.

"What's charming you like a serpent?" Nancy grunted, edging close and flinging the loose rope of her black hair backward and out of her face.

"Sh-h-h!" Flora grabbed at a shoulder and yanked her down. "You've made *enough* noise. Now they know—"

"Know what?" Nancy whispered, impressed.

"That they're being watched."

"Who's being watched?"

"Our deliverers."

Flora hunched herself closer to the big weather crack in what had

4

once been the outer parapet, and again stared intently downward. Nancy pawed her way alongside, stretched out her neck like a turtle, and peered outward through the hole.

"You've always said that someday our deliverers would come," Flora whisperingly confided. "Well, here they are."

Directly below, close enough to spit on, were two soldiers. Their horses were unsaddled, the pack was off the mule, and the animals were tethered to sagebrush clumps beyond. Their gear was spread about like they had slept there all night, and one soldier was lighting, with a sulphur match, a tiny fire of sagebrush at the base of the wall.

Nancy lurched from the broken mud parapet, rolled on her back, and looked upward at the wheeling gulls in the summer sky.

"Deliverers!" she chuckled wildly. "Golly damn!" And thoughts scudded in and out, and there was a pondering and a mulling of those talks with Flora regarding their plural trap. There couldn't be too much hope in a pair of soldiers. "Deliverers!" she laughed again. "When Bishop Earlington sees 'em, *they'll* be delivered back to Camp Floyd."

But Flora was not laughing. Nor had she stopped looking. The acrid smell of burning sagebrush already was wafting up over the wall. She hunched up a little on her elbows and, like a lithe animal, shook some of the tow hair from her eyes. "Speaking of bishops, Nan," she said earnestly, and in low voice, "that Provo bishop—Anselman's his name —came a-courtin' again last night. Did Father tell you he's due in again tomorrow?"

Nancy watched idly as the cloud fleece drifted with majestic certainty across the unanswerable blue world above. The nervous gulls, screeching plaintively, flung themselves at invisible air barriers, crying out their repeated defeats. "Father said only that Anselman was sitting in at tomorrow's court. Everyone, of course, knows it's *you* he's eyeing as a woman. But Apostle Cragg's the one *I* hide from. He's due for the Twenty-fourth of July celebration, and my mother makes me stitch every day on the new dress. For an apostle, I've got to look my fancy best. As a bishop's wife, what number will you be?"

"Fourth or fifth . . . who knows?"

"Golly damn, Flora—you'll hardly be important *at all*. Apostle Jonathan Cragg has at least *eight* wives! And do the town gals envy *me!* At our last ward conference, he took a real kindly interest. Said I was a pretty little thing, and chucked me under the chin. I told him I was more cat than human, and he laughed. Father Corey says if this luck holds out, I'll be living in Salt Lake by fall."

"Ninth wife of a pot-bellied apostle," Flora giggled. "Ninth wife of old Lofty Cragg!"

Nancy laughed. "Fifth wife of a bloated bishop!"

"Anyway, I'll be youngest wife."

"So will I, smarty!" Nancy lay quietly a moment. And then she turned and stared at her tawny-headed half sister. "What does your mother *really* think about marriages under the covenant?" she asked soberly.

"She thinks they're preciously important." Flora never turned from her intense eyeing of things below the wall, even though the stench of smoky sage now came in stifling gusts. "The only path to endless exaltation in the hereafter. The new and everlasting covenant. The great gift from the Prophet Joseph Smith. Time and all eternity. A most blessed privilege, says the Prophet Brigham."

"You know what *I* think?" said Nancy.

"I've a good idea," chuckled Flora.

"I'd like to spit in the eye of Apostle Cragg, and every other old stallion who comes a-courtin'."

Flora wagged her head knowingly. "That won't get you very far into heaven."

"Don't it give you fits to think of bedding up with some fat old man after he's spent the night dredging four or five other women?"

Flora pulled back. Her blue-eyed, freckled face was impishly appealing. "You should be ashamed to talk that way, Nan," she giggled. "Your fat old man's an apostle. You could live in style—in Salt Lake. Count your blessings!"

Nancy half smiled, and nuzzled close to Flora's shoulder. "You're an idiot," she said. "And I'm scared numb. I don't want any part of the Principle." . . . If only Flora knew the half thoughts that already poisoned! . . . "Your mother kinda favors it, huh?"

"Don't most women?"

"I don't think my mother favors it—like *your* mother. Mums has been twice in the covenant. She doesn't like Salt Lake. With what happened when she came off the plains, and all. About me being born in Salt Lake, and so forth. Mums talks little about it, but I think she's sorta sad about Apostle Cragg's having eyes on me."

"I forget, Nan, that Father Corey is really not *your* father."

"I love him as though he was," Nancy declared. "In his quiet, firm way, he's good to me. I never knew my other father. Never want to know him. I think Mother just don't want me to have any of the sadness she went through. You don't hear her hip-hooraying for the covenant."

"And you don't hear me either," Flora growled.

Nancy Corey nodded silent agreement.

Flora turned her attentions back to the hole in the wall, and their thoughts went silent. Then she started to laugh. "He's got the coffee water boiling. But his pesky fire nearly stifles me. Wanta take a look?"

"Naw—what's two soldiers? Camp Floyd's full of 'em."

"Yeh. But not the town of Ammon. Besides, I'm not too sure these cockies *are* from Camp Floyd. They're officers. Got shoulder bars. They're geared for travel. Pack animal. Maybe don't even know about Camp Floyd."

"If they did, they wouldn't be anywhere near Ammon." Nancy remembered the admonitions she'd endlessly heard from the pulpit. Latter-day Saints and soldiers had nothing whatever in common. Soldiers, without exception, were whoremongers and seducers of women. Soldiers had invaded Utah in '57. Their purpose, and the whole reason for Camp Floyd, had been to intimidate and persecute the Church and its people. Excommunication, and worse, was the instant lot of any Mormon girl who took up with a soldier. "They'll be scourged away from that wall when the menfolk discover 'em," Nancy laughed.

"Sh-h-h," Flora cautioned. "They keep hearing us. They keep looking up. Both good-looking. Peek out, Nan. Pick your man. I've already chosen the tall, sandy one." Flora silently studied the smoky scene below. Then she started giggling. "Know what, Nan?" she said.

"What?"

"He's dropped two eggs in the coffee water."

Flora rolled back from her vantage point, and Nancy hunched forward to the view. The July sun was bearing down hotter to her back and legs, although the lumpy, crumbly adobe, cooled deeply by the night, was comfortable to the touch. Nancy shut from her hearing the churning noises of the wakened town below and beyond. Her round face and brown eyes eagerly framed themselves in the weathered gully of the wall. Directly below her, squatted like an Indian, one of the soldiers stared in rapt interest at the dismal eye-stinging fire, at the battered coffee pot on its twin rocks, at the eggs boiling in its lidless interior. Through the noxious, stabbing smoke, she could see the mess gear strewn about the fire, the two tin plates, each with government biscuit, and the two scarred and dented cups waiting for the coffee not yet in evidence. It was clear the two men had spent at least part of the night at Ammon's wall, because the other soldier was strapping up

7

the blanket rolls, and busying himself alongside the saddles and grounded mule pack. The sun apparently was not yet hot enough to force them to their dusty hats, and she could see that the farthest one had mouse-brown hair—and neither of them, she somehow was glad to note, had burdened their chins with the ratty beards so prevalent in Zion.

Her throat caught a vile and stinging blast from the smoking fire, and she glanced down at the squatting egg-boiler below. With a spoon now, he was gingerly fishing for the eggs in the pot. Nancy suddenly stared with piqued interest. The man's black hair was as thick and curly as a buffalo's. But the amazing feature of it was a groove down the center of it as clean as a cleaver mark, and as noticeable as though he were wearing twin black wigs. She'd never seen a man so oddly marked.

He soon had the eggs on the tin plates. And then, most startling of all, he spooned ground coffee from a buckskin bag directly into the water that had boiled the eggs.

Nancy wriggled back to Flora. "Golly damn," she laughed delightedly. "He's making coffee in the egg water!"

"Aren't they the pair, though?" Flora giggled. "It's real wild fun to watch 'em."

Nancy's move back to view this time somehow managed to coincide with a puff of bitter smoke that strangled her and the fact that the men had heard an irritable amount of human commotion above them. Now they were both looking upward toward the noise. She fought to hold back, but the big sneeze came—and then two more—directly through the aperture, and almost down at the face of the egg-boiler.

"All right, you smart little bastards!" the man roared, making a jump for the black hair and contorted face above him. "Come down, and I'll knock your heads together!"

Nancy hauled herself out in alarm, and was quickly elbowed aside by Flora—who raised her tawny head to full view. "And *we'll* claw your eyes out, Mr. Soldier!" she taunted. "You know you're not supposed to be here!"

"Well, God alive, Ed," the egg-boiler called to his companion. "Look who *we* have for breakfast!"

Hesitantly Nancy raised her head. The other man stood up, staring like an antelope. "It's a Mormon maiden, Joel," he laughed. "No . . . it's two Mormon maidens, b'God!"

The soldier with the permanent part in his hair—the one called Joel —lowered his attention to his breakfast. Calmly he poured himself a cup of coffee, squatted on his hams, and went assiduously to work crack-

8

ing the shell off his boiled egg. "Probably both are wives to one of these mud-walled prophets," he grumbled without looking up.

Soldier Ed whapped some of the dust off his blue trousers with the flat of his hand and started forward for his own food. "Can I ask you spying Jezebels something?" he called, grinning up at the two women above him. "Is that big, thick wall to hold you *in* the harem, or is . . ."

"It's to keep the Indians out, you crusty devil!" Nancy heard herself screeching back.

Joel, with the peculiar hair, neglected his breakfast to stare up at the new voice, and the new girl. He smiled warmly at her, and in an instant she saw that his eyes were a matched blue to the mountain sky, and that they laughed out through long, dark lashes. Soldiering and travel had weathered his skin like Ute copper. He needed a shave, but his black mustache was still neatly a-trim. Best of all, he'd shunned those goaty beards so monotonously prevalent among the Saints.

"And it's to keep soldiers out, too!" she also heard herself adding.

Ed poured his coffee, took up his egg and hardtack, and squatted beside his companion. "Not if we want to come in, you noisy little crow," he grumbled.

"What've you got against soldiers?" said the man with the blue eyes and peculiar black hair. And to Nancy there was not a thing hateful or pugnacious about the way he said it, or about his merry, contagious smile.

"We got plenty!" Flora bellowed. "You're seducers and despoilers of young girls. You made war on Zion!"

"Come, come, you little plural puss," Ed growled. "We're not making war on anybody. And how the hell can I seduce or despoil you, if you stand cackling on that wall?" He swigged a draught of coffee, and went at the task of peeling the egg.

"You're from Camp Floyd," Nancy declared. "It's a . . ."

"We're *not* from Camp Floyd," said Joel, of the blue eyes. And he looked directly at Nancy and smiled again, this time wryly. "Why don't you stop screeching like a magpie, and come down and have breakfast with us? I'll keep Ed at arm's length."

Nancy laughed, and she no longer could be angry at this man. "I don't want any of the breakfasts *you* cook," she giggled.

"Then you *did* watch us. I *thought* I heard something on the wall; including mirth and comment."

"Egg-water coffee," she taunted. "Phew!"

"That's army coffee, my pretty face. And I hope you've observed that this is a mighty skimpy breakfast."

9

"If you're in the Army," said Flora, in quieter tone, "and you're not from Camp Floyd—where did you come from?"

"We've come a long way," said Joel. "All the way from the Presidio at San Francisco Bay." His egg was peeled now. He tossed the shells into the dying fire, took a swig of coffee, and looked contemplatively at the egg held between thumb and finger of his left hand.

"We wanted to see what you Mormons look like," Ed laughed, tossing the shell of his egg impudently at Flora. He finished off the hard-boiled delicacy in two robust bites, and picked up the hardtack for a more leisurely gnawing. "And now we see."

"Don't believe him," said Joel. "Nothing but seduction ever satisfies Ed. But if you'll come down, I'll promise to protect you. And you *don't* have to eat my cooking."

"I wouldn't," Nancy declared, watching with some repugnance the way he devoured the hen's egg without salt or pepper. To her, it really *was* a skimpy breakfast, and she felt a little sorry for the two men.

"What's your name?" Joel asked.

"Nancy."

"What's your friend's name?"

"Flora."

Flora glowered. "If that's anything to you," she added.

Nancy saw the impish perversity returning to Flora. Already there was a half smile on her face.

"How did you happen to get out of the harem?" Joel teased at her.

"We've never been in a harem," Flora snapped.

"We're half sisters," Nancy added demurely.

"You don't look much like sisters. Not even half sisters. But then, they tell me, plural wives are *all* called sisters."

"We're not plural wives," Nancy explained. "We're not married . . . yet."

"Good," said Joel, taking a neglected turn at his coffee. "Now stand up. Let's see what a pair of Mormon half sisters really look like."

"Yeh," said Ed. "Show us something besides hair mops, gimlet eyes, and mouths that spit venom at two poor, lonely wayfarers."

Without hesitance Flora rose to her feet, the wind whipping crazily at her ankle-length black skirt. She tugged at Nancy, but Nancy suddenly felt shy and reluctant.

"Well, damn it," said Ed, laying down his cup, "that's not bad. Not bad at all. But only God and the prophets know what's under those billows of Mormon homespun." He looked at Nancy. "Stand up, half sister. Let's see what *you* look like."

"Yes, Nancy," urged the blue-eyed Joel. "Stand up. Don't be afraid."

Nancy looked down at the appealingly kind face of the stranger. Never had she seen a face like it. Certainly this was not the breed of soldier she'd been warned against. Slowly, reluctantly, she rose up on her bare feet—holding ladylike to the skirts which a fickle and treacherous breeze was determined to whip high on her legs. Almost against her will she smiled back at the man.

Instinctively she knew he was impressed. "Now, let's start over—and be friends," he said. "Why don't you drop yourself off that wall? We've a few questions to ask."

"We don't dare," Nancy cautioned. "Father would flail us, if he caught us talking—"

"I dare," said Flora, scooping her flying hair out of her eyes. "Nan can stay up here, but I'm coming down. There're a few questions I wanta ask you."

Like the impulsive tomboy she was, Flora walked a rod or so up the wall and, as they had done so many times as youngsters, bellied down to the parapet. Clenching skirt-bottom between her ankles, she eased herself over the edge. Then, with the agility of a mountain cat, she hung by her fingers to the wall's adobe edge, and dropped to the earth below. Nancy admired the performance, though it was positively unladylike the way the breeze, in the drop, whipped her shapeless skirt high up her bare legs. The men, she saw, appreciated it enough to laugh and whap their thighs merrily. Ed hurried over to help Flora to her feet after the long fall.

"That was neat," Joel called up to Nancy. "Now it's your turn."

Alarmed, Nancy looked backward over the rooftops, into the walled village of Ammon. She was certain she could hear Martha Corey's voice above the human throb of the town—calling her back, in shrill falsetto, to the duties of a woman she so shamelessly was flaunting and shirking. "I—I—don't think I'd better—" she protested. "This is wrong—"

The man below held out his hands. "Come on, dark eyes! Your half sister made it. Let's see what the other half can do."

Nancy knew she was being tempted. One should guard against it constantly. But instinctively she knew too that without the pulsing joys of an occasional temptation, life itself could be flat and colorless. There was not the least doubt in her mind she could like this new man. And there was little doubt in her mind that Flora was impulsive, crazy, and an unreliable little fool. Desperate, like herself, Flora already had called these soldiers "deliverers." Under these urges, a person could be capable of anything. And Flora needed watching.

11

"Really, I shouldn't," Nancy protested halfheartedly. And really she knew she shouldn't. She *should* get the hell out of there. Get back to the house, where her mother was screaming. And if Flora didn't quickly get the hell out, too, to alarm the town. These nervy invaders would be scourged out of Ammon.

All these things, of course, were the right thing to do. She looked down again. Flora was smiling, and gabbing with the soldier known as Ed. The other stranger—the one she instinctively had chosen—was still beckoning her down. Wordlessly, and without further hesitance, Nancy walked up the wall. And, a minute later, just as shamelessly was finger-hanging to its edge. She let herself drop to the earth below.

She felt the firm grip on her elbows. She felt his easy strength lift her to her feet. He turned her around, and she was looking into the merriest blue eyes she had ever seen in her life.

"Now . . . let's start over," he said. His clipped New England accent, with its slurring of the "r" was strange to Nancy, but not unpleasant. His strength eased out as she settled to her feet, and he dropped his grip from her arms. "My name's Joel Walden Scott." He nodded to his companion, already immersed conversationally with Flora. "My nasty friend's name is Edward Albert Graham. We arrived too late last night to enjoy the hospitality of your town. So we camped outside the wall."

"You wouldn't have enjoyed the hospitality of *our* town," Nancy chuckled. The man's good manners had a way of putting one at ease. "You're a soldier, you know."

"What the hell you Mormons got against soldiers? I sense it in every town—even in Salt Lake City."

"The Saints just don't like soldiers, that's all. Can't forget that the Army invaded Utah." Nancy had heard the tales from childhood. She was seven years old, in '57, when the Saints, after harassing the Army in its advance to the mountains, had fled southward through Ammon, Provo, and on into the far southern settlements—leaving every home in Salt Lake Valley piled high with straw, and ready and waiting for the torch that would devastate their new cities. Only the men charged with duty of setting the fires were on hand when the Army entered. The Prophet Brigham had sworn that if the Army so much as paused, or molested one Saint's property or belongings, it would get nothing out of Utah but scorched earth—exactly as the Saints had found the valley, ten years before.

"Yes, I know the Army came to Utah," Joel said impatiently. "But that was years ago. It didn't misbehave. Its commander, Albert Sidney

Johnston, wouldn't let it. It didn't even pause in Salt Lake City. It went on south to Cedar Valley, and set up Camp Floyd."

"Floyd!" Nancy whistled derisively. "And do I know about *that* place!"

Joel chuckled merrily. "Then *you* were in the Army? What rank, young lady? Colonel, laundress, or temptress?"

She bit her lip angrily at the taunt, clamped hands to hips, and eyed him squarely. "No decent woman ever sets foot in Floyd. It so happens my father has a dairy farm at The Point. Sells butter and cheese to the Army. I work my turns at The Point—and that's as close as I ever wanta be to soldiers."

"Such spunk I like to see in a girl," he chuckled, his pale eyes dancing merrily. "You're smart in keeping away from them."

Nancy glanced at Flora and *her* soldier, and then at this other crazy man in blue. She grew mellow and warm again. "Guess all soldiers aren't alike," she sighed. "In spite of what Father says."

"Honestly, I can't see why you Mormons complain so much. Utah's never been shot up by the military. Even your hated Army—except for a small garrison—was pulled out of Camp Floyd, and sent east to the *real* slaughter of the Civil War. Johnston—your very worst enemy—was killed at Shiloh—as a Reb commander."

"Soldiers are just not our friends," she defended weakly. "They've made war on the Saints."

"Tush," he chuckled. "If I had a lot of time, young lady, I'd talk some sense into you." He looked soberly, almost tenderly at her, and spoke to her as to a child. "Many many things have happened since Johnston's army entered Utah. Many terrible things. Mormons have had it quiet and comfortable by comparison."

"But the Army's back again! And Father says its men are a bunch of drunken bummers!"

Joel's easy, hopeless shrug bothered her. She turned a worried glance toward Flora and the other man. The two had moved farther along the wall, and Flora was giggling like a wanton idiot.

He laughed again, and idly dug a boot heel into the summer's dry earth. "Connor's built up Camp Floyd with a little infantry and cavalry —but you mustn't hold that against *me*. I can see why his new fort near Salt Lake could be a stinger to you Mormons. But I didn't come in with *his* army."

"But you *are* a soldier."

"A defanged one, my pretty," he said. "As I've told you, I came from California. Edward and I are among you Saints without hate or malice.

So, in turn, you mustn't hate us. We've had a warm, friendly visit with your Prophet Brigham. We've a note from him to your Bishop Earlington. Neither of us, at present, are on active duty—although we *will* check in at Floyd."

She looked at him curiously. Here was a strange one.

"But first of all, we want to visit Ammon. It's interesting. A real walled town in America. Took a lot of guts and brawn to build this town."

"The wall was built when Walkara and his Utes were on the rampage," Nancy explained. "But now Utes are more pests than enemies. And the wall is tumbling down."

"What *I* especially like," Joel chuckled, "is what came tumbling down the wall this morning."

"Wait until Father Corey hears about it!" Nancy sighed. "We'll be scourged out of town . . . or called before the priesthood. I'm ashamed for both of us."

Joel lifted her chin and, with his left hand, deliberately and slowly parted the wild black hair away from her brown eyes and forehead. "Then your name's Corey . . . Nancy Corey?"

"That's what I'm known as now," Nancy replied, tingling deliciously to his touch. "But my real name's Brayton. Isaac Corey is my present father."

"That's too involved for me," he said, stepping back and eyeing her searchingly. "But I'll swear you're about the prettiest thing I've seen." He smiled. "Innocent like a fawn, bigoted like a priestess of Judah, and wild as a colt. What a frightful mixture you are, young lady!"

Nancy looked, unflinching, and unafraid, into the bronzed and weathered face of the young officer. This captain needed a shave, and he looked travel-weary and haggard from his travel. But he had no beard—again thank Jehovah. His mustache was black and trim. His eyes were blue like joy itself. He was not too tall, by her comparison. And his hair was black, and curly, and tufted curiously to each side. "Can I ask you a question?" she queried soberly.

"Fire away, my dear."

"What in heaven's name is the matter with your hair? I've never seen a man who could part his hair like that."

Joel's face reddened with embarrassment. "You don't like it?" he said.

"Don't know whether I do or not. Just odd, that's all. Just that I've never seen anything like it before."

"Nor will you again, my dear. I'm probably the only man living with a permanent part in his hair. A Confederate minnie ball at Chancellorsville did it for me. The man behind me was a bit taller. It parted his skull instead of his hair. But do you find my disfigurement repulsive?"

"I think it looks nice," Nancy said, a little sad and ashamed. "And you're sure not a bit like the soldiers they tell us about."

"And you're sure not like the Mormon girls I've been told about. You don't seem to be afraid at all."

A calm certainty now possessed her. Where had this man come from? Why had he come to Ammon? What special magic had brought her to him this summer morning? Would he go? Would she never see him again? "I was afraid—on the wall," she said. "But I'm not afraid now." Wide-eyed with wonder, she again stared to trembling at his face, at the strong, compact body in its travel-frayed army blues.

"Then, if you're not afraid," he said, "I'm going to ask you and your half sis to do us a favor. Will you—quick as we gather up our breakfast gear—escort us to your Bishop Earlington?"

Nancy writhed in laughter at the thought. The Corey girls, leading two soldiers to the ward bishop! Then panic swept through her like a wind of sickness. Soldier—Gentile—the tenets and teachings of the Gospel! Oh, no!

"Well . . . will you?" he persisted.

She thought again—this time recklessly. There was meaning to their visit. Flora was right. There was little time.

"What's the matter, Nancy?" he urged. "If you're afraid, Ed and I can go it alone."

"I'm not afraid," Nancy said resolutely. "I wouldn't be afraid to tell Bishop Earlington anything. I wouldn't even be afraid to tell Bishop Earlington the thing that's on my mind."

"And what, pray, is on your mind?"

"Well, I wasn't really hard hit with it, until I saw you," she confessed. It was impossible to keep from staring into the face of Joel Scott. She trembled nervously at the brink. "Flora and me were really talking hell talk, while we watched you from the wall."

"Hell talk?"

"The kind of talk no Saint should utter—especially a woman in Israel."

"Sounds like real spicy chatter," he laughed. "Do all Mormon women peek over their walls, and make hell talk when they see strangers?"

"They shy from strangers. Never as much as cast eyes on Gentiles." Her lips were dry, and they shook with the strange tremor now sweeping her. It couldn't hurt to be honest. And with him, she wasn't exactly afraid. "But we were casting eyes on you," she said, demurely trying to

15

hide the churn of her true feelings. "We even fancied you as deliverers."

"Only thing I'm interested in delivering is this note to your bishop," he laughed.

"And then—after that—you'll be gone," Nancy sighed.

"Oh, we've a chore or two—*then* we'll be gone." He looked curiously at Nancy. "Are you trying to wheedle a ride with us—or something?"

"Mormon girls don't wheedle rides with Gentile soldiers," she said. But, just the same, it was an idea.

"Glad I was hearing wrong," he laughed. "This child has no yearning for harem snatching."

"We don't have harems in Zion," Nancy argued. "It's called plural marriage."

"Well, whatever it's called, I've no hankering to meddle with it."

"That's exactly why we were casting eyes on you. You're a Gentile. You don't believe in the covenant. Maybe hate it. Your wife would never have to share you with another woman."

"You mean you're already worried about sharing a man?" Joel asked incredulously.

"I mean I'm in trouble."

"Oh? Then get away from me!"

"I wanta spit in the eye of Apostle Cragg. I'm hunting a way to escape these bearded old goats who wanta add me to their holy increase." The bitter words of her mother flooded through her recollection. The Brayton younger wife had ridden in the wagon across the plains. Her own mother—fat with child—had walked—while old Enoch Brayton tittered and made love to the fresh bride who rode with him. "Only a Gentile, who doesn't give a snap for the covenant, can deliver me out of my trouble," she sighed, and looked hopefully and hungrily at him.

"Well, don't try counting *this* Gentile in," Joel growled. "I'm here for a little information—not to get my throat cut."

"If a man married a daughter of Zion—and didn't seduce her," Nancy nervously tried to explain, "that ought to be different. I think—"

"Then stop thinking, you crazy little idiot!"

She felt his two strong hands clench her arms, and he shook her like a dog shakes a cushion. Only then did she realize what she'd been saying, and the tears came. Ashamed, she dared not raise her eyes to look at the face, now close, nor the look of surprise that must be upon it. "You must *really* be desperate," he said.

"I must really be crazy, like you say," she moaned.

He did not let her go. "Nancy," he said, with real tenderness instead

16

of anger, "I *am* what you call a Gentile—and I *don't* give a snap for your covenant. And I'm damned uncomfortable—because I'm not hunting any increase—holy or otherwise. I thought, at first, you had a lot of sense and courage. Instead, I find you a frightened, desperate, impetuous little fool—apparently willing to throw yourself away on a stranger."

"But I don't feel you're a stranger."

"No matter."

Now she was really weeping. "Had I felt you a stranger—I couldn't've talked this way. You're—"

"It still doesn't matter, my dear," he argued. "These things can't be built on expediency. You're a very attractive girl. You should never be added to any apostle's holy increase."

"Thank you, sir," she managed. "And forgive me."

"A man could like you a lot—if he knew you better. But I'm not here for the deliverance of Mormon women. I've other reasons for being here." He dropped his hands from her.

Nancy at last looked up. His dark and handsome face was suddenly hard, unsmiling. She felt now as though she were drowning in Utah Lake. "I was desperate. Carried away. For a minute I didn't know what I was saying. Never talked this way to a man before in my life."

"Well, deliver a chunk of this hell talk to your apostle. Just don't let him—or anyone else—rope you into plural marriage."

"You were asking me to take you to Bishop Earlington."

Joel was silent a moment. Then he smiled once more—and in the smile there was no trace of rancor or disgust. "On second thought, my dear, and considering all," he said, after another pause, "I don't think you're the one to take us to Bishop Earlington. I think it best my friend and I tackle this thing alone."

And then the humiliation and shame of her hasty and ill-timed effusion really caught up with her. The rebuff was gentle, but it revealed his estimate of her. Without a thought for Flora, Nancy turned from her soldier. Like a thing pursued by Walkara's arrows, unmindful of the broken glass and prickly-pears between the ground and her bare feet, she made a dash for Ammon's east gate.

17

II

IT WAS FLORA—FLORA, WHOM NANCY HAD ALWAYS CONSIDERED IRRESPON-
sible and giddy—who demurely led the two men to the fort dwelling
of Bishop Herschel Earlington. The bishop, like all other Mormon males
tall enough to follow a plow or mount a horse, was out in the harvest
fields which, in squares of green and brown, ringed Ammon like a
blocked quilt of hope and promise. The elder wife of the bishop read the
letter from Brigham Young, presented by the two men, and the result
was another Mormon miracle. Sister Earlington, all smiles and hearty acceptance, had given them cool buttermilk to drink, had sped a youngster
out to call the bishop, and had herself aided the men in putting up
their horses and mule in the stray pound at the south end of the cattle
run. The stray pound, entered by a three-rod lane, was completely ringed
by the sheds and corrals of the town dwellers, and at the town's very
center. And when Sister Earlington thus publicly gave her approval of
two young men who were both army and Gentile, Ammon's cackling
and gabbling women not only joined in their acceptance, but had
plenty more to cackle and gabble about.

Since the bishop, unfortunately, had taken the morning to go to the
Wasatch "bench" for cedar poles, it was late afternoon before he knew
of the two men who were visiting his town, with Brother Brigham's
blessing. By that time every interested female in town not only knew
of the young Gentiles but were anxious and willing to aid in any way
they could toward their strange project—that is, every female but Nancy
—who, closeting herself in the Corey hut, sweltering in her shame, was
keeping an anxious ear close to the window so as not to miss anything
of interest from the exciting babble outside. Martha Corey had filled her
in on whatever was lacking in the tittle-tattle. Nancy gave no mind to
the verbal blistering Martha alternately unleashed for her morning's
truancy. This had happened often enough. In morbid silence, in the
earthen-floored hut, she thumped the dasher into the churn until the

cream within the elongated barrel, under the onslaughts of her smoldering fury, became a dead and lifeless weight of yellow butter, heavy and viscous to the lift.

For long periods Martha Corey left her alone to her thoughts, while she gabbled with the other wives and neighbors over the strange and unprecedented interest a pair of Gentiles had in Ammon. By the time Nancy had drained off the buttermilk to the crock, covered the crock with muslin to protect its contents from the ants and crawlers, and had beaten and kneaded the last stubborn milk out of the butter, some of her inner agitation had drained out to dead remorse. But none of her interest in Joel Scott had diminished. She kneaded a batch of bread dough near enough to the window to tune her ear to what was happening. Occasionally she peeked like a cautious wraith through the muslin curtains at what was occurring outside.

The men, she knew, had an inordinate interest in Ammon. Why, she could only guess. Through the occasional appearances of her mother, the agitated voices she could hear outside, and her own window peeking, she'd spent the hours piecing together, and thinking on the strange things that were happening this day.

"He goes around with a notebook in his hand—counted each of the sixty-one cabins inside the wall," Martha had sighed worriedly. "He's visited the grist mill at the north wall. He wanted to know where the creek came from. We told him it flowed down Ammon Canyon, out of the Wasatch, passed center of town, and on into Utah Lake. He asked how the town got its name. We told him it came from the *Book of Mormon*, and that he ought to be a-readin' it."

And Nancy, like a rejected, defeathered bird, had allowed herself no active part to these goings-on. As she labored at her dough mixing, she knew that Martha's prating about "he" had meant the only one and important stranger in their midst. It was Joel who was walking Ammon with a notebook, and asking the questions. Edward probably had Flora up creek, exploring the willows. It was Joel who was the curious one. For the man's interest, she was certain, was as insatiable as his charm. That he took notes could only be flattering to the Mormon women, and the fact he was their visitor with full approval and permission of Brother Brigham and the Authorities, was enough to melt the usual Mormon reticence toward a Gentile. Nancy—jealous, frightened, humiliated—could only desperately wish she might elbow out a few of the quacking ducks who now surrounded the man, and be allowed, alone, to the telling of Ammon's story.

Her strong young hands flopped the heavy and flabby mass of dough over, and she slammed it angrily down to the flour-dusted board.

Martha's nervous head had bobbed on her neck like a hen turkey as, throughout the morning, she'd freshened the cabin with verbal samples of the weird happenings outside. There could be no doubt Joel and his notebook were stirring up as much interest among the women as would a daylight entry of the Three Nephites. To the sad and silent Nancy, even the stalest tidbits were something to be mentally devoured.

"Sister Earlington explained to him that a lot of the houses once stood out on the fields," Martha had said at one of those informative intervals. "That the Utes, in the big uprising, had caused us to fort up, and move our living—such as it is—behind walls. And then this captain wanted to know all about the walls. We told him they were built by the back-breaking labor of men, faced with the necessity of survival. He wanted to know just how, and we told him—that twelve feet of clay, six feet wide—had been tamped into wooden forms, and around pine poles set six feet apart. That no one would ever know how many aching backs it had taken to build the fort—but that it held off the Utes, and that was important. He must be a little odd, because he started drawin' pitchers of it."

The incessant bobbing of Martha's head had indicated how interestingly odd she had thought the man. And only Nancy, smugly, silently, had really known how much more than oddity there was about this exciting Gentile.

"We walked him between the houses and the wall, so he could see how we stored grain, wood, and hay, and shedded our animals. But that wasn't enough for his curiosity. He wanted to see the meetin' house, the square, the public and private corrals—even the stray pound."

And Nancy could see, from the window, that the soldiers' animals were tethered in the stray pound, and she knew, almost to certainty, that they would be sleeping at the bishop's house instead of outside the wall. She knew, too, that all these things about Ammon, and a plenty more, she could herself have told him—had she not spoiled it all forever by being such an impulsive, bird-brained fool.

"'Twas the courtin' scare that babbled me so foolish," she moaned aloud, when once more alone. Viciously she slapped at the dough. "Oh, God, I *can't* be—and I'm *not* gonna be—an apostle's plural woman! I'm not gonna be *any* man's plural woman! I'll run away with the Lamanites. I'll be a squaw first. I'll send myself to hell—and I don't care!" Two teardrops landed neatly in the middle of the dough. Without caring a damn, she folded the tears into the flaccid mass, lifted it high, and slammed it savagely down to the board.

As to her soldier, that was more than sorrow. Had she not bobbled her big chance, she, instead of a bunch of gabbling witches, could right now be telling Joel all he wanted to know about Ammon. He could know from her that the town no longer was in danger. That the Indians, presently feeding off the Saints like a voracious plague, would rather beg or steal than fight. She could be telling him that these Indians—or Lamanites—hadn't yet turned white like the *Book of Mormon* said they would, but they no longer were scalping Saints, either. That the walls of Ammon were melting lower with every rain, and no one cared. That industrious brethren, like Isaac Corey, were hoping and planning for new houses on the original townsite outside the fort. That there was so little danger now, even soldiers could enter Ammon, and be cordially received—or embarrassed by an idiot girl trying to run away from the "Principle."

Nancy shook the flour from her hands, wiped her eyes by a rub with her upper sleeve. Impulsively she turned from the table and its breadboard. Her bare feet plodded across the cool and earthy floor to the plank door. With floury hand she drew the iron bolt, opened the door a crack, and peered out across the town corrals. Under summer sun, in the stray pound alongside the horses, and stared at by a motley group of women and youngsters, was Joel. He had set himself up an easel and—without a thought, apparently, as to how strangely it might appear to his viewers—was sketching the walled town of Ammon. Nancy, like any other gawking Saint, watched him in wonderment.

Soldiers she had seen before. While she and her mother had slaved like drudges milking cows and bending over the foul-smelling cheese vats at Isaac Corey's dairy below the Point of the Mountain, there had been soldiers to see. Isaac, tireless worker himself, made certain that none of his four wives or any of his fourteen robust children ever shirked. He was a canny, clever man—but just and honest. His canniness was instantly apparent in any trading—horses or land—and the fact that he had established this dairy farm on the lush margins of the Jordan River, below The Point, and close in to the insatiable military demands of Camp Floyd. His impeccable record in the priesthood, and the fact that each of his wives took their seasonal turns at The Point and at Ammon, was proof enough he was a just man. He could neither read nor write, but his wives and those of his daughters who could "spell and cipher" took their just turns evenings, reading aloud from the *Book of Mormon* or the *Doctrine and Covenants*. One tenth of all his earthly increase never failed to go to the Church. Illiteracy alone had kept him from rising to the dignity and station of a bishop, a stake president, or an apostle. But Nancy, along with all his family kingdom, knew that Isaac eventually would be "called" to fill a mission.

It was at the dairy farm, at The Point, where she and Flora had seen and known the soldiers—the drunken lechers who came to the farm in the commissary wagons, or that wild cavalryman who had chased her horseback through the cedar groves. He'd followed her, frighteningly close, and howling like a Ute. But Nancy, like most Mormon farm girls, had ridden horses from the time her legs had been stringy enough to scissor one, and the little Indian pinto she was riding bareback that day had kept her virtuously safe from the madman at her back. And it was well for the cavalryman. Had he laid filthy Gentile hands upon her, he would have gotten his throat slit as certain as God lived. Isaac Corey, maybe with the help of Porter Rockwell, who managed the stage station ten miles north of The Point, would have seen that there was atonement. Mormon womenfolk were not to be defiled by Gentile soldiers. And among the Saints these matters were never taken lightly.

Thoughtfully Nancy wiped the flour from her hands onto her starched muslin apron. She stared out at her strange soldier, and the ache in her chest was like a throbbing wound. Amid the hubbub, Joel was still sketching, unconcerned. Probably with never a thought that what she had said was no stupid girl's whim; that she truly had been thinking heavy on it; that, for some reason, she had dared any peril to say it. Yes, soldiers she had seen before. But never had there been one, or ever would be, a soldier like this man.

He would go away, and it would be the last she would ever see of Joel. She would say "yes" to Apostle Cragg, or some other fat dignitary, and by that act, lift herself out of Ammon, drudgery, and maybe into the high circles so coveted by most every Mormon girl. But God—and maybe her own Mother Corey—knew how vile, wicked, and rebellious she was at heart. She wanted no part of the everlasting covenant, if it meant sharing her husband's bed with another woman. With a Gentile, she could never wear the garment of the covenant, and there would probably be nothing ahead but eternal damnation. But she wanted a Gentile. This Gentile. And she gritted her teeth like a clove press as she thought of it.

But her Gentile couldn't care less. For him she had almost offered herself into damnation—in this life, and the next. Unconcernedly he was sketching the odorous, rotting skeleton that was Ammon. Well, let him pack up his sketch bag, his notebook, and his coffee pot, and go on to hell alone! He was a soldier. And Isaac Corey could clearly and quickly tell you what a soldier was!

For Isaac had never allowed any of his womenfolk to go near Camp Floyd alone. Uneducated though his voice might be, it had cried out, from ward pulpit and family circle, the unbelievable things his keen eyes and sharp perceptions had shown him about Floyd. Past the sentries, and inside the gates, was military neatness and precision. Outside the gates, and beyond the sentries, was Hogtown, where liquor and lechery flowed endlessly in tents, mud huts, and clapboard brothels. Here were gambling and wanton women; here was the trail's end for Mormon girls who ran away into whoredom; here was the place where Ute squaws, in cedar-pole shacks, were sold by their men to the soldiers, at a bargain price over the white girls. Here was a place of filth, abomination, and disease, which only Isaac could describe. "I saw with my own eyes the burning," he had described it. "The squaws were rotting with disease, so Arrapeen decided to put a stop to it. He had his braves tie up every sick squaw. He built a big fire of dry cedar. And he burned 'em alive! Shoulda burned the white women, too. For I tell you, a Mormon girl is better off dead than to consort with a Gentile soldier!" Well, *she'd* never consorted with a Gentile soldier—but not because she hadn't wanted to. She'd have followed this strange new soldier like a Ute squaw, had he given her chance. But he'd rather sketch the tumbling walls of Ammon.

"Well, let him," she said, and slammed the door.

The door did not stay slammed for long. Nancy scarcely had gotten back to her dough kneading when Martha once more entered, with the usual sureness and dispatch—like any well-trained mare to the stall. Martha, this bony, leathery, shrunken little woman was Mother Corey the third—Aunt Martha to half brothers like Cove or half sisters like Flora. Mother Corey the fourth—Aunt Kirstine to Nancy—was a recent bride to Isaac Corey, a young Danish convert to the Church, only five years older than Nancy, mother of a new Corey boy, and at present serving her allotted turn with the dairy herd at The Point. For the fourth and final time, Martha snatched from off her rounded shoulders and corded neck the black knit "fascinator" she never failed to wear outside— summer or winter—and hung it on the peg at the back of the door. "When you set that dough to rise, Nan," she said, advancing brusquely toward the gray-ashed and tired old fireplace, "you'd better stir up some sweetcake. Millie gave me my share of the molasses this morning." She scratched herself casually and reflectively. "Them soldier fellows have sure set this town ga-thumpin'." Her gray-streaked, straight-combed head

23

peered into the sooted iron water pot hanging disconsolately from its crane over a fire that had all but given up. "You should see 'em, Nan. Flora's had a time with 'em. And the bishop's sure tooken 'em in." Martha grabbed a couple of chunks of dry juniper from the room's corner woodpile, and tossed them on the wearied fire.

"I saw them," Nancy said, patting the dough she'd laid to rest in the big pan. "I've seen soldiers. What's so strange or important about *these* soldiers? What they doing here? Soldiers are not wanted in town."

"Brother Brigham says it's all right. To give 'em every assistance, and show 'em every courtesy. That's what the note said." Martha Corey watched the tiny flame trails up the stringy juniper bark. The crackle and snap told her the fire was not too dead for further work. "Oddly, they're not attached to Floyd. They've been a week in Salt Lake. They're both finishing out with the Army, and headed east. The little captain with the funny hair is writing something about Mormon policy with the Indians. Seems most interested about how we forted up during the big troubles. He's drawin' a pitcher of our town right now. Wants to visit other walled towns. The tall one seems to be along for the ride, but the artist man with the funny hair is real educated. Lots of learnin', and seems sharp as a tack."

Idly Nancy peeled the flecks of dough off her fingers—fingers that were strong and agile because they'd gotten their strength and agility through endless hours of pulling teats on cows; by cording, spinning, dough kneading, and even the hefty work of the fields. "You seem to know a plenty lot about these soldiers, Mums," she said with a sort of sad flippancy, "but I bet you don't know how the artist man got his queer hair."

Martha turned, and looked questioningly at her daughter. "Do you?"

"He says it's a wound from the Civil War. Says a minnie ball creased his head, and that the ball killed a man behind him. Guess he's glad he's a little short. And he also boils eggs, and makes his coffee in the same water. I can add, too, that he's still a Gentile—for the time being, maybe, a soldier—and probably as evil as hell."

The dark, beady eyes of Martha searched and saw her own daughter's tears. Her head gave one of its odd, convulsive shakes, and she moved quickly toward Nancy. "So that's it," she said. "That's where you girls were all morning." She reached Nancy's side and peered quizzically at her. "If you saw these men," she said, "why have you been weeping and hiding? I sensed it all along, because Flora's jumping around town like a colt out of halter. And *you* lock yourself indoors. Did this man—?"

"No, he didn't." Nancy grinned weakly in spite of her tears. For a moment she sharply studied the homely face of this woman who was her mother. The drudgery, the caustic sorrow of two unhappy marriages were written there as plain as the signposts to hell. It made the woman's fretting over a daughter's turbulence seem a trifle ridiculous. "Flora and I watched 'em from the wall. They talked us into dropping down and joining 'em."

"And you did?"

"We did."

Martha snorted, and shook her head convulsively. "They must have been *some* talkers," she growled. "Or you were mighty eager to climb down with 'em. All the time you shirking your work, and me screaming lungs out trying to find you." She wagged her head sadly. "I'm ashamed of you, Nan. And I'm deep worried about you."

Mechanically Nancy shoved the pan of dough to the back of the table, and drew a clean towel over it to keep dust and bugs out during its rise. "Maybe you've got reasons to be ashamed and worried," she said, quietly. "I would have married this man. I'd have gone anywhere he says."

"I *thought* he was a fast one," Martha decided with conviction. "Snatches 'em off the wall! Of all the likes! Wait till Isaac hears about this!"

"Please, Mums," Nancy said, wearily. "It's *me* that's the fast one. So try to simmer down." She drew a knife from the table drawer. While her mother waited expectantly, she began scraping the dough scraps and flour to the center of the breadboard. "I'm just plain desperate. I don't want to marry into the Principle. Before I'll be a plural wife—I'll marry *any* Gentile. I can't stand these old stallions that swarm in every Sunday —washed down with tar soap—wearing boiled shirts and sweet-scented bear grease—smiling, and pawing, and fawning—hungering to add to their increase. They stammer out silly things—and, in the next breath, thunder about the glory of God and the heavenly hosts—and all the time their eyes, and their trembling, sweaty hands tell me what they're after. They come a-courtin'—while at home they've left behind their pregnant, tired women, and houses full of snotty kids. They want to add me to their increase. Father Corey thinks it's a big thing to match me up with an apostle. Or to match Flora up with a Provo bishop. But it ain't right, Mums! Flora and me have talked a lot about it. Father says it'll mean exaltation hereafter. But what about *here*—and *now*?"

"The Principle's not an easy thing to live," said Martha in kind concern. "Never was intended to be. I'll confess—with Enoch Brayton—I'd have done anything to get out of it—and away from him. Brayton was unfair to me as a woman, and cruel. But Brother Brigham was kind enough to take me away from him—and to give me to Isaac Corey."

"And Isaac Corey has worked you like a plowhorse ever since! You think I'm blind?" Nancy shrugged. "Even this may be easier than what you had at first. I'm not the one to say. But it's *all* bad. *All* bad." Idly she speared at a dough morsel with the knife. "When I see what the Principle has done—and is doing—to you—I'd rather die than be a plural wife."

"So you try to run away with a Gentile soldier," Martha said, leaning wearily against the table. "That's a *real* death."

Thoughtfully Nancy scraped the dough leavings into a tiny pile. "Truth is, the Gentile wouldn't have me. Never gave me a chance." She turned, and looked again at her mother. "He never insulted or molested me, so there's no need to tell anything about it to Isaac Corey. He was every inch a gentleman. But when I talked about my true and deep feelings, he quick showed me he wasn't interested. I feel like a real fool."

"And you are one . . . no mistake," Martha agreed. "Bad enough to throw yourself at a man . . . but a Gentile . . . and a soldier!" She blinked her eyes, and her head shuddered sideways. "You've been taught the Gospel. You've grown up in it. You know what's right. You know what's wrong. But it's a pain to an old, sick soul to hear her only living child tell how little she cares. Willing and anxious to throw yourself away on any bummer out of the unknown. Do you wanta cut yourself away from eternal glory? Wanta be a daughter of perdition? Are you as anxious and willing to live in Hogtown, like any other soldier's woman or squaw? Lord, Nan, I'd hoped better of you!"

"You make it sound as though I'd spurned heaven to choose hell." Nancy lugged the big breadboard over to the hearth and scraped the dough leavings into the sputtering and smoking fire. She wasn't sure whether she'd weep, or howl her anguish like some calf being mutated under the swift, sure knife of Isaac Corey. "You said yourself that the captain was nice. Educated. Sharp as a tack." Angrily she hung the heavy board to its hardwood peg on the clay-calked log wall. "He's not like the men of Ammon. He's not like the men who come here. Even *you* admit it. He looks happy. Our menfolk are not."

"Probably never did a real day's work in his life," Martha sighed defensively. "Our menfolk plow, and plant, fight pestilence, and try to wring a living from the earth. They're trying to build a kingdom, Nan. It's cruel, hard labor . . . not calculated to make a man gay. Our men *are* happy in their own way. But I guess it's hard for a young girl to see.

Especially when she wants to be as giddy and rebellious as a sheep in a ticking vat."

"I'm not mad at the Church, Mums," Nancy said. "But I *am* scared of these sanctimonious old bloats who are trying to marry me. Brother Corey's daughter is now old enough to be plucked for some old dodderer's eternal increase. No wonder the young men are sad. They get little enough chance for even *one* wife. Instead, they're sent on missions, while the old men gather in the virgins. Why I'd be proud to plow and plant alongside a man . . . could he be young, and happy, and full of hope. And—providing I could be his one and only wife. But who comes a-courtin' Nancy Corey? The old men—bald, fat, and slicked up with grease and courtin' scent. All they talk about is their holy increase, and the glorious covenant revealed by the Prophet in these latter days. I don't see any young men who *dare* come a-courtin' Nancy Corey. And I'll be a daughter of perdition, and the wife of a one-woman Gentile, before I'll be added to the increase of such a man as Apostle Cragg!"

"Many a young woman would envy your chance," Martha said weakly. "They're *all* looking to marry somebody high in the Church."

"Well, let 'em! Let 'em have *him!* You married Enoch Brayton because he was a president of the Seventies. Because he was close to the Prophet at Nauvoo!"

"I married Enoch Brayton because I loved him," Martha sighed again. "We were both young, then. And in the beginning, I was his only wife."

"And look where it led you," Nancy said. And she thought of this woman who was her mother. Heavy with child, she had walked the plains—while Enoch's newer and younger favorite rode, and giggled in derision. She looked at this graying piece of rawhide and sinew, who, loyal to the Principle, labored uncomplainingly in the plural harness with Isaac Corey, because God was not unmindful of her sacrifice, and because the other man Brigham had given her was just, honorable, and "magnified his calling." And that was it. Suppose her daughter somehow escaped the hungry clutches of Apostle Cragg, or some other sermon-spouting dignitary, and *was* lucky enough to marry one of the apple-cheeked young men before they sent him overseas to the field of harvest? As sure as God were in His heavens, this young man would later fall into the pattern—receive encouragement from the Authorities—and start gathering his own increase. That *was* the pattern. Few women escaped it. "I'll wed a Gentile—and I'll see myself in hell—before I'll be a plural wife to *anyone!*" Nancy suddenly shouted. "I'd rather be dead than face the life you've known! Talk about *hell!*"

Martha's head went into a quick twitching spasm. It stopped, and

27

she blinked wearily. "They're not all like mine, Nan," she said tenderly. "You're pretty, and at heart you're a good girl. It's hard for such a woman as me to blame you for what you're thinking. But to marry high in the Church can be an easy life."

"High or low," Nancy howled defiantly, "I'll be a plural wife to *no* man!"

Quickly Martha's thin and leathery arm went around the shoulders of her rebellious daughter. "I understand," she said, quietly. "I know just how you feel. I'll say nothing to Isaac. Anyway, he's at Millie's . . . and it's not his turn here. The soldiers will be at Bishop Earlington's tonight. But tomorrow . . . put on your shoes . . . and dress like Sunday. Walk around like nothing at all happened. Keep your head high. Don't be brassy. Don't be pushy. Walk around like any decent Mormon girl should. You're pretty, Nan. You're young . . . and not work-sunk. Maybe he'll notice you. Maybe he'll notice you . . . like the first time." She squeezed Nancy's shoulders reassuringly.

Nancy turned, and nuzzled comfortingly to the haven of Martha's arms. She might never again make time with this man Joel—but, thank God, one mother in Zion understood.

III

NIGHT TORE WITH FURY AT THE TOWN OF AMMON. THE CLOUD FLEECE which, during the day, had rolled with summer aimlessness, took on new determination from the lake winds, and piled high, dark, and urgent to the southwest. After the black wall of the gathering storm had blotted out the last furious glow of the dying sun, the distant stabs of lightning and low rumble of its thunder warned of the wet and noisy time ahead.

The children and the menfolk came in at the close of day. As always, they went about their chores—adding their own discord to the seething noise and clatter of the town. The walls, once planned to keep hostile humans from coming in, were now doubly effective in keeping a suffocating, noisy mass of humanity from breaking out. Bishop Earlington fetched in his load of cedar posts. His sons, like other loyal and helpful Mormon sons, unhitched the team, grained the horses in the fenced corral circumspectly set aside to the bishop's use. Isaac Corey came in with the other menfolk, gave his team to Cove, Flora's wild and erratic older brother, for feed and care, and went directly to Flora's mother—Aunt Millie—for food and bed. This week it was Isaac's turn with this particular Corey family. Other than a cheery wave as he, and Cove, and the smaller boys drove by toward the log house, neither Martha nor Nancy saw more of him. And tonight, for once, they were not sorry.

When Nancy went out to the milking—not too great a chore with only one family cow to worry about—the wind already was churning the air with dust, with bark, hay, and manure straws from Ammon's sixty corrals. Closing darkness brought zip and meaning to the distant lightning, and the low grumble of the thunder from the west told throatily of the distance and time yet separating them from the storm. Her heart thumped along with the squeak and rattle of the empty bucket on her arm as she glanced demurely but searchingly toward the town's stray pound. The soldiers' horses were still there, munching contentedly at the town's bounty, but the soldiers were gone. Joel's sketching easel had vanished from the public cattle run—and so had he. Backed by Brother Brigham's written introduction, they would be honored guests of the Earlingtons this night, with probably no necessity for boiling eggs at the town wall tomorrow morning.

Yes, and the best part of her own living could be tomorrow. She envied the Earlingtons, that they could be so especially singled out; to feed, wait on, and listen to the rich talk and interests of these men who had come so far. But tomorrow would come. And, with the help and connivance of Martha, she could somehow make it her day.

A minute later, while the wind eddied mischievously about the town, Nancy laid her head to old Gertie's aromatic flank, and the twin streams of milk, blasted from the teats by her strong young hands, were playing their own merry and hopeful little tune on the tin bottom of the bucket. Actually, her mother had been more startled than furious. And how could anyone who had fared as badly under the Principle as had Martha Corey ever be furious at a daughter who was set in her mind not to get into it? Tomorrow would come, and she'd try not to be pushy or brassy about it.

But before tomorrow would come, there were a few more reckonings with tonight. Come supper finished, and the chores which every Saint had his or her allotted share, accomplished for the day, Flora Corey made her usual nightly visit to the cabin of Nancy and Martha. By the light of the fire, and the wind-drafted candles behind them, the two girls toasted their feet on the wide rock hearth, and talked of the day. Nancy was secretive about the thing that had sped her in shame and terror from Joel; and she confided no part of it to Flora, or her plans for tomorrow. On the other hand, Flora, the impulsive one, had no such culpability against her, and no reason that was apparent to be ashamed. She had been rewarded with a joyful afternoon's truancy.

While Joel had made his notes, sketched his sketches, and talked himself out about Ammon, Flora had tendered his companion with a far less intellectual tour. They had strolled around inside the fort, inspected the woodpiles and careful-stacked hay against the wall, kept out of the way of noisy urchins, toddling babies, the plethora of town dogs, and the too many women with sin-hunting eyes and gossipy tongues. They had taken a fast look at the rows of log houses around the quadrangle, ducked under the wall at the north creek hole, and had followed the stream up past the grist mill toward the bridge and willow banks. Like any soldier, Edward had tried for advantage and, according to Flora, had been clouted for his pains—as could be expected from any virtuous Mormon girl. "He talked like a windmill," Flora confided. "But he's nonsensical, and a real laugh. He worried a lot about my bare feet, and wanted to lend me his boots. And he asked a million questions about plural marriage. Said he and Joel wanted to see the abomination first-hand." But back in town, Sister Earlington had quickly taken over. And when the bishop came, that was the end of any public availability to the soldier boys. Instinctively, Nancy knew that Flora, too, was anxious for tomorrow.

But tomorrow was not to come easily. Two hours after midnight the storm gathered its courage, and burst upon Utah Valley with a fury that was spectacular and deafening. Its lightning stabbed the earth in ear-shattering explosions, with only the more distant bolts rolling out in shuddering thunder. The Saints caught a real storm that night. In a land of ungentle thunderstorms, this one turned out to be a real pulse-quickener. And when the inky clouds had packed themselves into the deep-gashed canyons of the towering Wasatches, it was hell's artillery for certain.

And then came the rain, as though the lake itself had been turned bottoms-up. Ammon's corrals, and the quadrangle's streets, became quagmires within minutes. The animals laid back their ears in terror, while their slender legs sank deep into the mud. From her bed, Nancy could hear the drip of water from the earthen roof above, and knew that a cabin full of mud would be their problem with the dawn. Sod and earth slithered like syrup from off the roofs of Ammon. And before the rain stopped, shortly before daylight, the town's mud wall had melted a little lower, and was gashed afresh with the storm.

The sudden end of the fury reminded Nancy of Isaac's quick dispatch of a hog. When his sure knife found the gullet, there was the moment of howling chaos, but death came quick as the blood pulsed torrentially out of the arteries. And so did the tumultuous life of the night drain itself out, and the dawn of the tomorrow she had looked for came out of the east as pretty and as peaceful as one could wish. Lightning had cleansed the air, and left her valley deliriously alive with the life-quickening scent of ozone. A million tons of rain water had washed the valley clean, and with the first grayness of morning, the gulls were again wheeling overhead, crying their plaintive cry, as they searched for the free-washed worms, and the water-soaked insects of Utah's rich earth.

But inside the cabin, the storm had departed differently. The place was one huge and abysmal mess. Nancy's bunk, tucked high and close to the north eaves of the big room, had somehow come through dry and untouched. The only other room of the cabin, the bedroom, partitioned off with a willow wall, sacred to Martha, and more sacred to Isaac during his allotted sojourn, had caught a full share of water and mud. At daybreak Nancy could hear her mother's stirrings, as she had heard them during the storm. Dawn's inspection revealed a more interesting scene.

To cope with the drizzling streams pouring down from the earth-and-straw roof, Martha, probably by candlelight, had been forced to use whatever vessels and utensils were available to catch the water. The cabin's two chamber pots—Nancy's plain china one, and the larger, florally ornate creation that had ridden the Brayton wagon across the plains—had served most usefully through the storm. The wide wooden bed, a product of Isaac's thrifty craftsmanship, was spiked to the wall, and could not be moved from harm's way. So the big pot had been spotted atop the bed, precisely in line to catch the roily drippings from above. Nancy's little thundermug was doing a similar service in the center of the room, alongside the milk pans and kettles Martha had been forced to press into emergency service. It somehow stirred up the giggles in Nancy—her first look at the big Brayton pot, tinkling with falling water, on the exact side of the bed eternally reserved and sacred to the kingship of Isaac Corey. Martha, heavy-eyed from lack of sleep, and the havoc around her, could see nothing funny or even promising about the new day.

Less damage had come to the big room, and also less care about its leaks. Nancy, dry, warm, and satisfied even to her dreams, had not once

31

arisen during the storm—much less worried about plugging dribbles. But, as she left the sputtering Martha, to tour the cabin in her nightgown, there was no question about the big room catching its toll. The pan of dough, set to rise, and which would have gone into the two Dutch ovens for baking, was yellow with muddy water. The shelf of dishes, too, must now be washed before they again could be used, and the low spots in the earthen floor were puddles. But the logs and kindling were dry, and in her bare feet Nancy lugged an armload to the fireplace. Kneeling into its black cavern, she pushed aside the sooty spider, smoothed out the still warm gray ashes, and peeled enough cedar bark for a start. The sulphur match sputtered, but the fire caught, and she quickly piled on enough thin kindling for a good start. She drew the big, smoky water pot forward on the hob, and while the fire caught on with crackling vigor, she went back to the bunk to get into her clothes.

This took little time—for it was summer, and one didn't wear too much. But still, it was the garb of a mature woman, because Nancy was never allowed to forget that she was now fifteen. There were the long, fluted pants of maturity, and the white shift which hung down from the shoulders—ordinarily made of unbleached muslin, but in the case of Nancy, fashioned from those ever useful flour sacks—well bleached with many a tubbing. Over this went the shapeless muslin petticoat, and over that the equally shapeless brown "house sack" she had worn the day before. No shoes or stockings were necessary. It was summer. These were saved for Sundays or courtin' visits.

Nancy, because she had been reminded of it, and because she had no need to be reminded of it, knew full well that she was a mature woman. She knew, too, that she was a Latter-day Saint. She knew also that on the day she entered the Endowment House in marriage—or the great temple when it was finished—her garb as a Mormon woman would change in one basic essential. From that day hence, instead of fluted muslin pants, she would wear the ankle-length holy garment, as did every other Mormon woman who was "chosen." This solemn marriage—for time and all eternity—could not be taken lightly, and there certainly was nothing frivolous about the badge of the covenant, the underwear. But such fleeting thoughts, as she clambered with speed and dispatch into her clothes, were quickly smothered by a more panicky one. "Golly damn," she moaned. And then she shrieked, "Mother!"

"Good Lord, what's the matter?" Instantly, like a vision from the other world, Martha appeared in the bedroom doorway—wraithlike and slender in her rumpled, muddy nightgown. "What's wrong?"

"Just thought of something," Nancy said. "And I'm afraid to ask."

Martha relaxed. "From that yowl, I thought you'd stepped on a snake." Her head bobbed nervously, and she retreated back into the bedroom.

Nancy shook the dress down around her bare legs and petticoat, and followed her mother toward the door. "Did our Sunday clothes get spoiled?" she asked, almost in fright. "Did mud and water get into the drawers and the chest?"

"No, they're dry," Martha grumbled, "and small thanks to you. I work half the night keeping things out of harm's way—while you sleep."

"Then heaven be thanked," Nancy said, gaily pirouetting back toward the fireplace. She tossed a couple of heavier logs to the happy, crackling fire. "I'd set heart to dressing up this morning."

"You'd best set heart to *cleaning* up," came the naggy voice from the bedroom. "It'll take hours to come rid of this mess. I've told Isaac enough times about the roof. Now, maybe he'll take heed. And I hope he got a good wetting at Millie's."

"I'll catch the milking first," Nancy offered.

"Do that," Martha snapped.

A speedy trip to the outhouse, a sousing with soap and water at the washstand beside the back door, and Nancy was ready for her first chores. All water had been hauled from the creek the night before. She, nor no other woman in Ammon, failed to do that. It was one of the rules—born of experience and the Indian troubles—to always have food and water in hand at nightfall. By the time Nancy had finished her meager toilet, Martha too was up and dressed.

But the first thing Martha did was to drop Nancy's waterlogged and mud-begrimed bread dough down the hole of the back-yard privy. Even this added work of a new mixing failed to dampen Nancy's spirits as she swung out the door, bucket pendulumed from her right hand, headed for the milking.

The sun already was beating hard across the square, the air was like the glory of God, and the smell of the good earth was everywhere. She waved at Sister Bringhurst, on a similar errand, and wondered vaguely if the stupid roosters were going to crow their throats and gullets out. The soldiers' horses and mule were still in the stray pen, probably in mire, but the men, she was happy to note, had not shared the mire with them. Ammon's visitors had slept snugly and warmly at Bishop Earlington's. And the bishop's house had one of the town's few shingled roofs. Yes, the men had slept snugly and warmly—but old Gertie was a mess. It took two buckets of water, lugged from the roily and swollen creek which bisected the cattle run, and flowed squarely through the center of Ammon, to wash Gertie's flank and udder clean enough for a go at the milking. But Nancy had had experience. She could play tunes with a cow's teats. It was a fast milking.

The other jobs around the house, however, were not so quickly accomplished. Martha was always a tyrant when the house was in a mess. Everything around her had to be as neat as the Gospel's teachings. Everything this morning had to be scrubbed and put away. She scarcely allowed time for breakfast. The new mixing of bread had to go into the newly cleaned pan, for rising. A stew had to be put on for lunch, and a fresh new stir-up of sweetcake. Through it all Nancy began wondering if Martha weren't deliberately slowing down or road-blocking her resolve to look sweet for Joel. An hour and a half more of Martha's driving, and the sand in Nancy finally came up. She was a woman! The hour was frantically important! To the devil with all this scrub and shine!

Deliberately, rebelliously, she pulled on her newest stockings and her shoes. Over her petticoat she drew on the pretty blue ruffled Sunday frock—all finished except for a few bastings—the frock that was to be readied for an apostle's eye. While Martha protested this premature use of it, in favor of a second best, Nancy defiantly tied its ribbon sash about her slender waist, and pinned it with an artificial flower from the big chest. She combed back her long black hair, and nervously and quickly worked at its shine. Martha finally relaxed enough to pin a blue ribbon at the back, and hang it straight and gay. The blue bonnet, to match, would yet take days to finish. Today Nancy had no mind about going bareheaded.

As to the morning's conquest, she had not the slightest idea as to how it should be conducted. Not until she had let herself out the cabin door, to the bright new earth outside, did her thinking come to grips with the problem. First, she might walk past the bishop's door, casually say good morning to Sister Earlington, and start the comments with the weather. Or she could walk over and admire the men's horses, and there Joel might surely find her, still admiring. And then suddenly she looked in the direction of the stray pound. And, just as suddenly, she saw that the horses were gone.

She strode by the bishop's door, and there was nothing casual or demure about her panic. Her eyes were wide and searching; terror was in her heart. There, at least partially according to plan, she met Sister Earlington—but failed to start the comments with the weather.

"Good morning, Nancy," Sister Earlington purred. "My, but you look—"

"Where are they?" Nancy cried in panic. "Have they gone?"

"You mean . . . the young men?" The good sister nodded knowingly, and stared.

"Yes!" Nancy screeched. "Who else?"

"Why, they left a little while ago." Sister Earlington's smile revealed her thinking. "I had no idea you—"

Nancy was off to the east gate like a startled antelope. She passed the meeting house unnoticed. At the gates—now scarcely ever closed—she peered long and sadly at the muddy road ahead. A quarter of a mile eastward it forked—one direction southward, and through the fields, toward Provo—the other northward toward The Point, Camp Floyd, and Salt Lake. In this direction her brown eyes stared intently. Horses and wagons rattled and clinked their way out through the gateway toward the fields beyond—the men and boys on their empty, bumping vehicles staring in surprise and amusement at Nancy Corey in her Sunday best at this the muddiest of midweeks. To them she paid no heed—but she failed utterly to see her soldiers. Tears welled up in her eyes, and anger convulsed her soul. "Damn the storm," she muttered. "Damn that mother of mine."

She turned back, rubbed her eyes, and ran up the alleyway between the shed-encrusted wall and the east row of cabins. At her old familiar place, she yanked off her shoes, and peeled off her long stockings. Lifting her skirts, clutching her stockings, and leaving her shoes on the damp earth, she started one-handedly up the worn cleats of the ladder. A minute later she was atop the old wall. Its weather edge was ditched and pooled with water, but there were drier spots. But from here one could see. Once more she anxiously scanned to northward.

And then she spied them. Little blobs of darkness against the sage in the distance. Unhurried, leisurely, they rode along—behind them the head-tossing pack animal. She was certain it was Joel in the lead.

Joel was riding away. He hadn't even noticed her. And there was so much she had wanted to tell him.

IV

SINCE JULY 4 WAS ONLY CASUALLY IMPORTANT TO THE MORMON SETTLERS, and its programming and celebration left more or less in the hands of the military and those who doted on the martial fooferaw, it passed safely without an appearance of the "general authorities" from Salt Lake City. For Nancy Corey this meant only that there would be no Apostle Cragg to dress up to, to curtsy to, or to listen to his slobbering over the fundamentals of the Gospel. There would, however, be a ward conference before the summer was out and, since she knew that an apostle would of certainty preside, and knowing also in her heart that Apostle Cragg was not just playing musical chairs in his attention to her, she needed no convincing that the Lord's work on that day would likely be supervised by this same Apostle Cragg. Isaac Corey would then find a way to put this particular dignitary up in style—if things were crowded at the Earlingtons.

But July held also one other probability that the general authorities would shake the mothballs out of their chapel suits, to bless Ammon with a representative delegation. That event would be July 24—the most exciting of all Mormon holidays—the day commemorating the first arrival of the pioneer Saints in Salt Lake Valley—July 24, 1847. That was just eighteen years ago—and three years before Nancy was born. Zion's every town and hamlet celebrated this day. Ammon was joining with Mountain Grove and Pleasanton for a day at the lake. Apostle Jonathan Cragg, shining in scented grease and broadcloth, could just as likely be standing in his calling on that great day.

Not that the Fourth of July passed without a marking in Ammon's calendar. The Utes came in as usual for their patriotic handout. Bishop Earlington, with the help of his ward deacons and priests, saw to it that a tithing steer was barbecued in a hot-coal pit in the cattle run at the center of town. A platform was put up for the oration, and decorated with dyed cloth streamers and American flags. The military, of course, took the main hand this day. To the Saints this had no meaning so far as the accursed Gentile soldiery at Camp Floyd and the new fort now a-building east of Salt Lake was concerned. They might be the Army of the United States, but to the Saints, they were invaders, despoilers of women, and hell-raising drunks. The Saints invariably insisted on celebrating the Fourth of July in their own way, and resented any intrusion of the American Army of occupation in the observance.

"Connor's no Mormon lover, but I think the general's got sense enough to keep his men in line come Fourth of July," Isaac Corey had predicted. "If there's patriotism to be shown—let the Nauvoo Legion do it. We got our belly full of Johnston's army, and the invasion of '57. Now it's Connor—and *his* army. Johnston had the good sense to get himself killed in the war. But it looks like this Connor is holing in for a long stay."

Nancy knew that her father had at best partially forgiven Johnston, even without this general's atonement at the battle of Shiloh, simply because Johnston had established Camp Floyd. For Isaac had not fared badly at Floyd. Johnston, before leaving for California, and abdication of command to join the Confederates, had placed Camp Floyd under the leadership of Colonel P. St. George Cooke. That Cooke had personally led the famed Mormon Battalion on its epic march to California in the Mexican War, was reason enough for Isaac or any other Saint to hold no grudge. It was Johnston, with his Utah War, that had opened the wounds. It was this new and implacable General P. E. Connor who now was keeping them bleeding. Isaac Corey, like his fellow Saints, hated Connor, for the fort he was building east of Salt Lake City. It was a dagger aimed at the Church and its people. Isaac had another even deeper hate—Connor, in establishing the new fort, was drying up Camp Floyd, and all the lucrative trade that had been a part of it.

"This year, if he's got any sense," Isaac opined, "Connor will keep his Gentile soldiery in his new Fort Douglas, where they can handily watch Brigham the Prophet, and leave our own Mormon Nauvoo Legion to do the drilling and marching on the Fourth. It would give the Gentiles time to cool gun barrels from their own big war."

Nancy had little direct knowledge of the great war, which had torn eastern America to shambles. She did know that Cooke, with most of the army, had been withdrawn from Camp Floyd, to be thrown into the battles of the rebellion. The huge camp at Cedar Valley, near The Point, and guarded by only a token garrison, had become but a ghostlike reminder of the Mormons' own "rebellion" of 1857. With the Civil War going into four long years, the Saints had begun to rejoice in the fact that the irksome military fetters had been broken in the territory, and Mormon farmers already had commenced eyeing the glass, doors, and the furnishings of Camp Floyd as possible loot to enhance their own dwellings. But the wonderful feel of freedom did not last.

Peace had scarcely been established in the East when General Connor arrived with the new army. He was no Cooke. He loathed Brigham Young, and the underlying hostility of the Saints. He had quickly activated Camp Floyd again, and by the same token prospered its Mormon neighbors like Isaac Corey. But Connor wanted closer scrutiny of the thing he was guarding. Already he was clashing head-on with Brigham. Already he was hated lustily by the Saints. Already there was feverish work on the big fort—which he called Fort Douglas—on the high bench lands east of Salt Lake City. And already Camp Floyd had again commenced to dry up.

But aside from bands and military parade in Salt Lake City, and the raising of the flag high on Pioneer Square for all Saints to see, Connor matched Isaac's hope and prediction. He did have enough sense to leave the other Fourth of July celebrations in the territory strictly alone. Apparently neither he nor his soldiers had the stomach to mix it with the Saints on this day. Yet the Fourth of July in Ammon, as in every other Mormon hamlet, was still a day for the military. The military, however, was not Connor's despised army—it was the Nauvoo Legion. The Legion was shabby, awkward in drill, and made up of work-gnarled farmers. But it was one army the Mormons respected and revered—because it was their own. Though its assemblage was now allowed only on special days, the Saints could never forget that it was instituted by Joseph Smith the Prophet, that it had protected the Saints from the beginning, and that it had held Johnston's army at bay—until Governor Brigham Young, of his own volition, had allowed Johnston entry into Salt Lake Valley.

And so, on July Fourth, Ammon's tattered and seedy contingent of the Nauvoo Legion assembled half a mile up the creek for martial entry into the walled city. As usual Ammon dressed its best for the occasion, and its population was swelled by two hundred Lamanites—known on days other than the Sabbath as lousy, beggaring Utes. At dawn the anvils were blown, with enough gunpowder to rock the town. Nancy and Flora, with all the more agile ones, had hurried through breakfast and chores, to mount the wall and watch the parade as it came up the dusty road.

At nine A.M. everyone started shooting off guns—and it was a real patriotic din. The town's single cannon, lifted tenderly to its spot on the north wall, blasted its quick, fat charge—well wadded and without ball. The old fieldpiece rolled back on its spindly wheels, snubbed by ropes so the kick wouldn't lob it off the wall. Everybody cheered, and, with this noisy signal, the Nauvoo Legion started its march.

Nancy could see the soldiers, and hear the roll of their three drums, long before she could catch the feeble bleat of its single fife. But march it did, up the dusty road to Ammon. There was little of spit-and-polish in this contingent. Four of its troopers had served in the Mormon Battalion. These Battalion boys were today specially honored with horse mounts. The remainder was a motley crew comprising most of Ammon's walkable males, which were not many. Isaac Corey strode, out of step, with Isaac, Jr. and Cove, two of his grown sons—half brothers to Nancy. Isaac, Jr. was Adah's oldest, and already a high priest in the Church. Cove, in the complex Corey family pattern, was a son of Aunt Millie— which made him a full brother to Flora. But Cove was considerably more than that. His being a "Jack Mormon" would have been burden enough for the devout and faithful Father Isaac to bear, but Cove walked with the Legion as an insolent and incorrigible rebel three times over— to the Church, which he now openly denounced; to Brigham, whose perquisites in the Mormon pattern of love life had shattered Cove's own hopes for marriage; to the Legion itself because it was sworn to defend the Brigham he loathed, and the Church upon which he had soured since his abortive mission.

Nancy, who could still love the wild and rebellious Cove, in spite of the fact he was a Jack Mormon, felt that this probably would be a last march in the Nauvoo Legion for this errant Corey son. Even the kind and ever hopeful Isaac had grown caustic toward him and impatient. And Ammon's Saints were publicly wearied with this hellish and insolent traitor to the cause. But Nancy and every Saint present knew that Cove, with his scouting and Indian experiences on the southern rim, was as good a soldier as any of them. Isaac, in the parade, still proudly shouldered the caplock muzzle-loader he had toted across the plains. Cove, along with his more loyal half brother, was not averse to using today's occasion to show off the fancy Sharpe's rifles upon which the Corey boys had squandered their ready money.

By the time the fife could be heard, the fifty men were thrumping through the town's east gate. On the shoulders of these agrarian troopers Nancy saw every conceivable type of weapon. They were shabby, out of step, and bucolic. To any Gentile they would have appeared ludicrous. But the Saints knew their wants, they had their army, and this was a part of their life. This, as Nancy Corey and every other

39

Saint knew, was the Nauvoo Legion. This army—small at Ammon, but large in its aggregate—had been blessed and set apart to its task by Joseph Smith the Prophet. And this army had been true to its calling.

As a Mormon, Nancy shared Ammon's pride in its contingent to the Legion, and something fiercely personal in the Corey men who were partial to it, and lent it meaning. She could smile proudly at the bearded Isaac, knowing well the tireless faith and sinew he ceaselessly had given to it. But her heart, and her frantic wave, went out to the Corey son who represented the family's closest and most hurtful failure. Impudently, as he clumped past, Cove raised both hat and rifle. And he was grinning out at Nancy like an imp from hell.

The fire had burned all night, and the dressed steer had gone into its pit of glowing coals at daybreak. It was well covered and hotly stewing in its juices long before the Legion made noisy entry into the town. Followed by the village urchins, and its every barking dog, the tiny parade clumped and waddled its way past the meeting house and Bishop Earlington's, made a sharp right turn at the two-rod lane leading into the stray pound. The pound's back gates had been thrown open, and the Legion bleated and drummed its way into the more spacious cattle run—through which flowed the creek, and which was the town's center. All the cattle were gone—except for the butchered steer, cooking in its hot nest underground. Here was the speaker's stand, gay with cloth strips and bunting, and with enough chairs for the dignitaries. And to here followed every resident of Ammon able to walk, and every Indian wise enough to the Mormonee calendar to know that this was one of those rare days when Mormonees quit their stupid labors, and shared great heaps of grub with their Lamanite brethren.

By the time Nancy and Flora had gotten themselves off the wall and followed the stragglers into the big run, the army had halted, and had come to attention. Only the four veterans of the Mormon Battalion were struggling to get their nervous mounts in a proper line to the left of the stand. One of these veterans, Nephi Bringhurst, was having more than his share of trouble. His half-wild horse, throughout the parade, had humped and skittied with the noisy drums at its back. Now, facing the source of the tumult, it was laying its ears low, and waltzing erratically against the flanks of the more docile beasts on either side. Then came the thunderous boom of the cannon from the north wall, the shouted command, the ear-shattering ruffle of the drums, and the unmartial and ragged firing of the volley from every musket and rifle in the contingent. Behind the grandstand, Old Glory was going jerkily up the Liberty pole while the drums rattled and fife bleated to the occasion. In front of the stand, Nephi Bringhurst's panicked horse was bucking in ever widening circles, with Mormons and Indians scattering like quail to keep from being trampled by the maddened beast.

For Nephi, the staying alive on the long march with Cooke was as nothing compared with staying atop this spooked broncho. The shrieking Saints and Lamanites somehow managed to get out of the horse's way. Forty feet south of the grandstand, after three wild circles, and to the accompaniment of three drums and a fife, Nephi Bringhurst finally soared over the horse's head. With a mighty splash, he landed in the creek's center. And a couple of courageous young Saints lunged for the dragging reins of the snorting, farting beast.

This ended the noisy part of the ceremony, and Nancy and Flora giggled unfeelingly as the Saints hauled the soaked and battered Elder Bringhurst from the creek and up to the stand, where four chairs of honor had already been placed for Ammon's veterans of the Mormon Battalion. There was the usual confusion while the dignitaries, the local Legion captain, and the other three veterans of the Battalion were seated. As usual, the program began with an overlong prayer, this time by Stake Patriarch Uriah Ursenbach, who intoned God through his beard to bless the nation, the inspired authorities of the Church, the homes, the crops, the animals, and the holy soil of Utah, to which the Saints had so miraculously been led. Each segment of the petition was dwelt on with a length and fervency which, in the aggregate, amounted to quite a hefty request directed Godward. Nephi Bringhurst had already started drying out in the July sun before the Patriarch's prayer was ended by the usual amen in unison from the crowd. He was well dried before the speeches ended.

Since this was a patriotic observance, Judd Wickam, captain of Ammon's contingent of the Nauvoo Legion, led off with the main oration. Only difficulty was that Judd, while brave, and attentive to his calling, had a harelip. In spite of a straining of ears from the assemblage, the Saints of Ammon had difficulty in understanding whether Judd was praising his glorious country, or inciting the Saints to a second rebellion. But, like the Patriarch's prayers, even Judd's oration came to its inevitable end. The crowd dutifully applauded and, as a response, Judd led his army in three "hip-hip-hoorays" to the flag which hung disconsolately from the Liberty pole.

It was inevitable, too, that Seth Biddle would be caught in one of his epileptic seizures somewhere in the program. Fortunately Seth, cognizant of his sometimes dramatic difficulties, had remained far out in the perimeter of the crowd. The Saints graciously cleared a space where Seth could flop and froth undisturbed, and the program went on as usual.

It was inevitable too that Bishop Earlington should be called on for a few choice remarks. This task was filled by the good bishop most willingly. His "overhalls" of weekly labor had been exchanged for his shiny black suit of Sundays, and it was plain enough he was prepared for the occasion. In mood for the day he mentioned the Saints' necessity for respect to the flag, how the signers of the Declaration of Independence had been inspired by Almighty God to their task in the creation of this nation. He mentioned how the *Book of Mormon* stated that "this, the American continent, is a land choice above all other lands of the earth. And it behooves us, as the chosen people, to remember this." He spoke of how, eighteen years before, the pioneers had entered Salt Lake Valley. How, as loyal citizens of this great republic, they had hoisted Old Glory to Ensign Peak. He reviewed how wrong the American government had been in questioning Mormon loyalty to the flag; how wrong it had been in sending an army to Utah; how right the brave Nauvoo Legion had been in resisting. "After being murderously uprooted three times, after seeing our Prophet slain in cold blood, after being driven out of our cities, out of our homes, and onto the trackless deserts and prairies—we had a right to say 'we shall be driven no more!' The defense of home and loved ones, and the right to worship according to conscience, is every man's right. These things we have defended bravely. These things we shall continue to defend!"

But Zion's defense, and the unhealing wounds, were not to be the main points of Bishop Earlington's speech. There could be no question of his patriotic feelings when it came down to his real and closest love— the town of Ammon, and his beloved flock. "When President Brigham Young, in the face of the Indian troubles, ordered the Saints to 'fort up'—we of Ammon did it, and with a will. With Ute arrows over our heads, and with prayers in our hearts for our wives and children, we worked around the clock. It was a task, my brothers, to move our cabins into this place. No man here can forget the bruising labors that went into the building of this great wall. But brethren, *we followed counsel!* While other towns dawdled at the task, *we* forted up! Because we were attentive to our leaders and the task imposed upon us, God has blessed us. Not one of our people, through the thick of our troubles, died at Ute hands.

"I know this is a day for patriotic observance. But I also know that patriotism begins at the hearthside. And so, I feel it not amiss to use

42

this day to pass on to you some new counsel." The kindly, bearded man looked down upon his people, and spoke softly. "The Lamanites, as you can see here among us, no longer wear their war paint. The time of trouble is over. The walls no longer serve a purpose. Brother Brigham, on his last visit, was appalled at the way we live. 'God never meant for Saints to roll themselves up in a bee ball,' he said. 'The war against the Lamanites is over. The war against poverty, adversity, and illiteracy has only begun,' he said. Yesterday I received his new counsel.

"We are to go back once more to the building of our real city of Ammon—foursquare and beautiful as we had planned. The walls are to come down. Chapels are to be built. Houses are again to go up on the town lots. And with all my heart, brethren, I hope you will build new ones, rather than to move back these leaky, filthy, infested huts I see before me.

"And too long have our children tried to learn reading, ciphering, and spelling in our crude little school at the meeting house. The glory of God is intelligence, and the glory of our people shall be in their knowledge and their learning. You've heard Brother Brigham tell of the University of Deseret. Of the plans for the Latter-day Saints Institute, and of another great university to be built at Provo. He's said he'll scour the world, if needs be, to bring to Utah men of scholarship, and men of learning, to teach our Saints the things they'll need to plan and manage a millennium. He asks for new schools—equipped and ready—in every town and city. If the towns and cities have not men and women of sufficient learning to staff them, teachers will be sent from Salt Lake City—and the towns had better be ready to properly pay them. As bishop, and leader, I know I shall live to see these prison walls come down, and the new Ammon arise like a butterfly from its stifling cocoon. If all of us catch this vision, it will come—and it will be beautiful.

"In the building of our city, we are given time. In the education of our children, an immediate and desperate duty is laid upon us. By fall, we must have our school—finished and ready. We already have Brother Brigham's promise of the best teacher he can find!"

There were other points to the bishop's oration, but they were inconsequential. To Nancy Corey, and the Saints now crowded within the walls, the prospects of a new town, with real churches and real schools, came like an explosion of the cannon on the wall. Since August would normally be Martha's turn at The Point farm, Nancy would miss much of the excitement of the town's first building. But what the bishop had revealed was good, and important—and she thought of her own hit-and-miss schooling under Sister Wellington, at the drafty old meeting house. Sister Wellington herself could scarcely read, spell or cipher, and if they staffed the new schoolhouse with this stupid woman, all would be lost before it was ever started.

When the good bishop sat down, the program finished off with the speed of a slide downhill. Stomachs already were growling with hunger, and patriotism could safely be laid away for this July. Willie Tuttle, ward chorister, bobbing rhythmically like a cork in the lake, led the town in singing "The Spirit of God Like a Fire Is Burning" and "the Star-Spangled Banner"; Elder Philaster Fetterman, President of the Seventies, pronounced the benediction. The program was over. The legionnaires, including the Corey menfolk, stashed their muskets and rifles in their respective log shanties, and the covering was rolled from off the hot, savory, and well-cooked steer.

Though the Fourth of July had proven a bit more startling than usual, Nancy Corey, her family, and the town of Ammon, knew that the greatest time of all, for July, was still the Twenty-fourth—or Pioneer Day. This was a holiday everyone could sink teeth into. Signers of the Declaration of Independence, and George Washington's Minute Men, were long dead and distant—but there were still plenty of men alive who, with Brigham Young, had entered Salt Lake Valley in 1847. This was the day set apart by the Church and its people in remembrance of a new and inspiring beginning, after the drivings of Missouri and Illinois. And since the land itself was nothing before they came, and would remain nothing until it was touched by plow and water, every Saint through the past eighteen years, who claimed any part in the building of Deseret was, in their thinking, a pioneer.

To Nancy Corey, who thought much on these things, the definition of a pioneer was simple. Any Saint who had crossed the plains to escape persecution, or to build up Zion in these last days, was a pioneer. "Only people in Zion who are not pioneers are the children being born here," Nancy declared to Flora on the day before the big affair. "Everyone else is."

"What about Gentiles, passing through on their way to California?" Flora argued. "They've crossed the plains. But they're not pioneers. Neither is Connor's or Johnston's armies."

"Well, in that case, I guess you're right," Nancy hedged. "But, I'm a pioneer. You know that."

"You just said that children born in Zion were not pioneers. You were birthed in Salt Lake."

"But I was birthed the day after Mums arrived from off the plains. So I crossed the plains—inside my mother. That makes me a pioneer." And throughout her life she would always proudly claim it.

Though Mountain Grove and Pleasanton, the two neighboring towns, were joining efforts in observance of Pioneer Day—Mormondom's great Day of Deliverance—it was Ammon, riding with strength under its new birth and purpose, that spearheaded the affair. A great stretch of meadowland, on the east shore of Utah Lake, eight miles southeast, and in full and spectacular view of snowy-headed Timpanogos and the great saw-toothed Wasatches, was set aside as camp and picnic grounds. Some of the wagons, white with bowed canvas, or more flatly stashed with tents and camping gear, began arriving at the lake days before the affair. Isaac Corey, in prudent anticipation of the event, had a month before purchased at Livingston & Bell in Salt Lake City, four huge wall tents, exactly alike, to house his four families on the lake shore. He and the boys had stopped hauling rock for the schoolhouse foundation two days early, in order to set up the tents, and to be sure his respective families were comfortable. He had left The Point farm in custody of hired hands, so that Aunt Kirstine and child could share the day, and himself give meticulous abeyance to his reputation for fairness within his family kingdom. For those wives at the fort who had cows to milk, he squandered good money to hire Seth Biddle to take care of the family teatings and corral chores.

Seth, an epileptic, who was never sure of the time and place of his seizures, preferred to remain behind at the almost deserted town. A sensitive man, he knew his spells were a constant source of wonderment and amusement to the people of Ammon. He knew, too, that when they hit him, they hit him hard. With the shriek of a lost soul flung to the fiery pit, he would hit the hard earth. Frothing at the mouth, moaning like a pump organ, he would flop on the ground like an unhooked trout. Pale and shaken, when the fit had passed, Seth would wipe the foam from his trembling lips, and resume whatever he was doing before the seizure.

It was not uncommon, during Sunday services at the meeting house, for the sacrament and the singing to be held up while Seth frothed and flopped. But the Saints, and probably God Himself, patiently awaited out these interruptions to the worship. For Seth, despite his infirmities, was a good and honorable man. And the Saints always respected such things.

For Nancy, the most intriguing point about Seth, however, was the understanding or rapport he had built up with the animals he served.

They just as patiently waited out Seth's strange voyages into helplessness. She herself had seen Seth, one minute guiding a plow behind his horses, and just as suddenly fling the lines in the air, bellow like a goaded steer, and start his fish-flopping in the furrow he had just made. But at this first sound, Seth's horses would stop. Gentle and tolerant as God's own love, the beasts would wait in patience, while their afflicted master suffered through his time of travail. Some people got loads of fun out of Seth, but Nancy never did. The pity in her heart for this lonely, unhappy man welled up until she had to fight from crying. She had a deep regard for Seth, and an aching wonder why God had set a curse so awful on a man so good. In turn, Seth poured out his own love and favor on this pretty, brown-eyed daughter of Isaac Corey—by keeping Martha's woodpile stacked high beside the hearth, and lending every favor Nancy would allow him. But, while everyone else enjoyed themselves at the lake, he preferred to remain behind at Ammon. As a man sensitive to his condition, he dreaded the possibility of one of his fits spoiling the joy of others.

At daybreak on the Twenty-fourth, while the roosters of Ammon were still flapping and crowing out their amorous plans for the day, and town dogs were still answering the yips and bays of the coyotes out on the bench's sage, Nancy hitched Dolly the mare to the single-seated rig. Martha lugged out her clothes basket, stuffed high with picnic. Even the springs on the rig gave something of a sag when she thumped the covered basket down behind the seat. No two women could ever hope to eat the smallest portion of the grub and baked things Martha had spent days in preparing. "There'll be others that won't have so much," she had philosophically declared. "And there'll be guests and Indians to share it with." Nancy had sagged like the buggy springs at thought of who one of the guests might be. Three surrey loads had arrived from Salt Lake last night. So many that Bishop Earlington had been forced to bed down his visitors in the meeting house. The Indians, always with the Saints, gave her no concern.

As for Nancy and Martha, all they had to take out to the lake this morning were themselves, and this fat load of grub. Isaac had set the tents up, the bedding had gone out with the wagons, everything had been in readiness since day before yesterday. The Corey women, and what children had not gone with the loads, were free to come on to the lake whenever they pleased. It had pleased the other three families to get out a day early. Martha herself had fretted, and urged Nancy on the same thought. But Nancy, sad as a squaw at a Hogtown cremation, had felt no urgency. Instinctively she knew that the day set apart to the

Mormon deliverance would be the day she likely would be marked for delivery into the apostle's household. Fall, and after the crops were in, was a time for marrying, and the time when the Endowment House was busiest. As sure as certainty Apostle Cragg would arrive, smelling of courtin' scent, and boiling like a virtuous teakettle with sweet talk and sacred promise. As sure as certainty the apostle would have solemn session with Isaac Corey, and she would be one of this fall's lucky girls to don the garment of plurality, and step as high as the fort wall in the favors and standing of the Church. Many another girl, she knew, was envying her. It was no small thing in Deseret for an apostle to choose you out. In status, both earthly and in heaven, only a marrying to Brigham the Prophet could stand you any higher in Zion's esteem. Even this had happened in her own family, though Cove was the one who had caught the brunt of it, and had raised all hell ever since. Nancy, as she backed Dolly into the shafts, and snap-hitched the tugs, knew that she was almost as bad as Cove in her attitude, and that someday Jehovah God would strike her dead for the moanings she made, and the ingratitude she felt.

Martha already had briefed Seth Biddle on the chores to be done and, since they were the last of the Corey families to leave for the lake, the tending of Martha's stock and chickens was but the final added portion of Seth's duties toward the multiple households. Nancy was glad to get out of milking old Gertie this early morning and, since Seth was already invisibly at work in Aunt Millie's stable, considerably up the line, neither she nor Martha could wave the man goodbye. So, Martha gave final tug to her sunbonnet strings, adjusted the knit fascinator to her bony shoulders, and Nancy touched Dolly at the root of her tail with the buggy whip. They were off for the big day at the lake.

Others of Ammon's Saints, not affluent enough for such luxury of a hired man, were frantically going through their morning's chores, and Nancy and Martha waved gaily as Dolly and the single-seater sped them smartly down the streetway toward the town gates and the meeting house. By the clutter of rigs, hitched up and ready in front of the bishop's house, it was plain to see that things must be throbbing within. A big, noisy breakfast no doubt, with the Earlington's putting on plenty airs in serving it. Nancy's canny eyes checked over the rigs, and such of the drivers as were on hand. There was real Salt Lake class in the carriages driven by the Authorities. But Brother Brigham's fine coach, with its Negro driver, was nowhere in evidence. Apostle Cragg's rig, however, was there, and even Martha craned her skinny neck into a shudder when she saw it. The apostle, either from the government surplus at Camp

Floyd, or from some California-bound caravan, had purchased an army officer's ambulance. With its comfortable seats, ample baggage capacity, and canvas roll-up storm curtains, it was an ideal vehicle for any Mormon dignitary to get around through Zion. It had strength and serviceability equal to any Utah rut and road. It had comfort and, in its own utilitarian way, it had class. About it was the solidity and sureness of the apostle himself.

Almost in front of the bishop's house was the turn, which led past the log-and-mud meeting house, and out through the east gate. Nancy swung Dolly neatly around, peered sickly at the ambulance again, and stung Dolly's tail with the whip. The buggy leaped forward like the thrust of a cannon shot. Martha's flowered bonnet, tied under her chin, was safe and could not be lost, but she grabbed for it just the same. The little blue hat, matching the new blue Sunday dress she wore, went flying off Nancy's ribbon-tied black hair. It gyrated crazily in the air, cleanly missed the apostle's ambulance, and fluttered obliquely into the seat of one of the Salt Lake surreys. Dolly, saddled or in the shafts, needed little urging. She had broken into a good, smart lope, which took the careening buggy through Ammon's east gateway with enough speed and dust to be spectacular. Nancy, anger rising as her mind chewed away at the bad thought, never paused for the hat, but let Dolly run for all she was worth.

"Good Lord, Nan," Martha groaned as the wheels hit a chuck deep enough to wham the springs to their blocks. "Wanta strew picnic all the way to the lake? Slow down! Slow down, I say!"

The walled town already was receding in the distance as the buggy flopped, slid, and careened toward the lake road. "I'm not going to do it!" Nancy screamed back at her own thoughts.

"Then *don't* slow down! Go on—get us both killed!"

"I don't mean about slowing down," Nancy said, finally pulling firmly back on Dolly's lines. "I mean, *I'm not gonna ride in that flop-curtained rig!*"

"Oh, you mean the apostle's." Martha settled more complacently back to the cushion. Dolly slowed to a still vigorous trot. "Who said you had to?"

"How many other women has he hauled to Salt Lake in that wagon? It's like gathering in a crop—only *his* crop is females. Come fall, I'll be lifted up to its back seat . . . my possibles stashed in the baggage trunk . . . and I'll be yanked off to the Endowment House in Salt Lake . . . If he'd put glass in it, instead of roll-down curtains, it would

48

be a hearse for sure." She stared dully at the mare's sleek rump. "Anyway, I'm already feeling dead."

"You make it sound ghastly and creepy," Martha primly replied. "You make it sound as though he's a bad man—which he's not. It's a sin to rail like that about the Authorities. Jonathan Cragg is a servant of the Lord—and don't you forget it!"

"He's here to honey me up for marriage. He's here to talk blessings and promises to Father Corey. He's here to take me as a plural wife."

"He's here because it's the Twenty-fourth of July," Martha defended, weakly. "There's always one of the Authorities here on the Twenty-fourth."

"You think I'm wrong then?" Nancy asked.

The creak of the harness and springs was lively, but the grind of the sand on the wheels, and the monotonous clup-clup of Dolly's hooves, had a saddening rhythm to it. "No, Nancy," Martha said, quietly. "I don't think you're wrong."

"You really think," Nancy replied, as the panic welled up once more, "you really think he'll ask for me today?"

"I think it's very possible," Martha honestly affirmed. "And you look a perfect mess, with your hat gone, and your hair a-snarl. Why didn't you—"

"I'll look a worse mess—when they find me," Nancy resolutely declared. "Because I'm gonna drown myself in the lake."

The patchwork of green and yellow fields they passed as Dolly clupped and rattled them out to the lake road, existed, as every Mormon knew, solely through their united communal efforts at irrigation. Green squares, fragrant, and easy on the eye, were the summer crops, or the alfalfa—which the Saints called "lucerne," from which area their tireless missionaries had imported it. Another importation, from California and New Mexico, was the *garbanzo*, brought to Zion by members of the Mormon Battalion, and now profitably in crop by Isaac Corey at Ammon—only Isaac and his fellow Saints called them just plain "cowpeas." But Nancy was not thinking on lucerne or cowpeas. Without a pause, floundering in dismal imaginings, she wheeled Dolly southward on the lake road, past more of the fenced fields belonging to Ammon's Saints. Those fields, green and fragrant because the canyon water, once drained straight to Utah Lake, was still, through the summer, being diverted periodically to their furrows—those yellow because they were fields of grain, ripening and hardening for the Mormon blades of harvest.

On this day the workers and the harvesters were gone from the fields.

And Utah Lake, to whose shore they had been drawn, and in whose depths Nancy was now mentally dramatizing her drowning, was one of the rarer gems of natural beauty, long known to the Indians, and soon discovered by the Saints after their entry into Zion. Eight miles long, north and south, five miles wide, east and west; it drained the melting snows from the mighty Wasatches on the east. In turn, it was drained northward, into the great dead sea—its sweet water coursing toward its own saline death, through the very heartland of the Mormon holy land. Quick to acknowledge God's hand and miracle, and quick to recognize its striking geographical and spiritual symbolism, pioneer Saints had given to the willowed green stream its only possible name— the River Jordan. For, like the Israelites of old, modern Israel had escaped its tormentors and persecutors in the accursed eastern Egypt, had braved the wilderness with a latter-day Moses, and had found and made blossom its promised land. That their Canaan had striking similarities to its Old World counterpart was no accident of nature, but a design of Almighty God for His chosen people. No Latter-day Saint, treasuring any part of this miraculously tendered holy land, ever forgot these things.

If Salt Lake Valley was the Judea, Utah Valley, over the mountains to the south, and in another world, came nearer to being a second Switzerland. From any vantage point, but particularly from the walls of Ammon, or the margins of Utah Lake, the scene in its natural beauty, was nothing less than breathtaking. Timpanogos, mountain of a thousand faces, snow-pocketed and granite-chinned, was lifted two miles high—the rocky, eternal sentinel of an alpine valley meant for endless repose, but which, with man's coming, was never to know this repose.

But today, as Nancy and Martha rattled their way toward the great lake, the day, with its warming July sun, was as peaceful as ever they would know. Even Nancy, whose morbid imaginings had explored varied modes of self-destruction, was sinking, under the warmth of the sun on her bare head, into languorous apathy. Drowning was spectacular—even Isaac Corey would be sorry for pushing her into a marriage from which he alone would benefit. But in her dream she somehow retained to herself the miracle of omniscience. She somehow always stood apart, and watched with smug and juicy satisfaction the dragging of her young, slender, marble-like body from the cold and hungry waters of the lake. They were weeping the tears of shattering regret, as they should. But never was it the apostle, or Isaac, who fetched her dripping from the lake and laid her tenderly to the sands of the shore. Always it was a young man, with a mustache, dancing blue eyes, a strange part in his hair. In the dream, he, too, was shattered with regret.

Martha, in turn, could not help but be troubled as the rig bucked and rattled through the ruts and dust. It wasn't that she worried about any stupid thing Nancy would do, impulsive as she was. But, most clearly, the girl was sick with fear; frightened as death at what in all probability was ahead. Marrying time should be a happy time—not a thing that could stir you into throwing yourself away on a Gentile, or drowning yourself in the lake. But the things in her own two marriages, which her mind kept dredging up, were anything but happy. Then there was that affair of Cove's that had soured him on Brigham and the Church. Still, he was a man. It was the women who knew the true sorrows. In a sense, women were made for sorrow—though it shouldn't be. There was a real problem ahead for this girl, which Isaac in a lifetime would never understand. That she was headstrong and rebellious Martha could lay blame at her own door. Somehow, somewhere, Martha Corey had failed in the Gospel.

As for Nancy, she already had commenced to drowse under the warming sun. At moments she wished they had a top for the buggy. But Dolly herself knew that the driving hand no longer was firm. With good mare's sense she slowed to an ambling walk. She knew the lake road—every mile of it to the "bottoms." And this good mare's sense told her, when there was no prodding, to take her own easy time for any journey.

V

THE SAINTS OF UTAH VALLEY, ALMOST FROM THE BEGINNING, HAD USED THE choice and meadowed northeast margin of Utah Lake for their communal picnics. Emptying streams had fed the roots of a little grove of cottonwoods and, besides shade and mountain-fresh water, there were fragrant and level areas for tenting, and limitless amounts of grazing for the horses while they waited out the holiday.

The July sun was high in the sky by the time Nancy drove the rig into the camp area. Martha was lifted down from the carriage seat by Isaac, and Nancy turned Dolly over to two of her young half brothers, Stone and Fred Corey, of Aunt Millie's issue. Happy as the holiday, the boys backed Martha's single-seater into the line of wagons and carriages facing the four big Corey tents, and then staked the sweated and weary Dolly out to a mare's heaven of running water and high grass.

Even though a considerable part of the enormous Corey family already were fishing, swimming, or laying out vast quantities of food at the picnic area, it still took a little chunk of time for Nancy and her mother to greet what Coreys remained. Flora, as giddy and irresponsible as usual, was already where the younger men were—at the lakeside. Martha made certain that Fred and Stone did not fade away empty-handed. "Here . . . you young'uns," she demanded. "Lug Auntie's basket of grub to the eatin' spot!" And Auntie's command was heeded, though they dragged the big basket across the meadow at a barefoot run, while their quarter-mother's head bobbed in palsied concern.

Isaac Corey, with characteristic thoroughness, had made certain his family camp was snug and secure. Other Ammonites were sleeping in wagons, or on beds spread out to the sun and stars. Isaac—with most of the boys from the three families that had provided him boys—had brought the big prairie wagon to the picnic grounds a day before. Now the roomy tents were up, and the Corey section of the campground as shipshape and orderly as Isaac's thinking. Inside Martha's tent a canvas wagon cover had been neatly spread for a groundcloth. Her own quilts and feather tick were there, neatly piled, and ready to be made into a bed.

The sun made the tent uncomfortably warm inside but, after the fading out of amenities, Nancy took upon herself the duty of making up the bed. Martha, with no intention of being outdone by the other wives, had followed her picnic basket to the eatin' spot at the grove. As Nancy bent herself to the suffocating task of squaring up tick and quilts, she knew that Martha would be nervously and spasmodically at work, spreading out, for any takers, her great and hopeless feast. Nancy, not too young to be knowing women's feelings, sensed also the pathetic nature of Martha's offering. Of all Isaac's four wives, she was the only woman who had not presented him with increase, according to the Mormon celestial family plan, and the great and everlasting covenant. Her only child, a daughter, was the issue of another man. After Martha and this daughter had been spiritually and temporally severed from her first unfortunate union by the Prophet Brigham Young, and given to

Isaac Corey as a part of his kingship, she, in one part at least, had failed him as a woman. Her reproductive apparatus had responded to Brayton, but not to Corey. With her, Isaac's seed had been fallow and, without bearing a single child to his name, she could never hope to reign, here or hereafter, with the regality of the more fertile Adah, Millie, or even Kirstine, the last choice. Nancy, as she worked and perspired in the hot tent, half listening to the noisy tumult and shrill, happy cries coming up from lakeside, knew that Martha would be laying out double the plates they would need, chattering with the other women, as she equaled up her heaps of fried chicken and cold mutton slices with them, and hoping in her woman's heart that the sheer quantity and attractiveness of her offering would be accepted by Isaac and some part of his healthy and robust family. Nancy knew that Martha, as usual, would tote a lot of food home, or give it to the Indians. As customary, Isaac would honor his first wife, Aunt Adah, on such a public occasion. Most likely, the Corey children would dine closest to their respective filial circles. And anyone who imagined there weren't secret and open jealousies among polygamous wives simply didn't know polygamous wives.

In spite of her thinking on these and other things, Nancy's spirits could not but rise with the picnic's electric atmosphere. The howls of glee she was hearing through thin canvas, the robust guffaws of men enjoying themselves, and the shrill cackle of the women as they happily did women things came at her from every side. Her efforts at making the bed speeded up. She was humming softly to herself, and really anxious now to go on the hunt for Flora. Already all thoughts of her own promised drowning had vanished from mind. The only remaining thing to plague were the thoughts of poor, half-sick Martha, and Martha's picnic spread.

Suddenly, then, came realization there *was* a possibility Martha's efforts would not be in vain. Isaac could *still* be snatched from the first wife, to squat his lanky and weather-hardened frame at Martha's plates and fare. Should Apostle Jonathan Cragg decide to honor the Coreys by dining with a certain Corey daughter, Isaac would, certain as death, be basking at this near glory, by eating at the apostle's side. Nancy's heart all but stopped beating with the sudden possibility and probability of it. Once again she visioned herself as she sank, arms gracefully outstretched to heaven, into the cold green depths of Utah Lake.

"Well, you *finally* made it!" came Flora's giggling voice from the tent flap. "Thought you were *never* coming!" She sniffed the wilting heat of the tent, and brushed back from her eyes the drooping strands of her peeled-back straw-colored hair. "We got in yesterday afternoon. You've missed some wild fun, Nan!"

Nancy smoothed out the checkered quilt. "Haven't got a heart to it," she said mournfully. "Is Apostle Cragg here yet?"

"Haven't seen him." Flora hooked an arm around the tent pole, and did a gay half circle. "None of the bigwigs are here yet. Maybe he didn't get down from Salt Lake."

"Oh, yes he did," Nancy said. She patted the quilt, and with a sigh of despair, flopped down on the fresh-made bed. "He was at the bishop's when I left. His infernal captive wagon was there. There's a mess of bigwigs, Flo."

"Well, who cares? Get yourself out of this hot tent. Come on down to the lake. It'll soon be time to eat. And the captive wagon's yet to show itself."

Nancy sprawled out, and stared sorrowfully up at the neatly stitched seams of the canvas above her. A lazy hornet was whining like a grindstone as he stupidly batted his shoe-button head at the ridgepole. "Well, the wagon'll be here, don't worry," she said.

"Poor enough reason to lay in a tent and suffocate." Flora reached down a strong arm. "Come on, Nan. We go!"

Nancy lost some of her courting sorrows, and most of her intentions of drowning, when she and Flora reached the lake margin. They must have made quite a pair, because many a young male eye stared longingly and hungrily at them. A few of the boys waved, and a few spoke. Despite the fact that Flora saucily tossed back the banter, and Nancy nodded and smiled understandingly, that was as far as it went. The Corey girls were prizes, all right, but, like so many of the luscious plums of Utah, they already were spoken for—by highly placed church leaders. And there was a silent understanding to that effect. More than one ambitious young male in Zion had attempted to horn in on some church leader's choice for a wife, and had found himself quickly "called" for a two-year mission in Samoa. And if he refused to serve the Church, there were other ways of dealing with him. When any leader, from the Prophet down, started making eyes at a girl, the field was instantly and miraculously cleared, and few young men there were who stood brave or reckless enough to challenge. Cove Corey had made sad enough discovery of that fact, with his own loss in love to the Leader himself. Cove's discovery had come too late for any bravery or recklessness. And the oddity of it all lay in the fact that most of the girls, and plenty of their parents, seemed satisfied with this coveting for top choice. It was something indeed to be singled out by a high church leader. Only the

Corey girls, it seemed, and Nancy in particular, seemed indifferent, unappreciative, and openly contemptuous of the honor.

Nancy and Flora passed the fragrant Lamanites who, with unbelievable patience, waited in silent clusters for their own big feast when the Saints were finished, and continued their walk on down to the pebbly and sandy lake edge to watch the frolicking in the water—and it was a sight! Nancy missed the blue hat she had refused to retrieve, the sun beat hotly down, and she would have appreciated a dip—not a drowning—in the lake. The youngsters, in cut-down "overhalls," were having a riotous time, and their shrill cries and merry whoops made a happy clatter to the fun. The menfolk were "bathing"—it was not called swimming in Utah—but the women took no part in the sport. Grimly Nancy realized that the only way she could indulge in the lake would be to go ahead with her drowning.

As a Latter-day Saint it was clear enough to her why the women were absent from the lake's edge, other than to sprawl wearily around on the pebbly margin. First of all, it was unladylike to don one of those fancy knee-length bathing suits, and mix it in the water with the men. Secondly, there was that deeper matter of the holy garment. This peculiar underwear was ankle-length. Its style and fitting had been revealed by Joseph Smith the Prophet. Its full-limbed covering was protection to the body against both evil and mishaps, and a good Saint wore it for this reason, and because it marked him or her as a definite candidate for the celestial glory. It was tangible evidence one had entered the House of the Lord, and few ever allowed their bodies to be completely without this badge of glory, night or day.

Nancy knew how Martha handled the problem, when Martha bathed herself in the tin tub at home. First she would untie the strings, and peel down the upper half, and the bath would proceed that far. Then she would soberly remove the garment from one leg, to scrub and dry it. This skinny leg would be inserted in the clean garment, fresh from the line. With this as a secure pivot, the other leg would be stripped of the soiled underwear, scrubbed, and dried. Then the whole garment would be pulled on, pulled up, and properly tied. By this involved process, Martha would be clean from skin out, her holy covering changed, and with the miracle of never having cut her body entirely away from its spiritual protection.

So far in life, Nancy had not donned the garment—but she would—the day she stood in the Endowment House, in Salt Lake City—to be married to Apostle Jonathan Cragg, or any other Latter-day Saint male

55

who had honored his priesthood, magnified his calling, and chosen her as his celestial mate. Sometimes the thought of wearing this ankle-length spider sack, for life, and eternities to come, sent Nancy to her pillow in tears. And then she would be ashamed for her heresy, and pray that God might forgive her, and somehow condition her to the inevitable day she, too, could be a proud wearer of the garment.

Some of the males, in their lake bathing today, Nancy noted, were proud enough wearers of the garment. For the water they may have donned cut-down "overhalls," but they had not removed their celestial underwear. It hid their hairy arms and legs, came down wet and firm to wrists and ankles, and doubtless protected them from sin and drowning, but to Nancy and Flora these men made a ludicrous sight. They looked so much like big white spiders with blue diapers, that the sight of them sent the two girls into spasms of unholy laughter. "Angel chaps," Cove Corey heretically called the underwear, but Cove was a bitter Jack Mormon, and shouldn't be listened to. Yet Nancy knew that if she ever saw Apostle Cragg in such an outfit, she would run a mile to get out of his way. A little sadly, she knew, too, that when she was close enough to Apostle Cragg to observe him in this underwear, she would be wearing it, too.

Nancy got herself away from this suddenly depressing sight by walking to lakeside and watching the younger couples farther out, in home-made boats and jerry-built rafts. Then there were those out on the long, bobbing catwalk—some were fishing, others gazing out across the miles of blue-green water to the purple mountain range far to the west. Summer clouds drifted aimlessly above, but the sky was deep and green-blue like the lake. And the day, other than the under-thoughts, was something of a joy. All these young townsfolk and the spooning couples who had stolen back into the grove, or far out from the camping margins, she most desperately envied. Other girls might covet her place, but to Nancy it was the saddest thing of her life to even think of being "chosen."

By the time of their arrival at the picnic area, the place, ringed by the whispering cottonwoods of the grove, was another real sight. Every family had brought their wagon covers to spread across the fragrant grass, and, outward to the grandstand, it was a checkered sea of white and gray. Like a hundred clucking barnyard hens, the women of the families were setting out the food. "Yow!" Flora cried delightedly. "What a sight for Utes, or starving men!"

Nancy watched at the edge, her nose taking in the tantalizing smell, her eyes half searching the grandstand, and half measuring the scene of the immense and attractive array of provender spread before her.

"Quite a change from the days of the cricket famine," she laughed.

"This *is* a change," Flora agreed. "And now I know just how those hungry crickets felt."

"I'm neither man, Ute, *or* cricket," Nancy said, "but I'm starved." She looked out across to the women, with their bobbing sunbonnets, and the myriad of youngsters, including babies and toddlers, tugging at their skirts. At last, away up front toward the grandstand, she spied the Corey wives, and Martha's brown bonnet and fascinator. "There're the folks," she said, pointing. "We'll have to edge around to the west side. Can't trod across two hundred table cloths. We'll just have to buck the Lamanites."

With arrival of the Salt Lake dignitaries, the Pioneer Day picnic got off to its real and lively start. Their occupancy of the grandstand before the big meal was only for the briefest possible interval—chiefly for their introduction to the assembled Saints, the invocation on the food, and whatever announcements were in order. Then, while the patient Lamanites looked on from the margins, even the dignitaries joined the sea of food and noise, for this once-a-year time of remembrance and fellowship. The real oratory would come later, on a note of collective relaxation and full stomachs.

For Nancy Corey there wasn't a part of these picnic preliminaries that did not sweat her limp with terror. Apostle Jonathan Cragg was most certainly there—genial, smiling, and eye-searching the crowds for his latest choice in spiritual wives. "Lofty" Cragg was the affectionate nickname given to this high-minded and inspiring apostle by his fellow Saints and, when his benign countenance beamed down in sanctity and love on the Corey segment of his audience, Nancy knew, beyond question or doubt, that she publicly had been chosen.

Accompanying Lofty Cragg was a fellow member of the Council of the Twelve, one of the truly great apostles of the Church—Orson Pratt, theologian, author, mathematician, and educator. His brother, Apostle Parley P. Pratt, had been murdered by the Gentiles in Arkansas during the big troubles of 1857. As one of the ruling heads of the Deseret University, and guiding hand in the new ferment toward universal education among the Saints, there certainly was a realistic enough reason for Apostle Orson Pratt's visit to Utah Valley. But Nancy, already shaken by the portents so inseparably bound up in Apostle Cragg's presence, was ill-prepared for a new and unexpected shocker on the program.

For, calmly, as though it were an everyday occurrence, Apostle Pratt now proceeded to introduce Joel Walden Scott to the assembled Saints —Joel Scott, the very egg-boiling soldier to whom she had offered her life and hopes! She had completely failed to recognize him because of her intent interest in Apostle Cragg, and because he wore no semblance of military garb. Today he was dressed in a conservative black suit, but when he took off his soft black felt hat, to smilingly nod to the introduction, and she saw again those parted wavelets of black hair, there could be no doubt that it was Joel. "Oh, Father in heaven," she muttered, with her eyes closed, "save me. Please save me."

"Professor Scott is a young man," Apostle Pratt was saying, "but a man of rare attainment. Educated in the best schools of the East, with an enviable record as a military officer in the United States Army, he was on the way back to his home in Boston. After military service, it was his intention to join his own family interests in New England. But, as a writer, a sociologist, and a world traveler, Captain Scott had in mind an unbiased study of our people. Unlike other Gentile writers, whose only desire seems to be to debase our Church, and tear out our guts as a people, Mr. Scott, as an intelligent and fair man, came directly to us for advice and help in his project. And, as always, this help was given. You people of Ammon can attest to this co-operation. You were a part of it.

"Because an open mind and sympathetic attitude seems to be the rarest of virtues among the Gentiles, at least those with whom we come in contact, we, in turn, became interested in Mr. Scott. As an educated man he has a deep grasp on the New England concept of free schools. It is our intention, as Latter-day Saints, to copy this plan; to make education universal, and free of charge. This is a great task for any pioneer people to set themselves to do. There is a saddening lack of trained educators among our Saints, and it is taking all our efforts to overcome this lack. But the Prophet Joseph Smith is emphatic in his charge that 'this people cannot be saved in ignorance.' And that the 'glory of God is intelligence.' Though humble may be our beginnings, we shall never stop until the Latter-day Saints are known throughout the world for their scholastic attainments.

"Because the New England concept of free and universal education will be the model for this Zion we are building, we have had many deep and penetrating conversations with Mr. Scott. More remarkable, he has taken an equally deep interest in our problem. Even more generously, he has postponed his trip home for a year, to lend his own energies and experience toward helping us through this immense movement. And because you good people of Ammon have been so quick to respond in the construction of a new and decent school, and will have the building ready for fall entry of pupils, Professor Scott has asked to take personal charge of it. Your school will be a model for every other community in Utah to follow."

"Oh, Lord in heaven," Nancy muttered again. "Forgive and watch over me."

"I had no intention of burdening these introductions with a speech," Apostle Pratt was saying, "but I *am* excited about our plans, and proud of you good people of Utah Valley. Perhaps, after we have partaken of this tempting array of food, Mr. Scott can be prevailed on to say a few words—so that you may know what kind of a man you're getting."

Nancy by now was palsied with fright—but this was by no means the day's end for the Coreys. Beloved Bishop Earlington took charge from this point on, while the dignitaries shook hands around the circle and filtered out to their choice places at the great meal spread out on the canvas before them. But, in Mormon circles, not even a social event had beginning or end without prayer. And this day of all times, the bishop chose Elder Isaac Corey to come to the stand for the invocation.

The soothing and familiar voice of Isaac, importuning God to grant peace, joy, and comfort to His Saints, fluttered humbly out over the gathering. Nancy loved this good man, and the steadiness of character so apparent in his voiced grace to God. Somehow he calmed her frights and worries before this multitude, just as surely as at chair or bedside in the Corey home. After mentioning the sufferings, the privations, and the hunger the Saints had known in the past, as "times of testing," the courage of the pioneers they were honoring this day, and the gratitude "every Saint amongst us feels for bounteous harvest and prosperity we enjoy," he closed with a most proper blessing on the tangible evidence of this bounty—the food so generously spread below him. What Isaac lacked in learning, he made up for in sincerity, and his amen was echoed in unison from five hundred throats.

But, when Isaac returned to his place at the picnic, he brought with him Apostle Jonathan Cragg—to Martha's spread—and as Nancy inwardly knew he would. For Nancy the whole affair seemed to be moving with the inevitability of a ward play—with every act and actor marching in and out as though on cue. This thing could be no accident, she felt—that Isaac had been chosen to pray. Subtly, and by design, the drawbridge had conveniently been let down for Lofty Cragg's entry. Even the singular appearance of Joel Scott, minus coffee pot and uniform, seemed some dreamy and unreal part of the drama. But Martha flustered and jerked exactly on cue, Apostle Cragg touched Nancy's arm and smiled benignly, precisely as she knew he would. And when, with a windy groan, he bent his fat hulk to squat uncomfortably on the canvas beside her, there could be no doubt the familiar vision she'd had all day was become a reality. When Isaac gave up his proper place with the first wife, to join with his third wife's circle, Nancy and every Saint around them knew that Martha's providence had been vindicated and the Coreys signally honored this day.

Even the most minor part of the preliminary program somehow was not enacted without in some way or another touching Nancy Corey. The time had come for announcements, and in her worries she had paid scant attention to Bishop Earlington as he told about the musical program, races, and contests for the day. What again brought her suddenly alive was when the bishop, making the usual and customary notice of lost articles, suddenly was standing there—holding out her blue hat.

"Here's some young lady's pretty bonnet," he was saying. "It somehow, someway, got into the back seat of Apostle Pratt's carriage. Mr. Scott discovered it—and it doesn't belong to any of the ladies in *our* party. Too pretty a bonnet to lose. If it belongs to any of the sisters present—will that sister please arise?"

Martha looked expectantly at Nancy. Defiantly Nancy shook her head. She gritted her teeth in stubborn anger, and utterly refused to acknowledge the loss.

"Last chance, ladies! Last chance for the pretty blue hat! Who does it belong to?"

Martha dropped her serving in panic. Clumsily she struggled to her feet; her head rocking like a shutter in the wind. "Here!" she cried, waving her arm.

"Oh," the bishop called across the crowd. "Sister Martha Corey!" He beamed right neighborly at her.

"No," Martha shouted. "It's Nancy's!"

"Stand up, Nancy," came the persistent voice of the bishop.

Isaac imperiously beckoned her to rise. She hesitated. Then slowly she lifted herself. Such effort was a little too much for Apostle Cragg, and he allowed her to rise without the gallantry of his assistance.

"This is Miss Nancy Corey," the bishop cried—as if everyone present didn't already know the fact. "*She's* the one who lost the blue bonnet. Stay where you are, Nan! We'll send it down to you!"

As Nancy squatted once more alongside the apostle, and once more tried to turn her attention to the picnic, she knew now that she was only a rag of confusion. Her feet, not used to those infernal laced shoes, were pinched and sweaty. The sun was burrowing into her head. She'd lost her appetite for the food everyone else was ravenously attacking, and she was uncomfortable and full of prickly aches, as she sat sidewise on her haunches beside the Lord's disciple. The murmur and buzz that had gone out across the crowd at her public recognition, was enough to unnerve anyone. Martha just *had* to be thrifty, and save the hat. It would never occur to Martha that everyone there was probably thinking the accursed hat had deliberately been planted in an apostle's carriage. For herself, she would have died, and they could have thrown the hat in the lake, before she would have stood to claim it. Then she looked again at Apostle Cragg, purring like a contented tomcat, a plate, high-heaped with Martha's food, balanced on his fat right knee. Nancy wanted to screech with agony and terror. She wanted to get out. She'd been right about drowning herself. She shook her head at the proffered food, but took the plate reluctantly as Martha nervously shoved it into her sweaty hand. The tears came. She couldn't stop them.

And then came a firm tap on her shoulder. She turned, and through tear-bleared eyes, looked behind her. At her back was a pair of black broadcloth pantaloons, standing erect. Slowly she stared up the legs that filled them. The air went out of her as though the gasp were her last. The man looking down at her was Joel Scott. His eyes and his face were a-twinkle with a smile that sent her crazy.

"Here's your hat, Nancy," he was saying, as calmly as though it were everyday. "I found it in the surrey. Nearly sat on it."

And then, before she could even utter a word, he calmly set the little blue bonnet to the top of her black hair. She was too weak to rise or protest. Apostle Cragg, grimly at his food, paid them no mind at all. Either he was too fat to rise, too sure of himself to worry—or didn't know a miracle when he saw one.

"Th-thank you, sir," she managed to stammer, swallowing like a carp out of water. "I never expected to see that hat."

He looked down at her mischievously. "You didn't?"

She flushed red as pig liver at the thought, and its implication. Even *he* was thinking she'd deliberately planted the damn thing. She touched it nervously, arranged it straight, and looked up at him again. "I'll have you know the *wind* blew it off," she said defiantly.

61

He dropped to his knees on the canvas beside her. Apostle Cragg, on her right, was eating like a hog at branning time. So far he'd failed even to notice the Gentile at her left. "I know," Joel said, gallantly. "Whatever way it got there, Nancy," he said, with a warm chuckle, "I'm glad it did. I was wondering whether I'd ever see you again."

She wanted to tell him she'd done some wondering too. Instead she said, "Everybody seems pleased you're coming to Ammon, Mr. Scott."

"Are *you?*" he asked.

"What can I say?" she sighed. "After what's already been said?"

With thought and gaze on her disturbing visitor, Nancy had failed to notice that Martha's nervous eyes were watching them both. Isaac, taken up with the apostle opposite him, hadn't gotten around to his own noticing.

"We'd be pleased, Mr. Scott, if you'd take picnic with us," Martha offered. She reached automatically for a plate. "Set right where you are, Mr. Scott. I'll fix you up with everything."

And then it was at last that Isaac saw the new schoolmaster. "Eat with us," he said, smiling proudly at the fresh honor. "Do eat with us." He wiped the mutton grease from off his whiskers with the back of his hand. "On your right is Apostle Cragg."

Stupidly and unsurprised, the apostle looked up from his food, his mouth stuffed to silence.

"We've met, Apostle Cragg and I," Joel Scott said, smiling. "We came down from Salt Lake in the same group."

"And he just brought Nancy's hat to her," Martha added, by way of explanation.

The apostle swallowed noisily, and returned a greasy smile to the Gentile.

"Move over, Nancy, and make room for Mr. Scott," Isaac commanded, completely oblivious to the fact that Nancy would gladly have rolled over to make room for the man.

The Gentile's blue eyes roved admiringly over Martha's lavish spread. "I'm sorry—"

"Please *do* sit in with us," Nancy managed to say at last.

"I'm afraid I just can't," he said. "They've fixed me up with the Earlingtons. They're expecting me." He arose, and stared down again at the food, a little sadly. "I wish I *could* stay. But I just can't. Thank you so much."

Nancy looked up at him. He smiled again mischievously at her.

"So long, brown eyes," he half whispered. And then, a moment later he was gone through the noisy crowd.

"That's our new schoolteacher," Isaac said.

"Yes, I know," Apostle Cragg agreed before sinking teeth into another leg of Martha's chicken.

"Looks like a purty smart fella," Isaac added. "We gotta turn to, an' get him a decent schoolhouse."

The apostle nodded comfortably, and gave a masticating half-smile to Nancy on his left.

But Nancy wanted to laugh at both these muttonheads. Joel Scott was coming to Ammon to live. He was coming to teach school. Well— so be it! She lived in Ammon also. And what they did not know, was that no captive wagon would ever now haul her off into plurality. Never, so long as there was even a fighting chance for this warm and gracious Gentile. For she had deep feelings for him. And the feelings were sure and sharp. She'd seen and talked to him once, she'd seen and talked to him twice—and still the ache for him was there. It might be wrong, it might be the greased skids to hell, but Nancy Corey was setting her cap for this Gentile.

She glanced over at Martha. From the twitch in Martha's neck, Nancy knew her mother knew exactly what she was thinking about.

VI

APOSTLE JONATHAN CRAGG TOOK HIS FALL BRIDE FROM THE COREY FAMILY in Ammon, according to schedule, but not precisely as planned. Three days before the October conference in the tabernacle, the apostle's ambulance, complete with roll-down storm curtains and charcoal foot warmers, arrived at the new Corey public house, in the new and miraculously growing Ammon. The new bride was lifted up to the seat by the proud and singularly honored Isaac, her possibles carefully stashed in the luggage compartment by the grown Corey boys, and with Isaac aboard, the apostle took proud leave of Ammon for the thirty-mile drive to the Endowment House in Salt Lake City. The only shift in Apostle Cragg's plans was that the pretty and vivacious Corey girl who was to be his bride for time and all eternity was not the original choice. It was the lighter-haired Flora.

But in many ways it turned out a far better choice. Flora was every bit as comely as Nancy, had been trained every bit as well, was not half as mule-headed and stubborn—and certainly a lot less dangerous. This little girl had wit, vivacity, and charm. With a little coaching from the other wives, she would stand out like a glittering gem in the social circles of Salt Lake City. Flora was a real prize. And Lofty Cragg had no regrets whatever about the marital switch.

A bishop in Provo, however, had felt a bit piqued about the ruthlessness of this apostolic perquisite, and the sudden necessity of shifting his own hunt for a fresh bride. Then there had been the problem of overcoming Flora's own slight aversion to the Principle. This had proven not too difficult. Unlike Nancy, who on the evening of July 24 had with her two fists attempted to hammer the apostle's florid countenance into a bloody pulp, and at the picnic had brought endless disgrace on the Corey family, Flora had surprisingly proven more tractable. To begin with, Flora had been brought to womanhood in a family who truly lived and respected the Principle. Martha had had her problems with plural marriage and, in light of her own unfortunate experiences, could perhaps be forgiven for not training Nancy more clearly in the peculiar requirements of the celestial order. Just the same, Martha could not be considered blameless for Nancy's attitude toward it.

It was true that Flora had shown aversion toward Bishop Anselman, and had disgracefully flirted with most anything that wore pantaloons; yet in the end it had proven not too difficult to convince her of the honor and dignity that went with marriage to one of the Church's great ones. Unlike Nancy, she readily consented to kneel in prayer with Isaac and Millie, with Bishop Earlington, and finally with Apostle Cragg himself. Her brother Cove was the only person who roared out against plurality, and such speedy and fortuitous courtship. But Cove was a roaring Jack Mormon anyway.

Nancy and Martha, on the morning of July 25, had been banished to the drudgery of the dairy herd at The Point, and any feelings they might have had on the subject was missing. In the end, for Flora, the friendly and loving counsel about her, and the never failing answer which prayer always gives to the uncertain heart, all prevailed against any negative and apostate influences that might have come to bear. Flora actually appeared happy, and beamed like a true expectant bride, when she rode away in the Cragg ambulance on that early October morning. Thus, through the miracle of prayer, counsel, and proper family guidance of Millie and Isaac, was the good name of Corey saved this day.

All through this time of the new courtship, as Nancy teated cows and drudged at the cheese vats at The Point, she wondered at the persistency of Lofty Cragg's courtship, and if Flora's acquiescence might not have been a little more difficult to obtain had Edward, the other Gentile, showed up with Joel that day at the picnic. She had never unburdened her true feelings about Joel to her half sister. Flora may have sensed her hopeless love for the man as an inseparable part of her own rejection of the apostle; Nancy had no way of knowing. If Flora's decision to walk into the Principle had any connection with any unvoiced desire to clear the field for her and her Gentile, she assuredly had furnished no logical reason for the act. Nancy, amazed and perplexed by the rapidity of events and changes, could only love her half sister with all her own sad heart, and wish her well in the great adventure.

For the events and changes had come with a speed that shattered and frightened her. Had Joel Scott not miraculously appeared at the Pioneer Day picnic, it was not illogical that Nancy Corey might have stood at the altar instead of Flora Corey. Prayer and persuasion could have wrought the miracle in her own life just as certainly and just as easily as it had in the flippant soul of Flora. When Joel, with grace and tenderness, set the little bonnet to her head that day at the lake, it was as though he had actually crowned her queen of his life. And that act alone was the ingredient which nullified every move of man and God to make her the plural wife of anybody.

That day, as she stood and faced him, Joel had talked but few words with her. He had been kind, diffident, and anxious to get away. He had remembered her from that morning at the wall, showed not the least rancor for her brazen misconduct, and indicated only mild surprise that the bonnet had landed in his carriage. But there had been warmth in his smile and merriness in his blue eyes. And then he was gone.

Those moments had been enough to turn her life and wreck the day. She had sat down again beside Apostle Cragg. The food he ate with such audible relish turned her own stomach. After the fat meal had come the long program—with singing, and fiddle music, by most of the familiar amateurs of Utah Valley. Then the dreary speeches, by Apostle Pratt and Apostle Cragg. Joel Scott spoke less than fifty words —of thanks, and of promise for the future. But they were the one saving feature to this day of fear. He was coming to live in Ammon, and that—God be thanked for the miracle—was enough. She felt sorry for Apostle Cragg; she felt sorry for Isaac Corey; the answer to them could only be no.

After the speeches had come the games. And with the games had come Apostle Cragg. While the hungry Indians got their long awaited turn at the picnic, and while the audience spread out to the grass for the games and contests, she reluctantly had allowed the apostle to tow her out to the secluded edges of the grove. There was no hate in her soul that day for the fat little man; neither was there love. In spite of his fertile experience at courting, he had been clumsy.

"Let's sit down in the grassy shade," he had said.

This they had done. And, just as expected, his heavy arm came to rest upon her shoulders.

"You're a lovely girl," he had said.

"I don't feel lovely," she had replied, honestly enough.

"Are you afraid of me, Nancy?" he had asked.

"Yes," she had also honestly answered.

"You don't have to be."

"But I am."

His hot and sweaty arm had clutched her tighter.

"I have talked to your father."

"About what?"

"Nancy . . . more than anything in the world . . . I would like to have you as my wife."

"What do the other wives say?" she had replied perversely.

"Oh, they're willing." His mellifluous voice had dripped molasses at this point. "You'll like them. You'll find them very sweet and devoted women. They'll be kind to you."

"And what does Father Corey say?" Nancy had asked, her voice trembling.

"He has already given *his* consent." He nuzzled his hairy, sweaty face against her cheek. "All I need now is your consent."

She had struggled against the sensuous pressure of his arms and body.

"Nancy," he had purred, "I love you very much. May I announce . . ."

"No you may not," Nancy had growled, fighting now to get away.

"Why, my dearest? Why?"

"Because I hate your guts . . . you horny old stud!"

And then he had tried to kiss her—and the fury of hell had broken out in her. It was then he'd found her strong arms no match for his persistent clutch. When she arose, she'd literally lifted him with her. And then, with her free arm, she'd let him have it.

66

But that wasn't all. Everything that had churned her that July day broke out with the erupting fury of a volcano. Before she realized what she was doing, she found herself administering a thorough threshing to a man of God. Her claws already had brought blood to his florid face, and she felt her hard fists bite deep into his eye sockets and whiskers. And as a wise and prudent man, he knew when to retreat. The last she saw of Apostle Cragg, until October, was the apostle headed for the picnic grounds as though Lucifer himself were at his tail.

And her retreat from that bleak day had been just as final. Shaken, angered, and hurt, she had fled to the tent to sob out the ferments of her body and mind. She saw no more of Joel Scott, but when Isaac Corey realized the enormity of the disgrace she had brought upon him and his house, her retreat was turned into an explosion. Hurt and baffled by her act, the scene had been one of searing horror, with nothing but thin tent walls between Isaac's infuriated rantings and five hundred picnickers at the lake shore.

Martha, frightened and humiliated, had joined Nancy as soon as the debacle was apparent, only to reap her share of the family storm. "Am I harboring a nest of vipers and apostates?" Isaac had asked himself in helpless fury.

Martha's timid efforts to defend her daughter came like a sparrow jousting at a hawk. But when Isaac finally retreated to the smug and self-righteous circles of his other wives, he did so in complete ignorance of the real reasons for Nancy's dramatic spurning of her apostolic suitor. And Martha had bravely stood up to Isaac's withering blasts without once even hinting that there might be certain feelings between Nancy and the new Gentile in their midst. Too, since the new Gentile was smart enough to keep himself aloof from Mormon family problems, and in Isaac's unwavering faith there was no place for even a thought of such things, Isaac had retired from the fray with only the one pain in his breast—that his daughter had humiliated, and held up to public ridicule, one of the Authorities of the Church.

Early on the morning of July 25 the Corey family had broken camp. In silence Nancy and Martha had driven Dolly and the rig over the long miles back to Ammon. Next morning they drove the longer miles to the dairy at The Point. This token of banishment from Isaac's bosom was not lost on the other segments of the Corey family kingdom. He had always been a firm believer that hard work was the devil's surest enemy—and to the watching family audience, anyone as full of hell as Nancy rated toil enough to tame her.

And so Nancy, as she teated cows, shoveled manure, and bruted hay around the big log barns and aromatic corrals of the Corey dairy, was, in her exile, lost to direct contact with the great things that were happening at Ammon. It was the Corey boys, as they brought in their occasional loads of hay for winter stack, who bridged the wall of her isolation and kept her and Martha informed of the great and dramatic things that were happening at the town.

The walls of Ammon had literally exploded. The energy liberated and the enthusiastic response to the new task of restaking and rebuilding a community must have been a furious and astonishing thing even among a people already noted for their united efforts. The school, complete with stone foundation, adobe walls, glass windows, and solid wood floors, went up on its five-acre plat, in time for mid-September entry of its students. And, while Nancy slaved at The Point, and fermented like the cheese in the vats, Professor Joel Scott was at Ammon setting up the school that would be the new model to Zion.

Ammon's streets were regraded, according to original plan. The Saints, with holdings according to the plat, got many a fine and substantial house far enough along that they could move their families out of the fort before the wintry winds swept down from the Wasatches. Isaac Corey, whose canny trading through the years of Ammon's chrysalis behind the walls had given him choice parcels of the new Ammon far beyond his original stewardship, now set a new record for Mormon industry. As if to show the Authorities in Salt Lake City that he was the truest of true Saints, that he could follow counsel with zeal and obedience, in spite of pioneer difficulties, and the disgraceful recalcitrance of one of his daughters, he set his limitless energy to work in the building of a hotel and stage station on Ammon's new main street.

With all the Saints of Ammon caught up in their own plans and building projects, the problem of manpower to make a fast building of the Corey public house was an acute one. This, however, was ingeniously solved. Cove Corey in his weekly freightings had kept the two women at The Point informed.

In Salt Lake City this year, as for years past, were the hundreds of Gentiles encamped on Emigrant Square. These were the gold-seekers, headed for California, who, because of late start or misfortunes along the way had failed to make enough westing to assure them getting over the High Sierras before fall. The fate of the Donner Party, trapped in the Sierra snows some years before, had taught even the brashest of emigrants the lesson of either making the crossing by late summer, or camping it out until spring safely freed the passes once more. So every winter Salt Lake City's population was swelled by the colony of camped Gentiles—many of them in utter destitution. To partake of the Mormon bounty until spring, many of them joined the Church. From past experience with these new brethren, whose interest still remained more with gold than with glory, they had come to be called "Winter Saints." From the Winter Saints, or just plain Gentiles, it did not matter, Isaac Corey recruited more than enough help to not only lift his hotel to completion in a hurry, but to help himself and the boys get three dwellings under way in the new town. Nancy and Martha, at The Point, and miles from the scene, could only wonder why one of Isaac's families was thus so patently slighted.

"It's quite a place the old man's building," Cove Corey revealed. And it was Cove, with his frequent trips to The Point with hay and supplies, who kept the news-hungry Nancy informed as to Ammon's new birth. "It's got a big room downstairs, to feed the wayfarers. Upstairs there'll be rooms for 'em to sleep in. Next week I've gotta drive to Salt Lake—to pick up twelve wash bowls, twelve water pitchers, and twelve china peepots. Our father in Israel has ordered 'em from Livingston & Bell," Cove chuckled with his usual irreverence. "The place is jumpin' with Winter Saints and Gentiles. Everybody who can afford 'em, are using 'em. With store buildings and all goin' up, you'll never know the place."

"Has Father Corey forgiven me?" Nancy had asked.

"Oh, hell no," Cove had answered. "No more than he's forgiven *me*. But I think you did the right thing, Nan. Can't understand why Flora should be makin' time with Lofty Cragg. Never could stand his sanctimonious bladder-talk. Prates about love, and the great Mormon movement. Even a Jack Mormon like me can see what he *really* means. Where there's love, there's always the great Mormon movement—up and down. Last week Lofty Cragg came in from Salt Lake. This time he keyed his talk to the Gentile peril in our midst—but he never got too far from love and the Mormon movement, because all the time he was beamin' down the love of God on Flora—just like he used to do with you. Just like old Brigham did to *my* girl. I'm afraid Flo's a goner. I'm sure afraid."

And—come October—Cove was right.

All of Ammon applauded the choice of this daughter in Zion—all but her own blood brother. With Flora's taking to the garment with Apostle Cragg, Cove stood on Ammon's street, drunk, red-eyed, and belligerent—cursing Brigham and all the apostles—and daring any Saint to defend the faith with knife, gun, fist, or argument. No Saint in Ammon felt inclined to joust with this hellion. But, along with the patient and forgiving Isaac, they did pray for him.

Not until Flora was eternally married to Apostle Jonathan Cragg, and comfortably installed in Salt Lake City as wife number nine in the Cragg family kingdom, were Nancy and Martha allowed to return to Ammon. Back to Utah Valley with them went most of The Point's dairy herd, either to be sold, or to be distributed among Isaac's own several families. As Fort Douglas grew into a formidable military outpost, built swiftly and efficiently by General Connor just east of Salt Lake City, Camp Floyd was just as systematically dried up. And along with it was dried up the lucrative business Isaac Corey had built up with the military personnel formerly housed there. As an industrious and prudent man, Isaac found it necessary to seek a substitute for his collapsing venture at The Point. When Nancy and Martha arrived in Ammon they quickly learned what the substitute was—and, along with it, the part they were to play in it.

By late fall Ammon was as disorganized as a bishop with the hives. Half its population lived within the fort walls, the other half had moved into the new houses—by now in many stages of completion. Nancy and Martha were never allowed to settle back to the familiar and memorable little dirt-roofed cabin they had left so abruptly on July 26. Everything they owned had been hauled to the new and almost completed two-story Corey public house. And it was there they too were deposited.

"You and Nan will run the place," Isaac had told Martha. "You'll cook for the boarders. Nan'll wait on tables, keep up the rooms, do the washing, an' help you in the kitchen. Sisters Adah, Millie, and Kirstine all have families—an' a public house's no place for young'uns. So this is *your* job. An' I've told Brother Brigham that you're gonna run the best public house south of Salt Lake. See that you do it."

And that was the total end to any more girlhood antics for Nancy Corey. The slavery she entered at the Corey House not only gave her the quickest possible maturity as a woman, but made the former drudgery at The Point seem like a summer's picnic by comparison.

With possible exception of the schoolhouse, the Corey building was probably the most substantial structure in the new Ammon. The townsite still straddled the canyon watercourse, but half a mile north of the fort. Main Street, upon which Isaac and the more enterprising Saints had built or were building their business establishments, ran due east and west, and Nancy's astonished eyes gained quick realization that the town's active center would lie westerly of the creek.

The return of Nancy and Martha from The Point had been with Cove Corey, in a wagon loaded with freight. The last cow, horse, and chicken, even Dolly and the buggy, had been taken south to Ammon weeks before, and the two women had sat in brooding, stupid isolation at The Point farm, waiting for Isaac to return them from their banishment. So, when Cove, with the big wagon and four-horse team, finally pulled in for their reprieve, it was a welcome sight. But the trip home was a bouncing, uncomfortable nightmare. Fall rains and snow flurries already were upon them. The road was a pair of ruts, which drizzling rain had melted to bog holes into which the big-tired wheels slipped and slithered. It winded the big draft animals to move the heavy load even half a mile at a time.

The load, which Cove had picked up in Salt Lake City, was made up of crated glass for windows in the new town, nails, and hardware. The communal load of freight, only one of many that had gone into Ammon through the months, was a heavy one. With the weather now fiercely upon them, it might be the last load for a time.

With a less experienced hand than Cove Corey, the load might have been left till spring, abandoned on the lonely, fearsome road between the two great valleys. But Cove was a real "skinner." He was young, strong, and tough, with a herd-bull's voice that could be heard a mile, and that could shout down even Isaac himself. In spite of the fact that Cove flouted every principle of the Gospel, that he drank, gambled, and swore like the worst Gentile skinner alive, Nancy had warm and loving feeling toward this broncho half brother. He flaunted every good thing Isaac stood for, and his wild bouts with the bottle, and his helling and fighting, were an open disgrace. But with all his faults, he was still the main hand in Isaac's family kingdom. The great hope that Cove would overcome the hate in his heart, and try once more to settle down, had not yet materialized. Cove's bitterness was an irrational, hideous thing. Directed, in those first years, mainly against Brigham Young for the loss of his girl, in the southern settlements, to the Leader's own privileged choice, it had, like a cancerous and yeasty growth, spread to rejection and apostasy from the very faith itself. Cove was not the first young man in Zion to lose a sweetheart to one of the Authorities. Such incidents were common enough occurrences whenever one of the dignitaries went on the hunt for a new bride. But none of the losers had reacted more violently. In spite of all, Cove

71

still had a continuing interest in girls, but never again with a thought to wife. And always he was profanely contemptuous of the plural pattern—even though his mother, his own one-time sweetheart, and now a sister, were a willing and converted part of it.

Every animal he worked he gave the name of some dignitary of the Church—probably because such mockery grated Isaac's soul like perdition's own sandpaper. "Hi, Brigham—you old son of a bitch!" Cove would roar at a lead horse or mule, and punctuate it with a rifle-like crack of the long bull whip. "Get along you John and Heber! Dig asses, you Orson and Parley! Hi-yee—yupp!" And wagons moved when animal ears were warmed with Cove's profanity, or their tails blistered with the sting of his whip-shots. But this soggy, wet trip home took all the dexterity and skill of even a Cove Corey.

If one could have remained under hoops and canvas, the rain would have done no harm. Martha, who, deathly pale, was under siege of another abdominal attack, and she got what relief she could by lying flat across the jouncing boxes. At least she kept dry. But Nancy, young and strong, quickly found that she, too, would be needed, if ever the straining and salt-grimed teams were to drag them through to Ammon.

In mud and slush to her knees, with cold rain streaming down her hair and back, she helped Cove pull sagebrush, or shovel rocks and gravel into the chuckholes that would have mired them hub deep until spring. Over the bad stretches she would stride ahead through the storm, to spot the worst, while Cove's howls and whistles behind her kept the straining animals slowly moving the big load toward their little promised land. Through two wretched days, Nancy learned some of the misery that must have once been Martha's. And she was glad for her own strength—and glad, for this once, the poor sick woman could ride.

But Nancy herself never felt more dreary, or looked worse, than when Cove pulled the team and wagon into the new Ammon, and hauled it to its stop in front of the new Corey House. As he snubbed the lines to the drag-brake, Nancy looked around. Mighty Timpanogos already wore a fresh white crown of early winter, the storm had worried itself out, and afternoon's sun now at last was fighting with the clouds for sky space. But the chill of the wind was still laying the horses' ears back, and there was the nervousness of season's change in the air. From the noisy fever of building, and the chaos of lumber, bricks, and logs up and down the muddy roadsides, she quickly knew how desperate was this battle for housing.

72

She could see that Isaac Corey was far ahead in the race. His building, of fresh new adobe and mill-fragrant lumber, stood like a monument to his foresight and industry. It had shingles, and it had glass in the windows, and it had a long, wide porch—also shingled over. His three houses in the town, as Cove had described them, were not yet to final stages of completion, still they were far enough along to house three of his families. All three were exactly alike, each had a one-acre lot, with ample garden and stable area, and all three were in a row—on the second street south of the town's center. Cove, in the long drive south, had told Nancy all about them. The only variance from Isaac's obsession to fairness was the fact that Martha—as wife number three—had not been given a house and an acre. Her home for the remaining years of her drudging life was to be the Corey House. This would be her place, and her responsibility. Cove had also made this matter plain. And, as Nancy gazed a little sadly at the fresh new building, and felt the twinge of nostalgia for the little old hut at the fort, she realized how much she was a part of the new arrangement.

But September had brought another birthday. She was sixteen now, and a real woman. If her failure to become the ninth wife of an apostle was the cause of this new responsibility—so be it. It was worth it.

"Come on, Aunt Martha," Cove was calling. "You're home now."

Martha raised her pale and twitching head from her bed of sacks in the big wagon. "Lord be thanked," she groaned, as she reached out for Cove's strong arm. "That's as rough a ride as I'll remember."

Nancy lifted her muddy skirts, planted one of her soggy shoes on the big wheel hub. Nimbly she dropped to the red-brown ooze of the street. A moment later she was helping the sick and sinewy Martha down the wheel to Ammon's new ground, while Cove, with a grin on his hellish young face, said, "Easy does it," and edged Martha down the treacherous descent. With one mighty heave he sent Martha's bulging telescope valise flying through the air. It landed with a hollow thump on the fresh pine boards of the hotel's wide veranda. Martha shuddered and twitched at this manhandling of her belongings, and Nancy jumped with fright. In it were all the clothes and personals they had carried to The Point. With the ease and litheness of a mountain cougar, Cove dropped to the ground beside them. "Let's go inside. You gals ain't seen nothin' yet." He picked up the bulged and battered valise, and led the way.

The big room was aromatic and heady with the smells of newness— new pine, new plaster, new paint. If the building were Isaac Corey's monument, it was a man's monument—and it was instantly plain that whatever design it had had come up quick and solid from a man's mind. The room was angular, high-ceilinged, glaring in its white plaster, and stingily lighted and ventilated by two multi-paned windows at either end. Its severity was unbroken by any touch of frill or decoration, and even the stairway, leading up to the second-floor rooms, was of plain pine, hung to the north wall like an afterthought, without so much as a hallway entrance to it. The room reminded Nancy of a quick meal—solid fare, but tasteless.

"Looks like a dairy barn, with a hayloft overhead," was Martha's comment. Her swift eyes made quick appraisal, and she twitched uncomfortably. She watched an unknown painter as he lazily and methodically laid the whitewash to one of the spindly joists which supported the staircase. "Did Isaac remember to put chimneys in the place? How're we going to heat it?"

"See the little hole, up the wall, Aunt Mart?" Cove asked. "No more fireplaces. A stove goes there. With a pipe to the hole. We're fancy as hell. Another stove in the kitchen—for you to cook on. The old man figures he'll save a lot of wood that way. If that Saint down Provo way gets us coal in time, you won't even need wood."

"Where *is* the stove?" Nancy asked.

Cove grinned. "I was supposed to pick it up in Salt Lake this trip. But Livingston & Bell didn't have it."

"That's real nice—with winter comin' on," Martha grumbled. "And me about as sick as a woman can be."

Cove slid the valise across the new pine floor to the wall. "I'll fetch it next trip," he promised.

"That's probably in the spring," Nancy sighed, remembering their aching labors of the past two days, and glancing down at her mud-caked skirt and shoes.

"Anyway, the kitchen stove's up, and ready to go," Cove said brightly. "Come on, I'll show you."

While the unknown man wearily whitewashed the staircase, they followed Cove across the room to the door in the north wall. The kitchen, while small for what would be expected of it, was more cogent with hope and promise. A new six-hole Art Eureka range, black, ornate, and beautiful, sat there on its feline legs waiting for its first firing and use. Martha, who had suffered out a lifetime with drafty, dirty fireplaces, brightened perceptibly at this vision of her first cookstove.

"Ain't she a dream?" Cove asked, happily.

"She really is," Martha said. "Purtiest thing I've ever seen. I'm glad Isaac thought to buy it."

"Think *you* can run it, Nan?" Cove asked.

Nancy pictured herself, demure and desired, cooking a man's meal on its polished iron top. "I'll run it," she said with assurance.

"Well, you ladies'll have plenty of chance. There'll be lots of cookin' on this store-bought gimcrack. And from what I glean, the old man's snortin' and pawin' to get this place rolling."

There could be no question as to who had been chosen for the task. All of Martha's kitchen possessions had been hauled from the fort house, and stacked in heaped confusion on the big, newly built kitchen table. Along with the old, battered, and sooty utensils of deep and poignant memory were the new things Isaac Corey had amply provided for the new venture. Stacks of new china plates, cups, and saucers were on the shelves. A heap of new silverware was dumped on the floor in the kitchen corner. A new copper washboiler, a new crank-handled wooden churn, two new iron skillets, a teakettle, and a new assortment of pots and pans lay in confusion about the room. Nancy knew there would be work ahead, and was liberally reminded of it, but no women in Ammon would have better tools with which to work.

Their further downstairs tour revealed a pantry, with plenty of shelving, a room to do the washing, and a little apartment of three tiny rooms, for Martha and Nancy. Here had been dumped every other belonging of any importance from the fort cabin. The place was chaos, but it was rich with promise, and about it was the heady and exciting smells of new whitewash, and new pine. Two store-new iron beds—one a big one for Martha and Isaac, another smaller one for Nancy—were leaned to the wall, complete with new springs.

"Which is *my* room, Mums?" Nancy asked, suddenly delirious with joy.

"You'll take the far one," Martha said, almost brightly. "You'll have quiet and privacy there. The other one I'll fix up for Isaac and me, and we'll use this one for a sort of parlor. Just a step from here to the kitchen and the big room."

"Now let's go upstairs," said Cove. "A dozen more rooms up there."

In the dozen rooms they found a dozen iron bedsteads exactly like the ones in their own apartment, a dozen identical commodes, complete with identical china bowls, pitchers, and chamber pots. A dozen identical mirrors, and eight coat hooks for each room, completed the furnishings. One small, louvered window was allowed each cubicle, and all were joined to the long hall which drained downward by way of the staircase to the big, plain public room below. This was the Corey House. And not until now did Nancy have any concept of the labors that would be expected of her.

She would have traded any or all of it to have returned to the old house at the fort.

VII

AT THE PROSPECTS OF CLEAN, DRY QUARTERS IN WHICH TO LIVE, MARTHA visibly brightened. Her internal pains and even her swelling subsided enough for her to be useful in putting the new place in order. But it was Nancy who really stormed through the work.

In the time of this frantic labor, Isaac's visits were brief, and his conversation curt and authoritative. He did hire Seth Biddle for a few days to give the women a hand in setting up beds, juggling furniture, and cleaning up after the painters and plasterers. Old Seth proved a real and willing help—until the afternoon of the third day—when, unexpectedly he was hit by one of his seizures.

He and Nancy were in the act of lugging the huge and clumsy wooden box of bedding up the stairway, Nancy ahead at one end, Seth behind, pushing upward, and bearing a sizable share of the weight. With a shriek like the broiling of the damned, Seth's arms let go of the burden, his arms and legs started flailing like a runaway windmill, and the box and Seth went rolling backwards down the stairs. Unnerved and frantic, Nancy clung to the big box, but gravity yanked it mercilessly from her fingers, and she could only screech in turn, as, stunned and helpless, she watched it ride the writhing man to the bottom of the stairs.

A moment later, with strength born of fright, she was rolling the big box off the shuddering and frothing man. Martha, from the kitchen, had heard the commotion, and was beside them as fast as she could make it.

76

"Oh my God!" she in turn shrieked, at sight of the fantastic wreck. "What happened?"

In the strength of her frenzy, Nancy gave the box a last wild shove. It teetered and slid along the new plank floor. "He had a spell," Nancy sobbed. "I couldn't hold it." She stared at the twitching Seth, his purpling, gurgling head hanging over the last step; his legs uphill, his body shuddering in the faded blue overalls. "I think we've killed him!"

"What shall we do?" Martha groaned in desperation.

"Grab his feet. I'll take head and shoulders. We'll lift him to the table."

With the speed and strength of desperation, the two women dragged Seth Biddle from the punishing rack of the stairway and lugged him to the clean pine expanse that was to serve as table—long, heavy planks, spiked to tall sawhorses. There they held Seth while his eyes rolled and his arms and legs pumped wildly against their grasp. The sight of this gentle, kindly man, possessed by a demonic fury beyond his control brought tears to Nancy's eyes. With her apron she wiped the bleeding scratches on his cheek and neck. Carefully she blotted the froth from his twisting lips.

"Hold him tight, Mums," she said. "I'm going for help."

Her first thought, as she fled out the doorway to the veranda, was to find Isaac Corey. It was late afternoon. Likely he'd be in from the fields. It was also his week with Aunt Kirstine. Nearest doctor was Provo. In Ammon there was only old Mary Magdalene Mattise, the midwife—and fits were scarcely her specialty.

She looked down the muddy street. Plenty of townsfolk—but Seth, sensitive soul that he was, would never thank her for bringing them in. It was Isaac she needed. Isaac would know what to do.

With the easy, tireless sprint she'd known from childhood, Nancy started south along the wagon ruts of the wide space that eventually would be a street. Workmen and townsfolk at the raw, new houses raised their heads as she flew by. Unsurprised, some of them waved. Frightened as she was, she made no attempt to shout the alarm. Instead she headed for the second street south, where the new Corey houses had risen. The first one would be Aunt Kirstine's. Off to the southeast, under the cloudy, brooding sky of this day, stood the old fort of deepest memory. She could see it, but there'd been no chance as yet to visit it. Now her pumping legs, under her high lifted skirts, brought her close to the fine new school building. Classes were finished for the day; the children had gone home. And there—oh God help her—was Joel Scott! He was calmly standing, three steps up on the porch landing, and just as calmly

77

smoking a Mormon-forbidden cheroot. His head snapped up as he saw her. He took the cheroot from his mouth, waved it, and whistled. She slowed to a walk; stopped; and stared at him like a worried owl.

"Hello, stranger," he shouted, and started down the steps toward her.

"Can't stop," she said. But she did.

His fast stride was bringing him nearer.

"I'm going for help," she added. "Something terrible's happened!"

Now he was at the new and unpainted schoolhouse fence. Against all sense, she strode out of the street center toward him.

"I saw you running like a gazelle," he said, smiling. "What's wrong, Nancy?"

"Seth Biddle's fell downstairs. A heavy box landed on top of him. He may be dying. I was on my way—" A new and more comforting thought struck her. "Will you help?" she begged.

"Course I'll help," Joel said. He took one last suck at the cheroot and tossed it over the fence into the irrigation ditch. Without hesitance, he bolted through the gateway, leaped the ditch, and was at her side.

"Where do we go?" he asked.

"Corey House. Follow me."

A moment later the townsfolk were again witnessing Nancy Corey on the run. This time they were a little more surprised. Behind her, hatless and coattails flying, was the new and fancy schoolmaster.

When, breathless, they dashed up the veranda and into the door of the Corey House, the scene they found in the big room was quite different than expected—at least different from what Nancy had expected. Seth Biddle was not dead. He was sitting on the edge of the table, feet dangling over the side, lucid and conscious. Martha was solicitously, with towels and cold water, applying compresses to his bruised and battered head. She all but dumped the basin of water at sight of Joel Scott. She had expected Nancy to bring Isaac Corey, and her surprise was as apparent as a dog caught at a milk pan. Nancy, only now aware of how quickly events had changed her resolve, was herself panicked by the ease with which it had happened.

Seth nodded a cool and nervous recognition of the schoolteacher. "How are you, Mr. Scott," Martha said, deliberately wringing out the towel. "Brother Biddle had a nasty fall." She wrapped the wet towel on Seth's hair and forehead and pressed it firmly tight.

"That's what Nancy said," Joel politely replied. He stepped around the table to the injured man. "You feel all right, Mr. Biddle? Break any bones?"

"I'm all right," Seth answered, embarrassed. "No broken bones. Shook up a little, that's all."

"A miracle," Nancy sighed, relieved. "That big box fell right on top of him."

Seth slid gingerly off the table side and reflectively felt along the faded denim covering his legs. While Martha held the towel to his head, he tested his bruises by teetering on his toes and flexing his arms. Satisfied that he was still whole, he smiled warmly and gratefully at the two women. "I'm embarrassed," he said, honestly. "Bad place for a spell." He looked again at Nancy, and Martha peeled off the towel from his head and dropped it into the tin basin. "Feel all right," he said. "Let's get the box upstairs—like we should've done in the first place."

"Are you sure you're able?" Nancy asked, looking nervously at Seth's sweat-damp face and neck.

"Sure I'm able." Seth smoothed down his soggy brown hair with his hand, and stepped over to the big box near the wall. "Only this time the teacher's gonna help buck it. This is no work for a girl."

Joel Scott needed no urging. He moved to the clumsy box and hefted an end of it. Seth again accepted the back stance that had proved so disastrous for him.

"Mr. Scott'll spoil his good clothes," Nancy protested weakly. "I can handle the front end, easy."

"Let teacher do it," Seth growled, bending painfully to hook his fingers under the box's bottom edge. "Don't you worry about teacher's clothes. He don't mind. And you're no pack horse, Nan—even if Isaac Corey's trying to make you one."

"I'm a *good* pack horse," Joel chuckled, bending for his own finger grip. "Seth and I will have this thing upstairs in a jiffy."

A moment later the two men had bucked the box to a good lift. They hesitated while Joel turned his stance around to a new grip so he could sensibly walk forward up the stairs. Relieved and happy, Nancy watched while the fat load of bedding went easily and neatly up the stairs under the willing strength of the two men.

Seth and Joel had no more than deposited their burden, and were returning down the steps, when the front door opened. It was Isaac Corey. And Isaac was agitated.

His dark eyes stabbed at the room like an animal squaring off for danger. "Anything wrong?" he asked. "They said folks were running toward the house. A fire?"

"No fire," Martha answered, calm at last.

"It was *me* running," Nancy added. "And Mr. Scott." She nodded toward the two men on the stairs. "Seth had a bad fall. Down the steps—with the box of bedding on top of him."

"No harm, Brother Corey," Seth reassured. "Whammed my head. A few bruises." He strode down the remaining steps, with Joel Scott behind him. "But I'm all right. And the teacher and me got the box up without a speck of grief."

Isaac relaxed, and the worry went out of his face. "Well, that's a relief."

"If you don't mind, Brother Corey," Seth said, "I'll take off for home. Get a little arnica on these spots before they seize up sore-like. I'll come in early tomorrow and finish helping Sister Corey and Nan."

"That's fine, Brother Biddle," Isaac agreed, thoughtfully fingering his beard. "You go on home. Glad the hurts weren't worse."

Seth snatched his battered felt hat from its nail under the staircase, and went out the door. Martha gathered up the towels and basin and started for the kitchen. Isaac already was cordially shaking hands with Joel.

"I'm glad to get this chance to speak a word with you, Mr. Scott," Isaac was saying. "My young'uns say you're a fine teacher, but that you stand for no monkey business. They're gettin' a lot of good learnin'. An' I think teachers *should* be hard and tough."

Joel smiled. "I find the Corey youngsters very bright. They're good pupils, and you should be very proud of them."

"Hear that!" Isaac said proudly, beaming for the first time at Nancy. "I like hearin' good things about my kids. Now, if they act up, just whale hell out of 'em. Or tell me, and *I'll* do it. I want my kids to learn manners —along with their readin'. An' you're a man who can teach kids manners."

Nancy tried to keep unobtrusive and demure through the talk. By rights she probably should leave the room—and probably Isaac would get around to asking her to do so. But she wasn't going to leave until he ordered it. In the meantime she let her lowered eyes travel up the black broadcloth trousers of the man she so secretly loved. His vest was real satin-plaited, and the watch chain across it was close-linked, with engraved medallion, and likely of real gold. His clothes were fairly new, probably purchased in California, and certainly appeared like quality. No doubt he was the best-dressed man in Ammon.

"I don't believe it's necessary to whale pupils," Joel was saying. "Apostle Pratt and I both agree that firmness at the start keeps the rod in the corner, rather than on the backs of wicked little boys—and girls. Oddly, I find your Mormon children exceptionally well behaved. At

80

home, they must get a lot of good teaching with their religion. I'm certainly impressed."

"The people like you, too, Mr. Scott."

Nancy at last took courage to look up into the bronzed and now sober face of Joel. She saw a firmness there that could hold any rascal in check. And certainly she could be numbered with those who liked him.

"My type of teaching is more or less an experiment. It's a little early as to results. I hope I can set up a plan and pattern that will please and be valuable to your people, before I return East. Your leaders in Salt Lake City are most co-operative. I'm glad I came to Ammon. And when I go back, I'll never forget these handsome, wonderful children here in the valley."

"And we'll never forget you, Professor," Isaac said. "The kids here are lucky to get a teacher like you."

Nancy, left completely out of the conversation, and apparently forgotten in the salubrious exchange, was not out of it in mind. She remembered the day she'd watched Joel Scott ride away from Ammon. By his own admission he'd ride away again. In Mormondom, he was as different as a white-furred buffalo. As a Gentile, they accepted him because he had much to offer them. But also as a Gentile, let him get in the way of their theology, and he'd be picked clean as a Sunday rooster of any adulation he now possessed. But even at the thought of his going away she sorrowed.

"I've been thinking, Professor," Isaac was saying, "that you should have a decent place to stay while you're here. It's a little noisy at the Earlingtons. Probably they want you to night-teach their kids, when you should have a place that's quiet and restful. I'm proud of what you said about my own kids. I'm so prideful I want to do something real nice toward educatin' our Saints."

"You already have, Mr. Corey," Joel said. "You and your grown sons had the biggest hand in getting us a fine new school building in an amazingly short time. I—"

"But what I want to do is this," Isaac persisted. "In this new house is twelve smackin' new sleepin' rooms. You saw 'em yourself, upstairs. Now, pick the one you want. Stay here as long as you want. It's yours —without one penny of charge. An' my women will feed you as good as the Earlingtons!"

Nancy felt herself turning sick. Golly damn! Father Isaac must be blind as a mole and stupid as a wether ram! Can't he see, or sense, that to put Joel in this house is like—?

"It's very nice," Joel was calmly saying. "And you're so generous, Mr. Corey. I just couldn't—"

"Oh yes you can, Professor. I insist."

Golly damn, again thought Nancy, weakly. If this father of mine has *any* inkling of what's in his daughter's heart, he'll keep this man *forever* at the Earlingtons!

"I pay board and room at the bishop's," Joel was saying. "I'd be foolish not to want to move into this nice new place. But I'd not come without paying—the same as any other public guest."

"Father in heaven, help me," Nancy whispered in weak and frightened prayer.

"Let's put it this way, then, Professor," Isaac insisted. "I don't know what you pay the bishop for grub an' bed. I don't even care to know. But if you insist on payin'—an' payin' will make you feel more right inside—I'll make another proposition. You move your possibles over here next week. Pay my womenfolk just half what you pay the bishop. Is it a deal?"

"It's a deal," Joel said, and he clasped the rough hand of Isaac Corey to bind it.

"Father in heaven," Nancy murmured. "I'll try to be decent about it. I'll try so hard not to make You ashamed of me."

She looked around her at last. Martha was standing in the kitchen door, solemn and twitching. Joel started toward the street door, turned, and smilingly nodded at all of them. "So long, Mr. Corey. And thank you so much. So long, Mrs. Corey. I'll be enjoying your hospitality soon. So long, Nancy. I'm so glad I could be of help to you."

And then he was gone—back to his schoolhouse. And for Nancy Corey, life would never again be the same.

But when he was gone, Isaac Corey quickly again became stern and caustic. "Come here, both of you," he called. "Pull up chairs to the table. I wanta talk."

As Nancy seated herself beside her father, and across the table from her mother, she tried some quick imagining as to what was coming. Surely, now that Flora was married, and away in Salt Lake City, Isaac would not storm afresh over the Cragg affair. If he dared, out the door she'd go! Surely he'd not blame them because of the failure of the dairy farm at The Point. They'd slaved from dawn till dusk. The soldiers had been moved out. And Martha had returned from his angry banishment a sick woman.

"I want this place ready for business Monday morning," Isaac said.

"There's a heap to do," Martha said weakly.

"You'll have to do it. I've told Salt Lake it'll be ready. Keep Seth on the job. Work him hard."

"Seth's as sick as I am," Martha argued. "Reason he fell is because he had one of his fits. And I'd appreciate a little time myself to get better."

"Where's the pain, Martha?"

"Same place. Gut deep. And there's swelling."

"I'll tell Mary Magdalene to look at you. Tonight I'll get one of the elders, an' bring over some consecrated oil. We'll administer to you. An' God will bring a healing."

Martha's head twitched despairingly on her shoulders. "I hope so," she sighed.

As though Martha's problem were disposed of, Isaac went on. "Cove's bringin' all the grub in tomorrow. I'm givin' you two cows, for milk an' butter. As many more as you need. I've got a reed organ comin' over from Provo. A little music of nights will brighten up the guests."

"We need a heat stove to warm 'em up the most," Martha sullenly replied. "This is a mighty big room to keep comfortable—with winter 'most upon us."

"I'm still lookin' for a stove," Isaac said, a little peevish. "Stoves are hard to come by."

"How come you didn't cut a fireplace? Fireplace would at least keep their backsides warm."

"I'll get a stove," Isaac growled. "Now, what I want to tell you is this: This'll be a public house. All kinds of people'll come an' go. There'll be stages stoppin' here, going north an' south. There'll be travelers—Saints an' Gentiles. There'll be good people, an' there'll be hard people. If there's temptation, the Lord has told you, an' will tell you, how to deal with it."

Nancy looked at her mother. Martha made as though to speak and then subsided. It could have been an unframed protest against the moving in of Joel Scott, because, of the two of them, Martha alone knew her daughter's heart. Had Martha managed voice to this protest, Nancy wondered if she herself would have pleaded in favor of Isaac's generous invitation toward "the professor." At any rate, nothing whatever came out. And Isaac Corey, apparently, remained unconscious as to the degree he was abetting temptation.

"This place is to be run in accordance with the principles of the Gospel. We've got to think of the Word of Wisdom, which was laid down by the Prophet Joseph Smith. Prayers at the table. No smokin' in this room."

"What about tea and coffee?" Martha asked.

Isaac thought a moment. "I guess we'll have to bend a little there. Give it to 'em, if they ask for it, or insist on it. But liquor is another matter. This has got to be a temperance house. Still, all the Salt Lake houses sell spirits." He thought another moment. "Serve them none. But if, say, a Gentile insists—we'll have to peddle it to 'em in the bottle. In the back room is an unmarked case of Valley Tan whiskey. I insisted they send it down in an unmarked case, because Cove was hauling it. Be sure an' get a full dollar a pint for it. An' if you sell any of it to Cove, or give any of it to him, you'll hear from me.

"Charge no less than six bits for a room, fifteen cents for breakfast, and two bits for lunch or supper. Make sure it's cash money. An' no credit. You'll be pestered by Gentiles an' Winter Saints with no money. If they're Winter Saints, tell 'em to go to the bishop. If they're Gentiles, tell 'em to go graze on the prairie."

There was much more of admonition and counsel regarding the new and fearsome venture, but Nancy proffered little in the conversation. All she knew was that there was work ahead. Yesterday she'd balked at the thoughts of it. Today it was not work that terrorized her. She wondered if the change that had come upon her, and which churned inside her like a butter plug, could somehow be visible from the outside. Martha probably sensed it. But Isaac, laying down the rules of God and commerce, appeared to be as blind and blockheaded as a cedar post.

VIII

THE COREY HOUSE WAS FULL FROM THE START. ITS GUESTS, BESIDES THE transients who, because of mud and inclement weather, failed to make Provo before nightfall, or road-battered travelers from infrequent arrival of the stages, included those of a more permanent status. Two families of California-bound Gentiles, who had taken employment for the winter in the now booming town, and those Saints who had moved to Utah Valley and needed housing while their own homes were built, stuffed the place to capacity, filled every chair at the big table three times a day, and kept Nancy Corey and her mother laboriously occupied from daylight to dark.

Nancy's sick-sweet inner trepidation over the imminent appearance of Joel Scott as a permanent boarder was ended at the week's beginning, when the schoolmaster appeared with his first load of personal traps. He was standing in the downstairs public room when Nancy entered from the kitchen for the first labors of setting out Monday morning's breakfast. Expected as he was, she still nearly dropped the plates at sight of him.

"Well, here I am," he said casually, and the revealment alone was enough to blow Nancy apart like a haystack in a norther. "Am I too early to move into my roost?"

"Oh no, Mr. Scott," Nancy answered, clattering the plates to the long table. "It's upstairs," she managed to say. "I've got it ready. Let me help you carry your things."

"No, no. I've only a light load. I'll bring more over after school. If you like, we can just leave them downstairs, and I'll take them up later."

"I've fixed your room up," she added breathlessly. "It's ready. Follow me upstairs. I'll show you."

Trembling like an ailing heifer, she headed up the steps—unmindful of the two Corey House men guests who were heading down toward their morning habits and breakfast. They gave the burdened Joel, with his valise and foot locker, the curious stare always reserved for newcomers.

Joel seemed proud and happy over the little room, and pleased with the counterpane and extras Nancy had managed special for the place where her man would sleep. But after that, in the most casual sort of way, he'd hurried off—without taking breakfast. Yet, knowing he'd be back, Nancy spent this special day in shakes and shivers.

And so the schoolmaster came to the Corey House. It was well he'd timed his arrival early—for opening the House's doors to the public was like yanking a headgate in the big canal. For once Isaac Corey had underestimated an opportunity. Between stranded gold-seekers, Winter Saints, and new townsfolk, he could have stuffed a building twice its size.

But Nancy, for one, was grateful the place was no larger. The work was hard, constant, and as inexorable in its duties as salvation's own plan. The milk, and from it the butter, these people devoured in such vast quantities, had to be teated night and morning from the three cows now stabled out back. The eggs they consumed had to be gathered from the House's hen coops; from hens that had to also be fed, that they in turn might produce. The four hogs Isaac cannily had provided had to be slopped with the guests' table garbage which, when the hogs were fat and ready, would be fed back to them in ham, bacon, and pork roasts. The urine so copiously left by the guests in their chamber pots provided the lye which, when mixed with the grease from their dinner drainings, made the soap which kept them clean and washed out their dirty linen once a week. It was like a perpetual circle—only it took an immense and thankless amount of labor to keep the circle moving. And the sadness of it was that Martha no longer was the woman she used to be, or which Isaac still imagined she was. Valiantly the shrunken little soul struggled to hold up her share of the daily program, but only Nancy seemed to know what it was doing to her.

"Nan, it's like some fiend has claws inside me," she would confide. "I hurt—and I hurt awful."

"This place is too much for you—hot stove and all," Nancy would commiserate. "Father's *got* to get someone to spell you off. He's *got* to give us help. Aunt Kirstine should take over the cooking till you feel better."

Nancy complained to Isaac, and asked for help, but Martha suffered on in silence. On her more desperately sick nights, Isaac and the elders anointed her graying head with consecrated oil, and prayed fervidly for her recovery.

"Keep faith, and you'll get the healing," Isaac prophesied to her. "I promise you, in the name of Israel's God, you'll feel better on tomorrow's rising—providing you keep heart and faith on this anointing."

But the recovery, such as it was, seemed only ephemerally tied to the prayers. Anyone could see, were they inclined to lift their heavenly blinders, that the little woman was in trouble, and in pain. As to the needed extra help around the Corey House—because Martha complained none, she got none. The prayed-on promises of God were sustaining, but Nancy was finding that her own unstinting help in the day's drudgery was the blessing poor Martha could more readily understand and appreciate.

Both were finding that these were sad, hard days, and Nancy herself could not escape the conviction she'd been bitterly betrayed. She was sixteen now. Any townsgirl from fourteen upward, not half so pretty or well formed, would have been showered with beaux and friendship for these two vital courtin' years. But what was Nancy Corey doing? Feeding two long rows of cavernous mouths three times a day. Scrubbing the towels and napkins that wiped these mouths, and the sheets and cases that wrapped in the sweaty smelly bodies belonging to these mouths, and carting out their excreta in the mornings. Maybe she *should*, like Flora, have married the apostle.

It was the bishops, and the apostles, she reasoned, who had indirectly tendered her this unromantic life. When they had moved in, fawning and attentive, every young man anywhere near her age, had quickly moved out. She had found herself sacrosanct to the high holders of the priesthood, and taboo to the handsome, daring young devils who delighted the hearts of the less lucky young girls of Ammon. Like a bear at a beehive, she had been well stung when she upset it, and for her there had been no honey. Now she faced life as a working spinster. Endless drudgery was her lot—and "it's one hell of a lot!" she groaned.

A house full of guests, paying or otherwise, should make for warmth or friendship. But how could anyone know anyone, when the only moment you met them was to fill their surly wants? At night they fraternized around the reed organ—while she was washing their dirty dishes. True, this nightly fraternizing, with no heat stove, was comparatively short-lived. But, short or long, she, as a slavey, had little part of it. And, when they gathered at the long table, there was nothing glowing or sustaining in whatever social contact she had with them. Among themselves, they were polite and sweet. With her, they were anxious and irritable. Their gullets craved the mountains of food she could never be fast enough in getting to them. She smiled, and tried to be nice, but what they saw in her was an endless feed-belt, serving twenty places at once, and at the same time individually available. What she saw in them were two long rows of rubbery mouths—red, ugly feed hoppers that fed their bottomless viscera. Other girls her age had men friends, flirtation, and excitement. The romance in her life consisted of twelve bedrooms to keep clean, and twenty mouths and guts to plug with food three times a day.

The imaginative romance in her life, however, was quite a different thing. Denial was a thing distinctly apart from dreams. If Joel Scott had any inkling of the chaotic and desperate nature of her imaginings, he would either grab his horse and be gone, or would rescue her forthwith from slavery. Other than a natural warmth and politeness, inherently a part of him, he was giving her only the barest crumbs of encouragement. But so long as he remained close enough to look at, and to speak to, his very presence in the house remained the one frantic hope.

"Good morning, Nan," he would say at breakfast, and "Hello, Nan," he would say in the evening. Both of which were sparse, and scarcely different from what the others said. Everyone called her Nan, but still, somehow, when Joel said it, there was a special something about it. There was smiling in his eyes, warmth in the way he looked at her, and the "Nan" was always rolled out in a way that sounded like no other person on earth. She knew Joel liked her—with a special liking. He showed it, and she felt it. She knew he wished her well. But to one so deeply hungering—a taste was slim and agonizing substitute for a meal.

As for Isaac, and his promise of a stove for the big room, the pledge was falling just as short of fulfillment as was his prophecy of a healing to his ailing Martha.

"I've slogged my way from one end of Utah Valley t'other," he sadly confessed to Joel one night. "Ain't a Saint'll give up his heat this winter —even for good money. I'm ashamed of the chill of this place."

"No stove to be had, even in Salt Lake?" Joel asked.

"None t'be had. Cove ransacked every store. Didn't b'lieve him, till I went north an' tried for m'self. No freightin' from the East till late spring. But I'll find heat, mark you. I'll find heat if I have to rob the Lord by carryin' a stove out of the meetin' house."

But while Isaac hunted, it was far too chilly for much after-dinner socializing of the guests downstairs. Joel's after-meal diversion consisted of a leisurely smoking of a cheroot out on the veranda, along with the other like-minded Gentile addicts to the weed. In compliance with Isaac's strict orders regarding the Word of Wisdom, Martha forbade any smoking inside the building, and banishment to the veranda became a grumbling acceptance of an inflexible rule at the Corey House. From her work at clearing the table and tidying up after the diners, Nancy could hear Joel's pleasant voice, in clipped New England vernacular, discussing such national issues as the hunt for the murderers of President Lincoln, problems of reconstruction in the South, and even his own reminiscences of the great war so recently past, and in which he himself had taken so active a part. These conversations were with the travelers and Gentiles who smoked and, in her work, the things she heard were only fragmentary to her own mad rushes to and from the kitchen. But everything the man said, was, to her, dramatic and interesting, and she hung on every intonation of his voice, and every scrap and morsel that in her imaginings could piece together his wonderfully dramatic life.

He would have been amazed at the things she knew about him—his war experiences, his travelings to India, Europe, and California. Martha would have been surprised also to know that Joel *did* smoke in the house. Every day Nancy carried one or two cheroot butts out of his bedroom, where he had smoked them in his own silent leisure, while he read, wrote, or sketched.

The twelve upper rooms, being close to the roof, received benefit from whatever warmth evaporated upward from the hot kitchen, and whatever heat the daily sun could beat into the shingles and rafters of the roof. Until the deeper chill of night, the sleeping rooms were by far the warmest part of the house, and it was not surprising that the guests chose them in preference to the chilly discomfort of the big room downstairs. By morning they, too, were cold and cheerless—with one possible exception. Nancy Corey had come to the conclusion that the schoolmaster's room was the warmest, cheeriest, and most exciting place on earth. By degrees it grew into the hub of her universe.

Joel could leave all the cheroot butts he pleased, he could scatter ten empties of Valley Tan all over the place, he could leave his evidence of any man-vice he pleased, and the secret would remain forever hers. He could catch her some day alone in this room, make frantic love, and do unspeakable things, but never would she betray the man, or love him any the less.

Mornings were taken up with breakfast, washing, scrubbing, butter making, baking, and then the frantic drive to get the noon meal over and the clean plates back to the cupboards. It was early afternoon when she got around to making beds, and putting the upper rooms in order. By that time the last late sleeper had given up, the workers were at work, and the whole upstairs was ready and waiting for her vigorous hand. Always she saved Joel's room to the last. She hurried like hell's fury through the other eleven, that she might have precious minutes there to dawdle and dream amid the belongings and secrets of this man.

Ah, but Joel was the gentleman! His clothes were hung to the hooks with neatness and military precision. Shirts and underwear were folded neatly in the drawers of the commode. His books, of which there were many and of fearsome titles, were, with his notebooks and sketch pads, neatly arrayed along the plank shelf Nancy herself had helped him add to the wall.

It had been that first Saturday, with no school for Joel, and he had come to her. "Nan, do you think your father would object if I stole a plank from his lumber pile?" he'd asked. "If I could hang some sort of shelf to the wall of my room, I'd get those books up off the floor."

"Let's just borrow a plank," she'd happily agreed. "He'll never miss it."

So together they'd plundered the back-yard lumber pile for a board

—straight and true. Together, from the back room, they'd borrowed Isaac's saw, hammer, and drawknife.

"You too busy to help me put the shelf up?" he'd asked.

"I'd *love* to help you," she'd agreed. "Golly damn, yes." And she'd have helped lug planks and tools to his room if there had been a work-margin on hell itself. So, together they'd gone upstairs. Together they'd been in his room.

But it had proven no love tryst. There'd been none of the torrid happenings she'd dreamed about.

"Hold that plank straight to the wall, Nan," he'd cautioned. "Not having a spirit level, all we can do is guess our best, and mark for position."

And that was the way of the conversation, while she watched him work at fashioning hangers and braces for the shelf—holding the lumber while he sawed, trimmed, and rounded the corners with the drawknife. They'd laughed. They'd talked. And she'd marveled at his skillfulness and neatness in everything he did.

Afterward he'd carried down the wood scraps and the tools, and she'd swept up the sawdust and shavings from the floor. But through it all, it had been a glad Saturday morning. The door had stayed open, he'd laid no hands on her, and they'd talked of innocuous things—still there was a knowing that he liked her—maybe secretly loved her—and there was a knowing he'd found pleasure in her company. She'd lingered to help him put the many books to the shelf, but through it all he'd remained the gentleman.

But that *was* the special something about Joel Scott. He *was* the gentleman. Even if he loved her, as she loved him, he'd never come bulling at her with the devastating singleness of purpose of say a Lofty Cragg. There were restraints and niceties about this man that were rare to Zion. Openly and secretly he *was* the gentleman—and something *really* special.

Even in the so-called little things, she had surest proof he was a gentleman. Joel, for instance, had never forced her to the necessity of emptying his chamber pot. And that was the most consideration she had ever gotten from any Corey House guest. An early riser herself, in order to get the milking done, she had never yet caught Joel emptying his own pot. She could only surmise that he either had magnificent control, or made his own private exits to the back-yard privy.

Then there were the mementoes, the pictures, and the personal trivia of the man that made him so secretly desirable, and set her heart to galloping about the places he had been, and the strange and little-known world from whence he had come. His uniforms as an army officer, his saber, his pistol, still hung neatly from the wall hooks—reminders of an exciting world that had been his alone, and the manner of man he had been when first she had seen him from the wall. In the upper drawer of the commode were his personal jewelry, engraved cuff links, cravats, bat-winged collars, a gold nugget or two from California, and piles of other little items indicative of a traveler and a gentleman. For him alone she had provided, from the big and personal trunk, that lace-edged runner she'd fashioned with her own hands. He didn't know that he alone of the paying guests had such a fancy doily on the marble top of his commode. But every day she willingly and neatly arranged his shaving mug, razor, and mustache shears along its frilly top. And so far he had slopped few stains upon it. She watched it closely, because downstairs was another one to take its place.

The tintype photographs and hand-painted miniatures arrayed behind the runner were the most disturbing mysteries of the man and his room. Frowning sea captains, pompous military men, and spidery, laced-in women, looked out at Nancy as every afternoon she sat down on Joel's bed and wondered what it would be like in the world he had come from. The pictures didn't look too friendly, and she knew she would probably fit into his Boston life like a nervous sow in a parlor. But it was something one could think about.

The most worrisome picture, however, was the exquisite hand-painted miniature of that blond woman. She was every bit as lovely as anything in *Godey's*. Joel had a sister named Amanda—letters and another signed picture had made that plain enough. The troublous one definitely was not Amanda. Never had he said that he was married; his remaining in Utah Valley would argue against it; and the talk she'd had with him that first day would indicate that he was not. Unquestionably, then, the woman was his sweetheart. And because of her alone, Nancy kept silent around him, circumspect and polite in her few words with him, and anything but the pushy and frantic woman of their first brief meeting. But the female part of her could not but be ripe with anxiety. Every day Nancy nosed into his mail. There were letters from Boston and other New England cities, and from Bangor, Maine; from his mother, Amanda, relatives, and wartime companions. They spelled out his life and background, yet gave no answer to the riddle which obsessed her. In time she came to the conclusion he was too smart a man to leave love letters around for prying eyes. The Army made a man discreet and clever about his personals. The foot locker under his bed was ironbound, solid, and mysterious, and he alone had the key. But someday would come the answer; someday he would accidentally leave a letter or two. Maybe someday, while she was leisurely making up his room in the afternoon, he would walk in, and find her there. Anything could still happen; and maybe, from his own lips, would come all the secrets she so yearned to know. And the fact that Joel's was the only room she allowed herself to primp and dawdle in, it was inevitable, she felt certain, that someday, he again would meet her there.

The certainty, however, became less certain as the weeks slipped into early winter. Joel's day at the school was full-time and an exacting task. Saturdays, he spent full day astride his horse. When he did arrive, her duties as chambermaid were long over, and she and Martha already were driving themselves to get supper on and ready for the irritable and anxious guests whose gullets needed filling for the night.

Yet in spite of the unyielding pattern of the day, and the lack of opportunity, her planned and planted dream actually did happen, just as she knew it would. But even this probably would never have occurred had Brigham Young not been delayed in his winter trip south.

The Saints, in their early exploration of the Great Basin, had made some rather remarkable geographical discoveries. Utah Valley, in which the town of Ammon nestled, surrounded by some of the richest and deepest soils the basin provided, had been one of these immense and fortunate finds. The story of the exploring parties, under Apostles Parley P. Pratt and George Albert Smith, who in the early years had pushed south—over the lower rim of the Great Basin, into the lands of the Sanpetes, the Piedes, and the Tonaquints, was common knowledge to Nancy and the Saints of Utah Valley, and a first-hand experience to Cove Corey. While Cove's mission southward had come at a later date, and his whole life had been embittered about it, still he had talked to Nancy and Flora a little about the country's red mountains, narrow fertile valleys, and the winter climate that was balmy and free of the blizzards and snow so prevalent in the north. All the Saints knew of Jacob Hamblin. With his hand-picked missionaries to the Lamanites, he had done a masterful job of pacifying the tribes, converting them to the Gospel, and preparing them for the many other Saints who never failed to follow the glad tidings. The Indian mission had been a continuing thing from the start, and the special men to fill it had been young, courageous, and adventuresome. Cove was nineteen when they sent him southward to live with the Indians on the rim, and the settlements were well established. He'd come back with deep and endless respect for Jacob Hamblin, and an undying hatred for Brigham Young, the man who had sent him.

The probe into "Dixie," as it was called, began with the establishment of Fort Harmony, near Ash Creek. In 1852 Cedar Valley was settled, and towns, under tireless energy of the Saints, had rapidly followed. With the discovery of immense iron-ore deposits in the red mountains of the Cedar Valley, the "Iron Mission" had come into being, quickly populated by converts from the mining areas of Wales and England, and charged with the responsibility of making this rich find available to the greater community of Saints. Then came the farmers and the townspeople, to fatten Cedar City, Parowan; and, over the mountains to the warm, pink paradise of the Virgin River margins, they had built the winter havens of St. George and Santa Clara.

But here, still, and far out across the rim and the chewed-up world beyond the River Colorado, were the Lamanites—still in great numbers, still a challenge; an ever increasing responsibility with the rising of every Mormon town. "This growth's not without its turmoil," Isaac had explained. "It saps the patience of Jacob Hamblin and every man of his mission to pacify the Lamanites and keep them in check."

Actually, the greatest turmoil incident to Mormon colonization in the west had been centered in these promising settlements to the south. In spite of the great promises of the *Book of Mormon*, and the example and dedication of Hamblin and his missionaries, the tribes had swung like a pendulum—from utter dependence and subservience, to outright defiance and open warfare. Worst stories to come out of Utah's Dixie, things that Nancy heard discussed in lowered tones and discreet speculation, were concerned with the tragic fate of those Gentile immigrants who had found themselves trapped in Utah's Dixie, at Mountain Meadows, during the hysteria and indignities of the Utah War, and Johnston's invasion. That these Gentiles had perished was known and accepted. That the Indians had a hand in it was universally believed. That the Dixie Saints had also had a hand in it could not so easily be proven and, in the total absence of confirmation or denial, the Saints of Ammon could only darkly imagine and speculate.

Cove Corey who, as a gutty young man of scouting skills and fibrous endurance, had been called to the Indian mission five years after the massacre, had his own theories regarding the affair.

"Indians?" he'd snort. "You think Indians did that job? Hell, the Dixie Saints were in it up to their eyebrows! Mum's the word now—but someday the truth'll be known. And it'll not look pretty for the Saints!"

But by the time Cove had abruptly returned from the mission, and was giving voice to these speculations, what he said had no more standing in the community than the effusions of any other lying and mealy-mouthed apostate.

About all that Nancy knew about Cove's abortive mission to the Lamanites was that like any other Saint heeding the "call," he'd departed Ammon with the lofty aim of dedicating the good years of his life to the uplift and welfare of the benighted Lamanites along the rim. She knew he had crossed the Colorado to the lands of the Hopi and the Navajo. She knew that Jacob Hamblin himself had written Isaac about the fearless and devoted nature of this son he had given to the mighty work of Indian salvation and regeneration. She knew that Cove had departed Ammon devout, courageous, and filled with high hopes—at the age of nineteen. Two years later he'd returned a matured man, but an angry apostate.

She knew, too, that the reason for this change was not an uncommon thing in Zion. In one of the towns of Utah's Dixie, the young missionary had fallen in love with a Mormon girl. Cove apparently had expected to marry her on his release from the mission, and, because of it, even for the good of the Church, had utterly refused to take a squaw to wife—as so many of the Indian missionaries were doing. On his return from that last dangerous and sacrificial sojourn with the Hopis and Navajos, it was to discover that the darling who had promised to wait for him, had married herself high into the Church. She had become a winter bride to the much married prophet, seer, and revelator—Brigham Young himself. Cove had never been a hand to spell out the details of his crushed love. All Nancy knew was that he had tossed his *Book of Mormon* into the Virgin River, and returned to Ammon as one of the angriest men in Utah.

But that was Cove's problem, and it worried the other Saints not at all. Even in the matter of the Indian ferment, Saints took such things in stride. As long as Nancy could remember, turmoil and Indian uprisings were an ever present part of Mormon life. And the southern settlements, despite every problem, were one of the most promising segments of the new heritage. From that rich, warm land would come iron, steel, cotton, silk, grapes, and the more exotic fruits and foods of southern climes. The more favored Saints had discovered in it a place to hibernate away from the rigors of a mountain winter. Brigham Young regularly spent his winters there. As an added convenience, some of his wives had been located at St. George, and a temple was being planned for that area.

But this year the Prophet Brigham was late in getting his trip started southward. "Another Indian war has erupted in the Sanpete and Sevier

Valleys, under Chief Black Hawk," Nancy heard from the northbound travelers. "Saints there have been killed. And still that useless General Connor, from the safe walls of Fort Douglas, has refused aid in quelling the uprising! Instead of his army protecting the Saints, he's insolently using it to throw a provost guard around the church headquarters in Salt Lake City!" It was common knowledge that the Saints were getting no help from either the government territorial appointees or the military in their persistent efforts to get the State of Deseret accepted into the American Union. Instead, Connor was allowing to be published at Fort Douglas *The Union Vidette,* a scurrilous, insolent sheet, aimed like a mutation's blade at Brigham Young and the vitals of the Church.

President Young ordinarily managed to get out of Salt Lake City immediately after the October conference, but this year, because of these problems, and many others in ferment, early winter was upon him before he could start for the southern settlements. Because of this, and the vile and almost impassable nature of the roads, Isaac Corey's greatest dream became a living reality—he was overnight host to President Brigham Young.

It was Saturday night. The guests had been fed, and had dispersed from the chilly room. Joel, with two other Gentiles, were out on the veranda in the darkness, enjoying a little talk along with their smokes. Nancy was busy lugging soiled plates to the kitchen. It was then that the closed-in carriage, with its Negro driver, and two mounted horsemen, slogged to a stop in front of the House. Not until the men dismounted, and engaged Joel Scott in talk, was there the least realization as to who the distinguished visitor might be.

A moment later the great fact was made known to Nancy, when Joel burst into the room, smoking cheroot in his hand. Nancy, with a double armload of plates, was just turning from the table.

"Brace yourself, my dear," Joel said, smiling, his blue eyes alive with bright lights. "Brigham Young is here."

She looked at him incredulously. "Did you say—?"

"I said, Brigham Young. He's here! They're tying up the horses. I've told them to come in. They'd expected to make Provo, but the team's done in. You'll have to put up the Lord's dignitaries. And you'll probably have to feed them."

"Oh, golly damn," Nancy groaned, clattering the stack of plates back to the table. "What'll I do?"

"Tell Mrs. Corey in the kitchen, quick," Joel said. "Get her out here to meet her guests. I'll hustle up Mr. Corey while you do it. But, hurry, Nan. They'll be in here before you know it."

He put the cheroot in his mouth, took one calm puff, and took off, through the front door, in search of Isaac. And before Nancy could finish exploding the news to the sweating Martha in the kitchen, the visitors had scraped their shoes at the door, and were standing in the big room of the Corey House.

Both Martha and Nancy, palsied with fright and surprise, did the best they could in greeting the four men. Before them stood the President of the Church, and former territorial governor, Brigham Young. With him was his tall first councilor, Heber C. Kimball. Behind them were the two men who had ridden horse guard, whom President Young calmly and casually introduced to the two flustered women. Bishop Stringfellow, who smiled and nodded to the introduction, was unknown to Nancy. But not the long hair, long beard, and beady eyes of Orrin Porter Rockwell. He had often come in to The Point, knew the Coreys well, and doubtless had guided the men to the Corey House when it was apparent they could never make Provo this night. The big pistol, sagging from his right hip, and his reputation for quick and faultless aim, was evidence that the carriage of President Young had been well protected.

"This is a fine building Brother Corey has erected," President Young was saying. The square-jawed leader let his eyes rove approvingly about the white new room. He rubbed his short beard thoughtfully, as he eyed the long expanse of table Nancy had been in the act of clearing. "Brother Corey's certainly to be commended."

"He certainly is," President Kimball agreed. He, too, looked around him approvingly.

All four men appeared weary, rumpled, and obviously hungry.

"Please be seated, brethren," Martha managed to gasp, her head twitching. "You must be starved." In her panic, Martha couldn't decide whether to run for the kitchen or further pursue the amenities.

"We *are* starved," Brigham agreed. He gave the two women his famous smile, and they both felt better.

"We've sent for Brother Corey," Nancy managed to add. "While you make yourselves to home, I'll finish cleaning up the table." Almost frantically she again grabbed up the stack of plates and started for the kitchen.

"If you don't mind, Sister Corey," Brigham said, "I'd like to wash up. And I imagine the other brethren are just as soiled and rumpled. We'd hoped to make Provo tonight. A congregation of Saints are expecting us tomorrow morning."

"There's towel and washbasin in the kitchen," Martha was saying. "Just through the door."

"By the way, is the young lady *your* daughter?"

Nancy paused at the door as her knee pumped it open.

"Yes she is, Brother Brigham. That's Nancy, my *only* daughter."

"Beautiful young woman," mused the Prophet. "Beautiful little thing."

Nancy slammed on through the swinging door. In her heart was the same damned fright she'd experienced when Apostle Cragg had uttered almost the same phrase. President or Prophet, he'd not get a fresh crack at the Corey family!

And that was the beginning of that wild and laborious night. The night when Martha and Nancy, while the other already stuffed guests looked on in curiosity, cooked and spread another immense meal for the most illustrious man in Deseret.

It needed no prodding of the schoolmaster to bring Isaac Corey on the run. And, as the immense news spread itself about Ammon, it also brought Bishop Earlington and a roomful of other town notables. To the official party, one other was added, as quickly as he had fed and bedded the horses in the Corey stable for the night. This man was Green Flake, the Negro driver for the Young entourage. Democratically, he was seated at the table with Presidents Young and Kimball, Bishops Stringfellow and Earlington, and Elder Isaac Corey.

Martha and Nancy, in the immense task so suddenly forced upon them, could have used some additional Mormon womenfolk. But it appeared that the women were either frightened away by the almost unbelievable high rank of their visitors, or, Mormon-like, considered the gathering strictly for holders of the priesthood. And Isaac, so utterly overwhelmed by the sudden affluence, never even thought to call in any of his abundant crop of women. The paying guests proffered no help—content only to watch from the room-side or stairway. It was the half-paying guest, Joel Scott, who this night returned some of the Corey generosity. With a grateful smile, Nancy pinned an apron around his slender middle. And he alone washed all the dishes in time for this second setting; and washed them once again when the brethren had shoved back their chairs for Gospel talk.

By that time the matter of housing, too, had been settled, this time the Earlingtons lost to the Coreys. But, good-naturedly, the bishop was instrumental in having three of the guest couples who were Saints moved to his home for the night. Gentiles were undisturbed in their rooms—with one exception.

"I'll sleep in the pantry—on one condition," Joel chuckled, as he slopped the plates through suds made with Nancy's soap. "And that is, that your Brigham Young uses my bed."

And since it was the nicest room of the twelve, the Prophet of the Church did sleep that night in the schoolmaster's bed. Nancy, two rooms removed from the hasty pad she made for Joel in the aromatic little pantry, slept little at all. It had been an experience to rub elbows with him in the kitchen. It had been something to walk back from that hungry Mormon table, and find, in the kitchen, the one Gentile who could scorch her soul like a pitch fire. Martha, who in her illness, appreciated the generosity of his help, had showed heartening warmth and friendliness toward him. When he lit a cheroot, and poisoned the air while he sudsed the dishes and helped ladle up the food, she had made no semblance of protest. Nancy had giggled to herself at the anomaly of the situation, and prayed that somehow the telltale fumes would not reach the table where sat Isaac Corey and the Prophet of the Church.

Brigham Young himself had complimented Martha on the good food and the extra effort in their behalf. Martha in turn had counted in Nancy and the schoolmaster for their share in the mighty effort. Joel, minus the cheroot, and in shirtsleeves, had shaken hands again with the dignitaries, and told them the fun he'd had. And both Brigham Young and Heber C. Kimball had smiled at Nancy in a way that could not help but disturb her.

Porter Rockwell, veteran of many a night ride, had, after the big meal, mounted his horse and pushed on to Provo. To the Saints there, awaiting Brigham and his party with nervous expectancy, he carried bad news. The Prophet would tarry in Ammon for the night. He would attend Sunday morning church services in the smaller town, and move to Provo in the afternoon. For Isaac Corey, and Ammon in general, it was a great and sudden compliment. For the Saints of Provo, a vast disappointment.

So, when the conversation at the table had worn itself thin, and the weary dignitaries had sought their respective beds, Nancy, with heart thumping like a churn dasher, and with legs as wearily brittle as stick candy, had shown her schoolmaster to the veritable love-bed she had made for him on the floor of the pantry. "Good night, little friend," he had said, as by flickering candlelight he had arranged his personals alongside the great deep pile of quilts and blankets she had affectionately laid out for him.

"Good night, Mr. Scott," she'd said, as she backed out the door of the little room. "It was so kind of you to give up your bed."

His smile had been no less endearing in the exciting play of candle-light. "It's something for a Gentile to give up his bed to Brigham Young," he had chuckled.

"This one'll not be very soft—but it'll be warm," she had added, tarrying as long as she dared. "It *was* so nice of you to help us in the kitchen."

"You needed help, little friend," he had said, ever so kindly. "And I enjoyed it more than you'll ever know."

"And I enjoyed it more than *you'll* ever know," she'd honestly declared. She'd started to leave him to the tiny food-packed, candlelit room.

"Come here, Nan," he'd said.

Thinking the bed might be awry, or there was a forgetting of something, she had stepped back again.

"Did I ever tell you what a brave and wonderful little thing you are?" he'd asked, and his voice was strange and husky. "Did I ever tell you?"

"No—you—"

Next instant he'd pinioned her in his arms, the man-smell was about her, and he was kissing her tightly and savagely on the lips. But the kiss had been quick. There had been no tarrying as he shoved her from him.

"Go, Nan," he had said. "Get out! Now!"

But even in the crazy, flickery candlelight there could be no denying of what had happened, and what she'd read from his face. Silently, obediently, she'd backed out of the tiny room, and closed the door. She hadn't said a word. Even in her surprise, she hadn't said a word. She didn't have to.

After she had retired, trembling and excited, to her own bed, in her own tiny room, she heard Martha come into the little apartment. Martha, as always, had made her final tour of the House, and with it the final snuffing of candles and turning off of lamps. Then from behind the closed door, Nancy had heard Isaac enter, and knew that in the elation of his own triumphal hour, he had chosen to honor Martha's bed for the night. For an hour there was the soft murmur of their voices as they talked over the amazing things that had happened to them. And while Brigham Young slept alone upstairs, in the schoolmaster's bed, Nancy heard the creak of added weight on Martha's bedsprings. The drone of voices rose and fell in the darkness from behind the door. And then had come the rhythmic squeak-squawk of the springs—slow at first, with gradual acceleration; this music of the night. Nancy, already aching in the groins, and strangely frightened, felt the hackles rise along her spine, and the sweat start to the palms of her hands. She knew what was happening to Isaac and to Martha, and wondered darkly at the mystery of it. And when the wild, erotic ride was over, she could only imagine what it had been like. But she did know that in this night of Isaac's kingship, he stood as a proud and favored man. As for Nancy herself, she was limp as a rag, and sweating like a teakettle in her own bed. And, long after everyone else in the Corey House was asleep, she had lain awake—as wildly excited as a rabbit in the brush.

Next morning was the Sabbath—the Mormon day of rest. That is, it was a day of rest for every Mormon in Ammon except Martha and Nancy Corey. At gray dawn Martha was rattling Nancy's shoulders back to wakefulness. As Nancy lifted herself grudgingly to the day, she fought back at the remembrance of things, even as it began its inexorable flooding in upon her. She wanted to flop back to the pillow, and sleep forever. There never was enough time for sleep, anyway. Instead, she again lifted her weary eyelids, and looked at the tired and disheveled specter of her mother standing over her in the dawn.

"Best get your milking done early, Nan," Martha was saying. "Get some buckets from the kitchen, and go out the other door—so you won't awaken Mr. Scott." Martha's head twitched curiously from above her rumpled flannel nightgown. "And try not to waken your Pa." She blinked her own weary and sleep-hungry eyes. "I'll be dressed as quick as you are," she now whispered. "We've got a big hard day ahead."

"And haven't we though," Nancy grumbled, swinging her legs achingly out the side of the bed. Her yawn was as wide as Ammon's canyon, and she rubbed the sleep grit in her eyes with the backs of her hands. "Why don't Brigham cook his own infernal breakfast? Why don't he stay home with his wives? They'll—"

"Hush!" snapped Martha. "No more of that!" Like a tired witch, she waddled toward the door. "We'll do it," she said over her shoulder. "Now get into your clothes."

And once in her clothes, the day, with all its furious pace, was on for Nancy. The only difference to her on this auspicious day of the Sabbath was that her zip and speed came a little more grudgingly, and there was double the work ahead. Last night, she imagined, must have been a dream.

Isaac, with the quilts tucked carefully to his bearded chin as Martha's final offering to her man, was finishing out his sleep with the peace and certitude of heaven's own acceptance. Nancy looked curiously at him in the gray dawn, as she crept on tiptoe through Martha's chamber, to the work-world outside. Even his usually loud and resonant snores were muffled down this morning to something more like a contented pump of the bellows; trailing off in their rhythm in sighlike sounds devoid of tautness and worry, and rich in animal-like contentment. The night, Nancy thought, had been good for Isaac—but it had been a hell for her. And no Sabbath such as this could ever look promising.

Sometime during her milking, the schoolmaster rolled out of his makeshift bed, folded up the quilts neatly in the corner, and sought his morning smoke by leisurely walking the streets of Ammon, and away from Nancy and the heavy gathering of the priesthood at the Corey House. Breakfast for the regular guests came early, and first. While Martha slaved over the stove for the second session, Nancy watched for Joel—even while she cleared the table, washed the dishes, and set everything up again for another, more leisurely turn around for the really illustrious guests.

The day was a chilly one, and the mud-pocked roads were crunchy with ice, but, rather than hang around in a world still peculiar, strange, and probably now worrisome to him, Joel Scott had chosen this time for a long ride. The same stout little sorrel gelding that had carried him from California, he kept in the Corey House stables. Its name was Duke. And Duke had been given the stall next to Dolly. It was perfectly safe to bed him alongside a mare, even in a land where the sex act carried its most fundamental and ultimate meaning. Dolly was safe, because Duke had been long since deprived of his lights. But the love Joel held for his little gelding, companion of many a day on the trail, was shown by the care and attention daily given him. This Sabbath morning, while the Prophet had had breakfast with Ammon's notables, and then presided at the inspiring church service in the old meeting house behind the walls, Joel Scott was riding good old Duke north and east toward the snowy foothills—with probably a lot to think about.

And while everyone else in Ammon sang their songs of praise, basked in the aura of God's Prophet, and listened to the stirring sermons of the morning, Martha and Nancy slaved in the steaming kitchen, preparing a noon meal fit and worthy of God's Anointed.

Again the grumbling tenants of the Corey House were fed early, that the big table might again be spread for more important guests. As expected, Isaac, without a thought as to the extra burden, brought additional town notables home with him from church. Conversation at the big table was exciting and inspiring, but Nancy, busy as a filly dosed with Glauber salts, could hear only snatches of it as she wore a steady trail between the table and the kitchen.

It was plain to all that Brigham Young was pleased with everything

Ammon was doing, and both he and Brother Kimball watched Nancy with warm and approving eyes. The building program for the new town was commendable, a real following of counsel, and an inspiration for every settlement in Deseret. The new school building, erected so speedily and so soundly, met with full approval of President Young. And had Joel Scott been present, instead of horseback, he could have personally heard the good words that indicated that at least one Gentile in Deseret had won both approval and eulogy.

The projected new council house, and new meeting house, both to be commenced with the spring thaw, won the unqualified endorsement of Presidents Brigham Young and Heber C. Kimball. With the spirit of God and brotherhood that apparently, had been so noticeable a part of the morning's services, Ammon's sudden scrutiny by the Authorities had been nothing less than a triumph. And it was certain, Nancy was gleaning in segments, that the enterprise and hospitality of Isaac Corey had not gone unnoticed. He, whose daughter had married high in the Church, and who this day had pleased a Prophet, seemed to radiate the glory of his pride. To him, and to all, the meal was a benediction and a love feast. And long after the official party took final leave for Provo, and while Nancy and Martha toiled at clearing away the wreckage, Ammon's townsfolk talked over the miracle that had happened on this Sabbath Day.

It was late afternoon before Nancy could manage to get around to making up the sleeping rooms. As usual, Joel's room—the room last night graced by the Prophet—was the final one to get her attention. Even this day, with all its demands, there could be nothing leisurely about its attention. Unlike other days, there was no dreaming and tarrying. But, just the same, it was on this particular and harried Sabbath Day that Joel's key went into the latch, and it was the day that he truly caught her in his room.

Her repetitious experience as a chambermaid had given her an odd sensitivity to the personalities of those who occupied the rooms even for as little as a night. She could tell at first glance whether a room had been tenanted by a man, by a woman, or by both. There was an indefinable masculine smell to a man's sleeping room, and there were always the little signs. A woman, for instance, was seldom neat about her quarters. Both bowl and slop jar were usually full, and there seemed little female compunction to save work for any maid. Man's untidiness, on the other hand, was of a minor sort. Loose tobacco, spilled snuff, cigar butts, or an occasional empty bottle. For the most part, though, men had a sensitivity about the essential things not usually found in women. Even Utah's chill night air failed to discourage most male guests from going downstairs and out to the privy to urinate. And she had yet to empty the first slop jar for Joel Scott. He was a gentleman. Everyone knew he was a gentleman.

But last night his room had been occupied by Brigham Young—the most important and revered man in Zion. Here was a man who had access even to God's direct inspiration and counsel; a man to whom tens of thousands of loyal Saints looked for guidance in everything pertaining to the kingdom on earth, and the kingdom in heaven. When Nancy entered the room with her passkey she had anticipated something a little different about the chamber where the Great One had slept. What she might expect would be a little difficult to define—maybe the odor of sanctity, maybe angel dust, or a spiritual illumination such as one found at night on fireflies or toadstools. But there was no glow about the unmade bed. The indefinable odor about the place was that of a man—but certainly not Joel Scott—for the thundermug was full.

But time was too short, and the day too full, to think on these things and make comparisons. Under her swift ministrations the chinaware was emptied downstairs, rinsed from the well bucket, and tidily put back in place. Somehow she wondered, as she completed these essentials, if Joel would ever know that the Prophet, Seer, and Revelator had used the Scott pot to pee in.

The clean sheets she'd put into the bed for Brigham's use the night before were yanked out and replaced with another fresh set for Joel's use. If they glowed with any special illumination, or if any special blessing were inherent in their touch, Joel would never know the gain he might have had in the Prophet's presence. Tomorrow Brigham's sheets would be tubbed along with the others. When finally the bed was made, the room swept and dusted, and last trace of its illustrious occupant gone, it looked again, and felt again, like Joel the schoolmaster. The lacy runner was once more squared and evened; the tintypes and the miniatures smiled or frowned again across the room. The books were in place on the shelf, and she was wondering even more fiercely at what mysteries might be hidden so securely in the foot locker under the bed. She sighed like a wind moan in the attic, and was secretly glad the Authorities had taken themselves to Provo.

"Golly damn, what a day!" she groaned, as she took a last look about her, at the last room to be finished. Wearily she lugged her mop, broom, and duster to the hall closet. On the way back she again peered critically into this special of all places—Joel's room. The late afternoon sun cut a bright swath across the bed she so neatly had made—the iron bed honored above all others in the Corey House. She stepped into the room once more, and adjusted the lace curtains at the louvered windows, to cut a little of the glare. Physically exhausted, dreading the mealtime work yet before her, she started again to leave. And again there was that woman's picture staring smugly at her from the commode top. That damned smug stare.

Like so many other times before, she tiptoed guiltily to the door, and pushed it shut. Then she went back to the commode, picked up the little gilt-framed miniature, and carried it to the bed. It felt so good to sit down on the softness of the spread and quilts. She was *so* infernally tired, and the young lady in the picture, with her slender and aristocratic neck wrapped with pearls, was *so* eternally fresh and beautiful, it was infuriating. "I'll bet this little darling doesn't empty slop jars, scrub, nor cook," Nancy murmured to herself in deepest pity. "This fluffy doll is fresh, and full of life. I'm tired enough to die—and I wish that I *could* die."

Holding the miniature in both hands, and staring bitterly at the insolent, self-sure creature so delicately and beautifully a part of it, Nancy laid back to the bed with a sigh. Why did God bless some women with ease and luxury, and curse others with unending drudgery? How must it be in Boston, as compared with the muddy, chopped-up Ammon? She wriggled to comfort on the bed that had sheltered a Prophet, and sagged to its softness with another comforting sigh. It was obvious this lady's hands had never teated a cow, scrubbed a floor, or emptied a slop jar. "Lord bless the lucky," Nancy murmured to herself, and lowered the lady who smiled so tauntingly. "Even Flora, with her apostle, is lucky." With half an attempt at a yawn, and a flutter of lids on her brown eyes, Nancy's aching body finally betrayed her. A moment later it surrendered itself to sleep.

And half an hour later, when Joel Scott let himself into his room, that is how he found Nancy Corey.

He had closed the door behind him before he saw her, but he did not retreat. Instead, he leisurely laid his battered campaign hat and gloves atop the shelf, peeled off his heavy coat, and hung it to the wall hook. Not even these sounds of his presence awakened the sleeping girl. Amusedly, and with a smile, he walked over to the bed and looked down at his uninvited guest. Her blue woolsey house dress had worked up her young and slender legs, her neat little waist apron was in disarray, and her thick black hair was tumbled about her face and neck. Something caught in his throat at this vision of unspoiled wildness.

He saw the miniature that had fallen from her fingers. He frowned knowingly, picked it up, and replaced it on the commode top. He walked over, stood beside the bed, and again looked down in puzzlement at the sleeping girl. And then his eyes twinkled in hellish grin. Slowly he leaned over, and kissed Nancy on the left cheek. She stirred fretfully, but did not waken.

For a long minute more he watched her—this time soberly. Then he reached down, grabbed a handful of her hair, and tugged it gently. "Nancy," he said. "Nancy!"

She awakened. For a moment she stared uncomprehendingly up at him. Then like the spring blade in a jackknife she suddenly folded upward. Shame and terror were in her eyes. She rubbed at their persistent sleep with the back of her hands.

"Golly damn," she groaned helplessly. "Must have been slumbering."

"You were," Joel said, and sat down on the bed beside her. "I'd expected Brigham Young in my bed." He chuckled to himself at the thought of it. "Instead, I find Nancy Corey." He turned and looked quizzically down at her again.

Nancy moved to get herself off his bed. By sitting down, he had blocked her way. She subsided with a helpless groan.

"Don't know how it happened," she said, honestly. "I was tidying up your room. Flopped myself down." Helplessly she waved a hand. "I was tired."

"I can believe it," Joel agreed. "They work you far too hard. A girl your age should have schooling—not slavery."

"Schooling?" Nancy looked at him incredulously. "Why, I'm a woman!"

Joel nodded approval, and merriment danced in his blue eyes. "You're a woman, all right. But Mr. Corey should get you back in school, before it's too late."

Nancy pulled her knees up, hooked her hands around them, and smiled coquettishly at him. "It's too late," she said, with finality.

"Not if I could have anything to do about it," Joel said. "Around this place I watch you in amazement. You can cook, sew, weave, knit, milk—"

"Wait on tables, scrub, and serve as chambermaid," Nancy added. "I've never seen you watching me. It's hard to believe you've ever noticed me."

Joel chuckled again. "Without you hovering around the table at mealtime, we'd freeze to icicles in that cold and cheerless room. You may not know it, but you're as warm and friendly as summer sunshine. And your mother, too, is a great person, Nancy. Only we see less of her."

Thoughts of the abominable task of waiting on table suddenly confronted Nancy with the duties she was shirking. Martha would be worried and nervous, if not furious. "I'd best be getting back to my job," she said guiltily, and hunched herself as if to move. And then a thought struck her. Joel hadn't shown up at the table for either setting at lunch. Apparently he, too, was churned up, and having mental problems. She settled back, looked soberly at his handsome face and strange black hair. "You must be starved," she said, a little shakily. "Didn't get a thing to eat at noontime."

"Your mother fed me from the kitchen, after I'd unsaddled Duke. I'm certain now your mother really likes me."

"She should." Nancy relaxed to the soft bed once more. "I do, too." She remembered last night, and blinked with fresh astonishment. But he was still evading any mention of it. "For the help you gave me," she said demurely, "I'll always think highly of you." She sighed at the memory, and then at the darker thoughts, and the immensity of the Corey House task. "I hope Brother Brigham doesn't make a habit of calling on us. I think he also likes me—but I don't like him."

"I like him," Joel said. "I think he's a great leader. A great man. One of the most extraordinary characters of our time. Think of it—he slept in this very room!"

Nancy glanced at the side door of the big commode, and giggled at thoughts of the essential piece of chinaware behind it. That wasn't all Brigham had done in this room. "He may be a great man—and Father Corey thinks so, too—but I don't particularly like him." She looked impishly at Joel, and with knees clasped tightly, rocked herself on Joel's bed. "And anyway, I've slept here, too," she said.

"So you have." He lowered his eyes in merriment. "Brigham Young's added Zion's glory to the room. But you've added a certain decorative quality that's ah—deliciously disturbing." The grin faded. "So far, it's our secret," he said. "For the good of Zion, and my own neck, I hope we can keep it so."

"Don't you worry," Nancy consoled, suddenly feeling excitedly alive. "I'll tell no secrets. My sleep here was an accident." But last night was no accident. And she thought again of the many times she'd literally prayed he'd catch her in his room. "Any secret's safe with me."

"You say you don't like Brigham. That's odd, coming from one of Zion's fair daughters. Why *don't* you like him?"

"Because he's married plural. Because he tells the Saints to marry plural. And I hate the thoughts of marrying plural."

Joel thought a moment, and hunched his leg upward for comfort. "Yes," he chuckled. "Seems I've heard you say that before."

Nancy managed a ladylike blush. "Please forgive me for that day at the wall. I was young, giddy, and frightened."

"I imagine you had reason to be frightened. And I'm glad you're young—and I don't mind you, even when you're giddy."

"At the time I was being courted by an apostle."

"I know."

"He already had enough wives to insure his kingdom forever."

"Maybe he was just the marrying kind." Joel said it with a shrug.

"Marrying kind, all right," Nancy groaned bitterly. "I can't stand the thoughts of plurality."

"I glean that much." Joel chuckled knowingly. "I'm told you gave Apostle Cragg an emphatic no to *his* proposal."

"I nearly beat his head in," Nancy confessed sorrowfully. "Father Corey's never forgiven me for it."

"Well, that's one way of rejecting a suitor. There's nothing like telling them in a way they'll understand. But what's this about his grabbing off your half sister—"

"Flora? She married him. For time and all eternity."

"Is the apostle happy with her? Is *she* happy with him?"

"Flora writes. Says she's happy. That he's good to her. Just a case of adjusting yourself to the Principle, she says. I believe she's really happy. And she has it soft—as an apostle's wife, in Salt Lake City." Then Nancy stopped, and thought a minute. Yes, Flora probably *did* have it soft. By marriage she'd escaped drudgery. For her there was no more milking, no kitchen slavery, no duties as a public chambermaid. "She says she's happy," Nancy repeated.

"Are *you* happy, Nancy?" Joel asked, tenderly peeling back her black hair from her eyes.

His touch, like last night, was like an electric tingle before a thunderstorm. She looked at this strange man, and felt as though she would dissolve into the shadowy pool of her longing. "No, I'm not happy," she confessed. "I'm really quite sad." Her eyes grew suddenly wet as she looked at him. "I'm tired. And I'm confused."

Without further hesitance he took her by the shoulders, and pulled her to him. "Poor, wild little soul." He comforted, patted, and rubbed at her back. "Will they *never* stop imposing on you?"

She nuzzled to him. The man-smell of tobacco, and shaving soap, and horses, was heady and wild—like a storm across the mountains. Her own shoulders heaved with sobs. "It's all so hopeless," she moaned. "Wish I could die."

"What you need is to live, my dear," Joel said. "They've done every-

thing in hell's dreambook to keep you from living. How can they mis-
treat you so?"

Her own arms went around him, and he laid her back to the bed.

"My wild little rabbit," he murmured, and his lips pressed in upon
hers. "How I'd like to take you out of here." The weight of his shoulders
was suddenly upon her. "Since last night, I've never stopped thinking
of you."

She clung tightly to him. "I do so love you, Joel," she moaned pite-
ously. "I do so love you."

"And I love you," he finally confessed, kissing her again, savagely.

And then, womanlike, it came to her. "As much as the lady in the
picture?"

He raised, and soberly eyed her tearful face. "The picture you went
to sleep with?"

Then she remembered, and felt ashamed. "Yes. That's the one. Who
is she?"

"I'll tell you someday," he said quietly. "But not today."

"Do you love me as much as you love her?" she persisted.

"I think maybe I do." And again he held her tight, and kissed her
hotly, eagerly. "I think maybe I do."

They broke away. "Oh, Joel," Nancy moaned, her whole body quivering in impetuous pain, "what shall we do?"

"Afraid?"

She felt his right hand slide from her shoulders. While she panted like
a winded horse, it slid deliciously downward. "Yes, Joel," she groaned.
"I'm afraid."

The movement stopped. "Don't be, my little one." The hand was
already tugging impudently at her.

"We mustn't, dear Joel," she whispered in panic. And then suddenly
she realized that this was the very moment of her endless daydreams.
How many times had she sat in this very room, hoping this man would
break in upon her? And now it was coming, and she was as frightened as
a calf mired in a tule swamp.

It was the voice of Martha Corey that put an end to everything. It
came from down the stairwell—clear and frightening to the ear—not
impetuous, not loud. It called to Nancy, not in the shrill, imperious
tones of work-demand, or work-neglect, but in the animal-like horror
of anguish and pain. By the very prescience of the spirit Nancy knew
instantly something terrible was wrong. The first cry froze her rigid with
fright. The second call was weaker. "Oh, Nan! Oh, Isaac! My God! My

God!" And in that cry was all the fright and heartbreak since the world began.

Like an animal possessed, Nancy shoved Joel from her, and bolted upward. In fright and panic, she kneed her way toward the foot of the bed. Joel, himself startled, rolled out and to his feet. But Nancy, her black hair flying and disheveled, was already at the door. Alarmed, and ashamed, he followed the flying girl down the stairs.

Together they found Martha, blue and writhing, at the foot of the stairs—in almost the same spot where Seth Biddle had flopped out his own seizure. But Martha's thin body was not fighting out something decreed by heredity. Her decree had come from a woman's lifetime of frustration and drudgery. The once stout pump of life within her, weakened by overwork and strain, was spasmodically and furiously fighting a battle to save itself.

Together they picked up the little woman, and carried her to her bed beyond the kitchen. Nancy, her arms clasped to Joel's in the quick cradle-lift he showed her, was astonished at the lightness of the burden they carried between them. Nancy was wracked with sobs, and tears rolled untended from her eyes.

Already Martha was gasping convulsively as they stretched her out. Joel paused long enough to feel her wrist pulse, and to shake his head. "Mums," Nancy moaned. Tearfully she looked down into the strangely contorted little face. "Mums! Speak to me!"

For the second time in twenty-four hours, Joel sped in frantic search for Isaac Corey. Nancy knelt at the bedside, pleading with Martha to see her through the staring eyes, and speak to her through blue and rubbery lips that, troutlike, were pulsingly sucking and chewing for the last sustenance in the air of life. Then alternately Nancy prayed to the God of love to heal and spare this precious soul who so suddenly and unfairly had been struck down. Neither Martha nor God were, in this moment, able to give an answer.

Soon Isaac arrived, and the other women of the immense family were on hand in belated appearance. Bishop Earlington, also aroused by Joel, came quickly to the bedside of this stricken Saint. Seth Biddle, Brother Bringhurst, and many others were soon crowding the Corey House.

In the name of Israel's God, and by the power of the holy Melchizedek priesthood, Bishop Earlington and Isaac Corey anointed Martha's grayed head with consecrated oil, and together pleaded with God to save this woman's life, and restore her once again to health. But this time Jehovah God had other plans. For while they prayed, Martha, with a weary sigh, slipped away in death. And this woman, one of the most loyal and dependent portions of Isaac Corey's family kingdom, was gone—but, in the hopeful and sustaining pattern of a Mormon death, the time of her going would not be for long. In the joyous promise of the everlasting covenant, she now would await him "on the other side."

But there would be sorrow enough for Nancy in the days ahead. Not even the comforting words of the Gospel would make easier the pain of this earthly loss.

IX

THEY HAD CLEARED TWO FEET OF SNOW FROM THE GROUND TO BURY MARTHA Corey. Ammon's little graveyard, in the foothills half a mile north of town, had overnight been made a fairyland by the sudden whiteness of this Wasatch winter. The storm began the night she died, continued through her day of preparation, and had deep-covered Ammon's world by the time of her eulogies in the meeting house, and her lowering to the frozen world below.

To Nancy, there was more beauty than strangeness in a Mormon burial—but to Joel Scott, who remained close and helpful to the family through their time of sorrow, it was plainly enough that, as a Gentile, he was observant of the oddity of it. The other wives took over the duty of dressing this fragile, shrunken little sister in clean, new garments of the holy covenant—properly marked with the mystic symbols. Over the garment was placed the white and ample robe of the House of the Lord, and about her waist was tied the short, green apron of the covenant, embroidered with the celestial devices sacred to the temple ceremony. Tenderly, to her grayed head was placed the little cap, and the veil— which Isaac himself would draw across her tired face in that last, sad moment. Together they padded and quilted the inside of the new pine box Brother Bringhurst had fashioned overnight, and gently laid the body of the little woman into this simple coffin of dignity—because it had been fashioned not by some commercial manufactory, but by the hands of a sorrowing neighbor. Carefully they arranged her robe and apron. Cognizant of its deep symbolism, they settled the veil above her forehead, tastefully, and with a certain beauty, ready for the last act before the coffin's lid was screwed down, and she was hauled across Ammon's snow for the last time. Laid out, in her celestial robes, so deeply sacred in meaning to the Latter-day Saints, was the way Joel Scott saw her, as he stood beside Nancy and the weeping family, at the old meeting house behind the walls.

Martha, the quiet little woman, who had refused to be a bother to anyone, must have been surprised from her place of heavenly vision at the effort she was putting her townsfolk to in these days of her death and burial. Isaac did not lock his guests out of the Corey House, but in the matter of food and room service they were forced through these days of grief to forage for themselves. A road had to be beaten through the deep snow to the graveyard. The grave—exactly on east-west tangent, had to be chiseled six feet deep into the frozen earth of the Corey plat. Wagons had to be converted into sleighs, by hanging iron-shod runners to the hubs. That was the only way, on this day, that the neighbors could traverse the distance from the funeral to burial.

Brigham Young was fighting through the lower reaches of the storm, toward the sunny and salubrious Utah Dixie, and thus could not be in attendance at Martha's obsequies. The Deseret Telegraph was not yet in operation and, even if it were, Apostle Cragg and Flora could never have made it through the storm from Salt Lake City. But most of the Saints of Ammon were there. And Martha Corey, from her secure and certain place "on the other side," must have drawn a heap of satisfaction from this candid and honest display of neighborly affection.

Since Martha alone, of the four Corey wives, had no proper home of her own, the pine coffin was hauled by wagon-box sled to the old meeting house at the fort. Even though it was still morning, Seth Biddle had the two stoves of the old chapel going when Nancy arrived with the body, and it was warm, comfortable, and as cheery as church austerity and the circumstances would permit. All the Aunt Coreys, with sudden effusive love for the lonely and sorrowing girl, had tendered the hospitality of their own new homes—but Nancy would have none of it. She had stayed with Martha in the little bedroom of the Corey House, in silent, soul-wracked grief, while the other wives attended to the washing, dressing, and "laying out" of the pitiful thing that so few days before had been her mother. In corrosive mutiny against the heartless drudgery which she was certain had killed Martha, her conscience eating away in guilt for her own callous pleasure in the very hour her mother was stricken, she ignored the Corey House paying guests. They could do their own damned cooking, their own bedmaking, and empty their own chamber pots.

With all her soul, Nancy wanted to help in Martha's preparation for burial, but even in this last final act she was denied, and she resented it deeply. As a Latter-day Saint she should have understood and accepted the fact that these ministrations were of the most sacred sort. Until she had her own "endowments" in the House of the Lord, even the dressing of a corpse in the garments and robes of celestial glory was something she could not properly do. The other wives, who had been married for time and all eternity, and had been endowed with all rights in the House of the Lord, had such prerogatives. Had her own half sister Flora been present, Flora could have dressed Martha with propriety, because she too had entered the everlasting covenant. But Nancy, who knew her mother better than anyone who touched her, and who loved her with a depth beyond any of their perception, was denied even this simplest of ministries in the shattering moment of death.

But after they had gotten Martha into her strange garb, and into the coffin Brother Bringhurst had fashioned to her slight measure, Nancy furiously resisted all their efforts to prevent her riding with the body, in the sled, to the fort meeting house. With Cove driving, and Isaac beside him in the seat, silent in his grief, Nancy sat alone in the wagon box, tenderly steadying the box as the wide runners squeaked and yawed their way over the deep new snow. She even helped carry the coffin into the meeting house, and to place it on two sawhorses between the sacrament table and the high pulpit. Isaac unscrewed the lid, and while the two men stared silently and sadly at Martha in her rich and beautiful robes and apron, Nancy straightened the little face upon its finally relaxed neck, and arranged her oriental-like burial garb to a last woman's touch. "Oh, Mums," she moaned, pausing, looking down, and shaking her head. "I'll miss you so." And minus the gabble of women's voices, she could now cry freely, and without anger or restraint.

"We'd best go," Isaac said. "We're all nooning at Adah's. She's cooked up a big meal."

Nancy looked tenderly down at the pinched, gray-blue face. "I'm not going. I'm staying here with my mother."

"It's three hours before the funeral," Isaac gently persisted. "You've had little to eat, girl."

"Who can think of eating?" Nancy snapped back. "I'm staying."

"Very well, Nan." Isaac took one more sad look at the sleeping woman who had been his third plural wife. Silently he turned on his heel. Cove looked kindly down on Martha, pressed Nancy's arm with affection and reassurance, and followed Isaac down the chapel aisle and outside.

The old meeting house had few of the appurtenances of richness and luxury that mark even the most ordinary house of worship. Erected on the pioneer frontier, in times of stress and trouble, and with only the barest of materials available, it still had certain monumental qualities. Simple multiple panes of glass, though precious at the time of its building, spread in it none of the wondrous and delicate colors of stained glass. Its timbers and exposed rafters were straight pine poles, hauled out of Ammon's canyon, and barked and readied on the spot. Its thick, solid walls were adobe, laid up in fat squares, and from the same clay from which the town's wall had been fashioned. But the walls were cleanly whitewashed, and Ammon's Relief Society Sisters had tastefully hung colored hand-fashioned drapes to the many-paned windows. The building was stately because it was substantial, and honestly utilitarian. It had the warmth about it of venerable use. Its handmade benches were worn and dished from the constancy of their function, and the devotion of the Saints who had worshiped there. To the Saints of Ammon it spoke with a thousand familiar voices. Few there were of Ammon's brethren who had not taken stammering turn at its pulpit, for, among the Latter-day Saints there is no paid clergy. Every man had a part in its building, maintenance, and spiritual operation. Next year it would be supplanted with a new brick edifice in the new town. To turn away from it would be like turning away from an old, familiar friend. Inside, and even to Nancy on this sad day, it was warm, comforting, and healing. Aunt Adah's home was not *her* home. There'd be noise, bustle, questions, and conversation at the meal. It was better to sit out the hours here, where all was quiet, and she could whisper the things she wanted to say, alone with Martha.

So Martha would not be ashamed of her, Nancy had dressed her best for the funeral. Since to Latter-day Saints death should hold no mystery, and was simply a walking through the veil to the more familiar world they had known before birth, it was no customary thing to dress in black as a token of mourning. In Nancy as in Isaac was the built-in certainty that on the day they too entered the "other side" Martha would be there to meet and greet them. Death, to a Saint, was only the opportunity for a greater, more wondrous experience. Only the stupid and uninformed ever wore black. Nancy was dressed in her pretty blue dress that Martha had helped her make for the summer's picnic. On her head was the little blue hat Joel Scott had personally returned to her. These, with her outgrown gray coat, were the best and most attractive clothes she had. And Martha, who had left the worn-out husk that was her body, and was somewhere invisibly present, perhaps in this very meeting house, could see and approve of her daughter looking pretty and neat.

It was a strange little ritual. Nancy, as thoughts welled insufferably up in her, would move to the side of the silent Martha, talk about them to her, as though life could answer them, and, after wiping her damp eyes with the clean kerchief, she would walk to the first row of benches. And, as she sat, pondered, and waited for the new experience, she was certain that Martha was present, and that the whispers and the urgings were Martha's own words of concern and love. Alone, she talked with Martha over the matter of Joel Scott. And back again at the quiet of her sitting, she knew that Martha approved of the man, and forgave the error of that black Sunday. He was a Gentile, and because of him, Nancy had gone counter to the urgent teachings of her faith—but Martha understood. Even in this silent moment with her, only Martha could *ever* understand. And somehow Nancy grasped assurance. God overlooked a lot of things. Somehow, not yet plain, certain astonishing things could and would yet come to pass.

When the fires in the sidewall stoves began dying down, Seth Biddle came out from somewhere, tiptoed up the aisles, and laid new wood to their feebling interiors. Seeing the silent girl, in her familiar blue hat, sitting alone in the church, he tiptoed over to her. Nancy, wracked with deep thoughts, and deeper grief, had been oblivious to everything. The kindly man sat down beside her. Startled, she looked about, and, seeing Seth, she smiled.

"It's not an easy hour," Seth said, touching her hand. "But God will take kindly to Martha Corey. She was a noble woman."

"Thank you, Seth," was all Nancy could say.

"And all of Zion will know her daughter for these same traits," Seth said, prophetically.

Shunning the possibility of one of his uncontrollable spells desecrating the church, and turning a solemn hour for a dear friend into chaos, he arose, and tiptoed out of the meeting house. Nancy, oddly consoled, turned back again to her thoughts.

Not even this hour was solemn enough to make her forget or overlook the tragedy of Martha's life. Martha had filled every obligation as a good, loyal Latter-day Saint. As a wife, and as a mother, no voice could honestly be raised in complaint. In her quiet way, she had done the very best she could. It was in the way she lifted her head above a lifetime of drudgery, and the way she had borne her trials, that made her the noble woman of Seth's mention. To the two men in her life, Martha had been more slave than wife. And to Nancy, not even her mother's willingness to accept the bondage, or her meek and willing performance under the yoke, excused either of the men for the sinful way they had used her. It was from Martha's own tragic background that Nancy had fed her implacable hatred of the Principle. Even in this moment she would rather face a thousand years of spinsterhood than to enter into the polygamous trap.

She walked back to the coffin, and talked some more about these things to Martha. For Nancy knew, beyond any question of a doubt, that what had been taught her about the great world of spirits was true. These things were just as the Prophet had revealed. The veil between the present life and eternity was a gossamer thing. Spirits of the unborn, spirits of the dead, were everywhere about. Only the limited vision of mortality prevented one from seeing and conversing openly with them. These spirits were mindful and concerned with those who, in hard reality, must trod the earth for yet a while.

There were such things as guardian angels, illuminations, inspiration, and voices of comfort and guidance from those loved ones who were dead. One buried the body, but, until the day of resurrection, the spirit was free, alive, and ever so close. These things Nancy knew, and accepted. As to the divinity of the Prophet, and the truthfulness and reality of the cause, there was not the least doubt in Nancy Corey's heart. The only wedge in her pattern of belief was the Principle. One look at Martha, one single review of Martha's life, and no amount of praying could make her accept it.

Bitter irony of it all was that in delivering Apostle Cragg and the Principle over to Flora, she'd literally been the cause of her own mother's death. Physically, poor little Martha had been in no condition to face that drudging banishment to The Point, nor that double drudgery that had come with the Corey House. Isaac, blind to the strength and capability of a woman, and avaricious as a man, could be considered the monster and the devil in this final sad act. But Isaac was no more monstrous or devilish than ten thousand other industrious Latter-day Saints. In this thing Nancy could easily hate him. In a hundred other ways she loved him. In the end she placed most of the blame on herself. In this one question, at least, not even the world of spirits, her mother included, were yet ready or willing to give the answer. In this one thing alone was she confused. Martha whose body had at last found rest in the stout pine box, and whose spirit was hovering so warmly close, was not yet ready to talk this thing with the daughter who wept so imploringly beside her.

And it was thus, alone in the chapel, a half-hour before the first of the mourners filed in for the services, that Joel Scott found her. Nancy was completely oblivious to his presence, until he touched her on the arm.

"They told me you were here, Nancy," he said. "Your father was concerned about you."

"I stayed on for a last talk with mother," she said, simply.

He looked at her oddly. "Talk—?"

"Oh yes. She's very close. She's here with us now."

Joel looked down at the strangely attired woman in the box, and nodded knowingly. "I can believe it, my dear."

Touched by his kindness and understanding, Nancy turned and looked at him. He was again dressed handsomely in black, neat broadcloth. His strange hair shone dark and curly from its twin puffs. There was concern for her on his face, and her eyes took another swim in their tears. "It was nice of you to come, Joel," she said, tenderly touching his arm. "What about school?"

"I dismissed it for the afternoon. I had to come, Nancy. Remember, I was there when it happened."

Nancy thought for the thousandth time on the pain and humiliation of that Sunday afternoon. For some reason it seemed as though it were months back, instead of only days away. "Yes, I remember," she said, and looked down again at Martha. "She looks beautiful, don't you think? Just as though she's sleeping."

"Yes, just as though she's sleeping. You must have loved her dearly." With uncomprehending eyes he stared again at the white robes, the strange green apron, the white slippers, and again at the lifeless bluegray face with its odd little cap and back-folded veil. "Are all the Saints so dressed at death?" he asked. In all his life he had never seen anything quite like this.

"Only those who have been through the House of the Lord," she said. "Those, Joel, are temple robes. Only those who have received their endowments, and those married for time and all eternity, can wear them. Without them you cannot enter the celestial, or highest glory."

"These endowments—?"

"It's part of the temple covenant. You've seen the Endowment House —on the square—in Salt Lake?"

"Yes."

"It's serving this sacred purpose until the great temple's built. Then all the ordinances of celestial marriage, and salvation for the dead, will be done there."

A dozen questions regarding the oddities of Mormon theology sprang to Joel's mind. All he knew was that Martha was never dressed like this when she slaved over the hot stove at the Corey House. And Nancy, again in her comely blue, was as angelic and gentle a mourner as any dying soul could wish for. "There's beauty and mysticism in so many things you Mormons do," he said honestly. In the same instant he was thinking of the mysticism and beauty in Nancy herself. Half girl, half mature woman, gentle, constant, and yet a broncho to her own faith. "You look so nice today. If your mother could only see you, I know—"

"My mother *does* see me," Nancy corrected. "She's here, now, and beside us. And she knows you're here, too, Joel."

Suddenly there were sounds at the back of the church. The first arrivals of Ammon's townsfolk were entering for the services. Nancy took one last, tender took at her mother who was dead. "I'll miss you *so* much, Mums," she moaned in sadness. Then she turned, and grasped Joel's arm. "Let's be seated," she said. "And I'd be proud if you sat with me at mourning."

This was considerably more than Joel had anticipated, but the request from this girl was solemn and honest. "I'd be proud to sit with you," he said, and followed her down to the first row of benches below the pulpit.

And that was the first Mormon funeral Joel Scott attended. At the moment, lacking the spiritual divination of the people among whom he now found himself, he had no way of knowing that this would not be the last Mormon funeral he would attend. But this first one, of itself, proved a revelation.

Not until the Corey family had filled to capacity two of the wide wooden benches in the church center did Joel realize what a truly mighty man in Israel was Isaac Corey, and what a kingdom of Saints he was siring. If any of the three wives, Isaac himself, or any of the numerous progeny had objections to the Gentile schoolteacher's presence among them, they made no audible point of it. Because of his tireless efforts in building a decent educational system in their raw land, he knew he'd gained Ammon's respect and affection. That he could seat himself among the mourners at a funeral of the Saints, was a compliment to the fact that, as a Gentile, he was certainly unlike any other Gentile of their comprehension. His acceptance on the Corey mourner's bench and the fact that of late many Ammonites were already calling him "Brother Scott" were undeniable proof of warmth and standing. But this day, even alongside Nancy Corey, and in the very company of the venerable Isaac, Joel Scott was anything but at ease. He sensed that most of the congregation were staring at his neck. And had there been any warning as to the size and unity of the Corey mourning contingent, no pleading of Nancy's would have induced him to have thus sat up front.

But as the services, after much coughing and considerable stirrings and confusion, finally got under way, Joel's uneasiness settled itself into a new interest. Ammon's choir, made up of townsfolk, and directed by ward chorister Willie Tuttle, did a rather commendable job of the music for any pioneer community. In honor of the fact that Martha in very deed had made the long journey from Nauvoo, the choir chose for its first number that hymn of the plains, "Come, Come Ye Saints." Accompanying, on a wheezy reed organ that likewise had crossed the plains with the pioneers, was Mary Magdalene Mattise, who, as the town's midwife was as adept at tying into an umbilical cord as she was at any chord from the hymnal. Elder Urgent Mathews, uneasy and nervous in his Sunday suit, gave a short and worried invocation. Then the choir followed in a sad and poignant rendition of "O, My Father"— a song written by Eliza Snow, poetess wife of Brigham Young, former wife of the Prophet Joseph Smith, and a sad and sacred thing which brought copious tears to Nancy and the Corey mourners. This song, whose theme dwelt upon the pre-existent state, the existence before birth, and to whence the soul, liberated by death, returneth, held so much of the Mormon philosophy in its monotonous stanzas, and such a blanket of comfort to the bereaved, that it would be used at Mormon funerals for the next hundred years. Elder Bringhurst, as a close and beloved friend to Isaac and the Coreys, extolled Martha's virtues as a wife, as a mother in Israel, as a pioneer, and as a loyal Latter-day Saint, with such well-meant candor that the tears of Nancy and her family spouted afresh, and this in turn sent Elder Bringhurst back to his own seat weeping.

The choir's next rendition of another Mormon hymn was considerably more ragged. This gave the Coreys, and those of the audience who knew and loved Martha a chance to dry their eyes before Bishop Earlington went more directly to the heart of the mystery called death. Nancy could see that Joel Scott sat before this discourse with new respect and astonishment. The supernal faith of the bishop, the fatherly way he explained the simple change that Martha had gone through, and the eagerness with which she now awaited her loved ones on the other side, appeared as deep a surprise to Joel as it was a comforting and sustaining thing to Nancy. Again there was the allusion to the filmy veil which separated mortality from immortality—that would disappear in its entirety at death's day of mystery. In this hour Nancy was sure Joel gained an inkling to the meaning of the eternal family pattern, the marriage for time and all eternity, eternal progression, and the pattern of striving, through good works and obedience to the Gospel, to godship itself. Martha, of course, being a woman, could never hope to become a god. But, she had married under the covenant, had earned her right to the celestial glory, and could go on through eternities, hand in hand with Isaac, to share whatever measure of godship this good man would eventually be entitled. To a Gentile, or the uninitiated, these things were never easy to comprehend. But the unshakable faith, the strength Mormons derived from it, and the unity of their brotherhood were apparent in every move of their lives.

The choir sang another tearful dirge, "Sometime We'll Understand" —and the benediction was pronounced by no less than the dignified, bearded Stake Patriarch Uriah Ursenbach. As funerals go, it had been a long one, and thus an important one. Martha, if she were invisibly present, could never have realized the profound effect her example and labors had made on family and friends. But such as it was, the funeral took its measure of added time, while the Saints in the back rows filed past the open coffin, and on out the drafty side door. Nancy sensed that Joel would make the attempt to directly separate himself from the mourners and join the early exodus. But she held on to his arm, and he subsided again among the Coreys.

And when the time at last came for the family's last parting, the Gentile schoolmaster found himself with Nancy, Isaac, and the tearful group closest to the coffin. It was thus that Nancy held him to her until the very last. And, a little dewy-eyed himself, he watched Nancy whisper to the silent figure a last goodbye. And then Isaac, head bowed with sadness, pulled the veil down over Martha's gray face, and the lid went on the box for the last time. In that moment even the schoolmaster began to understand a bit of the Mormon symbolism.

In wagon-box sleighs, and a few cutters, they followed the covered sleigh containing the body to Ammon's cemetery. From the old fort, up past the new schoolhouse, which Joel watched with deepest interest, and across the main street of the new Ammon, they slid and squeaked their way to the graveyard on the hill north of town. The storm was gone, the clouds had peeled the sky back to the wild, bright blue of the mountains. To the east towered Timpanogos, white and venerable as any Holy Land prophet. To the north another great, high wall of granite was snowed to the whiteness of a celestial dream. And as the horses strained at the sleigh tugs, and they gradually rose toward the foothills, one could see spread out to the south like a pale glass window in a fairyland of white, the great sheath of Utah Lake. Under the weight of snow, even the sagebrush took on new and wondrous charm. Nancy was concerned with the abysmal storm which so deeply had marred her mother's burying. Joel, always affected by the breathtaking splendor of Utah Valley, was seeing the place with new eyes. He was glad he had, that summer's day, ridden in with the long absent Graham. He knew that, when his own time came to go East, he'd leave this place with regret. He looked at Nancy, squatted and bobbing on the quilts beside him, her little nose protruding from the once gay bonnet, and red with cold. Only too well he knew how much she stirred him. Somehow, out of this confusion must come some plans.

The townsfolk spread themselves in a great circle around the wet and frosty earth scar soon to house Martha Corey. The men laid the coffin beside the grave, and slipped beneath it the lowering ropes. Isaac Corey himself had asked for the privilege of dedicating Martha's resting place. And so, in the familiar voice, quavering at last with final grief, he blessed the ground made sacred to this mother in Israel, prayed God to hold it inviolate and unmolested "until the day of the great resurrection," when Martha's spirit again would be united with the earth shell she had so suddenly discarded. With a final blessing upon his own great family in its time of grief, he said the last amen. Martha's body was lowered, facing the east, to await in patience that great and unknown day.

When the brethren took up the shovels, for the final grim task of the day, it was Joel's turn to take Nancy's arm. Rather than let her face the agonizing ritual of the falling earth, he led her back to the sleigh. Her eyes, while red, had cried themselves out, and neither Joel nor Nancy had a word to say. Her little gray coat was an ill fit against the trim blue of her dress, and strangely out of place for a winter burial. He realized, as he led her away, that now the people were *really* looking. There was a bit of insanity to everything that had happened to him this year. That he could be so deeply concerned with a little Mormon waif, was something he would never have believed possible. He smiled at the thought of how concerned would be his mother and Amanda if they too could only read his thoughts and see him now. But he did have thoughts, and *he* was damn well concerned. It would be something to take a motherless Mormon girl East with him.

X

THE DAY OF MARTHA'S BURIAL SEEMED TO PRESAGE A TIME OF CHANGE IN
the Corey family. For a week or two the state and fortune of the Corey
House hung precariously in the balance, and Nancy's own problems
became more bitterly real. To manage the place, Isaac chose Aunt
Kirstine—and Aunt Kirstine was anything but happy about it. To give
up the comfort and status of her new brick cottage in exchange for
Martha's cell-like apartment adjoining the kitchen was no happy or easy
choice for the youngest of Isaac's wives.

Kirstine, a Danish convert to the Church, was an excellent cook, and
not at all afraid of work. But in Denmark the Mormon missionaries had
extolled the wonders of the new Zion in America's Far West, and she
and her mother and father, after baptism, had made the long and precarious journey to the promised land. Kirstine Overson, young, and filled
with dreams, had not anticipated drudgery as a part of her new life.
Her father had opened a little cobbler shop on South Temple Street, in
Salt Lake City, not far from the square and the new tabernacle. The
Overson Cobbler Shop in Zion was doing almost as well as had its
counterpart in Copenhagen. At the time Kirstine met Isaac Corey, on
a shoe-buying trip to the city in behalf of his family kingdom, she could
scarcely speak a word of English. But, after the visits of Isaac to the shop
were repeated, she needed no interpreter to tell her what this kindly-
faced patriarch was after. In Danish, Father Overson explained to her
that Mr. Corey was from Utah Valley, that he was probably very
wealthy and important because he had shoes made in dozen lots, and
always had good, firm American money to pay for them. Because everyone talked of it, because it was preached and practiced everywhere and
openly, the matter of polygamy was no particular problem. What *was*
astonishing was that Isaac Corey, a simple and uneducated farmer from
Utah Valley, had been able to snatch a pretty young bride from under
the very noses of the Authorities, with her parents' consent, and without

one of the dignitaries themselves getting first grabs on her for one of their own multiple brides. But the miracle had happened, and from the Overson Cobbler Shop to the Endowment House, it was less than two blocks.

Despite their differences in age, and difference in outlook, Kirstine Overson had not fitted too badly into the Corey pattern in Ammon. Without delay she bore Isaac a son, and in a marriage for time and all eternity, and in the doctrine of family kingship and eternal progression, that was commendably important. As the younger wife, and current favorite, Kirstine had not objected to the work and responsibility usually the lot of any wife in the plural pattern—and had not balked too strongly even to the seasons of drudgery and isolation at The Point. Not until the time came for Kirstine to take Martha's place at the Corey House did she flare up like a lynx kitty. This time it was a case of her being taken out of the fresh comforts of a new home, while the other two wives enjoyed the status of separate dwellings in the New Ammon. Her identity as the youngest and prettiest of Isaac's women would likely be lost, once she was cast in the ignoble role of workhorse at the Corey public house. Nancy was of the opinion that Aunt Kirstine's vociferous objections might have a deeper source—a normal but un-uttered fear that, once the new home was vacated, Isaac might receive a spiritual urging to seek another bride to occupy it. Too, the naggings and the scoldings that came out of Aunt Kirstine's suddenly acquired ill temper might have some basis in the fact that Isaac had promptly gotten her pregnant once more.

Nancy quickly found that any attempt to work in harmony with Kirstine was an impossibility. Try as she might, nothing satisfied the new cook and housekeeper of the establishment. Thwarted by the rock of Isaac's invincibility, Kirstine took out her frustration and disappoint-ment on those nearest at hand—usually Nancy. And Nancy's own record of implacable and successful resistance to the Principle helped her none. To lighten the work load that had killed Martha, Isaac hired Seth Biddle for the heavier chores, and, except for his fits, which Kirstine had little sympathy for, he was a great help. The more direct culinary aid came from a young Paiute squaw by the name of Itte-chey—better known to Ammon by her anglicized nickname of Itchy.

Itchy was no ordinary blanket Indian. In the early days, when Walkara and Arrapeen had carried on their nefarious traffic in slaves with the Spaniards of New Mexico and California, many a Paiute child had been purchased by the Saints from these wily devils, to keep them from the Spanish slave procurers, or the long ride to their ultimate doom. Like many another slave child, Itchy had been purchased to save her, taken into a family of Saints, and reared along with their own numerous progeny. Result was that Itchy spoke perfect English, dressed like an American, was an accomplished housekeeper and cook, and had her own testimony as to the truthfulness of the Gospel. Itchy took care of the washing, the churnings, the soap making, and helped Nancy with cleaning and dishwashing.

But no skill, accomplishment, or family tie were sufficient to blunt the thrusts of Kirstine's sharp tongue. In rattling Danish she would lash out at Nancy, Itchy, or poor Seth. At first Nancy bore Aunt Kirstine's verbal lacerations in grieving silence. But as the weeks sped on into the bitter blue cold of a mountain winter, with little or no mellowing of her half mother's hellish disposition, she commenced bucking up to the abuse. Nancy was discovering that jealousy had strange avenues in which to work; that Kirstine, perhaps feeling that in her own life she was trapped, hated Nancy because she was young, free, and newly desirable. In turn Nancy was also trapped—in her own small bedroom, hemmed off from the rest of the house by Aunt Kirstine's apartment, her abominable temper, and the frettings and tantrums of little Nephi, the smallest and newest contribution to the Corey family kingdom.

Joel Scott still continued to keep room and meals at the House, and in her own unhappy state, was ever more dear to Nancy. But Aunt Kirstine's pale, sharp Danish eyes were not blinded to the call of the flesh. What she saw in the looks of Nancy and the Gentile schoolteacher she neither liked nor approved. Let them be as much as three feet in proximity to another, and she would break up the collusion by intruding between them, or barking some order to Nancy that would speed her safely and busily away. To Itchy now went the duty of making up Joel's room. And so Nancy found herself safely shielded from at least this phase of Gentile danger. But even Aunt Kirstine could not be everywhere. And the snatches of conversation, understanding looks, and the sympathy she knew Joel felt for her in her time of trial were the only things that kept her from running away.

The complaints about her, with which Kirstine continuously nagged Isaac, were the intolerable burdens. To hear Kirstine tell it, Nancy was slothful, quarrelsome, and flirtatious—certainly venial sins in the Mormon calendar. In the frequent clashes with Isaac's fourth wife, Nancy invariably came out the loser. Nancy sensed, from Kirstine's evil verbal campaign directed to Isaac against her, and the now frequent lectures and tongue-lashings her father gave her, that Isaac's once warm love and sympathy were being rapidly eroded away.

But events were happening fast for Isaac, too—the culmination of which would take him far from the quarrelsome pattern at the Corey House. For President Brigham Young, now safely at the hearthsides of the wives who kept their houses open for him in the warm and gentle Utah's Dixie, had not forgotten Isaac Corey. Remembrance of the night the Prophet had spent under the Corey roof was manifested in more ways than one. At Provo, on the way south, Brigham had made it emphatically known, through proper channels, that Isaac Corey was badly in need of a stove to warm the tenants of his public house in Ammon. Within ten days had come this essential article, through the snow by sled and team. It was not a new stove—not even Brigham could have gotten a new stove on so short a notice, and in the middle of winter. But it was a good stove—a four-foot Bergstrom Emperor, made in Neenah, Wisconsin, that would take a real length of cedar log in one gulp, and turn out enough heat to keep the Corey guests happy around the table and the winter evenings at the reed organ. Possibly someone in Provo, Nancy imagined, would be forced to shiver out the winter, but the stove added mightily to the comfort of the Corey House, and was tangible evidence Brigham approved of all that Isaac was doing.

Within weeks came other evidences of this approval. Quickly as snow cleared, every Mormon town and outpost in the proposed State of Deseret was to be linked by telegraph—the new and much talked-of Deseret Telegraph system. For Ammon, the Corey House had been designated by Brigham Young as a station in this far-flung church enterprise. Already scores of men and women were in training in Salt Lake City, in the intricate pattern of the Morse code, to man these stations quickly as the wires could be laid.

A still greater compliment to Isaac Corey's steadfast nature, unwavering testimony to the truthfulness of the Gospel, and loyalty to the Authorities, came speedily on the heels of these other developments. The Church, under the prodding of President Young, at last got around to calling Isaac Corey to the mission field. In line with church policy and practice, there was no such a thing as pay or emolument for any elder's services as a missionary. No matter where anyone might be "called"— Europe, Asia, the South Seas, or continental America—it was up to the individual missionary to provide his own transportation, and to pay his own expenses while serving in the field. Honor and privilege of serving God and the Church in this great work of "the last days" was enough, proven by the fact that the Church never did nor never would have difficulty in keeping thousands of missionaries proselyting throughout the world.

That Isaac Corey's "call" was for the southern states, rather than to some more exotic spot on the other side of the world, did not lessen the importance of honor of the new charge now laid upon him. Even the Saints, in their insular kingdom of the Rockies, were not unaware of the devastation and misery the war had heaped on the Confederate States. To have a part in wooing these defeated peoples to a new life and the great cause was privilege and importance enough for Isaac Corey. In the true pattern of all loyal Saints, he accepted the "call" with alacrity, and began immediately to put his affairs in order for the many months he would be away from his families, and from Ammon.

In the sixty days Isaac was allowed for these preparations, Kirstine redoubled efforts to get herself out of the work-trap at the Corey House. Once he departed for his mission, Nancy reasoned, Kirstine's pattern for conduct would be set. There could be no mistaking that she hoped it would be something other than slaving over a hot stove to three times daily stuff a house full of hungry people with hot and steaming food. In this Kirstine was not at all successful. Pleadings, arguments, feigned sickness, real sickness, and the fact she was three months pregnant had not the least effect upon Isaac. Martha was dead, and he'd decided that this was the most logical and useful place for Kirstine. That was that. And it was up to her to resolve herself to it.

But resolve seemed painfully slow in coming to Kirstine. Meanwhile, with her carping tongue, and Danish epithets, she made life miserable for Itchy, Seth, and Nancy—particularly Nancy. Like Moses on the mountaintop, Isaac stood serenely through the minor turbulences in Israel. The new calling had made him a changed man—with an inner peace and an outer sanctity that was obvious to everyone who came in contact with him. Patiently, with God's love written all over his bearded and weather-beaten face, he listened out the complaints of Cove's helling, the petty bickerings of his women and children, and Kirstine's reiterations of her woes. To all, his counsel was brief, firm, and measured with exactness to the laws of God, and the revelations of His Prophet. Since Cove and Nancy had become the more continuous and pernicious thorns of his trial, they received the greater share of his judgment and counsel. But God had tempered Isaac's capacity for wrath. No longer did it thunder down on them like the storms and fires of Sinai. For the first time in their young lives, they could actually verbally defend themselves. It proved more difficult for him to keep his patience and austerity with Kirstine. "Martha managed it all right," he would remind her. "And few were *her* complaints."

"Maybe she *didn't* complain," Kirstine would argue. "But just the same it was too much for her. She's dead, you know. And it killed her."

"Martha was a sick woman. She died because she was sick. She died because the God of Israel had decreed her time."

"Maybe you think *I'm* not sick," Kirstine would groan.

"You're strong an' healthy as an ox," Isaac would remind her. "And the wee life inside of you should give no proper pause to a mother in Israel. Besides, you've Nancy, an' Itchy, an' Seth—they're husky help to you."

"Them!" Kirstine would explode. "A squaw, an epileptic, and a little wanton who's disgraced the Principle, and who makes eyes at every Gentile she sees! *Some help!*"

But against Isaac's resolve, and stubborn nature, it was like a gull beating out its wing and heart upwind. Kirstine remained at the Corey House.

Putting mundane affairs in order was only part of the problem Isaac faced in preparing himself to be a sharp-edged tool in God's harvest of souls in these the last days. Most any other man who could neither read nor write would have backed away from the challenge of preaching the Word from only the storage house of memory—but not Isaac Corey. If God loved him enough to single him out for the task, it was obligatory that a man do every whit in his power to prepare himself for the challenge. What Isaac hoped and expected of himself in sixty days appeared insuperable. But no Mormon elder ever worked harder in preparing himself to preach the Gospel.

The call had come without warning—but no matter, he must speedily learn to read and write. The very night of his call, he visited the boarding house to seek out the Gentile "professor." Most of the guests had left the table for their chambers, or had drawn chairs in huddles about the room. Others were dawdling over their food; and Nancy had already started clearing the table, and packing the plates back to Kirstine and Itchy in the kitchen. Joel was just rising to leave, when Isaac, like an ox yoked to a stubborn load, plowed determinedly into the room. Had not Nancy already been alerted to the great thing that had happened to her father, she would have backed away from one of his expected and frequent reprimands. Instead, he nodded and smiled at her, but made straight for Joel, at the table.

"Why, Mr. Corey," Joel said, rising, and extending a hand. "Good to see you."

Isaac pumped Joel's hand worriedly, pulled him back to the chair, and seated himself beside the schoolmaster. He wasted no time in getting to the point. "God has called me to a mission," he said simply.

"So Nancy has told me," Joel replied. "Between trips to the kitchen, she's been telling me some interesting things about the Mormon missionary system." His smile was friendly and understanding. "Congratulations, Mr. Corey. You'll serve your church well."

"You're wrong, Professor. I'll serve my church poorly. Unless I have help. I need *your* help."

"Mine—?"

"You've got to teach me to read and write. In sixty days."

Joel craned his neck in surprise. "I'm afraid, sir, that's an impossibility. It takes years—even when you're young."

Nancy, surprised at the conversation, hovered around the table's end, idly stacking plates while she listened. If Kirstine only knew Isaac were here, she'd be piling up complaints higher than the plates.

"Nothing's impossible," Isaac brusquely replied, "where there's a will, an' a man's prayerful about it." He looked around. "Nancy here could read me out of the Bible, *Book of Mormon*, an' *Doctrine and Covenants*. She's pretty good at readin', considering that she ain't had a lot of school room learnin'. But I've got a hunger to read by myself." The face peeking out of his beard was frantically appealing. "*I've got to read*, Professor! God's called me to a mission!" He grabbed Joel's coat sleeve. "Couldn't you give me lessons tonight?"

"Glad to, Mr. Corey—but it will take more than that. You just don't cure a lifetime of illiteracy in sixty days."

"What else must I do?" His voice was eager with hope.

Joel looked soberly at the missionary-elect. "I hate to suggest this, Mr. Corey. You might not like it."

"Suggest away. I've got to read."

"As you say, I'll help you nights. But you'll have to enroll in school. You'll have to attend classes, like the other pupils."

"With the kids?" Isaac's voice whispered it low, as if in fright.

"Yes, with the kids. There you'll get the fundamentals. Then at night I can *really* help you."

The thought of Isaac Corey desked and scratching slates with Ammon's youngsters—with his own youngsters—almost exploded Nancy with the giggles. *That* would be the sight. She was certain Elder Corey would reject this idea quick enough.

But in this, she was wrong.

"I'll start tomorrow," said Isaac. "I'll be at your school at the stroke of the bell. I helped build that school for the good of Zion an' the glory of God. I'll be proud, Professor, to take advantage of it."

Joel smiled, and in that smile Nancy read the astonishment and respect the schoolmaster was feeling toward his new pupil. "I'm afraid, though, Mr. Corey, that I'm not all through with my demands on you."

"Demand away, young man," Isaac said.

"You mentioned that Nancy here was a good reader, in spite of so little schooling. I'm going to insist also that Nancy go back to school."

Nancy let the plates slip back to the table. In fright and dismay, she sank to the nearest chair.

Joel looked at her and smiled like a rogue. "She's a comely young lady—but I'm afraid her education has had some sad neglect. I must insist you let me help her."

"You mean, I *also* go to class with the kids?" Nancy asked, suddenly sweating out the thought of her, a grown woman, knuckling to the desk with Aunt Millie's youngest. Joel could make a public ass out of Isaac Corey—but not Nancy!

"I mean that you go to class," Joel said firmly.

"Well, I just won't."

"She's at the marryin' time," Isaac protested. "Nancy's flipsy—but smart. But she's a grown woman."

"I know she's a grown woman," Joel chuckled. "And I know she's at the marrying time. But everybody needs schooling."

"True. Though it ain't like she was havin' a problem like mine. I've been called to preach. I'm goin' out to the world."

"Nancy's going out to the world, too," Joel said, quietly.

"But not to preach."

Joel spluttered joyfully. "Lord, I hope not!" When he sobered, he looked straight into the eyes of Isaac. "I'll help you—if you'll let me help *her*."

"Nancy's got her work. She's needed here. Just don't seem fittin' to me."

"I insist," Joel said firmly. "Nancy has too much work."

"I resist," Nancy declared. "I'm *not* going back to school."

"You heard her," Isaac said brightly.

"The girl needs help, Mr. Corey."

"All right, Professor," Isaac growled. "If, in sixty days, you can fix me so's I can read the Scriptures, I'll let my daughter Nancy go back to school to you." He looked cannily at Joel. "But not until you've got me eyein' the Word with understandin'."

"Not until then." Joel put his right elbow on the table, turned, and watched Isaac soberly. "You're giving me little time. At the end of sixty days you'll probably only be able to read and write simple things. But you're an intelligent man, Mr. Corey, and you'll be on your way. You can't expect miracles in sixty days. Still, from that time on, your learning power will increase and delight you."

"As a Saint, I have the *right* to miracles," Isaac declared. "I'll humble myself, even to goin' to school with children. An', because I humble myself, God will make me a good missionary. An', in the sureness of His promise, He'll make me able to read."

"I'm certain he will," Joel said.

"This woman's not going back to school!" Nancy insisted. "I'm not going to tote slates with children."

Isaac eyed her with the old parental fierceness. "You'll hold that impudent tongue, young lady," he roared. "I say you're goin' back to school—soon's I graduate! I say you're gonna do exactly what the professor here says! Now, quit your lip, an' your dawdlin'. Git them plates back to the kitchen. An' tell your Aunt Kirstine I'm here!"

And that is how Isaac Corey came to go back to school.

The town youngsters laughed at the bearded man. His own youngsters laughed at him—until he blistered their butts good and fancy. Loyally, courageously, he struggled through the alphabet and the numerals. Patiently Joel coached him nights. Tired as they were, Nancy, and Aunt Adah read hours of Scripture to him. But in sixty days the miracle *did* happen. The man's retentive capacity amazed even Joel Scott. His eagerness and attentiveness to detail made him the perfect pupil. And before Isaac departed for Salt Lake City, the miracle was assured. He could read and write. And Ammon was as proud of Isaac Corey, as Isaac was of his new accomplishment.

All through these weeks Nancy watched this tutoring process from the sidelines, surprised and delighted with the patience and skill of the schoolmaster in guiding one crusty Saint into the paths of learning; giggling as much as any other town youngster at the ludicrousness of a bearded patriarch sharing classes with Ammon's children. At the same time, she knew her own turn was coming, and the day of Isaac's departure was scarcely one to look forward to with much eagerness. It was gratifying to see the friendly warmth developing between these strangely different men. Joel had often expressed gratitude toward the Coreys for the gracious and comfortable manner they had housed and fed him. To help Isaac in so desperate a time of need was, Nancy knew, an eagerly accepted opportunity for partial repayment of a continuing favor. In such comments as "Ah, but that Scott is a sharp one," or "The gracious God of Israel brought this Yankee professor to Ammon for a purpose—for only he could have taught me to read," Nancy knew how pathetically grateful was Isaac for the friendship, interest, and expert help he was receiving.

However, and with all the factors to the contrary, she would not allow herself to think that God had brought the Yankee to Ammon for the sole purpose of tutoring Isaac. She was certain Joel Scott's winter sojourn in the town must be one of the weirdest experiences in his adventurous life. The man was handsome and desirable beyond anything she'd ever known and, anywhere else on earth, women would be tumbling over one another to gain his favor. But, here in Ammon, he was a Gentile—and therefore a creature to be watched and studied at a distance. That the town liked him there could be little doubt. For the things he was accomplishing, they already owed him much, but they were narrowly self-conscious in their repayment of the debt. Joel seldom missed an opportunity to be gracious and friendly, though there was nothing maudlin or fawning about his efforts to be liked. He attended their parties, their amateur theatricals, and even joined his rich baritone voice in their big dinner sing at Thanksgiving time. But about him, Nancy sensed, the Saints were still uneasy. He still was a Gentile, he was writing about them, he still sketched—and no Gentile did such things for any idle purpose. Nancy knew, better than any other person in town, that Joel's talented fingers were recording this winter's experiences. Why, she did not know, or particularly care. The main fact was that Joel seemed to be giving more to her people than he was receiving.

At social events the women of Ammon still were like mice so far as he was concerned. Even the well-married polygamous sisters were polite but aloof—simply because he was neither allowed nor cared to break the Sunday bread of sacrament with their husbands. With the thundered warnings of what happened to Mormon girls who consorted with Gentiles, none of the younger, attractive, and more eligible girls dared even come near him. Nancy was not too young to be observant of the anomaly of the situation—desirable Mormon lovelies, frightened at the sight of a young Gentile—yet perfectly willing to surrender themselves into multiple wedlock with some fat and shaggy Mormon elder—simply because the man was an Authority, or an important man in Zion. That even the handsome and eligible young male Saints were faring badly under the Principle was observable to anyone but the blind—but this problem was a Mormon one, and did not concern Gentiles. Only such females as Mary Magdalene Mattise, Ammon's midwife, who was too angular and homely even to find a place in some less particular Mormon harem, dared "shine up" to Joel Scott at a social.

Through the years Mary Magdalene had frantically tried to get herself hitched into wedlock, because in Mormon theology, an unmarried female had no standing—here or hereafter. Not only was this state embarrassing to Mary Magdalene, but to the Authorities as well. It was whispered that more than one Mormon male—old and well-married, young and unmarried—had been nudged by the Authorities to offer marriage to Mary Magdalene. It was common gossip that even Isaac Corey had received counsel in that direction. But Mary Magdalene, apparently, was for no man—and, unless there came a direct command from God or His Prophet, she would likely remain useful but unattached. So, instead of being a good wife to a good man, she had become a good midwife—on constant call to deliver each year's increasing crop of Mormon babies. Because no man wanted her, or would provide for her, she still lived in her little hut behind the walls of old Ammon. But to Mary Magdalene Mattise, the hunt for a husband had become a sort of desperate quest. Unhesitatingly she would have laid aside every warning of the priesthood, and every scruple of the faith, to have married even a Gentile like Joel Scott. Still, Nancy Corey, worried, overworked, and despairing, might just as unhesitatingly have done the same.

For, since the day of her mother's death, Nancy had lived under a maddening situation. Kirstine had seen well to it that she and the schoolmaster were publicly separated. With Itchy serving as chambermaid, and with the upstairs out of bounds to her, temptation could never engineer another tryst. She waited on Joel at the table, she could worship him from the other side of the room, but unless they were willing to delight the gossip-hungry ears of the multitude, they were never allowed the opportunity to talk about the intimate things Nancy dreamed about. Brazenly Nancy could choose him for a partner at a social, but most of the dances were by sets, with only occasional "round" dances, so even here any talk was fragmentary and self-conscious. But in spite of religious taboos, and the sin-hunting eyes of Kirstine, Nancy sensed an increasing warmth and closeness in even these moments. It sent her spiraling like a smoke cloud to the skies. She could not mistake the look in his eyes as he watched her at the table, or his "Thank you, my little Nan," as she leaned close to serve him. These things were obvious, could not be mistaken. They were also obvious, and a little worrisome, to Aunt Kirstine.

The greater gain had come during the nightly tutorship of Isaac Corey. If the big room were full, and there was singing and noise about the organ, the lessons were carried upstairs to Joel's room, and, therefore, lost to Nancy. But there were other nights, when quietness reigned beneath the lamps, and only one or two persons were on hand to read or doze. Then the two men would spread slate and books out on the big table and, happy to be near the huge and cheery stove, would do their lessons where she could observe, comment, and occasionally take part. At times, when the pestiferous Kirstine was not inventing tasks to keep her out of the room, she would draw a chair up beside Joel, occasionally touch shoulders with him, and smell the faint aroma of the cheroots he was never allowed to smoke in the parlor. Without the comfort of the big stove, these nights would have been impossible. For this important reason, and for his gift of gifts, Nancy blessed the name of Brigham Young.

As the day of Isaac's departure grew near, Nancy sensed subtle changes everywhere about her. The dreaded nearness of her own entry into school was frightening and humiliating enough, but it was as nothing compared with the charged atmosphere about the Corey House as Aunt Kirstine floundered against the implacable will of her husband. It was then Nancy began wondering if Joel might not have invented the whole idea as a means of her escape from a situation that was all but intolerable. For she was caught like a Sunday hen—between the creek and the ax.

Isaac, realizing that he at last could read, and not badly either, became more expansive, self-satisfied, and demanding. His tireless energy as a farmer and town opportunist became the tireless energy of a man with a new-found purpose. His winter work was automatically taken over by Cove and his several other full-grown sons—so that was no particular problem. What was difficult was Isaac's effort to cram a lifetime of reading neglect into the last few weeks of his theological preparation. It had been much easier to read the Scriptures to him, than to have him walk about among his families, with the *Book of Mormon* in hand, constantly demanding help for the words of Mormon Scripture which continued to stump him. In spite of his pathetic halts and failures, he was making real progress, and he now moved with the assurance and cocky pride of a farmer who had found gold in his irrigation sluice. Joel Scott had come to him like a miraculous visitation of one of the Three Nephites, and, like these ubiquitous visitors from the unseen world, Joel had left a blessing beyond any reckoning. The credit, of course, was to Isaac's innate intelligence and tenacity, rather than any gift from the schoolmaster—and Joel went to great pains to so indicate to his eager pupil. But Isaac was almost childishly grateful, and Nancy knew, beyond further doubt, that her father liked her Gentile very much.

Yet the change in Joel, in those final nights with Isaac at the Corey House, was just as pronounced and indicative. As Isaac grew more expansively self-satisfied, Joel retreated deeper into thoughtful silence. That he was fighting an inner problem was obvious enough. From his kind, soft words, and the way he found a dozen ways to touch her, or to press her fingers beneath the table, it was plain to Nancy that somehow the problem might have something to do with her. It couldn't be schooling, because that already had been grudgingly decided—and, if it were, he could just as well forget it. That it was something deeper, she intuitively knew, and she grew weak and steamy when her own secret thoughts boiled up like stew in a pot. Had there been any way to decently talk to Joel, away from the prying eyes of Kirstine, house tenants, and even the self-righteous Isaac, she was certain he now liked her enough to share the secret. He would never know how she longed to be even the tiniest part of his life, to share with him even the little problems. And, oh, there were so many questions she wanted to ask!

Final decision was that Isaac should depart for Salt Lake City, the beginning step in his great mission, on the first Monday in February. Could he have waited less than three years, the great Pacific Railway would have been completed through Utah Territory, and he could have finished the first leg eastward in comparative ease. But now it would be winter travel, horseback, and fraught with hardship, from Ammon to Salt Lake, and thence overland to the western terminus of the railway, somewhere in Nebraska. Cove would push a team and wagon through with him to Salt Lake City, and bring back a load of supplies. After a week or so in the missionary school at church headquarters, Isaac would be on his way to warn the world, and to point the way into the only true Church.

Since Ammon's new assembly hall consisted only of a snowed-in foundation, and a dream for next year, the big missionary farewell party for Isaac would be held in the old meeting house behind the walls—on the Saturday night previous to the departure. The chapel's benches would be pushed back to the walls, the big floor cleared, and the church would resound to the fiddle of Joshua Rowley, Mary Magdalene Mattise on the battered piano, and the thump of dancing feet on the church's squeaky pine floor. The piano, an ancient relic, had, like the organ, weathered the plains crossing. Next morning, with benches back in place, the Saints would break the bread of sacrament in the Sunday service. Willie Tuttle would lead in the sacred hymns, Mary Magdalene would accompany at the organ, and Bishop Earlington would preside over the worship. Since it would also be the first Sunday of the month

—Fast Sunday—breakfast would be forsworn, and the money given to the poor. The Saints would "bear their testimonies" to the truthfulness of the Gospel, and publicly acknowledge the hand of God in their behalf. This would be Isaac's time to rise and acknowledge the miracle that had come into his life, and perhaps bid another, more austerely final farewell to the people who were close to his life and heart. Next day he would be gone. And Ammon would miss him.

All these things, to Isaac, as to any departing Mormon missionary, were touchingly important. But to Nancy Corey they paled to insignificance compared to that strange and shattering hour on that Thursday night previous to the farewell. Thorough and persistent pupil that he was, Isaac had insisted on tutorship up to the very last. As usual, he showed up at the parlor of the Corey House when the guests had thinned out in deference to this nightly ritual. Luckily for Nancy, Kirstine and Itchy were preoccupied in the kitchen with extra baking for Saturday night's big party, and she could sneak unobtrusively to the table, beside Joel, while the two men labored through the process of learning.

But this night it was different and, when Joel's hand closed tightly around her own, from beneath the table, and remained closed, she already was warmed like a muffin by the premonition of things to come. Joel wouldn't let go. And that alone was enough to make a woman slither down to a blob, like a spat of butter in a skillet.

Outside of the warmth of his nearness, the faint smell of his tobacco, and the delicious wandering of his hand, the night started out casual enough.

One-handedly Joel spread out the slate and the *McGuffey Reader*—grade four. "When you first started out, Mr. Corey," he said, "I had my doubts. Didn't think you could possibly make it. Instead, I've found you the most apt, bright, and willing pupil I've ever known."

"I tried," Isaac said modestly. "I prayed a lot over it, too. But you're a good man, Professor. Without you whippin' me at it, I couldn't've writ my own name. I've been lucky knowin' you. Ammon's been lucky havin' you."

Joel squeezed Nancy's hand reassuringly. "I feel that I've been most lucky, too. But any credit for what you've done these past two months must go to you, Mr. Corey. You've worked very hard. You've a very alert and retentive mind. And now that you can read, a new world will open to you."

"You ain't no hand to brag about yourself, Professor, but I know you to be a sharp and useful man. You've done me a lot of good—an'

I'm not a hand to forget a favor. I know you'd argue, an' try to pass it off, if I tried to offer you money. So I'll not even try. But I do know you've been a blessing to me—an' you're a blessing to my town, an' my people. As sorta somethin' to keep you here, I've done a little thing. If you'll check with the bishop, you'll find that I've deeded to you the town lot opposite the school. It's a good an' close-in acre. An' Ammon's sure to grow into a first-rate town. The lot's yours, no matter what you do with it, or do with yourself. But we'd be proud to have you stay in Ammon."

Joel had straightened erect, and for the first time he let go of Nancy's hand. "I—I don't know what to say," he stammered. "I helped you because I wanted to. I want no pay."

"That I can believe," said Isaac jovially. "But the lot's yours regardless."

"It's so very kind of you, Mr. Corey. I—"

"Can blessings be measured out on scales? It ain't pay, man. I could never pay for all that's come to me. I can only hope that, since you own a little of Ammon, you'll stay around to help us make a town of it." Isaac chuckled, and drummed his calloused fingers on the slate. "Who knows? You might even decide to join the Church—an' become one of us."

"I'm leaving in the spring," Joel said, a new tautness in his voice. "I agreed with Apostle Pratt to stay this winter to help your people get started. And I do so appreciate your generosity and kindness, Mr. Corey. But my family's in the East. I've been away a long time. There are obligations I can't very easily shirk or sidestep. I must go."

And there, Nancy knew, she had it in finality. Their worlds were inescapably apart. The man would go East in the spring—and that was that. The shock of it made her want to go to her room and blubber it out.

"Well, you've fulfilled *your* part of the bargain," Isaac said, a little sadly. "We'll be sorrowful about seein' you go."

Nancy started to rise. Joel drew her back to the chair. Isaac saw it, and glanced oddly at the Gentile.

"I'll feel sorrowful about it, too," Joel said. "I've learned to like Utah Valley and its people a lot."

"Come Monday, I'll be gone," Isaac sighed. "I guess it'll be a real goodbye between you an' me. I'll be expectin' you at the farewell. An' you'd be right welcome at church, too."

Joel's hand again sought Nancy's. This time she sensed a tremor in his grip. The air about them stood expectantly and frighteningly still, like the pause before a crack of lightning.

"There's more to this than just a goodbye," Joel said. Nancy could feel his body tighten.

"It'll not be easy for any of us," Isaac sighed.

"Real point about it—is, that I want to marry Nancy."

Like a punctured wind bustle, the air went out of her. She commenced to sweat and tremble.

"I want to take her East with me. I want to give her schooling, culture—the chances and opportunities she deserves."

There was a hush, and, as Isaac's face reddened with surprise the air grew crackling with expectancy. Nancy felt her own face crimson like a garden beet. She hadn't expected Joel to blurt out anything like this.

"I wish you hadn't said it, man," Isaac said, slowly, thickly. "I respect you. I like you. I want you to find your place here in Zion. But Nancy's my daughter. An' she's a Latter-day Saint. You can go—or stay—as it pleases you. But, if you do go—don't be toyin' with any idea of takin' Nancy with you."

"I'm not stealing Nancy, sir. I want to marry her. I want her to be my wife."

"No matter to me, Professor," Isaac growled. "You're a Gentile. She's a Latter-day Saint. You're talkin' about takin' a daughter of Zion out of Zion! You're talkin' about takin' her thousands of miles away—to set her down amidst mobocrats an' persecutors! You think I've raised her up for that kind of life? She'd be better off dead."

"I love Nancy. I'd be good to her."

"No matter," Isaac snapped, rising to his feet.

Joel rose, bristling like a cock rigging for a fight. He looked sharply into the bearded face of his pupil. "Suppose Nancy thinks differently! Suppose Nancy's willing! Would you—?"

Isaac turned. "You wanta marry this Gentile?" he grumbled.

Nancy sat in the chair, shaking like a pan of clabber. "He's never asked me," she admitted, with fright. "But I would marry him, Father. I'd marry him in a minute." And then suddenly she was weeping. "I'd marry him—because I love him."

"What about this business of going East with him?" Isaac probed.

If this were a courtship, Nancy thought through her tears, it was of the strangest. This was no way for it properly to happen. She thought a moment on Isaac's question, and then Joel's hand was on her shoulder. "Joel's said nothing to me about it, Father," she sobbingly confessed. "But I'd go—if he wanted me." And then there were the familiar thoughts of this, the only place she'd ever known. "I'd rather stay in Ammon," she moaned. "But I'd go—if he wanted me to go."

Isaac looked at Joel. "I like you, man," he said, perplexed. "Wouldn't *mind* you in the family. If only you'd set your roots in Ammon, I'd pay no heed. I can see Nan's really takin' up with you—an' with her havin' a hellion's reputation for turnin' good men down. But 'twould take God Himself to see out of a woman's eye—they're that strange. So, if she's set on marryin' you, Professor—I won't fight you—providin' you make that marriage decent by stayin' here. But this I'm gonna say—if you try to take this girl East with you—now—or more sneakingly, after I've departed on my mission—you'll have *me* to fight. An' you'll find me a hard one, mister!"

"Why are you so set against me taking her East, Mr. Corey?" Joel reasoned. "I came from a decent and honorable family. I could make Nancy's life very comfortable—give her advantages she could never know here. I'd be good to her. I'm certain she'd be very happy. I can understand a father's desire to keep his family about him. But this is a marriage I'm proposing, sir. If Nancy's willing to go with me—I can't understand your unreasonable attitude about it."

"Well, maybe I can make it a little plainer," Isaac snapped. "We're Latter-day Saints. Nancy's a Latter-day Saint. You Gentiles drove us through four states. You murdered our people. You murdered our Prophet. You shoved us out on the prairies in the dead of winter. We walked those prairies, an' buried our dead there, until we came to these valleys. I can tell you, Professor, that there's a line of Mormon graves from here to the Mississippi River. We found our homes here—an' here we established our way of life. Still you damn' Gentiles won't leave us alone. In Nancy's own time you've shoved two armies at us. You've been a soldier. You know the contempt with which we're treated. But make no mistake, Professor—we're human, we're proud, an' we believe in what we preach. We also know an' recognize our enemy. You managed to shove us out of the East—but it'll take a hell of a bit of shovin' to git us out of the West!"

"But I'm *not* your enemy," Joel argued. "I understand your problem. I'm not making war. I'm not shoving. I'm asking—"

"You're a Gentile. You're talkin' of takin' a child of mine back to the land of our persecutors. You've stripped that land of Mormons as bare as a winter tree. There ain't enough of our people left back there to fill a jail. Yet your preachers an' your editors keep up their howl against us. While we try to build our towns an' farms an' homes, an' try to mind our business, in our own land, far removed, you label us as your enemy—

137

an' make war against us. Well, damn it, we're not stupid! We know our enemy—especially when he's got a bayonet shoved down our gullet! An' yours, mister, is enemy land—a land in which we have no friends. An' that's no place for a daughter of mine."

"Not even if she's willing to go?"

"You'd best not try it," Isaac said, coldly, deliberately. "An' that goes for in front of me, or behind my back." He stalked to the door, took his hat off the wall hook, and eyed first Nancy, then Joel. "I'm warnin' you, Professor," he said.

A moment later he was gone.

In spite of the fact that Joel's arm was still protectively about her shoulders, Nancy shuddered with fright and tears. Instinctively she glanced toward the kitchen door. As expected, Kirstine was there. The smug, happy smile on her evil face was evidence she'd heard it all.

XI

SO ISAAC COREY DEPARTED FOR THE MISSION FIELD. THE ROUSING SOCIAL IN his honor, and the Sunday night sermon he was asked to preach, were in themselves indicative of the respect, if not affection, in which he was held throughout Utah Valley. At sacrament meeting, on Sunday after-noon, he bore a testimony to the truthfulness of the Gospel that brought tears to the eyes of the assembled Saints. The attendance at all these events was flattering and, though Joel Scott was too ill-at-ease to be on hand, and preferred a wintry ride with old Duke instead, most of the townsfolk were there. As a Corey, Nancy could not properly miss her father's going away, but she felt as shaky and floppy as a shutter in the wind, and just as uncertain. After Isaac's blowup on Thursday night, Joel had kissed her in front of Kirstine—deliberately and with crush-ing warmth. Without another word he'd gone upstairs. She'd seen little of him since, and she'd lived out the weekend in weepy uncertainty.

But Isaac Corey departed without heaping further censure on their heads. Not once, public or private, did he mention his problem with the schoolmaster, and he was kind, and even affectionate, toward Nancy in those final hours. In spite of the fact that Kirstine, with malicious delight, had spread the news to the family, and thus, naturally to the town itself, Nancy grew more calm and sure of herself. Of course everybody in Ammon now knew that she had spurned an apostle to become the sweetheart to a Gentile. It was only natural they should feel sorry that such a good man as Isaac Corey should have to be tormented by an all-but-apostate daughter in the time of his going away. It was only natural, too, that Ammon's women and girls should snub her, and icily glare at her. Strangest reaction was the automatic release her acts now gave to the young bucks of the town. Since none of the Authorities had further claim on her, they could now smile at her and flirt with her. And since she had dropped so low as to admire a Gentile, they were free to do even worse things, once given a chance.

After Isaac and Cove drove northward, things once more became calm again. Four days later Cove returned to Ammon, and the letter, written in Isaac's proud new scrawl, told of his nice visit with Flora and Apostle Cragg, and his departure from Salt Lake City. He, with five other missionaries, was riding horseback to Fort Bridger. From there they would go by church wagon to the western terminus of the railroad. But Nancy sensed the calm could not last. Joel looked worried, and failed to bring up the idea of her going back to school. Inwardly, she hoped he never would. He said nothing more about his startling proposal of marriage and, under watchful eyes at the Corey House, slight opportunity was given—and this disturbed her more. As expected, it was Aunt Kirstine who finally brought this apparent calm into shattering eruption.

Nancy herself probably lit match to the tinder when she purposely dawdled with Joel at the table that night. With Martha gone, with tyranny, slavery, and hopelessness the inner and outer ends of her life, she hungered like a winter-starved whelp for any crumb of conversation the schoolmaster might throw her way. From Joel this night, as she shunned her after-meal labor to deliberately sit down beside him, she received his smiling kindness. But she had always received that. The smile that lit up his tawny face could light up her own soul like a kerosene torch. And, ah, what a gentleman; for kindness was an essential part of him. Tonight, for extra, he even pressed her hand. But again he was preoccupied and worried, and the amount of wordage she had with him was small. They never got beyond the barest friendly amenities, and certainly miles from love-talk or spooning, when Kirstine spied them from the kitchen door.

"Ged on vid your vork, you little apostate bitch!" she shrieked. "Ged dose dishes in here!" She finished off in a chattering trail of Danish invective that sounded like a barrel of horseshoes rolling downhill. The words she ended with were unintelligible, but the meaning was clear.

Joel again squeezed Nancy's hand understandingly, and grinned. "Seems I hear an angel's voice," he chuckled. "Your guardian angel."

"A voice all right," Nancy groaned. "But she's no angel." Reluctant, sick with disgust, she arose, and pushed the chair back.

"That witch should ride a broom," Joel said, also politely rising. "How do you stand her, Nan?"

Nancy commenced gathering the soiled dishes. "I *can't* stand her," she said, staring down at the shrill pattern of the oilcloth table top. "I *can't* stand her." Methodically she stacked the plates, unmindful of their load of steak bones and silverware. "I so miss my mother. Mums was gentle, kind; and she understood." With both her strong arms she gripped her high and rattling load for the kitchen. But she did not lift it. Instead, she bowed her head, and let her misery leak out in audible groan. "Oh Joel," she cried softly, without looking up. "Take me out of here! In God's name, please do take me out of here!"

Joel's hands pressed both of her shoulders. "I shall, dear Nan," he whispered close to her ear. "Try hard to be patient—for a little while longer."

But from the doorway, Aunt Kirstine's sin-hunting eyes were watching. The trumpet of her Danish voice was not far behind. "You fildy, conniving pair!" she howled. "And vid your fadder scarcely gone!"

"Aw shut up—you screaming buzzard!" Nancy shrieked back. "I've had enough of you!" She hoisted the load of plates to her belly, and made straight for Kirstine and the kitchen.

Embarrassed, but politely silent, the schoolmaster headed for the wintry porch, and the comfort and quietness of a cheroot.

But this night, for once, Nancy had really had enough. She dumped the soiled dishes on the scraping table. Without another word to Kirstine, volubly grinding in her native Danish, or to Itchy, mercifully silent in her patient and wonderful Lamanite way, Nancy headed straight for the apartment. This was the first time she'd ever deliberately shirked her job, and for once she didn't care a damn. When she reached her little chamber, she slammed shut the door, and flung herself, sobbing, to the bed.

There was commotion enough as she cried out her heartache, and Kirstine and Itchy drove themselves through the heavy tasks of night. Twice Kirstine beat feverishly on the door, and shouted for her to come back to her neglected tasks, but Nancy, in the darkness, refused to leave her room. The door, of rough slabwood, had no lock, but Kirstine had sense enough to give up without forcible entry.

As dutiful Mormon women, Kirstine and Itchy completed their heavy tasks, but when the little Indian finally took off for home, it was considerably later than usual. Eventually things quietened at the Corey House, and sleep came at last to the worried, unhappy Nancy.

And then suddenly she was awakened by the light in the room. At first she thought it was morning, and guiltily realized she'd been doing her sleeping fully clothed. But it was not morning. The light was from the kerosene lantern in Kirstine's left hand. In her right hand was the heavy iron stove poker. Kirstine was fully clothed also. Deliberately she laid the lantern to the dresser top. Before Nancy could rise, Kirstine was standing over her, staring down with enough malevolence and hate to shrivel a pine stump.

"You'll not ged away vid it," she muttered. "You laugh, and make disgrace vid the Principle! You make love to Gentile behind your fadder's back! You wanta be vun vife only! You tink you be vun vife only! You lazy bitch! Take diss, you damn apostate!"

With an insane gibber of Danish, she brought the poker down on Nancy's head with such force that the world exploded in light before the surprised girl's eyes. Stunned for a second, Nancy instinctively arose to protect herself, but before her mind could clear, the woman had rained half a dozen more shattering blows across her head, shoulders, and stomach.

As the blood rolled down her eyes and cheeks, Nancy howled her fury, and struck out for the sudden, shrieking menace that had come to her in the night. Instinctively she knew the woman was trying to kill her. There was no time to wonder what insane ferment of jealousy, hatred, and frustration had prompted the attack. But it was here, and now—and, unless she cleared head, and moved quick, she'd die.

But Nancy herself had the strength and litheness of a panther. The first blow had wrecked her ability to see and think clearly, but there was instinct in her arms, and capacity for defense. Suddenly she was coming at Kirstine like a maddened, wounded animal. In the rolling battle that followed, she managed a hold on Kirstine's arms that flesh-and-bone-twisted the fight out of them. Somehow, miraculously, the lantern failed to be upset, and the poker at last dropped harmlessly from the woman's hand before she could lethally finish the job. Then Nancy's mind and eyes cleared. Her ears could hear the frightened howling of Kirstine's youngster, in the other room, disturbed and wakened by the shrieking fury of the two women. By lantern light she could see the twist of hate on Kirstine's face, and the murder gleam in her strange pale eyes. Nancy wrested free her right hand from the deathlike grip she had on Kirstine's arm. Deliberately she doubled her fist, hauled it back, and swung with everything she had. The fist bit into Kirstine's nose and lip. A second later, Kirstine had landed on her buttocks in the corner.

Nancy shook herself like a stricken dog, pushed her wild hair, wet with sweat and blood, from her eyes and face, and reeled to the doorway. The lantern gleamed faithfully. Kirstine, from the corner, moaned, and shook her head. Little Nephi, from his crib in the next room, was howling as though panicked by the shades of hell. Nancy whimpered a minute, and clung to the door frame. Still whimpering, unmindful of little Nephi and his fright, she slowly and painfully made her way through the house, and up the stairs to Joel's room.

XII

STRANGE, WHAT THOUGHTS CROSSED A WOMAN'S MIND AS, STARTLED INTO accustomed early risings, one's eyes opened to the unfamiliarity of the room, and then one's whole body settled back to the sheets and quilts, knowing there was no necessity for bounding out of bed for the milking, the chores, and such. For this morning, it was Nancy's second awaking. Joel was gone early, to Fort Douglas, the room was as cold as a barn loft in a blizzard, and he'd insisted she sleep late. So, she fingered the blue and broken spots of her cheek and scalp, sighed with the luxury of it all, pulled up her knees, and turned herself sideways to the warm bed. It was something not to have to lug out mountains of ham, porridge, biscuits, and gallons of coffee to the breakfast gullets of the Corey House. Sleeping late, and lazily dawdling in bed, was a new experience. It was something to make the most of. And this was the Salt Lake House—not the Corey House. And it was presided over by Brother and Sister Townsend—not by Isaac Corey and his fiend, Aunt Kirstine.

One might wallow in this bed of rest like a calf in clover, but there were still the worries and the guilt. She was facing the side Joel had occupied, and she reached her hand to the pillow—still cupped and hollowed by his head. Her hand laid there a moment—and then, with another sigh, she wrapped her arm about the pillow and drew it affectionately to her. It still smelled faintly of Joel and his cheroots. And that was good. For this, small as it was, marked a bit of her possession of him.

Not that this was a good way to be married. It had happened wildly, and not at all as it should have, and could have. And the troubles she'd brought to Joel were like plagues of locusts—and by no means solved. A marriage should be a thoughtful thing, with warmth, and music, and friends, and heaped rich with great promise. But this marriage had been thrown together like a quick meal. Worse, it had been born in violence, loaded to breaking with physical pain and fatigue, and sure to bring reprisals that were frightening to think about. Joel's reputation as an educator, and his good name in Ammon and all Zion, were shattered. After the two of them had gotten the moaning Kirstine to her bed, and defied her by gathering up a bundle or two of Nancy's possibles from her bedroom, they'd saddled up Duke and Dolly, and started in the cold of night for Salt Lake. And what a journey for a bride! Cold as the snow-sweeps of Timpanogos! And also, what a bride! As battered and bleeding as a rabbit in a grist mill! And the marriage—tired, dilapidated, standing before a Protestant chaplain at Fort Douglas. It had violated every precept of her Mormon heritage.

Never could a woman love a man more than she loved Joel. Never could a woman be more appreciative of the sacrifice he so willingly and insistently had made in her behalf. But still it was a bad marriage. A hasty marriage. It saddened her to think it had happened so. Yet she knew she would never be sorry about its happening. It was her plain duty now to make certain Joel would never be sorry.

But, oh, the problems it had raised! Even at this moment, as she dawdled in a warm bed, trying desperately to unscramble the good and bad thoughts, Joel was out to Fort Douglas with the dawn—frantically trying to get them transportation by military wagon or horse train over the winter-bound Wasatches. This formidable thing must be accomplished before they could get into Nebraska, and to the new railroad that would take them to the wondrous East he had told her so much about. It would never do, he explained, to trust themselves to Mormon conveyance or custody, after what had happened, and knowing the feeling of the Saints toward Gentile ensnarement of womenfolk. But travel by winter, in and out of Utah Territory, even by experienced Mormon freighters and the military, was sparse and desultory. With spring and summer's opening of the road and trails, there would be traveling aplenty—freighters, California immigrants, thousands upon thousands of Saints making real the "gathering," and military trains loaded with supplies for the Fort. But this was neither spring nor summer. Chances for quick departure for the East were not the best, and she knew her Joel was worried.

And as Nancy hugged the pillow and sparred with her thoughts, she admitted she had no real stomach for leaving. Martha, after her miserable journey west from Nauvoo, had birthed her right in this city. And Martha, after giving a life for the cause, was buried in this land. The Mormon Zion, odd as it might appear to Joel, was home to her, and the only life she knew. Plurality she could hate—but never Zion and the Saints. She loved this land, because it was *her* land, and in all the honesty of her heart, she dreaded the leaving. Boston was a great city; it had its good life, its history, its ships, even his family's ships—but nothing it had, or no part of its promise, could ever take the place of Utah Valley, its lake, its mountains, and the familiar and beloved things. But go she must. And what Joel said—no matter what or how—she'd do it willingly, and as happily as she could.

They'd borrowed a ring for the ceremony at the Fort. Yesterday, at Livingston & Bell, he not only had bought her the real ring, of rich, pure gold, but new clothes, and the satin bride's nightgown to which she now nestled so luxuriously. She reached her lips to the ring of her troublous marriage, and kissed its yellow gold. Today she'd visit Flora, at her cottage on the Cragg plural row, West Temple Street. Flora would know she'd married Joel, but would never understand the wicked circumstances that had brought it about, nor their apostate's haste to flee Zion. She'd probably even tell Flora that she was not Joel's first bride. That Edna Reavis, the pretty lady of the picture, had married Joel when he went off to war. That along with wounds, and carnage, and suffering had come notice of Edna's death by typhoid fever, and his own helpless inability to reach her bedside. She could tell Flora that after Joel was invalided out of service, he'd crossed Panama to California, to heal both broken heart and body. Instead of seeking gold, he'd activated his commission in the military, and joined the man-depleted garrison at San Francisco Bay. And, oh, there was so much to tell her about his aristocratic and wealthy family, his home in Boston, the family ships he'd sailed on, and all the things she was going to see. And that even though Joel had now married twice, she, Nancy, was the only present and official bride. And for this blessing, and many more,

Flora would know of her resolve that Joel would never be sorry he'd chosen her.

And with these new thoughts of Joel, and this mental affirmation of her obligations, Nancy brought quick end to her ease and revery by rolling herself out of bed, and setting face to the stinging cold of the day.

With the room temperature what it was, and even the water pitcher iced over, she tarried none in getting herself dressed. But even through the speed of her toilet, there were those plaguing, fleeting thoughts—brought on by the very barrenness and discomfort of the room. For it was not at all like the new room Joel had so comfortably settled into at the Corey House. There was no shelf, loaded and stacked with the books he loved. There were no rows of his hanging clothes and trail-worn army uniforms; no metal-bound locker of valuables under the bed. All these, plus a good and honorable name, he'd left behind in Ammon. And all these had been abandoned because of her. In her shift, and unlaced shoes, she stood before the cracked mirror of the dresser, appraised herself as a red-cheeked, slightly confused bride, and rubbed some of the pitcher's ice on the bluish-red head welts Aunt Kirstine had given her.

Half an hour later, fully clothed for the day, she'd crossed the social room of the Salt Lake House, and had casually loped down the stairs. Her breakfast, she quickly found, was a noisy, embarrassing one. The table, presided over by Sister Townsend, was almost filled with a rough and noisy group of men. Experience had taught her the knack of spotting Gentiles—a few words of their conversation, coupled with their hard, pugnacious looks were enough. And this was Salt Lake's public house, and these were Gentiles all right. She knew, too, instantly, that they'd mentally pegged her as the new bride. Her bruised appearance was enough to make any of them stare in wonder. But they might have been a little less crude and salacious about it.

Sister Townsend, the ample-bosomed matriarch of the establishment, did all in her power to ease the embarrassment of a battered bride alone at a table of rough and noisy Gentiles. She personally served Nancy her bread, porridge, pork chops, and bacon. While Nancy got started at the robust breakfast, Sister Townsend hovered over her like a mother hen; smiling, talkative, and kind. Unmindful of the fact that coffee was forbidden by the Mormon Word of Wisdom, she poured Nancy a steaming mug full—and Nancy was glad enough to receive it. Yet in spite of the sister's motherly attentions, she was glad when the meal was over, and she could take her turn around the yard away from a dozen staring men. It was too cold to sit in her room, too embarrassing to sit downstairs with the men guests, and the upstairs social room barnlike and drafty; she donned the new padded winter cap, the new coat, and the new fur-lined muff Joel had bought for her travel East. A moment later she'd let herself out the door of the Salt Lake House to the wintry sidewalks of the city.

The smell of wood smoke, and the sick-sweet odor from the morning burnings of Utah's newly popular soft coal, were in the air. But the day was as crisp and snappy as the frozen snow beneath her feet. It was a little early to call on Flora, and there would probably be considerable time before Joel returned. In the meantime there was a city to see. With the easy, animal-like stride of mountain-born Mormon women, she headed north on Main Street toward the focal point of Salt Lake City— the great ten-acre square upon which would stand the Temple of the Lord.

At the main intersection with South Temple Street, Nancy paused. She shoved her warm and comfortable fingers deep into the luxury of the new fur-lined muff, and almost happily whizzed her steamy breath to the morning crisp of the air. The city, in spite of winter, was lively and astir. People, like herself, were walking the sidewalks. The clip-clup of the business drays, delivery wagons, and shiny new carriages taking merchants to their stores, and dignitaries to their offices were evidence enough Zion was prospering. Take away the humiliation of the past, and the imponderables of the future, and this could be a rare moment of great excitement. But there were laws and rules, rights and wrongs, hates and reprisals, and a hundred other dilutants and poisons to the joy and wants of living. She'd messed things up proper for Joel, and probably for herself. But he'd insisted on going ahead with their elopement and, on that score, she hadn't protested too vigorously.

Any other time she'd have walked the block and a half down South Temple to the cobbler shop of Aunt Kirstine's parents. This time the Oversons could burn in hell so far as she was concerned. But this coming meet with Flora should be a happy moment, even though it was likely that, by now, Flora would be so deeply converted to the everlasting glory of the Principle that her half sister's revolt and marriage to one of the handsome Gentiles they together had ogled from the wall would be nothing short of pure sin and apostasy. And the fact Flora's own husband was the fat Authority she'd basted in the nose not too long ago was no added comfort to her thinking.

In other years, too, she'd have walked down South Temple Street to gain entrance to Temple Square. But even after two years the south

146

entrance, through the great ten-foot-high walls, remained bricked up—Brigham's defiance to Connor's provost guard stationed across the street. So Nancy continued northward along the wall toward the more welcome area of the east gate. And it was a wall indeed. Its freshly plastered exterior hid the massiveness of its inner construction—of squared adobe bricks, set on a solid foundation of dressed red sandstone, and weather-capped at the top with a canopy of fitted sandstone blocks. There'd be no melting down of this wall, like the one at Ammon.

The ornamental iron gates of the east entrance were already flung open—not only for the Saints attending celestial marriages, or those standing proxy for the world's departed, in the sacred and secret ceremonies of "endowment" and baptism for the dead, but for the heavier wheeled traffic incident to the robust building program going on within the square.

The east entrance brought her alongside the yawning hole and granite block confusion of what someday would be the most holy of temples. When this great six-spired edifice was finished, the Endowment House would come down, and the sacred ordinances of the Gospel would be moved to their permanent and fitting place. Today the spot was only a tumult and a mess.

Here on this square was shattering reminder of what she, as a Mormon, had learned about the Church's frantic and frustrated efforts to fill its greatest obligation—temple building. There was the handsome first one the Saints had built in Kirtland, Ohio; stolen from them and desecrated by the Gentiles—the great temple at Nauvoo, Illinois, in which Martha had received her original blessings; also stolen from them by the Gentiles, desecrated, and demolished. There was that mightiest temple of all, once planned for the center Stake of Zion, in Jackson County, Missouri, but thwarted when the Saints were driven out—but which someday would yet be a living reality. She knew, because it had been prophesied, that there would come a time when the Church would blanket the earth with its holy temples, and that the world in that day would stand alongside their construction with the same wonder and awe she felt as she gazed at the chaotic promise in granite before her. And then she was remembering that this was no longer a promise to her. She'd discarded every right and promise for the Gentile she loved. She was leaving this center of Zion forever. In guilt and sadness, she turned, to pick her way through the immense confusion of Mormondom's sacred ten acres.

And on the west side of the square it was the same confusion—multiplied and intensified. The great new tabernacle, supplanting the smaller, simpler building which had stood in its place, now spread itself outward to the square like a gigantic tortoise. The temple, a dream for the millennium, might take half a century to build. The House of the Lord must, as a slow and exacting task, rise leisurely along with the skill and fortunes of the Saints. Not so with the tabernacle. Mormondom had outgrown the previous building. A place where Saints could congregate in one great audience for instruction, admonition, and spiritual fellowship was an imperative necessity.

Unlike the temple area, this place was swarming with workmen; and the urgency of its construction was everywhere apparent. Its great turtle shell, two hundred and fifty feet long, rested on dozens of pillars meticulously laid up in red sandstone. From these pilasters the great dome, made up of interlaced wooden girders, soared upward eighty feet, and spanned the entire area without a single support. Nancy, as she stared at the building in awe, trying nimbly at the same time to keep out of the way of the work crews, realized some of the mighty force that was at work in the minds and hearts of her people. This, and many another thing, she would sorely miss in Boston.

It was at the Endowment House, the only structure untouched and serving usefully amid the ferment at Temple Square, that she almost reeled with the impact of the thing she was doing to herself. This "little temple," just north of the great new tabernacle, and separated from it by a high wooden enclosure, lent little of itself visibly to Nancy. Its adobe construction exuded far more mystery than glamour, and about it was the same dismal grayness of a thousand other clay dwellings of Mormondom. Nor was there anything distinctive about its architecture. The center section of it was high, two-storied, and slant-roofed. On either side were one-story wings, but similarly shaped. Unlike the new Salt Lake Theater, a block south and east, there was little sign of elegance or eye-appeal in the Endowment House. To a Gentile, unacquainted with the mysticism of the Saints, it could be just another Mormon building—and an unpretty one at that. To Nancy, as to every other person Mormon born, it verily was the celestial doorway.

Until the Saints could build another temple, safe and secure from the rapacious Gentiles, the Endowment House on Temple Square must serve heaven to save a lost world. Hour after hour, in its baptismal font, the Saints underwent this essential water ritual for salvation for the millions who had died without hearing God's message of everlasting life. Within its sacred rooms, Latter-day Saints were being sealed for time and all eternity, one to another, and under the covenant which God had revealed to the Prophet. This for the living—and this for the dead. All was part of Nancy's life and belief. All this Nancy accepted without quarrel. It was the more disturbing revelation, wherein God allowed the faithful in the priesthood to espouse a plurality of wives, toward the same cause, and the upbuilding of the kingdom, that had stirred up her only resistance. This ordinance, too, went daily on.

Face to face with structural reminder of the covenant, Nancy turned a little sick with the thoughts of where this resistance had already led her. According to the revealed Word of God, she deliberately had rejected the only path toward eternal exaltation in the celestial glory. Deliberately, and in the black spirit of apostasy, had she rejected it. Worse, and against the warnings and admonitions of her father, she had married a Gentile, and with him was trampling her beliefs into the earth, and throwing away the heritage of a thousand martyrs.

The February wind whistled through the wooden lacework of the great tabernacle, and scurried the frosty snow against the high wood wall of the Endowment House—the wall so symbolic of the thing that had come between her and her Church. She freed a hand from the muff, and snugged the winter cap to her sore and bruised head. Then she slipped the hand back to the warmth and consolation of the muff's fur lining. Huddling in her sin, suddenly sick and frightened, she watched while a happy group of Saints came up the path, and paused at the wooden gate of the Endowment House. She spotted the bride and groom—the bride, rosy-cheeked, and smiling through her fright—the groom, huddled in overcoat, bearded, and blowing winter steam as he talked with the assurance of experience. The other members of the group, as they showed their bishop's "recommends" to the gatekeeper, and impatiently stomped the snow from their shoes, might be sisters, or other wives, or brothers or fellow friends. But it was a Mormon wedding party, and soon they were gone behind the wall, and into the ritual that would unite them from everlasting to everlasting. Like one pursued by a great sin, Nancy moved quickly on toward the north gate of Temple Square. A moment later she was gone from the haunting place.

Two hours with Flora added no soothing to Nancy's conscience, nor solution to her problems. The visit started out warm and congenial enough. Flora, surprised and happy, met her half sister at the doorway of her cottage on West Temple Street with the joy and effusion of a long separation.

"Come in, dear Nan, come in!" she cried almost hysterically, wrapping Nancy in tearful embrace, and hauling her across the threshold. "How glad am I to see you! It seems ages!"

"Does seem long," Nancy said. "And I'm glad enough for the two of us."

"Did Cove fetch you up from Ammon? Is my wicked brother in town, too?"

"No, Flora. Only your wicked half sis. I was fetched up from Ammon —but not by Cove. Let me shed wraps, and I'll tell you all about it."

While Flora lugged the coat, muff, and cap to the hallway, Nancy made a woman's quick appraisal of the nest Apostle Cragg had provided for his ninth bride. And there could be no denying he'd set Flora up in comfort, and considerable style. The house was new red brick. She'd guess it had at least five rooms, and with windows one could lift up and down. It had good eastern rugs on the floor, leather settees, and doubtless a real stove in the kitchen. There could be no question that Jonathan Cragg was pleased with the new bride God had given him. And judging from Flora's self-assurance, there was no question that she, if not also pleased with the arrangement, was at least satisfied.

"Sit down, Nan," Flora said from the doorway as she closeted the wraps. "Jonathan left for the church office not half an hour ago. You barely missed him."

For this Nancy inwardly thanked the God she had betrayed.

"But he always comes home for lunch," Flora assured. "And he always eats with one of us sisters."

Nancy, her thinking as bruised and disturbed as her head, made quick and inward resolution not to tarry long enough for any nooning with the man she'd rejected with a well-placed fist.

"Sorry, Flo, but I gotta cut this visit short," she reminded. "Don't plan on me for lunch."

Flora stepped back into the room, and Nancy began taking her own first good notice. She was trim and pretty as any woman could ever be at midmorning, but it was plain to see the apostle had wasted no time in getting down to the fundamental business of his family kingdom. It was a little odd to see a fat belly on Flora.

Flora's appraisal, in turn, was just as sharp and painful. "What's happened to you, Nan?" she asked, walking forward for closer view. "Your head looks like you'd shoved it in a rock crusher. Did a horse tromp you?"

"No," Nancy replied, bitterly. "Aunt Kirstine did."

"Aunt Kirstine?"

"With a stove poker." Self-consciously Nancy touched the bruises. "She's a madwoman. A fiend."

"But why, Nan?" Flora looked genuinely alarmed.

"She says I'm a fildy conniver. A lazy bitch. An apostate. And that I make love to Gentiles behind my fadder's back."

Flora gave her old-time happy chuckle, and flopped down in the leather settee across the room. "Wild dreams—Danish temper. You must have got her real mad." Suddenly she whooped with mirth. "She fixed you up mighty goot! You're a sight, Nan!"

Nancy sidestepped the laugh, and stared grimly. "No wild dream, Flo. I *am* a filthy conniver. I *did* make love to the Gentile—even after Father Corey forbade it. Not only did I make love to him—but I married him."

Flora reared up as though the thought had skewered her. "When?"

"Yesterday."

"Who?"

"Joel Scott."

"Who's Joel Scott?"

"Lord, Flora—you know who! The schoolmaster! My Gentile soldier at the wall! Handsomest Gentile in Zion! Don't try to tell *me* you don't remember!"

She slumped back, and sighed unhappily. "I do remember, Nan. But I'm sorry to hear it."

Nancy stared back in amazement. "You mean that, Flo?"

"Yes, I do mean it." And her look was no liar to the fact. "How *could* you do it? With Father on a mission, and all?"

"Because I love him, that's why!"

"First Cove," she said dismally. "And now you. This will kill Father."

"You don't seem to hear, Flora. I said I *love* Joel Scott."

But she wasn't hearing, and suddenly Nancy was sickened. Here was the very girl who had stood with her on Ammon's wall. The girl who so willingly had ogled Gentiles with her. The girl who, with skirts high, had dropped off the battlement to flirt with the strangers was now literally horrified at the disclosure she'd married one of them.

"You're in trouble, Nan," she was saying. "What are you going to do?"

Nancy's stare was straight and angry. "I'm gonna get the hell out of Zion. That's what I'm gonna do."

The shocker hit home, and Nancy was glad. For, whatever training and conditioning was necessary to the new order, it had not been wasted on Flora. From the pivot of her new vision she could see nothing amiss in marrying the man Nancy had rejected, and sharing this man with eight other women, but apparently she was seeing plenty of things wrong in Nancy's marrying a monogamous Gentile.

"Joel's at Fort Douglas now, trying to wrangle us a ride over the mountains. We're headed back to Boston."

Flora tried to rise, but she looked as though she'd been thumped on the head with a derrick pole. It pleasured Nancy to see her hurt.

"Oh, Nan, *don't* do it," she implored, finally coming to her, and quick to tears. "You're casting yourself into perdition, Nan! I beg of you to talk this over with Jonathan! Promise me you will? Please?"

But by now Nancy was in no mood to promise anything. This had been no happy morning. If even a half sister couldn't wish her well in marriage, if all she could do was piously predict disaster, she wanted none of Lofty Cragg's holy counsel. Wrong or right, she'd married Joel Scott. Wrong or right, she'd love him till she died.

They both finally had sense enough to back away from the impasse, but the gulf between them was wide and deep. Almost hysterically now, Flora started simple chit-chat about the other wives, the families, her clothes, the swirl of Salt Lake society, and her own hopes for the child that was coming to brighten another Cragg home. Nancy could see that all of Flora's old bumptiousness was gone and, in its place, a form of sanctity and assurance that was like an irritant to any Saint in rebellion. If the Cragg households were not one great happy family, Flora, by the casual and affectionate referrals to the other sisters who shared bed and board, was striving valiantly to make it appear so. Flora, the gay and erratic tomboy, had become just another plural wife. She was mouthing the platitudes and doctrinal phrases of Mormondom like every other plural wife in Zion. And by the girth of her belly, she had the appearance which so often went hand in hand with the Principle.

Suddenly Nancy was seeing that Flora was not too much different than Kirstine. Their adaptation to a way of life was at the expense of tolerance toward anything that differed from it. Plural marriage, she now saw, was a matter of utter conversion—because it *had* to be. If a doubt moved, or showed its face—shoot it down. Destroy it. To them, Nancy knew, she was the doubt. Willfully, deliberately, she'd flaunted the deepest sources of their conversion. They were right—and she *had* to be wrong.

It was easy for Nancy to terminate the visit. In that household, as in Aunt Kirstine's, she could never be known as anything less than sin incarnate. But, somehow, as she left, to trudge the snow back to the Salt Lake House, she felt better. Joel, luckily, could do most anything without being bowed down with guilt, or the weight of sin. He even dared snap his fingers at Isaac, and laugh at the gravity of apostasy. Somehow the warnings, and the inner prod of conscience, had little

152

meaning and less sting, when Joel was present, or even in her thoughts. She was humming to herself as she circled Temple Square, and headed back to the refuge and comfort of Joel's arms.

When she returned to the Salt Lake House he was there, as expected. What was not anticipated were visitors. With speed and new assurance she'd swept through the downstairs public rooms, ignored the staring and leering of the Gentile transients in their circle of stale smoke and stale jokes, and had gone up the creaking stairs like a blithe and unfettered spirit. Lifting her heavy coat and skirts for speed, she'd half run across the big social room, and down the narrow hall. At the bedroom door, while she fumbled for her key from the little muff pocket, she'd heard the voices of the men. The clatter of the key in the lock brought Joel to the door. He opened it, smiled at her, and kissed her. Then she saw the visitors—and her heart sank like a rock in an open well. In the tiny room, occupying its only two chairs, were Bishop Earlington, and Apostle Orson Pratt.

Joel's introduction of her to them was superfluous, but he did it anyway, and with nervy grace. "My wife Nancy," he said, with no outward trace of nervousness. "I'm sure you gentlemen know her."

The two men had already risen from their chairs. "Indeed we do," said Bishop Earlington, with no loss of kindliness or godliness.

"I know Brother Corey, your father, extremely well," said Apostle Pratt.

Frightened, and suddenly pale, Nancy nodded to the introduction. The bishop was familiar enough to her, but Apostle Pratt's dark, sharp eyes, probing out from under those shaggy brows, was a conjuration she did not relish. If escape were necessary, she hoped Joel would stay close to the door—and she'd be ready, and behind him.

"Please be seated, gentlemen," Joel was saying, with admirable coolness. "Nancy and I will sit on the bed."

For a moment there was silence—unbearable and painful. Joel again made talk—for Nancy's benefit. "The canyons are snowbound," he said to her. "May be weeks before any sort of express can get out."

"What about the military?" she whispered, in panic.

"That's what I'm talking about, Nan."

"Are the church wagons getting through? Maybe they'll—"

"Nothing's getting through," he said, gently, sadly.

"We wanted to catch you before you left," Bishop Earlington added. "I rode hard to overtake you runaways," and he even smiled as he said it. "I traced you to Salt Lake. And Brother Pratt and I have tracked you down."

And that was it, thought Nancy, trying to decide which one she'd hit first, when Joel signaled their getaway.

"Nan, they want us to return to Ammon," Joel explained.

Nancy was certain now the awful thing had caught up with them. "You going to atone us?" she asked in paralyzing fright. She was remembering the whispered stories of the Reformation. Of the frightening, sin-hunting campaign of her childhood. "You going to spill our blood on the ground for what we've done?" she moaned in terror. "Because, if that's what you're planning—don't let it happen to Joel! I'm the cause of it all! I brought it on! It's me! Can't you understand? It's me!"

Joel's arm was suddenly around her shoulders. He drew her to him. "Please, Nancy," he said. "Don't be frightened. Everything's all right."

"We plan no harm, Sister Scott," the bishop was saying. "We understand. We're not angry."

"We need teachers and educators in Zion," Apostle Pratt explained. "Your husband's been doing a great work in Ammon. We'd hate to see him throw everything up at this time."

And that, precisely, was what Nancy felt like doing—throw everything up. But, in spite of fright and queasy stomach, she felt reassured there'd be no bloodshed, and her panic subsided.

"I had Sister Wellington take over the school until Captain Scott returns," the bishop explained. "Our town so needs your husband. This has been the greatest, most promising year Ammon's ever had. We do wish he'd return. And we don't want to lose you, either, Nancy."

Nancy turned from Joel's embrace, and again faced the visitors. She detected no threat in what they said, and her worst fears subsided. "What about Aunt Kirstine?" she asked cagily. "What about my father? I've married a Gentile, you know."

"We know," said Apostle Pratt. And he smiled with kind forbearance. "Your husband's not the type of Gentile we worry about."

"I'm writing to Isaac Corey," the bishop said. "I'm explaining everything. I hope to prevail on Brother Pratt to write also."

"If necessary, I could have Brother Brigham write a word of counsel, on his return from the south," said Apostle Pratt.

"As to your quarrel with Sister Kirstine," the bishop gently explained, "these things occur in the best of families. It takes patience and forbearance to live in the family kingdom. I'm sure a way can be found to patch up the difficulties."

"She tried to kill me," Nancy muttered in anger. "She went at me with a stove poker."

"Women fights are not uncommon," the bishop said. "As head of Ammon's flock, I hear many things in confidence. Only last month the older wife of one of our most prominent brothers attempted to strangle the younger wife. She nearly did it, too."

"But I'm a daughter. I'm sharing no husband with Aunt Kirstine. And I'm sharing no house with her."

"The same problems prevail wherever women are concerned," the bishop sighed. "Daughters, mothers, plural sisters—women act strangely, and sometimes irrationally. There's no accounting for what they'll do. The only answer is prayer and patience."

"Golly damn," said Nancy. "I'd like to see anyone use prayer and patience on Kirstine! As for me, I'll never again live under the same roof with her!"

"I shouldn't think you'd have to," the bishop chuckled. "You have a husband."

Suddenly Nancy remembered, and she laughed at the absurdity of her worries. Joel laughed; they all laughed. And in one magic moment the air was clean and fresh again.

"I think you two should forget about fleeing Zion," said Apostle Pratt, rising. "At least for a time. Even if you *could* get through the passes, it's darn cold traveling."

"Don't worry about Isaac Corey. Don't worry about Sister Kirstine. Everything's going to be all right." Bishop Earlington also rose from the chair. "I'm going back to Ammon. I'm going to see that you two get a house of sorts to live in. I'm going to suggest, though, that you let me properly marry you."

"In the Endowment House?" Joel chuckled, rising. "For time and all eternity?"

"For time only," the bishop said, walking over and facing Joel. "You're a Gentile, sir. The privilege of eternity you'll have to work for. But you've a good start. And you've married one of Zion's most precious daughters."

"Thank you, Bishop," Joel said, cordially. "I agree with you about Nancy Corey. And I'll ponder this matter of remarriage."

The bishop smiled, and put out his work-calloused hand. "Now, what about coming back to Ammon?"

Joel smiled and gripped the bishop's hand. "What about it, Nan?" he said, turning to her.

But Nancy already was remembering—the funny old walled town, Timpanogos, the valley, the lake, the seagulls, the heady smells of Utah's spring and fall. She remembered the putting away of Martha, and the lonely grave. "Oh, Joel," she said. "Let's go back. Let's *do* go back!"

"Keep the school going." Joel shook Bishop Earlington's hand like a real friend. "Keep the school going. And we'll see you in a few days."

A minute later the apostle and the bishop were gone. Not until then did Nancy remember to peel off her winter cap and coat. And then, at last, with freedom's abandon, she threw herself into Joel's arms. "Oh, you Gentile wonder," she said. "You answer my heart. You answer my every dream. I'll love you and be true to you forever."

Tenderly he drew her to the bed, gently parted her dark hair past the bruises. "My little battle-scarred Mormon half sister," he murmured, kissing her. "How could *any* Gentile keep from loving you?"

XIII

AND SO JOEL AND NANCY SCOTT RETURNED TO AMMON, BUT WITH FAR LESS haste than the night they had fled it. With the necessity and urgency for fleeing Zion removed, at least for a time, Joel relaxed to the green pastures around him, Nancy joined in the mood, and they enjoyed with carefree zest everything that Salt Lake City could offer a nuptial pair in wintertime. The holy secrecy of the Endowment House, available to the much married Mormons was, of course, denied them. But, for this marriage at least, they scarcely felt the loss, and they were able to content themselves with winter rides on Duke and Dolly to the warm springs north of the city, to the lower canyons and foothills of the Wasatches, to Fort Douglas, east of the city, and a westerly excursion to the Jordan River and the great and spectacular dead sea of the Mormon holy land. At night there was dining in the little restaurants about town, all of them fighting for their bit of the general prosperity in the land, and usually presided over by European converts to the Church who, in accepting the Gospel and the "gathering," had brought their culinary skills with them. At night they also joined, as though they had a right to, the brightly lighted balls and gay parties at the Social Hall, and paid two visits to the magnificent new Salt Lake Theater. There, holding hands, and dressed in their new store clothes, they saw *Pride of the Market* and, two nights later, heard the reigning American humorist, Artemus Ward. For two hours Ward held his audience in stitches while he daringly poked fun at Mormonism in general, and their quaint marriage pattern in particular. Like the burrowing gimlet of a Utah bedbug, he drew Mormon blood, but the Saints enjoyed their welts because the scratching felt so good. It was Nancy's first introduction to professional theater. She liked it. There was no question about such things always having been a part of Joel's world.

At night there was the love, the intimacy, and the long talks about their diversely different childhoods; about Joel's voyages to India and to Italy on the Scott family ships; the great war; and the death, in battle, of Joel's younger brother, Edward. Little was said about the young wife who also had died through this time of bloody travail. Womanlike, Nancy wondered about the dead Edna Reavis, but, womanlike, she knew when to refrain from any such intimate prodding. Important thing, to her at least, was that with the wondrous and sudden decision to remain in Zion, they had at last become relaxed, happy, and deliriously in love. And that was the way lovers should be. Before them were problems—but they had a lifetime to talk them out, and to cope with them. Most important of all was, that before they left Salt Lake City, there no longer was any doubt in Nancy's mind that Joel loved her. As for loving him, there just never had been any doubt.

Bishop Earlington, true to his promise, made their return to Ammon easier, and devoid of embarrassment. They had no need to go near the Corey House, or to face again the wrath and censure of Aunt Kirstine. With the help of the now oddly sad and silent Cove Corey, all the personals of Nancy and the schoolmaster had been hauled to Martha's old house, behind the neglected, crumbling walls. Relief Society Sisters, under the bishop's orders and direction, had scrubbed, cleaned, and put in order the old sod-roofed shanty. When Joel and Nancy tied their horses to the hitching post, the first dwelling they were to share in their stormy marriage was ready and waiting for their occupancy—everything familiarly in place, even to Martha's ornate chamber pots. To Nancy, as Joel set her inside the door, the place was as familiarly and intimately real as though Martha herself might enter at any moment, hang her fascinator to the peg, and move into her own remembered pattern of living.

For Nancy there was no stove—only the immense and drafty old fireplace, and the soot and blackness of its hob, spider, and pots. But long ago she'd learned how to make do with such things. Here there were no memories of drudgery, heartache, and death. Here there had been no Kirstine with her hates and Danish babble. Here, behind the old fort walls had been a home since childhood, with every familiar and exciting memory. Bishop Earlington had chosen wisely, and had added depth and meaning to their marriage. She was glad beyond words he had trailed their flight to Salt Lake City. The hand of Almighty God was apparent in the provision and dignity of their return. She loved Ammon—old or new—as she loved Joel. On her knees she would remind God of her gratitude. All her life—in this hut or in a mansion— she would strive with all her woman's heart and love to never let Joel Scott regret his sudden taking her to wife.

The old house was intimate and familiar enough, but the walled town itself would never again be the same. Few families remained from the old pattern. From summer, through fall and winter, every family that could do so had relocated on their allotted acres at the townsite. There, most of them had built their new houses, at least to the point where they could winter in them. Others, contrary to counsel, had dragged their old fort huts to their town lots, and a majority of the remaining dwellings had been plundered of windows, doors, hardware, and anything usable for Ammon's rebirth. Probably the only reason Martha's house had not been plucked clean was the fact that Isaac had used it to house some of the extra hands he'd imported to erect and finish the Corey House.

Townsfolk were finding the old fort a convenient run for their livestock. Cattle, horses, and hogs now tenanted many of the doorless shanties. To Joel Scott, reared in the gentility and ease of the Scott homes in Massachusetts and Maine, it was an experience to see a horse or a cow moodily gazing out the open window of a neighboring house, or, instead of the tinkle of harp or piano, to hear the squeal of pigs, as they fought for comfort and position inside the once trim and useful little cabins.

But Joel and Nancy, in their honeymoon, were not completely alone in their sojourn with the Mormon livestock. The Bringhurst family still tenaciously clung to their log dwelling immediately to the north. Mary Magdalene Mattise, the midwife, still lived alone in her hut, because, in spite of her essentiality to the ever spawning community, the men of the town had so far been too busy erecting their own dwellings to give time to a fresh housing for the old maid. And the door latch to the midwife's old hut still, as always, was freely open. In similar category was Seth Biddle, who was perfectly content to live alone and remain alone in his neat little cabin across the corral. Two or three other families of Saints, of the less ambitious type, and one California-bound Gentile family, wintering in the valley, completed the human population of Ammon's old town. The big meeting house, of necessity, was still used every Sabbath, and one or two nights a week, until more favorable weather allowed the finishing of the new building. This fact alone made living behind the walls something more than just a barnyard sojourn. To Nancy, as she prettied up the cottage, and worked hard at her marriage, it would never have mattered how many horses, cows, or pigs she had for neighbors. To her, in the essential thinking of her people, home was where you made it.

At the gentle insistence of Bishop Earlington, Joel finally consented to another marriage ceremony, although Nancy herself had given the matter no particular thought. Ammon's Saints were not unacquainted with the circumstances behind Nancy Corey's elopement with her Gentile. Kirstine had managed to twist the story enough to indicate that it was she who had gotten the beating from the hands of the irresponsible, wicked Corey daughter. In light of Kirstine's pregnancy, months along and visible, she had little difficulty in enlisting sympathy. Convinced that a miscarriage was inevitable, from the violence of her experience, Kirstine had called in Mary Magdalene Mattise the very morning after Nancy and her Gentile had fled the scene. Either the midwife's herb teas and bed rest were efficacious, or Kirstine's constitution was built well enough to withstand the shock; the baby was saved for a later and more normal delivery.

What Nancy failed to realize was the usual distortion of fact when dozens of female tongues mulled juicily at the shreds of gossip. Absorbed in her own affairs, aloof in setting up a home, and half delirious with nuptial joy, she lived in complete ignorance as to the town's ferment concerning her. But Bishop Earlington, wise to his flock, and patient in the affairs of those he served, had already laid his own long-range plans for the Scotts. Acceptance of the Gentile and his Mormon bride was the earliest part of it. A Latter-day Saint marriage, even though not of the more solemn variety, would be a step in the right direction.

"We're getting married again Sunday afternoon," Joel announced that evening after school.

Nancy, setting the table, looked up in surprise. "We're already married," she said.

"Then we're going to be double-married." Joel stepped behind her, circled her middle with his strong arms, bent his head around her neat-combed black hair, and kissed her on the cheek. "Your bishop is bringing over his Mormon Bible, *Book of Mormon,* or whatever he uses, and you and I are going to be made one in the eyes of the Saints."

Nancy's hands relinquished the plates. She pressed them tight against Joel's fingers, and nestled into Joel's embrace. "We're already one. I'm not asking for any more prayer words."

"Me neither, my little Nan. But the bishop's sure it will do wonders for us. Anyway, there's no loss. And I don't mind. What difference could a few words make?"

"None whatever, Joel. You're my husband. I'm your wife. And that's the way I like it."

Joel squeezed her tighter, and affectionately rubbed his cheek to hers. "Well, this will give me a lot more spiritual leverage, you know. As a Mormon wife, you'll have to behave yourself."

Nancy laughed. "I'll behave myself."

Joel pondered a moment, and then chuckled. "It just occurred to me. This'll probably make me a Mormon, too, will it not?" Then he roared with laughter. "Wait until I tell this to my sis, and the family in Boston!"

But Nancy suddenly found herself pawing out of an icy lake. Joel a Mormon? Good Lord, no! That could mean other marriages. Other women. Then the facts of Mormon life came back to her, and her breath returned. "No, it doesn't make you a Mormon," she said. "And thank heaven."

"How you disappoint me, Nan," he teased, holding tight against her sudden squirming. "I thought it fixed me up in Zion. With the privilege of twenty wives."

"It makes you no Mormon!" Nancy fairly shouted. "You have to *accept* the Gospel—you have to be baptized by immersion! And don't you *ever* say another word about other wives!"

"All right, my little fire ball. Quit squirming. But the bishop is coming over with his marriage book this Sunday. You'll be pretty like a bride. I'll be sad and proper like a groom. You'll bake a Dutch oven full of those molasses cookies for the bishop and our guests. And after they're gone, we'll climb right back into our Mormon bed. Our second honeymoon."

"I'm still on my first," Nancy sighed, happy again. "And, for a schoolmaster, you're a bit crazy. Now, let me loose—and I'll feed you."

"But I'm not finished," Joel persisted. "I haven't reached the morning after, yet."

"And that will be Monday?"

"That will be Monday," Joel repeated. "We shall arise together, like any other double-married couple. But on this coming Monday morning, we shall go to school together. You shall not only be my wife—but you shall be my pupil."

"Oh no," Nancy said in alarm, squirming again. "Not with all those kids. They'd laugh their heads off."

"We promised your father. And I want to patch up some of your educational neglect."

"But we're married now, Joel!"

"That makes the reason more imperative. When we go East, I don't want you at any disadvantage, my dear."

And so Nancy Corey Scott, like Isaac before her, became a part of Joel's school. From the beginning she never was happy about it. For one thing, she discovered that the Joel of the classroom was a different Joel than the man of their intimate hours. In the matter of educating Mormons, he was all business. He never raised his voice, nor flogged a child, but every pupil in his crowded school held him in fearful respect. Here the martinet training of his army career was carried over into another endeavor. At the blackboard, with back to his audience, he could and would spot a mischievous miscreant. Without ever turning around, he would call out the boy's or girl's name, and in stentorian voice, order him or her to the discipline corner—to wear the dunce cap, the "stupid" sign, or to stand on one leg like a stork. His pupils swore he had eyes in the back of his head. They feared him. They stood in awe of him. There was no man in Ammon quite like Joel Scott.

Without recourse to profanity, in a voice packed with suppressed thunder, he could shrivel a troublemaker into limp fright with a vocabulary unmatched in Zion. On the other hand, he had the capacity to delight his audience with word pictures from the other side of the world. Scott ships had taken him to places these simple, ordinary youngsters could never hope to see. He had seen firsthand, and lived through, the bloodiest war in all history. To them he was a strange and different man—a man of tremendous and mysterious background—a man feared, held in awe, and loved. Under this peculiar sort of magic, Ammon's worst hellion quickly became as docile and devoid of fight as a March lamb. Even Nancy, who entered his school with the flippant sureness of her possession, quickly felt the sting of his discipline. Thirty minutes in the corner, on one leg—while the class ogled in amusement and Nancy hated the master's guts for the humiliation—quickly taught her that the business of learning in Joel's school was indeed a business. That night she argued about returning to his school—but she did.

Evenings, under the oil lamp, he helped her with her Latin and English grammar. His austerity and hardness were always left behind at the classroom. Once away from the prying eyes of his pupils, they walked hand in hand along the snowy road to the old fort. At night, in the little cabin, he was the relaxed and attentive Joel of their strangely churned-up marriage. But her career in his classroom was doomed almost from the start. The pregnancy was not long in manifesting itself. As her girth and worries increased, she not only began to fit less handily into a child's desk, but began to look less and less like a youthful prospect for Zion's first free school. By spring, before the school's term was over, even Joel was glad enough to drop her from his classes.

Not that her education stopped. Joel still tutored her, but with diminished enthusiasm. The more important segments of her learning began coming from the fort's lonely midwife, Mary Magdalene Mattise. The very day that Nancy first tossed up her breakfast, she realized the wisdom of more closely cultivating the friendship of Mary Magdalene. And as lonely and rejected as a featherless hen in a barnyard, Mary Magdalene had plenty of friendship to offer. It was only natural that when the wife and mother of the Gentile family at the fort went into the agony of a breech delivery of her baby, that Mary should hammer on the Scott door at one A.M., and beg Nancy to "lend a hand" to the problem. And it was that night that Ammon's midwife really discovered Nancy Scott. Face to face with the rawest of nature's dramas, the girl Nancy did not panic, or throw herself into useless hysterics. She was strong, competent, and unshaken amid the tumult of this painful and prolonged birthing. She went about the task with the calmness of Isaac or Cove assisting nature with the animals. Mary was vastly impressed with the girl.

Like all farm youngsters who had lived close to these things, nature's reproductive process was no mystery to Nancy. Because she herself already realized what was in store for her in the months ahead, she became an apt and willing pupil to anything Mary Magdalene might be willing to teach. In turn, recognizing real timber when she saw it, the midwife decided on that first night that Nancy Scott not only should be her understudy, but in all probability would be the one person to take her place in the birthing of the endless tide of Ammon's babies. In this supposition and near-prophecy, Mary Magdalene was more right than she could have imagined.

But the growing imminence of Nancy's own ordeal made Joel as nervous about the future as a bull with rump scabies. Every plan had been set for their departure East by June at the latest. Intelligent, quick to learn, Nancy had made great headway in her studies. Around his clipped and precise Bostonian diction, and the fact they had not mixed too freely with the townsfolk, Nancy had shed her Deseret drawl, word-murder, and slang to a remarkable degree. On this score at least Joel could present his Mormon bride to the family with some measure of confidence. It was her physical problem which shook him to the marrow. By June Nancy would be as round as a washtub. By June she would be in no fit condition to ride, either horseback or by jolting wagon, across the plains to Nebraska and the railroad.

Nancy knew, by the letters Joel occasionally received, and the worried look he wore for days afterward, that his family had not taken too kindly to his marriage among the despised and rejected Mormons. She knew how desperately he wanted her to make the best possible appearance on the day he introduced her to his own snobbish and genteel circle. Well, now, Nancy Corey Scott would make one hell of an appearance. The competent, lovely little Mormon lass he'd so bragged about by letter, would look like a cow bloated on ragweed, on that Boston day of days. As the weeks dragged along, and she grew ever more fat and misshapen, Nancy began to realize that even Joel must give up any idea of hauling her East. If the Scott family saw Joel this summer, it would be Joel alone.

With Isaac Corey far away in South Carolina, spreading the good tidings of the Gospel to the discouraged and defeated southern people, it was Cove and the older Corey brothers who managed the communal herds and farmlands of the family kingdom. Cove had his weaknesses, but in agrarian affairs he was as tough and sharp as his father. For a Mormon missionary, who traditionally must finance his own proselyting efforts, Isaac was far more fortunate than many who were "called," and who were forced to leave their families in desperate straits for years at a time. With Kirstine tight-fistedly and hard-headedly running the Corey House, and the older sons holding snug to the productive strings, polygamy for Isaac, economically at least, was a resounding success. The Authorities could always point to the Corey pattern as a model for anyone contemplating entering the covenant.

Inside this celestial symphony, of course, there were a few minor discords. Kirstine hated Nancy with enough venom to poison her forever. And Cove, moody, querulous, and wild, was no shining example of how a Saint should live. But in spring the Deseret Telegraph was extended throughout Zion and, through Salt Lake City, linked to the transcontinental lines which were crossing the continent. As promised, the Corey House was chosen for the Ammon link to the church-owned system. A telegrapher's desk, batteries, and rattling instruments were installed under the stairway in the public room, and a young trainee from Salt Lake sent down to man the station. Now, with the wheezy reed organ, the clatter of dishes, telegraph instruments, and Kirstine's Danish vitriol, there was a real cacophany of sound in and about the Corey House. All of Ammon, with the exception of Nancy and Joel, turned out to view the new wonder—which would keep the Saints informed as to the great Gentile world beyond and, through the fount of revelation and inspiration in Salt Lake, tie these same Saints ever closer to God. Nancy wanted to see these wonders as much as any person in Ammon, but, after the discord and the havoc, she dared not face Kirstine. To Joel, who had come through a war, there was nothing new or particularly exciting about a telegraph.

The other dissident problem in the Corey household, and a continuing yeast to the family ferment, was Nancy and her Gentile. Bishop Earlington, probably with help from the Authorities, did a creditable job of smoothing back Isaac's hackles in far-away South Carolina. Although Isaac never quite managed to scrawl a letter to Nancy direct, there was enough information filtering down from Aunt Adah and Aunt Millie and their respective families to indicate that Isaac would probably honor any sort of truce, so long as the Gentile made no attempts to haul a Corey daughter out of Zion. And Nancy, swollen like many another mother in Israel, knew by now how little danger there was from that source.

Outwardly, the Corey family was as placidly at peace as was Ammon itself. In Washington there had been an exciting roundup of the die-hard southerners who had murdered President Lincoln; in the Mormon settlements down toward Dixie, the Lamanites, under Chief Black Hawk, were forgetting their *Book of Mormon* promises by murdering enough Mormons to set the Deseret Telegraph to a real clacking. But in Ammon, spring came in with peace, promise, and beauty. And from there it walked into the real glory of one of those wondrous mountain summers.

With the first thaw, Ammon's Saints were out with horses, scrapers, and manpower to clean and repair every intricate foot of dams, canals, and ditches of their communal irrigation system. Then the plowing of the fields, with the gulls wheeling and diving to the fresh-turned earth, in search of the tender worms and grubs trailed out behind the laboring men and sweating horses. Towering above the awakening valley in the spring was mighty Timpanogos and the Wasatches, white with snow, and rich with the promise of enough precious water to leaf out the crops to harvest. But it was the town itself which really sprang to life. The Social Hall was started; houses were finished; new dwellings got their start. And in the manner of Mormon towns everywhere, the urge toward community beautification became a reality.

Cove himself hauled down from Salt Lake City the hundreds of Lombardy poplar seedlings, which were set out to the rich earth in straight rows up and down Ammon's streets. This particular variety of tree, imported from Europe by the tireless missionaries, seemed to thrive in Utah's soil, and already had become the most conspicuous feature of Mormon towns. The trees, green and fragrant-leaved, grew up straight as the finger of God. Many Mormon dwellings, of adobe, or logs, were ugly. But these became inconspicuous when the poplars were planted. The little Mormon hamlets, so drab and forbidding during winter's metamorphosis, became veritable temples in green when spring and summer broke ferociously upon the land. Each poplar became a spire and a steeple pointing upward to God. And Ammon gave every promise of being a Mormon model to the world.

"Wish I didn't like this valley so much," Joel said, one day in May. "I'm going to miss it when I go home. There's nothing like it in the East. There's nothing like it anywhere."

Nancy had expected him to announce the time of his departure, probably with his summer dismissal of school. But she knew now he must make the trip alone. It was no happy thought, and she did not press him for a decision. With freedom from work, and the opening up of the canyons, he took to riding Duke for days at a time. With his gun, blankets, and his army saddlebags stuffed with grub and sketch books, he'd set out for the mountains. Nancy, familiar enough to the independence of men, worried none about Joel's preoccupation with exploration. Joel, with the vast army experience behind him, was wise and trained to the saddle. It pleasured her to watch the real wonders of Zion grow upon him. The only regret she had was the fact that his child, growing within her, prevented her from joining him in his journeys to the wilds. And then she would remember that, were it not for this child, neither he nor she would have seen this summer in Zion. She knew when to let well enough alone.

Oddly enough, the schoolmaster appeared, outwardly at least, not to chafe at nature's disturbance of his summer plans. His excursions deep into Mormon country were, through the weeks, augmented with trips to Salt Lake City, and conferences with Brigham Young, and those apostles having to do with the sociological and educational aspects of Mormonism. As Nancy suspected, the material he was gathering, the sketching he was doing, and the earnest discussions he was having with Bishop Earlington and the Authorities concerning Mormon doctrine and history had for its purpose the writing of a book. Joel's increasing enthusiasm was contagious. His reputation and prestige in Zion gave him ready access to the intimate information usually denied the many Gentile writers and news correspondents who were continuously trying to pierce the veil of mystery which clouded and shrouded the peculiar faith. Newspapers were filled with the most sensational kind of stories regarding the Zion of the Rockies, with its harems, fanaticism, and sudden and mysterious death to dissenters. Joel's book, when and if written, would be only one of many concerning the American Mahomet and his kingdom of Saints.

"What a place!" Joel would declare. "What color, and drama! What an odd and different experiment in living! There's nothing in God's world can stop this people, because they've learned to work as brothers —because everything they do, they do together—because they stand in solid unity against a hostile world! Look at Ammon! The word's spoken, and, within a year, a new town emerges. I'm glad I came here. It's been an amazing, eventful year to me. Someday the world will know the Mormons for something besides their heresy and their polygamy!"

The pregnant Nancy could agree with Joel that the year had been amazing and eventful. As to his prediction about the future understanding of Mormonism, she was not seer enough to know that Joel would be wrong. The heresy of the Mormons might, in time, be forgotten— but its polygamy, never. She was happy that his sudden preoccupation with the Saints, their ways, and their beautiful land was delaying his decision to return East. For in her heart, intensified by the weight of the baby she was carrying, was the nagging thought that once Joel set foot in his own family land, he might never again return.

"The lore of this strange place is endless," Joel would enthuse, and then he'd tell about some other facet of interest he'd discovered or explored. "Take the Indians—or Lamanites, as you call them. It isn't only you Mormons who have an honorable history!"

"Do you know," he'd happily reveal, "that the Spanish explorer Escalante reached his most northern spot, nearly a century ago, and in this very valley? In his writings the Spaniard noted its beauty, its lake, and lifted the cross of Jesus among the Indians he found here. He called them Lagunas—or Lake Indians. Later you Mormons, coming in from the north, following such trappers as Provost and others, had identical experiences with Escalante—both aesthetically and spiritually. Like Escalante, you Mormons found these Indians quick and willing

166

to accept the bounty that went along with baptism. It was only when you Saints went industriously to work damming all the streams for irrigation, and fencing all the land for agriculture, that the Indians regretted their ready acceptance of God's new plan. And when Walkara shed his Sainthood, spat in the direction of Brigham, and swept his barbaric cavalry into the Mormon settlements, you Mormons learned in one bloody jolt what these valley Utes could be like when the promises of God and the *Book of Mormon* failed to cancel out what they considered a rape of their *own* holy land. Towns like Ammon 'forted up' in a hurry, as you well remember. The wars came. But they were one-sided. The Utes were battered, and Walkara died. Not until then did the Indians learn the real point of the thing. When they did, peace came again to this valley."

"Golly damn, you know more about it than I do," Nancy would exclaim, a little proudly.

"There are lots of things about it you probably don't know," Joel had boasted. "Remember the place where you had that picnic at the lake? The place where I set a blue bonnet to your worried head? Where you knocked a certain apostle into the middle of the new dispensation?"

"How can I ever forget it?"

"Well, that spot's very close to the place where Escalante set up his altar to evangelize the Lagunas. And, do you know something else?"

Nancy could only shake her head.

"There are literally mountains of coal and iron ore in the Wasatches. Nature has placed water, coal, and iron within mating distance. What's coming is inevitable. Our beautiful valley will almost certainly, someday, be ruined. In that far day, when our nation becomes of age, and these things are badly needed, the shores of Utah Lake will be dotted with iron foundries and steel mills—maybe on the very spot I delivered the bonnet. I don't know why Brigham sends his miners and foundry men to Dixie to get their iron. It's all here—because I've seen it. But, in that day when this place is really commercially discovered, our sparkling alpine valley will be fouled with smoke and stinging vapors; the gentle and serene lake will be polluted with the poisonous excretions from these steel mills and smelters; the fish life will die; and the Lamanites will vanish. I'm only a Gentile—and not generally known as a prophet. But there, Nancy, is my prophecy for today."

"It's a blessing," Nancy sighed, "that I can't see so far and dismally into the future."

While Joel studied Utah, and the ways of the Saints, Nancy studied firsthand Mormondom's most important and prolific by-product—

babies. In her trips with Mary Magdalene she grew accustomed to the animal-like wails and anguished howls of Mormon mothers in childbirth. For her no longer was the stark picture of water and blood a thing of horror. Under the midwife's competent tutelage, no longer was she afraid of the squirming, gasping ball of red and bloody flesh as nature forced its new life from the womb. After not too many trips she could, without nervousness, hold and help a baby as it squirmed its first way into air and life. She learned, from Mary Magdalene, how to tie the umbilical cord in two places, cleanly sever it, and how to dispose of the afterbirth. And after the birthing was over, she many times stayed on with the weak and weary patient, to help keep the child alive until strength came to it and to the mother. "You're a natural for this thing, and born to it," Mary Magdalene would compliment. As for Nancy, she was gaining a more certain and more abiding interest in this essential skill than from all the book learning and wise observations Joel could cram into her.

For children were born so long as there were love and mating between man and woman. Only squaws had the animal fortitude to tend to the essentials of their own painful deliveries. Mormon women needed help, just as she herself would be needing help within a matter of months. When she was younger, and a good deal stupider, she, like many another person in Ammon, had looked on Mary Magdalene as a queer and rejected old spinster. Now, at last, she was knowing this remarkable woman for what she truly was. Take away Mary Magdalene from Ammon, and what then? Bishops and apostles might be necessary and important healers to the spirit, but Mary Magdalene's ministry was twice as essential, though far less appreciated. In the time of woman's deep and lonely ordeal, Mary was there, lending courage through the pain and blood, tending competently to the basic essentials of life's greatest miracle. She held no degrees from medical school, her training had come from life's own experiences, tutelage of other midwives, occasional contact with real doctors, and the basic secrets learned from having lived among the Paiutes and Utes. These squaws, even Nancy knew, could still teach many a fact of life and healing to the white man, were he willing only to take the time to pause and listen.

Mary Magdalene, because marriage had been denied her, was, according to Mormon theology, basically shut off from greater rewards of eternal progression and the celestial glory. Since she was not married for time and all eternity, and could not reign a queen in a family kingdom, her position in the great hereafter must of necessity be that of a ministering angel. And that, Nancy was agreed, was a status this competent and useful woman already possessed on earth. Let the pains come, and the calls go out, and Mary Magdalene was there. And in that far day of judgment, if any human from Ammon deserved a just reward, it would be Mary Magdalene Mattise.

Through the strange months of her new life behind the wall, Nancy became an apt and willing pupil to this midwife. More than that, she learned to love and appreciate this good woman. She wanted God to bless her for her patience and for her skills. The day was not too far off when she herself would be desperately needing Mary. It was comforting to have her for a neighbor.

"About going East, I've decided to wait until next year," Joel announced one day in August. "By that time you'll be back in shape again, and we'll have our baby to show off in Boston."

"Our son," Nancy corrected.

It was a warm twilight suppertime, and every door and every window of the little cabin was open to catch what was left of the lake breeze after the high adobe walls had stolen their share of it. Nancy was not at all surprised by the decision. Joel was so engrossed in Zion you couldn't have pried him away.

"Our son," Joel finally corrected, helping himself to a slice of Nancy's fresh-baked bread. "I'm glad you know with such certainty, because a son would be very nice."

Nancy watched for the first boil on the coffee pot. The new stove, where sat the pot, was her pride and joy. Joel had traded a California-bound immigrant out of it, and shipped it down from Salt Lake. He'd erected it by setting it up on the big hearth, and elbowing its stack up the cavernous chimney. Except that Nancy kept her treasure immaculately blacked, it stood out in the room like an abscessed finger, and the strangest sort of concession to modernity. She arose from her chair, and patted Joel on the shoulder. "I'm as certain as I live it'll be a son. Mary Magdalene says it kicks and tumbles just the way a boy baby always kicks and tumbles." She left the table, and drew the coffee pot to a hotter spot on the stove's circled lids—beneath which burned a real coal fire.

"By next year at this time, he'll be husky enough to travel," Joel said. "And maybe by then they'll have gotten the railway through to Utah. Meantime, I'm going to play schoolmaster another winter. And settle myself down to writing some good things about you Mormons." He helped himself eagerly to one of the fried mutton chops from Nancy's new covered platter.

"That'll be a switch," Nancy opined. "As a Gentile you're *supposed* to write *mean* things."

The little cabin, so rich in memory to Nancy, was by now arranged and furnished in a way that would have delighted Martha. Besides the stove, Joel had a desk, and Nancy had new chairs, dishes, and utensils in plenty, and a real dresser with oval mirror for the bedroom. These Joel had no trouble getting in Salt Lake. The summer's California-bound travelers, in order to lighten wagons for the long haul over the Sierras would sell, for any piddling sum, the valuables they had hauled all the way from the East. Many of them, unable to find purchasers, just dumped their excess loads on Emigrant Square, and drove off without them. Salt Lake homes were being well furnished with treasured possessions of the Gentiles. But the old fort cabin, for Joel and Nancy, still had plenty reminders of the past. They still used the immovable bed, once sacredly focal to Isaac and his third wife. The floor of the cabin had remained earthen, and Nancy lived in a sort of suppressed terror lest some heavy storm might wash more of the roof mud down on the neat and refurbished interior. Kerosene lamps now supplanted the candles of her younger days and, above the desk where Joel worked so much at night, he'd fashioned a swinging hook to hold the essential light in any desired position. Because of the heavy cost of freighting, kerosene was expensive, and at times very scarce. But the wick lamps did not use a great quantity of the fuel for their clear, unsputtering flames, and the Scotts were frugal about this luxury.

But outside the cabin, the old fort was a mess. With the building of the brick chapel in New Ammon, and abandonment of the meeting house to decay and the scavengers, the old walled town's last community tie with the townsfolk vanished. More than ever were the remaining dwellings plucked for whatever they were worth in Ammon's new program of building. Into the shells of these once human dwellings moved the livestock that was taking over the fort. The big cracks in the walls were deeper, and more eroded with another year of weather. Where once was neatness, and the orderly and interesting voices of humanity, now there was only disorder and chaos, with the squeals and grunts of swine, and the bleats and bells of sheep and cows to shatter the memories of what once had been.

Besides Joel and Nancy, a few families still tenaciously clung to the habitable dwellings, including Seth Biddle, Mary Magdalene Mattise and the Bringhursts. But Joel swore that this year would positively end their tenancy at Old Town. And since the end of the school year would mark the time of their trip East, it was not too difficult to laugh at their predicament, and make the best of their brief sojourn with the animals.

But as fall advanced, and Nancy's time came more imminently near, their problems multiplied. Still, Mary Magdalene Mattise, Ammon's only competent obstetrical help, was but a stone's throw across the quadrangle, so Nancy refused to worry. Anyone facing a birthing could ask for no better, safer place to live.

Ammon's fall crop of babies was never heavier. Zion was growing with a velocity that would have delighted the Prophet. Plural wives were reproducing at a rate that would quadruple the population in less than a decade, and the town midwife was continuously on call guiding new Saints into mortality, and tying the cords that would set them loose to their destiny. In these busy hours Mary would have appreciated the competent help of Nancy Scott. But Nancy's help, of necessity, dwindled as fall advanced, her own abdomen swelled, and she felt the imminency of her own time.

So Nancy drank the vile and bitter herb potions which Mary Magdalene insisted were essential to easy delivery, resting occasionally in Mary's neat little hut, to listen with whetted interest to such clinical experiences the midwife might have time to recount between calls. Some of them were sobering and frightening, and many a time Nancy toddled her fat self across the smelly public corral, dodging sheep, pigs and cows toward home, and wondering if her first child would come out straight and natural. There was always the thought that it might be one of those messy, painful sessions that took all the skill of Ammon's midwife and, more often than not, ended in the death of mother and child. And then there were the worries of whether or not she ever *would* return to the slender woman in whom Joel had taken such fussy pride. Mary Magdalene had a Paiute tea that was supposed to guarantee a shapely return. It was brewed from unspeakable ingredients, and was potent enough to physic a woodpecker, but Nancy was desperate enough to take it regularly, and as prescribed. And always there was the wondering over the future, that nagged and disturbed.

That Mary Magdalene held the pivotal balance in this important phase of her life, Nancy willingly acceded. That she was only one of many women who clung to the same thread of dependency was brought forcibly home when Cove Corey, shaken and frightened, made those night visits to the two shanties in Old Town.

Nancy answered the banging of the door, and was relieved and happy at sight of the familiar face of Cove. It had been weeks since they'd had a word with one another, and always the wild and interesting Cove was welcome.

"It's my third trip, Nan, to Old Town," Cove said breathlessly. "Aunt Kirstine's in a bad way! Her baby's coming! And I can't find that goddamned midwife anywhere between the mountains and the lake."

"Mary was home this afternoon," Nancy said. "I myself talked to her."

"Well, she's gone now."

"Probably had a call. Come in, Cove. You look real shaken. Joel's here."

"I *am* shaken. Shaken as hell! Mother's at Kirstine's. I went back. Told 'em old Mary was gone. Kirstine's bellowing like a steer with a running iron up its ass. They said get the hell back, and find the midwife. I tried again. Went back and told 'em there was no midwife to be had. They said for crissakes then, to get *you*. That *you* were handy at birthing. So, get your things, Nan. This is *real* trouble!"

"But Cove, I can't!" Nancy protested. "You *know* about Kirstine and me."

"I know that Kirstine's having a baby!" Cove roared from the doorway. "And I know that you're the only other person in this valley that knows a goddamned thing about these things!" He looked at her angrily. "Don't waste time, Nan! Climb into this buggy with me! You want Aunt Kirstine to die?"

"No, of course not."

"Then grab your stuff. It may be too late!"

"Let me ask Joel, first," Nancy begged.

"To hell with Joel. He's only the schoolteacher. *My mother's alone with Kirstine!*"

But Nancy, knowing Aunt Millie would act wisely in any emergency, took the time to walk over to the table and confront Joel.

"I heard what Cove said," Joel answered without being asked. "Forget bygones, Nan. It's best you go."

"Then watch for Mary," Nancy said. "Quick as she arrives, tell her where I am—and tell her to get up to the Corey House as fast as she can."

And so, on that night, Nancy made the trip to the Corey House—a trip Mary herself could never have made any quicker. She was frightened and nervous, as Cove laid on the whip, and the buggy careened along the dusty road toward this one more errand to a bedside.

This was one birthing she gladly would have left to Mary Magdalene. But nature took no cognizance of priority, convenience, or personal feelings when it decided to dump a child into the world. Kirstine, in the savagery of the ordeal, needed help. She needed it desperately. In

172

the next awesome hour there could be no time for petty hates and wounded feelings.

While Aunt Millie looked on in amazement at Nancy's cool-headed competency, and followed without protest every order she gave, Kirstine delivered, by lamplight, and in less than two hours, her second child. It was a beautiful little girl; plump and dark-headed.

"Father Isaac will be proud of this child," Nancy said wearily.

Aunt Millie folded Nancy to her ample bosom, and cried as though it were a wake instead of a successful birthing. "Father Isaac will be proud of this other *child!* You're a marvel, my dear. Simply a marvel! What in the Lord's world would I have done without you?"

Kirstine, weak, and still in pain, smiled feebly. With hands creased and red from the bed ropes, she squeezed Nancy's arm. The tears that were in her pale eyes could not have sprung from hate. "Thank you, Nan," she sighed.

Nancy peeled off the gore-stained house apron, and smiled proudly. "Now I've another half sister," she said.

When Mary finally arrived, the ordeal was completely over, but with professional scrutiny she examined the mother, and she examined the now wailing child. "Couldn't have done any better myself," she grudgingly admitted.

To Nancy that was the highest possible compliment. And suddenly, if it weren't for the lively load in her own womb, she'd have turned a handspring with relief and joy. It pleasured her a lot, to have been this help to Aunt Kirstine.

Slowly, week by week, her own time gradually grew nearer. As to her monthly tally, she must have been a little muddled. She'd counted the child's arrival about the second week in November. In this fate proved her wildly wrong. Apparently she'd caught her trouble from the first shot in Joel's locker—for her drawbridge of destiny came down with a thud on that last week in October.

Thinking she had plenty of time, she hadn't begun to get her baby's possibles laid by and ready, her confinement necessities at arm's reach, or had even alerted Mary Magdalene. It was a nippy, cold Thursday morning. Joel was at school, and she was at the ironing board slicking up the starched things with the new set of sadirons he'd bought her for her seventeenth birthday. The pains, at first, were only whispers, and she paid them no mind as she hummed at the task of making neat and pretty Joel's shirts and the aprons to hang so precariously about her swollen belly.

She put the irons back to the stove top, and sat down a minute, as the pains hit her with a new and methodic sharpness. This helped; and, when she felt better, she went back to the ironing board. But when, in less than thirty minutes, the dam broke, and she suddenly found herself in an unspeakably watery mess, she knew it for what it was. Thank God Joel wasn't on hand to see her in this repulsive phase of the confinement. But time was now as short as the warning. Pains had started in real earnest—sharp, rhythmic, regular. She hurried into the bedroom and, grunting in her misery, stripped everything off the bed but the bottom sheet. Over this she spread the oilcloth Mary Magdalene had given her, and tightly pulled over it another sheet. From the dresser she hauled out the length of rope she'd hidden, and passed it through the foot slat of the bed, with the two knotted ends close enough for her to grab to and hang on to when the time came, and Mary Magdalene was on hand. Pains were now hitting her with enough cringing misery to bring groans to her lips, and she knew the imminent necessity of getting the midwife without further delay.

With what speed was left her, she went to the cabin door, opened it, and looked out to the bright cold day outside. The animals stared stupidly at her from their stance in the icy wallows of the big corral. She saw no one—human, that is. And the door to Mary's house, across the square, was closed.

"Mary-e-e-e!" she howled, exactly as Martha once had howled for her. "Mary-e-e-e!"

A chorus of ba-a-s came back from the sheep. And that was all.

"Mary-e-e-e!"

Again the sheep answered—as though hers was the one and only voice. And suddenly the pains hit her again—sharp and positive. She grew panicky.

From the door hook she grabbed her coat, and drew it frantically around her wet and soggy skirts. A second later, moaning with every step, she started across the square. Dodging the animals, she staggered toward the most important source of help in her life.

A hammering at the door of the midwife's hut made quickly real the reason her shouts had failed to nail attention. Again Mary was not home. Again Mary had failed her. Again Mary was attending some other woman in travail. And then Nancy remembered it was Thursday morning. It was the morning of the twice-a-week mail from Salt Lake. The few tenants of the Old Town were patiently and hopefully awaiting the mail stage at Ammon's new post office. Another stab of pain crumpled Nancy's legs. She had no control over the howl of anguish that came from her lips. And exactly as she'd so often noted in her own barnyard research, it was answered by the animals from the old corral, and with the barks of dogs, as though they were answering some distant wail of a coyote. It was no new thing to Nancy, this rapport of animals to the moan of pain or fear. Frightening thing was that it was *her* voice that agitated them. That in this moment, of all time, it was her to be alone with the beasts.

On her knees she reached up to the big wooden latch handle of the midwife's door. It gave with her lift, and the door moved open with her weight. And then, too, she remembered that Mary Magdalene Mattise made a fetish of no locks to her door, and, in this moment she was grateful. For, to the women of the little Mormon world around her, Mary Magdalene's door was never bolted, night or day. For the men of Mary's Mormon world, it was also unbolted, and Mary likewise had never ceased to make this fact known. But, so far as anyone knew, only the mothers in Israel had availed themselves of Mary's open heart and open door.

Inside, the room was still warm from Mary's breakfast fire. Nancy crawled across the hard earth floor toward the rocking chair near Mary's beloved reed organ. Another stabbing, paralyzing pain, that tore downward at her very guts, pressured out another shrieking moan. This pain changed Nancy's mind entirely. The moment of truth was here. Pains were too frequent now. She hadn't a chance of ever getting back to her own cottage.

"My baby's coming," she groaned and whimpered, clawing the earth floor with her fingernails. "God help me! *Oh, God help me!*"

With the next moment of relief, she turned her crawl to the other little room, and Mary's bed. Another pain laid her low before she could reach it. But even while the animals outside were answering her basic howl of life itself, she was moving once again toward the bed. And when she clutched its side, and raised herself to it, she saw its neatness; the circle-blocked quilt, tucked in at the corners; the pillow, rolled and covered.

There was no time to strip the bed, or find a tug rope. By the time she could crawl to the bed top, the pains had turned her into a howling, moaning beast. Frantically she tore at her skirts. Insane, panting and whimpering like an animal, she ripped apart her muslin shift and pantalettes. And for the next hour, like any Paiute squaw in a sagebrush retreat, Nancy Scott fought at the barrier of life itself.

Half conscious, half insane with pain, she suffered in solitude the bloody travail known only to the females of the animal world. It was odd the way those flashes of thought came in the lucid intervals between the spasms of her pain. There was Flora, whose boy baby had come with the help of one of Salt Lake's eminent physicians. They'd already christened him Jonathan Isaac, publicly, and in a Mormon church service. And in the nepotism of the hierarchy, his future as a leader of the Saints was already assured. She remembered Martha's telling of her own birthing—in a covered wagon on Emigrant Square, and in its own circle of heartache and broken promise. But, this birthing of Nancy Scott's son was as barbaric and fundamental as a calving in a barnyard. Through chattering teeth she cried to God for help. In between pains she shrieked for the closer, more human aid. Raging, panting, moaning, she cursed in lively fashion the vagary of fate that had taken Mary Magdalene away at the very time she was needed most.

But in the end Nancy Scott was her own midwife. In the loneliest, most helpless hour of her life, she was both mother and physician to her first child. But in doing so, she made a mess of Mary's bed and round-blocked quilt. Never, in all her lifetime, would she ever forget those minutes when she staggered around the cabin, clutching her gasping, quivering, bloody child in her hands, as she hunted among the midwife's personals for the surgical shears and thread to sever the umbilical cord.

Yet somehow she did it. And when the pain and terror had simmered down to weakness, she rolled the round-blocked quilt into a bloody ball, and dropped it off the foot of the bed. She found a clean quilt in Mary's chest, and pulled it over herself for the warmth she was needing. And wrapped in the tattered remnants of her own woolen skirt, was the son she'd delivered—alone and unaided.

XIV

MARY MAGDALENE WAS ANYTHING BUT CENSORIOUS OVER NANCY SCOTT'S fouling of the roost that eventful day. In fact she seemed quite proud of the fact that a baby had actually been born in her bedroom. It was more than she'd ever dared hope for herself.

It was Sister Bringhurst, on friendly call, who discovered Nancy Scott atop Mary's peeled-down bed. But Mary was only minutes behind her. The bloody quilt was burned, of necessity, and in memory of Nancy's second successful baby delivery in Ammon. Of the hundreds that were to follow, this one would forever hold the most vivid recollection in her memory.

But the competent Mary Magdalene took it all in stride, and was vastly pleased. "You're doing a real neat job of these things," she smilingly reminded.

"The first one was necessity," Nancy declared. "But this one was murder." Nancy touched a weak and trembling hand to young Joel Arthur. "But I guess he was worth it."

The baby may have been born at the wrong time, and in the wrong bedroom, but the schoolmaster likewise didn't seem to mind. After the initial shock of having to retrieve his wife and infant from Mary's house, and the frightening news that Nancy had faced the ordeal alone and unaided, Joel had settled down to the urgent necessity of getting used to being a father. It was no easier for him than for any other husband faced with a first child, and all the exigencies that go with it. There were the wailing nights, and the sick nights, which cut inexorably into his writing time, his sleeping time, and the efficient conduct of a classroom. There was the constant wonder of all first fathers at the discovery that the rubbery, red organism known as an infant, was little more than an animated funnel into which food was poured. This food, in turn, after going immediately through it, must be caught at the bottom end with equal constancy and diligence. He learned, as all first fathers do, that nature, in order to assure preservation of the species, had made the wail of the infant the most irritating and commanding of all sounds to the human ear. Night or day, it was impossible to let this sound go unheeded.

Nature had also made the human baby the ugliest and most helpless thing known to the animal kingdom. Born without hair, adornment, or any single point of natural beauty; without reasoning or intelligence, save the one instinct to suckle a teat, and a raucous bleat to indicate hunger or discomfort, it was certainly no thing of usefulness or charm. But from the red new-old face, which resembled nothing more than a cross between a sun-dried apple and a baboon's butt, Joel, like most first fathers, read from it new volumes and new wonders.

"He has your nose, and your blue eyes," Nancy would happily declare. "And that makes him a lovely child."

"He has your black hair and, I think, your warm and impish smile,"

Joel would say, gazing fondly down into the puckered countenance of his first-born. "And you said it would be a boy all along."

"Of course. I never for a minute doubted it."

And in the manner of all young couples caught in the inexorable pattern of the reproductive process, they imagined, dreamed, and told their little lies and compliments one to another, as mother and child slowly gained the strength to face the task of living.

In all this Nancy seldom wanted for help. Busy as Mary Magdalene was, her attention and interest in the child never waned. She'd failed to help birth it, but the child had come to life in her own room. To Mary this was more than a favorable omen. It made her a sort of Mormon godmother and guardian angel to the child. Young Joel Arthur's health and well-being would never want for vigilance or care.

And quickly as Itchy had heard of Nancy's dramatic confinement and new child, she'd deserted Kirstine at the Corey House to hurry over to Old Town and offer her help. She'd made up her mind to aid Isaac Corey's daughter. She intended to stay. And that was that.

"But Itchy?" Nancy had protested. "What will Aunt Kirstine do without you?"

Itchy had shrugged. "Who cares? She's too bossy. I like you. I always like you."

"But there's so much work to be done at the hotel! Aunt Kirstine can't do it all. She has the babies. You know that, Itchy."

"I know that. So I send another Indian woman. Friend of mine. She'll not like that Danish woman. But she'll work."

"There's really not much to do here," Nancy had argued guiltily. "I'll be as strong as papa's ox in a few days."

"No matter. I stay. I stay because I like you."

And stay she did.

Itchy spent nights with her foster family, but every day, at dawn, she was at the Scott cabin in Old Town. She milked the cow, slopped the pig, cleaned the house, and took care of the washing and ironing. To her endless delight, Nancy occasionally let her bathe the child. But such sudden idleness was a new thing to Nancy, and it taxed her ingenuity to find things to do.

Occasionally, while Itchy tended house, and watched with vigilance over the baby, Nancy would take off with Mary Magdalene in the midwife's ancient carriage, for one of the shorter sick calls. Always she timed these jaunts so there would be no neglect for little Joel, and with the self-reminder she must be back in time for the return of big Joel from the daily grind of the classroom.

And as the weeks advanced into deep winter there were other things at work pertaining to the future well-being of her child.

"Bishop Earlington says, in Zion, you just can't give a child a name, like you would a puppy dog," Joel chuckled one evening. "He says our baby should be christened, in church."

"That's true," Nancy agreed. "But I thought we were going to do it when we get to Boston."

"Probably will," said Joel. "In Boston I'll give you the choice—Unitarian or Congregational. But for the present, we're living in Mormondom. And when in Mormondom, do as the Mormons do—a Mormon christening. The bishop says you're now a mother in Israel. And when I think about your talents in brooding and birthing children, I just have to agree. Shall we bundle up our little waif this coming Sunday? Shall we take him to the new meeting house? Shall we get him prayed over in public, put his name in the Mormon book of judgment, and, just generally show him off to Ammon?"

"If you say so, Joel, I'd be happy and proud to," Nancy agreed. "I'd hoped you'd somehow see it this way."

"They're finding me the most amiable Gentile that ever hit this town," Joel laughed. "Half the people now call me Brother Scott."

"You don't object?"

"Hell no! I like it! Makes me feel homey and accepted."

To an orthodox Mormon, in Ammon Ward, the sight of an unbaptized Gentile assisting in the "blessing" of a child was an uncommon thing to say the least. The priesthood, of course, was represented by Bishop Earlington and one of the elders from the congregation, but Joel Scott clutched with them his fretting infant as the three men stood in the sacred circle, and the bishop intoned the prayer and the blessing that would officially mark his name in heaven, and set it imperishably upon the roll of the Saints.

After it was finished, tiny Joel Arthur was handed back to the proud Nancy. His father, a little nervous and shaken by the experience, joined her on the bench, to witness the naming and blessing of others of the latest crop of young Saints. After this came the confirmation ceremonies for those who had been baptized in the weeks previous. This prayer, on the heads of the candidates, was the final act to officially make them members of the Church. Most of the new members were children at or near the age of eight years, the accepted Mormon time of first accountability, although there were a few adults in the crop also entering the faith through this one and only door.

Nancy, as she jogged her baby into the slumber necessary to wait out

179

the long and tedious service, could no longer remain blind to the proselyting efforts the bishop and the ward brethren were using on behalf of her husband. The fraternal warmth, the pleasant conversations, the patient explanation of doctrine and history at the least sign of Joel's interest in weeks past were proof enough to Nancy that the bishop had great hopes of eventually bringing this Gentile schoolmaster into the fold. All this, of course, would have pleased Isaac Corey mightily. It did not exactly please Nancy. To fight it would be a betrayal of her faith. To abet it might hasten the day when even marriage to a Gentile was no longer assurance against the possibility of polygamy. It was a strange predicament for a female Saint to be in. Wisest course seemed to be to keep one's mouth shut, watch the signs, and rely on Joel's great fund of common sense.

After the confirmations came the sacrament, of broken bread and water, prayed over by the young "priests" of the Aaronic Order—on week days Ammon's farm boys of adolescent age. As a Saint in good standing, and without too many venial sins on her conscience, Nancy partook of the cup and the bread when they were passed to her. She was not surprised when Joel refused these holy tokens of the blood and flesh of Christ, served up in the new Mormon meeting house. She glanced across the aisle to where sat Isaac's wives and most of their children. Kirstine had loyally taken herself away from the press of duty at the Corey House. She had said little to Nancy since the night of her confinement, and seemed nervous and ashamed in her presence. As their eyes met again in curiosity, Kirstine smiled acknowledgment and turned her head. And, Nancy noted, she too partook of the sacrament.

Then came the time for the "testimonies." For another long hour Ammon's brothers and sisters in the faith arose to their feet and haltingly, and occasionally tearfully, told of the goodness of God to them personally, the miraculous healings, the visitations from "the other side," and their unshaken conviction that the labor of their faith and hand was indeed "the work of the Lord in these the last days" and that "Joseph Smith, the martyred one, was truly a prophet of the Living God." Others told of having seen with their own eyes one, two or even the full trio of the Three Nephites. Nancy had already explained to Joel the presence of these three bearded men, from ancient days, who had never tasted death. Their mission was to wander the earth until the millennium, strengthening faith, and doing little acts of charity wherever the need might arise. They would appear, leave a silver dollar, or a loaf of warm bread to a destitute Saint, and even had been known to miraculously plow a Saint's field when his horses were sick or strayed. After these acts of mercy, the Nephites would vanish as suddenly as they appeared. But from the stories one heard on every hand, and the testimonies so tearfully told in fast meeting, they were probably the three busiest men in Zion.

After the meeting, Aunt Adah and Aunt Millie came over to talk to Nancy and to take a peek at her first-born. They, with most of Nancy's half brothers and half sisters, were friendly enough, and Nancy proudly showed off to them the most beautiful baby in the world. Kirstine, making a fast and nervous exit from the church, never came near enough to either bark or bite. From the Coreys Nancy learned that Isaac was well, and laboring diligently to save a lost and wayward world. She gleaned that he was not too angry over her marriage to the Gentile, and that he, like the bishop, had great hopes that this fine and valuable man would eventually join the Church. Nancy knew, of course, that all this would be changed with next summer's trip to Boston. But that was far away, and the present good thinking on Joel was pleasurable. Joel, through all the family confab, had been monopolized by Bishop Earlington and some of the leading elders of the town. Nancy could see they were working hard.

In the carriage, on the way back to Old Town, Nancy was silent a spell, while she hugged the sleeping baby to her, and mulled things over in her mind.

"How did you like that long-drawn-out fast meeting?" she asked at last.

"Interesting," Joel said, apparently also deep in thought.

The winter road was a sad mixture of mud, snow, and slivery ice. The slipping and slithering of the buggy made it a problem to hold the baby so he might stay asleep. But the sun was out, and it was not too cold.

"It made me right proud to see you standing up with our son in the naming."

"I'm proud they asked me. It was a friendly gesture."

"But golly damn, those testimonies! I thought they'd *never* get through telling how good the Lord had been to them."

"Oddly, I felt like rising to my feet and saying the same thing. It's been a strange and wonderful year, Nan. And the same Lord who blesses all has blessed me. Look at that little rabbit you're holding, and you'll know what I mean."

Nancy did look down at the little rabbit, bundled tight and warm in the new christening comforter. The tiny face twisted hungrily. "I know what you mean," she said.

They thumped and rattled along the old road while Nancy also silently counted her blessings. It *had* been a good day.

"But didn't you get a bit wearied of the long meeting?" she persisted.

"Oh, it was long all right. It couldn't help but be long, because the people had a lot to say. And it's the saying that's important. Remarkable that, without a trained and paid clergy, a faith of such vital strength could be evolved and nurtured. I'm impressed with your religion, Nancy. I see in it a democratic thing, a faith of the common man, a drawing of strength from one another, the brotherhood of man truly at work. Other denominations have confessionals, where a man can whisper his sins to a priest, be forgiven, and gain back his strength. The Saints stand up like men, and tell it to one another. They may stumble in their words, and yaw like a clipper in a squall while they tell it—but tell it they do. I've heard a thousand polished sermons in my life—but I gained more this morning than I've ever gained from any of them, or all of them. You Mormons have a strange religion, Nan. There's an indefinable, mystic something about it. I'm impressed. I'm really impressed."

"I can see the bishop's sure been working on you," Nancy sighed. "He sure has." And she again fell into thoughtful silence.

In spite of the fact that Nancy had Itchy to help her through most of the winter and, as a schoolmaster's wife her household chores were not nearly so large as those families who operated farms and ranches, she still found herself as busy as most other women in Ammon. An interested and willing understudy to Mary Magdalene in the all-essential birthing process, she was more and more being recognized as a cool and competent nurse and midwife. There were occasions when nature decided on simultaneous confinements in and about Utah Valley and, while Mary Magdalene attended a woman in one area, Nancy was literally hauled by nervous and hysterical husbands to the bedside of their wives, and, like that night at the Corey House, forced into the necessity of attending these births unaided by the more competent and experienced Mary.

With the breeding and birthing in Ammon now at an all-time high, it was comforting to the townsfolk to know that the community actually had two midwives. So, through no particular efforts of her own, Nancy Scott grew into the profession which was to endear her to her generation in Zion. Mary Magdalene's fee for the service was five dollars—cash or usable goods. At first Nancy was reluctant to take pay for willing help, but Mary, fearful of a degeneration of an honorable profession, was vociferously insistent that Nancy accept her pay without apology.

"Even a veterinarian gets paid for birthing a colt," Mary would say. "If these many-married men can afford to get their women in the family way—let 'em pay a little to get 'em out of it. If they haven't got cash money, take molasses, flour, or wood. But be sure you get your full five dollars' worth. They'll not love you any the less for a willing taking of what's rightfully coming to you. Only when there's no man or money in sight, do you do it free. Them are the times when you rack up your pay in heaven."

Joel's great plan to give her a more general education became progressively more sporadic as he hugged himself nights to his own studies and writings, and it became increasingly clear that Nancy's time and interests more closely favored Israel's mothers in distress. He admitted she was a good reader; sharp, and quick to learn. Latin and the classics were beyond her, and her Mormon twang and slang were painful to a Bostonian—especially in the beginning of their marriage. But, by the twin process of Joel's getting used to it, and Nancy's own improvement through close association with an educated man, the verbal irritants gradually subsided. He drew strength and pride from her frontier hardihood and accomplishments, and she drew strength and pride from Joel's background and versatility. Both were learning that the process of human growth and development was not necessarily tied to the classroom.

By midwinter the mighty transcontinental railroad had pushed itself hundreds of miles eastward from the California coast, and westward to Cheyenne, in Wyoming Territory. There was a definite possibility one or both of the construction segments would reach far into Deseret by next summertime. The long awaited journey East could then be made, for most of the distance at least, in the comfort of a train coach. All this was exciting to both Joel and Nancy.

And then, with the baby only two months old, and January scarcely ushered in, Nancy Scott was again reminded by the unmistakable signs of another pregnancy. After three times heaving up her breakfast, she had to tell Joel.

"Looks like I've married one of those fertile Mormons," he groaned. "Or maybe it's these long winter nights."

"By summer I'll be fat like a barrel," Nancy moaned tearfully, "and practically ready again for Mary."

"Well, I hope to God this time she's around when it happens," Joel said. "Or do you want to once more try it alone?"

"I don't want to try it at all, Joel. You'll have to go East without me. You've married nothing but a brood sow."

"We'll worry about summer when it comes," he said, quietly.

Nancy could not be blind to his look of disappointment.

But Joel's disappointment could scarcely be called a heartbreak. At first Nancy construed his reticence to discuss their going East as a conscious effort on his part to avoid worrying her or hurting her needlessly. In time it dawned on her that he was enjoying his second year in Zion, that more and more was he being accepted as one of the Saints in Ammon, and more and more was he taking part in the town's social and community affairs. Always the sure sign of Mormon acceptance was the affectionate term "brother"—and Brother Joel Scott was no longer a Gentile stranger, to be eyed with suspicion. In the schoolhouse and new Social Hall he coached dramatic groups, and lent his fine baritone voice to choir offerings and musicals. The Saints, on the other hand, were discovering that he was a gay and good dancer and, by some magical divination, not at first apparent to Nancy, the womenfolk seemed released from their reticence toward him. At a time when Nancy was again bloated and uncomfortable with a new pregnancy, "Brother Scott" was finding new and exciting things to spice up his second year in Zion.

For some of Joel's switching to new endeavors, Nancy blamed herself. Many an evening she'd spent at the bedside of the sisters in Israel as they labored and strained to bring forth fruit to the great cause of the latter days. But in time her deeper fears took root. Meetings and obligations were taking Joel more and more away from his writings. His home studies were becoming more doctrinal than critical or sociological. The Mormon home missionaries had already made the Scott cabin a regular port of call, and the bishop and these visitors were welcomed happily and willingly into the house by Joel himself.

Now, at last, Nancy knew why Joel had become so acceptable to the Saints of Ammon. He was deliberately being converted to Mormonism. A prayerful, concerted program had been set up to bring him into the Church. The Mormon grapevine had spread the news. The warmth and affection he now received on every hand not only was flattering and acceptable to him, but was indicative that God had set His mark on this stranger in Zion.

"Reason argues against Joseph Smith being what he claims," Joel said to Nancy one howling March night, when it was pleasant to sit securely in the little log house, and let the Wasatch gale screech its own fury down the valley, or break itself into howling anguish across the still substantial clay buttress of the old wall. "A year ago I'd have laughed at any man's announcement that Smith was a prophet of God —that he'd talked face to face with deity. But this man is either what he claims to be, or he's the greatest impostor since the dawn of time."

Nancy, her knitting needles clicking furiously on a new black sock for Joel, had watched curiously as he, under the gusty, fluttering lamp-light, gathered a new strength to his conviction from the Prophet's own utterances in the *Doctrine and Covenants*, spread out on the table under his nose. His interest in writing about Mormons had somehow trapped him into the deepest kind of study about them. And it was a worrisome thing.

"Do *you* think he was a prophet?" Nancy asked cagily, staring so-berly down at her dancing steel needles, as expertly she guided them in forming the heel to the sock.

"I don't know," Joel said weakly. "I don't know."

"Another month, at the rate you're going, you'll be standing up in fast meeting, and declaring it so," Nancy said, glancing quickly up at him.

The wind moaned, rattled the windows. The kerosene light, from its bracket overhead, flickered nervously.

"*You* believe he's a prophet of God, don't you, Nan?" He asked it almost hungrily.

"I was born a Mormon," she said, dropping her needles and half-formed sock to the ball of black yarn in her lap. "Such things were taught me from my cradle days. I've never known anything else."

"But, Nan—do you believe it?"

"Seems reasonable." She went back at her knitting. She was in no position to fight him on this issue. "I've never had cause to doubt it."

"Take the *Book of Mormon*," he said. "Joseph Smith claims to have translated it from golden plates, hidden from the world for centuries, and miraculously delivered into his hands. You've either got to accept this version of its existence, or argue that an illiterate New York farm boy cooked up one of the most complex pieces of fiction in this gen-eration, and the most amazing religion and philosophy of our time."

"You'll accept it," Nancy sighed.

"Why do you say that, Nan?"

"Because Bishop Earlington and the brethren will convert you, that's why. I've watched it coming."

"Would that be a calamity?"

"Of course not, Joel. Mormon wives should be very happy to have their husbands get interested in the Church."

"I'm just beginning to get the feel, and some understanding, of the tremendous sweep of this thing you so take for granted. It has power to remake men, to charge them with a faith and conviction greater than life itself. This ignorant New York farm boy, may have put on earth a philosophic pattern that will someday remake the world."

"You *are* converted." Nancy sighed again. "They'll be baptizing you before long."

"You irritate me, Nan." He looked sharply at her. "At my every mention of Mormonism—which you accept and espouse—I sense an antagonism in you. Do you *hate* your Church?"

"Of course not. I'd have no other."

"Then, what *do* you hate?"

"You know what I hate," she said quietly, her hands suddenly trembling on the needles.

"You mean—?" he suddenly laughed uproariously. "You mean that I might join the Church, and take myself a dozen wives?"

"I mean that you probably *will* join the Church." She gave him a stare that would have withered a cactus. "But I'm just telling you, Joel Scott, that in the day you bring even one more wife to share your bed, I'll take an ax and chop the pair of you into chunks!"

Joel laughed long and wildly. "You're a rare bud for these parts," he chuckled at last. "That's why I fell in love with you, Nan."

Nancy did not laugh. "You knew how I felt about polygamy the first day I met you," she said, soberly. "I haven't changed, Joel."

Suddenly he was quiet and sober. "Don't worry, little one," he said, touching her arm. "You're wife enough for me. You're the mother to my children. And I love you more than you'll ever know. I'm not a Mormon yet. I'm only interested."

"But you stand a powerful chance of being one."

"Can't one be a Mormon without being a polygamist?"

"It's hard, Joel," she said, and tears came up with her sadness. "Men tire quick of one woman, here in Utah. And it makes a man damned happy to have God and His prophets sanction and make right the one thing any loving woman fears most."

XV

THE GIRL BABY WAS BORN DURING THE NIGHT, AND THIS TIME MARY Magdalene was in full and competent attendance. From the fresh warm sheets of Martha's old bed, Nancy could hear the midwife stirring about the kitchen room, talking in low voice to Itchy, so as not to wake Nancy or the baby from their needed sleep. But Nancy was awake, and the little red mite, at last breathing securely beside her, would be named Martha, in memory of the grandmother she would never see.

Joel, after as hectic a night as anything he'd known in war, had finally departed for school, secure in knowledge he was a father for the second time. Mary, in the usual way she took over, had barred him to the sidelines during the birthing. Nancy had long ago observed that in this, the most fundamental hour of a woman's life, Mary showed nothing but contempt for any man close enough for her beady eyes or sharp tongue. Any other time she would have rolled over like a friendly dog at anything in pantaloons, but this attitude quickly changed at the time of a birthing. She'd lock a husband and father outside without compunction. At the first groan of a woman's labor, Mary's hungry attitude toward men quickly switched to one of hate and disgust. Joel Scott was no exception. He refused to be thrown out of his house, but last night, whatever rest had been his had been taken on the old wall bunk in the big room, the bunk Nancy had occupied since childhood. Not until morning, and Mary Magdalene was good and ready, was he permitted to enter the little bedroom to view Nancy, and the tiny girl he'd sired.

Nancy turned painfully in her tight belly-bind, pulled aside the comforter, and peered in at the little withered face, the closed eyes. She had enough black hair, and was red enough, to be an Indian. Itchy herself had commented on her resemblance to a Lamanite. "My teeny papoose," Nancy sighed, smiling possessively. For this baby had been amply anticipated and provided for. Joel Arthur, bewildered, had been banished for a night and a day to the Bringhursts. The little red lacquered cradle in the corner was still set and ready for Martha's first occupancy of it—but Nancy, savoring the victory of her second ordeal, was not anxious yet to release her prize from the bed, even at Mary's insistence. She had two beautiful children. She'd remember more diligently to pray out her gratitude in the future.

It was so nice that her new prize was a girl, and there'd be no question about her being named Martha. At this, the Scotts' second public christening, it would not be the bishop who would mouth the prayer—it would be Joel Scott himself. In his precise Bostonese, he'd bless his own child—because he now had the right to bless his own child. And with the thought came remembrance of that morning in June, at the baptismal dam in Ammon Creek. That had only been four months ago, but much that was strange had happened in those four months. On that morning Joel, dressed in a faded pair of army blues, had walked willingly out into the pond. Bishop Earlington, smiling like a general with a great battle won, had greeted his protégé waist-deep in the chilly water with "this is a proud moment for me, Brother Scott."

Standing on the willowed bank with the other witnesses and spectators, and holding Joel Arthur in her arms so he too could see the immersion of his father, Nancy had watched God's victory with considerably less enthusiasm. "Joel Scott," the bishop had said, "having been commissioned of Jesus Christ, I baptize you in the name of the Father, and of the Son, and of the Holy Ghost. Amen." There had been no miracles in attendance when Joel was plunged by the strong arms of the bishop deep into the chilling waters of Ammon Creek. No angel chorus had sang as Joel walked dripping, and satisfied, toward her. And certainly there had been no singing on her part.

The following Sunday, with all of Ammon for witness, had come his confirmation. When the gift of the Holy Ghost was prayed down on his head by the victorious bishop, and he was publicly made a member of the Church of Jesus Christ of Latter-day Saints, there still were no heavenly miracles in attendance. But the testimonies that were borne by the faithful Saints that day were rich in the tone of victory, and well larded with the goodness and wonder of God and His prophets. Not until Joel himself arose and proclaimed the new peace and wonder that had come into his heart, did Nancy realize how truly and thoroughly had he converted himself. Since then volume after volume of Mormon theology had littered the house, and added to Joel's already hefty accumulation of books. Never, in her recollection, had a conversion been more clean-cut and sure. With the fire and conviction so apparent in all new converts, Mormonism had, in the months following, virtually become Joel's life.

As Nancy mulled the memories of this strange summer and fall, she again realized that Joel would never know the strange and uneasy transformation that had come into their lives. The Gentile of her first recollection had become an entirely different man. In the very home, first nurtured on near-apostasy, she was hearing the utterances, the platitudes, the familiar spiritual vernacular she'd heard from babyhood. To Joel the unfoldment of the Prophet's wondrous plan of salvation, the doctrine of eternal progression, and the proxy salvation of the world's dead, were new and ecstatic experiences. To Nancy they were as familiar as an old shoe. But the strangest thing had been to watch Joel give up such familiar vices as his beloved cheroots, and his occasional nip of Valley Tan, in obedience to the Word of Wisdom. When this happened, Nancy knew her beloved Gentile had become as rock-ribbed in the faith as Isaac Corey. In silence, with a lack of enthusiasm that was exasperating and baffling to Joel, she watched the transformation that never failed to occur in a conversion. She prayed God to forgive her the sadness she felt, and the darker thoughts that had a way of entering her mind.

The tiny new baby beside her, and Joel's conversion—they had been the Scott problems of the year 1870, and its summer in particular. The glory of heaven's unfoldment, and concern for her pregnancy, could be blamed for Joel's decision to postpone their trip East yet another year. "The transcontinental railroad will be completed then," he'd declared. "Next summer we can ride in cushioned comfort all the way to Boston."

Strangest thing to Nancy, but, oddly, not at all strange to Joel, had been his correspondence with eastern relatives. She knew, as did all Mormons, that the first sign of a true conversion, was the almost fanatical desire to pass on these wondrous things to others. Joel, apparently, had all the signs. For now his letters were full of preachments, revelations, and an obsessive urge to convert the Scotts to the new Gospel so mysteriously revealed in these the last days. When the Prophet had declared that his was a missionary church, it actually was an understatement. Nancy herself had grown up in an atmosphere charged with the responsibility of saving the world. Apparently Joel failed to realize, or no longer cared, what a shock his conversion to Mormonism must have been among the puritanical Scotts. With every newspaper in America consistently blasting Brigham Young, polygamy,

and Mormonism in general; with writers of books groveling in obsceni-
ties keyed to Salt Lake City; with politicians and preachers thunderingly
demanding the utter destruction of the Church and its people, Joel
Scott now took upon himself the patient effort of explaining his fall
from family grace as a step upward into the glories of heaven. Tirelessly
he was expounding the new philosophy and the wondrous peace that
had become his very life. From her surreptitious readings of his letters
to mother, sister, and cousins, Nancy knew that so far this program
had ended in utter defeat. Probably a good thing he *hadn't* gone East.
The Scott family would doubtless have tossed him out on his Mormon teehinder. As for her, now that he'd fouled his family nest, she
had not the least desire to face the venom that was certain to be
Boston.

Nor had they managed the move out of Old Town after all—simply
because Joel's conversion had set a new pattern to things. Isaac Corey,
by letter from the East, now turned sweetness and love toward his son-
in-law. He insisted Joel now accept the Ammon lot he'd deeded to
him. The whole Corey family would unite in building him a house on
it, and God would bless him throughout his stay in Zion. By September
Joel had decided to accept. It would be next year before Mormon skill
and labor could shape to completion the new dwelling. In the meantime Joel had put a wood roof on the cabin.

And as Nancy wrapped her arm about the waking infant, she was
glad that a solid layer of shingles would hold the storms secure from
the cradle and bed of young Joel and younger Martha.

As if reading her thoughts the tiny child fretted nervously, and its
little mouth, like the puckered top of a buckskin pouch, was showing
its first hungry movement. Nancy, clucking like a contented hen,
wrapped her arm about the precious bundle, and drew it close. She'd
taken real joy in this birth. In it was none of the fear and terror that
had ushered in her first-born. At the first sign of pain, Joel not only
had alerted Mary Magdalene, but had brought back with him Bishop
Earlington. The two men, with holy consecrated oil, had anointed her
head, and the bishop had "sealed" Joel's brief anointing supplication
with a prayer of great power and promise.

"I seal upon your head, dear sister, a time of only the briefest and
most necessary pain," the bishop intoned through his beard, as he and
Joel cupped hands upon the oiled spot of her black hair. "The child
shall be born normal in every way, shall grow up in grace and honor to
you, and shall be one of the most precious parts of the holy increase
that God has ordained to you and your husband as chosen vessels in

the kingdom. I do also promise your complete recovery from the mortal task of bringing this child into the world. And what pain you have, will be quickly blotted out in the joy you shall know and feel as a true mother in Israel." As Nancy jogged the awakening infant, she could not but realize the bishop had been right.

Other parts of the good man's prayer had touched more on future promise than present travail. "God has a great work in store for you, my dear sister," he'd said. "The skill of your hands, and the willingness of your heart, shall be the means of bringing countless souls into this world, of alleviating pain, of comforting the sick, and of setting an example of unselfishness and self-sacrifice that shall be a thing of pride and remembrance to generations yet unborn. These things shall be written to your eternal credit in the book of life, and in that great day of judgment you shall stand spotless and exalted before the Lamb. For God loves you, dear Nancy. And for your good works, so shall your fellow mortals love you."

And this prayer, four hours before little Martha was born, held in it much of the identical promise that had come with Patriarch Ursenbach's blessing. One of the functions of the patriarch was that of divination, as well as healing and fatherly counseling to the body of Saints. When Joel had decided to join the Church, there had been no halfway measures about it. After baptism, one of his first acts had been to petition for patriarchal blessings for both of them. "Your name shall be known for good throughout this land," the patriarch had promised Joel in the name of God. "Generations of Saints shall rise and call you blessed." When Nancy's time came for the bearded patriarch to pray in promise over her head, it was comforting to know that God had not been unmindful of her labors at the bedside of the mothers in Israel. "You shall be a healer, and a fount of solace and great strength all the days of your life." And last night Bishop Earlington had reiterated the promises. Amid prayers that were rich with promise.

Yes, her baby had come. That was good, and had given her mind's ease at this birthday. That the child she cuddled had been touched by God's finger, there could be no denying.

But still she was plagued with the strangeness of it all. On that far-off day when she'd first seen her Gentile from the wall, not even a patriarch's revelation would ever have convinced her Joel Scott would someday walk into the waters of Mormon baptism, accept the obligations and discipline of this strange new faith, lead himself and family into the praying ordinances of the priesthood, and actually administer to his ailing wife with the oil of consecration and healing. As Nancy

191

cuddled her child on this morning after, she could not but marvel at the things that had happened, and were happening, to Joel Scott. To a Saint, bred and born in the faith, such miracles should never be amazing or frightening. But they were.

Only last night, with her own ears, she'd heard Joel tell about his dead wife to Bishop Earlington. She'd seen the bishop, with sepulchral calmness and surety, lay his hand on Joel's shoulder and, as though it were the commonest thing in the world, counsel him to have Nancy, as soon as she were well enough, to be baptized, in the Endowment House, in Edna's name—and then have both these women sealed to him, as wives, for time and all eternity. The shrieking moan Nancy had given could have been a labor pain. But when Mary Magdalene cleared both men out of the bedroom for the grim business of the birthing, Nancy was not too sorry.

Now there was time abed to ponder these things—and many another thing. With all her heart she wished she could think better of Joel's conversion. She'd been taught that Saints always should rejoice whenever a lamb was brought into the fold—that even the angels in heaven sang for joy. If only her Joel would remain just a lamb in the fold, she'd willingly rejoice with the Saints and the angels. But men, once they entered the fold, were not too likely to stay lambs—and that was the ungodly fear of it all. She'd married a Gentile, and ended up with the eagerest kind of a Saint.

When her tiny girl commenced bleating in earnest, Nancy jogged her closer, and began getting positioned for the child's first feeding. Soon the horse face of Mary Magdalene was in the doorway. That crazy smile of victory was upon it.

"I've come to the conclusion God works in a mysterious way," Nancy said, a little bitterly.

"It's not so infernal mysterious," Mary grumbled, coming quickly to the bedside. "God just works, that's all." While little Martha yee-wawed out her first fundamental demand, the midwife yanked down the sheet and comforter. "Lordy, what a pair of lungs—for a girl!" Then she pulled the bowstrings on Nancy's nightgown, and thoughtfully kneaded Nancy's firm and pointed little breasts. "They'll be sore on the nipples for a little while, after this brat starts her tugging. But they feel all right to me. Let's start her with the right teat first."

Nancy positioned herself for the feeding.

"Yes," Mary growled. "God sure does work."

PART TWO

The Lascivious Cohab

I

THE SCOTT FAMILY KINGDOM, UNDER HEADSHIP OF JOEL AND NANCY, WITH an "increase" of only five children, was almost too modest to count in the spawn of eternity which was Mormonism in 1880. But time was on its side, and eternity ahead—and small as it was, the Scott kingdom was alive and vibrant with promise. Mormonlike, it hewed to the pattern, was solid in its thinking and, outwardly at least, stood rock-ribbed for conformity.

Like all other family segments in the great pattern peculiar to Mormonism, it relegated the inexorable movement of time into the cloistered divisions of "good" years and "bad" years. This cutting of time into sausage lengths was accentuated, if not credited entirely, by the wide swing of the year's pendulum between the bitterness of mountain winter and the almost ecstatic beauty of the highland summers. The weighing in of the year's qualities, insofar as it affected their lives, was quite another thing.

Take the year 1877. Nancy remembered it as starting out well enough, with the dedication of the first temple in Utah—at St. George, in the salubrious Dixie to the south—even before the great temple in Salt Lake City was finished. That was the year Joel had finally persuaded her to the necessity of their receiving the celestial "endowments" in the new and beautiful structure, and it may or may not have been the turning hinge of that sadly remembered time. Anyway, they made the trip, from Utah Valley snow, to the Rio Virgin Valley springtime, and, in the name of heaven's celestial glory, and family peace and unity, she had married Joel Scott for the third time—this time for time and all eternity. She also had been baptized in proxy for Edna Reavis Scott, Joel's first wife, who had died in Massachusetts in the war days. Nor was that all. She had stood in like proxy while this unknown woman was also sealed to him as a wife for the endless hereafter. This concession Nancy had been willing to make, so long as the battling for Joel's sole possession could be safely put away until after death. In the more timely present she was no more converted to Mormon plurality than on that first day she had met Joel. And on that far day, she would have cringed had she known her errant Gentile would someday wear with her the holy garment! But it had happened—in that mad, bad year.

For that was the year Brigham Young, Prophet to the Church, and Joel's friend and confidant, had died in Salt Lake City—after enough Gentile and federal harassment to kill any man twice as durable. That was the year they executed John D. Lee for the infamous Mountain Meadows massacre, and brought thundering down on the heads of the Mormon people a wave of hate and disgust unmatched in history. That was the year they arrested Porter Rockwell for murder, and the year that dear Isaac Corey, the foster father Nancy had come to love with all her heart, dropped dead atop a load of hay, toppled off of it, and landed under the wagon's wheels. They had buried him, amid the whole town's mourning, in the Corey plat alongside Martha.

In that same topsy-turvy year, with the Gentile world howling its hate and disapproval of everything Mormon, Mary Magdalene Mattise married Seth Biddle, in the Endowment House, and afterward spent more time taking care of him than in delivering babies. And that, of all years, was the one time Joel had chosen for his long delayed journey back home. This time Nancy was glad another pregnancy saved her the necessity of facing the aroused Scotts in New England, for Joel couldn't possibly have timed it worse. Congress already had passed its Anti-bigamy Act, the Mountain Meadows tragedy was being exhumed by the American press and clergy, and a Mormon in the East was an unwanted and despicable character. Joel's mother ordered him out of the Scott home, his sister Amanda refused to speak to him, and he'd returned to Utah an unhappy man. But not even this shattering experience had any visible effect on the unshakable "testimony" he never ceased to bear to the truthfulness of the Gospel.

But though 1877 had been put down as a bad year for the Saints, and for Joel, Nancy, and the Scott family in general, the year of 1880 had every evidence of being at the other reach of the pendulum—a good year. Isaac had been most generous to Nancy in his hand-scrawled will. Besides the Ammon lot, upon which Joel already had built a brick house —enlarged twice to house his eternal increase—Nancy had been given one of the Corey lake-bottom farms, two more town lots, and enough cattle and horses to assure that they were comfortably fixed above the average family in Ammon. Under Joel's direction, and to care for the needs of the fast-growing community, two additional new schools had been built, and he served in the dual capacity of principal to one of them, and superintendent over all three. At any rate, Ammon's school system was now a model for the territory.

This year, too, was a good one, because Nancy managed the entire year without any stirrings in her own womb—although she attended to the stirrings of many another mother in Israel. Since Mary Magdalene was now old, tired, and taxed with the problem of Seth, her answers to the eternal call were sporadic and based on whim and convenience. With Nancy's own affluence, the five dollars she collected for the chore had nowhere near the meaning it formerly had. But in this essential task, Ammon's townsfolk refused to allow her rest. There could be no such thing as turning down a woman in labor, and Nancy's family of five—from young Joel to baby Edward—were long since conditioned to this peculiar Scott problem. The older girls, Martha and Amanda, had been thoroughly trained to keep house and tend the little ones— Vernell and Edward—while her sprightly mare took her through the weird hours on the mercy calls that just had to be answered.

The year too was especially auspicious since a new President was to be chosen for the Church—probably John Taylor—the John Taylor who had stood with the Prophet Joseph Smith, in Carthage jail, on the day of the martyrdom. For three years, since Brigham Young's death, the Church had been ruled by the Quorum of the Twelve Apostles, of which John Taylor had been the senior and revered member. If Apostle Jonathan Cragg had secret ambition to fill Brigham's shoes in the exalted calling, he was discreet about it. Perhaps, if he had such a dream, he was helpless in abetting it—for he was in far-away England.

"John Taylor will be chosen to lead this church to its great and ultimate destiny," Joel declared. "Though if he is, he'll find the path just as thorny and rough as did Brigham Young." In this Joel, as usual, was right.

The other auspicious thing about this year of 1880 was that it was the Church's jubilee year. "Fifty years ago, in New York state, Joseph the Prophet re-established the Gospel of Jesus on earth," Joel said. "It started with six members in 1830. Someday it will fill the whole earth."

"Are we going to the jubilee conference in Salt Lake?" Nancy asked, her interest suddenly aroused at the hint.

"We certainly are," he said.

"Do we take the children?"

"I doubt we'll do much jubileeing with five children along."

"And to that I agree," Nancy sighed. "Jody's eleven years old, and plenty able to tend to all the chores for a week; and Marty's ten, and

196

a good woman of the house. She's always handled the smaller ones when I've been called out. She'll have no trouble managing this time. I'll tell Seth and Mary to look in."

This year the usual "conference weather" for April did not hold, and spring had made its entry, mild and warm. Nancy, up to the day they left, had been worried on that score, and with good reason. The tendency for rain, heavy frosts, and even snow to usher April in had spawned the term "conference weather" throughout Utah Territory. Joel, still youngish, in spite of ecclesiastical sobering and family banishment, was jovial and whistling as he went at the task of packing the surrey. His smart, matched team of black geldings, always meticulously groomed by himself or Jody were, on the dawn of the third day of April, hitched to the fringe-topped rig, already carefully loaded with two telescope valises, and Nancy's bandboxes stuffed with new hats and gloves for the occasion. Young Joel, whining a bit because he was being left home to keep company with the cow, the other two horses, the pigs and the chickens—and the schoolroom, which only his father seemed to have privilege of deserting—expertly harnessed up Gus and George. Father and son soon had them hitched to the carriage, and ready.

There would be no camping, as Joel had decided to make the long run to Draper in one day—staying overnight there at the public house, and continuing on to Salt Lake City the morning following. The Mormon-owned Utah Central steam railroad could be boarded at Draper, but Joel had made plans to drive the whole distance. Besides conference attendance, he had many visits to make pertaining to the business of the Utah Valley schools, and he would need the team and rig. Nancy had sensed he wasn't averse to showing off his flashy team and fringe-topped surrey, and it was doubtful even the apostles or the Gentile Governor Avery could boast anything finer than Joel's high-stepping blacks.

Young Joel, brown-eyed and black-haired, was allowed to drive the rig and horses up the lane from the stable and carriage house, and around to the hitching post in front of the Scott home. And then, in the early morning, on the ditch bank beneath the poplar trees, while the horses nervously yawed and chomped, the five Scott children lined up for tearful farewell. Nancy, weeping like a widow at a burying, got down the line from Joel and Martha to Amanda. When she came to daughter Vernell, age five, and son Edward, age one and a half, who bobbed and sagged from Vernell's hand, the ordeal was too much. Nancy grabbed up the baby, smothered him with kisses, and burst into a frenzy of weeping.

"I'm not going," she howled. "I'm just *not* going!" She turned and looked furiously at Joel Scott, who was patiently leaning against the hitching post. "You go on without me. I'm not going."

Joel grinned. "What will I do with that surrey-load of dresses and hats?"

"Well, it's neglectful, inhuman, to leave your children this way! I just can't, Joel." And she was off to a fit of weeping, which was promptly joined by the whole Scott tribe.

"Lord and little fishes," Joel said, slumping hopelessly. "Morning's no time for this caterwaul." With patient forbearance, he looked at Nancy. "I thought we'd agreed on leaving the children home? I thought you wanted to get away for a little while."

"Can *you* go away and leave them?" Nancy moaned.

"Yes," Joel said impatiently. "And so can you. Kiss 'em good, and hop into the seat. The sun's up, and it's getting late. They'll be all right."

"Joel, I just can't! I've never been away like this before. I can't see how you can be so hard-hearted."

"I'm not hard-hearted," he said, hopelessly shaking his head. "We planned a trip. We've packed for ourselves alone. We're going. I've made reservations at Draper, and at the Walker House in Salt Lake. I thought this would be something interesting and enjoyable. Instead it's a damned funeral."

"You go, Joel," Nancy whimpered. "I just *can't*."

"Can anyone *ever* understand a woman?" he growled, throwing his arms in the air, and starting for the horses. "We'll both stay home. The trip's off!"

"Why couldn't we take the kids with us?" Nancy suggested, her voice suddenly alive with new hope.

"Yeah!" said young Joel.

"Whee—that would be fun!" said Martha.

Joel stopped, whirled, and looked at her hopelessly. "We planned it for you and me," he said angrily. "We packed only for you and me. There are one hundred and fifty thousand people in Utah Territory, and at this jubilee, Salt Lake City will be bursting at the seams. I reserved a room for two at the Walker House. Not for seven. You must be out of your mind." He turned to young Joel and sharply commanded, "Drive the team back, and unhitch 'em, Jody. The trip's off." Angrily he strode toward the gate.

With little Edward in her arms, Nancy followed him. "Joel," she said, contritely. "You're right about it." He turned. "I want to go, and I want you to go. And I can see now that to take our whole tribe's impossible." She smiled at him through her stupid and foolish tears. "But couldn't we just take the baby? The others are old enough to manage. I could stand it if I had little Eddie along."

"Little Eddie will hobble you for sure," he said. "Tie you down."

"He'll be no problem at all."

"But we'll have to pack his clothes. We'll have to take along milk and food and dry pants and—"

"It'll only take a jiffy to get him ready."

And so, after a considerably longer time than a jiffy, Edward was made ready for the jubilee trip. The sun was up and at their backs when finally they got away. But as they jogged smartly up Ammon's streets, and westward out of town, Nancy felt a little sad from the second parting, but still she was relaxed, and at peace with herself and her good and patient Joel. Spring, sharp, crisp, and wildly alive, was everywhere about them. The stately poplars were already bursting furiously into leaf. The sky was blue like turquoise. It was a good time to be alive.

"I think Ammon's the most beautiful town in Utah," Joel said looking happily about and waving a gloved hand at a familiar face among the early risers. "You ever see old Timp more loaded with snow? There'll be plenty of water for the crops. It'll be a good year."

Nancy smiled. He talked more and more like a Utah villager.

They wheeled past what had once been the Corey House—enlarged now, and called the Ammon Hotel. At Isaac's death, it had gone to Kirstine, who promptly had sold it and moved back to her own home in Ammon. Several strangers were on its veranda, but none of them could ever have resemblance to a young man who once had stood there of evenings to calmly and reflectively smoke his cheroots. The man was older now, the cheroots were gone, but in spite of his durable shift to Mormonism, he was still hers alone—at least for this life. They'd been blessed immeasurably, and no woman could ever ask for a better husband. He loved her, he loved his children, and she loved him with a constancy beyond his ability to know or even guess.

She drew deeply at the winy air of Utah's April, and smiled happily at the tiny son sitting between them on the seat like a real man. "Yes, Ammon *is* the most beautiful town in Utah," Nancy sighed. "I'll never cease to love this place."

"I fell in love with it when it was only a walled fort with a sassy woman on top. But it's the valley, and the mountains, and the lake, that gets at you."

"Not the sassy woman?"

"She still gets at you," he chuckled, holding tight and down on the lines of the morning-spirited Gus and George. "And she's still sassy."

"I'm sorry about this morning, Joel," she said contritely. "And I know we've got an awful late start because of it."

"Not so important," said Joel, airily retreating. "Nice to have Eddie along. He's getting an exciting eyeful, watching everything. I guess it would have been good to have the rest of the kids, too. I'll take the older ones to Salt Lake with me one of these days. Good for youngsters to know how the other half of the world lives. If my family weren't so damned narrow-minded, I'd take all of us back East. Mother threatens to give my share of the Scott money to Amanda and her children. She thinks I'd use it only to advance the detestable, unspeakable cause of Mormonism."

"Wouldn't you, Joel?" Nancy asked.

"I don't know," he mused. "I'd want enough of it to educate my children. But I'm not too discontented as I am. I never want to live any other place than here."

The horses, at lively trot, had already pulled the surrey past the west end of town. Joel and Nancy both glanced back at the twin lines of poplars, which were the town's mark of distinction, receding in the distance. The spring rains had settled the road dust to a damp, spongy cake, which squeaked interestingly along the rolling wheels, and made for the most pleasant sort of traveling. For an April third, it was a rare day.

"But you've lived so many places," Nancy said. "You've known what it's like in the East, in California—even in Europe and India."

"Home's where your heart is, my dear," Joel reminded. "When I was a young boy, in Maine, I remember skating up the Penobscot River from Bangor. Visiting my uncle's shipyard. Listening to the men of the sea. And planning that someday it would be my life."

"What an odd life you ended up with."

"That I'll agree. But I saw, and knew, those other lives." He pulled the animals to a resting walk, and mused a moment. "I remember in California—riding a horse around trees so big that no one would believe you when you told them. I thought then that raw, bustling, beautiful California was the only place on earth to live. But, as I told you, home is always where your heart is."

"My heart's here," Nancy sighed.

"So is mine," he said. "And you know it."

Joel chuckled happily as the team settled themselves to the long, slow grade toward Pleasanton. He lazed a while before he spoke again.

"In the beginning there were a lot of Saints who thought California was not only the proper place for Zion, but the predicted one. Many Saints apostatized—particularly those who, under leadership of Samuel Brannan, had migrated to California by water."

"Brannan himself was an apostate," Nancy added. "I've heard all about *that* scoundrel."

"Well, when I first saw Salt Lake Valley, and the choice Brigham had made, I couldn't help but feel Sam Brannan had been right in urging the Leader to move the Saints to the coast. It was not until I'd studied this thing called Mormonism that I realized how truly wrong Brannan had been. Suppose the Church *had* moved on to the lush, rich lands of California? It would have gone into disintegration along with those seaborne Saints. The Church has had to sharpen itself on adversity, Nan. Hard as the decree, Brother Brigham was right in telling the Saints to leave gold-digging and mining strictly alone—to the Gentiles. He was right in settling them in a place where they'd have to scratch for a living. He was right in trying to insulate them from the Gentiles. It made the Saints strong. It made them self-reliant. But now the great man is dead. Now, with the railroad, the Gentiles are moving in, elbowing hard. For our people I can only see a strange, hard time ahead."

Little Edward, sound asleep by now, and uninterested, was rocking and rolling to the carriage seat like a round-bottomed water gourd. Nancy, smiling down at him, wrapped a steadying arm about the boy. "You know more about Mormon history and doctrine than most apostles," she added admiringly.

"I ever tell you I met, and personally knew, Sam Brannan in San Francisco?"

"You don't seem to care *who* you know," she laughed. "Brigham preached that Sam was a thief. That he'd robbed the Church. I never knew you consorted with thieves before I married you."

"You'll never know the thieves and rascals I've consorted with. You should see the waterfronts of the world—Bombay, Naples, Marseilles! You should see the bestiality that war can reduce men to. The hardness of men one to another. The callous indifference. The putrid, maggoty wounds. The stench of death." He was silent for a moment. "Sam Brannan's a model of virtue compared with some of the men I've known."

"And you'll never guess how you amaze me. The way you're always popping up with these wildly interesting bits."

Joel smiled. "When I met Brannan he was the richest man in California. He owned buildings, saloons, stores, and San Francisco's newspaper. You know, he started out as printer and newspaper publisher. He told me he'd published the Mormon *Messenger* in New York City. I learned a lot about Mormonism from Sam—though he'd long since given up the faith. It was through him I became interested in riding to Utah and seeing first-hand this strange sect and its people."

Nancy laughed. "At least we've one thing to thank Brannan for. Without Sam, you'd probably never have come here."

"Perhaps not. But you know, Nancy, I think I was predestined to seek out the Church, and to seek out *you*. Isn't that part of our belief?"

She nodded vaguely, and clung tighter to Edward through the jouncing ruts.

"Sometimes, now I, too, am a Saint, I get a hankering to go back to San Francisco and talk once more to the errant Sam. I might have some influence with him. He may be California's richest man, and a wild one, but he was also once a great leader of our people."

Nancy never ceased to be awed by Joel's terminology since his conversion. It never seemed odd for any other Saint to speak freely of "our" people, but somehow, even after these years, Joel had never quite shed the Boston inflection of speech, the polite gentility, the mannerisms that had first endeared him to her as the gallant Gentile. To her, somehow, he never would quite belong to this generation of Utah sodbusters she'd been so inseparably tied to since childhood. "I think even *you* would have a rough time making a Saint out of that tithing thief. I understand the Church has sent missionaries to him—many times."

"Might take some doing at that, Nan." He smacked a line down hard to Gus's rump. The team jumped alive again, and the carriage clipped merrily over a solid, drier stretch of road.

Again Nancy marveled at her Joel, and the sweeping change the years had made in his outlook. He was a talented, brilliant writer. She'd read enough of his words to know. But his great plan to acquaint the world with the Mormons, at least as he saw the Mormons, had foundered in failure and despair—simply because he'd written the wrong way. A hundred books a year were being turned out about the Mormons—all of them sensational, salacious exposés of the peculiarities of their faith, and their system of marriage. Any author could spend a week in Salt Lake City, turn out a hasty manuscript on the horrors of polygamy and the treasonable attitude of the Saints, and be reasonably certain of immediate publication by America's publishers. Nobody, anywhere, wanted to hear anything good about Mormons. Joel simply had written the wrong kind of books.

"Isolation of the Church and its people probably saved it from falling apart through the Gold Rush," he was saying. "But the railroad and telegraph ended Brigham's blessed isolation once and for all. Troublous times are upon us. The vultures are in our midst. There's a real storm gathering, Nan."

"It all started with those scurvied judges, federal appointees, and the army they've kept here to guard us," Nancy opined.

"And it's likely to be finished by them," Joel prophesied. "We've had eight years of squeeze between Judge James McKean as chief justice, and the military—but that's only the beginning. I read now where the federal government has taken over the territorial penitentiary. Maybe we'll all be jailed before they're through."

"You're safe, Joel, so long as you only have one wife," Nancy laughed. She picked up the sleeping Edward, pulled his little cap down to shade his eyes and face, and cradled him lovingly in her arms. "As I see it, the whole war between Gentiles and Saints is over polygamy. They're withholding statehood to Utah, until Mormons abandon the practice. President Young's last arrests were because of it. The present jailings of the Authorities, and all the uproar in Congress stems out of the government's decision to stamp it out. As you know, by now, Joel, I've never been much in favor of it, either."

On this touchy subject, at least, Joel had long since learned when to be silent. He had his eyes on the high poplars of Pleasanton up ahead. There they would stop for a little rest, and a little water for the laboring horses.

"The divorce and lawsuit of Ann Eliza Young against President Brigham Young, in his last years, and this stupid Miles polygamy case they're dragging through the courts, haven't helped the Mormons and their cause." Nancy said it with the bitterness and disgust that always came to her when she thought of it.

"Can't you see, Nan, that the anti-Mormon movement, federal, judicial, and Gentile, blow these things up out of all proportion to further their own nefarious campaign?" Joel patiently explained. "It makes sensationalism—it enlists public support—it makes Mormons look ridiculous."

That ended all talk until the surrey pulled into Pleasanton.

Under the shade of the poplars, at the town's public watering trough, the horses took their rest, drink, and a treat of oats from their nose-bags. While Joel daintied his handsome animals, he made small talk with other Saints who were gathered at the spot for the same purpose. Many of them, too, from as far south as Provo, and even from the southern settlements, were on their way to Salt Lake for the conference. The journey over The Point, and on up Salt Lake Valley to the city, would certainly no longer be a lonesome one.

And while Nancy used the pause to make a comfortable little bed for Eddie on the back seat of the surrey, she marveled again at these twice-a-year—April and October—travels of the Saints to Temple Square. It was a little like the pilgrimages to Mecca Joel had told her about, where tens of thousands of devout worshipers of another faith gathered in the holy city for spiritual strength and uplift.

This was by no means her first trip to conference. Like every other Mormon child in Utah, she'd made the familiar journey on so many occasions that they all faded to one in her recollection. She knew Salt Lake City would be jammed to overflowing with Saints from everywhere. She knew the hotels, public houses, and even the parks and squares set aside for camping would be just as tightly packed with Mormon pilgrims as would be the great new tabernacle. Nancy, like most Mormons, looked upon conference time as the happy, exciting time. If the Authorities, from the pulpit of the tabernacle, fed them with the bread of faith and spirit, that was only so much added gain. Conference was a time of rejoicing, of fraternizing, of worship—in Mormondom's Mecca by the great dead sea.

At Nancy's insistence, their next resting stop was at what had once been the old dairy farm at The Point. Little was left of it, but to Nancy even its ruins spoke in lowered talk of memory. The Jordan River still made its loop, and flowed its silent way northward through the willowed trough. But the barns were down; the old rock house only a burned-out shell. A year after Isaac had abandoned the venture, a wandering band of Utes, as a last defiant gesture against the land-grabbing Saints, had set fire to the property. Any other thing usable, or of value, had been carted off by neighboring Saints to go into their own houses and barns. Cove Corey had inherited it as part of his share of the Corey holdings. This, with many of the choice lots of Ammon he'd gained at Isaac's death, had gone to buy Cove's liquor and to pay his gambling debts. Who owned it now, Nancy could only wildly guess. But in looking at the ruin, she could remember a lot, and in the remembrance there was a sadness.

Not enough time remained from the day for a close view of what had once been Camp Floyd. Across the valley, from the high roadway, as they climbed back up to The Point, they could see the pocked and roofless ruins of what had once been the Army's hope of holding the rebellious Mormons in check. Connor's masterpiece of threat and intimidation, Fort Douglas, had done a far better job, simply because it commanded the heights above Temple Square. Jack rabbits and coyotes now could freely cross Floyd's weedy parade ground, and its roofless adobe walls were melting back again to Mother Earth. "I'll bet every house in the valley's south end is wearing roof timbers and glass windows from good old Floyd," Joel mused as he looked out across the deathlike ruin.

"Wonder if they moved Hogtown up to Fort Douglas?" Nancy said.

"They've got a reasonable facsimile. Only it's less than half a mile from Temple Square. And they no longer use squaws."

Because of their late start, and their nostalgic tarryings along the way, it was dark before their weary team pulled them into Draper. Here many of the southern Saints put their teams and vehicles up at the livery barn, and continued on into the city by steam train. But Joel was still determined to keep his team and surrey with him, and he asked for only their overnight care.

In spite of the fact that their room, in the made-over residence serving as inn and lodging house, was drafty and infested with bedbugs, Nancy was glad that Joel had reserved it in advance. Conference rush was on. The little town was glutted with pilgrims, and public accommodations were totally inadequate for this twice-a-year traveling boom. Already Nancy had foretaste of what Salt Lake City probably would be like when they arrived. The fiftieth anniversary of the Church, the jubilee conference, would definitely not be lacking in attendance.

As compared to their first day's travel, the drive from Draper to Salt Lake City was an easy one. Though the road was carrying plenty of northbound pilgrims, it was wide, and hard packed. The geldings, pampered with a good night's rest and oats seemed tireless along this good stretch of highway. The carriage, rolling at a sharp clip, passed many a slower vehicle. And for April, the day was perfect.

When Joel started them north on Main Street in the bright and prideful city of the Saints, little Edward stared at the new sight in bug-eyed wonder. It was his first visit to the city, and the maze of horses, buggies, wagons, high buildings, and glass-fronted stores apparently were overwhelming to the little boy. Even Nancy was trembling with excitement —for this was the great city—the hub center of everything that pertained to the life and well-being of a Saint. Joel, considerably more calm, headed straight up Main Street for the Walker House. But he never made it.

Flora, dressed for spring in flouncy white, and carrying an ornately fringed pink parasol against the April sun, had been window shopping for her last-minute conference specials. She recognized Nancy, and she recognized Joel, as the team and surrey clupped alongside her point at the sidewalk. Nancy heard her wild screeches first, as she followed them along. Flora never waited for Joel to make a decent curb stop, but dashed into the street after them. Joel finally worked the horses into a vacant place at streetside, but by then Flora had somehow managed to mount the surrey step—in spite of yards of white skirt, and the parasol that worried the geldings enough to make them lay their ears back and pull hard against the lines in Joel's gloved hands. And somehow Flora managed to fold the damn thing down before the animals bolted. In the next minute she'd squeezed into the seat beside the three of them, and, weeping furiously, had her arms about Nancy Scott.

"Oh, Nan," she moaned wildly. "It's *so* good to see you!"

She spied the Scott child, tucked between the adults like an afterthought. "And this is baby—?"

"Edward," Nancy added.

Edward, his blue eyes circled in terror at the effusive half aunt who had invaded the carriage seat, backed shyly from her, and bent himself to hide behind his father's back.

"Is this the last one, Nan?"

"I hope so."

"And how are you, Joel?" Flora asked.

Joel finished backing the nervous team from the curb, pulled outward on the lines to guide Gus and George once more into the wide expanse of Main Street, and smacked their rumps sharply with the lines. The surrey darted forward and northward. "I'm just fine, Flora," he said. "You're looking beautiful." He eyed her merrily, from fashionable white dress to the folded parasol in her right hand, which she was using to steady herself in the careening carriage. "I always did say the Corey half sisters were the prettiest pair of girls in Utah." He looked impishly at her. "But two halves are not supposed to make a pair."

"Always too involved for me," Nancy laughed.

"I'll skip the mathematics also—but accept the compliment," Flora said. "You're looking fine and handsome yourself, Joel."

"And how's Apostle Cragg? He hasn't been down to Ammon for ages. For that matter, neither have you."

"Jonathan's fine. But he's in England, you know. Heading up the British mission, and church immigration. We miss him terribly."

Nancy had the wicked impulse to ask Flora which of the wives had gone with the apostle overseas. Or was he looking for a new and younger one from the English crop? Instead she said, "We're up for conference, Flo."

"Certainly you are," Flora said. "And the city's jammed for the jubilee."

"I've reserved a room for us at the Walker House," Joel explained. And the smart blacks had already stepped off enough of Main Street to bring them to within a block of the hotel.

Flora flung her head up coquettishly, defiantly. "You're coming home with me! You're staying with the Craggs! I've a whole house to myself and my little family. Plenty of room. We can talk ourselves silly over old times."

"But I've already reserved at the Walker House," Joel repeated.

"Some other Saint will be glad to get that room. It hurts to even think you'd desert kin to hunt a strange place in Salt Lake. We'll have a grand visit."

And so it was they stayed in an apostle's home for the jubilee. But even in the moment of decision, Nancy couldn't help wondering, in light of that other visit so long ago, if the Scotts would be half so welcome if Joel had remained the Gentile.

The Cragg house was still ample, in spite of the fact that Flora's little family had totaled out at six. The children were quietly well-behaved, polite, and handsome. Their lean toward pudginess unmistakably marked them as the apostle's issue. But the Scotts were better housed at the ninth Cragg home than they could ever have hoped to have been at the Walker House. For a plural wife, Flora had it exceptionally fortunate. As a midwife, Nancy had visited enough plural shacks and shanties to know the difference. So pleasant was the visit that now she wished with all her heart the other children might have shared with Edward the opportunity of meeting their Salt Lake kin.

Joel, anxious to confer with Salt Lake educators, and transact what business he could before Tuesday's opening of the conference, took off as soon as they were comfortably settled, and amenities were over. It would be late in the evening before he returned, and Nancy and Flora used the time to catch up the skeins of their own diverse lives.

On her first visit Nancy had come away convinced Flora had made every compensatory adjustment necessary and incidental to successful living under the covenant. This trip she was certain of it. No longer was there any tension between her and Flora. Joel's acceptance in the Church, and his manifold activities in behalf of it, had changed all that. Now even a monogamous wife could talk to a polygamous wife without strain, and with the affection of a close and mutual girlhood. As wives in Utah went, and as Nancy had plenty opportunity to observe, Flora Cragg was well kept, fortunate, and from every appearance content. There could be no denying that, as youngest, and probably prettiest, she had been the apostle's favorite. Apparently she'd satisfied Jonathan Cragg enough to halt his propensities for further wife hunting. This accomplishment had given Flora the flippant poise which women assume when they are particularly sure of themselves.

Flora had laundresses to handle the washing, her milk and groceries were delivered daily, with only the necessity of making her wants known. A rawboned Scandinavian woman convert, just feeling her way into the English language, took care of the cooking. "Elena handled everything before little Matey Thorpe arrived," Flora said. "Now I have to divide their duties, and try to keep them both busy." Matey, brown-haired, shy and winsomely pretty, was also a recent convert—but from the British Isles. Apostle Cragg, humanitarian that he was, had taken a special interest in Matey. She was an orphan who had attended his lectures on the faith, and had personally been baptized into Mormonism by him, so Flora explained. More than that, Jonathan Cragg had paid into the Perpetual Immigration Fund the entire cost of her passage to America, and had guaranteed her a job in one of his own households. Nancy early detected that Flora was a bit irked that the branch of the Cragg household chosen had been hers. But Matey, unobtrusive as a mouse, attentive, and polite, would be a treasure to any home. Yet Nancy's woman instincts sensed the unvoiced worries in Flora's heart, and it amused and pleased her mightily. Conscience and memory reminded her of how close Flora's life had come to being her own, and her smugness subsided. She'd survived as her man's only wife, and it was wrong to gloat, even in silence.

But not until this visit in Salt Lake City did she realize the gravity of the national crusade against Mormon polygamy. Because she was one of the most prominent of the plural wives, and an active participant in the Utah women's counter-protests, Flora was not at all reticent in bringing Nancy up to date on the storm that was gathering over Zion.

"Repeatedly they deny us statehood," Flora declared. "Polygamy must go first, Congress demands. With that kind of a provision, we'll be known as Utah Territory until the end of time. This is the everlasting covenant they're tampering with. It shall stand forever. And all hell shall not prevail against it."

A little smugly, Nancy's thoughts took a hoop-roll back to the attitudes of their girlhood. She accepted another helping of tea—rare and forbidden in Mormon households—and sugar cakes from Matey's silently proffered tray. Flora seemed willing and anxious to forget a few things. Nancy sipped her tea like a lady, and nodded understandingly.

"The first thrust at us—or 'test' as they called it, came nine years ago, when they arrested President Young, and a number of the Authorities, under the anti-bigamy laws Congress had cooked up against the territory. Luckily, Jonathan was traveling for the Church, or he might have been rounded up as a common criminal like the rest. 'Lewd and lascivious cohabitation' was the term the federal grand jury worked into the indictments—punishable by ten years in prison. If Utah were only a state, instead of a tightly controlled federal territory, they'd never have gotten away with such nonsense."

Nancy nodded. "Joel says that's the reason they refuse us statehood. State's rights might tie their hands in dealing with the problem."

"Problem!" Flora snorted. "You mean war—against the women of the Church!"

Nancy looked at her half sister. Time and good living had added a mite of weight, but Flora was still a handsome woman. It was understandable why, with her natural ingenuity and charm, she'd managed to hold favored place with her apostle. Comforting it was to realize that neither Flora nor herself were being dealt with too badly by time. And, in this land of marriage-ferment, these things were important. "But it's the Mormon *men* they're arresting and hauling into court," Nancy argued perversely. "And they've had rather small luck in keeping them in jail."

"Nancy, you just don't seem to realize the scope or the implications of this thing."

Nancy took another sip of tea, and gave her half sister a lofty smile. "I guess not. Not being a plural wife, I sorta get out of touch."

"Well, you'd better get *in* touch," Flora sighed, "because every woman and every man in the Church is going to feel the weight of the crusade before it's over." There was a defiant glint in her eye as she looked at Nancy. Her own tea and cakes were going neglected. "They'll never stop plural marriage, Nan," she said, patiently and firmly, "because it was set upon this earth by the Prophet Joseph as the everlasting covenant. But they're going to try hard—ever so hard. Jonathan says the new persecution being rolled up for us will make the days of Illinois and Missouri seem like a dream of contentment. Why do you think the federal men are taking over the territorial penitentiary?"

"They're not going to lock up the *women*. 'Twould take a lot bigger jail than that to house the plural wives of Utah. And by golly damn, they'd need another just as big to bed 'em down for the babies that keep a-coming."

Flora nibbled at her cake, and then laid her plate and cup down to the serving table. She cocked an ear to the noise in the back yard, where the youngsters were playing. Apparently impressed that Elena and Matey had them competently in hand, she turned back again to her major worry. "The Gentile women of America have united against us, Nan. I'm a lot closer to this thing than you are, and I know. You recall the Boston resolution?"

"Only vaguely," Nancy confessed. "I know there were mass meetings in Boston, because Joel's mother took an active part. You know how *she* hates Mormonism."

"I've heard," Flora said. "Well, the resolution as published and circulated demands that Utah never be admitted as a state until polygamy's abandoned, that the right of women to vote be rescinded in Utah, that every man and woman living in polygamy be immediately disfranchised, and to disfranchise the offspring of all plural wives. But that isn't all, Nan—and this part may be the important part to you and Joel—they demand that the public schools be taken entirely away from the Mormons, and staffed with Gentile teachers. If this idea carries, Joel, in order to teach, will once more have to become a Gentile."

"Small chance," Nancy laughed. "Not even Father Isaac could be more caught up in the spirit."

"Well, then, even *he* can suffer—can't you see? But this thing's not by any means confined to far-away Boston. Two years ago, timed along with this eastern agitation, the non-Mormon women here in Salt Lake, held a mass meeting at the Congregational Church. They drew up a petition to Mrs. Rutherford B. Hayes, wife of the President of the United States, deploring the practice of plural marriage, begging her to prevail on her husband to begin a determined campaign to stamp it out, and to deny statehood to Utah until it *was* stamped out. Oh, Nan, there's a lot to it! They raised unholy Ned because our territorial representative, Apostle George Q. Cannon, was allowed to sit in Congress, when it was a known fact he had four wives. I doubt there were three hundred non-Mormon women behind this so-called mass meeting and petition, but the ugly thing they did went far beyond their numbers."

"I heard more about the Mormon mass meetings that followed," Nancy said. "We had 'em down in Ammon and Provo."

Yes, she remembered the mass meetings, and her own reaction at the time. Thousands of Mormon women, caught up in a marriage system she'd never understand, defending with their honor and their lives the right to practice it. If America thought Mormon women didn't condone their unnatural servitude, and were anxious to be released therefrom, it should take a close look at the female commotion that went up and down Zion two years ago. Nancy had shocked her Mormon sisters by refusing to sign.

"We met at the Salt Lake Theater—two thousand of us," Flora said proudly. "Sister Cook presided, Sister Bane acted as secretary. As an apostle's wife, I couldn't stand out too prominently at a mass meeting, but I served on the committee, and worked like mad. Theater was absolutely jam-packed. And after it was over, there could be no doubt as to where *we* stood on this issue. In the petition, signed by thousands of Mormon women, we reminded Congress of the misrepresentations that had gone out, even from Utah; that they must make no laws abridging the constitutional right to worship God according to the dictates of one's conscience; and that, as wives and mothers we be accepted and respected. It was a tremendous thing, Nan."

"From the worries I hear on every hand, I'd say it hasn't done a startling lot of good."

The English girl, Matey, silently entered, and commenced gathering up the now neglected plates and cups. The firming of Flora's lips at sight of her, and the way her still bright and blue eyes studied the trim and appealing little figure, seemed to Nancy a measuring out of a menace in the Cragg household. From outside she could still hear the shrill squeals and chatter of the children, but in her earnest discussion of polygamy and its problems she'd all but forgotten Edward.

"I didn't mean to dump my child on you, Matey," Nancy apologized. "Is he all right, and a good boy?"

"Oh, he's most all right, ma'am," Matey replied, with her intriguing little accent from Britain. "And he's a very good boy. He's riding the lawn swing with Florinda and John, and having a merry time of it." Her gray eyes squinted with her winsome smile. And Nancy knew then how decorative and useful an addition Matey would make to any Saint's family kingdom.

"Well, you call me, if you need me, Matey. Or bring the boy in if he gets tired. He's had quite a day."

"I shall, ma'am." And the smile was charm itself.

When she was gone, Flora pondered a moment, as though to talk about the girl, but shrugged and went on with the more general problems of Mormon polygamy.

"With the hue and cry going on across the nation," Flora said, settling to fresh ease on the sofa, "it's next to impossible to get the Mormon side of the story heard. Most damning things of all come right out of Salt Lake City. Let a Mormon squabble with a plural wife, and the news is telegraphed around the world. Look at that Miles case."

"Joel and I talked about it on the drive from Ammon. That, and Brigham's public bout with his Ann Eliza."

"One of John Miles' plural wives—Carrie Owen, *a convert from England,* became jealous of one of the other wives, Emily Spencer. She told a fantastic story to the federal officers, and then all hell broke out in the newspapers across the nation. At one time she declared that Brother Miles had decoyed her from her home in London, brought her to Utah, and forced her into an unnatural wedding ceremony, to a man already married to two other women. Then she claims she was taken to the home of Angus Cannon, and there cruelly outraged in the name of religion."

"Seems to me these wife-hunting brethren would avoid a lot of trouble if they'd marry their brides before bringing them to Utah."

Flora looked sharply at her half sister. "As a Saint, Nan," she said wearily, "you know that's impossible. Marriages under the covenant can only be performed in the House of the Lord. Someday, when the Church has dotted the earth with its holy temples, such a thing will be possible."

"That'll be the day," Nancy chuckled.

But Flora saw no reason for laughter. "This English-born Carrie Owen, in her lawsuit against Brother Miles, dragged celestial marriage through the mire, and made the Church a laughing stock before the world. President Daniel H. Wells, former mayor of Salt Lake City, former general of the Nauvoo Legion, and a high authority in the Church, was sent to jail because of the sensational antics of this woman. They subpoenaed President Wells to the federal court hearing the Miles case, as the man who allegedly had performed the plural wedding ceremony at the Endowment House. He answered all the court's questions freely, until they demanded he also reveal the details of the ceremony, the clothing worn, and all the things which Saints consider most sacred. These things President Wells utterly refused to answer. For this honorable stand, they hustled him off to the penitentiary."

"I read in the papers about Salt Lake's celebration when President Wells was released. Must have been quite an affair."

"Well," sighed Flora, "it should have served notice on the world that the Saints are united in their fight to save the Church. His escort from the penitentiary became one of the biggest parades in this city's history, with bands, marchers, floats, and his beloved Nauvoo Legion all taking part. The great tabernacle was literally packed with thousands upon thousands of Saints, at the public reception held in his honor. Seven bands of music sat with, and accompanied the tabernacle choir, as it sang its praise to this courageous man. For one day at least, Carrie Owen was forgotten." Flora arose, nervously, walked to the front window, and looked out on the wide city street. She turned, sauntered back to the couch. "After stirring up this hornet's nest of filth and blackmail for the Church, Carrie Owen has gone East to carry on her troublemaking. For her part in the betrayal, she was given a federal job in Washington, D.C. *The Deseret News* says she's now writing a book aimed at exposing the Church."

Nancy thought of Joel's long, abortive effort to get anything published that might favor the Church. "The book should have a fat sale," she said. "Public can't get enough of that kind of stuff."

"They're pouring it at us, Nan. Hot and heavy. What does Joel think about this Reverend Joseph Cook, in Boston, who demands the government remove all danger of polygamy, by wiping out the Saints?"

"Well, Joel's mother is well mixed up in these anti-Mormon movements. Probably backing this Boston preacher vocally and financially. You see, Joel's had no luck whatever in peddling his beliefs to his upsnoot family. Sorrows because of it, too."

"I'm doing some sorrowing, too, Nan. If men like President Wells can be jailed for their beliefs, my husband, as an apostle, is not any the less safe. Seems to me the holy principle of celestial marriage is on trial before the world—and that we're powerless to present the truth in our own behalf."

Nancy toyed thoughtfully with the tassel hanging from the little table beside her. "Flo, forgive me for asking this, but I can't help but wonder how it is in *your* life. As a plural wife, you appear happy—and certainly you're well taken care of. But are you *really* happy? Do you have the same jealousies and hurts with the other wives, that Father Corey had in *his* family kingdom? Can a woman really adjust to this sort of thing?"

Flora laughed. "A woman can adjust to most anything—especially if she has to. I'm not sorry I married Jonathan. He's human. He has his faults. But he's been good to me and my children."

"He also has other wives," Nancy reminded.

"True. And I'd be a liar if I said that all was serenity in the Cragg kingdom. Several of his wives I can't stomach. Others I deeply love. At school our respective children mix it a little, and it takes tact and patience to unsnarl some of the little problems. But, once you're used to it, Nan, it isn't bad."

"But it just can't be *that* easy."

"No, Nan, it isn't. Before I got accustomed to Jonathan and his ways, and the glares and sarcasm of his other wives when he moved *me* in, there was many a time when I was ready to flee back to Ammon. I'd remember our talks about the Principle, and how you alone had the nerve and courage to fight out of it. But all of that passed with earnest prayer, with time, and with the children. The first time you and I talked together in this room, I'd prayed myself into full belief and acceptance. It was later the real tests came. But I overcame them, Nan."

"The real tests?" Nancy probed. "What were the real tests?"

"Oh, as I look back on them now, they don't lump up as anything very important. Just a woman's natural possessive nature. And the little hurts. You just learn to share, overlook, and forgive, that's all. And probably the most persistent thing has been the everlasting problem of being the youngest, and the favored wife. It's one of the hardest parts of the plural covenant to be forgiven this thing."

"I don't mean to carp about this, Flo, but it still seems to me plural marriage amounts to one thing—making the best of a situation over which a wife has little control. She has to fit her life to a certain pattern, in which she has only one vote. Instead of romance, and a partnership with her husband, she has to adjust, compensate, tolerate, and pray. I still don't think that's the way a marriage should be. And I'm glad I've thus far been able to keep free of the Principle."

Flora smiled loftily, and tossed her head. "Be glad while you can, Nan. Because it *can* happen—even to you. My life with Jonathan hasn't been particularly romantic, I'll agree. But it hasn't been a bad life, either. Adjustment, compensation, tolerance, and prayer—yes, indeed. But they'll come even to the most romantic and exciting of marriages. You're still a little smug about the Principle, Nan, but don't ever lose track of the fact that you live in Utah. That you're a part of Mormonism. And in spite of the fact that the Saints are cursed and criticized around the world, they *are* practicing plural marriage, and will *continue* to practice it. It's woman's nature to own and possess. But there's never been a man born who isn't a polygamist at heart. It isn't only possible but probable that Joel will get that roving eye—especially when it not only is sanctioned but urged by the Church. You may squash his talk about the Principle, Nan. But it will take a better woman than you are to squash his thoughts."

Nancy cocked her head defiantly, and managed a laugh. "Mary Magdalene, before her marriage to Seth, offered herself to Joel in the Principle." Nancy chuckled mirthlessly. "I don't have to tell you that he spurned her."

"Don't be a blind little idiot, Nan. When and if Joel decides on plurality, he'll grab off some fresh young little chickadee. And you'll suddenly find yourself making the same adjustments and allowances daily facing the thousands of other plural wives. And for the sake of your loved ones, your children, and your Church, you'll line up with the rest of us in defending the Principle to your last breath."

Flora had probed mercilessly at the black thoughts Nancy had lived with for years, and they growled back at her like any aching tooth. Then suddenly she panicked with fright. "If Joel should ever dare pick another wife," she snarled, "especially a younger and prettier one, I'll wring her damned neck like a chicken!"

Flora smiled knowingly, and again walked to the window. It was late twilight now. She turned and looked condescendingly at Nancy. "My, my—where's the smugness and the bravado now?"

"You'll never hear me defending the Principle," Nancy grumbled. "I still hate it. I think it's damnable."

"You don't have to defend it—yet." Flora again walked back to the couch.

"I never shall!"

Flora smiled and shook her head.

Nancy, nettled and angry, said, "What would you do, now that you've so accustomed yourself to plurality, if Apostle Cragg suddenly decided to get a younger, more attractive wife?"

"I'd react precisely like Nancy Scott. I'd wring her damned neck like a chicken."

"Aha!" Nancy laughed triumphantly.

"As a matter of fact, you're going to *help* me wring her neck, Nan." Flora beckoned. "Come over to the couch, so I don't have to talk too loud."

Nancy moved, in the darkening room, to Flora's side. "What's up, Flo?"

"I've got to banish this Matey Thorpe to somewhere. I know Jonathan enough to be certain his bringing her to Zion was not altogether for the salvation of her soul. When she looks at me with those wide and innocent gray eyes, I want to crawl out of sight like a bedbug. I feel this little doll knows that one day soon, at the Endowment House, she's going to upset my reign as favored queen of the Cragg family kingdom. Nan, I can't sleep. I'm going crazy."

"Well, by golly damn!" Nancy sighed, a little sadly. "But there's nothing I can do!"

"Oh yes there is." Flora leaned close, and half whispered. "I've written Mother. She's agreed to accept Matey."

"Aunt Millie?"

"Yes, she needs a girl, a lot more than Jonathan needs another wife. I want you and Joel to take Matey back with you."

"You think that'll stop your apostle?"

"It'll be a good try. And at least I'll get the girl out of this house before I lose my mind with worry." She looked beseechingly at Nancy, and for the first time in years, Nancy saw tears in Flora's eyes. "Please, Nan," she implored.

"I'll have to talk this over with Joel. He's the boss. He's the driver."

"You've got the surrey. There'll be room."

Nancy, shaken and upset, could say no more.

"Good grief, it's practically dark!" Flora said, rising. "Let's get the lamps lit, and the kids in. And Elena should have supper cooked and ready by now."

When Flora arose, Nancy watched her dully as she scurried about, lighting the ornate lamps. When she was gone from the room, to gather the family, and to get the household moving normally again, Nancy leaned back to think. There was no envy in her heart for Flo's position as an apostle's wife. It was something to know that, but for a few flukes of circumstance, she too might have occupied the same frame of existence. It hadn't been easy to buck the Principle, but she'd done it, hard and furious. And so far she'd won. She had Joel as evidence and prize. Moreover, in spite of Flo's dire predictions, Joel hadn't looked with hungry eyes at any other woman. Flo could have her precious apostolic life. She wouldn't trade places with her for all the glories of this world or the next.

Joel, anxious to confer with Salt Lake educators before the city was hopelessly tied up in the affairs of the great three-day conference, had dinner elsewhere, and did not get back to Flora's house until late evening. By then all the children, including little Edward, were asleep in their beds. Nancy felt that Joel had missed a rare evening. The Cragg "supper," competently cooked by Elena, and unobtrusively and politely served by Matey, proved an elegant treat.

"It really isn't much," Flora apologized. "If you'd have dropped me a line you were coming, we'd have had something quite nice."

"You're certainly putting yourself out for us, Flo," Nancy said. "I sit here wishing Joel could have managed to be here with us." She let her woman's eye rove over the snowy linen, the sterling silver, the special dining room for serving, and the competent help Flora always could have at her elbow. This was so different from Ammon. She couldn't blame Flo for wanting to show it off. Even the perfect manners and behavior of the Cragg children were strange contrast to the noisy, relaxed table when Joel and her own brood sat down to eat. While she was here, it would pay her to learn and observe a bit of the city ways. For she was impressed—vastly impressed.

On Tuesday morning, April 6, the jubilee conference of the Church got under way at the great new tabernacle. Though conferences were regular twice-a-year features of the Mormon pattern, this one was particularly significant in that it marked the fiftieth anniversary of the Church. Nancy, nor any other Latter-day Saint, was allowed to forget, especially at this time, that the Church which would someday fill the whole earth, had its humble start April 6, 1830, at Fayette, New York, with six members. Now the huge domed tabernacle could not begin to hold the crowds from all over Zion. Though Mormonism had a considerable way to go before it would fill the earth, it had made a heady start.

Most of the apostles, with the exception of those who, like Jonathan Cragg, were filling essential posts across the sea, were on hand to preach the word, and to bear their own testimonies to the truth and essentiality of the Gospel in these the last days. Nancy and Joel, knowing the Church had been ruled by the Quorum of the Twelve Apostles since the sad and sudden death of Brigham Young, three years before, went to the sessions fully expecting the long awaited announcement as to Brigham's successor. They nor no other Saint questioned who it would be. John Taylor, the apostle who had stood with Joseph Smith in Carthage jail during the martyrdom, was the senior apostle. This would not only automatically assure his accession to the presidency, but would also make certain the Church would forever be managed by old men, rather than the more fearless and virile youths of the Prophet's day.

But the Authorities decided to wait until the October conference to confirm John Taylor in the presidency—reserving the jubilee sessions to a time of general rejoicing and appraisal of the Church's amazing strides over its first dramatic and turbulent half-century. Apostle Orson Pratt saw to it that Ammon's schoolmaster, now he was a Saint in good standing, occupied a seat in the section reserved for the ruling elite—in the high stand behind the pulpit. Back and beyond this area, in rising tiers of seats up to, and surrounding the great organ, was the choir of four hundred voices. The organ itself, its pipes lovingly fashioned of seasoned pine from the mountains of Utah's Dixie had, through the fortuitous circumstances of good organ-building and the unmatched acoustics of the great dome, already become famed as one of the most superb musical instruments on earth. Nancy, who sat with an apostle's wife, in a special reserved section down front, was not quite as exalted and favored as Joel, but it didn't matter. In this building no one was slighted. Every word of any given speech could be heard equally well from any portion of the building, and every majestic note of music from choir and organ, was acoustically perfect to the ear of any Saint fortunate enough to squeeze into the tabernacle.

For three days the building reverberated to the sermons and songs of a Mormon conference. This time, however, there was a difference. Proud of their fifty-year achievement, the leaders thundered out their hopes for the future. But, more important, the Mormons made this conference significant by a real borrowing from the more ancient Israelites.

Convinced, through revelation, that they were of Israel, through the very loins and seed of Father Abraham, the Saints long ago had copied every Israelite custom that would fit their pattern, or was mentioned in Holy Writ—even to the peculiarities of ancient Hebraic marriage. At this conference, they borrowed once again—this time the biblical jubilee practice of the forgiveness of sin, and the rescindment of debt. As an altruistic example to the flock, the Church led out by forgiving the Saints who were deeply in debt to it; such debts as advances made from the Perpetual Emigration Fund, or tithing arrears. The Church held notes against its people for hundreds of thousands of dollars. To set the pace for the speedy freeing from bondage of every poor and worthy debtor in Utah, the Church offered willing cancellation of its own debts to any of its worthy poor, in return for a like example of faith and altruism from the merchants and moneylenders throughout Zion whose tentacles of debt might be strangling the good efforts of its citizens. Joel and Nancy, vastly pleased by this generous example of the Church, were not so sure private business would as wholeheartedly go along. But spiritually, the jubilee turned out to be a time of remembrance. Not a soul who attended the stirring sessions of that memorable week, went away without the feeling of vast pride in the progress of his

Church, the shattering importance of its message, and an honest resolve to be a more loving brother and a better Saint.

And when the time finally came for Joel's decision as to whether Matey Thorpe could ride in the surrey to Ammon, Joel, spiritually at peace with the world, filled with the message of the sermons, and the brotherly kindness so thoroughly implanted, could not help but be expansive and hospitable. "Of course she may ride with us," he said. "There's plenty of room. We'd be more than glad to have her."

Joel, vastly pleased with the attentions he'd received from the Authorities in Salt Lake, and the fact they at last seemed to be cognizant of his sacrifice and work on behalf of village education in Utah, was in exuberant spirits throughout the trip southward. Nancy, aside from the spiritual uplift of the sermons and music, the satisfaction from her close personal visit with Flora, and the fact little Edward could meet and mix with some more of his cousins, was not in an especially joyful mood as Joel's fine horses sped them homeward. Again they stopped overnight at Draper, and by that time Joel and the young girl, Matey, were well acquainted.

Joel had been to England; had visited Liverpool, Matey's own town. In their discussion of this far land and its places—Matey in her odd and winsome dialect, Joel in the sharp and still strange vernacular of New England, Nancy felt completely shut out of their conversation. She could teat a cow, tie an umbilical cord, and tell a hell of a lot about Utah, but these things were no part of this talk. Matey, sunny as usual, showed no resentment whatever in Flora's connivance to get her out of Salt Lake and into her mother's hands. "Oh, that would be jolly," Matey had said, when finally it was decided Joel would take her. "Often I've wondered what it would look like over the mountains."

"You'll find it the most beautiful place in the world," Joel had predicted.

"I'll get my things packed forthwith." And Matey did it, as happy as a bird in a fresh-ploughed field.

At their various stops, Joel handed Matey down the surrey steps with plenty of flourish and politeness. And it was these little things that stirred Nancy's resentment. By the time they reached Draper, she'd built up a festering dislike for this happy, delicate, competent youngster who had so much to talk about.

At Draper there was only one room to their reservation. So Joel slept in the surrey, and Nancy and Matey shared the big bed together. By then Matey had practically taken over little Edward, and there could be no question that Edward in turn liked Matey. Through the long miles she amused him, played with him, talked with him, and was attentive to his every whim. For long miles, on the back seat, she let him sleep out his naps with his head cradled on her lap. And Nancy, though edgy, could scarcely be rude to anyone who showed love and attention toward her own kin. Certainly she'd wanted no Matey Thorpe for this return trip to Ammon—but she'd gotten her. One just made the best of it, that was all.

The weather held exceptionally good for the entire trip, and Ammon was never more beautiful than when they pulled into its wide and shady streets on the afternoon of the second day. The cherry orchards were a-blossom, and the stately poplars were already wearing their summer's green. Matey's gray eyes opened like auger holes to everything about her. "So different from England," she sighed.

"I told you 'twould be pretty—and you'd like it," Joel said confidently. "Take a look at those snowy mountains. See if you don't think it the most startling sight in the world."

"Oh, I love it," she purred. "I know I'm going to enjoy living here."

"Give another month, and it will *really* be classic." Joel started the horses again, and the carriage moved east on Main Street. "Are we going home first, Nan?" he asked.

"No, we're not," Nancy said with finality. "You forget that Matey's going somewhere else. Take her over to Aunt Millie's. Then home."

II

AS THE DAYS OF SPRING, LOADED WITH THE PROBLEMS OF A BUSY HOUSE-hold, and the unwanted but continuing problems of other households, passed along into Nancy's time of living, she could look back on the jubilee trip as a most happy and eventful experience. It was good to go to the city, to observe the new customs, and at least absorb enough of the grace and polish one encountered to chisel away at the rougher edges of country life. Through the Ammon Co-operative Store, Nancy ordered tablecloths, napkins, and antimacassars similar to those Flora had used with such elegance in her home on West Temple Street. At least she described them to the clerk, and hoped to heaven there would be some similarity to the original, when and if they finally arrived.

From the time of her return Nancy put a strict halter on the noise and manners of her own brood. Not that they had never been exposed to good manners, for Joel had always set an exemplary pattern, but out of his sight they could be lax and perverse. Now she took a hand in correcting the youngsters at the table. Over and over she insisted they say "Thank you," and "Yes, ma'am," and "Yes, sir," whenever the occasion required it. She hoped that in the day the Cragg and Scott families came within spitting distance of one another, that the Scott children, even if country-bred, would not suffer too much by comparison. But in setting up the new regime of grace and gentility, she suffered—and so did the children. "I think Mom's gone crazy," was Jody's comment. And freckled-nosed Marty could only shake her head in amazement at the queer things that were happening since Mother's return.

It had been good to immerse oneself once more in the dynamic activities of the Church. The dramatic words from the pulpit of the tabernacle not only stirred the spirit to greater endeavor, but gave one a truer perspective and a greater understanding of the vitality and destiny of the Latter-day Movement. Nancy had come back from this conference resolved to pay stricter attention to her religious duties, and, for the sake of her family, if nothing more, to set a more perfect example before them of a true and devout mother in Israel. In line with the jubilee theme, she canceled out the debts of the eleven Ammon families who still owed her five dollars apiece for delivering their respective children into the new dispensation.

It had been good to meet and get acquainted with Flora once more. It had washed out the bitterness of that other more caustic and critical visit, when she'd confessed to Flora her intentions of fleeing Zion with her Gentile. But that had happened so long ago. Joel, like every other convert under the mesmeric transformation of the Church's spiritual conversion, had long since shed every trapping of his Gentile days. Now, even though Flora was married to an apostle, and moved constantly in the public life, Nancy could eye her straight and unwavering; she could hold her head as high as any Cragg. And on this evened-out basis, the old love and friendship had, in a measure, returned to their lives. The only disturbing note to that rich and happy trip, had been Flora's shedding Matey Thorpe to the Scott custody, and the lethal nearness of this British elfin through the miles of the trip's return. But

Matey had been delivered to Aunt Millie's and, other than an occasional glimpse of her at church, nothing more had come of it.

While in Salt Lake Nancy had bought new clothes, ogled the new furniture at the Church-owned Zion's Co-operative Mercantile Institution—shortened by everyone to the simpler ZCMI—and purchased a lot of the needed household supplies so far unavailable to the Ammon Co-op. She'd even squandered fifteen dollars in church scrip on a leather surgical kit to house the essential instruments necessary to help bring children into the world.

With the arrival of Dr. Horace Middy, a Thompsonian physician with enough medical schooling to make him competent, Nancy had hoped her own years of midwifery would be at an end. That was two years ago. Mary Magdalene, old, arthritic, and dedicated to the care of Seth, would answer only nearby and occasional calls. The women of Ammon, Nancy quickly found, had been slow to tender themselves in this delicate and embarrassing hour to the hands of a strange man, no matter how competent. Dr. Middy's practice, at least in obstetrics, had grown a lot slower than had Nancy's. And then there had been that problem of momentum. A great portion of Ammon's women bore children with clocklike regularity. No sooner was the womb back in condition than a fresh seed would be planted. And Nancy, who had guided the earliest child to its first bleat, was insistently expected to tend the latest one—and the doctor of the town be damned. So, until Ammon women were more willing to accept Dr. Middy at their birthings, Nancy's trim little buggy and fast horse were just as familiar to Ammon on this essential errand as had been Mary Magdalene's before her. And still hoping that 1880, the good year, would at least show the beginning of the end to her midwifery, Nancy had purchased her leather professional kit to tide her over to the day that her full time and attentions could be given to her own family.

In such fashion did the fall of this good and auspicious year roll around. The solid winter previous had left plenty of snow in the mountains, and the Utah earth had again produced in abundance. Granaries were fat with the rich harvest. Saints were smug and self-satisfied with their new prosperity. The summer had been one of green beauty, and there was no question but what the smile of God was upon His people.

The fiftieth year had brought some serious thinking into the Church, along with the certitude and acceptance of its material prosperity. Its people, to all intents and purposes, were united in their determination to fight back at the calumny and criticism heaped upon them by a hostile press and pulpit. Since the return from the jubilee conference, Joel had more deeply dedicated himself to religious study and good works. At times Nancy grew irritated with the fact that it was like living again in the household of Isaac Corey. At Joel's insistence, they had family prayers in the morning, the blessing on the food at mealtime, and family prayers at night. Joel's late reading of Scripture and Mormon doctrine had not only made him a theologian of repute, but an eloquent speaker who could deliver the Word in a way that shook any backsliding audience to its sinful marrow. There could be no question that he was a marked man in the Church. And, if he kept on in this inspiring manner, it was only a question of time until he would rise to the top.

Nancy wondered about this fervor, and was as vaguely disturbed about it as any of the other striking changes that had come over her Gentile in the years of their marriage. Throughout this splendid summer, and into the fall, she failed to know the answer. And then, at the October conference, in Salt Lake City, John Taylor at last was sustained as Prophet, Seer, and Revelator to the Church—to at long last fill the vacant shoes of the mighty Brigham. In light of the spiritual steam generated by the April conference, Nancy was a little surprised that Joel had not suggested or insisted they likewise sit in on this second historic meet. A week later, she knew exactly why.

Sister Melinda Cheshire, second wife of Elder Alpheus Cheshire, lived in a new three-room adobe out on the acreage which, in the days of the walled town, had been sage-land, and a free and accessible walking area to Walkara, Arrapeen, and their troublesome Utes. With the rebirth and growth of Ammon, this newly resettled farming area had become known simply as the East Fields. Here the Cheshires and other ambitious Mormon families had established neat and prosperous homesteads for themselves extending outward almost to the town of Mountain Grove. Brother Cheshire, like so many Saints before him, had first tried housing his plural wives and families under one roof. Quickly he'd learned that if he were to preserve any semblance of saintly serenity, he had best make a change. So, and again like so many Saints before him, he'd built identical houses for his women, on separate plats of land. Throughout both these arrangements, Brother Cheshire's seed had been exceedingly fertile. Sarah, his first wife had presented him an increase of four children—two of them delivered by Nancy Scott. Melinda, in only four years, had added three to his family kingdom, and Nancy had attended all her birthings—including the last, and most recent.

It was on the second day of Melinda Cheshire's confinement. Nancy had finished her follow-up call. Mother and girl baby were doing well, except for that pesky caking in Melinda's left breast. It was late fall twilight when Nancy tossed her leather kit into the seat of the buggy, climbed in, touched Bess's tail with the whip, and started rattling her jaunt westward toward town and home. For fall, it was not at all cold. What frosts there had been this year had been only occasional, but enough to turn the orchards and the poplars into a fantastic pattern of gold and reds. It had been a pretty year all around. She'd never known it to be so pretty.

Preoccupied with her thoughts, and the wild and lavish paint of color surrounding, she was letting Bess find her own way home. And with water, stall, and oats so imminent, Bess required no guidance or urging. The buggy rattled merrily westward, and occasionally Nancy waved to a Mormon brother or sister as she passed their neat little houses and yards. Not until she reached the new stone bridge over Ammon Creek did she notice the couple. The man and girl, arms entwined about each other's waists, were sitting on the bridge's stone coping, backs to the road, and staring down into the creek. For lovers to choose the willowed and romantic seclusion of the bridge or creek-bed was nothing new. In her travels about the valley, she'd seen more than one pair in that very spot. But as she topped the big, wide bridge itself, a vague familiarity made her take a second look. And what she saw was enough to make her topple over the dashboard. It was Joel—and another intense look identified the girl—Matey Thorpe.

Not even the rattle of the wheels had disturbed them. And Bess had pulled the carriage over the bridge before Nancy could haul the hungry and anxious mare to full stop. But stop Bess did. With a sob of fury, Nancy piled out. Oddly, as she did at every call and emergency, she grabbed up the leather midwife's kit without thinking. It was in her hand as she strode back up to the top of the bridge.

So intent were they in their conversation and love-making, they did not even turn until she was actually within arm's reach. By then her rage was whistling out like stream under a pot lid, and she was like a panther ready to spring. When Joel did look around, to actually observe who was stalking him, the look of blank amazement on his face gave him the look of the village idiot with his finger caught in a cracker barrel.

"Well, Nan," he managed to stammer. "This is Matey Thorpe—we—"

"I know who it is, you damned lecherous, conniving pair!" Nancy shrieked.

Matey languorously turned around and smiled innocently. "How are you, Mrs. Scott?" she added before Nancy could start the grim business of killing her.

224

"Nancy," Joel said, fighting for his poise and assurance, "let's all go home and talk. I've some things I want to tell you."

"What home? You'll not come into my home! You'll not bring that English harlot anywhere near me or my children! If you do, I'll kill you both!" Tears and moans of rage were coming, and she couldn't stop them.

"Oh, Nan, let's be sensible!" Joel said. "Let's talk—"

"Sensible! And *you* outrage me like this! Why, you—!"

And then, like a windmill, Nancy Scott went into action. Moaning like a wounded beast she commenced flailing them both over the head with her heavy leather kit. They both put their hands up to defend themselves from the murderous onslaught, but they were sitting wrong way to the bridge for any effective defense. Matey started screaming like a seduced cat, and Joel's voice quickly turned from reasoning to bellows and roars. But the blows came; they came hard, and without mercy. And then finally, with one mighty lunge, Nancy charged. She caught them both in the middle of their backs. Flailing the air, shouting and screeching like crazy, they both went face forward off the bridge coping, and into the waters of Ammon Creek.

"I hope you drown—the pair of you!" she shouted after them.

Sobbing, still clutching the leather kit by its broken handle, Nancy limped down the bridge side and into the dusty road. The carriage was gone. Bess, her mind on oats, had little thought for human tangles. Bess had continued along the familiar way.

Half running, half walking, moaning and hysterical, Nancy followed the errant mare, far in the distance. Thank God, she thought, it's darkening. People can't see me in this state. But her world was shattered. This was the end. Only place to go was home. And somehow, by following Ammon's back streets, she made it. When she got there, Bess had pulled the buggy up to the lane gate, and was patiently waiting to be unhitched and led to her stall and oats.

III

IN THE ENTIRE SPAN OF THEIR MARRIAGE, THIS WAS THE FIRST NIGHT JOEL had willfully absented himself from home because of family differences or misunderstanding. Professional journeys to Salt Lake, pack trips to the mountains, and that long trip back to Boston had taken him from the family circle for varying lengths of time. Even in these secure and understanding intervals he'd been sorely missed. But never was the shattering impact of his absence more sorely noted and felt than this night Nancy spent alone in her bed.

In the helpless anger and humiliation that kept her in sleepless tossing, and sogged her pillow with tears, Nancy probably would have stripped off his hide and quartered him, had he decided to return home. But even the delicious privilege of flailing out her hates and hurts upon him were denied. In her bedroom turmoil, she kept her ears attuned to the familiar footsteps on the gravel outside, the turn of his key in the lock—but those sounds never came. By the time her sleepless night died out to an aching dawn, her anger had subsided. Only the hurts, the deepest kind of hurts, remained.

When she'd first stumbled into the house, the youngsters had quickly noticed something was wrong. While they eyed her in silent surprise, she'd gone to the bedroom, flung the broken medical kit into a corner, and peeled off her coat and hat. After touching up her hair and drying her eyes, she'd tried for a calm entrance into the living room. To keep things moving she'd ordered Marty out to the kitchen, to start the evening meal, and young Joel to drive Bess back to the corral, and get her unharnessed and fed. It had kept the older ones from asking questions. The younger ones had been unimpressed.

Dinner had consisted of warm-overs, and a place was dutifully set for Joel. At the questions of where father was on this fall night, all she could say was, "He may be late . . . leave him some dinner in the warming oven." Biting hard on her trembling lip kept her somehow from a slobbering breakdown in front of the youngsters. They'd accepted her plea that she was ill—because she'd probably looked it—and her fast after-dinner exit to her room had been made without too much comment or concern. As to the dishes and the evening cleanup, Marty and the smaller girls had, because of their mother's frequent calls away from home, long ago mastered that particular problem.

But the children, in their innocent minds, could never know the devastation and horror that walked with their mother into that bedroom. Nancy had changed to her nightgown, because it was habit, and there was nothing else to do. But no bed is ever lonelier than when its man is gone. She'd tried to steel herself to the fact that it must be forever—but somehow, when it came to the final, desperate resolution, her courage ended up in a flood of tears.

She knew, beyond any question of doubt, what it was Joel wanted the three of them to talk over. The thought and substance of it never ceased to infuriate her throughout the wracking night. For months, probably ever since spring's ride down from Salt Lake, Joel had likely been keeping company with Matey Thorpe. Joel's politeness and animation, and his courtesies toward the girl, had given an intuitive warning—but she'd dismissed the thought when they had dismissed Matey at Aunt Millie's. She should have known that men cannot shed their manly arousals as easily as they do their dirty socks. Throughout the summer, she'd been so taken up with living, and other women's problems, that she'd stupidly never given second hearing to her first worries. And the cleverness of Joel and his hussy had made it no easier to discover that another Mormon romance had started along its inevitable path toward acceptance and sanction. The thing she'd seen on the creek bridge was the culmination of her deepest fears, and the greatest shock of her life.

The ease with which Flora had removed her household menace and planted it in the Scott garden made her furious enough to claw the plaster off the walls. And what the hell difference was there between Jonathan Cragg and Joel Scott when a tender little English twig minced and swayed before them? It was a case of here's a *real* bud—first pluck, first bloom. And now Joel—her Joel—the Gentile she'd once married to keep out of plurality—would come up with the pious decision, now that he was a good Mormon, to add Matey Thorpe to his holy increase. And he'd expect her to consent; to love and cherish him still. And this, like the others before it, would be for time and all eternity.

No, by hell, there'd be *no* sharing of this man she'd married! When he came sheepishly crawling in for the verdict, it would be Nancy Corey or Matey Thorpe, not both, and the celestial glory be damned!

And then the inevitable next thought paralyzed her with fear. The choice would, as sure as God lived, be Matey Thorpe—because that was the way men were constructed. A man could be a perfect husband and a model father. He could sire a family and love them. He could sleep with the wife; be tender to her; cherish her. Then, let some mincing young thing strain the buttons on his pants, and a new chase was on. It was nothing to leave a familiar fireside; nothing to desert the bed of his first love; nothing to walk away from his children. Men were hunters —all of them. Thousands of wrecked homes around the world were proof of it. But only the Mormons put the stamp of divine approval upon it. Apostle Cragg had married Flora; he would have married Nancy; Isaac Corey had married Kirstine Overson; it was done every day, and with the sanction of the Church, and the blessing of God. But when the inevitable came, and Joel Scott was forced to decide between Nancy and Matey, Nancy already knew, in the middle of her tears, what the answer would be. The other choice was to share him. And oh, God —this world or the next—she *couldn't* do that!

With the sleep she so desperately needed chopped and ground out to nothing by the twin burrstones of futility and despair, Nancy rolled early from her soggy bed, and had breakfast prepared for the youngsters as soon as daylight rousted them from their own more comfortable sleep. Jody was old enough, and had been conditioned by his father, to feed the horses and milk the single family cow, and Marty had long ago fitted herself into the routine help and smooth operation of the Scott household. Not until Jody, Marty, and Amanda had seated themselves at the breakfast table did they take notice that things were not quite normal this October morning.

"Where's Father?" Marty asked, looking across the table at the wearied Nancy. "Did you call him for breakfast?"

"He'll not be here for breakfast," Nancy said, straining for a smile. "He didn't get back last night."

"He didn't take out Gus and George," Jody said.

"He's not driving *his* horses," Nancy answered, casually as she could.

"Oh." And the boy shrugged, for all the world like his father. "Will he be at school?"

"Perhaps. Maybe later. You'll probably see him there."

The explanation sufficed. And an hour later the three youngsters had departed for their classrooms.

Little Vernell lacked a year of being school age, and baby Edward, who needed a lot of help in dressing for his day, were fed at a later sitting, and were too young to ask questions. But as the morning rolled on, and Joel failed to appear, Nancy grew increasingly nervous and panicky. Over and over she rehearsed in her mind what she'd do and say when her errant husband walked through the door. In the end, she finally decided on the silent treatment. Let the man do his own explaining, and, after he'd talked out his say, be ready to cut him down with the answers. But then, again, she remembered, there really were no answers. Everything she knew she'd say was only part of the venom distilling out of the hurt and humiliation that was grinding her down through this night and this day. By afternoon not even the chance of eyeing him out was granted her. Joel made no effort to return.

Vernell and Edward had been put to nap, and by now she'd reached another weeping frenzy. And then, at long last, a buggy pulled up to the hitching post. Out from under its cover stepped a man. But it was not Joel. It was the aging and now bent figure of Bishop Earlington. In this hour, the bishop was the last person in the world Nancy Scott wanted to see. But even this unwanted errand must have some link with Joel, so she blotted her eyes with the soggy handkerchief, touched the wilted puffs of her hair, and met the bishop at the door.

"Hello, Sister Nancy," he said with nervous geniality.

"Come in, Bishop Earlington." When he'd gotten himself somewhat feebly across the threshold, she reached out for his overcoat and hat.

"Nice day." Clumsily and laboriously, while she held his time-tired hat, he worked himself out of the coat.

" 'Tis a nice day," she said, knowing well that, by the very act of surrendering his coat, the old man had come loaded for talk. "We've had some beautiful fall weather, I think." She hung the hat and coat to the wall hooks. He was still standing, teetering thoughtfully on his spindly legs, and clawing at his gray beard when she returned to the living room. "Do be seated," she said.

"Thank you, Sister Nancy." He flopped wearily into Joel's soft stuffed chair, and sighed contentedly. "The old legs ache a little—even ahead of the weather. How're those fine children of yours?"

"They're fine," Nancy reiterated, growing edgy at his reluctance to get down to the reason for his visit. Wearily she flopped to a chair. "The devil with the weather and the kids," she suddenly blurted. "Have you seen Joel?"

He pondered a moment, while she fidgeted. "Yes, I have," he said at last. "Joel asked me to come and see you."

Again the anger flared up in her. "What's the matter? Hasn't he two legs? Hasn't he a voice to speak for himself?"

"I'm sorry, Sister Nancy." The bishop again fingered his beard, and then rubbed his arthritic thighs with both his hands. "These things are always distressing."

"Well, it distresses me to think he's so cowardly he can't do his own talking. Where did he stay last night?"

"At the hotel."

She flayed herself by perversely hoping he'd gotten the same upstairs room he'd once tenanted. "Does he want his clothes sent over?" she asked tauntingly.

"Sister Nancy," the bishop said patiently, still slowly rubbing his legs, "you and I both know Brother Scott's no coward. He's asked me, as his bishop, to help him in a delicate and difficult situation. I—"

"Delicate and difficult is right!" Nancy leaned her head back and eyed the silvered patina of the cream-colored paper she and Joel had chosen for the room's ceiling.

"Brother Scott's coming to talk to you, but he's asked me to see you first. He'd like to talk to you tonight, but he'd rather not do it in front of the children."

"You mean he's ashamed to talk it in front of his children!"

"I don't mean that at all, Sister Nancy. These things are just not for children's ears. He suggests you meet him at the hotel. He'll have the other young lady present. And the matter can be settled privately and maturely—as it should be."

Again she struggled to cap the volcano of her anger. "Well, you can tell him, Bishop Earlington, that I'm not leaving my house to discuss any extra-marital love life with him—or his mistress!"

"She's not his mistress," the bishop calmly and patiently explained. "Brother Scott wants to marry her."

"Oh, he does, does he? Well, isn't that convenient?"

"Many times these things come as a shock." He clawed his beard again. "May I suggest then, Sister Nancy, that you send the youngsters to the neighbors tonight. The three of you then sit down to this matter, here in this room, prayerfully and maturely."

Nancy thought a moment, and shook her head. All the seraphs in heaven could never persuade her into sharing Joel with another woman. "I'll send the children away," she said at last. "I'll hear Joel out on anything he has to say—and in this house. But I warn you, Bishop, if he brings that other woman with him, I'll chop her into kindling sticks! I'll not have my house defiled with her presence."

"It's his house, too, dear Sister Nan," the bishop reminded.

"Not if he's decided to make Matey Thorpe a part of his life! This house is the home nest for me and my children. I look on this other woman as a hawk and a menace. If she dares come near this place, I'll fight her till the blood comes. And if Joel takes up with her—I'll fight him out the same way."

"Have you never been converted to the Principle?"

"Never! I saw my mother's life destroyed over it!"

The bishop fingered his beard, and looked at Nancy through sad and rheumy eyes. "This *is* difficult."

"I *had* my chance at the Principle, Bishop—before I ever married Joel Scott," Nancy explained. "I could have been an apostle's ninth wife, if I'd have wanted plurality. I folded that apostle's beard up under his tonsils the day he tried to put plural paws on me."

"I think I heard something about it," Earlington said modestly.

"I married Joel Scott because he was a Gentile—because he had no use for the covenant. Then you converted him. You baptized him. You changed his views, and his attitude toward life. You made a slobbering, self-righteous idiot out of him. And now you come into my house to try to talk me into joining with him in the holy estate of polygamy. I'm beginning to think *you're* the monster in this thing, Bishop! I'll not cave in your head—but I'd like to. But I can tell you this—no matter how much I love Joel Scott—I'll live no plural life with him!"

Plainly Bishop Earlington was appalled at what he heard. He'd lifted himself erect in the chair, and had started to slowly stroke his aching legs. "I had no idea you were so bitter about it, Sister Nancy," he said, weakly. "I knew your dear mother. I knew Martha had a difficult time of it, and some reason to be bitter. But I can't recall her striking out at the Church and its beliefs, or any refusal to be converted to its teachings."

Nancy shrugged defiantly. "Some women meekly swallow their grief. Some women bury their heartache, and accept the yoke without protest. My mother was a selfless, sacrificing, noble woman. To her, submission, and humility under the load, were a form of godliness."

"They *are* a form of godliness, dear Sister."

"Well, I'm not at all like my mother!" Nancy growled. "I'm not accepting any double yoke! My mother's dead—because she was selfless, sacrificing, and noble. Well, I'm none of these things. I'm alive! I'm full of fight! And I intend to stay alive!"

"I have to laugh when you deprecate yourself this way," the bishop chuckled. "In all of Ammon there's no more selfless, no more noble woman than you are, dear Sister Nancy. The people of this town depend on you; worship you. Joel and Nancy Scott have come a long way in the Church. You're both choice spirits in the eyes of God."

"Then let God and the Church keep polygamy out of my life!" Nancy shouted. "I'm not converted to it! I've no intention of becoming converted to it! Why persecute *me* with it?"

The bishop remained thoughtful and unruffled. "I've lived a long time, and through some of the darkest hours of the Church. I've been a confidant, arbiter, and counselor to my flock for many years. I'd be a liar if I maintained that plural marriage was an easy thing to live, or, that in every case, it's well ordered. Of all marriages, it's the most difficult to adjust to, and to maintain in love and unity. It takes unselfish and courageous people to live it, my dear."

"Then I'm just not the type."

"I don't know whether you are or not, Sister Nancy," the bishop continued. "But time and experience has convinced me that there *are* certain types of people who just cannot be converted to it. For them, it's always best they stay out of it."

"Then you can plainly see I'm of the breed that should stay out of it."

"I'm not convinced either way on that score, my dear. But I *do* know that rebelliousness can be conquered, that love and understanding *can* wipe out jealousy, and that prayer and an open mind *has* wrought many a miracle. I love Joel and Nancy Scott more than either of them will ever know. An hour of great decision has come into their lives. Your husband is deeply troubled, and he's come to me for help. There's nothing in the world I wouldn't do for either of you. I hope you know that." The honest look in his moist blue eyes was the nearest thing to reprimand for Nancy's outburst.

"Joel's troubles are his own doing, Bishop Earlington," she said more quietly. "I just *can't* accept, or tolerate, an endless life of suffering—brought on because of his carnal appetite for some younger woman. You can cloak it with all the spirituality you want, Bishop, but to me it's still only barnyard lust."

Slowly, methodically, Bishop Earlington's veined and knotty hands began searching his coat pockets. While time beat awesomely and hopelessly about them, he slowly drew out his worn and well-thumbed *Doctrine and Covenants*, and his steel-band spectacles. With the precision born of practice, he hooked the glasses to his nose and ears, halved the little book at the proper passage, and cleared his throat. "All I can do is quote you the words God, through Joseph Smith the Prophet, said regarding it," the bishop explained. "I can well see that you and Joel have a lot of talking and praying to do before this new marriage will ever work out." He found the page. "This is what the Prophet wrote:

"'For behold! I reveal unto you a new and an everlasting covenant; and if ye abide not that covenant, then are ye damned; for no one can reject this covenant, and be permitted to enter into my glory' . . . 'verily I say unto you, if a man marry a wife, and make a covenant with her for time and for all eternity, if that covenant is not by me, or by my word, which is my law, and is not sealed by the Holy Spirit of promise, through him whom I have anointed and appointed unto this power— then it is not valid, neither of force when they are out of this world, because they are not joined by me, saith the Lord . . . they cannot therefore, inherit my glory . . .'"

The bishop eye-searched the long revelation for the appropriate passage, found it, and settled down. "'And again, as pertaining to the law of the Priesthood,'" he read, "'If any man espouse a virgin, and desire to espouse another, and the first give her consent; and if he espouse the second, and they are virgins, and have vowed to no other man, then is he justified; he cannot commit adultery, for they are given unto him; for he cannot commit adultery with that that belongeth unto him and to no one else . . . and if he have ten virgins given unto him by this law, he cannot commit adultery, for they belong to him, and they are given unto him, therefore is he justified.'"

The two children were awake by now. Little Vernell had made it to the doorway, and was standing there in her rumpled nightgown, and baby Edward was fretting in his crib. The bishop gave up his reading from the revealed Scriptures; folded up his glasses to his pocket. "I can only suggest you read carefully, and prayerfully, the entire 132d section of the *Doctrine and Covenants.* Take your youngsters over to a neighbor, and leave them for the evening, and I'll tell Joel that you'll see him."

"I'll see Joel," she repeated, "but alone."

"Alone." And Bishop Earlington arose on his arthritic legs and stuffed the little book into his pocket.

Little Vernell made a dash from the doorway and grabbed Nancy's ample skirt for a hiding curtain as her mother stood up from her chair. With a benign smile, the bishop patted the youngster on her curly black hair.

"You have beautiful children, Sister Nancy."

"Thank you, Bishop. We think we have, and we love them so." She managed something resembling a smile. "I'll get your overcoat and hat." She turned, and towing Vernell along with her, headed for the closet.

233

When she returned, the bishop was teetering thoughtfully on his skinny legs. "Please forgive me for being so rude," she apologized, holding the coat for his long arms. "I'm just terribly wrought up. It's come as a real shock."

The bishop hunched the coat to his bent frame, and smiled understandingly at her. "I know," he agreed. "And I've probably been of little help to either of you. These things come. They're sometimes hard to understand. But please *do* read the revelation. Please *try* not to be angry with one another. Just sit down and talk it out. Whatever comes, Sister Nancy, I'm sure it will be for the best."

A minute later he was gone. And Nancy, as she dressed and tended to the wants of her babies, was again weeping like a spring rain.

Soon after the bishop had left she heard the bell from Ammon's First Ward School, across the street, clang its exuberant sound of dismissal, and minutes later the three older children were tumbling and shouting about the house as though all was well, and the world had not yet quite caved in upon them. A bit of cautious probing revealed that Joel had not been seen by them—not at their school at least. To them, there was nothing alarming about that. His duties could have led him to either or both of the other two schools in the growing town. And Nancy herself could have approximated the same guess. She'd nervously watched the school from the window most of the day, in the hope of even seeing a glimpse of the man she alternately hated and loved.

She pushed the youngsters into their chores and fed them early. In dressing them for their evening stay at Seth's and Mary Magdalene's little house up the street, she kept as casual a front as possible—vaguely hinting that their father would get back from his unexplained business, to pick their mother up to take her to some other vague point of unexplained business. If the older children were suspicious of this excuse, or their mother's obvious depression of spirits, they made no comment. They had no particular objection about going to the Biddles. When Seth was not strangely ill, he turned his whole life into entertaining them and making them happy. And Mary, who played and sang wild and happy songs on the reed organ, and let them make candy to their heart's content, loved the Scott youngsters as though they were her own.

Nancy's silent prayers, as the whole family of them, at turn of dusk, started their walk to the Biddles, was that, for this night at least, any Ammon babies that may be readying themselves for exit from the town's near-thousand wombs, would please reconsider, and crawl back. This time, at least, fate had a greater, nearer claim on Nancy Scott and Mary Magdalene. And to hell with the birthings!

Mary was a little surprised to see the whole Scott clan walk up her pathway, but she welcomed them effusively. She grabbed up Edward, the toddler, in her skinny arms and carried him inside.

"Mary," Nancy said, when all of them were inside the new little house, "I've got to impose on you tonight."

"You call this an imposition? Glad to see all of you. We'll have a real hoedown."

Young Joel already was in tow of Seth, and they had headed for his little shanty workshop.

"I'm leaving the whole family in your care for a while," Nancy explained. "Joel and I have some business to transact in confidence. Little children have big ears."

"I think I know what it is, Nan," Mary half whispered. "You look as though it had hit you hard."

"Harder than any human will ever know," Nancy said, fighting back the pesky tears. She looked sharply into Mary's homely old face. "How did *you* know?"

"Nan, in this town, there're lots of people with big eyes. The only way a man could keep court with a chickadee in Ammon, and not be observed, would be to do his courting under a rock."

"Damned funny that everyone knows but me!" Nancy growled, her anger flaring.

"S-h-h-h!" Mary cautioned, looking around at the youngsters. But they already were preoccupied with the treasures of Mary's parlor, and Marty already was pumping the treadle on the reed organ. "It's always that way, Nan," Mary consoled. She put Edward to the floor and, still in his little overcoat, he started his own toddling across the rug.

"*You* could have told me," Nancy moaned.

Mary folded her in her skinny arms. "Nobody wants to hurt those dear to them, Nan. I figured that all men have these spells, and a lot of 'em get over their extra-marital erections without serious consequence. I thought perhaps it would be so with Joel—and anyway it was only gossip. And I'm not a hand to pass gossip along to anybody." She patted Nancy's shoulders affectionately. "Is it the little English girl at Millie's?"

"That's her. Matey Thorpe. I caught the two of 'em spooning—on the creek bridge. Mary—the shock of it has nearly killed me. I damn near beat their heads in—and I shoved 'em both into the creek."

"Good!" Mary chuckled, holding her at arm's length. "Very good!

Cold water's a quick cure for a premature erection. And a dash of it won't hurt what ails Matey, either."

"Joel hasn't been home yet—but he sent Bishop Earlington this afternoon. Joel wants to marry the girl."

"That figures."

"Joel's coming back tonight, to talk it over. That's why you've got the Scott kids on your hands."

"Is he bringing Matey Thorpe?"

"If he does—I'll wring her neck like a chicken."

"Good. Very good. But she's quite a chicken—from what I hear."

"Well, I'm ready for it. And I've got to get back. It's going to be a tough, sad night for me."

"I'd hate to try to advise you in this, Nan," Mary continued in low talk, and confidential. "When the hunt's on, you just don't turn men away from it. The mating appetite is stronger than life itself. Only weapon left you is calmness, and good judgment. Try to keep from getting riled. Don't be rash or impulsive about it. Try to remember it's woman's nature to love one man, and it's hard for them to believe or understand that the man can love more than one woman—and at one and the same time. As a midwife, you of all people, should know this fact by now. If Joel's got an explanation, try to hear him out. Reason with him. Don't fight him. It's the last—and only—weapon you've got. Just remember, Nan, that half the women of Utah have faced the problem you're facing tonight. In Mormondom, it's a man's world—and don't you ever forget it!"

"Who the hell will ever let you forget it?" Nancy groaned.

It was dark, Nancy had the lamps lit and a comfortable fire in the stove, before she heard the sound of Joel's footsteps on the gravel outside. Her impulse was to go to the door to meet him, but she stayed beside the lamp and the table, knitting, her steel needles going at furious pace. Back on the shelf had gone the *Doctrine and Covenants*, and with it the revelation God had given Joseph Smith regarding plural marriage and the everlasting covenant. She'd read every part of its rambling and stentorious passages, as she'd promised the bishop she would, but still it had left her unconverted to the Principle.

Joel's key rattled in the door, exactly as it had a thousand other times. She bent her neck to the knitting, and her needles clicked furiously. It was another black sock she was fashioning, to the familiar size and shape of Joel's foot.

She heard the door squeak familiarly on its weathered hinges, heard him fumble in the entrance hall as he hung up hat and coat. And then he stepped into the room. "Hello, Nan," he said.

"Hello, Joel," she replied, bent her head, and turned a course with her needles.

Awkwardly, nervously, he fumbled with his soft chair. She knitted wildly and defiantly as he dragged it around exactly in front of her. Wearily he dropped into it.

Nancy looked up. She saw that he looked as haggard and used-up as she was. And there were two purpled and broken bruises protruding from his black and curly hairline. She dropped her eyes toward the half-finished sock.

"I sent the bishop," he said.

"Yes."

He was silent a moment, and one could hear the tick of the clock, and the click of Nancy's steels above that awkward silence.

"Well, Nan," he said at last, "I guess I've hurt you. Hurt you a lot."

"That you have, Joel."

"I didn't want to hurt you. Please believe me."

"Then why did you?"

"These things happen," he sparred futilely.

"So does murder—and disease—and death. But why to us, Joel? We love one another. We've a family. So much to look forward to."

"All I can say, Nan, is that my affection for Matey just grew. At first I thought she was sweet and interesting. I enjoyed talking to her. She was so innocent and naïve. I found myself seeking excuses to meet her. Before I knew it, I was in love with her."

Nancy sighed, and dropped the knitting to her lap. "Weren't you mature enough to back out of the thing, Joel? Aren't you mature enough to back out of it now? You've a family of precious children. You've a wife who loves you dearly, and will be loyal to you forever."

"I can't back out, Nancy," Joel explained. "It's gone too far. And please try to believe that it has nothing to do with any change of my feelings toward you *or* my family."

"Have I failed you, Joel?"

"Certainly not."

"Then why are you hunting?"

"You make it sound like a willful desertion—which it is not. This thing just came into my life—grew—and there it is."

"Meaning Matey Thorpe?"

"Nancy, I love this woman. I want to marry her. I want your consent to add her to my holy increase. To take her into the celestial covenant with us."

"Oh no!" Nancy groaned, dropping her knitting to the floor, and burying her head in her hands. "Please God, no!"

"I've talked to Stake Patriarch Ursenbach—I've talked to Bishop Earlington."

"Naturally they say it's all right," Nancy sobbed. "There's always divine approval for any and every hot-lighted woman-hunter in Utah." She looked up at him pleadingly. "But you, Joel, of all people!"

"I'm no different than any other human, Nancy," he said, the glint of anger coming to his eyes. "I believe in the teachings of the Prophet Joseph Smith, and the practices of the Church. I know your feelings on the subject of plural marriage, and how touchy you are about it. All our married life I've been very careful not to antagonize you on the subject. But fate has taken a hand in our affairs. A time of decision has been reached. It's being faced every day by hundreds of other Mormon women—and with a lot more grace and understanding, I'd say. I'm in love with Matey Thorpe. Under the laws of God, and under the sanction of the Church, I want to take her into celestial marriage."

Nancy eyed him coldly. "Suppose I say no."

Joel bowed his head. Across the familiar twin tufts of his thick hair, Nancy could see the sharp bruises she'd put there. For a man in love, he didn't seem so buoyant or sure of himself as in the days of *her* courting. But then again she wasn't Matey Thorpe. Or maybe she'd flailed some of the buoyancy out of him.

"You can't say no," Joel said, quietly and sadly.

"Oh, can't I?" she growled defiantly.

"It's gone too far, Nan."

"What are you trying to tell me, Joel?"

"I've got Matey in trouble. She's in the family way."

Nancy sat erect, as though stabbed by one of her needles.

"You stupid ass," she said derisively. "And I thought you were a smart man!" Her tears had stopped, and she snorted in defiance. "What does our bishop say to *that?*"

"He doesn't know."

Nancy rocked and laughed hysterically. "You may fool Ammon, you may fool the bishop, you may fool me," she taunted, "but remember, God's big eyes are upon you!"

Joel looked up at her again, and this time there were tears in *his* eyes. "Nancy, I'm in trouble. Deep trouble."

"You certainly are," she growled.

"I've *got* to marry Matey Thorpe. I've *got* to have your consent."

"You must be real stupid to think you'll get it."

"Then I'll take her away. I'll flee this country."

"Back to Boston, I suppose?"

"Perhaps."

"They'll love you for that. The Mormon—the polygamist—arrives with a fresh bride. I never quite made it. But it doesn't matter. I'm only your first wife. I only mothered five of your children—which you seem damned-fired willing to desert for a little pecker-teaser from England."

Joel's look at her was half angry, half frantic. "I don't *want* to desert you or my family! I want to stay here in the old and familiar pattern. I—"

"But you don't mind busting the pattern. You don't mind at all!"

"Nancy, I love you. And I love my children."

"I can see that," she taunted.

"I also love Matey Thorpe."

"I can see that also."

"Then don't drive me out. Here, in this land, I've found peace, and a way of life that satisfies me."

"You've also found a few other things, I'm judging."

"Nancy, you were born a Latter-day Saint," he said, sadly and solemnly. "I'm a converted Latter-day Saint. What I'm asking is something accepted and understood by our people here in Utah. There's nothing unusual or uncommon about it. I've sinned, and I regret it, but I shall never desert this other little woman I've found the capacity to also love. Neither shall I ever desert you, or my children, whom I also love. I'm asking only the thing which other Mormon men so commonly ask—which Isaac Corey and thousands of other good Saints have asked. It's simply that a plural marriage will save us all. In the name of God, Nancy, and all that's precious to both of us—please find it in your heart to give your consent to the bishop for this marriage! Please be big enough, and brave enough, to do this thing!"

"Why don't you be big enough, and brave enough, to dump Matey Thorpe—and come back to the wife and family you claim to still love?"

"Because, Nan," he said patiently, "I also love Matey Thorpe."

Nancy tried to retrieve her knitting, but the needles had slipped from their loops, and the yarn ball was halfway across the rug. She gave up, bowed her head, and held her eyelids tight and shut with her left hand. The things Joel had said had shocked the grief out of her. It would never be in her capacity to understand how anyone, Joel no exception, could decently love two women at once. There was simply no logic to his statement that he loved Nancy Corey and Matey Thorpe at one and the same time. But somehow, illogically as it seemed, these multiple loves were prevalent enough in Utah. Within days and hours she delivered babies from the same man's seed, and seeded to more than one wife. But oh, the catastrophic thing that Joel had brought upon his own marriage! Plurality was certainly and logically a way out, and maybe the only way out. But it was a mighty poor way, in her estimation. No plural marriage could rightfully be consummated without a first wife's consent—although she was certain there were plenty of cases where this nicety had never been bothered with. But Joel, even in his deep and inextricable trouble, had hewed to the law of consent. He was crawling to her for help. She had his life and destiny in her power. If she said yes, another bride would be taken over the marriage altar at the Endowment House, little Matey would be accepted in Ammon, and even first wife Nancy could hold her head up without censure or disgrace. A few eyebrows might be lifted when Matey's first baby came, but even that was not too uncommon in plurality, and, in Zion, even God forgave these things.

On the other hand, if she said no to Joel's frantic plea, the turn of the card could, and might be, infinitely worse. Mary was right—you just don't turn men away when the mating hunt is on. She knew her Joel. He had a streak of honor up his back a foot wide. On the same basic urge and promise that had nearly *taken* them out of Zion in the beginning, Joel would back up his mistake and defend Matey Thorpe to the last. And the gain? Another Mormon desertion. Another fatherless family in Ammon. As for herself, much as she loved Joel Scott, she wanted no more of him. He could have his mincing Matey, and be damned to both of them. But the children? She just couldn't break a man publicly and spiritually, just for the sake of being contrary.

"Nancy," Joel said at last, "I must ask you again—and this will be for the final time. Will you please, for the sake of all of us, give your consent to this marriage?"

She let him suffer a moment more. "I'll give it, Joel," she said.

"God will bless you for this, dear Nan," he said, considerably more brightly. "You've an understanding heart."

"I've no understanding heart," she growled. "And God will never bless me—because I hate this thing you've done to me." She swallowed hard, and wiped a moist eye with the back of her hand. "I'm giving this consent only for the children. As for me, I want you to take this little slut you're so anxious to marry, and get out of my life forever. When you marry her, don't bring *her* here, and don't *you* come here.

Take her to Provo, or Salt Lake. Plenty of plural husbands keep families in different towns. But just don't bring her within eye-shot of me—because I'll wring her neck like a chicken!"

"What about my job, Nan?"

"Get yourself another one!"

"Who'll support you and the youngsters?"

"I'll support me and my youngsters! I'm a Corey. Father Isaac left me a little. I'm a midwife. We'll not starve."

"You make me feel as low as a worm."

"You *are* as low as a worm!"

But when he was gone, and she'd picked up the youngsters, and at the same time emptied her heart to Mary, she wept out another long and heartbreaking night.

IV

WHEN JOEL SCOTT AND MATEY THORPE STARTED NORTH FOR SALT LAKE City, the back of the surrey was well packed. Besides Matey's little trunk, that had come with her from England, and Joel's metal-bound chest, that had crossed the seas and continents with him, the wedding rig was fatly stuffed with his saddles, guns, books, and manuscripts. In his pocket was the "recommend," written in the hand of Bishop Earlington, and signed by him—and which constituted the Mormon passport into Endowment House or temple. This most necessary document vouched for his worthiness to enter the House of the Lord, the circumspectness of his sainthood, and implied, at least, that his present wife (or wives) were in agreement to his present addition to his family kingdom.

Aunt Millie's family, who had already given a fair daughter into the Principle, were on hand for the early morning farewell. They alone waved off Joel's carriage as his high-stepping blacks headed it out into the long road, toward the city, and the celestial marriage that would unite the two for time and all eternity. The October weather had turned cold and blustery, but the clouds, still loose and vapory, were cogent reminders that the storms were not yet ready for their first downwind thrusts into Zion. Nancy, at home, trying to explain the strange and sudden journey of their father, was not on hand for any farewell. There was nothing uncommon about such lack of enthusiasm on the part of established wives toward these plural additions and adventures of their husbands. Occasionally, in those rare polygamous homes where love and understanding had washed out all traces of jealousy and fault-finding, one or more of the older wives would accompany the wedding party, and even stand as willing witness to the ceremony. But Nancy was not one of those rare women. Hurt, humiliated, crushed by the speed of calamitous events, she wished the pair of them nothing but total misery.

Her children, nor no one of the town of Ammon, yet knew that Joel Scott was not likely to come back. They did not know that the things he stuffed in the back of the surrey were the personals which went with a man, and stayed with a man. Before picking Matey up at Aunt Millie's he'd harnessed the blacks, and packed the surrey, before dawn. The youngsters were not allowed to realize that the warmth of his kisses and the fervency of his farewell were in the nature of final, lasting ones. He'd agreed with Nancy that this was the better way. When it came to her own farewell to Joel, outside, on the ditch bank, in the red dawn, it was a hard and bitter thing to take.

"Nan," he said, quietly, and earnestly, "I wish it weren't turning out this way."

While the horses chomped, geed, and fretted, she looked down to hide the tears, and said nothing.

"Please, my dear, try to believe, that I love you deeply. That I love my children. And that love will always be an inseparable part of me."

"It should be, Joel," she said quietly. "We've never given you any cause for change of heart."

"Please do try to understand that a man's love can take many facets. That a division of that love is not necessarily an indication of a weakness of it."

"That's a little harder to believe," she replied, stiffening.

"One of the greatest things the Lord has taught His Saints is the infinite and endless nature of love, the infinite and endless nature of the family pattern. I wish you were more in agreement with me, Nan dear. It would be *so* much easier for both of us."

"I think you'd better go, Joel."

"Will you and the children be all right?"

"We'll be all right."

"I'll send you some money. I'm expecting a draft from the East."

"You'll need it to set up your new bride. We'll be all right."

"Try not to think so hard of me, Nan. Pray to understand."

Then suddenly, impulsively, as of old, he swept her into his strong arms. She struggled, until she felt as though she'd cave. And then he kissed her, and the strength of her life drained out. For one short second, all was well again, and she was on the cloud to glory. And then he released her, and she wept and swayed, and watched him clamber lithely to the carriage seat.

He turned to look at her as he grabbed the lines, and thumped them hard to the tails of the blacks. But in that morning's instant, as the carriage rolled away, she saw his face. There was pain in it for what he was doing. And there were tears in his eyes as he looked at her.

To gain strength, she looked away, determined to watch him no more. But the rhythm of the hooves, and the carriage-rattle of his going away, beat into her ears like a fading storm.

When it dawned on the elders of Ammon that they had lost their schoolmaster, and in the middle of a school year, there were questions and worries, which Nancy parried as best she could. When word came that he'd taken an important teaching post at the Latter-day Saints Institute in Salt Lake City, pride in his accomplishment and promotion offset some of their sense of loss. For the town, and educationally at least, Joel Scott had builded well. Three free schools, operated out of tax monies and school lands, were his monuments to the town he so abruptly had left. And to Ammon, long conditioned to the plural pattern of marriage, it did not seem odd or unseemly that the schoolmaster now maintained two households. He was simply needed in Salt Lake City for greater things.

Nancy's need in Ammon was just as basic, and far more important. For, as long as the night-rhythm of Mormondom continued—and there seemed no clear sign of its abatement—the babies would come. And when the babies came, the Saints still insisted Nancy Scott be on hand to meet them.

The winter storms came, and the snow, the sleet, and the howling gales. For Nancy it was not alone the cold that was bitter about this winter. She kept faith with her duties to the women of the town, she tried as best she could to explain the new order of things to her worried children, and in her heart she felt as bereft and deprived as the day they had buried Martha Corey.

243

That the same vicious pattern that had broken her mother should, by the quirks of fate, be visited upon her, was almost impossible to believe. She who, to avoid polygamy, had deliberately and willingly married out of the faith, was now as securely trapped in it as had been Adah, Millie, Martha, and Kirstine. Since Mormons counted time from the pre-existence, to earth-life, and into the hereafter—Joel now had three wives securely cornered in his family kingdom. She herself had been talked into the sealing of Edna Reavis Scott, the Massachusetts bride, to Joel, at the time her own temple marriage had been solemnized, and she had put on the garment of the celestial order. Little Matey Thorpe was now the third woman in his life. And, damn her lousy soul, she hoped Joel would gag and choke on *this* bride.

In the explosive heat of Joel's new mating, and Ammon exodus, little or nothing was said about keeping any bond of recognition alive between the two Scott families. In the first few months after his departure, Nancy was able to convince herself she hated him enough to care little whether she ever saw him or heard from him again. But memory, familiarity, and habit had too many ingredients of hard perversity ever to be willed down and talked down. And they had voices that whispered out of every corner of the house or town, and that talked more boldly and tauntingly out of the darkness of the night. In her travels about the valley, she tried to avoid any nearness to the crumbling ruin and wreckage of what once had been the old Ammon. Few of the houses remained standing, most everything usable had long since been hauled away, and the great wall of their very first acquaintance had melted lower year by year. But no mere resolve could keep her eyes and thoughts turned entirely from it, whenever its visual nearness broke upon her. Still walled within its confines were the scenes and experiences of her childhood, her dreams, romance, joys, frights, and sorrows. These things were the grist of which life was made, and only death itself could will them down. She was glad when the snows came and covered the old ruin.

And about the newer town it was almost the same. Joel had become such a substantial and inseparable part of it that it seemed impossible to believe he no longer could be seen walking, erect and soldier-like up its sidewalks—graciously tipping his fedora to the townsfolk, or chucking some familiar youngster under the chin. She never walked or drove Ammon's streets without half expecting to see Joel drive his high-stepping blacks and surrey down Main Street, or watch him ride the aged but brush-sleek Duke in easy gallop, and witness the polite and friendly wave of his hand in acknowledgment to the friends and townsfolk who had come to love and respect him. He doted on horses, and was inordinately fond of showing them off. There was no denying that her Joel had been something special in a man. And in a land where men, special or not, were seldom the sole property of one woman, she began to realize now how stupidly foolish she'd been not to have anticipated and prepared for the inevitable competitive struggle to hold him for herself. As the lonely months went by, it became less easy to hate and censure him for doing what was already a most acceptable and ordinary thing in Zion.

She could never pass the veranda of the Ammon Hotel without being stabbed like a knife with its memories. Other owners had enlarged it considerably from the old Corey House, though time had made it more slatternly in appearance and operation. It still housed the telegraph station, and was still Ammon's stage stop, and, next to the post office, the focal point of the town. It still fed its guests in the old public room Isaac had designed, though she doubted, from the drunks who frequented the place, that the Word of Wisdom was any longer its guiding policy. But, upstairs, its rooms were probably as little changed as her memories of the place. The sharp-tongued but efficient Kirstine had probably long since been forgotten. After selling the place, following Isaac's death, she'd lived on for two years in Ammon, and in the family pattern. Wearying of that, she'd sold her home to an eager buyer in the rapidly expanding town, and joined her parents in Salt Lake City. Family gossip had it that she was being courted anew, this time from the circle of the Authorities, and had every likelihood of switching out of Isaac's holy increase into the bewildering pattern of some other good man's hope toward godship. But it wasn't Kirstine, or the memory of Kirstine, that taunted Nancy out of the walls of the old Corey House. It was Joel, and the twin wigs of his black hair, the easy, fascinating manner of his conversation, the patience he'd shown in teaching Isaac, his forbidden cheroots, and the sweeping impetuosity of his love-making that even yet sent her wildly a-tingle. She, herself, had practically kicked him out of Ammon. Now she was realizing that he was as much a part of the town as the town itself.

And then there were the schools he'd pioneered and built, and, for which the town forever would be in his debt. Across the street from the Scott house was the first and most important one. Never could she look at the building without associating it with her vanished man. How many times had she seen him standing on its foolish and useless little porch? How many times had she waved across at him? How many times had she sent him on his short way, to his deep and dedicated task, with a housewife's hasty kiss and pat of affection. With him gone, nothing in her life would ever be right again.

But it was at night, in the loneliness of the dark, that the unbearable specter of his absence reached her like a knife to the heart. One didn't share the same bed with a man for twelve years without erecting a structure of memory that would last out a lifetime. No longer could she hear the deep and raucous man-breath of his sleep. No longer could she reach out and touch the whiskers of his face, or run fingers of affection through the curly softness of his odd and peculiar hair. No longer could she wrap an arm around his firm and sinewy body, fold herself into its contours, and know what it was to hold and possess a man who was near and dear to her. Gone now were those intimate intervals when they melted, with deep sighs, one into one. Not till now did Nancy realize how truly happy she had been in the life that had been given to her with Joel Scott. In the deepness of the night, aching with loneliness, hungering with all her flesh, she blamed herself through her tears. Why, in God's name, hadn't she shown him more appreciation for the joy he *had* given her? Why hadn't she told him, a hundred times a day, how much she loved him? Why did she not realize these simple things before? One never misses the water until the well goes dry. She'd willfully and forever dried up the well. Had she shown, and gratefully delivered to him, all he could ever have desired in a wife, it was not so likely he would have hunted elsewhere. And then, of all things, to deliberately banish him out of her life!

It was easy enough to hate Matey Thorpe for what had happened. At first, it had been easy to hate Joel Scott. For Matey this acrimony had a durable quality. With the closing in of winter, and the long, hard, dark months that went with it, the hate she had felt toward Joel wore ever more thin. Nancy longed to see his face, feel his body, and talk to him again. She longed for the peace and security she once had known, when this home in Ammon had been enriched and livened by the sound and touch of his presence. In the deep of the night she prayed God for a reconsideration; to somehow find a way for his return.

In the explosion and acrimony of his departure, nothing had been said about letters, and Nancy's pride was too deeply wounded for her to be the first to write. With the children conscious of only an echo of the strife tearing mercilessly at their parents, it was easier to keep the flimsy bridge of the written word still intact and usable. And for Nancy, when a packet of short notes, in Joel's familiar hand, arrived—one for each of the children old enough to read—she was glad. They merely told the youngsters that their father had been called away by duty for a while, that he loved them very much, and for them to do their chores and school work willingly and uncomplainingly, and to mind and love their mother. He reminded them about their prayers, and the necessity of attending church. He told them he was living in a small wooden house on east South Temple Street, and gave them the exact number so they in turn could write. With no sense of shame, and in the best Mormon tradition, he announced to them he had taken another wife; that she was kind, and good, and sweet, like their own mother; and that she was to be known to them as "Aunt Matey." And likewise, in the best Mormon tradition, the children were neither shocked nor visibly dismayed by the disclosure. For what shreds of comfort she could gain, Nancy purloined all the notes, after the children had gone to bed, and read and reread them by the lamplight of the night.

This easy correspondence between Joel and the children, urged and encouraged by him, continued throughout the winter. And then, in one of the packets, there came a short note for Nancy, that made her happy enough for tears. It told about the excitement of teaching at the big Academy, of the notable men with whom he was associated, but that he missed the intimacy and warmth that he'd known in pioneering the schools of Ammon. Most important, he missed Nancy, and the happy brawl and turmoil of his family. "I love you, Nancy," the letter concluded. "Don't ever lose sight of that fact." And that sentence alone was the one buoy she needed to keep her afloat in the sea of doubt that had been drowning her.

The note she penned in return was friendly and newsy. Pride kept her from any maudlin revealment of the love she likewise felt for him, but no trace of rancor or censure went with her note. And that was the beginning of the warm and friendly correspondence that helped to make life bearable for Nancy throughout that long and deathlike winter.

The letters confirmed one thing she'd anticipated and expected— the reprisal of Apostle Jonathan Cragg for Joel's merciless demolishment of his own marital hopes. In Ammon, and throughout all of Utah Valley, Joel Scott had risen to the top in public esteem. When he spoke at church, the building was packed with listeners, and the eloquence of his sermons, and the brilliance of his reasoning, had made him a marked man. "Brother Scott will be an apostle some day," one heard on every hand. And in some instances, the ante was even raised to "Wouldn't be a bit surprised if this fine man followed John Taylor in the presidency." Before the discovery that Joel had gone the whole Mormon distance, Nancy could not help but take comfort and pride in these offhand predictions, and certainly it was an experience to share with an audience his fervor and eloquence. But now, in Salt Lake, things were changed. Like any farm boy who had stolen a bishop's favorite, he suddenly began to feel some unexpected bumps and rocks in the road to eternal glory. Under the fury of apostolic disfavor, Joel was still a marked man, but in a different sort of way. No positions of trust or importance were offered him. No public recognition was accorded him. Not a single pulpit in Salt Lake City was ever graced by his eloquent and handsome presence. He was a schoolteacher, not a public leader, or voice to the new dispensation. And they never let him forget it. Nancy half expected to hear that he'd been called to some long mission in the Fiji Islands, or some equally obscure place, while Lofty Cragg re-wooed his British discovery. But not even the honor of a mission was accorded him—probably because Cragg wanted no other man's leavings. But it was plain that, because of Joel's violation of the unwritten rule of apostolic perquisite, he would now suffer out his time in church obscurity.

In late May Joel's first-born in the plural pattern—a boy—arrived. A good Salt Lake physician attended the confinement—not a midwife. And for some oblique reason, Nancy felt a little hurt that she'd not even been asked. She would never have gone, of course. She would have died first. Still, Joel, of all people, knew she was a skilled and competent person in such things. They named the child John Radcliffe Scott. With Ammon and all of Zion engrossed in breeding and birthing, few there were who took note of the fact that John Radcliffe came a bit early according to the count.

More to be wondered at was that, only three weeks after John Radcliffe's advent, Amanda Scott Radcliffe arrived from Boston, accompanied by Commodore Nathan Radcliffe, her husband. They had come to inspect the hornet's nest of Mormondom firsthand, and Amanda's recalcitrant brother in particular. With the correspondence strained and infrequent between them, they had the idea Joel still lived in Ammon. Nancy, cleaning house on a Saturday morning, and in her dirty worst, met the Bostonians at the door with broom and dust pan. They had left their luggage at the hotel and, after inquiry, had walked the dusty blocks to the Scott residence.

"I'm Joel's sister, Amanda," the woman had said, by way of introduction at the door, "and this is my husband, Commodore Nathan Radcliffe. You're Joel's wife, Nancy?"

"Yes, I'm Nancy. Please do come in. And please forgive my appearance. I'm cleaning up after a family of kids, and I look a mess." She tossed the broom and dust pan to the hallway corner.

Nancy took the commodore's hat, gloves and coat, and the gloves and coat of Joel's handsome sister. As she deposited them to the hooks and table of the hallway, she tried to make herself look less like a peasant by snatching the towel from off her head.

"Please be seated," she said, cordially, once she'd gotten them into the living room. "I'll see if I can't scare up some of the youngsters. Joel has real sweet children."

They both sat uneasily down, and she could see that there was a worry between them. "Yes. I should like to see the children," Amanda said, "but first, could I ask about Joel?"

The commodore yawned, and touched his mouth with the back of his hand. "The man at the hotel said he no longer lives in the town," he said, in a weary idiom strange to Zion.

Amanda showed plainly her disturbance. "But he said Joel's wife and family still lives here. And directed us to the house."

Nancy, already distressed by their sudden, unannounced appearance, and wounded anew in the vulnerable center of her pride, said, "Did he tell you *which* wife, and *which* family?"

"I—don't follow you," Amanda said.

Nancy took a sudden dislike to both of them; to the world they came from, which she had never seen, and could never understand; to their obvious snobbery, and more obvious dislike for the world Nancy more intimately knew. She wanted to punish them; punish them for hurting her. "Well, by now you should know that in Utah there are many wives —and many families. Visitors who don't understand these things usually ask *which*."

"You don't mean—Joel—?"

"I do mean Joel." Irked and defiant, Nancy threw herself into the nearest chair. Now she didn't care a snap how she looked, or what kind of an impression this household made on these well-dressed creatures out of another world. "I mean that he's got another wife. That he's got another family. That he's living with them. That he's a polygamist."

They couldn't have looked more shocked if she'd crowned the pair of them with a length of stovewood.

"Oh my God," Amanda said, shutting her eyes with a convulsive shudder.

"Incredible!" said Commodore Radcliffe.

"And he hasn't told you?" Nancy continued to probe.

"Good Lord *no!*" Amanda replied, her eyes still shut. "This will kill his mother. This will *absolutely* kill her."

"Where *is* Joel and—ah—this other household?" the commodore asked, leaning forward intently.

"In Salt Lake City," Nancy readily answered. "You could have seen him there—and saved yourselves the long trip to Ammon."

"No," Amanda said, opening her eyes to reality once more. "I'm glad I came to Ammon—to you first, Nancy. I don't think I could have stood the shock of finding such a thing."

"It's a shock—but you'd get over it." Womanlike, Nancy eyed this older and only sister of her husband's. Amanda's coat was heavy, richly fur-trimmed, and satiny inside. Her gray traveling suit, while a little out of press with the heat and the miles, was well tailored, and obviously expensive. She had Joel's hair—without the unique part—but there was gray in it. However, her eyes were slatey-colored, not the wild sky-blue of her brother's. And there was certainly nothing of merriment in them.

"You're not divorced—or living separately?"

"I'm living separately, but I'm certainly not divorced. I told you—Joel is a polygamist."

"I knew he'd gone overboard on this Mormon binge of his. But it's impossible to believe he'd become a polygamist. Not Joel." Amanda drew a handkerchief from her crocheted bag, and dabbed at the sadness in her eyes.

Nancy stared deliberately at the woman and, when she had her squirming again smiled wryly. "Lots of Mormons are polygamists."

"That I know," Amanda sighed. "It's the horror of the world."

"Part of the Mormon binge," Nancy added.

"I just can't fancy Joel as a polygamist," the commodore said, stretching his long legs. "How many wives has he?"

Nancy, now thoroughly wearied with both of them, eyed Amanda's husband critically. Joel hadn't particularly liked him, and neither did she. His preened blond mustache and goatee, the starched and cuffed shirts, the once well-pressed blue trousers, and the claw-hammer tails to his morning coat disturbed her sense of country disorder. She knew, without his ever telling it, that he loathed Utah. And like any other woman in the Principle, she found herself swinging pugnaciously into the fight against these uncomprehending Gentiles. "So far he only has two," Nancy said, defiantly. "But he's still a comparatively young man— a devout Mormon—and who knows?"

"Incredible," said the commodore.

"It's just impossible to believe that such a change could have come in Joel." Amanda sighed. "It just isn't like him."

Nancy said, honestly, "I agree. It's quite a change."

"Did you convert him to Mormonism?"

"No. Joel converted himself. He was a Gentile when I married him.

I've loved him, and been a good wife to him, as a Gentile, *and* as a Mormon."

"But," Amanda asked, leaning forward, "what did you think when he decided to embrace polygamy? When he decided to add—?"

"It's none of your business what I thought," Nancy snapped angrily. "I'm not probing into *your* family life!"

"Oh, I'm sorry," Amanda apologized. "You must forgive me. I'm simply shaken to the bones."

"I can see that."

"You can't imagine this unbelievable change in Joel. He was *such* a promising young man. So brilliant. Such a wonderful, secure future. And to trade it all for a philosophy, and a way of life, that's loathed around the world. It's already broken his mother's heart. And this will probably kill her. Have you any idea of the sacrifice he's made for this strange cause?"

"Have *you* any idea of the sacrifice other people have made for this cause?" Nancy sharply returned. "It's a religion of sacrifice. And it *could* be that Joel has found his happiness in it." She could hear Edward fretting and stirring from his nap. His first lonely bleat gave her the chance she wanted to get out. "Will you excuse me a moment?" she said. "My baby's awake."

Abruptly, without waiting for their answer, Nancy arose and marched through the hall to the back bedroom. When she returned, five minutes later, with the now smiling youngster, she could see that her visitors had at last mellowed through their first moment of truth. She set Edward down to his feet but, seeing them, he clung safely close to her skirts.

"This is your aunt and uncle, from far away," she smilingly told the child. But Edward made no move to fraternize.

"What a beautiful little boy," Amanda crooned. "Looks something like Joel. But I must say his really handsome features come from you, Nancy."

"Thank you. His name is Edward."

"Named after our youngest brother," Amanda said. "Edward, who rode proudly off to war—and never came back." She held out her arms and clucked appealingly. "Come to your Aunt Amanda, Edward," she crooned. But Edward teetered hesitantly, and hung on to Nancy's skirt.

"How many children do *you* have?" Nancy asked.

"Four. Three boys and one girl. They're all practically grown up. The oldest boy is already in Scott shipping. We're real proud of him." She smiled warmly at Nancy. "You have more children than just Edward here?"

"I have five. The others are outside. Older ones working in the garden. Younger ones out at the barn or haystack. Let me see if I can round 'em up. I'd like very much for you to meet Joel's children." Without waiting for an answer, with Edward tagging clumsily behind her, Nancy went to the kitchen door. With the precision and skill of her girlhood, Nancy blew a two-finger whistle that carried far, and with authority. She shut the door, and returned to her visitors, Edward still tumbling along behind her.

"I'll not apologize for their looks, when they come in, because the youngsters have been digging hard in the dirt. But they're good children—and a great help and comfort to me."

The whistle worked magic on three of the Scott youngsters. Vernell, the little one, elected to remain outside, in the more comfortable world of make-believe. In spite of the heat, their dirt grimy hands, and the garden dust on their faces, the children looked good to Nancy, and she presented them without apology.

"The young man is Joel—Jody we call him—the man of the house, in his father's absence. The tall young lady is Martha—named after my mother. We call her Marty. The other little lady is Amanda—your namesake in this family."

"What perfectly *beautiful* children!" Amanda squealed, as though she meant it.

With the good manners Joel had instilled into their lives, the children shook hands and curtsied all around. Nancy could see that Amanda, at least, was impressed. If the commodore hadn't wiped his hands so soon after young Joel's strong grip of friendship, she could have tolerated the man. The earth was not unclean, and there was nothing degrading about her children working in it. But when this feathered dandy drew his handkerchief to wipe away her son's sweaty contact, she knew she would hate him to the day of her death.

The youngsters went back to their tasks at Nancy's dismissal.

"I'm so glad to meet the children," Amanda said. "You certainly must be very proud of them."

"I am," Nancy said, honestly. "And now, I'd like to serve you some tea. You must be weary after that long stage ride."

"Kind of you," the commodore replied. "But we lunched at your town hotel immediately on our arrival."

"Thank you, dear Nancy, but we must *really* pass it up."

"You're staying overnight, of course. I'll fix up a nice room for you."

"Can't even do that," the commodore said, yawning again. "We've already engaged a room at the hotel. And we're leaving on the morning stage for Salt Lake City."

Rather than press the point of her hospitality, Nancy felt more like telling the commodore to go drown himself in Utah Lake. The sooner he was gone, the better she'd like it.

"I dread to visit Joel in Salt Lake City," Amanda said.

The old hurt returned. "I can imagine you do." Nancy sat down again, and hung on to Edward's hand while he see-sawed happily upon it. "His other wife's name is Matey. Matey Thorpe Scott. She's an English convert to the Church. They have a little baby boy. And his name is John Radcliffe."

"Complimentary to *my* family name," the commodore said.

"I would say so," Nancy said, vaguely. "I'll write out their address for you. And try not to be too hard on Joel. He doesn't like to have his judgment questioned."

"What judgment?" Amanda snorted. "It's a shame and a disgrace! And I shall tell him so! I can't understand a man walking away from a beautiful family like this—to take up residence with another woman. And so blatant about it, too!"

"Joel's teaching at the Academy, in Salt Lake."

"No matter. His place is with his children—wherever they are."

With Joel's children already strategically and geographically separated in Zion, the question was interesting, but unanswerable, and Nancy felt no urge to comment. She got up, went to Joel's big desk, and wrote out the hated Salt Lake address. For once she would like to be there; to watch the Scott family explosion, when these Gentile Bostonians got their first view of polygamy firsthand.

And so they departed, and summer moved in the swift and swinging round of seasons into fall. Not until then did she learn to what depth Joel's star had really plunged. Apparently Amanda and her husband had been anything but pleased with Joel's complete and unequivocal embracement of the Principle. Undoubtedly, from the granitic certainty of his testimony, he not only had defended his faith, but every peculiar and misunderstood tenet of it. He'd never been a hand to back down on anything, especially when pride and judgment were questioned. Whatever happened, it had destroyed him in his family.

Even Nancy was not blind to the anomaly of the thing. Had Joel gone East, and wedded in the more approved Scott style, he could have enjoyed any amount of extra-marital experiences, so long as he acknowledged only one woman as wife. Even a child or two on the side, so long as paternity was not openly avowed, could probably have been taken in

Scott stride. But to publicly admit and publicly defend a polygamous marriage, especially a Mormon polygamous marriage, was much too shattering for the Boston concept. If Joel wanted this sort of mire to wallow in, it was his—to enjoy alone.

The news Amanda carried back East with her apparently didn't quite kill Joel's aging mother. Nancy learned, from Joel's sad little letter, that a family caucus had been held, the attorneys and trustees called in, and he'd been disinherited; cut off from the Scott family fortune, according to his mother's new codicil, with a bequest of one dollar. The total estate, upon her death, would go to Amanda, her husband, and their children. Nancy had no idea of the size of the Scott fortune, and cared less; but with ships and shipyards, it undoubtedly meant an immense and crushing loss to Joel. Whether the new and everlasting covenant was wrong or right, whether the Church's maintenance and defense of it was good or bad, Joel Scott had paid a heavy price for his acceptance of it. Nancy wondered if Joel, in the secret chambers of his thoughts, didn't rue the day he'd ridden a horse into Utah Valley. Was any religion that made a man a laughingstock before the world and sweated him into poverty worth this price? Knowing her own comfortable and comforting way with Joel, she was certain that the immature and fawn-eyed Matey was of little help in talking Joel back into fresh esteem in the face of these new and shattering problems.

If the Scott family was appalled by the threat of Mormonism, and decisive and merciless in their action against it, their thoughts and acts were only a faint echo of the wave of anti-Mormon sentiment that was violently sweeping the land in this second winter of Joel's exodus from Ammon. President Rutherford Hayes, in his December message to Congress, was adamant that the severest measures possible be immediately taken against the hated sect. "Polygamy will not be abolished if the enforcement of the law depends on those who practice and uphold the crime," the presidential message clearly stated. He would meet this threat head-on "by taking away the political power of the sect which encourages and sustains it." Specifically, he said, "I recommend that congress provide for the government of Utah by a governor and judges or commissioners, appointed by the president and confirmed by the senate." If, on the other hand, this act of completely dumping and abolishing Utah's constitutional form of government proved too rough or high-handed in a democracy, he suggested, as an alternative: "I recommend that the right to vote, hold office, and sit on juries in the territory of Utah be confined to those who neither practice nor uphold polygamy." Nancy, nor no other Saint sensitive to events, could mistake this clarion call for government to move with speed and severity against the Church.

Nor did the retirement of President Hayes and the election of President Garfield make any appreciable change in this sentiment. The new President, in his inaugural speech on March 4, 1881, made plain his plans and hopes in that direction. It was the duty of Congress, in his judgment, "to prohibit within its jurisdiction all criminal practices, especially of that class which destroy the family relations and endanger the social order." The assassin's bullet which struck down President Garfield before he could decently get his executive program formulated neither slowed nor stopped this anti-Mormon pattern in Washington. Chester A. Arthur, who succeeded the fallen President, was just as quick to urge "vigorous measures against the plural marriage system of the Latter-day Saints."

By now the press, and the pulpits of the nation were literally screaming for action. Everything was advocated, from public whipping posts to death, from imprisonment to castration, from hot-iron branding and disfranchisement to banishment to the heathen islands of the Pacific. The Mormons, in their peaceful and industrious Utah, had suddenly, and once again, become the greatest menace to civilized society.

Even the most optimistic Saint knew that in this winter of hate and worry, Congress would act in some way against them. In this they were not guessing wrong. On March 14 Congress answered this public clamor with the Edmunds Act—passed it with an overwhelming majority, and quickly made it a law.

Actually, it was an amendment to the anti-bigamy law of 1862—but with new and strange teeth. It defined polygamy as a crime. "Every person who has a husband or wife living—who hereafter marries another, whether married or single, and any man who simultaneously, or on the same day, marries more than one woman . . . is guilty of polygamy." Penalty was $500 fine or five years imprisonment, or both in the discretion of the court.

Polygamous living was defined as "unlawful cohabitation," and punishable by fine and imprisonment. The law excused from jury service those who were living in polygamy, bigamy, or unlawful cohabitation. It was lawful also to challenge any prospective juror who believed in the practice, without even the necessity of having lived it.

Section Nine of the act carried real teeth against the Mormon threat. It declared all registration and election offices vacant throughout Utah Territory. Duties of said registration and election officers were to be performed by a board of five commissioners, appointed by the President, with the advice and consent of the Senate—not more than three of whom were to be of one political party.

Both Joel and Flora had been right. Nancy, now that she too was a polygamous wife, was entering the worry, just as Flora had said she would. It was as plain as daylight that America's press, clergy, and government were united against the Mormons. It was plain as daylight why Utah had never been granted statehood, and, that before such a thing would be possible the territory would suffer the brutality and relentlessness of a governmental crusade to stamp out the Principle. And it was just as plain now why the territorial penitentiary had so abruptly gone into federal control.

V

AMMON'S WILD AND PULSING SPRING WENT INTO THE GOLDEN LETHARGY of mountain summer, but the pain of Joel's leaving was lessened none by time. The vindictive anger, and even the humiliation and hurt, at having been trapped into the polygamy she loathed receded further and further into dimness, but the ache of his absence was like the Prophet's allegory of the two-edged sword which severed both bone and marrow. She needed Joel; the children needed Joel; and no amount of recrimination and prideful argument would ever fill the vacancy of this loss.

In the support of herself and the youngsters Nancy felt as smugly sure and independent as a mother turkey with her poults. The fertile acres Isaac had left her at the Ammon "bottoms" was a choice piece of Utah Valley, and was farmed for her on shares by the Corey sons, along with the other Corey ranchlands. There was enough income from this source alone to keep food in the family's mouths. And in spite of the efficiency and willingness of Dr. Horace Middy, the Thompsonian physician, enough of Ammon's productive mothers in Israel still demanded Nancy's services to keep her steadily on the hop from house to house. The Gentile campaign against polygamy was having not the least effect on the flow of babies from these unions. The springs and featherbeds of Zion were never busier. With Joel's leaving, Nancy had augmented her bedside fee by an additional charge of one dollar for each post-natal visit she made to mother or child. Such unheard-of charges had no appreciable effect on the insistent demand for her services, and the additional income, in cash, or usable produce, was more than enough to make ends meet in the Scott household. And Nancy, with Bess and the buggy, still rattled around Utah Valley in the capacity to which fate had trained her. But, without a visible and tangible man in the house, any kind of living was poor living.

Old Town, now that everything usable had been purloined from it, was melting down into a sog heap. When the children, or their children, grew old enough to be interested, Nancy knew it would be difficult to convey to them the fact that this melting heap was once a lively, pulsing town. Even the new Ammon, with the snows of winter and the rains of summer, had taken upon itself an ageless quality. Already the town looked as though it might have had its beginnings generations ago. The stately poplars had, by now, taken on the warts and grayness of age. In few places were there any evidences of the raw newness so apparent in the town's explosive birth. In one year an adobe or wooden house, in Utah's elastic climate, would look as mellowed in time as anything surrounding it. Probably, to the youngsters, the town appeared as though it had always existed. They would never have the capacity to picture a barefoot girl, on a twelve-foot clay wall, making clumsy flirt with a Gentile soldier who boiled his eggs in the coffee water. But, though incomprehensible to others, the time, the scene, and the memory of those days, were poignantly real and dear to Nancy. With Joel gone, and the busy press of time, they flavored her thinking in every move and act of her life.

Like any other polygamous wife in Ammon, she was a member of the Relief Society, went to church, partook of the sacrament, and listened to the word of God as delivered by the laymen and unpaid clergy of her ward. And she insisted that every one of her five children attend church with her. At times she bit her lip, and wanted to scream, as some of Ammon's brethren, mistaking a stirring in the genitals for inspiration and God's holy love, would urge the whole world to choose out the desirable sisters for holy increase, and discover the heavenly wonders of the everlasting covenant. Those were the times when she wanted to grab up the eleven-year-old Martha and at least get *her* out of earshot and eye-range of *that* zealous Saint. And then she'd worry guiltily, and about the future, and her confusion, and her implacable hatred of the covenant. But one thing was certain, if any polygamous elder ever had the temerity to even make eyes at Marty, her first-born daughter, she'd ax him into slivers.

On the other hand, and in spite of the specters, the heartache, and the doubt, Ammon was a good place for any man or any woman to live. Always now she tried to cast aside the reactions and the attitudes which any Saint in Zion took for granted, and to try to see things about her through the eyes of her lost and beloved Joel. What was it about this valley that had so captivated him—enough to change his own lively and promising destiny to another obscure entity in Mormondom? It encouraged her to know that the first and most poignant reason had been her, Nancy Corey. If he married thirty women, she could always console herself with the fact that she'd piqued his interest enough to have had first hand in this destiny. But there had been more—and that, of course, was the valley itself. He'd loved this place from the very first hour of his entry. And in his penal sentence with his second choice, in Salt Lake, Nancy was certain he loved it still. The town, too, with its kindly and peculiar people, had likewise grown into this love. He may have seen the world, or been bred in Boston, but Ammon was Joel Scott's town. His had been an exciting and useful hand in fashioning it—and one just did not put these things aside.

As a midwife, with Bess and the buggy, she knew her valley and her town as did few humans in it. But among many other things, she could thank God for Joel, and the sharp appreciation he'd given her of the valley of their joint destiny. He'd told her of its magnificent mountain back country, the Swiss-like glory of its green sweep to the lake. She'd told him of its people, their quirks, their color, their humor, and their heroics. Together, with enriched and quickened vision, they'd seen their valley and their town through eyes of tolerance, love, and real understanding. And while it lasted with Joel, this had been a precious and wonderful thing.

But even with Joel gone, habit prevented any dimming of this perception. Many a time she'd rattled home from a case, loaded with experiences—humorous, tragic, or sad—aching to share them with Joel, who alone of all Ammon's people could appreciate them.

Together they had savored in delight the characters of the town, whom she, of few people, met intimately in their homes. There was Brother Eggerson, who slept with all three of his plural wives in one family bed, and managed to keep all three of them regularly pregnant. There was Brother Bissell, whose apple orchards now produced enough cider to keep his barrels perpetually full, and aged by time, sharp enough to keep him wildly drunk between Sunday services. As a speaker he was almost as eloquent as Joel, and with a conscience that could make any sinner heed. In the winter he'd roll a barrel or two of this cider out into the yard, for a thorough freezing. Then, with a long auger he'd bore a hole from the bung, into the ice block's center. There the distillation of the unfrozen alcohol, with unique and piquant apple flavor, would be drained off and bottled for future use. This applejack was the sharpening basis to many a Bissell sermon.

There was Sister Plush, a Mormon handcart pioneer, who had lost her husband in the terrible disaster on the Sweetwater. Alone, in her little house, lovingly supported by the ward fast offerings and the Relief Society, Sister Plush saw and talked constantly with the spirits from the other side. To walk into her cottage was to go into a wraithlike world. Always there were several plates at her table, and she carried on an animated and illuminating conversation with the visitors which she alone could see and appreciate. Her house was Ammon's most important port of call for the ubiquitous Three Nephites. These bearded strangers, from another age, were regular visitors at the little home of Sister Plush. And, every month, at testimony meeting, Sister Plush would tell all of Ammon about the spirits she'd met and mingled with.

Then there was Brother Proctor and his double rupture. It was amazing how, with this intimate impediment, he could manage to keep two women regularly pregnant, but somehow he managed it. In his walks about town he was a good deal less successful. In this, gravity apparently worked against him, for his lower guts had the acute and painful tendency to work themselves through the rupture gates and into his scrotum. It was nothing to see Brother Proctor on the sidewalk, howling and writhing worse than Seth Biddle. The only remedy to his unfortunate condition was unique, but it had to be done quickly—and that was to stand the good brother on his head. When these seizures came, any bystanders would be urgently enlisted to this all important task. And Ammon had gotten accustomed to seeing Brother Proctor, head down, legs in air, while his fellow townsmen shook his guts out of his scrotum.

"These are the things which make a town," Joel had told Nancy. And now more than ever could she agree with him. But to her there had come one qualifying addition. Joel, too, had been, and was, an essential part of this town. Ammon missed him. And oh God, so did she!

One other essential ingredient in the basic structure of Ammon, as in every other close-knit Mormon town in Utah, was that humble quality of brotherliness—a quality Nancy accepted and took for granted, because she'd never known anything else, but a virtue Joel had analyzed and marveled at from the day he'd made her town his own. The brethren might argue and battle furiously over the small things, but on the big and important issues of their collective lives, they stood to the world with a united front, and hands clasped as one in Mormon fraternity. On Sundays they prayed together, sang together, and broke the bread of sacrament together. Not only did they take their "turns" in the watering of their fields, but they likewise took their "turns" in the capacity of their universal priesthood, to guide and exhort from the rostrums of their chapels. This was "the church of the people, operated by the people, without paid clergy, and actuated by love and brotherhood," which Joel had so often described, and so literally embraced.

But always there was so much more than these observable virtues in life's pattern for this Utah Valley town. Nancy believed, along with Joel, that it was the friendliest place on earth. In play and relaxation, as in labor and worship, the community was as one. In the present settlement, as in the clay-walled Old Town, the dances, the socials, and the holidays were shared by anyone and everyone who cared to take part. From her earliest recollection, the Twenty-fourth of July—Pioneer Day—had been celebrated as a traditional time of picnic and festivities, either at the lake shore, or in the cool and shady pine groves of Ammon's rugged and spectacular canyon. This year the choice was the canyon and, as her parents had done before her, Nancy gathered up her children, and at daybreak, they joined the procession headed up the creek road and foothills into the mountains. With a family of the size and turbulence of the Scotts, Bess and the buggy were completely inadequate. So, the day before, Nancy had borrowed a Corey team and wagon. The handling of this cumbersome and uncomfortable wheeler, along with its unfamiliar team, she gladly left to young Joel, who was as adept and skillful with horses as his father.

As in almost every other year, the Authorities would be represented by one or more dignitaries from Salt Lake. This time, as so many times in the past, Apostle Jonathan Cragg would be on hand to lend both sanction and spirit to the occasion. Nancy knew this because of Flora's letter. And Flora, and, perhaps some of her family, were coming along in the apostle's entourage. There was nothing especially unique about Apostle Cragg's choice of community picnics for this day. Whenever he was not serving his church in some other part of the world, Lofty Cragg made every effort to share this day with Ammon. He liked Ammon, he enjoyed showing his favoritism for the town, and the most beautiful bride in his personal collection had come out of this valley town. His visits, on Pioneer Day at least, had become sort of traditional.

For Nancy and her family, there was no sense in delaying their trip to the canyon to wait on any official party from Salt Lake. The bishop, the stake president, and even Aunt Millie's family had the close and immediate claim on Apostle Cragg the minute his carriage showed itself around The Point, and little likelihood the apostle or Flora would care to stoop to the discomforts of a borrowed and bumpy wagon for the five-mile trip up Ammon Canyon. Anyway, the picnic was for the youngsters, Nancy reasoned. She had planned, and baked, and cooked for their day—not for any prospective visit with Lofty Cragg or Flora. She was not so sure she even wanted to see Flora, after the crafty way Flora had planted that serpent in the Scott garden. As for the apostle, if he still suffered from his deprivation, she was one party who could feel genuinely sorry for him. That was one increase she wished the Lord had somehow seen fit to favor him with.

Half a mile within the canyon was the "flat," a wooded section of rare beauty, through which raced the cold and tumbling waters of Ammon Creek. The stream had plenty of fighting trout, and already the early arrivals, and those who were making more than one day of the outing, had fat strings of fish to prove the wisdom of an early dipping of the line. From the valley floor, rich with the sounds of roaring water, the flutings and cries of the mountain birds, and the reassuring voices of happy humans, the walls of the canyon rose abruptly, towering, and almost overwhelming into the high crags of the Wasatch wall. As one climbed upward into the granite wilds, by way of a trail negotiable only afoot or by horseback, the chasm narrowed into sheer walls and the wildest beauty imaginable. From her young days, Nancy had known Ammon Canyon like an open book. And Joel himself had found it one of his favorite spots to ride, explore, and sketch. A few miles above the decorated and noisy picnic area, the canyon split into two forks, and, along with it the watercourse. If one had the capacity and endurance, he could climb out and over the rugged Wasatches, and into Weber Valley, by following the north canyon draw to its end. To travel the south canyon, through rich pine forests, upward into the immense flats and pockets of the aspen groves, eventually brought one to the backside of Timpanogos, and the living glacier descending from its crest, which fed both Ammon Creek and its larger branch, the Provo River. In fact, a ride over the rocky feet of the mountain's glacier, brought one down into Provo Canyon, and outward again into Utah Valley. Nancy had ridden it, Joel had ridden it many times, and it was just as well known now to Joel's children.

But Joel's trained mind had seen many more things about Ammon Canyon and the mountainous back country not even yet apparent to the stolid, agricultural-minded Saints of the town and valley. He'd taken cognizance of its mineralized and timbered areas. He'd patiently explored the little-known caves opening out into the canyon's high mountain walls. "When those caves are better known, they'll be a wonder to the world," Joel had said. "Inside they're a veritable fairyland. Stalactites and stalagmites, row on row, like organ pipes. Pockets of fantastic beauty that will take your breath away. Places for men to hide, where only God Himself could discover you. Those caves are stupendous!" Nancy had been forced to take Joel's word for it. She'd never visited Joel's discoveries. And few other Ammonites seemed to even be aware of their existence. At the picnic today, in Joel's beloved canyon—it seemed a shame he could not be here again to enjoy it with his family.

But his youngsters, like those of most plural families, were resourceful and enterprising. As so often happened, one of the sisters—Sister Jones this time—was nearing her time. The minute Nancy made her appearance at the picnic ground, she'd been spirited away by the good sister's anxious husband. "I'd be obleeged if you'd take a look at Sophia," was Brother Jones's way of nailing her. And so, for twenty minutes Nancy had asked questions of Sister Jones as to the peculiarities of her case, felt her abdomen with an expert and revealing touch, and reassured the woman as to her prospects. When she returned, the Scott children had the tent up, the tarpaulin spread out, the fire started, and baby Edward safely guarded to the canvas, out of reach of bugs, stinging nettle, and rock-hiding rattlesnakes. It was moments like this, when Nancy looked at her handsome youngsters, that the Mormon concept of the family eternal, had believable glory and substance. She had not the least doubts that these children were living entities before they were born, just as the Prophet had revealed. That the family pattern, in its deepest love and meaning, would be reunited after death—a marriage and a kingship, with Joel Scott at its head, with herself at his right hand—for time and all eternity. Eternal progression, as the Prophet had revealed, and as the Church ceaselessly taught, was a noble and breathtaking concept of endless love, and endless increase. The only discord she'd ever felt, or ever would feel in this mystic wonder, was about the other queen; the claimant for Joel's other hand. Yet plenty of Mormon women accepted and lived this phase of the Principle, without tearing their hearts out, or destroying their husbands. Somehow God had put this block of granite in *her* path, and in *her* thinking. Not even prayer or fasting could blast it out.

"Gee, I wish Dad was here," Jody said, as expertly he laid the ax-slivered kindling to the blaze.

"I do, too, Joel," Nancy said honestly, and half dreaming. "With all my heart I do." Deliberately she jarred herself out of any such reverie. With expert eye, she looked around at the Scott camp. "Did you water the horses, and grain 'em, before haltering 'em out?" she asked.

"Of course I did," Jody replied.

"That's fine," Nancy said with proper parental authority. "Rules are that all families picnic at their own camp circles. At two P.M. everybody assembles for the program and speeches. We eat again before dark. Then the music and the dancing."

"Mom, *we* know that," Marty said tolerantly. "We've read the program."

And before the day was over, it turned out to be quite a program.

As expected, Apostle Cragg arrived at just about the time the nooning got under way. One sensed a dignitary had arrived, by the wave of electric excitement which swept the family camps up and down the canyon. Nancy, busy with her own picnic circle, made no effort to go hunting out the Salt Lake visitors. But like everyone else present, she knew something important had happened, because even the crickets and the birds seemed momentarily to stop their chirping.

"Shall I go and see who's here?" Amanda asked.

"Yes—but be careful—and hurry back," Nancy said, stirring the paste she'd made from the slivered and precious chocolate into the kettle of warm milk on the fire coals. "We're about ready to eat." She knew Aunt Millie and family were here, expectant, and with picnic and plates for the visitors. And should they choose, any one of the town's notables, would make quick claim on them before they could ever begin to make an up-canyon stop at the Scott camp. There was no call for her to spread out extra plates. But she *would* like to know if Flora had made it.

She looked at baby Eddie, sound asleep on one edge of the big canvas tarpaulin. He was worn out with the excitement. She really ought to bed him down in the tent. She looked again, and smiled. He was content. Leave him alone.

From the same big basket Martha had so often dragged to the picnics, Nancy hauled out the ready-cooked eatables. Had the man she'd married been here, there would have been trout and bacon in the pan, but, with philosophic discount of the loss, she'd packed the crocks with fried chicken, cold roasts, and that new and fancy salad made from boiled potatoes. When, with Marty's help, these gustatory satisfiers were exhumed, dished up, and laid out to the spread of the tarpaulin, from the same cavernous depths of the ancient basket came the mince pies, the ground-cherry pies, and the apple pies—followed by the fat and high layer cake she'd sat up half the night baking, and at daylight had slathered together with fresh whipped cream. The jolting wagon had shaken it down to its basic layers, and the white filling hung disconsolately about it, but with knife and spoon she reformed the contour, and it would probably taste about the same. All through this preparation, there was the merry banter with the neighboring camps, as they, too, went through this ritual of hauling out the grub. It was noticeable that the dozens of youngsters had abruptly broken off their noisy and ribald play, to retreat to their respective family circles for the big feed. By the time Amanda returned, the Scotts, in turn, were anxious and ready to demolish Nancy's offering.

It was a bug-eyed and almost hysterical Amanda who came dashing into camp. She stopped, fought for breath, and looked as though she'd explode.

"Is Apostle Cragg here yet?" Nancy asked. "And Aunt Flora?"

"I dunno," Amanda managed to say.

"Well—"

"It's Daddy! He's here!"

Nancy dropped the plate to the canvas. "Where?"

Amanda pointed down the canyon. "Down there. Shaking hands with ev'rbody. He says that he'll be here in a minute."

The older youngsters let out a whoop of joy, and Marty was off like a wild deer down the roadway, closely pursued by young Joel. Nancy, fighting for her own strength and composure, put a loving and protective arm about Amanda.

"Was Daddy—was Daddy—a-alone?" she asked.

"Couldn't tell. Too many people. I had to sneak in behind."

"Shall I fill your plate, sweetheart? Or would you rather wait, and eat with Daddy?"

"Oh—I'd rather wait. I'll bet he's hungry. And it's been a long time since he ate with us."

"It *has* been a long time," Nancy sighed. "Such a long, long time."

Vernell, the silent one, came up from the creek bed with a double hand load of pretty rocks. Nervously, Nancy took the time to admire them and to wipe the little girl's nose. It had come, as she knew it would come. Joel was here—maybe to step back into the place he'd vacated in his family. But if Matey was here—what then? The same acrimony arose in her, sharp-edged, and undulled by time. What must the first wife do, when the second wife steps into the family circle, unwanted, and unasked? Now that Matey controlled the man, as young and reigning favorite, it was a little late to again shove her into the creek. "For the children's sake—for Joel's sake," Nancy murmured to herself, "I'll try to be polite and civil."

Nervously, and with trembling hands, she went at the task of laying out more plates on the ground-level spread. She smiled tolerantly as Vernell tried to help. She should have brought more picnic. Joel had an appetite like a Wasatch bear. She hoped to the good Lord there'd be enough food.

A moment later she heard a clatter of hooves, and the shrill shouts of the older children. Around the bend in the canyon road came the sleek and familiar picture of the geldings, Gus and George. With whistles and whoops, young Joel was driving—and, on the surrey seat, between his son and his daughter Martha, gay and happy as ever, sat their father, with an arm around them both. The back seat of the rig was empty. His plural wife was nowhere to be seen. God be praised, he'd come home at last! And he'd come home alone! Nancy, now standing erect, and vibrating like a tea bell, felt dizzy enough to fall face flat into the picnic. She caught herself, wrapped an arm around Amanda, and waved with the frantic joy of a schoolgirl.

A moment later he'd leaped from the carriage seat and, while the youngsters put the rig and horses to rest alongside the wagon and more complacent Corey work-team, Joel made straight for Nancy. A second later he'd wrapped her tightly in his arms. For a full minute, while Amanda and Vernell looked hungrily on, and baby Edward obliviously slept at his edge of the tarpaulin, they held one another wordlessly tight. And then he kissed her, full-mouthed and starved. Misty-eyed, still trembling, Nancy felt herself flowing in to him, and she did not care.

He broke away, looked into her face, and his eyes grew merry again. "It's been a long time, Nan," he said.

"It's good to have you back," she whispered. "We've all missed you so."

She had a thousand questions to ask him—some casual, some personal, some intimate, and some of them perhaps explosive. All had been set churning within her by his sudden and unexpected appearance. But they'd have to wait. This was no time to sort them out. He was back, this moment, with her and her children. That was enough.

"We thought you were Apostle Cragg," she said, laughing.

"Oh?"

"I sent Amanda to find out if Flora was with him. Instead she found you."

Joel laughed merrily. "Would you rather have the apostle?"

"You fool," she said, snuggling close. "You forget that I *had* my chance with the apostle."

"And it was on the Twenty-fourth day of July, if I remember right, that he really whetted himself up for his courting."

"And it was also on the Twenty-fourth day of July that I unwhetted him." This casual talk of courtings unsettled her. They broke their embrace, and she held his arm while they both surveyed the spread of food before them.

Joel gathered up both the little girls—one in each arm—and kissed them heartily. "Well, you weren't wrong about Lofty Cragg being here," he said, hugging the youngsters as he talked. "He came up the canyon ahead of me. But I don't know whether or not he's here to look for another bride. I've played hide-and-seek with his carriage all the way from Salt Lake. He's not overly cordial, you know, and I made no point to seek him out."

"Let's forget about him," Nancy urged. "You're just in time for lunch. Here, girls, you can sit right next to Daddy."

"And, I'm hungry as a wolf in a mine-shaft." After he'd set the youngsters to the canvas, he leaned over and grabbed a chicken leg, gnawing at it with happy content. Amanda took off to join Jody and Marty.

"We'll eat, quick as the kids get through with the horses." Nancy went back, happily, to setting out the food.

"You were wondering about Flora," Joel said, his mouth thick with chicken. "She's here, too—with her two oldest youngsters. Our paths crossed at Bishop Earlington's. The bishop, you know, couldn't make this picnic. He's so old, and sore, and lame."

"Poor soul," Nancy said, dusting off Joel's plate. "I worry about him."

"Flora and the apostle went from the bishop's directly to Aunt Millie's. Their party was well ahead of me coming up the canyon road. I guess they're still down below, shaking hands with the Saints." He flung the chicken bone far out into the creek, walked around the wide spread of canvas, touched Vernell's hair, and knelt down beside his sleeping little boy. "Great gods, but he's grown," he murmured. "He's a handsome lad, Nan. And he looks more than ever like you."

Nancy watched while, tenderly, he bent over and kissed the little forehead. Edward stirred restlessly, but did not awaken. She shut her eyes with sheer joy. This picnic had suddenly turned out to be a wonder.

Soon Jody and Martha were with them, tagged in with Amanda.

They were lugging the three watermelons Joel had brought up the canyon in the surrey. By the time they all had squatted down to the rich spread of food, it was a talkative, wild, and noisy meal. The news had spread that the schoolmaster was back, and, one by one Joel's Ammon neighbors dropped by the Scott camp to shake his hand and welcome him home. Result was that they were much too late in getting through their nooning. The program was started, and the four older youngsters had hurried along to hear it, before Nancy could get things in order and she and Joel could saunter along down the canyon toward the music and the oratory. Edward was awake now, and tugged affectionately from Joel's hand.

Brother Urgent Mathews served as master of ceremonies, in the absence of Bishop Earlington. Joshua Rowley and his fiddlers furnished the music; and they would likewise liven up the dancing after sundown. The bishop, who had been a familiar part of every gathering and picnic within the years of Ammon's recollection, was sorely missed. But Apostle Cragg, who himself had become something of an Ammon tradition, set the day and tore the heart with his eloquence.

The wagon and handcart pioneers were especially honored with a little wrapped gift from their appreciative townsfolk. With all her heart, Nancy wished Isaac and Martha could have been present in the flesh to line themselves up with their friends and neighbors in this token of remembrance to the sacrifice these noble souls had made in the name of brotherhood and religion. And again, in the eerie pattern of another time-dimmed picnic, Joel Scott was asked to speak to the Saints of Ammon. With the same becoming reluctance he was hauled to the stand, and the murmur of joy that went up at his presence fed Nancy warmly in the esteem with which he still was felt by his brethren. This time it was no dwelling on the hopes he had for Ammon in an educational way, but rather a reminder of what Ammon had accomplished through the years. Scarcely a family was present whose children did not know "the professor" in the classroom, and had not sweated out their learning under his firm but understanding guidance. Apostle Cragg, who sat firm-faced and undemonstrative beside the fashionably dressed and still favorite Flora, had all but thwarted Joel's future in the big city and the Church. But he had no power whatever to blunt or deprecate the love of Joel's neighbors and friends. As before, Joel's words were few, but they were rich in remembrance and appreciation for all that Ammon had come to mean to him.

"Your talk was wonderful," Nancy told him, after the crowds had broken up for evening meal, and she and Eddie could join him for the walk back to camp. "The best oration today. Ammon likes you a lot."

"And I like Ammon," he said, taking her arm to guide her along the brushy mountain path. "I've had my fill of Salt Lake. Up there even my shoes seem to be mismates."

Nancy was on the verge of asking one or more of the intimate questions plaguing her, but she resisted the impulse. Joel was honest. He'd do his own talking in proper time. Instead she asked, "You plan to come back to Ammon to teach?"

"I've been asked."

"Do you want to?"

"You know the answer to that, Nan. Of course I do. This is home to me."

They walked in silence for a moment. The sun, like a great patient reddish lamp, still lit the canyon mouth to the west, but the high wall of granite and jack pine on either side threw their shadows, already deep and dark, to the wooded floor below. Soon the little valley would be alive with a thousand lanterns, like fireflies in the summer night. There was magic in it for Nancy, and its mystic pattern had been enriched beyond utterance by the return of Joel. Their talk was close to the edge, and she parried with her thoughts before speaking again.

"If you came back to Ammon," she said cautiously, "what about your two families?"

"That would have to be decided. They only asked me today."

She clung to his arm as he guided her along the brushy, spooky pathway. They were silent again as they listened to the roar and tumble of the stream, the metallic chitter of the crickets, and the twilight flutings of the night birds. To her other hand clung little Edward, overawed by the mystery of the dying day far from home. Their slow walk was measured to his brave and tiny stride. It was Nancy who decided, resolutely, to break the barrier.

"Little John Radcliffe must be quite a boy now," she said at last.

"He is, Nan," Joel said, with almost pathetic eagerness. "A fine and beautiful boy. He walked before he was a year old, and talks a torrid streak. You'll see him tomorrow."

"Tomorrow? I thought he was in Salt Lake!"

"Oh no. I brought Matey and the boy down with me."

Nancy cringed with fright and despair. She tried not to transmit the paralyzing wave of it to the arm that clutched her polygamous husband. "Did you leave them at Ammon?" she asked, dimly.

"At the Earlingtons'."

"How come you didn't bring them to the picnic?"

"Matey didn't feel up to it, after the long ride. She's in delicate condition."

"Family way again?"

"Yes. But her time isn't yet."

"You're sure? A long ride in a jolting carriage can sometimes bring a baby in a hurry."

"She'll be all right. A little rest is what she needs."

"But why did you attempt the trip, Joel? That's no good for the woman *or* the child."

"I wanted to get out of Salt Lake. The place hasn't been good for me, Nan. Your Apostle Cragg has done everything in God's kingdom to hurt and discredit me. I think you must have caught the idea by his looks when Ammon's townsfolk shouted me to the stand. He'd as soon have shared it with a rattlesnake."

"I know," Nancy agreed, sadly. "Even Flora acts strange and standoffish. Lord knows, she's got little enough reason."

With the slimy plot she'd foisted on the Scotts, thought Nancy, it was certain Flora should be the last person to stiff-arm the half sister she so callously had betrayed. Instead, if she couldn't radiate love and joy, at least she should be grateful.

Little Edward, struggling bravely against the shadows and the rocks, at last decided to seat himself on a large boulder for a rest. Joel chuckled. "Come on, son," he laughed. "You need a horse." He kneed down in the pathway, exactly like he used to do. "Climb on, Eddie. You can ride me home to oats." Gleefully Eddie climbed aboard Joel's broad back, hung on to the shoulders, and Joel's hands became the secure stirrups. Once again they resumed the walk, nodding cheerfully to townsfolk, as they passed the evening fires of their camps.

And that was the way it was in this polygamous world, thought Nancy. And she tried not to let the bitterness of it lash out in the acrimony that would destroy every sweet moment of Joel's return. But there was no use dodging the issue. The trap of polygamy had inevitably, inexorably, sprung shut upon her. She, the one woman in Ammon who had hated the Principle, dodged the Principle, refused even to sign a Mormon petition in its defense, was now caught tight and sure in its endless web. How, in heaven's name, did one adjust to it? How, in honesty, could any woman share her man with another, and feel happy, reconciled, and secure? In this canyon were scores of wives who, outwardly at least, seemed not to mind it in the least. How and where did they get this serenity? These things she was seeing with her own eyes—and still her eyes remained blind and hostile to whatever it was that made it work.

And now, for her, as a polygamous wife, the inevitable had happened. Joel hadn't said as much, but he'd brought Matey to Ammon for her acceptance. He loved Ammon, truly, fiercely. He'd gotten his craw full of Salt Lake, its petty jealousies, and intrigue. And the Boston hurt was still upon him. He wanted to return to Ammon. He wanted both his families together. He was anxious to set up the polygamous family pattern one saw on every hand. If not two women in a house —at least one week at Aunt Matey's, the next week at Aunt Nancy's, and so on, for time and all eternity. And both issues of the Scott children would accept this arrangement as commonplace as did all the other youngsters in the town. But could *she* accept it? And if she did, could she *ever* know happiness again?

"I'm distressed and worried about what's happening in Salt Lake," Joel was saying. "Things are firming up since the passing of the Edmunds Act into law. The streets are beginning to swarm with deputy U.S. marshals—and they're hard-looking characters—toughies and gunmen from every riff-raff mining camp in the West. They're being hired by the dozens, coached for whatever's coming, and getting ready for some sort of campaign against us. It will start first in Salt Lake—but none of us are going to escape it."

Little Edward, imagining his father a horse rather than a worried polygamist, prodded him with his heels, and they continued their walk through the gathering dusk.

"What's worrying the Authorities is the fact that some of the bitter apostates of the Church have joined ranks with the federal judges and marshals, as informers against their former brethren. Anti-Mormon newspapers, from the Gentile town of Corrine, to Salt Lake City, are pouring out their vitriol. There may be a little quiet spell before hell breaks loose. The judges, the marshals, and the wardens at the penitentiary must get their machine well oiled and ready. Congress has provided the legal backing, even though the provisions of the Edmunds Act itself are blatantly unconstitutional. All I can say is, God help our people, and our church! That's one of the reasons why I want to get out of Salt Lake, Nan. I want to be near my families when the storm comes. I want to be close enough to see them, while I look for the enemy's eyes."

Again Nancy could scarcely believe that the devout Mormon who uttered these words, could have once been the Gentile army captain who had dropped in to the walled town to sketch it and study it. "I'd think it good strategy to keep the families separated," she said. "Marshals could never make a polygamist out of a man unless there were more than one wife around. And any wife would lie about it for her husband's sake."

"Nancy, I love both my wives. I love all my children. If and when the time comes to test that love, to fight for it, I at least want them near me."

And there she had it. The thing she most feared in life was upon her. In the name of himself, his love, and his church, he was asking her to knuckle down to the Principle—to accept Matey into Ammon. To share him every other week. To accept plurality, like her neighbors. And if she didn't? Where could she go? What could she do? What about her own fierce love for the man? What about five children he'd sired, and who loved him as deeply as he loved them? If the government was going to stop the practice cold in its tracks, why hadn't it stopped it five years before?

Arriving back in camp, they found that Jody and Marty, probably with limited help from Vernell and Amanda, had a cheerful fire going, and the lanterns lit. Joel lowered himself, like a good horse, and Edward clambered off.

"Horses have been grained and watered," Jody said pridefully.

"I've always said we had a good man in Jody," his father declared.

"Jody *is* a good man," Nancy added. "Don't know what in the world I'd have done without him."

Jody grinned happily, and proudly thumbed out his overalls straps. Joel made no comment.

"It'll be fun to eat supper by lantern and firelight," Nancy quickly added. "Come on, girls, let's get the cooking going."

And it *was* fun. The old-time fun they'd known as a family, before the Principle had divided them. In the happiness and unity they felt, Nancy all but forgot the bitter thoughts that had disturbed her. They stuffed themselves with food, they told stories about the campfire, and they sang—as scores of other Ammon families were doing by the lights and fires of the canyon party. Above them, in mystery, blackness, and solitude, towered the broken and jagged walls of the Wasatch. In the wonderful parties commemorating Pioneer Day throughout Zion, with the joy and brotherhood they symbolized, it seemed incomprehensible to Nancy that even the Gentiles could see it in their hearts to unleash their war of hate upon this people—as Joel so darkly had predicted. In the happiness she felt in once more seeing her family together, she postponed most of her own thinking about the peculiar Mormon ques-

271

tion of plurality. This was her problem, this was the Church's problem, this was a problem for the Saints to solve. Please, Gentiles, for once in your lives, leave us alone!

In honor of their parents, and the father who so miraculously and unexpectedly had returned from exile, the children conceded to Joel and Nancy any claim they might have had to the tent. Jody, manly and fearlessly, rolled himself up in a blanket, Paiute fashion, alongside the dying fire. Marty sought her bed on the soft cushion of her father's surrey. The other three youngsters, little Eddie included, settled themselves noisily down in the high and protective bed of the wagon. As in every man's family, catcalls, jokes, and weird noises came from the different segments of the Scott picnic area, until sleep finally silenced the tired and happy youngsters. And then, far into the night, Joel and Nancy, once more together beneath the intimate covers of their own marriage bed, listened to the shouts, the singing, and the merrymaking of their townsfolk. This night was something to remember. Her own problems Nancy shelved for another day's solving. Joel was here—and beside her. Joel had his arm around her, and there was peace, mystery, and contentment in the night.

"You've been a good wife, and a good mother, Nancy," Joel whispered in the darkness. "You've been good for me. And I love you."

"I love you, too, Joel," she said.

And nothing in the devil's arsenal, and nothing in God's good world, could ever alter that fact.

VI

NANCY NEVER QUITE MUSTERED ENOUGH FIRMNESS TO HER RESISTANCE, AND Joel Scott and Matey stayed on in Ammon. Before Joel started his fall term in the Ammon schools, they had managed a down-payment on the house that Isaac Corey had once built for his youngest bride, Kirstine—and Joel settled his own youngest bride therein. As a co-operative plural wife, Nancy shared her furniture with Matey and, with what they shipped down from Salt Lake, the second wife was adequately set up in her household. A week later, Nancy delivered Matey's child—a little girl. The birthing of this child was a supreme ordeal for the child's Aunt Nancy.

At first Nancy utterly refused to heed the call, even at Joel's frenzied insistence. "Get Mary Magdalene," she'd demanded. "I just can't do it, Joel."

"You think I'd burden you with this, if there was any other way?" Joel pleaded. "Mary's sick, old, and utterly refuses. Says she wouldn't come anyway—that it's good for you—that plural wives should help one another."

"Well, you can tell Mary Magdalene to go to hell—and that I said so!" Nancy angrily declared. "What's wrong with Dr. Middy?"

"Nothing—except that he's taken Sister Ranson to Salt Lake for an expert's help on that maggoty leg of hers. I'm desperate, Nan. Aunt Millie's alone with Matey. The baby can come any minute!"

"Great God—why is it *I'm* always caught in the middle of these things?" Nancy screamed. "Nobody *ever* seems to be around when they're needed most! I even had to deliver my own child! My first-born child! Maybe 'twould be good for Matey, if she also delivered her own child."

And then, in this moment, was one of the few times she'd ever seen tears in Joel's eyes. "Nancy," he pleaded, "this just doesn't sound like you. You're a competent, respected midwife. A woman's having a baby. Her life—and the baby's life—is in danger. I'm asking you, as a hundred other humans have asked you, to attend this birth."

"And it happens to be *your* child, and *your* woman," she moaned. "I just can't, Joel. I just can't." And now *she* was weeping.

"Please, Nan?" he implored.

But finally, like any other good, dutiful plural wife, Nancy went to the assistance of another member of the family kingdom. Only by biting her lip on this travesty of her girlhood resolve, and by forcing herself to look on Matey as just another woman in trouble, was she able to force herself through the ordeal. But the baby was a hefty, healthy one. For a little girl, it squawled strong and loud; and was a credit to Joel. Matey proved good, co-operative, and, in her peculiar British way, mildly sweet. Nancy had always maintained that one really got to know the real woman when the birthing pains and screams were upon them. Matey grudgingly measured up. In an oblique and inexpressible way, Nancy came to sort of like her. By now, with this final act of knuckling under to the Principle, she knew she would always have to acknowledge and tolerate her.

So, in the tried and true pattern of Isaac Corey, and the many other stalwart brethren of Utah who had found the best and easiest ways to make the plural pattern of marriage tolerable and workable, Joel Scott set up his twin households in Ammon, alternating the weeks of his life to each wife and each family. There were still many polygamists who, either exceedingly brave, or exceedingly poor, maintained all their wives under one roof. Experience, however, had long ago indicated the hazards and the explosive possibilities where more than one woman shared the same man in the same house. As for Nancy, even though she could respect and tolerate Matey as a person, it was hard to grudge her even an existence as a second wife. And had Joel attempted to house the pair of them under the same roof, one or the other would likely have gotten her throat cut.

That Joel Scott now openly lived under the covenant, and maintained two households for everyone to see, neither shocked nor surprised the town of Ammon. At least two thirds of the brethren likewise lived their polygamy in the open, their breeds of children mixed and mingled, and, for Zion at least, it had become an accepted and acknowledged way of life. Actually, for Ammon, it was a matter of pride that the converted Gentile had gone "whole hog" for the doctrine of Mormonism; accepting without reservation every tenet and restraint maintained by the faith. To Nancy, it was a little saddening to see the ease with which the children slipped into the polygamous pattern of their friends and playmates. Not only did they accept the fact that their father spent every other week in the home of Aunt Matey, but they even seemed to store up their joys and interests toward the festival weeks when Father Scott was intimately in their midst. They seemed to give more heed to his correction, his guidance, and his love, than when he was present to the full-time job. The affectionate perceptions which absence always sharpens, became a constant and observable thing under the new pattern. Joel's demands and discipline had a way of sticking. Mother, who was always around, handy, and seldom missed, had less success. The only other virtue Nancy was willing to grudge to plurality was that, even with the inhuman aspects of the plan, it was better than those years without Joel at all. And to the children, half a father was decidedly better than none.

But to Nancy it seemed some sort of travesty that the years Joel chose to enter the Principle were the very years that an aroused populace and government had set their determination to stamp it out. The

Edmunds Act, with the new congressional Tucker Amendment, was every bit as lethal as Joel had predicted. The territorial representatives to Congress, Allen G. Campbell and George Q. Cannon, irrespective of the fact that they were duly elected by the people of Utah, were unseated by the august body, and their offices declared vacant, because of their public acknowledgment of more than one wife. Hundreds of other polygamous officials throughout Utah were being turned out of office with like impunity.

In the elections that followed, to try to get suitable Gentiles, or Mormons without taint, to preside over territorial affairs was a sudden and new problem. Joel, as always, was asked by Ammon's new mayor, John F. Willey, to take over the supervision of voting and registration for the town. He came home to Nancy, white-faced and angry. The task he'd assumed was impossible.

"This is worse than I ever could have imagined, Nan," he said, and dropped wearily into his chair. "Take a look at this." He handed her a sheaf of papers.

"What are they?" she asked.

"This is the oath every voting officer has to take, and every Mormon has to sign, before he can cast a ballot in this territory. It represents the disfranchisement of this people. And, by God, I resent it!"

Nancy glanced down the many vicious, intimate, and patently unfair *Whereas's* to the oath itself. On this she gave a closer scrutiny.

> And I do further swear (or affirm) that I am not a bigamist nor a polygamist; that I am not a violator of the laws of the United States prohibiting bigamy or polygamy; that I do not live or cohabit with more than one woman *in the marriage relation,* nor does any relation exist between me and any women which has been entered into or continued in violation of the said laws of the United States prohibiting bigamy or polygamy, and, (if a woman) that I am not the wife of a polygamist, nor have I entered into any relation with any man in violation of the laws of the United States concerning polygamy or bigamy.

"And every person in Utah has to swear to that?" Nancy asked incredulously.

"If they want to exercise their rights as a citizen to vote, or to hold office!" Joel furiously roared. "All it means is that most of the Saints can no longer be citizens. All it means is that I can no longer function in any capacity whatsoever that might benefit my town. All it means is that you, me, and Matey, have had all rights as a voting citizen high-handedly taken from us."

"Why can't the Gentiles leave us alone?" Nancy moaned, exactly as had every Mormon from the beginning.

"Lord, Nan, you don't know the half of it! This new Governor Murray's a Mormon-hater. Every commissioner, every judge appointed to the territory come here with one avowed purpose—to knock the props from under Mormonism. The flood of anti-Mormon books is nauseating. I've tried for years to get a few honest words published about this people. But anything libelous, untrue, trashy, or sensational has no trouble finding a publisher. And the newspapers! Led by that lying, scandalous *Tribune,* now raising hell in Salt Lake, the nation's press is crammed with the sort of things that turns a nation into a holy war. Hundreds of thousands of dollars are being subscribed by the Christian denominations throughout America, for the non-Mormon churches of Utah. But it's the real brotherhood displayed by these sects that get you." He rummaged through the stack of papers and periodicals in his hands. "Here's one I note from the *Chicago Interior,* a Presbyterian organ:

"Let the lands and tenements of the Mormons be thrown open to original entry by civilized settlers . . . Let it be understood that the army will keep out of the way in Utah for four years, and that the use and occupation of Mormon property for one year is to give a pre-emption title. There are enough young men in the west and south who are seeking homes to finish up the pest, fumigate the territory, and to establish themselves in ninety days after the word 'go' is given."

He hunted out a current and well-thumbed copy of *The Methodist.* "They've taken away the Mormon vote, now they want to take away the Mormon lands and homes. Here's another, in similar vein." He opened the periodical to his marked place. " 'We could, if we had the courage and the purpose, check Mormonism, at its central seat, by the use of the simple and perfectly natural system of colonization . . . The thing to do is to put Christian [Gentile] voters into Utah, and the threatened adjacent territories, in such numbers as to just simply outvote the Mormons . . . Ten million dollars, wisely expended, would probably settle the Mormon question.' "

Nancy smiled, in spite of the gravity of the situation. "What if, when all these Christians, or Gentiles, get to Utah, they in turn join the

Church? I remember what happened to *one* Gentile who came to Utah. And you oughta hear him now!"

"It's not particularly humorous, Nan," Joel said soberly. "This Gentile-Mormon is worried. I see nothing ahead but trouble and heartache."

And in that election, and the elections to follow, Joel Scott was denied the right to serve his town and his nation. And as long as the oath was operative, neither he, his wives, nor most of his townsfolk could ever cast a ballot as a free citizen.

The climate of hate, which press and pulpit had catalyzed into this stringent and unparalleled congressional action, began erupting in every part of America. "It's one thing to vent spleen in mass meetings and resolutions against this sect," Joel would protest, "but it's another thing to turn public violence on our missionaries, and our converts who are trying to live as decent citizens throughout this nation. It's no longer safe for a Mormon outside Utah. And Lord knows, it's anything but safe here. Look what's happening to our Saints in the south!"

"I'm glad Father Corey finished his mission there before *this* trouble," Nancy would declare. "He'd have defended his Church and his plurality to the last gunshot."

"And he'd have been shot!"

For it was not at all uncommon now for the irate Gentiles to unlimber guns against the Mormon missionaries and converts in their midst. The southern states, never hesitant about using mob hysteria and lynching to settle their problems, were now generously using these tactics against anything that smelled of Mormonism. Tennessee, especially, was fast becoming a state of death for any Saint who dared show his face there. The Henson family, in Tennessee's Decatur County, because they were baptized Mormons, were fired upon by a mob, and driven at gunpoint out of their homes. The next day, at Cane Creek, in Lewis County, another mob stormed a Sunday morning church service, poured volley after volley into the house where it was being held, and, when they departed, three Mormon missionaries were dead, and the wounded among the little congregation lay writhing and moaning in their blood and pain.

And as if by a signal, these atrocities opened wide the reign of terror against the Saints; the crusade which Joel had solemnly predicted.

In Utah it started with less violent dramatics than in Tennessee, but the results would be vastly more consequential to Joel Scott and his fellow Mormons. Under the provisions of the Edmunds-Tucker Law, and the "plurality oath," the territorial judicial system was quickly emptied of every Mormon judge and barrister. Gentile federal appointees just as quickly took over. And since no Mormon of even the remotest polygamous leanings could serve on a Utah jury, the machinery for convictions was as efficient as it was sure.

"I thought they'd use Salt Lake as their base of operations," Joel stormed. "But these farcical kangaroo courts are being set up in Provo, and every other part of this territory. Looks like none of us are going to escape."

The tough-looking federal deputy marshals who, for the next few years, practically took over the Ammon Hotel were matched only by the rough Gentiles and apostates who moved into every vacant house they could find, or pitched tents and hauled camp wagons onto the vacant fields west of town. For the first time in Ammon's history a town marshal had to be appointed to attempt some curb on the drinking, carousing, and brawling which now disturbed the once somnolent and peaceful little town. And for the first time in her life, Nancy felt uneasy about making her mercy missions alone at night. The swaggering bullies who now packed gun and star as federal deputy marshals were not present in Ammon because they loved its people. They were there to get the "cohabs," the bounty that went with the getting, and Mormon women could just as well be a bonus in the deal.

"Don't ever go out at night without this thing beside you," Joel cautioned, as he handed her his Colt revolver, fully loaded. "These men are the scum of the West. They've been hired in for a nasty job— because they're nasty and ruthless. If any one of them ever comes close enough to lay hands on you or your horse—shoot—and shoot to kill. Because, if you don't, God help you."

In the beginning, as through all the bitter and turbulent years to follow, these strangers in Ammon remained strangers. They were not long in learning that the brotherhood of Saints, and the towns and cities of Utah, were a deal different from the hell-roaring mining camps and cow towns where they had first notched their guns and gained their reputations as toughies. The Saints closed their ranks against these invaders, just as surely and tightly as they had against the mobs of Missouri, Illinois, or the army that had been hurled against them in '57. In attempting their first arrests, the deputies ran into one frustration after another—the main one being the mighty Mormon bulwark of silence. There was not a Saint in Ammon who did not know the name and address of every polygamist in town, his wives, and his progeny. But any Saint would have died piecemeal rather than reveal one iota of information to the judges or the ruffians who had come to destroy his way of life. Nancy probably knew the plural scene more clearly and accurately than any person in Ammon, because she literally had a finger on its pulse. But for one who so loathed the practice privately, she would defend it publicly, just as certainly as any converted Saint around her. The gentle characters of the town, like Seth Biddle, Brother Eggerson, Brother Bissell, Sister Plush, the ruptured Brother Proctor, and even the aged and cantankerous Mary Magdalene, had been pushed from Ammon's sidewalks and interest by this drunken and noisy set of strangers. Nancy told them nothing. And the Colt revolver rode with her at night.

If the judges expected to pierce this wall of silence by aiming at the weaker side of plurality—the wives themselves—they were doomed to quick disappointment. The women, like Sister Nellie White, who was hauled into the Third District Court, just was not talking. She was silent when she was sent to the penitentiary in May, for contempt of court, and she was just as silent when, in frustration, they finally let her out in July.

When Apostle Rudger Clawson was hailed into court, he fought back with everything he had. President John Taylor and Apostle George Q. Cannon were subpoenaed to court for testimony. Through the failure of testimony to convince even a Gentile jury, the apostle was discharged. But not for long.

Three days later the deputies arrested Lydia Spencer, as a plural wife of the apostle, and a new trial was ordered. Lydia refused to testify against her alleged husband and, like Nellie White, was sent to the penitentiary for contempt. The humiliation of it, however, was too much for the apostle. At his insistence, she was finally induced to admit she was indeed a Clawson wife. In seventeen minutes of deliberation, the jury convicted Clawson. Judge Zane, of the Third District Court, sentenced the apostle to four years in the penitentiary and an $800 fine, for polygamy and unlawful cohabitation. Lydia Spencer was released, but the Gentile judge denied bail to the prisoner, and the penitentiary doors clanged shut on her illustrious plural husband.

"They're canny and clever," Joel declared. "The pattern emerges. They get the woman. To save her from disgrace and imprisonment for refusal to testify, the man confesses. And these judges are tough as hell. Big fines, long terms. And, when we Mormons get out of jail— then what? Do we murder every wife but the first one—and all the plural children? Or will they take care of that while we're in jail?"

"Sounds a little drastic to me," Nancy couldn't avoid adding, in view of the way she felt about plurality in general.

Joel would only sadly shake his head at her, as though reproving her for her smugness in being the first wife. And the look of his worry would quickly make her sad. For the years had now become troublous ones. No man, or his families, knew where lightning next would strike.

The crusade in Utah Valley lagged none with what was happening elsewhere in Utah. The "cohab" hunt, well planned, well organized, was on in earnest, and as the brethren and their wives were hauled from their homes, night or day, by surly, brutal marshals, passed through the well-oiled legal machinery, and on into the penitentiary, the Saints began to realize the magnitude and ramifications of the government's war upon them. Ammon's "court of no hope" was seated at Provo, the larger town ten miles south, county seat of the new Utah County, and the city where the Church had already started building the great college in honor of the dead Brigham Young. It was to here that Ammon's "cohabs" and their wives were hauled off by government hack and team. Well guarded by swaggering, gun-packing deputy marshals, they were hustled before judges, sentenced quickly, and without the privilege of a decent farewell to their families, hauled north by guarded hack to the penitentiary at Salt Lake City.

To face the jail sentence was bad enough, but the fine tacked on simultaneously by these conscientious judges and their juries, consisting entirely of Gentiles and apostates, was enough to break the heart and back of every Saint unfortunate enough to be caught in the toils. The fines, running anywhere from $200 to $3000 were usually more ready money than most the brethren had ever seen. So along with the convicted Saint went his farm, home, and everything else he had slaved for in this land of promise.

"They're out to break the Church; they're out to break this people," Joel would roar through his weekly stay at Nancy's. "A lot of the brethren are going into hiding. Some of them heading for Mexico. I'm going to stay and fight this thing."

"And you'll get your head battened in," Nancy opined. "This thing's too big to fight, Joel—and you know it."

"I've never run away from a fight in my life."

"Well, you'd be smart if you ran away from this one. They got Brother Chandler the other day. And he was a two-wife Saint."

"And another thug collects his bounty."

"Well, my suggestion would be to stop this fight talk. Stay away from Matey for a time. At night they could be watching both our houses."

"Spoken like a true and selfish first wife," Joel said bitterly.

And to this Nancy had no answer. Because what Joel said was secretly true.

The cream of Ammon's earliest convictions under the Edmunds-Tucker Law came from the homes of those brethren who had maintained all their wives under one roof. All the marshals had to do was scoop up every man and woman in sight, and the courts and judges did the rest. If no man was present, the women were tried. If the women were unco-operative and refused to talk, which most of them were, they were jailed for contempt of court. If the man wanted to prevent his wife or wives from serving a long and drastic sentence, he had but to show himself, confess his polygamous leanings, and take the long journey to Salt Lake.

Brother Eggerson, who had slept with his three wives in one big bed, was one of the first to discover how quickly and how cleanly the marshals could empty that Mormon bed. But Brother Eggerson, who, like Joel and almost every other polygamous male in Ammon, had furnished himself an "underground" apartment in the miles of limestone caves of Ammon Canyon, played out his cohab soliloquy with interesting variations. The three wives were hauled off to Provo. In the pattern of most Mormon women, they not only refused to admit their mutual sharing of bed and man, but refused to talk at all, and quickly drew the drastic penalty for contempt of court. But Brother Eggerson, free at last, decided not to budge from his canyon hideout. It was something to have a chance to recuperate from this prolonged rutting with three women in one bed. He just let them go to jail, while he rested.

The next year, 1885, dawned with Joel Scott still a free man, in spite of his tendency to "talk up," and his belligerence against the new plague of locusts that had come upon Zion. Nature gave Nancy's womb a rest for yet another year, but not so with Matey. The third child, a boy, was born to her in March. It, of course, had to be named Joel—making a final total of three Joels in the Scott household. This still continuing flow of infants in Zion now offered the most fertile source of evidence to the deputy marshals and their new coterie of apostates and informers.

For one thing, the government had finally been forced by the sheer magnitude of its task to give up the jailing of Mormon women. The very persons whom beneficent America had set out to save from wedded servitude utterly and uncompromisingly refused to open their mouths in aid of the great goings-on in their behalf. Like bright-eyed martyrs, they walked their singing, praying way into jail, with never a word that would help the marshals in ferreting out their cohab husbands to face the courtly music for their own sins. To house every polygamous wife in Utah would require a penitentiary twenty times the size of the present one—and even now fifty masons and builders were constantly employed expanding it merely to fit its male tenants. Too, they could jail five thousand Mormon women, and not one of them would lift their finger to save themselves. It was frustrating.

It had been comparatively easy for the marshals to knock off those polygamous "harems" housed under one roof. But to sort out the women and families who lived in separate houses, according to the men they served and loved, proved quite another matter. The Mormons knew who was who in plurality, but the government bounty hunters did not. And to every inquiry, at every house, they received the same uncooperative silence, and the same granite-like stare. The Mormon "underground" had become just as smooth and workable as the federal machine, with its Gentile judges, juries, and hired deputies. To convict a cohab, one had to catch him. Thousands of them had lit out for other western states, territories, and Mexico. Realizing now that the problem tackled was a big one, the judicial and apprehensive machinery had been extended into Idaho and Arizona. The territorial penitentiary at Yuma, in Arizona Territory, was already so stuffed with Mormon cohabs that there was scarcely room for Arizona's real criminals. And with the flow of Mormons away from Utah reaching a discouraging figure, this could only be the beginning.

In the little towns, by watching the pregnant women, the babies as born, and the doctors and midwives, the deputy marshals were able to nab the more loyal cohabs who preferred to defend their families rather than flee the scene. They were now abetted by the little fringe of apostates and Winter Saints who had been counted in on the wages and bounties in return for the intimate information they possessed, and which was impossible to coerce or frighten out of the loyal Saints. Nancy, because of her peculiar knowledge and profession, was a constant target for the deputy marshals. She knew every wife, baby, and father in Ammon—and half the towns around. But it would have taken the devil and his minions to pry a word out of her. By night she carried the loaded Colt, and had no inhibitions about using it. By day, and in her household, she had perfected her technique. Let her once observe a marshal or an informer coming up the path from the gate, and she was ready for him. Before he could complete the knock at her door, it would fly open, and her amazed visitor would receive a pan of dishwater or pig swill straight to the face.

"Oh, I'm sorry," she'd apologize. "Just emptying my slops. Didn't know anyone was here." And it was amazing what a dishpan of water or a bucket of swill could do in toning down the swaggering officiousness of these pests.

To Nancy, as to every Saint in Ammon, it became a big war, with their own endless and private little battles. The Saints themselves, harassed and frightened, were serving their cause with courage and distinction. The apostates were something else. Like that morning Nancy met Cove Corey in front of the Ammon Hotel.

She'd been shopping for some Sunday hair ribbons for Martha and Amanda, and almost passed Cove before she realized who he was. Time and dissipation had already made an outward stranger of him. They both paused, turned, retraced a step, and looked at one another.

"Why, Cove," Nancy said happily. "You've come back at last!"

"Hello, Nan," he replied, his bloodshot eyes sheepishly looking down. "Yeh, I'm back. But not for too long."

"Where you staying?"

"Here at the hotel."

"But it's full of feds. They're as low as rattlesnakes. Come over to the house. You can stay with us."

"Sorry, Nan. But I'm working with these men."

"You?" She was not sure she'd heard right.

"Nan," he said. "I've always thought a lot of you. I've always had level talk with you. And you're gonna get it now. I'm no longer a Mormon—and I hate what it stands for."

She looked at Cove's red and droopy eyes. The day was early, but already Cove was sweaty, and smelly with booze. "What does Aunt Millie, your mother, say about this?"

"Hell, she knows about it. I've been a lot of places since I saw you last. California, Virginia City, Pioche. I've made money . . . lost money. Now I'm back making a dollar. And it pleases me."

"Have you been to see Aunt Millie? Does she know you're here?"

"Good God! She'd broom me outa the house! You forget, she's a plural woman. You and me are plural kids. What I'm doin' won't exactly please her."

"And it pleases me even less," Nancy angrily retorted. "Oh Cove, cut it out! Break away from this gang of bummers. Ammon's *your* town. Remember?"

Cove yanked the Bull Durham and papers from the pocket of his greasy shirt. Reflectively he creased a paper, shook some tobacco in it. Holding the little sack in his right hand, he teethed the tag, pulled it tight, and dropped the sack back to his pocket. "Guess you didn't hear me right, Nan," he said slowly, almost casually. He rolled the cigarette, tongued it, and pinched tight its ends. "I told you I was no longer a Mormon. I hate every goddamned thing connected with it. I'm here to do my bit at knocking this polygamy in the ass. And it pleasures me to do it." He put the cigarette in his mouth, and deliberately struck a match on the seat of his pants. A pair of pants just as worn and dirty as his shirt, and weighted low at the hips by a scratched and scabrous gun belt and holstered revolver. He lit the cigarette, took a leisured puff, and flipped the match out into the roadway. "Once upon a time, if I remember right," he said, above his lip-drooped smoke, "you were a little piffed at polygamy." He laughed nervously, and too loud. "I hear even your schoolteacher's built himself a harem. How do *you* feel about the Principle now, Nan?"

"After what you've just told me—and considering why you're here—what do you expect me to say? How can I even talk to you?"

"Don't have to, Nan," he said. "That's your business. But I'll say this before I go. I'm not here to turn guns on my own family. The town's full enough of game without that." He blew a load of smoke through his nose, and gave another phlegmy laugh. "Not that I owe them any loyalty, considerin' the fact I once owned quite a slice of this town—and now who the hell's got it? My brothers—half brothers—cousins—and half the goddamned breed of our old Isaac Corey. Funny, ain't it, Nan?"

"Not too funny," she said. "Everyone knows why you didn't hold on to it. Father Corey loved you, was loyal to you, and saw that you had your share when he died. I've always believed you could have been a great man. But I'm not proud of what you're saying and doing today, Cove!"

"Well now look, Nan," he said, confidential. "I'm gonna show you a little Corey loyalty, by giving you a word of advice. I'm not here to make war on my kin, I'm not here to make war on you, but I'm sure's hell here to make war on Mormonism and polygamy. To you, I say this, because I'm fond as hell of you. Tell your teacher-man to follow the leaders. He's bein' watched . . . and he's gonna be knocked over . . . if he don't get wise like the big boys in Salt Lake."

Nancy tried to make sense of the lethal warning Cove was trying to whisper out to her. "What's happening in Salt Lake?"

"Oh my God," Cove chuckled knowingly. "Everybody from your President John Taylor down has hit the grit. You notice *they're* not taking any raps in the penitentiary."

"Rudger Clawson did, and a few of the apostles."

"That was in the beginning. The Church has used a lot of tithing money buying up Hawaii and Samoa, and great hunks of the other islands of the Pacific. Where has John Taylor, Lofty Cragg, and half the Authorities departed to? To Hawaii—the tropical paradise of the Pacific. They loll under the palm trees, while the lesser Saints rot in jail for the Principle. Other apostles and even the lesser prophets have gone to other islands, equally desirable and far away, or have been sent to the cities of Europe, or any other place where they're good and plenty out of range of the cohab hunters. And have they deprived themselves in this hour of dire stress? Jesus on a broomstick, what a laugh! They've taken along their younger and favorite wives, to dawdle with while Zion falls apart. Maybe you don't know that Lofty Cragg took Flora with him to Hawaii? Maybe you don't know that the Church is now being governed by epistles from the Hawaiian-livin' hierarchy? Maybe you don't know that you couldn't find anyone above a ward bishop in Salt Lake right now? It's things like this that pisses me off against the Church. John Taylor may have caught a bullet in Carthage jail—but he's goddamned gun-shy *these* days."

"You *are* bitter, Cove," she said. "And I feel sorry for you."

"Well, sorrow no more, little Nan," he growled, dragging the last of his cigarette. "I'm out to lend my grubby little hands to this last big bust. The government's set its mind to knock out polygamy—and they're gonna do it. I'm here to do what I can to push things along." Disgustedly he flipped the cigarette butt to the roadway. "Just be warned, Nan. Get that teacher of yours either out of the Principle, or out of Utah. When it hits, it hurts."

Nancy narrowed her eyes at Cove, the turncoat. For the first time in her life she wanted to whack him square across his dirty mouth. "Did it ever occur to you," she asked, "that you wouldn't be here, if it weren't for the Principle? Your own mother was a second wife."

"Well la-de-da," he chuckled flippantly. "And who the hell cares now, whether I'm here or not?"

"I'm really sorry for you, Cove," she said.

But when she left him, her knees were weak, and she rattled and trembled like a corn frond in the wind. There could be no doubt Joel Scott was marked, and in mortal danger. And there was no doubt about some other things Cove had said. President John Taylor *had* fled to Hawaii. And damn few Authorities were being jailed these days!

VII

COVE'S BITTER DECLARATION THAT THE AUTHORITIES HAD ABANDONED THE lesser Saints in this, one of the darkest hours of the Church's existence, heckled Nancy Scott unmercifully through the worried months ahead. To her, there was plenty of evidence that, denied the satisfaction of jailing the church leaders, there was no lessening of the zeal in trailing down, by every evil and diabolical scheme, the common Saints who stood convicted almost from the moment they were taken into custody. And one of the greatest sources of her worries was Joel himself. Instead of availing himself of the underground, or fleeing the town altogether, as did his more wise and cautious brethren, he took on a reckless and belligerent attitude toward the crusade and the imported and domestic dregs of humanity who were executing it in the name of the government he'd fought for.

Nancy who, more than any person in Ammon, realized what this storm of harassment and persecution was doing to her town, and all of Zion in general, was more frightened now than any moment in her life. With Joel's tendency to fight rather than hide, and his openly defiant visits with both his wives and households, on alternate weeks, could only mean his eventual arrest and imprisonment. With all her heart she wished that a few of the Authorities would exhibit some of Joel's guts and cool courage. Those common Saints around her, who were dragged off to the crowded horrors of the territorial penitentiary, and whose homes and substance were going into the insatiable machine now crushing them, needed a decent example of leadership to give them the courage to live through this dark hour of despair and humiliation. She herself had never been in sympathy with the Principle, and probably never would be. But she was a Latter-day Saint, and any abuse and persecution aimed at the Church was aimed at her. Mormon people had suffered enough at the hands of their enemies.

So, like the most converted of her polygamous sisters, she fought back at these new invaders exactly as they were fighting. As Flora had so accurately predicted, she signed her name to a second great petition, along with the thousands upon thousands of other polygamous wives. In her heart she knew President Cleveland would treat this appeal exactly as had his predecessors. And Congress, as always, would ignore it, file it, and forget it. She answered the deputies who stormed her door with dishwater or hog slops full in the face, and their startled interrogations with the bland answers and stone face of her sisters. In her mercy errands to the now worried and pathetic mothers in Zion, she still packed the loaded gun and a willingness to use it. And this fact seemed to have permeated the thick skulls of those drunk devils at the hotel. Apparently they knew that, much as they'd like to wring a few facts out of the wiry, peppery little midwife of Ammon, she was a cat to tangle with. And that her shooting was just about as quick and sure as was their own. So far, on her night rides they'd left her alone, following her only by horseback, at a safe distance. In her daytime rides she was not afraid.

But a greater mystery was why they hesitated to move against Joel. Perhaps it was the fact that even in their foggy thinking, they realized that as a former captain in the Army, and a wounded veteran of the great war, he'd stood up and been counted for his government as tangibly, and probably a lot more valiantly, than had they. But more than that, Nancy was convinced both she and Joel had a friend at court. Poor, bitter, and unhappy Cove—her half brother who had translated his own hurts at the hands of the leaders into apostasy and revenge— was probably the voice who made these things known to the vermin with which he was associated, and probably the one reason only why Joel Scott had not yet been taken into custody. Poor, dear, kind Cove. In her bedside prayers she never missed thanking God for his presence in Ammon, and God would bless him for what he was doing, for her and Joel.

But in her heart she knew that neither Cove Corey, nor God Himself, could long keep the vindictive, searching hand from Joel. With Ammon relegated to practically a city of women, and not even enough men to stand Brother Proctor on his head and shake down his rupture, Joel Scott walked to school, to church, and to his polygamous homes, as defiant and as sure of himself as the day he had moved into the withering fire at Chancellorsville.

"Why in heaven's name don't you lay low for a while?" Nancy pleaded. "Cove says you're a marked man. And there's nothing wrong with taking to the underground. Everyone else is doing it. Every church leader's gone. In fact the Church is no longer governed. It's just drifting to its doom."

It was Joel's week with her and the kids. He sat in his easy chair, just as he always had long before Matey Thorpe and the deep troubles. He laid down his copy of the viciously anti-Mormon *Tribune* and smiled tolerantly at her, as he always had. "The Church is *not* drifting. It's being governed—from above and below. I'll admit these are black and difficult times, but the Gospel of Jesus Christ will endure above the petty hates of men, and this unconstitutional and unwarranted crusade by those who represent our government. Sometimes I think your faith is shaky, Nan."

"It *is* shaky." She grasped her forehead with both hands, and leaned back in despair. It was a relief to get the kids to bed. Even *they* drove her frantic of late. "I don't see President John Taylor on hand to lend counsel and courage."

"John Taylor's an old man. They'd like nothing better than to break him on the rack. It's wisdom that he keep out of their reach. Joseph Smith was surrendered by his brethren—and you know what happened."

"So the Authorities take off," Nancy said bitterly. "And the *little* men get broken on the rack. You like it that way, Joel?"

"Of course I don't. I don't want to see anyone hurt or broken. That's not the American way."

"Sometimes I think, by your defiant attitude, you'd welcome being picked up and sent to jail."

"I'd welcome nothing of the sort. But I'm not going to turn tail and run, either."

"Well, the leaders have," she sighed. "There's no one guiding the Church. There's discouragement everywhere. Menfolk are in jail, or in hiding. The women are left to fend for themselves, and somehow scratch out a living for their families. And those that are having babies —and *can't* work and provide! A few years ago the Saints were prosperous and secure. Now, everywhere is bitterness, heartache, and poverty. I talk to these poor women, Joel—and I know." Pity of it was that somehow, through it all, and the menfolk jailed or in the underground, there still were babies. And those babies wailed out to the cohab bounty hunters the unmistakable evidence that somewhere there was a man around. All the deputies had to do was trail Nancy Scott and old Bess. "Brigham Young never would have paddled off to Hawaii. He'd have stood up and spit in the eye of every fed who dared make a move against this people. And I can tell you, Joel, that unless there's some heartening evidence of leadership pretty soon . . . your vaunted and defended Principle will go. And very likely, the Church."

"I've given up trying to convert you to the Principle, Nan," Joel said patiently and tolerantly. "But I *can* assure you the Principle's *not* going to go. It's the everlasting covenant—and it means just that. It was revealed by God Almighty, through His Prophet, to His people. And all the powers of hell are not going to prevail against it. To abandon it, because Congress has passed a few stupid and unconstitutional laws against us, would be to repudiate God and the Holy Writ. To repudiate it would be to make homeless widows of our women, and bastards of tens of thousands of our children. And the Church is not going to go, either, Nan. I've come to know that this is God's work —the restored Gospel of Jesus Christ—preached with the simplicity, power, and authority as of old. The Church will not vanish from the earth."

"But its leaders have," Nancy tartly replied.

She didn't want to be argumentative with Joel—and him facing worries, and problems, and maybe jail. But it had always seemed to her that, in plurality, the Church and its people had been saddled with a real problem. As she saw it, not until lately had the Principle been rough on the men. It had *always* been rough on the women. The women suffered the consequences; they bore the kids; and many a one that she knew earned the living for herself and her polygamous family. Joel could never know her own thoughts of those lonely nights—when she knew that he was exercising his polygamous prerogative in Matey's house only four blocks away. Joel was hurt, defiant, and defensive of the Principle. He had another wife, whom the government considered a concubine. He had three children, whom this same government had labeled as bastards. And call his intercourse with Matey by its every holy and divine name—it was known to the judges, and the deputies, as "lewd and lascivious cohabitation." It was true that neither Joel, nor Isaac, nor the bishops, nor the revelations of Joseph Smith had made much headway in converting her to the Principle. She honestly felt the Church would, and should, abolish it. There'd be suffering if it did. There'd be a lot more suffering if it didn't. It was a mixed-up mess. No wonder the leaders had ducked out of it.

"You think the Church is wallowing through this crisis, without guidance," Joel argued, almost as though in answer to her thoughts. "It just isn't so, Nan. John Taylor's ill, and old, but he still has hold of the reins. Have you ever wondered what has happened to President George Q. Cannon, his first counselor?"

"All I know is that they threw him out of Congress because he was plural."

"Well, he's in the Utah underground. And he's taking care of the Church's interests. I saw him and talked to him, secretly, only a week ago."

Nancy looked at Joel, and wagged her head sadly. "He'd cheer a few discouraged Saints, if he'd show his face, and raise his voice in their behalf."

"And they'd nab him, quick as he did. The posted bounty on George Q. Cannon's scalp is five hundred dollars. They'd love to get him."

"What a comedown for a congressman," Nancy sighed.

"What a great and courageous man he is," Joel argued.

"I wish I could see it your way, Joel. But he's hiding, and silent in this crisis. You're not hiding. You're standing up—defiant-like—for the things you believe in. It's Joel Scott who's the great and courageous one. At least that's the way I look at it."

Joel rattled the *Tribune,* and scanned it quickly. "Well, here's a little case in point—and from this very scurrilous sheet. You moan because the leaders are not present. Well, Apostle Lorenzo Snow showed his face last week in behalf of this people. Quickly as he did, the *Tribune* gloats, he landed in the penitentiary. Only the Lord can help George Q. Cannon, if *he* reveals himself."

"Only the Lord can help Joel Scott, if he doesn't *quit* revealing himself," Nancy groaned.

But in February they had even the illustrious Mormon apostle, George Q. Cannon, in custody. With the fat bounty for his capture, they pursued him into Nevada, where he was attempting to flee to San Francisco, and thence to Mexico, to join the Mormon expatriates in that nation. Marshal Ireland made the arrest, loaded him on a Utah-bound train at Winnemucca, and almost got his bounty into Ogden. But when the train neared Promontory, the ex-congressman and church leader somehow managed to evade his captor, jumping train as it slowed down at that point. A special train, loaded with soldiers from Fort Douglas, was dispatched out to lonely Promontory and again apprehended the unarmed prisoner. It was a great day, throughout America, when this presiding elder of the Church was finally hauled into Salt Lake City, and fed through the judicial grinder.

Joel Scott's day in court was a little slower in coming, but Nancy, nor no other Saint who dared pause long enough to observe, could doubt it was just as inexorable and just as certain. The night Cove

Corey chose to visit her for the final warning—a night deliberately chosen during Joel's alternate week at Matey's—Nancy knew the end of her once peaceful world was at hand, and as sure as death itself.

Saints of Ammon, and every other harassed community, had their own coded door knock—three staccato knuckle raps, repeated three times—which, until the feds penetrated even this secret, served instantly to identify any stranger at the door as friend or foe. The rap at Nancy's door that night was no Mormon knock, so she shouldered Joel's heavy gun belt and loaded revolver, went to the kitchen for the bucket of pig swill, and returned to the front entrance hall. The knock had grown impatient by then. It was no Saint at the door, she was certain, because the code was not there.

In the maneuver, perfected by practice, she flung open the door with her left hand, while she clung securely to the pail of swill. Then she advanced one big stride toward the dark figure silhouetted in the doorway, and let him have the slop full in the face and shoulders.

"God a'mighty!" Cove roared in surprise. "What in hell are you trying to do?"

"Oh, it's you, Cove!" She dropped the empty bucket, and stared in surprise at the dripping figure on the doorstep. "I—I—was just emptying the swill."

"That's for damn sure," he said. "I caught it in the teeth. What the hell you trying to do, Nan?"

She laughed in spite of herself. "I'm protecting my household, you stupid jackass! And if you'd been a friend I'd have known it! But step inside. I'll try to clean you up."

She knew this would be some job, the moment he moved into the light of the hallway. He was more bewhiskered, red-eyed, and dirty than ever she'd seen him before. And the swill's grease, water, and table scraps added nothing to his cleanliness.

"You can rid yourself of that gun," Cove said. "I'm not here to shoot it out with you."

She hung the belt and gun to a hallway coat hook. "Come on into the kitchen. Let me swab you down. You look a real sight."

In the kitchen, by lamplight, she dried off and blotted her half brother with a dish towel. Not even the sour smell of the swill could obliterate the equally sour smell of the stale whiskey, which, vaporizing from pore and fabric, was the sure mark of the compulsive souse. He did avail himself of the washbasin, soap, and water. Although this was more than she'd willingly do for any other cohab bounty hunter,

Cove was still her half brother, something special, and she sorrowed for him.

"Let me fix you up with some of Joel's clean clothes," she offered. "He's got plenty of shirts, underwear, and pants. He wouldn't mind a bit. And yours look mighty tattered, Cove."

"Goddamn it, Nan," he said. "I'm willing and anxious to swab the pig feed out of my whiskers, because you put it there. But damned if I'm going to outfit myself in Joel's clothes."

"Why?"

"Because I'm not here on any brotherly visit. I've got something to tell you that you'll not like. And anyway, God would send a bolt of wrath through this very roof, the minute I put my apostate leg into Joel's holy underwear."

"Not so loud, Cove!" Nancy half whispered. "You wanta wake the whole family? Let's go into the living room. There you can tell me what's on your mind." Inside, she beckoned him to Joel's chair by the still warm stove. Wearily she dropped into her own chair near her sewing table. "Now, Cove, what *is* on your mind?"

Deliberately, but with trembling fingers, he drew the little bag of tobacco, and papers, from his shirt pocket. Nancy was relieved to see that even though his filthy shirt was damp, it had been swabbed soon enough to prevent the moisture reaching his "makings." Not until his long and trembling fingers had rolled the smoke, and he'd teethed the drawstring, lit the pinched end of the cigarette, and drawn his first puff did he bother an answer.

"I warned you about getting teacher out of sight," he said at last. "And that's more than I'd do for any other cohab."

"I know it, Cove," she said, sadly. "But Joel's no man to be scared down. He was an army man. He thinks to go underground is a disgrace."

"Well, he'll have plenty of time in jail to preen up on his pride and courage."

"I've begged him to light out, and save himself."

"You just haven't begged hard enough." Cove leaned forward, and squinted his eyes for emphasis—exactly as had Isaac Corey. "This drive to break up polygamy is no waltzing contest, Nan. I've always liked you a lot. I've liked you a lot more than Flora, my natural sis— because you had guts to buck the Principle. But as long as you're in it, and for it, I'm your enemy, Nan. The day Brigham, the blue-ribbon stud, took my woman into his harem, that was the day I chucked my celestial crown and set my heart to fight this thing. Now that the big push is on—I'm in it, and for it. I sing hallelujah every time the jail door clangs shut on a cohab."

"You call it the 'big push,'" Nancy said. "I call it a terror, and an inquisition. A bounty hunt, that's what it is. They used to pay a bounty on coyote pelts and Indian scalps. Same thing now. So much a head for a cohab."

"Exactly, Sis." Cove blew twin strings of smoke from his nostrils, and smiled wickedly. "Greatest bounty hunt in history. And it's only begun."

"You're my own family, and special to me, Cove. You're a real Mormon pioneer, because you rode across the plains as a child, in the wagon, driven by Father Corey. You know what the Church stands for, what it has suffered in the way of misunderstanding and persecution. I can't understand how you can feel this way."

"A good friggin' by Father Brigham would open any man's eyes to understanding. But I wasn't the only one. How many young men in the Church have lost their sweethearts to the big studs of the hierarchy?"

"You're a bitter, vengeful man."

"You're right, Nan," he said, rising. "But I've made one hell of a big exception with you. I've warned you about your teacher. I've done all I can for him. Now, I tell you once again, you'd better hide him, and hide him quick. For he's a gone cohab. And when a devil like me can't save him—it's hopeless for Jesus and the angels."

"Thanks, Cove," Nancy said. "I know you've done all you can."

"Just remember, Nan, that once he's in court in Provo, he's on his way to the big house. I'll testify against him, because it's my job. I like you, more than you'll ever know. But Joel Scott's nothing particular to me. And there's others'll testify. Some of the Saints of Ammon who served in jail while their leaders bask in the sun of far-away Hawaii are a bit disillusioned as to Mormonism, and the Principle. Up at the big house, they've done a little thinking along with their sweating. They're being released as material witnesses. And what they've got to say will put your schoolmaster and every other fightin' Saint behind bars for a long stretch."

"They ought to revive the Nauvoo Legion and drive the whole pack of you wretches out of Utah! I agree with Joel, the Saints should rebel and put an end to this mockery in the name of the law." Nancy wanted to shriek with the hate that filled her soul.

"By God, you *have* changed in regard to the Principle." Cove laughed, opening the stove door, and pitching in his cigarette. "Don't tell me you *favor* polygamy?"

"Of course I don't!" she groaned. "What I hate is the horror of this man hunt!"

"Well, if any of the Saints think rebellion's gonna help, they'd better think again. Government put a stop to the Nauvoo Legion three years ago. Let enough of the brethren come out of underground long enough to shoulder a gun, and they'll get their asses shot off by the army regulars at Fort Douglas. The government's playing for keeps, Nan. And you'd better remind teacher of that fact."

"Joel knows," Nancy moaned. "But I'll remind him." She followed Cove toward the doorway. "All I can say is that your crusade's the most cruel and inhuman thing the Saints have ever had to endure."

Cove looked over his shoulder at her, and hellishly grinned. "But it works! God a'mighty, how it works!"

And when they took Joel, it was a strange thing. When he failed to show up at Nancy's house, she reconciled herself to the thought that he'd decided to stay on past his week at Matey's. And Matey, in turn, was of the opinion that he was taking his normal turn at Nancy's. What neither of them knew was that he'd been hauled off to Provo, jailed overnight, passed through Judge Stone's court, convicted of illegal cohabitation, fined $500, and sentenced to six months in the territorial penitentiary.

With Cove, and the help of the local Mormon dissidents, there apparently had been enough testimony to convince the court of Joel Scott's polygamous conduct without the necessity of going through the judicial travesty of attempting to force either of his wives to testify against him. The government hack, loaded with convicted Mormon cohabs, had gone through Ammon at night, and its guard had allowed him no chance to even bid farewell to the wives who were not yet even aware that he was gone.

VIII

NANCY HAD NEVER REALIZED THE SCOPE AND MAGNITUDE OF THE GREAT, heartless, and impersonal machine that had taken over the affairs of Utah until she visited Joel Scott in the penitentiary. The big gray pile of rock and adobe, south and east of Salt Lake City, reminded her of the medieval turreted fortresses portrayed in the family picture book called *The Crusades.* With the constant additions necessitated by the unprecedented demand on its facilities, reminding one of the bulbous protuberances of a mud-wasp's nest, Nancy and Matey could see the fortress a mile away, as the tired Gus and George drew the surrey over the well-used road toward their anxious reunion with their man.

No matter how close one got to the thing, it was still ugly and depressing to look at. Not even the American flag, hoisted high on the pole above the corner guard tower, to remind inmates and visitors alike who was now true boss in Utah, seemed more belligerent than decorative. And when they entered the big wooden building, added like an afterthought to the outer area of the twenty-foot wall of the fortress, timidly moved into the "visitor's reception room," and faced the gimlet-eyed prison matron who manned its desk, they learned what reception was, in its most negative sense.

The hard benches of the room were filled to overflowing with the dozens of female visitors, who, availing themselves of the one visit allowed a month, and who already had bothered and irritated the matron. Timidly, clutching the big boxes they had stuffed with baked foods for their man, they approached the desk. "What can I do for you?" the matron snarled, from whiskered lips.

"We'd like to see a prisoner," Nancy said, frightened and nervous.

"Male or female?"

"Male."

"What's his name?"

"Joel Scott. He's in for cohabitation."

295

"And who are you?"

"Nancy Scott—his wife."

"Who's the other woman with you?"

In line with the coaching of Joel's letter, Nancy answered, "She's Matilda Corey—my sister." Only by such subterfuge could a polygamous convict hope to worry out a visit with an "unlawful" wife. Even this did not always work. And those men with sizable harems were hopelessly defeated from the start. Nancy could not miss the snort of disgust and disbelief from the whiskered matron. Apparently she'd given up trying to fight this particular Mormon custom because she scribbled down both their names as eligible visitors.

"You'll be allowed thirty minutes each—and one at a time. I'll call you when the prisoner can be seen. Which of you is to go first?"

Nancy and Matey eyed one another, and the thoughts of both flushed the faces of each.

"Well?" snarled Old Whiskers. "I've not got all day! You're not the *only* visitors!"

Then Matey, big-eyed and timid, spoke the words Nancy had been waiting for. "You go first, Nan," she said. "You're the wife."

"All right, wife first," the matron trumpeted. "Find a seat. I'll call you."

Joel Scott's two wives stepped obediently out of line, so that the next polygamous visitor could come to grips with the matron. But to find the seat was the nearest thing to an impossibility. Every inch of space on the hard benches was occupied by sad-faced women, just as anxious to see their husbands as the Scott sisters from Ammon. Like dozens of others they edged into standing space near the wall, and not too far from the stove. The weather outside was blustery, cold, and already they were chilled from the long and exhausting drive.

"We might as well set our bundles down, Matey," Nancy said, with a cheerfulness she did not feel. "By the looks of this hen party, we've a long afternoon ahead."

To Nancy it had been hard enough to raise the $500 for Joel's fine, but this queuing up before authority was a humiliation she could scarcely endure. To ride out a woman's life in the Principle, one's mind had to have two compartments. For one thing, and standing forlornly beside her, was the very cause of all this hell and sacrifice. Had Joel been able to keep his penis in his pants, and not contaminated and periled a happy and successful marriage, his first and legal wife would not be clamoring for a penitentiary entrance on this cold and cheerless afternoon. The normal woman's instinct would be to hate Matey, fear

Matey, and be jealous of Matey—and Nancy was guilty of all three.

On the other hand, and from the other compartment of her mind, she could never look at the delicate-skinned English girl, with fawn-like eyes, without getting the feeling she was more daughter than wife and menace. Take away the humiliation and heartbreak of Matey's forced entry into the intimate circle of her love and life with Joel Scott, and she could have liked Matey very much. Matey had a soft, ingratiating way about her that got to the heart and conscience of any normal person. And now these very qualities, under the merciless scourging they both were taking, had turned to an innocent, forlorn dependence as irresistible as it was touching. "Take care of little Matey and her babies, as best you can," Joel had written from this bestial prison. Well, this day she could tell Joel, that she had done all that and more. She'd divided her food with this second wife, she'd helped nurse Matey's children through grippe and whooping cough. She'd kept the hate compartment well sealed through every moment of it. Instead she'd turned an understanding heart to the same ache of parting that was in this woman's breast, had comforted her through the nights and days of their mutual sorrow, had tendered her loving-kindness, under-standing, and material help. Nancy Scott had been a true Latter-day Saint, and an honest and decent sister to Matey in the plural pattern. And not only had Matey long since forgotten that shoving into the creek, but had turned love and gratitude back to Nancy. Only with two compartments could a woman's mind live with polygamy. There was still a fighting back of the black thoughts in every day of Nancy's life.

Nancy had imagined that hours on end would be consumed while each sad-faced female in the room went, one at a time for the allotted thirty minutes with her man. She soon learned that a penitentiary visit was scarcely that private and intimate. Before she and Matey could do much talking about the inadequacy and discomforts of the place, the far door was opened by a trusty, in a zebra-striped prison suit, and the room was suddenly filled to suffocation by half a hundred women and a few men, whose visits with inmates had been terminated. Many of the women were weeping as they went outside into the chill air, and the men didn't look any too happy. There was no joy or fraternization in this dismal place. What conversation there was came up in the cautious undertones of humiliation and despair.

The room cleared, as the visitors went out. The weazened little pris-oner, in stripes—probably a Mormon cohab himself—waited obediently and silently at the door while the matron scanned her list, and the new visitors waited expectantly, and in hushed silence, for their turn.

The names were called, and as the woman at the desk read them off, the visitors arose from their seats, and took their place in the long line forming at the far door. Nancy and Matey listened intently until the matron snapped, "That's all for this visit." The trusty opened the door and led the procession outside and to the prison's big gate.

"Might as well grab ourselves a seat," Nancy said. "This place'll be filled up again in a few minutes."

They hauled their heavy and cumbersome packages to the bench, set them on the floor for footrests, and dropped gratefully and wearily to the freshly vacated seating space. They had driven all night. It had been cold. And there'd been little joy to be had in it.

Together, and in the best tradition of plurality, they talked and drowsed as the room again filled to smothering capacity. After an almost endless time, filled with small talk, deep thought, and the trivia of their wait, the far door again opened. Once more the familiar weeping, funereal exit, and the expectancy of the new call. The line was well formed, and Nancy already despairing, when at last came the masculine trumpet of the matron's voice.

"Mrs. Joel Scott—to see Joel Scott."

Eagerly Nancy jumped to her feet and grabbed her big package by its strings. Then she saw the sadness on little Matey's face. She bent and kissed her. "It won't be long," she said. "I'll tell him you're waiting—with another big package."

A moment later she'd joined the line. And with a few more names, the call was terminated. The weazened man in the zebra suit opened the door to the blustery cold outside, and she followed him, with the others, to the fortress gate.

An ugly federal guard, armed with rifle and side arms, watched them suspiciously, as a second guard, from the inside, keyed the big lock, and then swung wide the giant gate built of cross-timbers thick enough to discourage any knife or saw. They moved inside, only to face a second gate—thicker, heavier, and even more secure. When the first big gate was swung shut and locked behind them, they stood patient, and a little frightened, in this walled enclosure, while trusties, in prison uniform, relieved them of their packages for inspection, scribbling names of the owners upon them as they took them into custody.

Nancy was certain the kindly-faced old man who took possession of her big package was a cohab—and probably a bishop. For, when he asked for the recipient's name, and she told him "Joel Scott," his eyes flashed friendly recognition. She knew he yearned to talk, but this was prison. "Its contents?" he blandly asked—as though the guards would not soon enough know.

"Food for my husband," she said. "And a blanket. No hacksaws."

His face lighted with a quick smile. "It will be given to the prisoner, after the visit." In reassuring half whisper, he added, "I'll *personally* see he gets it. Your husband's one of the great men of this wretched place."

Not until every package was taken, and the crowd silently scrutinized by the guard, rifle in hand, was the second big gate swung open, and they entered a large wooden building, down the center of which were two long tables, with corresponding benches on either side. "Visitors will seat themselves at the tables," the guard called, once they were inside. "Right-hand benches, please. Prisoners, when they enter, will seat themselves opposite. Thirty minutes will be allowed. All conversation must be conducted in normal tone, so the guard may hear. There will be no touching of prisoner across the table whatsoever. Understand?"

There was a scurry for the benches. Nancy, still trim and agile, made a quick run for a bench nearest the far door, where the men most likely would enter. Not until all were seated, and the scowling guard had walked once around the room, was the door thrown open, and the convicts allowed to enter for the precious minutes with their loved ones.

And the thing Nancy witnessed seemed unbelievable, unreal. The very sight of half a hundred men, clad in their garb of ignominy— jumpers and pants, horizontally striped in black and white—was like something out of a dream. They marched in orderly enough, but it was a pathetic sight when they broke ranks to eye-search the visitors for the one face and smile of their yearning. For only one monthly visit was allowed these men, and Joel already had spent thirty days of his sentence.

She saw him, and in the same instant, he saw her. A world of affection and a world of words passed in the smiles of recognition and endearance that passed between them. With a shock, she saw how thin and haggard he looked. The twin tufts of his once black hair showed under streaks of gray. He closed the short distance between them in a few rapid strides, and was talking even as he wormed himself to the bench at the table's end, where Nancy had already grabbed advantage over her fellow visitors.

"There's little time, dear Nancy," he was saying, even as he seated himself, "and there's much I want to tell you."

"I brought a big package," she said, happily. "There's food and candy in it. And the blanket you mentioned."

"God only knows how they're needed, my dear. Thank you so much."

"Matey's here, too," Nancy added, striving to be heard above the suddenly droning monotone of a hundred voices, all just as frantically trying to get in their allotted words, while the guard circled the tables, listening, and watching sharply for any infraction of the rules. "She has a package just like mine."

"How good of you both to come. I've counted the hours for this visit. I was afraid you'd not be able to make it. But you did." The blue eyes looked at her across the table. There no longer was merriment in them. Joel's immediate annoyance was the voice and elbows of the fat little prisoner on his right, even as Nancy was annoyed by the voice and elbows of the prisoner's fat little wife on Nancy's left. The whole picture was grotesque—the long line of prison zebras, faced by an equally long line of women and men visitors, and all raising one mighty voice of pandemonious uproar, as a million thoughts endeavored to cross the table in one immense roar. The whole thing was one of barbaric cruelty, and Joel was striving along with the others to be heard.

"First of all, Nancy, and while there's time to say it, I want you to know how much I love you." The blue eyes of Joel were swimming in tears. She felt his knee touch hers, and she moved her legs as close and tight as the wide distance between them would allow. This had to do for the embrace and the kiss so stupidly denied them. "It takes a place like this to make you realize how much is lost or missing. How I've been blessed in you, Nan!"

"I love you, Joel. I'll always love you." And now she was weeping like a summer shower. "You look thin. They feeding you?"

He managed a smile. "Well, for breakfast we get our pint of coffee —no cream or sugar—a potato boiled the night before, and a slice of bread. For lunch, our pint of coffee, our slice of bread, a minuscule chunk of boiled beef, or a bowl of the swill they call soup around here. At night we get tea and bread only. When I get out, Nan, please feed me!"

"I'll cook you up a big batch of hunter's stew. You always liked hunter's stew." Above the vocal clatter she almost had to shout it, and, with the shouting, what she said sounded ridiculous. She looked about her at the planked wall room, its repellent austerity. "This *is* an awful place."

"Nan, I'll remember this hole until the day I die," he said. "It's like being locked into a communal tomb, with every corpse clawingly alive.

Its twenty-foot walls are high enough to shut out every view of the mountains and the valley—saving only our tiny patch of sky—straight up, and a million miles away. Much of the open ground in the enclosure, where prisoners might stretch, walk, and breathe, has been wiped out of existence by the cell houses that have been made necessary to cope with the hundreds and hundreds of farcical convictions under the Edmunds Law. This place is so crowded every bunk now sleeps two men. They've stuffed this place with the men who man the farms, the shops, and the industry of Utah. What little work there is to do here is begged for, bribed for, in order to keep a man occupied and to prevent him from going insane from the sheer necessity of standing perpendicular throughout the long day because there isn't room for benches to seat him. The new elite in Utah is the trusty. There are so few of those positions available, they carry a high cash price to the wardens and the guards.

"Should they allow you, as a visitor, into the cell house, I'd not let you view it, Nan. It's a disgrace and an abomination to think that honorable and decent men have to face anything such as this in the name of justice. At five P.M. after our slice of bread and tin cup of tea, we're locked into this unventilated, unheated bedlam of despair. The bunks are tiered three high—two men to each bunk. Here the men attempt to wash the vermin out of their clothes, and to dry them while they try to sleep. But sleep? My God, what a travesty!

"The walls of these asylums are built of heavy planks, spiked together. And between the seams and interstices of these planks are housed the ten million bedbugs who now dine royally on the best blood of Utah. At nine P.M. the lights are doused, and every man has to be silent and in his bunk. And promptly at nine P.M. come the bedbugs for their nightly feast. They tear and riddle themselves into your flesh, and they swell up, fat and red on the blood they've stolen from you. The men groan and fight and twist and turn as they suffer out another night of this barbaric onslaught. In barracks of soldiers, in prison camps of war, in the foc'sle of the ships I've traveled, I've never seen anything to match the verminous disgrace of this hole. There isn't a man in this compound whose body isn't an itching mass of sores. Look at this, Nan." He drew up the left sleeve of his zebra suit to show her a skin that looked pimpled, wounded, and purple enough to have been lashed and beaten with a curry comb.

Nancy shook her head in horror at Joel's arm, and pictured in her mind what the rest of his body must be like, and the agony this man was enduring in the name of his religion. "Oh, Joel," she wept. "Why didn't you run away, like Bishop Earlington and the others? I was so afraid this would happen. I think this is terrible beyond words."

He lowered his sleeve, and looked affectionately at her. "Nancy, to a man whose family name goes back to a signer of the Declaration of Independence, who has faced death and carnage as an officer in the Army of his nation, and whose pride and honor as an American citizen has always carried with it a keen awareness of his obligations, this thing comes as a shock, and a humiliation hard to bear. I believed before I was arrested, and doubly so now that I'm jailed, that this polygamy crusade is a violation of every principle and right of an American citizen to worship God according to the dictates of his own conscience. This constitutional guarantee is a part of the heritage of every American citizen, and I saw no reason to abdicate in the face of any set of men who'd steal this right from me. I've tried to be a good citizen, I've fought for my country, and I've harmed no man. That is more than I can say for the carrion who arrested me and hauled me off to jail—or even for your own half brother, Cove, and the Ammon apostates, who testified against me in that farce called a trial at Provo. These things hurt, because my children will always know me as a criminal.

"But some day, Nan—maybe in generations to come—they'll point back to me, not with shame, but with pride. I share this vile, unnatural spot with many a noble soul, Nan. Every one of us has been given our chance for freedom. A few have taken it, but mighty few."

"Your chance?" Nancy asked, anxiously. "They gave you a chance?"

"A paper to sign. All one has to do is repudiate plural marriage. Cast away every wife but the first one. And make bastards of one's children born under the plural covenant. There are a few other niceties—such as pledging, under pain of returning to the penitentiary, that never again will you be guilty of illegal cohabitation."

Nancy, keeping an eye on the stone-faced guard, as he circled the tabled bedlam of the room, tried hard to think through this one. Here was a chance for freedom; for Joel to toss over the tribulations he so willingly had assumed; for the two of them, along with the only recognized children under the law, to resume the precious life they once had lived. But knowing Joel, and knowing the Mormon pattern he also had willingly assumed, she knew that he would rot and bleed to his death before he'd sign any such abdication. It was as confusing as it was saddening.

"I'd like to see you free at any price," she said. "I'd love you, and welcome you home, no matter what you did or signed. But I think I can see how you feel about it, Joel. And I'm proud of your character and your courage." She paused a moment, and looked tenderly at him, longing with all her soul to cross the wooden barrier separating them and crush this man into her arms. "Joel," she said, sadly. "I still can't understand why the leaders of the Church are not in here with you; showing by their example that they are behind you in this struggle."

"But some of them are in here, Nan!"

"And most of them aren't."

"Rudger Clawson and Lorenzo Snow are here. I talk to them every day. I serve with them at the Sunday worship they allow the Mormons once a month. Oh, they're noble men, Nan. The example they show under adversity has convinced me, as never before, that we're fighting the Lord's battle. And, in this thing, *we shall win!*"

Nancy could never be sure of this—not after her talks with the traitorous Cove, and the shock of this visit. The nation was behind this drive, and Joel, nor no other dedicated Saint, as yet seemed big enough to stay it.

"Now that we have President George Q. Cannon, and his fine son, Abram, locked up in this place, I'd say we have a pretty good representation of the Authorities in this penitentiary. I'd also say that the Church and its people are being directed just about as much from here, as from Temple Square. I'm in good company, Nan, and proud to share my prison stay with such men as these. Please worry yourself no more regarding those leaders in exile. Someone *must* be free, if this work is to go on."

Joel would never understand, and she promised herself never again to bother him with the inequities of leadership. Just the same, it would be warming to the heart if fat old Lofty Cragg could squirm out a few months with the bedbugs.

"We've got characters here, too, Nan—just like in Ammon. There are a few murderers sharing our company, a few clowns, and all the imbeciles and insane they can gather up around the territory. I find there's no insane asylum in Utah, so they commit them here, to howl, rant, and scream day and night. It's a good thing they allow the prisoners no knives or forks.

"You'd never believe this, but they've got tiny doghouses, called sweatboxes, set up at various spots. Inside these crates, staring out like animals, solitarily confined, are the incorrigibles, the insane that the inmates and guards can't batter into submission, or the poor sick devils too diseased to share the once-a-week bath, the washrooms, or the cell houses. There's not a doctor in the place. Nothing but sadistic, snarling guards, and hundreds of decent, upright humans, who'd rather live out their long sentences in the most inhuman and disgraceful penal institution in this nation, than degrade and renounce the tenets of their religion, and abandon those whom they love and cherish. We're both living through an odd page of history, Nan. If fate prevents me from writing about it, I hope someone else will have the inclination and the courage. Maybe one of my sons—or their sons."

"These things are not going to be forgotten, Joel," Nancy reassured him. "These are times of sadness that will be remembered and wondered at." She hesitated to say more, because there were so many kinds of sadness in this thing. The sadness the men felt, in being hounded and caged like the lower beasts, was not necessarily the type of ache felt by the women caught in this insane muddle. Nor could a first wife have the same type of hurts from it as, say, a second, third, or fourth wife. Each had her own peculiar sadness—and it was a sadness that was working and souring at Zion like yeast in heat.

"If our captors, the judges, the politicians, the preachers, and all those behind this inhuman crusade, weren't so blind and stupid, they'd realize the futility of trying to change a man's conscience by locking him up," Joel was saying. "History has proven that only the weak and the useless break under this sort of thing. When a man goes to jail for conscience' sake, it forges that conscience into the unbreakable steel of the martyrs. We may be dirty, vermin-infested, and housed like rats in a burrow—but in our hearts we're clean, and we know it, and even our captors are beginning to know it. I never felt surer in my faith than I do in this hour, Nan. Within these walls are the great minds, and most noble souls of this Latter-day movement. My own bunk mate is Aurelius Miner, a graduate of the State National College of New York, with a degree in law; a member of the bar at Columbus, Ohio, and the State of Michigan; admitted to the bar of the Supreme Court of the United States; one of the truly great barristers of Utah. Now he's a cohab; a convict. Because he would not betray his church, or sign away his rights as a citizen under the Constitution, he's been disbarred by our infamous Judge Zane, and committed to a long sentence in this house of infamy. But make no mistake—in trying to break him as a human, they've made a greater man of him by far. And so it is with every Saint in here. We draw brotherhood and strength from one another; we look up to the sky, and praise God for this time of our testing; we know better than ever the meaning of this Gospel we espouse; and this penitentiary, instead of being the Mormon meat grinder planned and hoped for by our enemies, is only kneading the convictions and courage of this people into a cord of strength that all the furies of hell can never break."

To Nancy, it still was confusing. In her visits to the run-down homes of Ammon, with their frightened and furtive-eyed inmates, she'd detected little of this mighty surge of spirit which a penitentiary, biased courts, and inhuman and cruel feds had brought to Utah. From what she'd seen and experienced, the Church and its plural marriage was being hit a shattering and irrecoverable blow. The men might emerge from here bright-eyed with conviction and purpose, buoyed up with the strength of martyrs, but when they returned to their neglected and abandoned homes, or tried to recover their lands and possessions confiscated by the government courts, there'd be little to shout hallelujah about. And Nancy sensed there'd never again be any picking up of the dreamy, secure, and smug pattern of plurality as it had been known through the years of her childhood, and the years of her own close and uncomfortable experience with it.

"But though our testimonies are strengthened," Joel was saying, loud-voiced enough to be heard above the bedlam of this mad room, "that doesn't necessarily mean our hearts fail to resent the injustices and outrage of human decency of this foul place." He smiled, and the purging of himself through talk seemed to have helped him greatly. "To think that the thing that first intrigued me to Ammon was its high walls. Now I never want to see another wall. And when I get out, I'm going to dedicate my life to breaking down every wall that exists. I'm not fool enough to think that any man can come out of a penal institution unscarred. My military record, for which I've taken considerable pride, is now forever canceled out and clouded. My family, as dedicated members of the Boston Guardians, discovered my name among the lists of convicted polygamists in Utah. Amanda sent me a scorching letter, addressed to me here, accusing me of putting my mother to bed with an illness that will probably kill her. I wrote back to those narrow-minded bigots, that I was proud to be a Mormon cohab, and proud to serve a penitentiary term for my religious convictions. I told them that, since they'd stolen from me the inheritance that was due me, I wanted none of their pity or their censure. In short, and politely, I told them all to go to hell."

The guard reached the prison doorway in his rounds, lowered his rifle butt to the floor, and with his left hand pulled out a fat silver watch. "Time's up!" he roared. "Visitors leave by the far door! Prisoners will line up, facing me."

"Oh, Nan," Joel groaned, above the sudden noise of the risings. "God bless you for coming. Try and make it again next month. Take care of my dear children. Tell them their father never ceases to think of them."

"You'll get the package," Nancy said, hurriedly as he arose to go. "I'll tell the children. And Matey's coming in. She has a package too."

"Nan, I *do* love you," he said, his blue eyes suddenly wet with tears. "And I love you, Joel. I miss you so much."

Then there was nothing more that could be said. The fifty men, in their striped garb of servitude, were lined up two abreast. Visitors, Nancy included, tried to wave to their loved ones, but not a head could be turned in recognition. When the guards marched them out, it was the visitors' turn to clear the room for the next repetition of the sad and noisy drama.

Back in the now crowded reception hall, Nancy stayed with Matey until her name was called, trying to answer Matey's own frantic questions as to Joel. After the second Mrs. Scott had joined the line, under the false name she'd been forced to use to gain her own visit, Nancy wearily sat down in the seat Matey had vacated.

Then, quite suddenly, the matron called out, "Mrs. Enoch Brayton," and a dumpish little woman, package under her arm, joined the line now almost ready to move.

"So, Enoch Brayton, my father, the man my mother divorced, is in this place," thought Nancy. And she eyed the sad and ragged little woman with sharp interest. The little old soul could very well be the plural wife who had made Martha's own share of plural hell. "So, my own father's here," her thoughts repetitively nagged. And there was a little sadness to her thinking. Other than a curiosity as to what he might look like, he could go to hell before she'd seek his company. And for what he'd done to her mother, she hoped the lice and bedbugs would chew him well.

Under the trusty's guidance, the line moved out of the room toward its own little taste of hell. She had half an hour to wait and think. But instead of thinking, she buried her head in her hands and sobbed out the ache in her heart.

IX

THAT WINTER OF 1885–1886, THE TIME OF JOEL SCOTT'S SOJOURN IN UTAH'S penitentiary, saw, along with its strange succession of events, a further tightening of the judicial screws on the Mormon Church and its still unregenerate polygamists. The Edmunds-Tucker Act continued to bat itself around the halls of Congress, with new and novel amendments tacked on with every blast of indignation against the Church and its people. About the time that Joel, wan, thin and ill, was released from prison, the new program being debated was a complete liquidation and dissolving of the stubborn sect. This, with an intensified bounty hunt on the cohabs, and outright governmental seizure of the Church's properties, should once and for all put end to that malignant cancer known as Mormonism.

Obdurate fighter that he was, Joel had tried for an appeal of his own case, with hope of carrying the thing upward to the Supreme Court. For him it proved futile. Not a chance was given him to test the constitutionality of the crusade. Other cohabs of higher standing in the Church were doing a mite better with their appeals, but all of them were forced to nest down in the vermin while their cases were being retried. The judges appointed to Utah were as dedicated in their task as the marshals. Bail and writs for Mormon prisoners were not to be a part of this crusade.

The new year of 1886 started with a few promising signs for the beleaguered Saints. A desperate hope was pinned to the governmental appointment of Caleb West as governor of Utah Territory. His promise to review the complicated Mormon question was strengthened by his personal visit to the penitentiary, to interview the louse-bitten cohabs incarcerated there. Caleb West's appeal to them was impassioned and earnest. All he asked them to do was obey the law, renounce polygamy, sign the pledge, and they could all go home. Not one cohab, including Joel, accepted the offer. Apostle Lorenzo Snow answered Governor West in the same tone as the others. "Well, Governor," the bearded elder stated, "so far as I'm concerned personally, I'm not in conflict with any of the laws of the country. I've obeyed the law as faithfully and conscientiously as I can, thus far, and I'm not here because of disobedience of any law. I'm here wrongfully convicted and wrongfully sentenced."

Joel later told Nancy that he himself answered the governor by reminding his honor, "I've stood for the laws of this nation from the beginning. I fought through a bloody war to sustain those laws. I hold that the Constitution of my beloved country upholds the laws of God, and the right to live in conscience within the religion of my choice. I'm here because I've dared to stand up for the things the Constitution and Bill of Rights guarantee to me. I've broken no law, and I'm unjustly convicted. And you can do whatever you want with your damned paper. *I, for one, will not sign it, if I have to rot in this hole for the rest of my life!*"

And from this first port of disappointment, to the end of his term, Governor West put his shoulder to the wheel of the judicial crusade, and did all he could to see that the penitentiary ran to its full capacity, by a ready refill for every cohab who stepped out at the finish of his sentence.

It was rumored John Taylor had secretly returned from Hawaii, ill, and resolved to die in the holy land of the Saints. If so, he remained well hidden among the uncommunicative and sullen brethren. Highest cash reward was posted to any bounty hunter lucky enough to make the big coup. And there was real zest to the search.

Against the planned escheatment of the Church's properties, and the intensified man hunt throughout the entire West for any fugitive cohabs, there was the great and humane side of the drive. Loudest laugh among the Mormons was the opening, on Fifth East Street, in the heart of Salt Lake City, of the great Women's Industrial Home, as a place of refuge for the Mormon polygamous wives. Mrs. Angie F. Newman, of Lincoln, Nebraska, had conceived the idea that if Mormon women could only be provided means of escape and protection from the horrors of plurality, the Mormon problem would be solved quickly and easily. The home was planned as a sanctuary—with love, conveniences, and no questions asked—for any Mormon woman who entered its always open door. The idea, publicized throughout America, quickly caught on. Thousands upon thousands of dollars poured in from churches and generous-minded individuals everywhere throughout the land. A huge congressional appropriation was added, and Mrs. Newman quickly learned what it was to have a philanthropic dream taken over by the politicians. Public funds were set up to provide fast and confidential night or day escape from the Utah horrors for any woman who desired to use the home's comforting and generous facilities.

Upon his return to Ammon, Joel Scott followed the progress of the home with amused interest, because he was certain some part of the Scott fortune had gone into it. "An abysmal flop!" he laughed. "They've set themselves up to receive a swarm of Mormon women escaping the Principle. Not a single Mormon wife has gone through the portals of escape. All they've gotten are a few old freeloaders, who never *were* Mormon wives, but just weary of servicing the soldiers at Fort Douglas. These women never did have a windfall to compare with this." And as Joel announced and predicted, the home was a failure from the start.

But the crusade was successful enough. New and ingenious teeth were added to it continuously—such as the government's refusal to naturalize Mormon converts coming from other lands, and the announcement that any cohab who had served prison sentence and was further guilty of "lewd and lascivious cohabitation" with a former plural wife would be remanded back to prison with a sentence stiff and long enough to keep him out of circulation for the better part of his studding prime. All a plural husband had to do to gain this new governmental generosity was to be caught in the domicile of any of his known polygamous wives. All one of these polygamous wives had to do was to get fat with child, or birth one, and back to jail went the head of this particular spiritual kingdom.

Joel, bitter, sad, and worried, endeavored to fit himself back into the normal pattern of Ammon. But there no longer was any semblance of a normal pattern. The once happy children who had crowded the town's three schools had, through the forced fleeing of their parents out of Zion, dwindled to but a fraction of the former number. And these children, nervous, furtive-eyed, and afraid to speak lest they betray their parents into the hands of the marshals, were the poorest sort of timber for the educative process.

Except for the deputy marshals, and their disreputable hangers-on, and the Gentiles who were moving in to take over from the distressed Saints, the town of Ammon was practically deserted. The wild, drunken orgies at the hotel Isaac Corey had built to the glory of God and His people kept things lively enough at night. But only the housewives visited the stores during the day. On Sundays the church services at the new chapel were carried on regularly and with the same old sincerity, but were attended almost entirely by women. And always there was a fed or two at the hitching rail, guns slung low on hip, rolling their endless cigarettes, and telling their lewd stories while they tirelessly watched the church for the wanted men.

It was safe enough for Joel to accompany Nancy and the family to church, because, according to law, Nancy was his only recognized wife, and the feds knew this. Let him drive Matey and his other family to church, and the story would quickly have been different. For this reason, most of the men had vanished to the underground, or had followed Bishop Earlington's example, and fled with their families to other states or Mexico. In spite of Joel's efforts to restore his town to normalcy, and in spite of his faith that a Supreme Court decision as to the unconstitutionality of this merciless assault on the Church would change things overnight, there was a blight and a rot throughout Ammon and the other towns and cities of Utah that was destroying and reducing to nothing the faith and industry of a people.

Nancy was watched, because she was a midwife, and went where babies were born. Joel was watched, because he had a prison record as a cohab, and there was money to be had if he was caught with some woman other than the gun-packing midwife he was legitimately married to. Every man, woman, and child in Ammon was suspect. And only a blind man could fail to see that it was killing the town.

Joel, in his own plural pattern, and up until the time the government had upset it, had been as loyally conscious of his obligations, and as meticulously punctual in executing them, as Isaac Corey could ever have been. Now his visits to Matey's house were weirdly executed, and entirely nocturnal. The long leisurely stays of alternate weeks, as set and sure as the calendar itself, came to an abrupt halt after his return from prison, and it was made painfully certain he would be quickly returned unless the pattern of his living was monogamous in every detail. No dime novel was ever richer in intrigue and inventiveness than Joel's badger game with the feds.

Any night he could be observed walking nonchalantly and leisurely up the path, and into the front door of Nancy's house, opposite the school building. But when darkness came, and on those nights promised to Matey, he would let himself through the kitchen trapdoor into the cellar. From there he would sneak through the outside door to the yard, crawl across it, belly down like an Indian to the potato cellar, where he would traverse its length. This brought him out below the garden, and almost to the corral. Then, by making his way across lots, and with the vigilance of a fugitive murderer dodging the law, he eventually landed in Matey's back yard—and *her* cellar door.

The dogs he encountered in his nocturnal safaris were almost as great a problem as the feds themselves. Jody's dog, Rags, while quick to learn that barking at the master's knee-and-elbow traversing of the back yard was a thing not to be tolerated, still could never learn that the game was one of marriage survival rather than some wild antic for Rags's own benefit. The dog now considered that his part of the game was to worm along with Joel, but with the annoying habit of licking Joel's face and hands while doing so. To tie the dog up, where he could not identify the back-yard prowler, was to set up a nervous baying that touched off dogs for a mile around, and was sure to alert the sensitive ears of the watching and waiting marshals that another cohab was on the prowl. Joel wanted Rags put out of the way. Jody's plea for the dog prevailed. So the polygamist not only got his knees and elbows dirty, but his face licked, when he made those nightly visits to his plural wife.

Rags, a dutiful animal, could be induced to return when Joel crawled under the back-yard fence into the lots of his neighbors, but the neighbors' dogs were neither so friendly nor so dutiful. They barked and raised hell with the dark intruder, as they pleased. And Nancy, with ears as sensitized as any plural wife in town, could mark Joel's progress in the night by listening to the canine uproar of her neighbors. She felt certain that sometime the dogs must eventually betray Joel Scott into another arrest. And then she took comfort in the fact that other dogs were barking, and other cohabs in Ammon had come out of hiding, and in defiance of every law made against them, were on nocturnal prowl toward their forbidden women.

Sometimes Joel returned, dirty, dark, and angry. "The damned feds are watching Matey's house tonight," he'd growl. Nancy would get an added night with her husband, an added steal from the calendar, but the added worry for his future. And the future of her own household made it hardly worth the gain. She never could manage to be half as sorry for Matey as she was for Joel. Any way one looked at it, it was a desperate way to be married.

But it was not the dogs—pests that they were—that were to betray Joel Scott. It was the normal results of any nocturnal meet of any man with a woman. When Matey whimpered out the confession that she had missed a period, Nancy was worried. When Matey threw up her breakfasts and began to bulge in the familiar place, Nancy knew that calamity indeed had struck.

This time, not even Joel Scott was anxious to face down the law and stand up and slug for the Principle. The feds had gotten as wise as the Saints were clever. Nature was their greatest ally. Babies had ever been the Mormon proliferation, and no amount of jail could ever keep the brethren from crawling into bed with their women. Once through the legal mill, every wife of the cohab was known and listed by the marshals. To deny paternity was to see the woman shipped off to the women's correctional institution in far-away Detroit. To admit paternity was to again open wide the gates of the penitentiary, with a sentence that would take the cohab out of circulation for a good part of his productive years. Never was Joel Scott in more desperate trouble.

"I could hide in the canyon," he suggested, but without enthusiasm.

Again Nancy faced him, while he sweated out his problem in the easy chair. She was sick and weary of the whole unhealthy, secretive mess. "Yes, it's a *nice* place in the winter. Thirty-foot snow. We'd find you a bundle of bones, come spring."

"Nan, I hadn't expected this to happen. When Matey told me she was going to have another baby, it was a shock, I can tell you."

Nancy snorted. "The law of gravity. That which goes up must come down." But she was worried and sad, and didn't feel like joking. "Matey told me last month. I've known it for a spell."

"What am I going to do?"

She looked at her husband, and shook her head. Was he weak? Afraid?

"Golly damn, Joel," she sighed. "For a man who's always known the answers, you *do* sound strange. Only thing *I* know, is how things might have been. To me you've always been the most important man in Ammon. You've brought more to this town than any living human. If the law weren't constantly on your tail, you'd be the one person to bring order and courage back to this sick community. But you're whipped and boxed in, like any other cohab. And what I see is not the Joel Scott I married."

"Things are confusing. And some of what you say is true." He looked at her earnestly, and a little sadly. "But I'd hoped you'd be on my side, Nan."

"I *am* on your side, and always have been. But I'm tired of it all. Bewildered and discouraged. And wondering where it's going to end."

"It will end all right," Joel consoled. "Never you fear. This is the Lord's work, and it's not going to be put asunder by the devil and his minions."

"That I've heard since I was born," Nancy answered wearily. "But Matey's fattening up for a baby. And when the baby comes—maybe before—you're going back to jail."

He looked as though she'd clouted him square in the face, and she was sorry. The shock of being sent back to that pest hole would unnerve any man. Joel actually was no weakling or coward, but he knew, and she knew that a penitentiary term this time, and for the repeated offense, would be a matter of years, not months. Some of his children were coming into manhood and womanhood; others were helpless and dependent. All needed him desperately. Even Nancy, who bitterly resented the tangle Matey Thorpe had brought, reeled back at the thought of Joel again facing jail.

"I swore I'd never knuckle down to hell, injustice, and oppression," Joel said, sadly. "But they've got me. There's nothing left for us to do but to get out of Utah."

The past year had been one of trial beyond endurance, but this, the end of the road, was the saddest time of all. Gone was Joel Scott's bravado, the fighting trim of a man who once dared strike back at cruelty and injustice. It was hard to believe that the beaten cohab, stewing in his worries before her, mouthing the familiar spiritual platitudes, could ever have been the impish, insolent, adventurous Gentile who had swept her into a marriage that had promised freedom and deliverance from the horror of polygamy. And where had this marriage brought her? Right into the middle of the worst polygamous mess any woman could imagine. She'd known few happy moments since the second bride arrived. Now, Joel Scott, erstwhile Gentile, was only another pathetic cohab dodging the bounty hunters. He'd become exactly like the thousands of others throughout Utah who, without bothering to button up their pants, were diving out windows and sneaking out back doors, in their fleeing exodus from the misery they'd heaped up for their women. Nancy wanted to weep out the pain she felt. But this she'd done a thousand times—and the pain was still there. Instead she looked Joel honestly and squarely in the eye.

"I'm not getting out of Utah," she said. "You go. You've got to go. If you don't, you'll rot behind bars for the rest of your life. But I'm not going, Joel."

"Nancy, I'm not going without you. We could all leave together. Clear out of this fantastic nightmare." He leaned confidentially, eagerly close. "The fleeing Saints have found a spot in Colorado—San Luis Valley— they've some towns going there already—Manassa, Sanford. We'd be safe there, Nan."

"You'll not be safe anywhere, Joel. Government's set its mind to nail every Mormon man who sports more than one woman. You go to Colorado, to Boston, or to Mexico. Quick as you can get away. But don't count on me. I've done nothing wrong. I've broken no law. I'm staying right here in Ammon. And I'll spit in the eye of any fed who dares bother me—or, better still, blow his can off."

"I'm just not taking off alone, Nan."

"Then stick around. They'll probably give you back your old bunk at the penitentiary."

Joel winced, probably at thought of the bedbugs. But the old hurts had come up in Nancy, and she didn't care.

"Where I go, I want my families," Joel argued.

"They've probably got a real neat penitentiary in Colorado. Just hoist the plural flag over there, and see what happens."

"Other Mormon wives have fled with their husbands."

"But not *this* Mormon wife. I'm just not going, Joel. I'm not fleeing. I'm not moving one step from Ammon."

"What about Matey?"

"She's *your* chickadee. I'm not married to her."

"I'll have to get her out of the state, Nan. If she has her baby here, it'll be disastrous. You *can't* hide a baby."

"That's for sure," Nancy grumbled, as she fought back a tear.

"Then this is it," Joel said. "I'll just have to take Matey and her youngsters. I'll go on to Salt Lake, as though nothing were wrong. Matey can join me there with the kids. I'll have train tickets for Colorado. Will you help Matey pack, Nan?"

"Gladly."

"This seems an awful thing to do."

"It is. But I'm getting used to it."

"I'll get established in Colorado. And then I'll come for you, Nan."

But Nancy, fighting back tears, could not answer. Instead she arose abruptly and headed for the bedroom. He could cross lots to Matey's. Let them finish out the night in talk—or whatever else they did to finish out the night. It wouldn't be the first or the last time Nancy Scott would cry herself to sleep.

And this time, instead of marching off to jail like a true soldier of the cross, Joel Scott hit the grit like any other hunted cohab. Matey's pregnancy was not far enough along to excite suspicion, especially after flouncing the swelling over with ample show of skirt and coat. As Joel had suggested, there was none of this fleeing hand in hand. His early departure for Salt Lake was accepted by the marshals as a routine occurrence. And certainly no significance could be attached to the little English woman's travel to the city with her three youngsters.

Apparently their fleeing of Utah occurred without hitch or delay, for two weeks later came Joel's letter from Sanford, Colorado. They had arrived. Joel had prospects of a teaching post in the Colorado schools. At last he was safe, and free from worry.

That night Nancy Scott really cried herself to sleep.

X

SPRING ROLLED INTO THE SADDEST AND MOST FRUSTRATING SUMMER OF Nancy's life. A pall of gloom had settled over her town and valley and, with the going of the men, the life and vitality of the community was drained away like juice from a cider press. Crops rotted in the ground, the wheatfields dried out and withered under the sun and, except for what the more energetic women could glean, they went uncut and neglected. Ammon had become a city of waifs and females. Only those men who hid out in the canyons, to make their nocturnal visits to bed and hearthsides, and those who somehow managed to convince the feds of no polygamous intent, were near enough to count.

Independence Day passed with only a desultory firing of guns by the older youths of Ammon, and the drunken debauchery at the hotel. Pioneer Day, July 24, had no semblance to the rousing picnics and celebrations that had so consistently marked the happier years. This was a time of sadness. And the rot of uncertainty and paralysis had spread itself everywhere through Zion.

And then, over the telegraph, the day after the quiet and gloomy Twenty-fourth, came news that President John Taylor was dead. The venerable head of the Church, who had stood with the Prophet Joseph on the day of the martyrdom at Carthage jail, and who himself had been grievously wounded by the mob that had cut the Prophet down, had quietly met death in the home of Brother Thomas F. Rouche, in Kaysville. As had been his wish, he had died in the home of friends, and on the ground of his beloved Zion. Most of the Saints had imagined he was safe from the crusade, in far-away Hawaii. And though the tidings of this loss was sad and worrisome, there was uplift in the thought their leader had actually dared return, had brashly ignored the high rewards for his capture, and had shown the courage to finish out his life in Zion. With John Taylor's death went the greatest bounty prize of all.

Under the Edmunds-Tucker Law the Church of Jesus Christ of Latter-day Saints had been dissolved as a religious corporation, and the attorney general of the United States had been directed, under that law, to institute and prosecute proceedings to forfeit and escheat to the United States all property in excess of $50,000 belonging to the Church. To Nancy, to Joel, and to every other Saint, this meant only one thing —the intent of the Gentiles, backed by law and government force, to utterly wipe the Church from the face of the earth. Since the Church, to the Saints, was the veritable work of God restored in these latter days for the salvation of the world, the crusade could only mean a cruel, rapacious, and hell-inspired conspiracy bent on the destruction of everything they had stood for, suffered for, and died for. To be hounded like animals, humiliated, and jailed for their religious beliefs was one thing that could be personally endured, in light of the great cause; but to see the very government—built on the rock of the rights of man, including the unquestioned privilege of every man to worship God according to his own conscience and belief—arbitrarily dissolve the very church which God Himself had restored, and confiscate its property—this represented to them a conspiracy of intolerance and injustice without a parallel.

Joel, with unshaken faith in the Constitution and Bill of Rights of his country, had maintained that once these harsh decrees of a hostile Congress were properly tested in the courts, that logic and justice would blast them to pieces, or at least expose them for what they were—an ill-conceived and unjust sword of persecution against a national minority. Only difficulty was that the wronged parties, once they showed faces for a court fight, found themselves summarily thrown into the penitentiary, and their rights blocked by as vicious a set of judicial appointees as ever disgraced a nation. A few appeals, including that of Apostle Lorenzo Snow, managed to get through to the Supreme Court. That august body refused to pass on the legality of the conviction, the appeal was dropped back to the lower courts, and the patient apostle remained in jail with the vermin and the bedbugs.

With President John Taylor's death, the church government, that is such government as remained, passed back to the headship of the Council of the Twelve Apostles. With a fat price on the head of each of these twelve notables, once they showed their faces, and with them scattered in exile over four continents, or languishing in jail, this was a time of trouble indeed. As best they could, and with what little tithing money was left after the long and vicious siege the Church and its people had endured, they fought valiantly in the courts against this merciless confiscation by decree. The fact that the government had already dissolved the Church as a corporation handicapped the legal battle immeasurably. In the courts, packed with non-Mormon juries, because Mormons had already been denied the right to serve, it was a hopeless cause from the start. The only thing left the harassed apostles and their floundering cause was to appoint trustees among themselves, and deed the Church's many properties back to individuals and wards, and break up the ownership of the Church itself into such a maze that it would take the attorney general a lifetime to appropriate everything God and the Prophets had named for the good of man.

Temple Square, and other church edifices, in Salt Lake City, the mecca of Mormondom, was deeded to William B. Preston, R. T. Burton, and John R. Winder, who acted for the Church as a Presiding Bishopric. And through this mess and tangle of hates, acrimony, and injustice that was destroying her town, her valley, and her people, Nancy remembered the words her high-minded Joel had thundered from the pulpit before jail and the mailed fist of the crusade had silenced him. "I expect to live to see the day when the minorities of this nation will be protected, rather than persecuted. I'm convinced I shall know the time when the weight and power of government will be used in nobler cause than to outrage, intimidate, and jail those of its citizens who think differently, worship differently, or seem racially strange to the great self-righteous and smug majority who make up this nation of mine."

Nancy had never been as optimistic about Joel's predictions. She doubted, now he was buried and silenced by exile, and his Church was being governmentally torn asunder, if he himself felt quite so sure.

As for herself, the mental battle to live in two worlds was rending her apart with the same methodical thoroughness of the judges and the marshals. Her own fight with the Principle was strictly a personal one. She could derive no fiendish enjoyment out of seeing fathers and husbands torn from their families and hauled off to jail, as did the Gentile press, politicians, and preachers. Polygamy, as much as she personally abhorred it, could never be as bad as the anarchy, desolation, and spiritual void with which the government was attempting to replace it. In her own short lifetime she had seen Utah made over from a sagebrush wilderness into an Eden of beauty. Regardless of what the Gentiles thought of it, the Mormon life, with its family pattern and brotherly endeavor, was a good life. Before this awful curse, greater than any devastation of crickets or famine, had come into the land, there had been happiness, laughter, and spiritual meaning to everything in their lives. Here, as in every society, there had been a trodding on toes, injustices, and some wrongs, but the flaws, as she saw them, were of minor consequence when weighed in the pattern of security and the sense of cause which had fashioned a commonwealth out of a wasteland.

Of the Mormon creed, and everything it stood for, plurality was the only phase of it she could not accept or believe on. But plenty of other Saints did. And perhaps the only reason she couldn't digest the Principle had come through some fault in her own conversion. Certainly she saw no need, as did the Gentiles, to destroy the whole Church because of some unpopular or unbelievable portion of its philosophy. Maybe, in the great sweep of life, it *was* necessary to put an end to polygamy, but it made no sense to her to kill the patient just to excise an ulcer. And what were Congress and President Cleveland in their harsh intensity to destroy this thing, and break up the Church, going to do with ten thousand fatherless bastards, many thousand husbandless wives, and a great and vital faith ruthlessly destroyed among this people? Were drunken deputies, fanatical judges, Gentile juries, penitentiary, and that imbecilic female home in Salt Lake City the only substitute the American people were able to give for the prosperous commonwealth and the way of life it was destroying?

But now that Joel was once more gone out of her life, she had come to feel that her own personal bucking at the Principle had been just as stupid and devoid of victory as that of the government's. Twice, now—willingly, almost with alacrity—she'd banished her man, because he'd found it possible to share a love and loyalty with another woman. The thought of her sharing her own great love with more than one man was an outrage to her senses. Yet Joel seemed perfectly capable of loving Matey Thorpe, without any diminishment that was apparent, of his love and tenderness toward her, or the children of this first union. If she lived to the age of the Three Nephites, she'd never understand this strange quirk in men.

She needed no convincing that men were naturally polygamous, and women naturally monogamous, and that was the way God had created them. Instinctively, every woman wanted her nest, and her man, inviolate. Instinctively, man had tolerance and loyalty toward the nest, but with an interest and ability to keep more than one nest going. It was normal for every woman to want her man to herself, and her nest alone. It was normal for her to resent anything that threatened the security of this nest. Therefore, in fighting back at Matey Thorpe, and the peril she represented, Nancy felt she'd acted normally and naturally.

But the oddity was the alacrity with which women went into this thing, and the endless succession of women constantly petitioning already married Mormons to take them on as added brides. It was said that the Prophet Joseph Smith, and Brigham Young, were besieged by hundreds of young girls, anxious and willing to share the luster of these great men in plurality. For every yes the Authorities made in wedlock, they were literally forced to say no to scores of hopefuls. These women who so willingly accepted the Principle, and so devoutly fought for it, were either on a higher plane spiritually than Nancy Scott, had somehow been miraculously converted to the sharing plan, or were hypocrites and liars at heart. These things, to her, had been the everlasting puzzle of Utah polygamy.

But the state of her own feelings as the months wore on was no puzzle. This time, as at every other time when Joel was gone, she missed him as though the best part of herself had fled with him. Once again she had literally kicked her man into Matey's bed. And just as poignantly now as at the first time, she was suffering the tortures of the damned. Pride was one thing. Love that transcended even human frailty and heartbreak was quite another thing.

As a first wife, her marriage and the legitimacy of her children were recognized by law. The Edmunds-Tucker Law had reduced Matey's claim on Joel Scott to something less than zero. Through the eyes of the law, at least, Matey's life with him was concubinage, immoral and illegal, and every child of the union had been born into bastardy. To Nancy there not only was a sense of satisfaction but a warming smugness in the prior and total claim the judicial crusade had given her. But it was one thing to count your buttons, she bitterly had learned, and another thing to darn pantaloons when the man who wore them was nesting elsewhere.

Joseph Smith, by making the natural polygamous urging in the male acceptable under God's law, had started something whirling that all the marshals and judges in the nation could never stop. Saints claimed, and the Church taught, that plural marriage was a revelation from God Himself. Until the Church, in the name of God, repudiated the practice, plural marriage would be a part of it, and all the laws and judges and marshals under heaven would never succeed in abolishing it. Penitentiaries could be filled and emptied a thousand times, government could dissolve the Church, break it up in a thousand pieces, and chase the Saints to the world's end, but, so long as any segment of its universal priesthood remained, and the law stood unrepudiated by divinity itself, there, and endlessly forever, would the practice and the Principle remain. This, then, was a holy war. And tragic thing about holy wars was the fact they were never won—except at the price of complete and unconditional extermination of one side or the other.

For Nancy there was an aching sorrow about the war, in the fact that whichever side won, she would lose. It lacerated her pride and shook her confidence to know that Joel would as willingly die for Matey and her children as he would for Nancy, and those he'd sired by her. If the Church won, which she knew was doubtful, in spite of the cozy reassurances of Joel and the Authorities, she'd have Joel divided by as many wives and nests as he felt inclined to establish and service. If the government won, she'd have a dead husband, a jailed husband, or an exiled husband. For her there was no winning either way.

But regardless of Mormon courage to stand up to the war, and Joel's bland certitude and conviction, she had never been convinced the Authorities were playing the persecution game straight with their beleaguered lesser Saints. There were too many, like Apostle Jonathan Cragg and his favorite Flora, who were fulfilling their duties a suspiciously long way from Utah's center of misery. Too many of them had gone away with their favorite wives, to Europe and the lush and peaceful islands of the Pacific, while ordinary Saints hid out in caves, or rotted in jail. If all twelve of the apostles, and all seven presidents of the Seventies, and at least two hundred and fifty of the five hundred bishops were swatting lice and bedbugs in the penitentiary, or trying to keep warm in a limestone cave, Nancy's own testimony to the Gospel would have been materially strengthened. But that was her own private view of Mormonism through the dark days of the great crusade.

Joel's letters from Colorado were encouraging in the fact that he'd found immediate employment in the schools of San Luis Valley. He and Matey had set up a little home in Sanford, and his first letters were nothing more than torrential pleadings for her to leave Ammon and join them there in the peace and serenity of their exile. There was nothing serene and peaceful about her own life. Trailed and frightened constantly by the feds, as they followed her for evidence toward new convictions, needing the money from her professional work to feed and clothe a large and insatiably demanding family, she was wearied and nerve-wracked beyond endurance. In the ache of her heart and the tears of loneliness she shed to her pillow at night, Joel would never know how close she'd so often come to abandoning everything and following her cohab into exile.

When it became apparent that his pleadings were having no effect upon her willingness to join him in Colorado, the urgings became less frequent. And for Nancy, this was even harder to bear. The fact that Matey and her family were being supported by the town schoolmaster in full public acceptance and style, while she sacrificed, slaved, and dodged feds day and night to support Joel's only legitimate brood, was as infuriating as it was humiliating. She could never cease loving Joel with every fiber of her being, and she missed him deeply and tenderly, but the monstrous thing he'd saddled to her marriage was more than even a patient woman could bear. If she stayed in Ammon, she'd have labor, heartache, and drunken feds to endlessly face. If she went to Colorado, she'd have labor, heartache, and Matey to face. Take the pick. Lose either way.

But wherever the marshal-dodging cohabs could get near their women, they kept them well fertilized—and this was true of Ammon. Somehow the babies kept coming, and, in spite of her mortal fear of the accursed feds, Nancy's task as midwife showed only the nominal slackening due to Ammon's population decrease. The town itself, from all appearances, was one of females and children. But somehow—miraculous to one unversed in the Mormon underground—the babies arrived, regularly, as the seasons. Nancy was certain that until Congress added castration to the Edmunds-Tucker Law, the government was fighting Mormonism uphill.

Why her own tragic brush with the law had to occur at the little house of Elena Christoferson was something she would never understand to the end of her days. Elena was only the second wife of Ansel Christoferson, both of them Swedish converts to the Church, neither of them very fluent in English. But apparently the Christofersons had digested well the visions and revelations of the Prophet, as recorded in the *Doctrine and Covenants*, for Ansel had gone the full distance into plurality.

But Ansel also was a mountain-born Swede, and no bounty hunter had yet laid his sadistic hands on him. Nancy knew he'd made himself comfortable in one of the limestone caves in Ammon Canyon—as did a lot of other hardy cohabs—but Nancy, as a loyal Saint, kept this and every other secret pertaining to her people in the silence that so baffled the judges and the marshals. Ansel, with the ubiquitousness of the Nephites, who still silently and loyally stalked the land, managed to slip out of his canyon retreat for an occasional meeting with his three wives. At least Nancy, who delivered the babies, was certain this was so, although she saw no more of Ansel than did the feds. What she did know was that Ansel was a marked and wanted man.

It started, just a little before midnight, when Ansel's oldest son, Peter, by Greta, the first wife, came tapping at Nancy's door. It was the familiar tune. "Aunt Elena's about ready. Her pains are regular. My mom's with her. Can you please come?"

In her nightgown, she'd dismissed Peter for his ride on horseback home to the Christofersons', where another baby was fighting entry into the Mormon world of woes. She'd washed the sleep out of her eyes from cold water ladled into the kitchen washbasin, and dressed hurriedly. As she went out the back path into the fall-chilled darkness, she carried her usual accouterments—in one hand her leather obstetrical kit and Joel's heavy gun-belt and loaded Colt, and in the other hand a lighted kerosene lantern. Familiar with every inch of corral, stalls, and carriage house, she tossed the gun and kit on the cushion of the single-seater. A minute later, with practiced hand, and talking in the half darkness, she'd hauled old Bess unwillingly from her stall, crossed through the hay-fragrant barn with her, and had backed her into the shafts. Then, by lantern light, she'd flung on the harness, collared the shafts, and had snapped the tugs to the singletree. She tied the lines to the buggy's whip post, opened the big door, and led the chewing and nervous mare, with her buggy, out into the darkness of the lane outside. Patiently Bess waited while she went back, blew out the lantern, and hung it to its wall peg. A moment later the mare and buggy were taking her on another too familiar call of duty—with Nancy wondering, in her sleepy way, why it was most women got their pains at night.

Since the Christofersons lived north of town, it was necessary to cross Ammon's Main Street. As usual, the only sign of life in the blighted community was the noise, music, and hilarity at the Ammon Hotel. But in her night excursions she'd gotten used to this brand of Gentile frivolity. They had good reason to celebrate. They'd all but driven the Saints into despair and dissolution. But what they would never understand was that dear dead Isaac had built the hotel they so noisily were contaminating. That a young girl had known the ecstasy of love and courtship in the very rooms where their whores were making a public travesty of the great moral cause to which the government had engaged them, and for which it was paying them. It was a dark, moonless night Elena had chosen for her delivery, and Nancy, as she paced the mare northward, could only hope it was dark enough to discourage any of the feds from following her. Only God, with His night-seeing eyes, would

322

know whether she was getting out of Ammon's center unobserved. She touched the worn handle of Joel's gun for reassurance.

Elena's house was a neat little adobe, surrounded, like most Mormon houses, with a stately row of poplars. With the Scandinavian knack for neatness and beauty, Elena had bordered the picket fence of her plural nest with fragrant lilacs, and had even extended the high bushes up either side of the long path leading through the yard to her front door. From the street itself, the house was virtually hidden from view.

The Christofersons, along with fate, had not given her too great a margin of time. Greta, Ansel's first wife, was waiting for her at the gateway. Knowing only too well the relentless march of birthing, Nancy hooked Bess's lines around the whip socket, and while Greta's practiced hand found the halter rope on the mare's collar, and tied the animal to the hitching post, Nancy jumped from the buggy, pushed the gun far back to the right-hand side of the seat, and grabbed up the obstetrical kit.

"I vass afraid maybe you not make it," Greta said. "Elena's lost the vater."

Nancy, in the darkness, crossed the little footbridge across the irrigation ditch, and followed Greta up the path. It occurred to her then, as it always did, that a few of the hostile Gentiles should observe the sisterly help Mormon wives gave each other when trouble hit the plural households. Wives cared for one another in sickness, and they buried one another in death. No wonder the great sanctuary for Mormon women, in Salt Lake City, was still vacant and untenanted by those it was built to save. Plural sisters were too busy at home, helping one another through this black time, to give any thought to such handy means of escape.

And so it was at the Christofersons'. Ansel, the man responsible for this complexity, was, for safety's sake, hibernating like a bear in the mountains. But the women of his household were on the job. The two other wives had the moaning, groaning Elena spread out on a clean-sheeted, hard-top bed, with tug ropes handy to help her along. A fire was going in the kitchen range, water was on and warm, towels and clean sheets within reach, and all of Elena's previous progeny dispatched to the other houses while this fundamental and barbaric event took place.

As usual Nancy gave her patient a reassuring pat on the cheek, and the good smile that always lent courage. She undid her kit by lamplight, washed her hands, and crisply and confidently ordered the Christoferson women through the next dramatic two hours. When it came, it was a boy, and Elena felt rewarded for the ordeal. After a sisterly cup of tea with the women, Nancy closed her kit, and started down the pathway to the mare, the buggy, and the prospect of still getting a little sleep from the night.

Yawning with real fatigue, she untied the mare, hooked the short rope again to the collar, and wearily climbed to the seat. She snapped the line to the mare's rump, whirled the buggy around sharply in the road, and relaxed as Bess clup-clupped toward home. And then her spine was suddenly sharp and prickly with the wave of terror that often hit her alone, and in the dark. As she always did, she reached over to touch Joel's gun for reassurance. In the darkness her hand glided around the leather flutings of the seat. The hackles of her neck rose higher, as she realized that only her kit was there. The gun was gone!

She sparred with her memory. Had she forgotten to bring it? Bess, glad to get going again toward home, was rolling her cheerfully through the darkness, while she sweltered in her panic. And clearly, she now remembered. She'd toted it out, as always. It had been on the seat when she went into the Christofersons'. Either it had dropped out, or it had been stolen. And then she saw the men—and she knew where the gun had gone. One man, afoot, had already stepped out to the roadway. Two more, on horseback, had ridden out of the line of poplars on either side of the road, and were already flanking the buggy.

In anger and terror, she whacked the mare's rump with the lines. But it was too late. The man up front already had grabbed the bit ring. The riders were alongside. She felt the buggy sag, as one of the men landed in the seat beside her. Paralyzed with fear, she tried to scream, but the other rider had grabbed her hair, yanked her down to the seat, and a sweaty hand was clapped over her mouth.

The ugliness and bestiality of the attack sent her into squirming frenzy. She lashed out with the strength and fury of a cornered wildcat, but the men who had her pinioned in the rocking buggy were hard and experienced. The one thing that might have saved her—her voice—was shut off tight enough to choke her—first by the man's hard, wet hand, and then by a rag or bandana handkerchief that was nauseous with the stink of dirt and sweat.

"Our midwife's a bit ructious," laughed the man who was gagging her.

"Her goddamned claws are like meat hooks," growled the other. "These Mormon women are half cat anyway."

With her knee she caught him under the chin with a blow that would have staggered an ordinary man. For answer, he grunted, and pinioned her wrists cruelly behind her back.

"They say they howl like back-yard cats when they're being screwed," laughed the man at her head.

"Trouble is, Jim, you don't listen enough for the howls. These Mormon women are being screwed aplenty—by somebody. The Swede's just had another baby. This little lady's just clipped a cord and buried an afterbirth. Another little Mormon's been birthed this night—right under our nose. The baby's Swede papa sneaks into town, diddles his women, an' disappears before we can lay hands on the horny sonabitch." He bent low over Nancy's face, and even through the dirty gag, she could smell the whiskey that apparently was numbing him to her threshing feet and legs. "Listen, midwife," he said, "we're gonna ungag you long enough for you to tell us where old Christoferson hides. Tell us, an' we'll let you go. Scream, and we'll kill you."

She felt the gag loosen. With one superhuman effort, she kneed herself against the buggy cushion, so she might roll off the seat and free herself enough to screech for help, then she'd fight until it came. But a hand went over her mouth again. She tumbled from the cushion, but they had her by the hair, the arms and the ankles—pinioned tight in the buggy box, with the now frightened mare bobbing and churning around like a ship in a storm.

"Hang on to the bit," yelled the man at her head, as he frantically bent over her. "Don't let the goddamned horse run away!"

"Let's get this fighting bitch out of the buggy," growled her interrogator. "She's tearin' it apart. I'll sit on her, Jim. You slip the gag back on. Then you jump down. We'll drag her out. Christamighty, she's a terror!"

"Well, for crissakes hold 'er, Jess. Plug 'er windpipe, an' let me get myself out of the rig. Watch 'er—she's strong as Brigham's ox."

"You tell me that? Hurry up, Jim. To the ditch bank. We'll match to see who gets first crack at her."

"Don't forget me up here," came the voice up front. "I been holdin' this fractious horse."

"You keep on holdin' that fractious horse," laughed Jim. "Leastwise till we git this fractious wildcat in the proper Mormon position on the grass."

"There'll be no cat howls when *you* screw her," the man laughed back. "Mormon women are used to something sizable."

In black fury and almost insane fright, Nancy squirmed and fought at the strong arms that had her pinioned. But it was useless. She felt herself being dragged bodily over the sharp sills of the buggy, and, in her struggles, it was like being threshed with the dull edge of a mattock.

While the man Jess clutched her shoulders and dragged her brutally from the carriage, the other man hung securely to her legs until she was hauled out far enough to drop free of the wheels. Her scraped legs and hips hit the hard road. Pain and shock of it told her they had her close to where they could use her.

Until the other man could get himself out of the buggy, and to her, she gave her handiest assailant a wrenching fight with flailing legs and a back battering of the head that came very close to freeing her. But even a close victory was not enough. A second later, the two men had her pinioned in the dusty roadway. Try as she might, she couldn't prevent them dragging her across the road's hard ruts to the grassier margins of the ditch bank, in the hiding shadows of the poplar row.

"Shall I turn the horse loose?" yelled the man up front.

"Hell no!" Jess called back, panting hard. "Wanta arouse the town? Pull the goddamned horse an' buggy over to the tree line. Round up all the mounts, an' tie 'em. While you do it—we'll get the midwife ready for a miscarriage."

"Hadn't we better find out from her where the Swede hides, before we doodle her?" asked the man called Jim.

"Naw. Pull off that blab, an' she'll only start howling. After a good Mormon massage, she'll feel more relaxed—an' maybe more like talkin'."

"This is gonna be real gay," laughed Jess. "Two men holdin', with one man friggin'. It'll be the craziest delivery this midwife ever had. Wish Oddy would get them damn horses tied. I've a hankerin' in my pants."

Silently, frantically, Nancy called on Joel, and Jesus Christ, to aid and save her, before these drunken beasts forever defiled her. Thoughts of what was coming sent her into frenzy. The frantic shouts welling out of her lungs made only slobbery gurgles in the dirty handkerchief. It was too late to tell them about Ansel Christoferson. They were going to ravish her in the night, on a ditch bank—with even this escape denied her. With the strength of a goaded mad woman, she once more commenced to writhe and squirm.

For answer Jess's fist caught her full and brutally in the face. He hit her again, and a million lights danced bright and wild.

"What the hell you doing?" Jim growled, still holding madly to her shoulders as they thumped the ground.

"No use. This cat's full of fight. I'll knock her goddamned head in, if she don't quit squirming."

Nancy felt his free hand tugging and ripping at her skirt. The blood had started running down her cheeks, but she fought to free her legs, to kick the teeth out of this monster.

"You dirty polygamist bitch," he growled. "I'm weary of fightin' you. This'll quieten you!" His free fist caught her viciously hard in the stomach. The single blow pumped all the air from her lungs. She wheezed for breath like a leaky bellow.

"I feel like screwin'—an' I've got no mind to fight for my screwin'. If you don't quit battlin' me, I'll kill you!"

She felt a great chunk of her skirt being ripped from her body, and she lunged out again. Wildly she fought to breathe and live once more. Her answer to this were vicious clouts to head and body by the madman trying to crawl atop her.

"You said we'd draw for first chance," said the man at her shoulders.

"You guys can draw—but I'm gettin' on! Jesus—she's as crazy as that Mexican chick at Laredo. I may have to break both her goddamned legs."

"But Christ, Jess, you could at *least* wait for Oddy to put up the horses."

"Wait hell! I'm vibratin' all over!"

The exuberance of his pounding fists was driving Nancy out of consciousness.

And then, above the pain, the wild and shooting lights in her eyes, and the whistle and ring in her ears, she could hear other men's voices. The voices were weakly distant, querulous, but they were not of the two who were forcibly violating her.

It was faint, faded in and out as she battled for consciousness; but someone else was talking to the man with the horses. And then she knew the voice, and the joy of it whimpered itself into the dirty mouth gag.

"It's Cove, for crissakes!" laughed the man at her shoulders.

In the throb of her pain, Nancy quit fighting, and waited.

"Just in time t'join our party," she heard Jess laugh insanely.

"Who's the woman?" she heard Cove demand.

"Why, the midwife. Just delivered another Mormon bastard to the Swede. Now she's gonna deliver us!"

The silence dug deep, and ominous.

"You filthy swine!" she heard Cove suddenly howl out in the night. "You goddamned rotten, filthy swine!"

There was a burst of gunfire. And it was at such close range the flash of it penetrated the wild and streaming lights of her vision. The great weight shuddered, moaned, and rolled off her. Another gun spoke, almost at her head. Three more shots stabbed and barked into the night. And with them, the last fight went out of Nancy.

She felt someone fumbling and tugging at the mouth gag. Consciousness returned enough for her aching body to resume the fight.

"It's me, Nan," she heard Cove's voice at her ear.

And then the gag came off her mouth, and she sucked desperately at the free and clean night air.

"What in God's name are they trying to do to you?" Cove asked. She tried to answer. But could only bawl like a baby.

And then her sore and pain-wracked body was lifted, tenderly, carefully, and she felt as though she were soaring like a gull.

The familiar quilted leather of the carriage seat came out of the blackness to touch the ache of her head and body.

"Lay quiet, Nan," she heard Cove's voice. "I'll tie my horse to the back of the rig. You'll be home before you know it."

And she was home before she knew it—because the dream was long, and full of strange remembrance. Through it she walked, young, free, barefoot, and the earth beside the stream was rich in green, and wild with the ecstasy of spring. Sometimes she cried, sometimes she laughed with the exuberance of love and living. But the important thing was, she never walked alone. For the stream beside the willowed margin was like the creek of Ammon, until one looked close and drew away. Its water was as dirty as the earth's first runoff, and it was deep, and filled to squirming with strange reptilian life that repelled and sent one cringing. But if one didn't look, or try the filthy flood, there was fairness about, and safety. For the earth under her bare feet, as she walked, hand in hand, was warm, aromatic with spring promise, and caressing to the feet. She was young, and giddy, and crazy like a colt, in that first walk with Flora. And they talked nonsense, and the wild worries they'd always had. When Martha grabbed her hand, she was older, and Martha's sad eyes were lit with a new sweetness and dignity. "You've been a good woman, Nan," Martha reassured. "Come with me." And then suddenly there were shoes on her feet, and she walked again, hand in hand, with Joel. And Joel wasn't worried, and the look of wild mischief was back in his eyes. She pulled him to a stop beside the willows, looked at him, and waved her head with fresh conviction. "I love you, man," she said. "I'll love you to the day I die." And he said to her: "I'll love you longer than that . . ."

She was home and in her bedroom when she awoke. It was daylight, she could hear the roosters crowing, and Cove was gone. But Jody and

Marty were there, sitting on each side of the bed, and they were bundles of fright and worry.

Nancy reached out a sore and aching arm to each of them. "You're good children," she whispered.

"We've been here waiting for you to wake," Marty said. "Aunt Millie's in the kitchen, cooking breakfast."

"Uncle Cove brought you here," Jody said, looking as though he'd weep in spite of his man size. "You were bleeding like a stuck hog. We were scared. Uncle Cove said he couldn't stay."

Marty threw herself down upon the bed, wrapped an arm about Nancy, and sobbed uncontrollably. "Oh Mother," she moaned. "How could they do this to you? You're so kind. So sweet. Never harmed anyone in your life."

With aching arm Nancy patted and reassured her near hysterical daughter. "These are troublous times, sweetheart."

"Uncle Cove killed the two men, and bad wounded another," Jody said, his voice a-tremble. "Town's in an uproar. Now the feds are riding after him."

"God bless Cove," Nancy sighed. "I hope they *never* catch him."

"Well, they'll need some swift horses. Cove's a tough man. Fast rider. They think he's headed over the mountains."

"And it's all my fault," Nancy groaned, patting Marty's thick black hair. "I wouldn't have brought this on Cove for anything in the world."

"None of this would have happened, if it weren't for this damned polygamy," Jody half shouted. "I hate the word, and everything about it. Look what it's done to Dad. Look what it's done to you. I feel like buckling on a gun and blowing the world apart!"

"I've never heard you speak this way before, Jody."

"You don't know me, that's all."

"Well, I feel the same way," Marty agreed, still snuggling to her battered and bruised mother. "Jody and I have been talking about it while you were asleep. That is, when he wasn't up town watching the posse form."

"The marshal will be here to talk to you," Jody said. "I told him I'd let him know when you were able to see him."

"Don't let him come yet," Nancy fretted. "It's all a dream, a horrible dream."

Jody arose, walked around the bed to Marty's side, and looked down at Nancy with real seriousness. "Let's go to Colorado," he said. "Let's get out of this town. Let's get away from Ammon. Suspicion, hate, dogging—and now this. This town's a stink. Marty and I have had all we want of it."

"Yes, Mother," Marty pleaded. "Please. Let's go to Father. He needs you. You need him. And we miss him so."

"She's right," Jody said. "Let's get the family out of here, before they wipe us all out! Because, if you don't get out—I'm going. I'm sick of it all. I'll follow Uncle Cove. Feds and Saints both hate him now. And that's a good way to be."

Nancy's head throbbed. She struggled for clear, clean thoughts. But the crisis was here. The youngsters were concerned. Once, in the days of its peace and serenity, she'd loved Ammon. But now, as Jody was saying, it was evil and fraught with peril. She'd had more than enough. She should have followed Joel's first pleadings, and gone with him. Now, an awful thing had happened. In saving her, Cove had killed, and become a hunted man. Suddenly, like one of the stabbing pains, it hit her. She wanted Joel. Oh, how she wanted Joel!

"We'll go," she said. "We'll go. Quick as we can get out of here."

XI

JOEL WAS WAITING AT THE SANFORD STATION LANDING WHEN THE DUSTY little train chugged and grumbled to a stop, and the weary, rumpled Scott family dragged their luggage down the car steps to meet their exiled cohab. It had been the first train ride for any of them, and their two sleepless nights showed plainly in red, cindered eyes, wrinkled clothes, and a final apathetic lethargy.

Frost of fall was upon the dead, flat earth of Colorado, and their breath steamed out like whistling vapors from the high-wheeled, wide-funneled little engine that had struggled through the days and nights in getting them from the nightmare that was Ammon. In the time it had taken Nancy to grudge out a sacrifice sale of the home and farm to the avaricious Gentile buyer who, with others of his ilk, was trodding the heels of the marshals of the polygamy crusade in grabbing up bargains from the fleeing Saints, her lacerations and bruises had healed and faded out. Memory of that night of horror, and what it had cost poor Cove, would never so easily heal, and certainly never fade. It had taken some stubborn resolve not to reveal the whole black episode to Joel by letter. Had she not decided, with the children, to flee Utah, it would have been different. She was glad now she'd spared him this helpless, useless anxiety. There'd be time and occasion in the weeks ahead to confess the reasons for her sudden surrender to exile.

But the flat gray San Luis Valley, already faded out to the first rimy call of winter, was an anemic substitute for the mountains, lake, and poplar-lined towns of Utah Valley. Her first studied eye-search through the car windows, at dawn, and the closer view of the shacky town of Sanford, at journey's end, were reminders enough of her loss. Yet Joel was here, arms outstretched, and smiling. She dropped the battered valise she'd dragged down the car steps, and melted, hungrily, willingly, into his embrace.

"I've missed you, Nan," he said, and his kiss left no doubt he meant it.

"I've missed you, too, Joel. And I've needed you so." She was crying a little. But that could be expected.

The children had dropped their apportioned share of the luggage and lunch boxes to the wooden platform and every one of them, little Edward included, had ignored their father to move up front and stare wide-eyed and tremulous at the hissing, belching locomotive.

"You look tired, girl," Joel said, eyeing her with concern.

"It's been a long hard trip. We had to cross the mountains by team and rig to reach the western terminus of the Denver & Rio Grande. They've still got a lot of steel to lay before they reach Salt Lake. And, with five excited kids, there's been little sleep. Glad am I to reach Sanford, I can tell you. And I'll welcome any bed you'll give me, Joel."

Joel looked at her sadly, and a little embarrassed. "I'm afraid you're in for another tiresome little ride, Nan. The house I have for you and the youngsters is in Manassa. I'm driving you there. There's plenty of quilts in the spring wagon."

"I thought we were to live in Sanford?" she asked in surprise. "Couldn't you get a house in Sanford?"

"No," he said.

Whether he was lying to save her embarrassment, she could not tell, but, even in her disappointment, she'd not press this nerve. Yet it did seem strange that Matey was not on hand for the greeting; that neither of them were proffering so much as an hour's rest to this travel-frayed segment of Joel's kingdom.

331

"A lot of sickness in Sanford," Joel was saying. "I wouldn't want to expose the youngsters."

Sickness my teehinder! Nancy thought. Matey has a roof, and beds. And I wouldn't contaminate her domicile *too* long. "What kind of sickness?" she asked, striving hard to button down her anger.

"Scarlet fever and measles."

The kids, all five of them, had made their way through measles. But scarlet fever was a new one. "I understand," she said. But she didn't understand—not yet.

The bell clanged wildly and noisily on the morning air. The locomotive hissed and belched importantly. The conductor was officiously yelling "All abo-a-rd!" to nobody within vision, and soon the train was rattling its way out of Sanford on its road bed of new steel. Not until the last of the wonder had departed did Joel's children cluster around him for the hugs and kisses that were their due.

Jody and Marty were as disappointed about their short visit to Sanford as Nancy had been. But, old enough to understand the peculiarities of the times, their protests were not too vociferous. They knew that the law's exigencies often forced the separation of Mormon families, and, in them, there was none of Nancy's first-wife jealousies to plague. A moment later they were loading the Scott luggage aboard the spring wagon, and, big and little, crawling under the quilts Joel had provided for their comfort.

Though tired enough to fall off into the roadway, Nancy insisted on taking her proper place on the high seat with Joel. That he avoided Sanford's one main street, with this strange, outlander portion of his family, and cut out of town by way of the back roads was understandable to Nancy. But to her it was as humiliating as it was unexpected. And now were rising some new and disquieting thoughts. The very reason for her exile, as she'd understood it, was to find the freedom from harassment and the peace of mind no longer allowed the Saints in Utah. Was it possible that here, in far away Colorado, the same conditions prevailed? Were the Mormons in Sanford and Manassa hiding their plurality under the flimsy and easily penetrable cloak of outward respectability? Had the long and searching finger of the crusade reached into the last hope of Mormonism—the far-distant underground? Had she sacrificed everything in Ammon, fled her life's homeland, only to meet the same feds, the same officiousness, the same cruelty, the same necessity for hiding and covering? She wanted to ask Joel, but the answer would come soon enough.

"The Saints of Sanford have only recently built the town," Joel was saying.

"I wouldn't know," Nancy said testily. "We saw little enough of it."

"First settlement was called Ephraim, at the juncture of the Rio Grande and Conejos. But the land was low and swampy. There was a lot of sickness. So they moved up here a year or so ago. Now it's called Sanford. And its neighbor is Manassa."

Nancy looked outward, with jaundiced eye, at the sage, greasewood, and alkali stretching to the low blue mountains in the distance. "You'd hardly call *this* low and swampy," she grumbled. "And you can just bet any town with the name of Ephraim or Manassa would be a Mormon creation."

"I doubt the world will ever know how many towns the Mormons *have* created. Colorado can thank the hardy Saints for colonizing and bringing into production *this* wilderness." Joel emphatically stung the rump of the right horse with an expert touch of the whip. The wagon lurched forward, and the youngsters, oblivious to the dark, sad thoughts of their parents, laughed and howled with glee.

Nancy wanted to howl, but not with glee. Any colonization of this barren waste that she could think of, even with Mormon doggedness and industry, could be laid with certainty at the door of a hostile government. Any person, Saint or otherwise, yielding an inch of hard-won Ammon for this treacherous and forbidding land of heartache, would be either fool or fugitive. And in her case, she was convinced by now she was both.

She thought again about the town receding in the distance. "Changing Ephraim to Sanford, and moving it up into the sagebrush, hasn't done much for its health, judging from what you say."

Joel turned and looked curiously at her. She knew he was perceptive enough to sense her credulity, and to know she was fishing for information. "This is scarlet fever and measles, Nan. The lowlands bred malaria and lung fever. When the epidemics are gone, this valley will be a real healthy place to live."

And then Nancy's own perception told her Joel's bragging on this wilderness was only his own valorous bit of rationalization. He was reading her well, as he always did. He wasn't unaware of the shock she'd suffered in comparing this land to the Utah Valley; of Sanford to Ammon. And come to think of it, his letters had mostly extolled the industry and courage of the exiled Saints in building up a new commonwealth, with little boasting on the scenic or cultural aspects of the new land they were attempting to subdue.

"The Mexicans, who live mostly in the hill areas, and along the Rio Grande, brought the sickness. They have lots of smallpox, measles, and scarlet fever. Quite a Mexican population in the valley. I'm enrolling them in the school. They're turning out to be real bright pupils."

Vaguely, as the wagon bucked and jounced her tired body in the swaying and rocking spring seat, Nancy wondered if the other exiled Saints were doing worse. Those who had gone farther south, and on into Mexico, would really know what it was to reconcile the peculiarities of Mormonism with an already established residential population of another faith. If what she sensed were true—that the cohabs were still on the dodge, even in exile—she'd made a fearful mistake in fleeing Utah. Must one move to the Hawaiian Islands to find the peace and security the Saints once had known? She realized her decision to join her husband had been a sudden, impetuous thing—brought on by the brutality and terror of that night. She recalled—now it was too late —that Joel's letters of the past months had shown little urging for her to flee Zion, and that she'd announced her coming without realizing he, too, might be facing some problems.

With gloomy foreboding, she again tried fishing. "Manassa, I take it, hasn't been hit by the sickness?"

The children, under the quilts in the jouncing wagon box, were laughing and chattering like a crate of magpies. Joel waited for a break in the noise before answering. "I don't know of any cases in Manassa," he said. "The kids should be a lot safer there."

"How about Matey and her youngsters? Are they down with it?" "No."

Joel's discomfiture showed the worry that was his, and told Nancy her shots were hitting home. She decided to bide a time before the real unloading. There was no sense in adding to this man's misery by any sudden revealment of that ugly affair in Ammon; that Cove Corey's bloody massacre had been for her good name and for her honor. Oh, there was so much to tell him! But tired bodies made tired and irritable minds. And as it was, there was trouble enough for all of them.

"What about school?"

"I dismissed it when your telegram said you'd arrive this morning. Wanted to get you and the youngsters located." He drove in thoughtful silence for a moment. "I know what an ordeal this has been for you, Nan," he said. "Things are not just as I'd like them, and I'm sorry."

"Is there a school in Manassa?"

"Yes. Such as it is. We'll have a better one next year."

The raucous sound of the children behind them was dwindling as their tired bodies gave up to the sleep they so desperately needed. Wheels of the wagon plowed new dust furrows in the prairie road as Joel took his family into deeper exile. Nancy knew she was faced with the pioneer necessity of making do with whatever one had. This wasn't Joel's fault, and she knew it. In the eyes of the law, he was just another cohab. And to hold any measure of respect through this merciless hunt seemed a remarkable accomplishment. His great mind and tireless energy had enriched Ammon. Sanford, or any other unpromising hamlet where he might hang his hat and saddle, would know and realize the blessing of his presence. As for her, she'd fled to him because she needed him, and the protection of his presence. She hadn't come out to Colorado to raise hell with Joel Scott, or further censure him for the misfortune and humiliation into which the Principle had led. She wrapped a reassuring arm around the swaying body of her man. She'd be glad to see Joel, if their meeting were on the outer perimeter of hell.

When the horses and wagon finally pulled them up the cloddy, unkempt street of Manassa, and delivered their weary souls and bodies to the clapboard shanty that was to be their home, Nancy felt a lot less reassured. To force five children and a pair of adults into three small rooms would take some doing. The funky smell and general filthiness of the place told of the hours of cleaning necessary to make it livable. There hadn't been time to repaper or paint, and the walls and ceilings were peeled, smoked, and as dingy as Aunt Adah's cellar. Even the children shrank back at the prospects of what was ahead. And Jody was making plenty of man-grumbles about it.

"It'll have to do until we can get something better," Joel said by way of apology. "Furniture's as crummy as the house, but it's the best I could do on short notice. There's little choice in San Luis Valley. Mexicans make good chairs and tables out of hides and reed. Their peddlers come in occasionally. First one comes along, we'll junk these atrocities."

"How I wish I had my kitchen stove," Nancy moaned, as she took another jaundiced look at the legged monstrosity that must serve her cooking needs through the weeks ahead. Those good American dollars she'd brought along were going to find sudden, providential use.

Joel and Jody went to the store for groceries, flour, and soap. There was a lot of whining and grumbling from the children as Nancy and Marty made up beds on bedsteads and floor for their first sleeping in this strange and foreign land.

When Joel returned, his arms loaded with provender, Nancy took instant note that his face was pale, that his mouth was drawn at the corners, and that the old ferocity had returned to his wild blue eyes.

"Don't you feel well?" she asked, alarmed.

"I'm all right." He dumped his burden to the table.

Jody came in behind his father, a sack of flour on his shoulder. Proudly, like a man, he dropped it easily to the floor, brushed off the white marks on the shoulder of his coat, and took off again for outside.

"You look sick," Nancy persisted.

Joel looked around the tiny room, unsmiling. "I'm not sick, Nan."

"You'll feel better after a bite to eat. I'll whip up some lunch in a hurry. And there's a mess of picnic grub left in the hamper. I'm worse than my mother used to be. Fixed a lot more than we needed on that train."

"Can't stay for lunch," he said, looking wildly at her.

"You can't stay—?"

"No. Got to take off right now."

"You coming back to sleep with us tonight?"

"No, Nan. But I'll be here tomorrow."

"You frighten me, Joel. What's wrong?"

"Nothing to worry about, Nan. I'll see you tomorrow afternoon. I'll drive over right after school."

But a moment later, after he'd climbed in the wagon and driven away, Nancy knew that something *was* wrong, and there *was* something to worry about.

When Jody returned, she nailed him for the facts. "You went to the store with your father. What happened while he was out?"

"Nothing happened," Jody said, snatching a meat sandwich from the table. "What *could* happen in *this* stupid place?"

"Did he talk to anyone?"

Jody took three chews and a big swallow. "The old man in the store. And, oh, yeh. He did talk to a couple men in the street. They knew him. Probably friends."

"Did you hear what they said?"

Jody looked at her in surprise, and stopped chewing. "No. I didn't hear what they said. Wasn't interested. Why?"

"Well, they weren't friends, I can tell you."

After Joel was gone, the youngsters, utterly wearied by their long train trip, and the rough and unexpected wagon journey from Sanford to Manassa, napped out the late afternoon in whatever makeshift beds that could be made up and provided. Though Nancy felt as though the last grain of energy had been ground from her, she still was determined to do what she could to make their Manassa pigsty at least livable. With arms dead and lifeless as tree stumps, she gave the whole place a slicking up with the broom, and scrubbed out some of time's accretion in the tiny kitchen. So devastating was the wave of self-pity that engulfed her, she could not help but weep openly as she worked. It was well that Jody again had gone out, and the youngsters had finally given up and left her to this bitter mood alone. They, too, hated the place. She knew that. But theirs was the youthful capacity to bounce back to a situation, and they'd find some measure of satisfaction as soon as they developed friendships, and discovered whatever there might be of interest to young people in this seedy, isolated town. As for her, she was as certain as the deadness in her body, she could never reconcile herself to Manassa. Tearfully she flailed herself for ever having left Ammon—for listening to advice, for sacrificing all, for even recognizing such a thing as Mormon exile or underground. She'd married a man, raised a family to the best of her ability, and she'd done no wrong. By what peculiar twist of circumstances had she come to the point of hiding in a burrow like a panicked rabbit?

At least she'd thought she could hold her head high and walk out into her voluntary exile unafraid and conscienceless. What she'd imagined was a simple joining of her husband for safety's sake, had taken on a sinister and frightening mystery that was as baffling as it was discouraging. Not by accident had Joel refused to show his family in Sanford, had hauled them out by back street, and hidden them in this town, miles away. His nervousness and secretiveness told her plenty, without the necessity of waiting for the more candid explanation that was sure to come. Most fearful thing of all was the feeling this was no sanctuary to the exiles. Colorado, in the endless hunt, had become only an extension of Utah. The sadistic, drunken, officious feds were probably as thick and relentless in the San Luis Valley as they'd become in the other far valley she'd fled. Joel should have told her. And then she remembered that her abrupt decision to flee Zion had given him no chance. And she wept some more at her own stupidity.

But there could be no question now about trouble in Colorado's cohab centers. Something Joel had learned, or been warned about, at the Manassa store, or in the street, had sent him back to Sanford in a hurry. There was a mystery in this thing that plagued and frightened.

Weary and saddened as she was, she managed a little more cleaning, and all the unpacking, before the grumpy family stirred back to their senses. Out of the provender Joel had brought in, she cooked up a simple meal of bacon, fried potatoes, and some minute biscuits baked in the unpredictable oven of the dirty, smoky stove. It was a moody, quiet, utterly discouraged family that sat down to eat by lamplight.

And then came the rap on the front door. Nancy turned from the stove, beckoned to the competent Marty to take over, and, with sick, queasy twisting in her stomach, she crossed the rooms to answer it. She wished now she had that bucket of swill or dishwater she'd always kept handy for the feds, but she did move the lamp to the little table along-side the door. It would light any hostile faces, and a little burning kerosene had been known to stop the nocturnal prowls of these ver-minous bounty hunters. Not until she'd backed a chair conveniently close, and anchored her own stance so that her foot could block a full swing of the door, did she open it a crack, and peer out into the Colorado darkness.

"Who do you want?" was her impolite answer to the last vigorous knock.

"Are you Sister Scott?" came a man's voice from behind the barri-cade. "The plural wife of Joel Scott?"

"I'm the *first* wife of Joel Scott," she growled. "What the hell do *you* want?"

"We'd like to speak to you a moment."

"Who's *we?*" Nancy demanded, still unyielding at the door crack.

There were two men; they were laughing, a little embarrassed. Nancy could see a nose, a beard, and a pair of eyes staring at her from the darkness.

"Well, I'm Bishop Goode, of Manassa Ward," said the man at the door crack. "With me is Bishop Janning, of Sanford. We'd like to speak to you a moment. May we come in?"

Nancy sighed wearily, relaxed, and swung open the door. "Forgive me for being sharp and cautious," she said. "And do come in."

The two men entered, hats in hand. She was impressed and frightened by the portentousness of two bishops descending out of the night. The fact they were as nervous as she was, helped a bit in calming her.

"You're wise in being sharp and cautious, Sister Scott," said Bishop Goode of Manassa. He stepped over the threshold, followed by the short, fat little man who tended flock in the neighboring town. "These are troublous times."

"May I take your hats and coats?" Nancy asked, with new politeness and civility, and closing the door behind them.

"Thank you, Sister Scott. But it's just a short, friendly visit. We'll keep our hats, and just sit down a moment."

She motioned them to two of the three rickety chairs in the dimly lighted room. They both laid their hats on the floor beside them, both clasped their hands, and smiled sanctimoniously out at her. Nervously she sank to the hard bottom of the third chair.

"You've brought your family with you, Sister Scott?" asked Bishop Goode.

"Can't you hear them?" Nancy said. "They're making a lot of family noise in the kitchen."

Bishop Janning at last got himself into the conversation, with thick, phlegmy voice. "How many children do you have?"

"Five."

The bishop from Sanford showed quick worry and perplexity at this confession. And Nancy again felt tension descend on the room. "Would you like to meet them?"

"Later, perhaps," said Bishop Goode.

"It's so nice of you to visit us on our first night in Manassa," she said, trying a smile.

"We do try to visit all our people, at every opportunity," said Bishop Goode.

"We think a lot of Brother Scott," added Bishop Janning.

Nancy smiled again. "Everybody does. They worship him back in Ammon. He's a great teacher."

"And he's doing an equally great work here in the valley," Bishop Janning assured brightly.

As Bishop Goode leaned forward, the feeble lamplight played the miracle of changing his beard from dark ominousness to cherubic brightness—at least on the lighted side. Still it wasn't the changing quality of his beard that worried Nancy. Bad news was coming. She just knew it.

"Sister Scott," he began, "the very fact Brother Scott is a respected public figure, and essential to his community, is our reason for visiting you tonight. These are troublous times."

"That I know," Nancy agreed, impatient at his repetition of a thing of which she already was aware.

"The witch hunt started here about a month ago. Colorado state authorities have had our towns under surveillance for some time. Now the federal marshals are here." His whiskered sadness reminded her vaguely of a constipated airedale. "We hate to be bearers of bad tidings on your first night in Manassa, but—"

"What you're trying to say," Nancy cut in testily, "is that you want me and my children to get the hell out of here! I've known it—felt it—from the moment I stepped off the train!"

Bishop Goode flopped back, nervous and cowed by the good sister's outburst. "We weren't trying to say it in exactly that way," he said, wearily.

"But you *are* trying to say it?"

"What we *do* mean," added Bishop Janning, with cherubic smile, "is that Brother Scott already has a wife and family in Sanford. They're accepted everywhere as his wife and family."

"And another wife and family is one too many," Nancy growled, her anger rising.

"It raises all sorts of complications—especially at this time."

"It could send Brother Scott back to jail," Bishop Goode added.

"And it's already proving very embarrassing to Sister Scott," said Bishop Janning of Sanford.

Nancy clenched her fists until the fingernails bit flesh. Her urge was to break a chair over the heads of these sanctimonious night toads. "There's one question I want to know," she said, her voice trembling with hurt and rage. "Did Joel Scott send you here?"

"No," said Bishop Janning. "He knows nothing about our coming."

"Did Matey—Sister Scott to you—send you to visit me?"

"Sister Scott talked out the problem. But we came of our own volition. Safety of our Saints is of deepest concern to us. The Authorities have counseled us as to our duties in this matter."

"To hell with the Authorities," Nancy snapped. "All I can see is the dirty, underhanded work of Matey to keep me away from Joel."

"You're not the only wife that's having these difficulties," Bishop Goode counseled tenderly. "We're making places for them, fast as they arrive—"

"Did Matey tell you I'm the *first* wife," Nancy argued. "That I'm the *legal* wife? That my children are Joel Scott's only *legal* children? I'll bet she didn't!"

"It wouldn't make any difference," Bishop Janning defended.

"The hell it wouldn't!"

"Sister Scott and her family are known and accepted in my community," Bishop Janning patiently explained. "It would be a little difficult and embarrassing for him to substitute another wife and family at this time. You don't seem to understand. In Colorado, we just can't practice plurality openly."

"I understand all right," Nancy suddenly shrieked. "You sanctimonious old goats are willing enough to get into the Principle. You may be in hiding—but it's your womenfolk who do the suffering."

"I served *my* time in the penitentiary," Bishop Goode reminded. "I understand your husband did likewise. It isn't easy for any of us—men *or* women. Not to be circumspect and above suspicion at this time would be disastrous."

"Well, now that I've heard your holy advice, let me tell *you* something. When I married Joel Scott, he was a Gentile. I married him because he *was* a Gentile. I married him to keep clear of the Principle— because I hated it. I married him honorably, as his first wife. Every child I have is legitimate, and accepted so by the law. I've done no wrong. I've broken no law. I'm weary of hiding in the shadows, creeping around in the dark, and being beaten and assaulted, just because I'm married to a converted Mormon. I want you solicitous bishops to know that I'll plant myself and my children where I damn well please, and look the world in the face with a clear conscience. And that if I want to go to Sanford tomorrow, and set up my household, I'll do it. If I want to stay in Manassa, I'll do it. And both of you can do anything you want to about it!"

"And having your way, Sister Scott," said Bishop Janning, "you'd be willing to send your husband back to prison, and destroy your husband's other family?"

Nancy thought a moment. It didn't concern her much as to what might happen to Matey and her unwanted tribe. But to send Joel back to prison—that was something she must *never* do. She heard a rustling behind her, turned, and there in the shadows was Jody and Marty. Strung out behind them, like startled little owls from the nest, were her other children. How much they'd heard of this sickening conversation, she could only guess. The fight went out of her. She felt weary, and ill enough to vomit.

"To keep circumspect, and above suspicion, as you call it," she said contritely, "where do you *send* your unwanted wives and children?"

"We have no unwanted wives and children," said Bishop Goode. "But until God sees fit to clear the air of hate and suspicion, we're sending our plural families down to Beulah."

"And where's Beulah?"

"It's over the border into New Mexico, near Abiquiu. On the Chama River. We've a real colony going down there."

"Then why not send Joel Scott's *other* family to your precious colony?" she argued. "In this house is his *legal* family. We have prior right to his attentions as a father and a husband."

"In the eyes of the Lord, all plural families are legal," reminded Bishop Goode.

"And this present family is already a part of our community," the Sanford bishop also reminded.

And then suddenly Jody was striding into the center of the room. And just as suddenly was Nancy seeing again the Joel Scott she once had known. This new man had the same aristocratic dignity; there was character and conviction in his sober young face. He towered above the squatting bishops.

"We don't like your Sanford," he growled. "We don't like your Manassa. Father can stay where he wants to. Aunt Matey and her family can live in Sanford forever, for all we care. I hate your plurality, my sister hates your plurality, and my mother hates your plurality. We're going to get away from it—some way. You don't have to worry about us. I'm taking my mother and my brother and sisters out of here—tomorrow!"

For the first time Nancy saw in her own family what she'd observed for years in other Mormon families. The older children, forced by the exigencies of divided parenthood, developed self-reliance and mature capabilities in their earliest years. How many Mormon sons, who seldom now saw their fathers, were supporting their mothers and immediate kin in plurality? How many daughters of tender years were mature women in the endless work of keeping these households going? How much had she depended on Marty and Jody now, and in the years past? They were tempered, trained, strong, and willing. And now they were mature. God had been good to her. The fears vanished. For once she felt secure.

"Thank you, Jody," she said, her pride soaring with sudden wings of joy. She walked to this new Scott man, put her arm around him, and faced the bishops with fresh defiance. "You've said what needs to be said, Jody Scott."

"We'll clear out of their damned wards," Jody was promising. "We're not knuckling down to this."

Both bishops were stunned by the outburst. And as they struggled uncertainly to their feet, it was plain to see that both were cognizant of a need for some drastic spiritual advice and guidance to this second family of Scotts. But they were looking full face at an angry young man; at his sharp-tongued, unconverted mother. This, they saw, was not the time for it.

"I think we'd best be going," said Bishop Janning, worriedly fingering his hat.

Bishop Goode clawed at his beard helplessly. "Yes," he said, "I think we should."

Jody, stiff and inflexible as a ramrod, glared on in silence. Nancy, beside him, made no attempt to mitigate or correct his outburst. Behind her she could hear the stirrings and heavy breathing of her children. The whole room was stickily tense.

"Good night, Sister Scott," said Bishop Janning, trying at last for a smile.

"Good night, Brethren," she said, a little more warmly.

The handshakes—for her alone—were quick and nervous. At the doorway there was a fumbling as they donned their hats. The bishops took off into the night.

And when they were gone she turned a proud smile at Jody. "They'll be praying for us *this* night," she said, and looked around at the youngsters crowding the doorway.

"Amen," Jody chuckled. And the voice sounded exactly like his father's. He shoved his hands importantly to pockets, and teetered on his heel. "Goodbye, old Colorado!" he laughed. "Our stay was short and sweet!"

The tenseness went out of the room. Everybody grinned. It was real nice to have a man in the house once more. It was real nice to have the children on her side. But not until this moment did Nancy realize how utterly weary she was.

XII

THE TOWN WAS BEULAH. AND BY WAGON AND HORSES, IT WAS A WEEK AWAY. Whether its name of Beulah was meant as the allegorical term for Israel, the sweet promised land where trials would be in the past, or whether it was named for one of Mormondom's plethora of wives who were finding escape and security there, Nancy had no way of knowing—and for this time, at least, cared less. All she knew was that the Mormons had taken over La Puenta, on the Chama River, near Abiquiu, renamed it Beulah, and Joel was taking her there.

The big wagon, packed with a month's provisions, slithered, bucked, and chattered as it ground the dusty miles southward. In less than half a day from Manassa, they had crossed the state line into New Mexico

343

near the Mexican town of Antonito. Constantly, to their right, were the slate-blue peaks of the San Juans, and every stop for water or rest was in hamlets occupied by Spanish-speaking natives. And even these natives, polite and courteous as they were, looked on the traveling Mormons, with their preponderance of women and children, with amusement in their eyes. Jody and Marty, on the fast little Spanish horses Nancy had bought them in Manassa, brought up a chattering and excited rear guard to the Scott wagon pioneers of the cohab decade. The three smaller children had their choice of sharing, in rotation, the driving seat with their parents, or the more solid comfort of the wagon bed, where Nancy had made them a snug little den, padded with blankets and quilts, where with the wagon cover pulled over their heads, they could sleep and talk in cozy comfort. Two other wagons stretched out for a quarter of a mile behind them, one from Manassa, and one from Sanford—visible evidence that the problem of excess wives was not altogether confined to the Scott family.

It seemed wholly fantastic to Nancy, as she rode in moody silence, that less than two weeks from the time she'd relinquished her home in Ammon, and abandoned the town of her childhood, that she'd be sitting on a thumping wagon, headed down desolation's trap, into New Mexico. Discovery that she and the children were excess baggage in Colorado, and a source of embarrassment and danger to Joel, had stirred up enough sullen anger in her to send her back to Utah by return train. It had taken a lot of talking, with the bishops and Joel present, and in which the older children mixed freely, to bring about this decision to hole in for the winter with the cohabs. Joel, embarrassed and hurt by the turn of events, argued long and earnestly against any return to Ammon—especially after Jody filled him in on the horrors of that night, and Cove Corey's murderous fight to save her. "Please, Nancy," he'd begged. "Now that you're here, stick it out a while. By next year I'm certain the hunt will be over. Then we can all return—unafraid, and with our heads up. And I need you, Nan. If you stay in Manassa, we'll make the best of it, in spite of what the bishops say. If you winter in Beulah, I'll drive you down there, and I'll come down as often as school will let me. When school's out, I'll spend all summer with you and the kids. Let's stay as near as we can to one another, until this thing blows over."

She hadn't believed it possible, but, undeniably, she was on her way. And only the fact she lived in cringing fright of Ammon and its bounty hunters, the fact she desperately loved and needed Joel in any measure he could give her, and that she believed with him that the crusade must certainly end soon, had induced her to chuck pride and remain in the underground. But even with that decision made, and much as she'd wanted to, she couldn't endanger Joel by remaining in Manassa.

It would have been sheer pleasure to root out Matey, and the smug priority she'd gained for herself in Sanford, but doing it would have placed her at cross-purposes with Joel, and wiped out any public acceptance even a first wife and her family might have had from the Colorado Saints. Lord knew there was enough trouble and heartache in this thing without stirring up any more. But it was the adventurous appeal of a wagon trip into New Mexico—Grandfather's Mormon plains journey lived again—that had won over Jody, and fired him and the children in favor of the idea. When Joel agreed to take time out from school, and personally accompany the little expedition, Nancy, with all her reluctance, was voted down. Horses and saddles were bought, the wagon was packed, and they'd headed for Beulah.

And now, as they rolled deeper into the lands of the Spanish-speaking race who had claimed the ground long before the greedy Americans or harassed Mormons, Nancy had plenty of time to think over the strangeness of her own life—with its high points of happiness, with its low points of despair. This was certainly not the peace of Ammon, nor the paradise on earth toward which all Mormons strove to the last breath of their bodies. But this was life, and it was wise in any Saint to take and accept whatever life was willing to give. This couldn't go on forever. There *must* come a better day.

As Joel rocked and teetered in the seat beside her, she knew that these were hard, cruel years for him. If the Gentiles could only see how wrong was their picture of the lascivious Mormon cohab! Joel could still stand proudly, and a little arrogantly, but most cohabs looked like beaten dogs. All had paid a full, desperate, and degrading price for their religious adventure. What this crusade had done to the courage, self-reliance, and material possessions of the men who had conquered a wilderness was incalculable. The tragedy it had wrought upon their loved ones would be written into Mormon hearts for generations to come. It was a black and solemn time in their history. Nancy knew she never could reverse or erase the events that had brought its abrasive and scabrous tentacles into her own life. Joel loved Ammon, and the good free life as much as she did. Joel was into this thing up to his ears, and there was no turning back. Joel had suffered, as she had suffered. She loved him now, as deeply as the day she'd married him. She'd try and quit her grumbling. She'd try hard to weather out the storm with him.

"There's one thing about Beulah," Joel was saying, as the weary team lazed them along the twin ruts that served as road, "it has little to fear from Indians. And the Saints have little to worry about the Navajos or Apaches. These tribes have made it rough enough for Mexicans and 'Americats,' but Jacob Hamblin and the missionaries have taught them that Mormons are their friends. Incidentally, these Indians practiced plural marriage long before Mormons were even heard of."

"I hope they're as happy with it as *we* are," Nancy said, thinking how weary were her buttocks in this long ride into polygamy's haven.

There was an ancient feel, a brooding sense of mystery to this land across whose scarred, strange face they were hunting sanctuary. Joel had assured her they would see Indians before they arrived at Beulah— possibly roving bands of Navajos, or the more gentle Lamanites of the pueblos, whose towns and villages grew more numerous in the southern country. So far they had met not a single Lamanite of any tribe, and the cliff houses, and decaying ruins, indicated only the more ancient and departed peoples of which the *Book of Mormon* spoke. The fact that Joel allowed Jody to strap on a six-shooter as he rode, and which swelled the young man with pride, stemmed from thought of meeting some possible immediate danger, rather than any peril of the phantoms that walked the brush and patch woods of this mysterious land. As a Mormon, Nancy knew the veil between mortality and mystery was as thin as spider-silk. In and out, among the living, walked the spirits of the departed. God, prayer, or any sudden miracle could change the mortal eye to see this strange world of the unborn and the dead. Many a Saint had publicly and privately testified to having walked and talked in this waiting land of the immediate beyond. But under the brooding blue haze of the day, the shadows and starlit skies of night, so inherently a part of this highland country of New Mexico, this world of spirits seemed uncomfortably close. Even the Mexicans they encountered, in their mud villages, were like no other Americans Joel or Nancy ever had known. Always they were smiling, generous, and polite, but about them clung an other-world quality as mysterious as their land. Their older men looked like patriarchs, their younger men moved with the stealth and sureness of the wraiths of the night. One instantly sensed their soul-deep religiosity—as deep in their own way as was that of the hunted Mormons who eyed and tried to understand them. Their adobe churches were dark, mysterious, lined with strange images. The effigy of death, in the coffin at the altar, was their constant reminder in mystery of the unseen world about them.

"These are Gentiles," Joel explained, "but like no other Gentiles on earth. Under the cross, and the flag of Spain, they penetrated north from Mexico into this hostile land, in similar mass movement to that of our own Mormon pioneers. And these Mexicans were pioneers—of superb quality. They fought the land, and they cajoled and battled the Indians, for this privilege of living. In the bloody Indian revolution of a century ago, the Mexicans were utterly defeated, their priests massacred, their churches destroyed. Contact with their mother country was cut off, and those of these people who were not annihilated were isolated and hemmed in by the savage Apaches and Navajos. Though they intermarried with the pueblo tribes, they retained their Christianity, and embellished it, in their isolation, with a liberal dose of pagan imagery and demonism. Because they, too, have suffered, they, in turn, are tolerant of us and our suffering. They allow us to live among them, without turning the sword upon us—unlike the Gentiles of my own immediate Protestant faith. I say, God bless them for their gentleness of spirit and goodness of heart. You and the kids will be safe in Beulah, Nan."

"I just don't feel safe in any part of this country," Nancy said. "At night, when we camp, we huddle like rats in a nest. Your Mexicans may be gentle, and full of God's love, but they look mighty strange and sinister to me. Even the kids think so."

"This is the land of the Penitentes. These people live the sufferings of Jesus until it shows in their faces, and actuates their very lives. During Passion Week they go to the hills, scourge themselves, mutilate their bodies, drag heavy crosses, and re-enact the crucifixion in its every bloody detail. It's said that actual dying on the cross is not uncommon. I saw this stark drama only last year, and I'll never forget it."

"Did they crucify a man?" Nancy asked, astonished.

"No, they cut him down in time. But he was a bleeding mess." Joel drove on in silence. "I have to agree with you, Nan," he said at last. "There're ghosts in this land. But they're not the sort of ghosts the Saints need have fear of."

The fourth day of their wearisome journey brought them into the mud town of Tres Piedras. And it was there that Bishop Janning caught up with them. As usual, the two wagon groups of Saints had wheeled into camp for neighborly solace, and mutual protection—this time a hundred yards north of the little Mexican village, and close to the single stream for the watering of stock, culinary needs, and a general cleaning up after the day's dust and wind. The bishop's horse, from the unmerciful pushing it had gotten on this frantic ride south, was lathered and stumbling with fatigue.

As the fat little man rolled from the dusty saddle, Jody caught up the weary animal and led it to the stream for water and feed.

"Thought I'd *never* catch up with you," the bishop said as, beating the dust from his clothes, Joel brought him to the campfire. At the edge of the circle, and before Nancy could beckon or invite him to share supper, he turned to Joel, and his face was solemn. "Brother Scott, I've bad news for you."

"Bad news?"

"Your baby's dead. Your family's down sick."

Joel gulped, stared, and lowered his head. "Scarlet fever?" he said, as if afraid.

"Yes, Brother Scott. Scarlet fever. It's raging in Sanford."

"The babies were ailing when I left," Joel sighed. "Matey thought it was only a sore throat and a cold. And now—"

"This week it seems like most every family in Sanford's been hit. Our children are dying like flies. I've got to get back."

"Sup with us, Bishop," said Joel. "Stay with my family tonight, while you catch a little sleep, and rest your horse. And perhaps you can prevail on Brother and Sister Chester, our neighbors, for them to travel along with my wife and children to Beulah. You know; sort of get them set up for housekeeping there. I'm heading back for Sanford—quick as I can saddle." He looked sadly and helplessly at Nancy. The firelight played on his weather-bronzed face, and Nancy saw the tears in his blue eyes. Sight of it all but caved her in.

What she saw was one of the imponderables of her life as a Saint. Joel Scott loved this baby, by another wife, with the same parental ferocity shown toward the children of her own issue. His baby was dead; his other children probably dying. This was a fact neither logic nor wishful thinking could whisk away. Joel had been hit a blow that staggered him. He'd suffer more before this thing was over. And this same blow had hammered closer to her than ever she could have imagined. As a family, they were one, in plurality, or out of it, and that was something not to be denied.

Joel continued to look at her soberly. When he spoke, it was slowly, with lips that quivered in the firelight. "I know it's asking a lot, Nan. But God's put a heavy need upon us for you. Could you—could you— find it in your heart—to come back with me?"

Nancy shut her eyes as she sparred with her thoughts. "I can't take my children back to this danger, Joel."

"Didn't mean that. Bishop Janning will arrange for Brother Chester to watch them close into Beulah. Jody's as good as any man you'll ever

348

find. Marty and Vernell are smart enough at taking care of things. I need *you*, Nan. I need you as I've never needed you before in my life."

"Would my going back endanger you, Joel? Remember, I'm on my way to Beulah because of the feds."

"You'll be Matey's sister. It'll not be the first time you've been Matey's sister."

Nancy thought a moment. She looked long and sadly into the fire. She glanced up at the solemn round face of the bishop who had ridden so hard and so far. She peered steadily and kindly into the tear-clouded eyes of the man she'd love and serve as long as there was breath in her body. "I'll go with you, Joel," she said at last.

The Spanish ponies Jody and Marty had ridden into New Mexico were pushed out of the state and northward with all the speed that could be driven or coaxed from them. Nancy had packed the saddlebags with a little dried beef, biscuit, and whatever eating scraps had been left over from their last meal at Tres Piedras camp. After admonishing the children as to their duties on the remainder of their wagon drive to Beulah, a circle of prayer, by firelight, joined by Bishop Janning, but with Joel himself giving voice to God in solemn plea for the safety and health of his living children, and a tearful kissing all around, Joel and Nancy set off into the night. The bishop accepted the wisdom of staying overnight in camp, to rest both himself and his horse from the merciless and forced ride south from Sanford.

But when they arrived in the town, dirty, and wearied to exhaustion, baby Sybil had already been buried, and the other three children—Joel, Caroline, and John—were dying.

Matey, driven to point of hysteria with grief and worry, welcomed Nancy with a fervor that was pathetic. But it took only one glance of Nancy's practiced eye to realize that the neat little frame cottage Joel had provided Matey in her exile was truly a scene of tragedy. In the shock of being wheeled out of Sanford as excess baggage, Nancy in her bitterness had been skeptical of Joel's mention of the epidemics that were gnawing at the vitals of the Colorado Saints. One look at these red, fevered, screaming children, and all doubt vanished.

Tired beyond words, but with all the skill and knowledge she possessed, Nancy fought for the lives of these children of the second wife. Side by side, Matey and her together, lugged cold water from the well, bathed and sponged the fiery bodies of the little ones, begged and coaxed them to swallow the healing herb teas Nancy brewed for their benefit. Undaunted by the virulence of the epidemic that was scourging the town, Joel Scott and Bishop Janning anointed the heads of the little ones with consecrated oil, prayed upon their fevered bodies for God's healing and saving power—not only in the Scott household, but in the homes of other stricken Saints. But in spite of every care and skill, in spite of every importuning on deity, death had set its grim hand upon the children of Matey Scott.

On the second afternoon of Nancy's arrival, little Joel died. Nancy had scarcely finished with the washing and dressing of this three-year-old for burial when Caroline, Matey's beautiful little girl of four, slipped out in death with scarcely a sigh. By then, with only one child of the entire family left feebly alive, Matey was all but insane with grief, and required as much of Nancy's care as had the children.

That Matey also was three months along with another child was another complication and worry. Joel, gray in face, reeling with fatigue, looked as though the world's end had at last caught up with him. Nancy felt that the sudden tragedy of this thing was more than she herself could bear. In this hour she was learning one thing for certain—in death and sickness, all women were sisters. And she was ashamed for the evil things she'd thought about this little woman with the strange talk.

From the slender store of medicines in the kit she'd brought north with her, she found the paregoric bottle. Into two glasses, she divided its contents. "Drink this," she said to the bereaved parents, each in turn. When at last they were stretched out on their bed, and finally oblivious to the death and sickness in their midst, Nancy Scott turned the last of her waning strength, all the skill she possessed, and every heartfelt prayer she could utter through her tears, to the saving of Joel's firstborn by his English wife—John Radcliffe Scott—the handsome boy of five, and last remaining child.

The fact that half the households of Sanford were stricken with scarlet fever or measles, that death was not alone in the Scott family, and that fear of contagion had gripped the community, there were few who felt willing to turn out to this second funeral of the schoolmaster in a week. Bishop Janning, like most Saints called to that office, was proving himself a true man of the people, and therefore, in the eyes of his brethren, a true man of God. Fearless, he walked among his sick flock, blessing, comforting, and lending strength in this hour of trial. The town's plain little chapel was almost empty for the services over the two little pine coffins. Other dignitaries of Sanford Ward were there, along with those of the townsfolk who had no children, or were old enough to no longer fear contagion. But there was nothing in this sparsely attended little service in Mormon exile to compare with the massive turnout at

Martha's and Isaac's last rites. With the rate of death now prevailing in the town, it was hard enough to get coffins built, let alone round up the reluctant townsfolk for a few final words.

Joel's dead children, though born under the covenant, were still under the Mormon age of accountability. Being therefore sinless, and too young to accept on their own of the temple endowment, they were not clad for burial in the celestial dress accorded Isaac or Martha. Nancy had laid them out in their regular Sunday clothes, the tearful Joel had lifted them into the pine boxes before hauling them in the spring wagon to the meeting house. Because of the epidemic, the lids were screwed down tight in the Scott home, and the coffins went to their burial unopened.

Neighbors had scrounged up a few fall flowers. These, with the floral leftovers from the many previous funerals, sweetened up the meeting, and lent a wisp of comfort to the parents. There was the invocation by a ward elder; the dirgeful singing of "O, My Father" by an off-key soprano; a kindly, fatherly, comforting sermon by Bishop Janning; more singing by the soprano; and then the benediction. From the bishop's remarks, there remained no doubt in Nancy's mind about the high standing of Joel Scott in this Colorado community. Here they had come to respect and love him as had the people of Ammon. Joel was a good influence for any town. Sanford was lucky to have him.

Through the service, short as it was, Nancy's mind kept wandering over the vague worries, and the disconnected and patchy areas of her thinking. She hoped the woman left with little John would sponge him regularly as ordered. She hoped, for Joel's and Matey's sake, this child would live. Going through her masquerade as Matey's sister—transparent enough to the knowledgeable Saints—she patted the sobbing little woman, even as she thought selfishly about her own children, alone and courageously driving through the wilds of New Mexico. She prayed God, in her heart, that her own precious flock would be spared the scourge that had all but wiped out Matey's issue. Instead of censure, she now was grateful that Joel had sped them out of Sanford. If her own children escaped, it would be from the fact Joel's fears had been as providential as they were inescapable. She'd seen the deputy marshals of Sanford, in her quick little journeys to the store for drugs and sick-bed supplies. The same swaggering, officious sadists one could observe in any Mormon town. There had been, and still was, reason enough for Joel to walk with care, even in exile. Still, the feds had one item of credit to their blacklist of crimes against this people—they had kept her and her family out of Sanford and its sickness. Unknown to them, they'd

351

probably saved her own children's lives—and for this she could forgive them a bushel.

She was ashamed for the way she drowsed with weariness, even as she sat the mourner's bench with Joel and Matey. But they should know she was tired, tired, even though her heart was right with them. No woman living could burden her soul with rancor in face of the ineffable sadness of this thing. A child was a living part of you. In or out of plurality, when it died, some of you died, and was buried with it. But in spite of the sorrow, her mind sparred with the inconsequential things —things like the never ending mystery of Joel's change from a carefree young Gentile into a burdened cohab, sorrowing in exile for a child born under polygamy. Then there were the little things, like the time, at the penitentiary, when Matey had posed as *her* sister. Now it was Nancy's time to pose—praying all the while that the feds of Sanford would somehow fail to detect the falsity of it, and leave poor Joel alone in his shock and in his sorrow.

When the sad little meeting finally came to its end, the townsfolk carried out the tiny coffins and slid them carefully, side by side, to the bed of the wagon. Loyally they followed this unfuneral-like hearse, driven by a ward elder, to Sanford's busy little graveyard. The mourners —Joel, Matey, and Matey's sister, Nancy—rode in a neighbor's surrey. At the cemetery, it was Joel himself who dedicated the graves.

In this tragic little pageant, as the man she loved prayed over three graves—one freshly filled, two freshly opened—Nancy herself broke into shuddering sobs. The prayer, in its beginning, was the usual Mormon plea on God to make holy the ground, to receive the loved ones, to protect it forever against defilement and molestation "until the resurrection of the just." And then, in the voice of a strong man, quavering in unanswerable grief, came the real prayer.

"Oh, God my Father, receive, and accept, my little ones. Let them be beautiful and precious unto Thee, as they have been beautiful and precious unto us, their parents. Help to blot out of our hearts the bitterness we feel, that these innocent loved ones should be struck down in our exile, far from their natural homes, dying needlessly because of the hates and persecution of men.

"Strike this dagger of oppression, death, and destruction from the hands of the great nation we all love. Bring soon to this hallowed and precious America a time when tolerance will reign, and justice will truly prevail. Take away from the high places that evil urge to use soldiers against citizens, to fling armed and rapacious might against fellow Americans, for the sole reason that these fellow Americans may think differently, dress differently, wear skins of another color, or be guilty of the high sin of disagreeing. Please God, protect the minority against the majority, whoever they may be, wherever they may be. For the different American, the little American, never had greater need of Thee."

XIII

BY SOME MIRACULOUS CLAIM ON GOD'S MERCY, URGED AND AIDED BY prayers and around-the-clock ministrations of the two wives, little John Radcliffe Scott survived the epidemic that had all but wiped out Matey's family. The shock, the tragedy, the horror of this loss was never more apparent than upon the return to the empty little house that once had rocked and vibrated to the noise of happy, healthy children.

Nancy's anxiety to return to her own youngsters was made doubly poignant by the scene of sickness and death about her, but she feared to leave Matey until some of time's healing could return a measure of poise and confidence to the distraught mother. Nancy, too, was fearful for Matey's physical condition. Her pregnancy was far enough along to be a real danger should the devastating blows of past days edge her into a stillbirth. Besides, this little woman desperately needed that child, alive and healthy, to bridge some of the irreparable loss she'd suffered.

"I don't know what Matey would have done without you," Joel, in his gratitude, constantly reminded. In honesty, Nancy didn't know, either. The English girl was as trusting, helpless and ingratiating as a frightened and worried puppy. In this crisis she seemed to have turned her entire life over to Nancy, to the point she seemed more daughter than second wife and rival.

In every decision she sought Nancy's advice. In food, medication, sickroom procedure, she followed Nancy's directions explicitly, willingly, with never a hint of protest. If jealousy or resentment were any part of Matey's life, there was no hint of it in face or actions. Instead she seemed glad and grateful for Nancy's presence in the household, and anxious to subordinate all or any part of it to the healing competence of wife number one.

As Nancy fought to save a sick child, salvage a household, and restore balance and sanity to a woman struggling out of the valley of the shadow, she was struck by the odd fact that here, in Matey, was the true picture of what a plural wife should be, according to the pattern she'd understood from childhood. Matey was humble, without guile, willing, loyal, and in every way gave deference to the senior wife in the plural household. It would have been easier for Nancy, and a shoring up of her own convictions against polygamy, had Matey been resentful, cantankerous, or covetous of Nancy's standing in the household. Instead, her good will and acquiescence only added to the puzzle. And how could one hate a person so desperately in need, whose disposition was genial, whose thoughts were sweet, and who radiated love and respect in every breath?

But not even Matey's problems, serious as they were, overshadowed Nancy's concern for her own children. Brave young Jody, who wanted so to be a man like his father, had been tendered the responsibility of driving the wagon loaded with her own precious brood into another mysterious and dangerous segment of this accursed Mormon exile. For all she knew, they, too, might be sick or dead. And the anxiety she suffered plagued her own thoughts and dreams through every hour she was away from them. Joel, too, in spite of his more immediate travail, appeared a little worried about them, in spite of the assurances he gave her to the contrary.

Nancy was maddened with the thought she had no right to expect Joel to tear himself away from this troubled household, in its most desperate need of him, to take up the return journey through the wilderness of New Mexico. "Find out if any of the Saints are going south in the next few days, and I'll tag along with them," she desperately suggested. But the season was late, the Sanford Saints were immersed locally in trouble, and all Joel was able to get was the nebulous promise that someone might possibly take off for Beulah in a week or so. From Manassa came the same uncertain response. But each day of her Sanford stay forged more solidly Nancy's resolve to get back to her children. Either she could make the demand on Joel to take her, or hazard the trip alone. In deference to the miseries fate had already piled upon him, she had no heart to force this issue with Joel. At first opportunity, she'd saddle up the Spanish mounts, ride one, lead the other, and slip out with only a note to mark her departure.

It was the night that John was well enough to sit up with them and have supper at the table that the kitchen window rattled with the gravel thrown against it. Joel's face, happy one moment with the joy of seeing his son well enough to eat, instantly grew drawn and grave with a flood of worry.

"Nan," he whispered, "while I buckle into my gun, you hide in the pantry. Whoever it is, I'll bring them in the front door. Listen well. If it's feds, you slip out the kitchen door. If the corral's free, grab a horse, ride south, hell for leather. If they've got us tightly watched, wiggle out afoot. Make for Manassa, and the old house there. I'll join you when I'm free."

As Nancy dropped to the floor, to crawl for the pantry, she took one quick look at Matey. The woman's face was white with fear, but her lip was buttoned down with determination against hysterics. The girl had learned to be a real Mormon wife. As she crawled across the floor, Nancy heard the determined strides of her husband, as he went to the hallway peg for his gun. She was well inside the tiny room, with its sourish lacteal smell of a thousand milk skimmings before she heard the opening of the front door.

The time seemed endless, and she feared for Joel's life and safety as she waited out his interview with whoever it was outside in the darkness. Joel would never be a man to be taken by surprise, and he could handle himself at gunpoint or with fists. But if it were a pack of deputy marshals, he'd be helpless. Neither she nor Matey might see him again—unless it were in a coffin, or in the zebra stripes of imprisonment. She could hear the murmur of Matey's voice as, like any other worried mother, she led the pale and frightened John back to his bed.

Nancy had just about made up her mind that Joel was captured, and was herself ready to flee the pantry and head for the yard, when at last she heard the men's voices. The front door was opened again. Nancy stepped to the pantry doorway and listened intently. Talk she heard seemed jovial, and she could detect nothing querulous or officious in the conversation. She heard Joel speak, and strained for identification of purpose or topic in the other man's voice before bolting out the door to the horses. And then she sensed a familiar ring to the masculine gabble in the parlor. The hellish, chuckling laugh bit deep into memory. There was no mistaking. It was the voice of Cove Corey.

Instead of ducking out the back door, Nancy headed straight through the house to the men.

At sight of Nancy, Cove folded her into his arms, held her tight, and muttered "Half sis!" He kissed only the top of her head, but she knew it was not an effort to hide a whiskey breath, for now he was nuzzling her affectionately with his whiskers. "They've got you way t'hell and gone out here," he said. "And I've come way t'hell and gone t'see you."

"Oh, Cove," Nancy murmured achingly. "I thought you'd gone forever."

As an alert and dutiful Mormon wife, Matey already was pulling down the window shades. She lit another parlor lamp, and the seeing was better.

"Cove wasn't sure of the house," Joel added. "He wasn't sure of me. But never was a man more welcome."

Cove ignored him, held Nancy out at arm's length, and grinned. "You're skinny, Nan. Don't teacher feed you?"

She looked at his whiskers, the frayed buckskin shirt, the saddle-glaze of his leather Navajo pants. All her life she'd known how special she was to this broncho in the family. And now she was thinking of all he'd risked and, in this moment, still was risking. Her tears threatened to turn into a real bawl. "You're not looking so fat and lardy yourself," she managed to say.

"I'll put another plate on," Matey added happily. "We'd only just sat down to eat. I know you're starved."

"Yes," Joel said brightly, touching Cove's sleeve. "Please sit with us."

Cove shrugged off Joel's bid at friendship. "I'll set with you," he grudged. "Because I *am* starved."

Joel tried again. "Can I be the first to acknowledge our debt to you, Cove? Nancy's told me all."

"Don't wanta talk about it, teacher," he snarled. "Not a fit thing for us t'rag about—'cause I'd start with a few questions. Maybe questions like—where th'hell were *you* that night?"

Joel, still unshaken, looked at him, kindly, soberly. "Nevertheless," he said, "I'm grateful, beyond any words I can utter."

"Well, don't strain yourself utterin'," Cove grumbled. "I'm not here t'see *you*. I'm here t'see Nan. So climb down off your pivot."

"No man could have done more than you've done," Joel persisted sadly. "No man could have given more."

"Cut it, teacher!" Cove snarled. "Cut it, I say!" He looked toward the kitchen, and began following the retreating Matey. "Your hymn's affectin' my appetite. Let's eat, damn it! Let's eat!"

And when they reached the kitchen, Matey already was setting out the other plate. She heaped it high with hunter's stew. But Cove paid no mind whatever to the second wife, as eagerly he slid into the chair.

Throughout the meal Cove's attentions were all for Nancy. She knew

356

how much Joel wanted to talk on the deeper things. She knew how much he wanted to express in some way the gratitude, and even love, he felt for this rough stranger out of the night. But there was no talking on the matter. Cove would have none of it.

Yet even in its limitations, the meal was a break from the mournful atmosphere about the house. Little John finished out his supper at bedside, with Matey herself helping him, explaining to the child about their weird visitor, and comforting him. Other than that, Cove's rough and affectionate thrusts at Nancy made the meal memorable, and almost gay. When Nancy revealed to Cove the relentless tragedy toward this household in the week past, he sobered, and shook his tousled head, but was non-committal. She sensed he was racking up blame against Joel for this, as well as every other mishap and tragedy that had befallen the Scotts in their hours of trial. In this, she was glad both men kept their silence. She was glad Joel remained the gentleman, in spite of Cove's churlishness, and that he maintained an attitude of warmth, kindness, and courtesy. Still it was amazing enough for tears that Cove would chance it, to search out, in this far place, the sister he'd befriended at point of death. There was no question how Joel felt toward a man who'd defended his helpless wife's honor at gunpoint, and had killed to save her from worse than death. But poignant as they were, there could be no talking on these things.

Yet when it came time for Nancy to tell about her own immediate problems, with the youngsters lost to her in New Mexico, Cove instantly came alive again, and talkative.

"My God, Nan!" he declared. "Let's get down the line and find 'em! That's wild, bad country!" He glared angrily at Joel. "What th'hell's the matter, teacher? You should be down there—watchin' out for your kids!"

"Joel *was* down there," Nancy explained. "He came up here to bury three of his other children, Cove. Both our families are in deep trouble."

"That's polygamy for you! Double and quadruple the families—halve and quarter the husband and his duties toward 'em! Got any ridin' horses, Nan?"

"Two. Spanish mounts. They're pretty good."

Joel looked frantically at Cove. "Could you," he suddenly implored, "would you, take Nancy south to the youngsters?"

"Christ afire, yes, I would and could!" Cove snapped. "Someone shoulda gone long ago! I've a good horse. Nan better take both her mounts. And if you don't mind, teacher, I'd like to get started in the dark. Don't fancy bein' caught in Sanford by day."

He looked fiercely at Matey. "Could you, as wife number two, bag us some vittles, get us some blankets out of your celestial treasure chest, and maybe a pair of teacher's pants for Nan? Sis and me are damned good riders, but we might git empty and chilly."

Again, at the parting, Nancy was grateful Joel, in any emergency, was ever the gentleman. In Cove's goodbye things got a little tense and sticky. "You're a good man, teacher," Cove said, eye to eye, "and everybody in Mormondom likes you. As for *my* likes, I can take you or leave you. I liked you a hell of a lot more before you saddled Nan's life with another woman, and started breedin' a second batch of kids."

"I'm sorry, Cove, if you don't like me, or approve of what I've done," Joel said, quietly. "I like *you* a lot. To the day I die, I'll be grateful to you. You're a brave and good man."

"Honey words mean nothin' t'me," Cove growled. "But the happiness and welfare of little Nancy does! You better be good to her! You better treat her right! You better give her the love and consideration she deserves. Brigham didn't appoint me her guardian angel—but I did! If you don't treat her right, I'll make crowbait of you—if it's th'last damn thing I ever do!"

Nancy, half frightened, half amused, didn't expect Joel to back down, and he did not. He smiled back at Cove, unruffled. "Nancy knows she's got a good guardian angel in you, Cove. Not even Brigham could have made a better choice." He put out his hand to Cove. "We thank you, with all our hearts."

And Nancy looked on in surprise as Cove responded. The two men actually and solemnly shook hands by lamplight.

Five minutes later Joel was saddling the horses in the darkness, while Cove, hiding in the willows with his own mount, half a block south, waited for Nancy to join him. Matey brought out the blankets, and the saddlebags stuffed with grub. Joel made neat bedrolls, strapped them back of the cantles, flung on the bags, and led the sleepy horses out of the stable. And there, in front of Matey, he gathered Nancy into his strong arms. "God bless you, Nan," he said. "You've been like an angel of God in this household." He kissed her fervently and held on until she broke away.

"So long, Joel," she said, a little saddened at parting, but still as anxious as Cove to get away.

"Kiss those precious youngsters of mine," Joel admonished. "I'll pray constantly for all of you. We must stand steadfast through all our trials, Nan."

And then Matey flung her arms around Nancy, and in kissing the second wife, Nancy did something she'd never expected to do. At last, with the agility of younger days, she stirruped her left foot, and swung her right leg over the man-saddle. It was shameful to be so anxious to get away—but she was. She squirmed uneasily while Joel haltered the spare animal to a right saddle ring. A moment later she was headed out into the darkness.

In spite of the anxiety regarding the children, a worry that pressed in upon her every waking moment, and chopped her sleep into fitful segments, the journey southward by horseback seemed ever so much shorter than when she'd rolled it by wagon and team. With Cove Corey along for company, had she been less troubled in mind, it could have been an adventure. The mountain air was winy and wild, the high valleys were riotous with the reds and golds of fall, and Cove seemed to fit into the wilderness as though a part of it.

Not that there weren't somber overtones to his presence—and a perpetual ache to Nancy—but in other ways it was like a return to the days of her youth—those far days when she'd scissor a horse with Cove and Flora, to ride off, like carefree Utes, into Ammon Canyon or the Wasatch foothills. Sobered by the vicissitudes of being hunted, forced by necessity to stay away from saloons, gambling halls, and human habitation, Cove had become like his old self. He still was bitter, hard, alert, and fiery—but once on the trail, a lot of the traits that made him feared of men fell away, and it was a delight to travel with this strange wild man.

Trail-wise and saddle-hardened as an Indian, Cove avoided the settlements as though a plague were upon them, skirting widely into brushland and foothills. It was a tiring experience to ride with Cove, because their stops were measured by his own weariness or hunger. He possessed the uncanny faculty of sensing another rider's presence on the trail long before the other wayfarer hove into view. Not one person was met face to face, though, from side thickets or canyon draws, they watched many a rider or wagon go up or down the lonely road. Nancy was certain Cove's training with Hamblin on the rim, his own natural trail sense, and the sharpening of his faculties in exile would make it hard for a strange posse, no matter how competent, to track him down, or take him into custody. In Cove, both Mormons and Gentiles had lost a good man.

Nancy had known, all her life, that she was something special to Cove. Toward him there was a fondness in her heart that brought tears when she thought of the price he was paying for his loyalty and love for her.

More than any member of the family, good old Isaac had recognized and defended the better traits of the rebellious son, and had forgiven his weaknesses and his excesses. Had Isaac lived long enough to have straightened out Cove's thinking, mellowed his feelings toward the Church, and kept the fatherly bridge open for Cove's own retreat from a young man's fierce hungerings, Nancy was certain the story of Cove's life would have been written a little differently in the Lord's tally. Tragedy of it all was that she herself had been the cause of this last awful thing—this happening that had closed the doors of humankind forever against him, and made his return to home and people impossible. She shuddered to think what her end might have been without Cove's timely and desperate intervention. God must have sent him in answer to her frantic prayers. Saints would never understand him, the law would call him a killer, and try to track him down, but God, Who had used him as an answer to prayer would, Nancy was certain, forgive, and look upon Cove Corey with the same love and gratitude that was in her own heart.

For this strange journey he seemed to have shed all the diffidence and truculence of his behavior back in Sanford. He talked endlessly, hungrily of the early days of Ammon and the walled town. It was a delight the way he could peel back the accretion of time in both their lives to the easy, dreamy, adventuresome stretch of childhood, and it was a joy to reminisce as they rode through northern New Mexico like a pair of ubiquitous ghosts.

On this journey southward, since Cove was in talkative mood, she tried gently to pry back into the bitter segment of Cove's own youth. She didn't get far.

"Do you really think you lost much in the girl Brigham married?" she probed.

His answer surprised her. "Let's forget it," he said at first, and then mulled the thought a moment. "Aw hell, I guess not," he finally chuckled. "A few years back, after the old stallion had gone to his just reward, I tracked down the little gal he'd stolen from me. She's no longer a little gal, I can tell you." He laughed uproariously. "She's as wide as a barn door."

The horses clumped and bobbed along the lonely road. Nancy shifted herself for comfort in the unaccustomed and chafing harshness of Joel's trousers. "Then why so bitter toward the Church and its people?"

"I'm bitter about polygamy—not the people. I'm bitter at the Church because it allows it and preaches it. I had my gut full of it when Brigham took my woman. Whatever she is or was, she was mine, and I had the right to make my own mistakes—and Brigham had no right, just because he was top man, to take her from me. I had a double gut full of it when Flora became the ninth bride of Old Windy Butt. And you've had your gut full of it too, Nan. Why don't you be honest about it?"

The conversation, Nancy could see, had gone quite far enough. She retreated into silence to watch for first view of the Chama River they were seeking.

"Have you ever thought of shaking the teacher? Of running away from him? Of letting his little English muffin have him alone for time and all eternity?"

Nancy looked at him in surprise. "No, Cove, I haven't. Your talk's strange. Why do you ask?"

"Because I know you. You've had a rotten deal in plurality. You're sick of it now. When you get double sick, just let me know. You're lookin' at the one man that'd love to help you out of it."

"I'll stick, Cove." She bit her lip grimly as she said it.

"You any idea where your teacher's sendin' you? Where your kids are now? Where Beulah—this land of excess wives—is?"

"The bishops said it was a little Mormon town."

Cove looked at her with amusement, and swung himself sideways in the saddle so he could impudently hook a right knee over the horn. "Little Mormon town, huh?" he laughed. While he leisurely bobbed with the horse, he drew his tobacco sack and papers. With relaxed casualness he rolled himself a smoke. "We skirted La Madera this morning. When we cross these hills, we'll come out at El Rito, and the valley of the Chama." He took a heady draw at the cigarette, and blew the smoke thoughtfully skyward. "We're aimin' straight into the tribal grounds of the Jicarilla Apaches. And a battleground since God knows when for Apaches, Utes, and Navajos. Your Beulah happens to be within spittin' distance of the spot where the Jicarillas took the measure of Kearny and Doniphan, and all but wiped out every American and Mexican in the valley. In that land there's been Indian fightin' for a hundred years. And so the Mormons make little old La Puente over into Beulah, populate it with unwanted females and kids, in the middle of Apacheland, and leave their trust in God. Only an angel would go where Mormons fear to tread. But when you told me you and your teacher had cut your own kids loose in Apacheland, it give me real shudders."

Nancy closed eyes in quick horror. "You scare me, Cove."

"Don't mean to do that. But since teacher didn't tell you, I think you should *know* the score. That's why I've pushed us pretty hard on this ride."

"They never even *hinted* at danger," Nancy groaned, nudging the horse to faster walk.

"Probably no danger t'worry about. And that we hope. But if Beulah stays safe, it's for one damned good reason only—and that's because it *is* Mormon. If the colonists were 'Americats,' they'd probably be scalped within a week. But because Jacob Hamblin lived with 'em, dealt justly with 'em, and taught 'em that Mormons loved Indians rather than hated 'em, the Navvies, Apaches, and most the other tribes have left Mormons pretty much alone. They consider 'em as friends. Let's hope they're still considerin'."

With her worries already steaming like a hot kettle, Nancy insisted on pushing ahead with speed. By early afternoon they'd dropped down from El Rito, and headed straight across the sage-land valley to the Chama. Over the river, and missing ancient Abiquiu by seven miles, was the refurbished Mormon town of Beulah. They had to ford the river to come upon it, but, even at first sight, Nancy had to agree with Cove—it was one hell of a town.

Like everything else she'd seen in New Mexico, whether it were Indian pueblo or Mexican village, Nancy saw nothing more in Beulah than a cluster of squared mud huts. But even from a distance, she could make out clothing hanging on the lines—and that in itself was reassuring. So long as Mormon women could do their washing, there was some certainty they'd retained their scalps.

"You go on in, Nan," Cove said, squinting casually at the town. "I'll wait out here for twenty–thirty minutes. If anything's wrong, signal me, or get the hell out here. From where I'm settin', I can see women and kids. And where you see women and kids, things are normal in Mormondom. If you find everything's all right, don't bother to come back. And if you don't come back, I'll mosey along toward the Pecos."

"Can't you come in with me, Cove?" Nancy begged. "I'm sure you'd be safe. And I know the youngsters would like seeing you."

"Not this time, Nan. I see no sign of Indians. But it ain't Indians I'm a-sceered of. I'd just as leave not be recognized by Saints, or for any Saints to know I'm in this vale of grief. But I'll come back, Nan. I've gotta soft spot in my heart for you. And if teacher don't treat you right, he's gonna have me to reckon with! Now, get along to your kids!"

Nancy eyed this wild son of Isaac Corey as he relaxed in the saddle to roll himself another smoke. His buckskin pants were soiled, saddle-glazed, and patched. The shirt, under the frayed leather long jacket was in need of a tubbing, and there was nothing fastidious about the way he kept his whiskers. Here was a hunted man, and the big Colt hanging handy and heavy from his well-stacked gun-belt hinted he could and would be a dangerous man to mix with. But no one brother in the immense family kingdom old Isaac had sired could ever claim half the affection she held for good old Cove. Oh, she owed him so much! And in spite of worries, her journey south with him had been a delight. At final thought of his leaving, she wanted to cry.

"So long, Cove," she managed to say. "You've been a real brother to me."

"God, how I hate that word 'brother,'" he growled. "Everybody in Mormondom's a 'brother.' I wanta be something special to you, Nan."

She puckered her face, but the tears rolled out like the squeeze of milk from the whey. "You *are* something special to me. Don't ever you forget it."

"I'll never forget it," he said, and smiled out at her with pathetic endearance. "So long, Nan."

Her mind see-sawed between two worries as she guided the two horses down the clay trail toward the town. Uppermost, of course, was her prayer that the children had made their own lonely trip safely, and without the sickness that had scourged the family at Sanford. The other was the pitiful, lovable specter of Cove, that would haunt her as long as she lived. It was murderous the way life could drag its helpless humans over the rocks. She pushed Tony, her little Spanish mount, and Juan, the horse she was towing behind, to a heady gallop, for the quickest possible meet with the problems ahead—even while with genuine reluctance and sorrow she was pulling away from the man behind her, leisurely smoking out his promised wait.

No Mormon plural sister ever swung into Beulah as strangely and abruptly as did Nancy Scott. Ordinary entrance to the town was from across the Chama ford, and straight in by the wagon road. Like an Apache or a Navajo, Nancy came in by the back way, in a cloud of dust, and by way of the gullied and ancient horse trail. In Joel's breeches and coat, she looked like a man, as she peeled herself from the warm and trail-powdered saddle. But she was a woman, all right, for even through her dust and travel grime, she went frantically searching and asking for her children.

She found all five of them at the old hacienda—all perfectly well, none of them sick—but the entire tribe, with all their belongings, crowded into one tiny room. They'd just finished lunch, on the rickety little table one of the sisters had provided, and all of them were present for the wild and ecstatic reunion that followed. They had endless questions to ask her, and she had endless questions to ask of them. They laughed wildly at their mother, in her rough and dusty man-garb. Repeatedly, one after another, even to the grown youngsters, she folded into her arms, and poured out her affection and relief at sight of them. And then she remembered. "Get my horse again, Jody," she said.

"What's the matter, mother?" he asked. "Going back to Colorado?"

"Just up the trail a little way. I forgot something."

But as she rode back along the old trail, filled with the excitement of telling Cove he'd guided her to the greatest assurance she ever could have known—the safety and well-being of her children—she knew that the amenities had pirated a lot more than the allotted time. Perhaps he'd still be there—and he'd be glad to hear the good news.

But he wasn't there. And Nancy rode back to Beulah with a new sadness.

XIV

NANCY'S FIRST RESOLVE WAS TO GET THE FAMILY OUT OF THAT ONE-ROOM cell. The nameless Mexican, who anciently had built the hacienda, not only had constructed his house for time and all eternity, but probably had been murdered by Apaches or Navajos for his pains. Like all upper-class Mexicans of the landed caste, the house had been his castle, as well as the ostentatious and visible mark of his station. Rectangular in shape, its adobe walls three feet thick, it looked more like a fort than a dwelling. Other than slits, once probably for defensive purposes, there was not a single window to the outside. Inside the small-scale fortress, however, the nameless Mexican had done better. All rooms of the rectangle faced inward to an open courtyard, or patio, with at least one door and one window per room. But the nameless Mexican had likely rolled twice over in his grave at the strange use to which his big house was now being put.

Every room was stuffed to capacity with women, and/or their bawling, brawling offspring. The only time men were seen about the place was when one or more of the Mormon husbands, living singularly in southern Colorado, loaded a wagon with supplies, and drove south for a short and fertile visit with his other wife or wives in plural status— at the strangest of all Mormon communities known as Beulah.

When Nancy discovered the conditions of the town, and the fact that not another foot of space was available to her and her family, she was furious. This was the final straw, the nadir of Mormon polygamy, a disgrace, and an insult to womankind. Every mud hut in town was crammed to capacity with women and children, and it took only a day to realize how utterly futile was the hope of moving her family out of that crowded room into some sort of dwelling. The next day she and Jody rode miles horseback, even into Abiquiu, stopping at every house they saw. Mexican natives smiled, were courteous, and answered her requests with tolerant and eloquent shrugs, or songlike, in a language of which she had utterly no comprehension. She could see, too, that the Mexicans themselves were acutely plagued with the same problem of overpopulation and shortage of space. At the Indian pueblos, it was even more hopeless. The natives stared with stolid indifference at the agitated white woman and, without as much as a grunt, turned their backs.

Inside the hacienda, it was bedlam. All cooking had to be done in the center of the patio. Since more than a dozen families stuffed the place tight as a sausage gut-sock, this was a problem indeed, and with promise of more aggravation when winter set in. To save bickering and hair-pulling among the frantic and frustrated women, a communal system of cookery had been set up. Supplies were pooled for the good of all, and meals were prepared in communal kettles and pans by the sisters taking their turns for the chore. The cooked food, doled out in proper share, was lugged back to the separate families.

"Mother, could this be the United Order?" Jody asked. "The United Order which God revealed to the Prophet Joseph Smith? Where Saints would have everything in common? The system all the Saints are some-day supposed to live?"

Nancy looked bitterly out across the ferment of women, with their children—screeching, tumbling, wailing, and getting in everyone's way. "No, Jody," she grumbled. "This is only some of the 'order of misery' the Prophet saddled on the *women* of this church. I'd hate to think God revealed *this* as a way of life!" Her critical eyes were telling her that at least four of the women in the hacienda were far enough along in their pregnancies to guarantee four more winter problems for her. If this were true for the hacienda, what must it be for the town in general? And long ago she'd come to the conclusion that women would somehow manage to reproduce, even if fate hung them up like the bats in Ammon's caves.

What appalled her about the place was that nowhere in the town was there such a thing as an organized school. The ragged Mormon urchins, all of them, were running around in mischief and confusion. Here were her youngsters—alert, bright, children of the schoolmaster —denied the right to continue their education, in a land that apparently even God had forgotten. She could see now that it was a mistake Joel had not accompanied his family all the way south. Certainly, unless he were as callous and as indifferent as other Mormon men she'd seen and known, he'd never have allowed his family to be thus pickled in this vinegared crock of misery.

Her first letter to Joel, carried north by one of the visiting brethren of the plural status, made known to him that Cove had gotten her through to Beulah, and that all the children were safe and well. And then, for the first time in her life, she finished out a letter to him in stinging criticism. "The place is impossible," she told him. "It's crowded, ugly, and a bedlam of noise and ill tempers. There is no semblance of schools or town government. Beulah is exposed, in the middle of Indian country, and Cove says that the only thing that stays the hands of the Apaches and the Navajos is that these Indians are not in the habit of fighting Mormons. But that could change—and where are the noble husbands and fathers to defend this place? Or maybe it isn't worth defending—and a few less wives and children in Mormondom doesn't matter one way or another! What you'd better tell your noble bishops of Sanford and Manassa, is to *send no more families down that lonesome trail*. There isn't room here for another woman or child. We live like ants. We are forced to share our food in common with others. You tell your bishops to get provisions and warm clothes to these poor people. Tell them to send a crew of able-bodied men to build houses before winter comes.

"As for me and my children, Joel," she wrote, "unless something's done for us quick—*we're getting out of here!* I've discovered that over the hills, southeast from here, is a town called Española—and at that town there *is a railroad*. I've enough money to buy us tickets to somewhere—but that somewhere, I can promise you, will be away from this hell, and away from any man or group of men who say that I, or any members of my family, have to live like rats and animals for the sake of polygamy or religion. This isn't a good place you and your bishops have sent us to, and I don't usually carp and criticize—but this time, Joel, I've had enough!"

Before Joel's answer came, it was discovered she was a midwife, and her hands and time were suddenly filled with problems. And then the Mexicans were hearing of her and, diffidently, and with fright, they came to her for help. Soon she was delivering babies, and nursing and treating every sort of disease and complaint, in mud huts, and single rooms, gringo and Mexican, throughout the valley of the Chama. "*Angel de Merced*," the Angel of Mercy, the Mexicans were soon calling her. And to the Scott door came food, tokens of silver, and the precious mementos these dark and kindly people insisted on sharing with her in their gratitude. The other plural sisters of Beulah were quick to treat her with awe and respect. They exempted her willingly from the round of public chores, and preserved her almost as a precious essential which God somehow had seen fit and willing to send into their tortured midst.

The letter she received showed a sad and chastened Joel. "I had no idea you were being sent into such a place," it said. "I've lodged a complaint with the bishops about the conditions in Beulah. They've promised to send no more families south, and that they will do all they can to get some brethren down there to build houses and make things easier for all of you. It seems, my dear Nancy, that I've not been at all good for you. When I married you, I promised to do everything in my power to bring happiness into your life. As now I look back, I can see that, more often than not, I've done the opposite. I accepted the Gospel, because I was truly converted to it. I'm still trying to live it as a decent, honorable Saint should. We have both suffered—sometimes it seems endlessly—in this thing. For the Gospel's sake, I've given up family, fortune, and respect. Your sufferings have been different, but no less acute and heart-rending. Cruelest thing of all was my forcing you into the Principle, when you were not converted to it. And now, just as stupidly, just as unconscionable, have I sent you and our children to this outer world of Mormon exile.

"Don't think, my dear Nancy, that I'm blind to the injustice that has been done to you. Don't think I've forgotten that, from my earliest introduction to Mormonism, you've been my first love, and my first wife, and that you cannot help but feel keenly about the awkward and insufferable position I've gotten you into. None of us can turn back the past, or change one iota the things that are done and gone. In Manassa events happened so suddenly; in Sanford the destroying angel has decimated the place, and my own immediate problems made me blind

367

to yours. All I can say now is that I feel a new day is dawning. I feel certain that the new President of the Church, Wilford Woodruff, will find a way to induce the government to call off its hounds of persecution, so that all of us may once more return to normal lives again. If you can find it in your heart, Nancy, to forgive, forget—and hang on yet a while—God has promised me in my prayers that things will change for the better. Please, I beg of you."

Even a slender word from Joel was enough to take the fight out of her. With this man for a husband, she'd been wholly trapped, and she knew it. She'd convinced herself it was for the children's sake, when she'd followed along with Matey's marriage and usurpation—in the assumption that, at least legally, Joel was hers. But she knew now, as she'd always known, that this was not altogether so. She'd probably have followed Joel if there had been no children. Things could have been ever so much easier, had she not been cursed with the capacity to love so deeply. So, once again she knuckled down—and decided to hang on yet a while.

But the promised change for the better did not come. The bite of late fall became the gales and snow flurries of winter, and not a single work crew of men Saints showed up in the Chama Valley to make the lives of these isolated women and children any easier.

Marty proved herself a real woman in this crisis, with Vernell fast growing into her shoes. They took their turns at the cold and drafty outdoor cook job at the hacienda—a job made a little easier when Nancy and Jody dragged in jack-pine poles by horseback, and, with hammer and saw and precious nails, set themselves and enough willing women and kids to the task of erecting a cook shack in the center of the patio. They could only roof it with brush, but it kept the old iron stove and dish tubs out of the weather.

All but the most querulous and pouty of the women now deferred to this wiry and officious little midwife out of Ammon. But someone had to take a hand in this hopeless circle that polygamy had set adrift in the lost lands of New Mexico. She was convinced that nothing in God's annals could be as chaotic and unprincipled as a town of manless women, with themselves and their children mixed and mingled, and with uncertainty and frustration hanging as the dark cloud over them. It was like wiring together the tails of fifty cats, and hanging them over a clothes line. She refereed their constant arguments over children, food, and obligations in the female community. She listened to their complaints, and barked her orders like a sergeant in Connor's army. She even laid a doubled fist or two on a feminine chin or two until those with fight in them began to realize the necessity for co-operation and order in this strangest of all segments of Zion. She insisted they purify the open well with quicklime. She argued for cleanliness. She delivered their babies. She nursed the sick of Beulah. And she came to realize that a person could live most anywhere on earth, when one was needed.

But she, probably more than any woman present, could realize how difficult this winter would be. Only thing that kept the little community alive were the occasional wagonloads of supplies brought down from Colorado by those of the Saints who had not yet forgotten their surplus women and children at Beulah. And from this came the most difficult problem of all. The families who received these loads of food and warm clothing usually fought to hold the treasure for themselves. To force them to divide it was the cruelest of the many burdens Nancy faced. But it had to be, or face the danger of the less fortunate ones tearing it from them like famished, desperate beasts. The food that was to last the Scotts through the winter months had long since been shared with others. What was deeply humiliating to Nancy in this despised job of Beulah boss was that Joel had failed to send or bring any more of these necessaries to them.

It was now, more than any other time, she thanked God for the skills Mary Magdalene had bequeathed her. Mexicans had babies quite as regularly as did Mormons. It became more pleasure than duty to serve these humble, kind, and generous families. To them, in their desperate need and isolation, she had come as the Angel of Mercy. Unlike Mormons or Gentiles, she never had to hint or degrade her services by asking for pay. Their gratuities, given to her like holy offerings, was a willing and happy sharing of whatever they had to share. After tending to the frantic needs of some dark-skinned sister in her mud hut, Nancy would go out to mount her horse, to find, tied across the pommel of her saddle the twin bags, heavy with red Mexican beans and redder chili pods. For her services she brought home ground maize for *tortillas*, sorghum, and whatever else these grateful natives could offer to this gringo woman who gave so graciously of her time and skills, and asked for nothing. This food, made up into *chile frijoles* and *tortillas*, which Nancy taught Marty and Vernell to make, became one of the great aids to Beulah's survival through that awful winter.

But more important to the immediate needs of the Scott family, was the fact that the Mexicans allowed no wants to the animals in the stable Jody had built for them at the south end of the hacienda. The two riding horses were absolutely essential to Nancy in the obligations so heavily laid upon her. And Jody made good use daily of the team and wagon. By donkeyback, rain or snow, the Mexicans somehow kept the Scott stable well supplied with hay and barley. But more than that, these observant natives saw to it that each of the children of *Angel de Merced* had his or her own burro to ride. And one grateful Mexican, of more than usual means, after Nancy had saved his wife from imminent death in a precarious confinement, personally brought to Nancy, Pedro, a magnificent horse, with Spanish saddle and bridle, silver-trimmed. With tears of gratitude in his eyes, he'd insisted this splendid gift be hers.

And it was amazing how she caught on to their lovely, musical language, and how she began to understand and appreciate them as a people. At every opportunity she took her own children to visit them, and soon Marty, Jody, and Vernell were talking Spanish like natives, and had struck up real friendships with the handsome Mexican young people of their own age. Nancy was a little ashamed at the thought, but she'd come to enjoy the free, easy, happy atmosphere of the Mexican homes in preference to the humorless, grim, and Gospel-tidy world of Mormondom that pressed in so oppressively from every side. Perhaps it was the difficult, bossy pose she was constantly forced to assume that killed her joy in the female sphere of the celestial order, but it did seem that, tolerant as they were in the concept of marriage, they were petty enough in their ordinary acts and thinking. It was a relief to ride over into the Mexican world, where God was just as deeply worshiped, but where smiles, civility, and politeness were everywhere in evidence in spite of poverty and suffering. Strangely, the Scott youngsters too seemed to have found their greater companionship with the Mexican families outside the smothering chaos of Beulah.

Nancy used her every effort to organize some sort of school, at least for the smaller children. It appalled her to see her own youngsters, along with the many other children of the town, so crassly denied the education that was their right; so completely abandoned to mischief and neglect. Halfheartedly, two of the sisters who could read and write, agreed to conduct a daily class, but lost interest in it after two weeks of endeavoring to bring into line the maverick tendencies these seemingly forgotten youngsters had so quickly acquired. To Nancy, it appeared, the women were far better equipped to breed children than they were to teach them. And so, in their own tight little room, partitioned at night by sheets and blankets, Nancy, whenever time and duties allowed, forced her own grumbling brood to put their noses into whatever school books they'd thought to bring south with them.

But her own hatred for Beulah, and all it represented, grew no less as the months went by. The mention Joel had made of the sacrifices he'd been forced to make—not only in that first letter, but the later one that had promised his visit for Christmas—rankled continuously in her thoughts. True, the Gospel had cost him dearly. It might have cost him a lot less dearly, had he not so assiduously embraced the most controversial of its principles. But, as he said, this was all in the past. Yet there was one thought that would not down. What if, on that mad flight from Kirstine into marriage, they'd managed to clear Salt Lake, and made that journey into the East? What if Bishop Earlington and Apostle Pratt had failed to visit them at the old Salt Lake House, and their urgings back to Ammon had never been heard? One thing for certain, there would have been no Matey Thorpe; there would, for them at least, have been no polygamy crusade, no fleeing into exile, no Sanford, no Manassa, no Beulah. She might have adapted herself to the role of a well-kept wife to a wealthy and successful shipowner in an illustrious and upsnoot Boston family. Jody and Marty would now be attending exclusive schools for young men and young women, and the younger children would be having the best in education that money and position could give them—just as were their Gentile cousins at the present moment. And it was there the thought stuck—to revolve like a waterwheel in her brain.

Jody and Marty thought their mother slightly addled when one day she packed the saddle bags with food, and insisted that Jody saddle up the three horses for the longest winter's ride they'd yet taken in New Mexico.

"Where we headed?" he asked.

"Española."

"That's a day's ride, Mother!"

"I know it. We'll make it there by tonight. Come back tomorrow."

"But it's cold enough to freeze carbuncles into wheel wedges!"

"I know it. It's good for carbuncles."

"Well, what's the point?"

"No point at all. Just want to look a few things over. Vernell and the youngsters will be all right overnight. You just get the horses saddled, and you and Marty bundle up well."

But there *was* a point to her journey, and some of the reasons for it she carried in the knitted bag, which she took with her to the only private spot in the hacienda—the privy outside the wall.

By lamplight, long after the children were asleep in the crowded little room, she'd written the letters. Española was the nearest contact with a railroad. And where there was a railroad, there were the mails—and, in desperation's necessity, escape. The one letter, penned in anger and sorrow to President Wilford Woodruff in Salt Lake City, told the whole and incredible story of Beulah, and the unhappy families exiled there. She cared not how much this revealment might disturb the new Prophet, Seer and Revelator to the Church. She'd meant it to scorch his tail a-plenty—and now, in the privy, she'd not even bother to reread it. But the second letter was touchy, and different. She settled herself to whatever comfort the privy's left hole provided, glancingly made certain the door was latched and, in the dim and aromatic light, drew the letter again from its unsealed envelope.

It was written, in Nancy's firm little hand, to Joel's sister Amanda, in Boston. A little self-consciously, it reminded Amanda of the visit she once had made to the Scott home in Ammon, of the children she'd fussed over, and taken such pleasure in meeting. "Dear Amanda," Nancy had penned in desperation, "these children, denied even the right to schooling, are living in the wintry wilds of New Mexico, like lost and forgotten animals. This terrible polygamy crusade has driven Joel into hiding from the law, and has left his families scattered and helpless. My pleading is not for him, nor for myself, but for his children. Martha and Joel (they are truly handsome) are entering manhood and womanhood. They are bright, quick to learn, and real helpful in every way. But I'm so frightened for them, and so sad. They have no school to go to, and nothing but poverty and hard work. I want them to grow up educated, like their father. And it would kill me if they grew up and married into plurality.

"Please Amanda, I ask you, and it is very hard for me to do this—would you consider taking these two fine children of mine into your home in Boston? They do need schooling, and I wouldn't want them to be hurt under the Principle, any more than they have already been hurt. They've been taught to be polite. They can earn their board and keep, and they will be willing and not grumbling about it. I have a little money from the property I had to sell on my fleeing Zion. I'll pay this, and send more, as soon as I can earn more—because I'm real handy as a midwife, and can make my living at it.

"I'm sick with worry for fear you will think unkindly of me. Please don't. And I pray that you will feel in your heart to do this thing for Marty and Jody. Their father, who lives with his other wife in Sanford, Colo., doesn't know that I have written this letter."

Nancy sat on the hole a while and, in shame and sorrow, had a good cry. Then she slipped the letter back to the envelope, sealed it and, after putting it alongside the Church President's scorching epistle, in the bag, she finished her toilet in shakes and trembles.

The ride to Española was a long one, and a cold one. Jody, already toughened to Mormon manhood through the responsibilities he'd assumed because of his father's prolonged absence, was able to take the trip in stride. Upon him had fallen the endless responsibility of keeping the hacienda and less fortunate houses of Beulah stocked with firewood. As the nearest thing to a man in the town, this had turned out to be a full-time job. But he'd grown into the New Mexico winter, and could take a lot of it. Even Nancy, who had braved many a wintry gale and snow to care for her sick ones, had developed her own weather endurance. But with Marty, less inured to the hardships, this lengthy and wearisome ride was not without its discomfort. Nancy made it worthwhile to the girl when at last they reached the town.

On the long ride Nancy was prideful of her two older children to the point of weeping. It had been no easy thing to knuckle down and abjectly beg favors from Joel's high-keeled family. Proud as he was, he'd probably roar like a castrated bull when he found out what she'd done. But what Joel seemed to be blind to, in his own troubles, was the fact that these two older youngsters were ripe and ready for the inevitable plucking. Marty now was past the age she'd been when Jonathan Cragg had come a-courtin'. And Jody was a year older than Marty. All the fury in America hadn't changed the plural urge in Zion one whit—except to make the Principle doubly difficult to live. Even with feds at their heels, apostles, bishops, and elders were still plucking off brides to add to their holy increase. And never—unless the Church itself decreed otherwise —would the practice of plurality cease, no matter if hell itself moved into the persecution. And therein was the stupidity of the governmental meddling, and the danger to her own children. She knew she was being a poor example of what a Saint should be, but thoughts of Marty marrying some bloated polygamist, and Jody entertaining the popular notion of acquiring a harem of his own, was appalling beyond endurance.

Then one could no longer ignore the possibility that either or both of them might grab off mates from the native population of New Mexico. The Mexican *señoritas*, whom Jody had come to know, were flash-eyed and comely. There was handsome charm to the young men who already were looking politely serious at Marty. Marriage, in either case, would mean nothing but a mud hut in this accursed valley. Yet even that was endurable and acceptable—in preference to polygamy.

The important thing was to save them from *all* perils—if she could. What they most needed was the basic education such as had been given their father—not a lifelong sentence to mud-hut poverty, or an indoctrination into the plural wonders of the celestial order. Oh, especially not the latter.

Smart kids they were, and handsome. Basically, and at present, they seemed to have no particular love for the covenant, and the heartaches and troubles it entailed. But that was only for now. They'd not yet been heavy shook with the mating urge. And one should never forget that of all the plural prospects to enter Utah, the educated, intelligent Gentile, Joel Scott, would have seemed the least likely. The spirit sometimes worked its wonders fast and furious.

Joel's promise of a change for the better had failed to make appearance. Plurality was still being practiced, babies were still being born, and the crusade was still driving Mormons into the poverty and humiliation of exile. As for her, she'd chuck pride and wriggle in the dust like a lizard, if somehow she could save her children from this stench called Beulah. If the eastern Scotts could find it in their hearts to help in this hour of testing, she'd be proud and happy she'd knuckled down to them. Their father, in spite of his Mormon disgrace, was entitled to something from the Scotts. And Marty and Jody would bring disgrace to no one.

The man at Española station assured Nancy that the trains carried the mail, and the postmaster readily accepted the letters. And too, he agreed to forward any mail that might come to her by way of Española, on to Beulah by way of the occasional and unpredictable burroback delivery up the Chama to Abiquiu.

At the town's general store, and with unshakable faith in her dream and in the future, Nancy took enough of her American money to outfit both young people in nice traveling clothes, shoes, and what she thought they might need in Boston. With no inkling of their mother's tight-lipped connivance, they were perplexed and surprised with her sudden decision to dress them up for the bleak wintry season in Beulah. Jody only grinned as the clerk did his best to fit him out like a gentleman, but Marty, dark-haired and pretty, was feminine through and through. She laughed her joyous little laugh, and cavorted and swirled in the flouncy new skirts. And Nancy grew misty-eyed at her loveliness when peeled out of the funereal sacks of Mormondom.

Afterward they hauled all their loot to the frame hotel, and all three of them had a fancy-cooked dinner there. Early next morning Jody scrounged the town for a burro and pack saddle. On it went a substantial load for Beulah. Most useless part, of course, were the fancy clothes. But there would be real need for the bags of corn, for the beans and bacon that kept strange company with those Boston togs on the long miles back.

Within a month Nancy received a courteous note from President Woodruff. The Church was cognizant of the suffering of its Saints in this time of great trial, and everything possible would be done to alleviate the misery and hardship at Beulah. The bishops of the San Luis Valley in Colorado were being apprised of the conditions Nancy had mentioned, and would doubtless act with dispatch. Since the bishops in Colorado already knew of these things, and the road northward was already closed with snow, Nancy dropped the letter in the privy, and did all she could to hold Beulah's polygamous horrors together until spring.

But the one letter she wanted, the jackass mail failed to bring. And after the weeks passed with no answer, she began to reconcile herself to the sickening fact that her dream was not to be.

The Indians came, bands of Navajo and Apache, riding the trails in dignity and disdain, on their way to the agents for winter allotment. These proud men and women, though obviously enough they hated the whites, were not begging Indians like Utes and Paiutes. Prayer circles were held in Beulah for the safety of the settlement. With no men around to defend it, Nancy figured that only God's lightning could save the town in case of attack. And if God had any particular concern for the plight of His outcasts at this place, He'd have provided the men, the food, and the shelter to make it livable.

Then, when all hope had about died in her, and within ten days of Christmas, came that firm, crisp envelope from Amanda, still smelling faintly of the sachet powder that had made it sweet for the beginning of its long journey. As soon as she'd snatched it from the Mexican mail carrier, Nancy retreated to the noisy and oppressive hacienda, and out its back way to the solitude of the privy. Without lifting her skirts, she sat quickly down, and, with trembling, fumbling hands ripped open the packet. First thing to fall out was a bank draft for five hundred dollars. The letter was friendly and sympathetic. "Joel's family, here in Boston," it said, "will never forgive him for the disgrace he has brought upon us. My heart aches for you, dear Nancy, for what you have been called upon to endure because of my brother's acts. We are heartily ashamed of him, and for what he stands for.

"Please know that the seeming harshness of this judgment does not, and cannot, be extended to you and your family. It has been my pleasure to meet you, and to sit with you in your home. You are the legal, honorable wife of my brother. Your children are Scotts, and I know they must be everything you say they are, because I had the privilege of meeting them when they were younger.

"Feel no shame in what you have done, dear Nancy. We would be happy to take young Martha and Joel with us, here in Boston, until you can find a way to get out of that awful land of misery and isolation. You are right, they *must* have schooling, and we will do our best to enter them into the good schools we have here. I mentioned the probability of their coming to Boston to my own children, and they are excited and thrilled at the prospect of meeting and getting acquainted with their western cousins.

"I'm glad you have mentioned none of this to Joel. So long as he can find joy with his Colorado concubine, in preference to his true children, he deserves no consideration. Please do send Marty and Jody on to us. It will do them a great good to see how the non-Mormon world lives. And it will be a happy adventure for us. Enclosed is a bit of financial help in our joint secret. If you need more, just let me know."

A bank draft in Beulah was as useless as teats on a ram, but the letter, considering the circumstances, was a kind one, and somehow lifted much of the shame and humiliation out of the transaction. She would let Jody return the check, uncashed, to his Aunt Amanda of the East. She had enough hard American to get the kids there. For twenty minutes, in the aromatic isolation of the privy, she bawled like a baby.

Red-eyed, but happy, she finally let herself out, and headed for the crowded little room at the hacienda. Jody was out with the horses and wagon, wood-hunting. But it was probably best she tell Marty first. What a surprise was in store for the both of them! And what a parcel of work there was now to do!

XV

FOR NANCY, THAT CHRISTMAS IN BEULAH-LAND WAS MORE LIKE A WAKE than a holiday. Up to the very hour of their departure for Española, Marty and Jody had slaved like grownups, that their mother and brother

376

and sisters might have something other than complete destitution for the remainder of the winter. Excited as she was over prospects of her journey into the wonderland of the East, Marty tended to every chore she could think of. Precious grease was turned into soap; everything was washed clean; a set of stockings was knitted for the family around; everything mendable was taken care of by her fast, competent young fingers. Jody's task had been even more formidable. Every waking hour of those frantic days had been taken up in hauling wood for the hacienda, with double certainty the stack was high for the tiny fireplace in the Scott family room. Providing all of Beulah in so short a time was a task completely impossible for one pair of hands, but he allowed no neglect for the more helpless, sick, and crippled of the exiled women. If for nothing else, these accomplishments alone were proof enough to Nancy that the eastern Scotts were getting something a little special out of Zion.

For all its faults, Nancy was certain that plural marriage stole little from the character of its offspring. Large families, and prolonged absence of the male parent, threw heavy burdens and unprecedented responsibility on the older children. With the hefty work load, always incident to plural families, the older daughters became little mothers to the younger fry; and older sons, in most cases, the very brawn that supported their own immediate segment of the polygamous progeny. The self-sufficiency and competence of Mormon young people, Joel had often said, was an amazing thing to behold. To this, Nancy was always willing to agree. She was certain that in the day the crusade ended, and the task of building Zion once more could be resumed, it would be this handsome new generation that would do it. As for Marty and Jody, they indeed were something special.

Four days before Christmas she put them on the train at Española. Since the town was only a railroad flag stop, the farewells had to be said briefly—which only added to their poignancy.

It was bitter cold when the train blew steamingly and noisily into town. The long morning wait was over. Whistle and bell put velocity into a segment of time. The station agent wasted no part of this time in getting the valise aboard the baggage car. And while Nancy and Marty fluttered through the moment, Joel and the conductor heaved the fat-stuffed carpetbags up to the car's open vestibule. The train—even its conductor—seemed pantingly anxious to shed themselves of everything that was New Mexico—winter, worries, and Nancy Scott.

Even Jody, showing the same adventurous propensities as his father, now appeared as eager to leave as he did self-conscious and fidgety in his new Boston clothes. The tears of his parting were mostly Nancy's—

though the bear hug he gave her was no light or casual thing. "I love you, Mother," he breathed in her ear. "I ever tell you that?"

"Not very often," she said, trying for a little gaiety.

"Listen well, then—because I do. Someday I'll pay you back for all this—the work and the sacrifice." He kissed her hard on the lips, and then broke away, and strode up the steps.

"Just remember what I've told you!" Nancy called frantically as he grabbed up the two carpetbags. "Just show your father's family the kind of man you are!" He smiled at her with a Scott smile, and walked on into the warm and steamy car. Jody was a man, all right, Nancy knew. And if he had a tear at this parting, he'd shed it from the train seat.

With Marty there was more slowness and reluctance. "I just *can't* leave you, Mother," she moaned. "Not like this. It's not right!"

"Tush," Nancy said, once more trying for a smile. "Just remember what I told you," she said again for Marty's benefit. "And write often."

"Oh, Mother," she groaned, throwing both arms around Nancy. "I'll miss you so!"

They clung to one another, swayed, and blubbered like a pair of fools. But that was quickly broken up. The conductor, with a watch in his hand, and hardness in his heart, growled, "That's all, ladies." His free hand whacked them both across the back. "Aboard! You're holding up a train!"

They kissed again, and both were bawling as Marty dragged herself like a limp mop up the car steps. Brusquely, importantly, the conductor waved his arms. He swung aboard, and the train lurched forward. Nancy, blowing winter steam like the slim-bellied engine, ran alongside, waving her handkerchief frantically at the weeping Marty.

"Write often," she called again. But the train was rolling. The train was on its way. For good or ill, her kids were headed for Boston.

That night, in the tiny Española hotel, Nancy cried herself to sleep. But next morning she packed the two burros that had carried the kids' luggage from Beulah, and made ready for her own lonesome journey. Instead of carpetbags and valise, the jackasses were again loaded with corn, beans, and bacon. With the two burros, and the two horses with empty saddles, haltered and strung out on the trail, Nancy started back along the cold and snowy return. Sending her own flesh and blood away had been no easy thing. She prayed God, as she rode, that it might prove out to be the right thing. That somehow she might find courage to confess this brash act to Joel. And oh, too, that God might somehow soften his man's heart to the shock of it!

In the nights before they left, she had tried desperately to prepare her children's minds for the Gentile world they were entering—a task made difficult by the fact that she knew so little about it herself. She'd seen to it that each of them had a Bible and a *Book of Mormon*, and had reminded them of the necessity of remaining steadfast to the faith against every wile and subterfuge the Gentiles would use to confound and confuse them. She'd cautioned them to remember that, in spite of the plural complexities of the faith, that Joseph Smith was in very truth a Prophet of the Living God, and that the thing called Mormonism was indeed the restored Gospel of Jesus Christ. As she told them these things, she had longed for the presence of Joel, with all his eloquence and persuasion. But had he been present, there likely would have been no jaunt to the East, and no particular necessity for briefing the children on the essentials of the Gospel. One did the best one could, whatever the emergency. And this, always being her own homely creed, she'd done her best. But the parting had been no easy thing. The days ahead would be as sad as a wintertime burying.

At Española she'd found enough popcorn for the kids to have a Christmas treat, by stringing the poppings prettily out on thread, or fashioning them into balls stuck together with molasses. She'd found a bit of red paper there, too—enough for garlands to festoon the dismal little room. For their own immediate gifts, she'd bought fur-lined mittens all the way around, including a big, warm pair for Joel—if and when there was a chance to get them to him in Colorado.

In spite of the gifts she'd brought from Española, and the party staged for the youngsters by all the sisters at the hacienda, with its good will, but dirth of real merriment or treats, this Christmas was the saddest one Nancy Scott had ever known. With the two older youngsters gone—having their Christmas on the train—with the general air of hopelessness everywhere about her, even the attempts to smile through the season were enough to make one weep.

The Mexican natives, in their dark little church so gaudily decorated, and so haunted with saintly effigies, held a Christmas mixture of solemnity and gaiety that was somehow touching and beautiful as compared to the almost austere observance of their Mormon neighbors. Outside the adobe structure a shed had been built to ward off the snow flurries. Under the shed was an amazing replica of the stable, complete with tethered live sheep, a donkey, and the manger wherein nestled the Christ child. As a practical-minded midwife, Nancy was glad the literal-acting Mexicans had decided to use a lifelike doll instead of someone's real live baby for the nativity scene. But for three nights it was beautifully alight with hundreds of candles. Nancy took Amanda, Vernell, and Edward to the church and its Christmas scene. There *Angel de Merced* and her own children were happily and effusively received by everyone from the padre to the lowliest family. Small gifts and trinkets were pressed into their hands, and the charm and goodness of heart of these kindly people lifted Nancy's own heart once more to the graciousness of God, and reminded her once more of the fact that even in squalor there was great beauty.

And when she returned to the hacienda, it was to find that her Mexican neighbors had filled her own manger with a Christmas present of new hay and barley. And the next night, amid the prolonged native festivities, amid singing, and the popping of Mexican firecrackers, she delivered a baby boy to a little native woman, in a little native mud hut. Naturally he was named Jesus Christ—Jesus-Cristo Lugo. And Nancy, sad as she was, found uplift and a little joy, in the fact that God had seen fit to make her useful.

Still, in her own heart, she was resolved there would be no second Christmas for her or her family in Beulah. If Joel's life henceforth was to be with Matey, in Sanford, so be it. If rapings, beatings, loss, and poverty would forever prevent a return to Ammon, so be it. If Sanford and Manassa were too close in proximity for the two Scott wives, so be it. No husband, no bishop, no God, no angels would long keep Nancy Scott and her remaining three children in this blighted highland wilderness of New Mexico. She loved Joel, and she loved the Gospel, but not enough to forever knuckle under to this needless humiliation and deprivation. From Joel she asked nothing, other than loyalty and a sense of protection. She'd made herself a good hand at supporting her family, and Joel's protection through this hard winter had been as ephemeral as God's promise to confound the Gentiles. There were other communities in the West. Babies were born there. Come spring, she'd bid Beulah and its snarling polygamous sisters a happy farewell. If the Church and their husbands had decided to let them perish—let them perish. Martyrdom was the seed of sainthood. But for Nancy Scott there'd be no martyrdom. She was clearing out.

But in the meantime there was a cruel winter that had to be fought through—made doubly difficult by the lack of communication and desperately needed supplies from the mother towns in Colorado. Snow had packed the mountain passes northward, and no Mormon hamlet in deepest Mexico could have been more effectively cut off from the world. It was then that Nancy Scott blessed the names of her Mexican neighbors. She had calls now, even from Abiquiu. And without the homely gratuities, in beans and corn, from these kindly, appreciative folk, Beulah itself might have perished.

It was useless to try to communicate with Joel by way of the northern passes into Sanford, so Nancy tried sending mail by way of Española, around the long northern railway circuit to Salt Lake, and thence down into Colorado—and it worked. Her first letter, by the long route, not only explained how she was doing it, but at last carried the confession that Jody and Marty had been shipped East. "When I first came here," Nancy revealed, "Cove had warned me that Beulah was in danger from Indians. He was wrong. The *real* danger is starvation and neglect. This place is a disgrace to the Church, and to those who even thought of it. With no schools, with the necessity of nesting like rats in one room, with want and suffering our constant companions, I feel I was justified in tossing pride aside, and writing to your sister. Amanda was kind about it. The children are gone. I thank God for it. My only wish is that there might be some way to do the same for the little ones."

Joel's answer, as she had expected, was a furious one. This letter, as with all the other ones, she read in the only intimate and private spot at the hacienda—the back-yard privy. "I can understand your feelings, dear Nancy," it said. "No one knows better than I, that sending my family to winter in New Mexico was a tragic mistake. In addition to your sad little letters, the Church from Salt Lake has censured us most severely. We've tried to get through, but cannot. Much sickness is still with us here in Sanford and Manassa. I, myself, at Christmas time, tried it by horseback, failed, and have been flat on my back with la grippe and pneumonia. These, indeed, are tragic times for all of us.

"In spite of any amount of suffering and neglect, Nancy, I am still appalled to think that you would belly-crawl to my family for help. I feel humiliated and disgraced by what you've done. You couldn't wait a few months until we could get through to you. And apparently you are incapable of clearly analyzing a situation.

"This question I ask you. What is the *real* cause of all the misery we are suffering through? It springs from the fanatical Gentiles who are determined to destroy us as a church and a people. Why am I in Sanford, and why are you in Beulah? Because of this merciless crusade against anything and everything Mormon. Again I ask you, who is behind all this? Where does Boston, and the Scotts stand in our desperate battle for survival? My own family's money has been poured into this crusade of extermination. My own family has disowned, disinherited, and kicked me out because of my religious beliefs and my way of life. And now, you Nancy, of all people, add to my burden of heartache, by crawling to them for favors, *by sending my own children into the camp of the enemy!* What do you think these two children will be like when we see them again? What will it avail us to have brought them up in the heritage of the restored Gospel of Jesus Christ, and have them return to us a pair of Mormon-hating Gentile snobs?

"Through the years, Nancy, I've overlooked and condoned some of your apostate attitudes and postures. But this time, you've betrayed me, and betrayed your Church. All I can do is pray for you."

Bitterly, furiously, she crumpled Joel's letter, and tossed it to the lost and aromatic depths of the other privy hole. "What the hell have *I* overlooked and condoned?" she moaned. "What I did, *had* to be done, you pious, plural prig! They may come back Gentile snobs—but they'll come back *alive!* Or do you care whether or not they live?" For twenty minutes, in the little room, she sobbed as though her heart would break.

XVI

WINTER SLIPPED INTO ONE OF THE COLDEST, MOST STORMY OF SPRINGS IN recollection of the natives of upper New Mexico. And, with the advent of the first warming days, the unprecedented snows in the canyons, and on the mountains, northward, sent floods down the Chama and across the lowlands. The waters were just as effective as the snows in blocking aid to the sick and discouraged colony of Beulah. As for Nancy, she wrote no more to Joel. Two more letters came. Their tones were softer, almost apologetic, but Nancy's ire was up. When she saw the schoolmaster, that would be soon enough to talk with him. She'd been wounded, and there was no hurrying in this heal.

She'd made her own plans. Joel or no Joel, she was pulling out with her family as quickly as the Chama went down, and it was safe to travel. In the meantime, she delivered her spring crop of babies, coached her own children in their ciphering and letters, and got the old wagon greased and packed, ready for the day she'd blow out of Beulah. And when she went, she was resolved, it wouldn't be by way of Sanford or Manassa.

The crazy, unpredictable weather held through March, and into the Lent and Passion Week of the Mexicans of this strange valley. And then suddenly, unbelievably, to the natives came the transformation. The joy went out of their hearts and off their lips. The mystic hour of death and crucifixion was upon them.

She'd been visiting a Señora Martinez, not far from Abiquiu, had delivered the baby boy, and night was slipping into morning before she'd mounted Pedro for the long ride home. But *Angel de Merced*, in this, as always, had not been forgotten. Behind the cantle of the saddle was a load of red beans and dried beef that would bring new hope to the women of the hacienda. Hanging from the horn was her priceless instrument kit. She was weary to the bones when she started the long ride, and lazed, half asleep, as wise old Pedro chose his own way.

And then, suddenly, she came alive. The chanting, the moans, the shrieks came from over the hill. Instantly thought of Indians came to mind. She reined Pedro to a stop. Cautiously now, in the dim light, she eased the horse off the trail and into the shadows of a clump of cedar trees. It was none too soon. On the hill, above her, human figures suddenly hove into sight. And then, with a fright that paralyzed her, she realized she was not alone. Another horseman was already sidling toward her.

"Don't scream, Nan," came a familiar voice from the darkness. "Don't let 'em panic you."

"Cove!" Nancy said, with relief and joy. "You scared me!"

"Sh-h-h!"

Obediently she wrung the hysteria out of her voice, and down to a whisper. "But how did you—?"

"Your kids said you'd gone babyin'. Toward Abiquiu. I was comin' to find you, when I ran into this."

"Indians?"

"Hell no. Not this time. Penitentes. Stay here. Be quiet. You'll see something."

"But, golly damn—to find *you* here, too!"

"Was hopin' you'd be smart enough to duck outa sight," he whispered, as the parade of men drew closer on the trail. "You were. This thing ain't exactly for Mormon eyes."

And then, in the pale light of dawning, she saw and understood what Cove had meant. This weird processional, as slowly it rocked past her, was an eerie, unearthly vision that chilled her with terror. What had frightened, as it rocked and bobbed over the hill, was a huge wooden cross, dragged along by a Mexican stripped to the waist, his back a mass of bleeding wounds, his crown of the barbed and lethal thorns of desert cactus. The long parade moved only as fast as the bloody, tortured man could drag the heavy cross. Behind him, like horror's chorus, were his consorts to the agony of Golgotha—chanting and praying, as they slashed and beat themselves across their bare backs with stranded whips, tips set with cutting edges of stone and steel.

"Gory sight, huh?" Cove whispered, as the suffering column moved alongside.

"Wouldn't have believed it. They're killing themselves. They're bleeding to death."

"They'll bleed a hell of a lot more before they plant that cross. Good thing they're occupied, and their thoughts are on God—'cause I wouldn't want 'em to crucify us for lookin'."

Nancy watched in morbid fascination, patting the nervous Pedro to keep him quiet. "They going to hang that man to the cross?"

"You bet! I've heard they sometimes get so carried away they forget to cut 'em down in time—and the crucifixion comes out for real."

"Well I hope they cut *this* man down in time—because I know him. It's Señor Lugo."

"You mean you know the man who's Christ?" Cove whispered.

"Delivered a baby at his hut, only a few months back."

"A real Christ child," Cove chuckled.

"Where will they do all this?" Nancy asked, alarmed.

"Somewhere between here and Abiquiu. They'll lacerate themselves for three days. Oh, they make a real gay social of it. But let 'em. I've come for other purposes."

After the strange procession had wended its bleeding way into the dawn, Nancy and Cove pulled their horses back onto the trail. For a time, thinking hard on what they had seen, they rode in silence.

Cove was first to speak. "It scrambles me to see what people'll do in the name of religion. Here's a group—we could call 'em fanatics. They're just ordinary, kind people. You know 'em as such. Suddenly, in the name of God, and for the glory of the Church and the Kingdom, they start cuttin' each other up, and whalin' hell out of themselves. We think it's odd. But nothing's odd, when it comes to religion. Take our Mormons. Kindest, most generous people in the world. Got themselves wound up on plural marriage. And they'll let the world cut 'em into stew meat before they'll give it up. Both Penitentes and Mormons will die

384

for their principles, odd and queer as these principles are. Nobody from the outside's ever goin' to change 'em—that much I'm now convinced. If the Penitentes ever quit beatin' themselves with whips, and Mormons ever quit beatin' themselves with women, it'll be only when some Big Voice on the inside tells 'em to stop. Even then it may be damn hard for either of 'em to stop."

It was daylight now, and Nancy could take surer look at the weary, whiskered traveler beside her. His buckskins were travel-shined, frayed, and dusty, but about him was a fresh and youngish exuberance, like the old days. It was good for her to see Cove Corey at this time. She smiled across at him. "Oh, for the sound of that Big Voice," she sighed.

"How was the winter at Beulah?" he asked seriously.

"Worst winter of my life, Cove. No Indian trouble. It wasn't that. Main wonder is we didn't freeze, or starve. I was desperate. Sent the older kids East. Joel hates me for it. But I'm glad I did. Now typhoid's broke out. We got a good, clean well at the hacienda, but little else. I tell you, I'm scared. Plenty scared. I'm getting me and my family out of here, Cove. I really am."

"You can bet your rights th'hell you are! We're goin' to Taos. In Taos they don't ask too many questions. Taos has always been free and easy. Plenty people there who are on the dodge. That's where we're goin', Nan. Quick as we can hit the grit."

And that day they finished packing the Scott belongings, and doled out to the hacienda sisters that which wouldn't fit into the wagon's tight load. And that very same day they braved the flooded Chama and its quicksand with horses and wheels. The two older youngsters swam their animals across like veterans. Nancy carried little Edward with her in the saddle, as she let Pedro find his own way over. Cove, adept and nerveless animal handler that he was, got the wagon across with but little wetting to its load of Scott personals. The somber, forgotten sisters of Beulah looked on in sorrow at the sudden loss of their tough and competent little midwife. Except for the humble Mexicans along the Chama, there was little sorrow in Nancy's heart. For her it was goodbye Beulah. It delighted her to give it back to the Lord.

They doubled south on the old road to Chamita—the road Nancy had followed into Española the day she'd put Marty and Jody on the train. But at Chamita, Cove swung their own little train north toward Ojo Caliente. All the way, voice-starved and aching for real talk, she harped on about those two children now missing from the family. Cove listened well, and tried to tell her that what she'd done wasn't stupid at all. But there had been the letters from Marty and Jody. The kids

had admitted they were confused, and a little frightened by Boston and
its strange new turmoil. And they were homesick—but only for Ammon.
But who wasn't? Still, and most important, they were being treated
with dignity, respect, and as part of the strange Scott family. These
fears and worries stretched out to a lot of talk. It was Cove's willing
listening, his assent and approval, that made Nancy begin to feel again
like a normal, wanted human.

"Hope your coming into Beulah won't stir trouble for you," she said
as they bumped and creaked along in the shabby little wagon.

Cove laughed. "Your plural sisters there'll probably think I'm your
dear lost husband, come to haul you back to the land of promise."

"Some of the sisters *know* my husband."

"Then th'hell with 'em. When we get to Taos, neither of us'll have
much to worry about. Meantime, we'll camp off the road at night. I'll
make myself scarce around the towns, and whenever we meet strangers
on the road. You're a good horse wrangler. You can handle the load
while I sweat along outa sight."

Amanda and Vernell insisted on continuing their ride horseback.
Eddie was asleep on his little bed on the load behind, and Cove, whenever travel solitude permitted, rode with her on the spring seat—his
horse lined out at the back, with Pedro—saddled and instantly ready
for its sharp-eyed and vigilant rider.

That night, five miles north of Chamita, and in a wooden draw a
mile from the road, they made first camp. Cove's gun knocked over
a pair of cottontails. He skinned the rabbits, and broiled them into a
succulent treat over the little fire. Later, when the youngsters were
safely asleep in their warm bed in the wagon, Nancy and Cove sat by
the fireside, watching the spooky dance of its light on the brush and
cedar trees around them. Cove had unharnessed and unsaddled all
horses but his own, and had fed them a bit of the provender they'd
brought along on the tailgate of the wagon. Down the bank gurgled and
spewed the little upland stream that had served their camp so well. It
was a time for thinking. It was a time for talk.

Nancy, her own heart full, again poured out the heartbreak of Beulah,
and most of its problems, on Cove's willing ears. Somehow it didn't
seem too odd to be sitting with an outlaw, in the middle of New Mexico's nowhere, talking troubles. She'd made few real and intimate friends
with the carping, jealous, pious sisters of Beulah. And in the matter of
her own problems, she'd kept her own silence with them. Result was
that they had feared and hated her—and for her good, and their good,
Nancy was content that this should be so. But in that sort of thing there

could be no intimacies; no purging of heartache in talk. Cove, being a silent man himself, and a good listener, caught everything that had been pent-up in Nancy through the months.

After he'd heard her out, he thoughtfully tossed another clod of root wood to the blaze. "Knockin' my way around this southwest for the winter, gave a lot of time for thinkin'. This, with what I learned for myself, brought me to the thought that, for both of us, Taos is the best place."

"Why *us*, Cove? Would *you* be safe there?"

"That's where Taos has the advantage. I'm not the only troubled man there. From long time back, when American trappers used the town to peddle contraband without runnin' afoul Mexican jails and taxes, Taos has been free and easy for them who don't exactly fit normal in the lands of the civilized. I've a job there, Nan. And I've a house for us. If you're willin', we can sure make a go of it."

Nancy sat up in surprise. "Cove, you talk kind of crazy. Sort of as if you're courtin' me, or something."

He looked at her fierce-like. "Is that crazy?"

"Why yes, Cove. You're my brother!"

His laugh was edgy and bitter. "Like hell I'm your brother! And you ain't my sister. I've a right to court. It's high time I did!"

"You *are* crazy," she laughed in turn. But her throat was taut. The laugh, coming out a little hysterical, came nearer to being a scream.

"Quit sayin' I'm crazy," Cove growled. "*Your* name ain't Corey. It's Brayton. Remember? Isaac Corey's not your father. Enoch Brayton's your father. My mother's not your mother. There ain't a drop of Corey blood in your veins. I'm not your brother. You're not my sister. You're a separate woman, and apart. And I'm glad it's so. 'Cause when we were kids, I had special feelins' for you. And now I think on you as my woman —night and day. It ain't wrong for me to love you, Nan. To think on you tender, and special-like. Honest to God, it ain't!"

"I'm not so sure about that." Shock of it had knocked her flat as a cellar door. She tried to think. Only stupid thoughts came out. Cove's revealment was like a blast of birdshot. What he was saying, was true, yes. But always, and without thinking, she'd considered herself a Corey girl. Cove's sister. And now, with one push, Cove had turned everything over like a bucket of milk. "I've never thought on *you* this way," she said feebly.

"It's time you did, Nan."

"But you forget! I'm married! I've got children! I've got Joel—"

"The *schoolteacher*," Cove groaned. "He sends you down to Beulah, with a little flour and bedding. What th'hell else has he done for you this winter?"

"He couldn't help it."

"Maybe so. Maybe not. But he's managed well with another woman. He's sleepin' right comfortable with her right now, while you spread blankets in the wilderness. Hell, Nan! Let's not pretend. I've known you too long for that. You've hated polygamy from the start. So have I. Your teacher, after he'd joined the Church, couldn't wait to beef up his plural increase. You know, in your heart, what it's done to you."

"But I married him, Cove. Can't you see?"

"It ever occur to you that, had you and me got married in the beginnin', you'd never have had to face plurality?"

"None of what you're trying to say *ever* occurred to me!"

"From the first, I had eyes on you. From the first, I had plans in my heart. Then along comes Lofty Cragg and the teacher. Knowin' you, and your attitude toward the Principle, I worried none about the apostle. Only thing that made me bilious was when Flora took him on. But your teacher was different. That was the loss that like to killed me. I could see, like everyone else, how bad gone you was on him. I couldn't talk my true thoughts without bein' the ass. Suppose, about that time, Cove Corey *had* come a-courtin' Nancy Corey? You and everyone else woulda laughed me outa town. Bein' sensitive-like, I folded up my camp, turned wild, and finally got th'hell out. But don't think that stopped my thinkin', or my lovin'. When teacher took on his English puss, and knowin' what it was doin' to you, I had my own battle to keep from killin' him. Now I'm concludin', Nan, he's dragged you through this thing plum far enough."

In the firelight, Nancy looked at him in silent amazement.

He bowed his tousled head to the fire, and sighed. "Didn't think a tellin' of my love for you would blow out your canister."

"Well, it's done just that, Cove," she said, still frightened.

His eyes were suddenly looking at her tenderly. "I'm sorry, Nan. Honest to God, I'm sorry."

"Please say no more," she groaned, her own eyes now damp. "I can't talk about it. Please go away, Cove. Please leave me alone."

Without another word, Cove arose, walked to his horse. With the ease of an Indian, he swung himself into the saddle. Without another glance at her, he rode off into the darkness.

For an hour she sat like a drunken Ute, staring moodily into the fire. It was a time for talk with the voices of the soul—but the voices said nothing. It was a time for converse with the unseen spirits around her, but they glided wordlessly about the firelight, through the cedar trees, grimaced silently, and were gone—like the voiceless thoughts that traversed her weary brain. Then she remembered, it was her second night without sleep. She shuddered like a stricken dog, arose, stretched her tired arms. It was a chore mentally to face up to the simple task of laying out her bedroll.

Careful not to wake the sleeping youngsters, she dragged her roll, and Cove's roll, back to the fire. Plains-fashion, she set out the beds, either side of the dying fire, and her saddle became her head rest and pillow. Cove's bed would be ready for him when he returned. For herself she wasted no time in seeking the hard but beckoning rest of the blankets.

Yet tired as she was, sleep, coy and reluctant, could not be coaxed. How could sleep come, when the night was lit with ten million stars, when her brain swarmed with thoughts, like fireflies on a summer night? Above her stretched the mystery of the universe. Around her, in this little wagon camp, was the unsolvable riddle of life itself. The unimaginable magnitude of the sky she stared at, its billion glittering stars swept across like trails from a dusty broom, was enough to frighten wits from even a sane person. Each twinkling light, from feeblest to brightest, was, as Joel had explained, a ball of immensity—billions, trillions of miles outward in the uncharted nowhere. "I am Alpha and Omega—the beginning and the end," God had thundered to the Prophet in words of fire. "Worlds without number have I created." And with all these other worlds to create and mind; worlds without number as she was plainly seeing; no wonder God sometimes was slow in getting around to the real needs and worries of simple folk!

In the wagon she could hear a stirring and a whispering, as her little ones grew restless in this spooked and pulsing night. They were talking together the mysteries of their own precious little souls. She thought of those sad sweet days, when Ammon was young, untortured, and a haven for crazy, reckless dreams. How could she have known that the wild broncho she'd always looked on as an older brother was secretly sweet on her? How could she have guessed? True, there'd been no hiding of the fact Isaac Corey was not her true father, but still he was the only father she'd ever known, and he'd treated her a full equal with his own natural children. And in the family pattern, Cove had always been to her as a brother; or at least a half brother, and that was fairly close in plural families.

Stupid as it seemed now, it just simply had never occurred to her, until tonight, that Cove could have loved her in any other way than as a brother. There'd never be any denying she'd always loved Cove. How could anyone help but love Cove? But now she was ground to sleeplessness with another worry. Had she actually loved Cove as a man apart? Suppose she and Cove *had* tossed aside the brother-sister masquerade twenty years ago? Would they have made out in marriage? There was a reasonable certainty they could have done so—at least if it had happened before she'd met the Gentile. And that spawned another question. Life had long ago forced her to the conclusion a man could love more than one woman—and at the same time. What if a woman loved more than one man? And at the same time? Maybe, unconsciously, she'd been doing that very thing!

But poor Cove, what a price *he'd* paid, and still was paying, for the kind of love he'd only tonight revealed! And all the time she'd been of the thinking that his deep and secret mooning had been for the long lost girl who, in the beginning, had set him at loggerheads with the Church, and blasted him out of the priesthood. Maybe even this mystery was only another strangely turned phase of the multiple loves of Mormondom. She could never be sure. As for her, she was lost. As lost, unnumbered, unnoticed as any weak star in the immensity above. Would she ever know the answer? Would she ever know the answer to *anything?*

Throughout the long night, Cove stayed away from camp, and his blankets remained as Nancy had laid them. Confused, frightened, sad, sleep came to her only when the desperate fatigue of her body forced it. When she awoke, numb and aching, the morning sun already was stabbing through the cedars.

Cove had returned. Red-eyed from his own sleepless night, he was squatting at the fire like an Indian. Coffee pot was boiling. He was roasting a fat sage hen on a smooth-peeled willow stick.

His lined, whiskered face looked at her and smiled. "I flushed the bird at dawn. 'Tain't the tastiest morsel on earth, but I bet you've et worse in Beulah. Anyway, sage hens come already seasoned."

"Seems like I just went to sleep," Nancy said, hinging upward, and yawning out the creaks in her sore muscles.

"Then you done me one better. I never slept a-tall. Rousted out the kids when I rode in. They're dressed. Down the creek. Playin' Ute, I suppose. If you'll roll out, I'll spare you some coffee. And if you'll trot up here sharp and smart, I'll spare you some of this hen."

Breakfast, around the fire, was happy, congenial. The youngsters, oblivious to the fact anything special was tugging hearts and conscience of their mother and this strange uncle who seemed to appear only when there was traveling to be done, gave no thought to Cove's red eyes and haggard appearance. They'd seen him around Ammon that way many a time. But by now, their diffidence toward him was gone. To them he was amiable, full of mischievous horseplay, and, with his sagging hip-gun, a rare and exciting man to know. The chattering around the fire, and at the saddling and breakup of camp, showed no hint of the deep talk of last night.

Once more Amanda and Vernell rode ahead. And Nancy was delighted and relieved, not only that Cove had decided to return, but in the fact he once more chose to ride with her on the wagon seat. Again they followed the familiar road, with the high and ragged line of the San Juans to their left. Talk through the morning was little more than chit-chat, or gay reminiscences of a better day. Not a hint was made of the somber things that had chewed their thoughts the night before. It was near noon before at last Cove observably sobered, let the silence grow again upon them. Once more Nancy realized he was thinking hard on the hurtful question. Then suddenly for her, the fright and uncertainty returned. She closed her eyes while the wheels ground the red earth. She kept them closed while the wagon bobbed and thumped to the shocks and dips of the road.

"I've done a lot of thinkin', Nan," Cove said, at last. "A lot of it, since last night."

"So have I," Nancy replied, her eyes still closed.

When her eyes came wide again, Cove was methodically rolling himself a smoke. Not until the graceful ritual was finished, and he'd made his first deep drag at the cigarette, did he speak again.

"Straight ahead, and over the rise, is Ojo Caliente. You'll want to water the stock, and you'll want to noon there. Ten miles above Ojo Caliente, you'll find a road that forks t'right. Follow it to the Rio Grande crossing, and it's only a short spell from there into Taos. Should you decide after all I've said, to go on to Taos, you'll find the town an ancient, pleasin', interestin' place. Like most Spanish settlements, it has a public square, or plaza, in center of town, where people loll, siesta, and generally forget such problems as Brigham's doctrine, and the claws and fights of polygamy. The little house I've chose is only quarter-mile from the square—north, up the road toward the Indian pueblo. I'll leave the key to it, for you, at the Don Fernando Hotel. Hotel's on the plaza. And Nan, if you take me, along with the house, I promise you'll never regret it. I'll walk straight. I'll work hard. I'll be good to you and these fine kids. And, incidentally, in Taos my name is Bill Hardesty—not Cove Corey. I'm Bill Hardesty—out of Oklahoma Territory. And I've never even seen Utah."

Nancy, afraid to speak, had watched the salty rime rise on the horses' rumps as they tugged the sandy grade toward Ojo Caliente. "You talk as though you expect me to go into Taos alone," she said, as finally he paused for another drag at the cigarette. "You're staying with us, aren't you, Cove?"

"No. It's best I don't. I feel deep enough for you, Nan, to capture you right now, and drag you off to that little Taos house. But that's not goin' to be my way. I'm a hunted man. I'm not the best choice. But I'm still askin' you to choose."

"You're hunted only because of me," Nancy said, sadly. "And you're a good man, Cove."

He smoked a moment in silence. "Let's put it this way. I feel I'm no worse choice than your teacher."

Nancy gulped hard and was silent.

"But I'm not gonna push my feelings in this. I've thought a lot on it. My big decide last night, after seein' the fright on your face, was for you to make your own choice."

"I'm sorry I was so jumpy, Cove. It came so sudden like."

"You were as shook and rattlin' as shot in a wallet." The cigarette hung limply from his lips as sadly, soberly he stared down at his rough and ragged boots. "This I'll tell you," he said at last, the smoke clinging idly and forgotten as he talked. "When you come to the Taos turnoff, stop the wagon. Send the kids for posies. Do some hard thinkin' over what I've told you. Pray if you wanta. But don't ever forget my deep love and hunger for you, Nan. For at that pause comes *your* big decision.

"If the little house, and my waitin' for you in Taos, ain't enough to make you swing horses across the Rio Grande, then just you continue straight north, straight on through Tres Piedras. Two days more, and you'll be in Sanford, tryin' to make your peace with teacher, and clawin' the plural eyes outa the British bitch who walked off with your husband. Choice will be yours alone to make. You'll sit in this wagon, all by yourself, lookin' hard at that fork in the road. I'll not be on hand to urge for myself. And teacher'll not be on hand to argue you back into polygamy."

Cove stopped the wagon, and they both sat still and silent, watching the two youngsters leisurely ride ahead. Holding the lines in his left hand, he took the wilted cigarette butt from his lips, shook his head, sighed, and with thumb and finger of his right hand, flipped it over the horses' heads and into the roadway. He handed her the lines. She saw that his sleep-hungry red eyes were tortured, and filmed with tears. Not a word was spoken as he stood up, stretched, and toed himself over the side and down the wheel hub to the ground. She waited sadly, silently, as he untied his horse, lashed on his blanket roll behind the cantle. Then he swung gracefully into the saddle. The big, black animal danced restlessly as he pulled alongside. He shook his head, and smiled at her though his wet and bloodshot eyes.

Then he pulled the nervous animal close enough to reach her. She leaned to him. They kissed.

"So long, Nan," he said, as the anxious horse pulled him away.

"So long, Cove. You're so good, and so kind to me."

He swung the big black, and cut across the brushy knoll. They both were waving a little crazily as he dropped down the other side, and out of sight.

For a full minute she just sat there, as helpless as Seth Biddle in a furrow. A lot of her had taken ride with Cove Corey. Poor, kind, dear Cove. The unvoiced things she now suddenly wanted to say! She swallowed hard; swabbed at her own tear-damp eyes with the back of her hand. At last she clucked at the team. The horses laid forward in the traces. The wagon again began moving uphill.

Ten minutes later the strange, sad little caravan was pulling into the Mexican town of Ojo Caliente. Here there was water for the horses. Here there'd be lunch with the unworried youngsters.

And then, suddenly, there were the bells; the wild, free bells that wakened Eddie wide-eyed from his sleep behind the seat. It was the crazy Mexican bells. From the little church of another faith. The exuberant din of them was fairly shaking the town.

And then Nancy remembered. This was Sunday. This was Easter Sunday. The bells were happy. The bells marked Christ's rising from the dead. The bells were special. They rejoiced for that great and wondrous deliverance from the tomb.

PART THREE

Family Kingdom

I

IT COULD HAVE HAPPENED NOWHERE ELSE IN THE WORLD. NOT EVEN THE
most sanguine and appreciative citizen could have predicted that a
simple and spontaneous encomium, uttered in the city council by one
of Ammon's dignitaries, could have gone into resolution, been picked
up enthusiastically by the public and, rolling out across Utah Valley,
emerge as the astonishing spectacle of this day. For Joel Scott was no
young hero, returned from the wars, to be pinned out with glory. Joel
Scott was old, plagued with arthritis, and limped with a cane.

Nancy Scott, while she managed without a cane, had her own share
of bone aches. She felt the twinge of those aches, and reminder of
those infirmities, as she lifted a heavy leg to the running board of the
automobile. Vernell, plump, good-natured, and smiling, helped her up.
Before stepping through the car doorway to her spot beside Joel, on
the rear seat of the big open-air limousine, Nancy took care not to snag
or soil the bottom of her white satin gown. It was hard for her to believe
that she, who once could scissor the wildest horse, had a groan coming
when she settled with Joel to the soft cushion of the throbbing car.

Now they were handing in Matey Scott to share the seat of honor.
There was some satisfaction to knowing that age had likewise dealt
inexorably with this little woman. Matey hadn't fattened. She still didn't
tire easily, or get drowsy, but she was as shrunk and wrinkled as the
weather side of a dried apple. Yet both women, once they had settled
to the cushion, primped hair like fresh maidens, evened their white
satin gowns across their knees, and received the great bouquets of red
and white roses they were to hold. And they did it with real smiles, and
real joy.

"We carry them in our arms, or in our laps?" Matey nervously asked.

"Laps were made for baby holding and pea shelling," Nancy laughed.
"I'm hugging these fragrant posies to my arms."

All around them were the excited, anxious voices of relatives, friends,

397

and the townsfolk who had gathered at the parade's beginning, out of friendship, or out of curiosity. Joel already had removed his tall silk hat, and was nodding and smiling to a world of well-wishers on this, his own amazing day. Nancy, excited and curious as always, peered up ahead. The guard of honor, from Ammon's local American Legion Post, were shouldering their rifles, and holstering the flags. Ammon's silver band struck up "The Stars and Stripes Forever," the silk-hatted state dignitaries in the governor's car, up ahead, became suddenly and stiffly alert at the first martial strains of the band. The marching units strutted off, the governor's car began to move, followed by Mayor Garland's limousine. Then the bunting- and flower-bedecked vehicle, carrying the Scotts, pulsed, throbbed, and fell into the line of parade.

"Just can't believe this is all for me," Joel said, to no one in particular, and wagging his head in the glory of it.

Nancy looked at him and smiled. Time had whitened the Professor's hair, unbelievably widened the unnatural part of it, until they were mere whirly tufts to left and right. His mustache hung slightly limp and bedraggled. But, thank heaven, never had he worn a beard. For, in Zion's olden days, that's all one ever saw.

And Nancy now knew, just as certainly, it never could have happened anywhere else in the world. Where had there *ever* been anything like Scott Day—especially in these busy, modern times? The great and terrible World War was over, and on its way to being forgotten. American doughboys had been home from France six years. One scarcely ever saw a horse and buggy any more, and Utah Valley was stretching itself into a lively center for iron and steel. Everybody and everything was in such bustle and hurry. And then, just when you'd begun to think this new and whirling world had forgotten you, the miracle had happened. No wonder the Professor had been taken and shaken by surprise. It was a strange and touching way for a town to honor a citizen. And where else in the world would one see the honored one, with both his plural wives in the back seat of the limousine, receiving music, cheers, and praise, as though nothing at all were different about it?

These youngsters, waving from the sidewalks, and even their parents would never know what Ammon was like in the old days. To be sure, Mormonism was here, defanged and safe enough now to be respected and accepted around the world—but the pioneering was gone. This New Day, Nancy knew, had its beginning with the Manifesto—that strange and sudden declaration from President Wilford Woodruff, in 1889, putting end to further plural marriage. Whether divinely inspired, or expediency's only answer, to the Saints who were suffering everything short of death for the Principle, it had come as unexpected as a bolt out of the blue. And as Nancy fixed her smile to the public, and nervously arranged her roses for the ride down Main Street, she was remembering a lot of things that were tied to that far day.

Old as she was, she still ached and sweated at the humiliating way she'd driven out of Cove Corey's life, to crawl back to Joel in Colorado. She could have taken that road to Taos. Probably she *would* have taken that road to Taos, could she have known the desperation and necessity Cove had placed in her choice. For Cove had never returned with the Saints to Zion. No person in Ammon, no person who had ever known him, had ever seen his face again. Alive, or dead, he'd gone in his own pathetic and mysterious way. But the ache of Taos had never left her. To her death she'd always feel that Cove had been given in needless sacrifice to the Principle he'd loathed. Only the fact that Joel Scott was father of her children, and the tender thinkings on him that would not down, had made her face away from Cove on that long ago day. And it was the Manifesto that had kept sorrow and shame from completely burning her out. With the Manifesto, the cohab crusade had ended. With the Manifesto, the feds had disappeared, and suddenly the world had been bright and free of fear once more. Like thousands of other exiles, they had returned to Utah in poverty. For the Scotts it had been the pioneering all over again—this time with strangers owning most of the land.

Oh, there had been those who had questioned the divinity and rightness of the Manifesto, and who still questioned it. Their voices had been loud, and embarrassing to the Church. God, through the revelation of His Prophet Joseph Smith, set up the new and *everlasting* covenant, they howled. By what right and authority could Wilford Woodruff set it aside? If God says it's all right in 1888 to take a plural wife, why is it wrong, and subject to excommunication, for a Saint to take a plural wife in 1889? And if this be a lost cause, and with no further meaning, why did God and the Church lead us into such humiliation, and let us suffer so? These were questions that were asked then, and probably would be asked for a long time to come. But Nancy had never been saddened by the Manifesto, or by the questions. No more polygamy. No more Sanfords. No more Beulahs. Her children had been providentially saved from any choice under the Principle. And she'd cared little how many hungry-eyed Saints there were who fretted over it.

There were, of course, the thousands of Saints, like Joel, who had been living plural at the time of the Manifesto. But the government had been satisfied. The government had returned the Church's escheated property, called off its bounty hunters, emptied the penitentiaries. With the granting of full statehood to Utah, not even the most avid congressman, clergyman, or editor had stomach to deal with the tens of thousands of Mormon bastards they had made, or the thousands of husbandless wives. So, gladly, and probably wisely, they had let nature take its own course. The pre-Manifesto Mormon cohabs, like Joel, had gone on living with their plural wives; many of them begetting a fresh crop of plural babies to the glory of their eternal increase. Since it was Church-forbidden, they had taken no more wives. But they didn't need to. They had enough. And Joel had been as punctual about his duties toward his women as old Isaac could ever have been. Every other week had been Nancy's week, even into senility. No man, under the circumstances, could ever have been more fair. Half a husband, and a whole father to her kids, had proven infinitely better than none.

And if the Ammonites, in gratitude to a steadfast and eminent citizen, had chosen this September day as Scott Day, the very Lord Himself had apparently looked down upon their choice with favor. The sky above had the blue serenity of a benediction. The late gulls wheeled and turned in the unseen and unfelt eddies which, high over the earth, were combing the few clouds out to long fleece streamers, readied for the weaver of all time. Timpanogos, drained by summer of her snows, stood stark and waiting in her gray-blue-purple sky-coat for another mountain winter to drape her yet once again with the whiteness which beneficently, and through another summer, she would distill into the life juices for the valley towns she loved, and who, in turn, loved her. But while she waited over them in serene and expectant faith, the only hint below of season's close was the golden yellow of the poplars which even the town's ebullient business growth had not as yet erased from Ammon's Main Street. The Lord had warmed the day with summery sunshine. Lawns of those Saints who still kept residence on Main Street were still green. The street was jammed and milling with the townsfolk who had turned out coatless, and live as springtime, for this day of special history to the town.

Nancy, smiling and nodding with Joel and Matey to the friendly calls, cheers, and applause greeting the slow-moving cavalcade, was at the same time striving with all her might to connect the new with the old. The Corey House had vanished into the four-story Ammon Hotel. The short-lived opera house, that had burned so spectacularly one night, was now the brightly lighted Lyceum Theater, with a different movie every week. Where once carriages, stage coaches, and wagons had bucked the dust and mud to Provo and Salt Lake City, there were now gravel and pavement—and automobiles could chug off in an hour the mileage that would have taken two days of hard driving. One block north were the rails of the Los Angeles & Salt Lake, connecting the once insular Mormon world with California and the East. Two blocks south was the Denver & Rio Grande roadbed which now fully hooked Utah to Colorado and the Middle West. And down Main Street, beneath the very wheels of the automobile now rolling the Scotts to their day of memory at the Ammon Tabernacle, were the tracks, and above them the trolley lines of the Orem Electric, whose big red passenger cars sped almost hourly up and down Utah. "Golly damn," Nancy sighed to herself, "time can sure stir a lively porridge."

This, of course, was progress and confusion—the story of every town in America. It bothered and worried her, as it did every other oldster. She could never get out of mind the things of Ammon as they were. At her insistence Eddie had once driven her in his coughing and chattering Ford in search of the walls of Old Town. Fenced residential lots and new houses covered the acres where the walled village had stood. In memory of the spot where she'd howled out her birthing pains in solitude, and delivered her own first child, a townsman had erected a two-car garage. Only part of the wall remaining was a melted nub of the fort's corner nearest the spot she'd stood to heckle the Gentile soldier boys below. The town merchant who had that big and bothersome chunk of adobe in his back yard, would never know that, to one person at least, it was just as significant a memento to Joel Scott as the new and modern Scott High School, a few blocks north of where the parade now was moving.

But now Nancy's thoughts were forced back to the more realistic things of this day, for the entourage, and the townspeople themselves, were converging upon the immense and beautiful new Stake Tabernacle —pride of Ammon. For one solid block, before reaching the still green lawns of the great building, the street was lined, either side, by Ammon's own school children. Each child held a white carnation, probably brought in by Orem Electric from the greenhouses of Provo or Salt Lake City. As the limousine of Joel and his two wives ran the cheerful gantlet of smiling children, each child dutifully tossed his or her posy into the laps of these three old folks of another day. Joel's smile was broad. He was bewildered with pride, and the graciousness of the act. Nancy tried to smile, but she could only sniffle and bawl. She looked over at Matey, and Matey was sniffling and bawling, too.

As the automobile, in the final block, slowly filled with fragrant tribute from the hundreds of children, there wasn't much else one could do but weep. When finally it rolled abreast the lawn and entrance walks of the tabernacle, the Ammon Silver Band was playing loud and martial enough to chill the blood and prickle the spine. The band had taken stance, along with the American Legion honor guard, on the lawn, and up and down the walkway leading to the building. The bright red uniforms of the musicians were noisy as the music. Men of the Legion unit, in olive-drab service uniforms, were less spectacular, but they made up with polish, precision, rifles, and flags what they lacked in scarlet hue and blaring horns. Because Joel was a veteran of the Civil War, they too had come out to honor him on this special day. Nancy, as she climbed out of her bed of flowers to follow Joel, could not but compare this military guard with the Nauvoo Legion, of a day these boys would never know. She wondered, too, how many of these young veterans of that great overseas war, that war to make the world safe for democracy, had any realization this ancient veteran of another war to make America safe for democracy was denied a veteran's pension because he'd served time in a penitentiary. But she was always getting strange thoughts—and this was Utah, where lots of strange things happened.

The band played, the people cheered, and the young veterans clicked heels, and thumped the rifles they had borrowed from the National Guard. The Professor, a little shrunken in his long-tailed coat, but walking, even with a cane, as a soldier should, passed these accouterments of honor, and up the path toward the steps and doors of the great building. Nancy and Matey, in white satin, still hugging their armloads of roses, followed their man, Mormon-fashion, up the steps.

Inside, with its gallery, organ, and choir loft, Ammon's tabernacle compared favorably with that great first building on Salt Lake's Temple Square. The governor and the mayor had preceded them, and shook their hands as they were escorted to their special seats behind the speaker's dais. Outside they could still hear the band playing. Inside, they watched with amazement while the capacious building swiftly filled itself to capacity. A substantial area up front, in center section, had been set aside for the Scott family, and even Nancy could admit that Joel had sired a real sizable family kingdom. Both she and Matey could smile and nod to more than a hundred familiar faces, in Scotts of four generations. The school children, who had thrown the posies, dutifully but noisily filed into their designated places down front, but on either wing. And from the side doors, came the mass of humanity who comprised the townsfolk, and visitors from every part of the state. These, mostly, were men and women who had known Joel Scott as their schoolteacher, or had been associated with him in education. Nancy could only shake her head in amazement at that sea of faces. She couldn't have imagined there could be that many people who loved, respected, or even were interested, in Joel Scott.

But this day everyone seemed interested in Joel Scott. And when the quieting music from the great organ muffled out the noise and movement below, the mood for the day was set. Every one of Nancy's and Matey's living children had come to Ammon for this great tribute, and, with them, their children, and their children's children. Not until they buried Joel would there be a greater or more certain family reunion. Even Martha and her husband, Dr. Joseph Norvall, and a sizable delegation from the Gentile corner of the family, had thought enough of this hour to be present. And Nancy drowsed on this reminder of the gains and losses of her strange and turbulent life. Joel had been right—at least partially right. Marty, pretty and desirable, had swum headlong into the Massachusetts upper crust; had married and stayed there. She'd never worried her bright little head over Mormonism as a way of life, but neither had she forgotten her family and her heritage. The years had brought the letters and the visits. And today had brought her home again in pride to Dad—with her children, and her grandchildren.

Jody was here, too, and, academically at least, a greater professor than his father—but only academically. Still, not even Boston or Harvard had made Jody turn his back on Zion. He'd had enough stubbornness to remain a Saint through it all, returned to take a post of honor on the faculty of Brigham Young University, at nearby Provo. Married in the Church, respected in the academic world, Dr. Joel Scott, Jr., now gray as his shrunken, arthritic father, had been a source of pride and wonder to the schoolmaster of Ammon. And Nancy, as she waited out the organ music, was smug in the knowledge that all had not been loss in that far day when she'd put two frightened youngsters on the train at Española.

Nor would one slight the other children or grant them less, even in one's thoughts. Lively as both Scott families had always been, not a child had ever brought stain or dishonor on the name of their father—and that was something to chalk up, here and hereafter. Her own Edward published the Ammon *Chronicle*, which, come next issue, would likely be stuffed with this day's happenings. And Marty was not the only Scott girl who had married well. All of them—including the three daughters God had sent Matey as final comfort for her Sanford loss—and her own Vernell and Amanda—had been wed to men whom no mother in Israel could ever point with shame. Doctors, merchants, tradesmen, farmers they were, but the kind of men even God could welcome into a family kingdom. And as for John Scott, the boy whom she herself took secret credit for saving to Matey out in Colorado—John was another real pride to Joel. A top Salt Lake lawyer now, he'd sure and certain be a judge someday, and even perhaps run for state's office—like his illustrious father. This then was the crop. And here today, with their children, and their grandchildren, they were something indeed for two old women to see.

But there was no Bishop Earlington now to start the ceremony, or make the invocation. It was a lisping elder from Ammon's Third Ward —Joel's own ward—who made the customary dedication of the meeting to the Lord. With that cleared away, the purpose and function of it was quickly keynoted by Mayor Garland.

"We've gathered here in remembrance and honor of a distinguished citizen and a revered friend. As a town, and a community of people, we've chosen and set aside this day, and have paused in our daily pursuits, to try, in some measure, to express our gratitude to this great soul for his long and beneficent ministry to Ammon and its people. Five generations of this town have sat in his schoolrooms. His wisdom, counsel, and inspiration have been beacon lamps to greatness for many of the most illustrious men and women of this state. Today these former pupils of his—from every walk and profession of life—have remembered the beloved schoolmaster of their youth—to acknowledge with love the homage due this man.

"Joel Scott has devoted a lifetime—from young manhood to old age —well over half a century—to the building of good and decent lives, and good and decent citizens, in Ammon and the great state of Utah. He has labored for you and for me, for our parents, and their grandparents, their children, and their children's children. And in this hour we arise to call his name blessed.

"Professor Joel Scott holds the record of having been in the school profession longer than any other individual in our state. To us he's given his 'full measure, pressed down, and running over' . . ."

There was so much more to Mayor Garland's eulogy that Nancy felt her pesky drowsiness creeping over her, no matter how hard she fought it. Joel was alert, leaning on his cane, bent forward with pride, and anxiously drinking in every word of public appreciation. Matey, who never seemed to be bothered with drowsy, tired spells, was, as usual, wide-eyed and chipper as a young poult. But long talks and sermons, no matter of earth-shaking consequence, warm rooms, and any gabble of voices, were one-way journeys into somnolence for Nancy and her tiredness. And, Lord a'mighty—this was Scott Day—she was slicked out in satin and posies—thousands of people were watching her—and she was batting a pair of leaden eyelids like a night-weary owl!

Bishop Garland had a few anecdotes to tell about the Professor and his schoolroom, and the loving humor of them brought chuckling response from the audience. Nancy could have told a few herself—and some that were more tragic than funny. But this wasn't the day for it. But the tales did claw back into the memories of Ammon, and a long hop farther back than even the mayor's recollection. Mary Magdalene was gone, Brother Eggerson who had kept his three wives in one bed with him was gone, as was Brother Bissell and his applejack. Sister Plush no longer entertained the Three Nephites in her little hut, and long gone was Brother Proctor and his double rupture. True, there was another generation of characters to amuse and leaven out the loaf of Ammon, but Nancy was a little tired now, and didn't get around much. Still, the sea of faces before her, was proof that plural or otherwise, the Ammon Saints had bred well, and Zion should never be ashamed of this mighty crop headed onward through time and all eternity.

There was no denying Joel Scott was a great educator, and he'd done a pretty fair job of fathering out his own kingdom. But Nancy, too, was gleaning her own kernels of satisfaction as she clung to her sweet-smelling roses and studied the people. For they were *her* people, too. This, of course, was modernity, and no one ever called in a midwife. But even with her dim eyes, she could pick out a hundred of the feminine oldsters, who'd held her hands, and she'd held their bellies, while they'd groaned out their babies into the problems of their own earth life. She'd thumped buttocks, and wrangled to first air, half a thousand others in that audience on Scott Day. And that was a mite for any woman to do, and hell of a mite more than Matey had *ever* accomplished!

And now the governor was talking. And even the audience knew this was something extra special. He wasn't politicking this time—he was talking Joel Scott—and it made one proudlike to hear the words. After the Manifesto, and the government had called off its bird dogs, Joel had made Utah Saints sit up and take notice. His talent as a writer had blossomed into three fat historical studies of the Mormon people, and a theological treatise that was still being used in the Church schools. Though these books were all published in Salt Lake, rather than the eastern presses he'd so fervidly courted, the governor himself felt well enough on them to publicly praise the works and the man. And then, too, Joel's platform eloquence, and his keen knowledge of the issues, had won him two terms in the Utah legislature. The state had not yet reached the point of being ashamed, in public, of its polygamists. Of Joel's political record, the governor was especially lavish in praise. But even this great moment, and so long as the man talked, had soporific effect on the tired eyes of Nancy. She looked at Matey. And Matey, of course, primly alert, showed not the slightest signs of drowsiness.

Nancy glanced at Joel, bending out of his batwing collar to the words like an anxious eagle. And then she tried to stay awake in the mulling wonder of a few more things. What, for instance, if Joel Scott had never met Nancy Corey? What if he'd finished his Utah stint, returned to New England, and resumed the family career which the Civil War had so acutely disrupted? What if his yen for adventure and travel had drained itself out to conservatism, and he'd settled down to some family shipping office, or, as an educator, staffed some eastern college? What if Unitarianism, or Congregationalism and family respectability had been his instead of the Mormonism that had stained the family escutcheon and broken the collective family heart? What if he had married only one woman, and perhaps only dallied or kept discreet silence on the other sexual escapades, and been free to raise voice with the other fashionable Gentiles in vituperation and holy horror against the Mormons and their peculiarities of marriage? What if the wealth that was his due had been chosen ahead of the poverty, humiliation, and disgrace he'd known as a disinherited and rejected black sheep out of the noble and circumspect Scott fold?

And as Joel, even in this moment, sat here, stiff as a ramrod, and silent as a corpse—what were *his* thoughts? Were there twinges of regret for the position and affluence he'd traded for a life that other men had considered pointless and quite stupid? Had a schoolroom, Mormon acceptance, and celestial marriage been a fair enough trade for social standing and aristocratic consequence? Or in accepting and working at the Mormon pattern, had he bartered a comparatively small thing for something immeasurably larger? These were things to conjure with. But no amount of hard thinking was enough to keep Nancy Scott sharp and politely alert. The governor's droning voice, even up the middle of its eulogy, made her drowsy and bat-eyed. And there was still the reception, the dinner, the ball!

And then, suddenly, the great man of the state was finished. The time had come for Joel himself to take the stand. Not often was applause heard in a Mormon place of worship, but this day was an exception, when the withered Professor stood soldierly erect, before the people who loved him.

For a moment Joel just hung on to the rostrum, and wept unashamedly. When he'd gained control of himself, he cleared his throat, and tried a smile. To Nancy it was all sort of touching.

"My children," he said at last, "let this be my funeral."

The great throng was silent.

"You've given me my flowers, in a manner to enjoy. I can see them . . . touch them . . . smell them . . . and be alive to appreciate them."

In part, Nancy had her answer concerning Joel. The other answers would somehow come out, like marriage—in time, and in eternity. She closed her eyes again, and listened to the voice—a little weaker, but still resonant, still eloquent . . .

"I love you, my children. And no feeble words of mine can ever voice the gratitude I feel in my heart for this . . . the crowning glory of my life. It pays for every loss and every sacrifice I've ever known. It's the answer to every hardship. No man living has ever been more abundantly blessed . . ."

Yes, Nancy thought, this is the recognition, and this the payment. It answers the hardships. At least for Joel. Bravely she opened her eyes to the man at the dais, and the throng he faced.

"My life is lived. Its span of allotted years are behind me. If, in this hour, and by your presence here, you so say that this life of mine has been lived in justice, usefulness, and fairness toward my fellow men, I can face my Maker unafraid, and with joy in my heart. When the hour is named for me to go, I'll go gladly, and without fear. God will bless you, my children, for what you've done for me this day . . ."

Joel always did have a winning way. Joel always had a gift of gab when it came to facing an audience. 'Twas well he'd kept them with his age. But Nancy had lost a few of her gifts with the years, and she knew it. 'Twas eternal hell to be pooped and drowsy—even when your own man was talking. There was still this big day ahead. And 'twas infuriating what a lick of energy Matey still had. 'Twas infuriating what difference even a few years could make. Matey never seemed troubled about keeping *her* eyes open.

But drowsy as she was, Nancy could still smile. A little smugly, she eyed the worn and nicked band of gold on her veiny finger. Joel Scott had bought that ring for her on that long ago day. That band of yellow gold, out of Livingston & Bell, in early Salt Lake, had been heavy enough and tough enough to wear itself through the years. 'Twas proof, to her at least, that she'd been first in Joel's choice. And for that fact alone she could always wear a proud grin. Matey might be younger. Matey might have grabbed herself half a husband. But, slick and dulcey as she was, what else could she claim? Could she have mustered enough wallop and guts to hold Beulah's town of women together for a winter? Could she look out over Ammon, as at this minute, and say, "In this town I birthed a thousand babies—helped a thousand of Joel's grateful admirers into the world?" You bet she couldn't! And that little stunt of wife number one had been done, for the silent note of God and His recording angels, over those same generations the mayor had prated about. But frightened husbands, nowadays, go for fancy doctors to tend their moaning women. And it's just as well. Babies no longer are Zion's constant industry. And a soul can get damned tired of birthings.

Nancy, floating pridefully in her own remembered glory, wasn't even aware Joel had finished. It never occurred to her that the great audience was standing in his honor. For her, it was that infernal drowsiness again.